PLAYING A GAME OF GHOST STORIES

GIVES

A STRANGE BIRTH

TO

FRANKENSTEIN

THE OMNIBUS COLLECTION

I saw the Pale Student
of the Unhallowed Arts
Kneeling beside the thing
He had put together.
I saw the hideous phantasm
Of a man stretched out,
And then, on the working
Of some powerful engine.
Show signs of life, and stir with an
Uneasy, half vital motion——

MARY SHELLEY

London:
PRINTED FOR
ROBERT DWIGHT BROWN & ALLONYMOUS BOOKS
2025

I0649252

ALLONYMOUS BOOKS
A Division of Chi Xi Stigma Publishing Company, LLC

ISBN 13: 978-1-931608-70-1 — *Playing a Game of Ghost Stories*
ISBN 13: 978-1-931608-72-5 — *A Strange Birth to Frankenstein*
ISBN 13: 978-1-931608-73-2 — *A Strange Birth to Frankenstein (Omnibus)*
ISBN 13: 978-1-931608-75-6 — *A Strange Birth to Frankenstein (Omnibus)*

Copyright©2025 Robert Dwight Brown
Collection Copyright©2025 Robert Dwight Brown

All Rights Reserved

Includes the following Novels and Short Stories (Complete):
FRANKENSTEIN;
   or, The Modern Prometheus – Vol. 1-3 by Mary Shelley, 1818
THE BURIAL a Fragment by Lord Byron, 1819
ERNESTUS BERCHTOLD; or, The Modern Œdipus – Part 2
   by Dr. John Polidori, 1819
THE DEATH BRIDE by Friedrich Laun,1813
   (English translation by Sarah Elizabeth Utterson, 1813)
THE VAMPYRE by Dr. John Polidori, 1819

Includes the following Poems (Complete or Partial):
CHRISTABEL by Samuel Taylor Coleridge, 1816
THE PRISONER OF CHILLON by Lord Byron, 1816
PROMETHEUS by Lord Byron 1816
PROMETHEUS UNBOUND by Percy Bysshe Shelley, 1820
DARKNESS by Lord Byron, 1816
MONODY ON THE HONOURABLE DEATH OF RB SHERIDAN
   by Lord Byron, 1816

Without limiting the rights under copyright reserved above, no part of this publication may be reproduced, stored in or introduced into a retrieval system, or transmitted, in any form, or by any means (electronic, mechanical, photocopying, recording, or otherwise) without prior written permission of the copyright owner.

This is a work of fiction. Names, characters, places, and incidents either are the production of the author's imagination or are used fictitiously, and any resemblance to actual persons, living or dead, events, or locales, is entirely coincidental.

We acknowledge the corrections made to *Ernestus Berchhold* made by D.L. Macdonald and Kathleen Scherf in their University of Toronto Press edition.

Table of Contents

Preface

At first blush, these two volumes are merely a collection of classic Gothic Horror tales from the 1810's, over two hundred years ago. One is extraordinarily famous: *Frankenstein; or The Modern Prometheus*, the first science-fiction novel. One is ordinarily famous (in vampire circles): *The Vampyre*, the first novel featuring a suave, seductive member of the undead. The remaining three: 'The Burial: A Fragment', *Ernestus Berchtold; or The Modern Œdipus*, and "The Death-Bride" are so obscure they are barely known out of academic circles. If these volumes had been published by a university press, they would a 'merely' be a collection of stories, perhaps with annotations from scholars, but a collection nonetheless.

The unique factor linking these stories together they were all conceived and/or written in 1816: the Year Without Summer. After reading "The Death-Bride", from a French translation of German ghost stories titled *Fantasmagoriana*, Lord Byron proposed playing a game of ghost stories. During this game, he wrote "The Burial: A Fragment", his personal physician Dr John Polidori wrote both *Ernestus Berchtold* and his plagiarism, *The Vampyre*, and Mary Shelley, the step-sister of his lover, wrote *Frankenstein*. This now becomes a special collection of stories linked in both time and space.

What you hold in your hands is not 'merely' a collection of these inextricably linked stories, it is *the* story of that long, cold, lightning-fuelled volcanic winter at the Villa Diodati on the shore of Lake Geneva. This is *the* story which I am telling in my own Gothic Horror-styled ghost story, interwoven throughout the rest. Mary Shelley, Lord Bryon, Dr John Polidori are *Playing a Game of Ghost Stories*, which gave *A Strange Birth To Frankenstein*!

A conceit in historical fiction, whether the medium is literature or cinema, is that liberties must be taken. These liberties include, but are certainly not limited to, combining multiple characters into one and contracting the timeframe and/or locations the story takes place in. The story of the haunting of the Villa Diodati includes only five people (six if you count the toddler, William), so one could easily have been tempted to turn one character into two or three, but I have not chosen that exercise that obscene option. The second liberty is the contraction of time. Through journals, diaries, and letters written during these three months, we know when certain stories and poems were begun and when or if they were completed during their stay at the Villa. I have taken the liberty of contracting the timeline of the writings into a little over two weeks (for the *Playing a Game of Ghost Stories* volume), instead of the three months and beyond that the actual writings took. And while Percy Shelley rented a nearby home, I have Percy, Mary, and Claire stay in the Villa Diodati for the entirety of their visit. I have also taken a fourth liberty common in historical fiction: creative licence to fudge the facts and outright lie. Sorry... not sorry (well, kinda actually).

A NOTE ON QUOTING SOURCES: I have included a bibliography of the sources that I have utilized to produce this book, including the full (and partial) texts written during, shortly after, or at very least inspired by the "Year Without Summer". During the debate between Percy Bysshe Shelley and Lord Byron about galvanism, I have the characters quote many contemporary (to them) and near contemporary sources. While strict rules to counter plagiarism are to utilize quotation marks, I have chosen not to. My reasoning is simple. As this is a novel of historical fiction, I feel these quotation marks in the character's dialogue distracts from the readability of the prose. When we naturally speak quotation marks are implied, so I imply the quotation marks by changing the font to the Century Old Style typeface.

A NOTE ON MODERN SOURCES: I have attempted to include sources as contemporary to the events of 1816 when humanely possible. In the modern age of the Internet, I have been amazed at the sheer number of contemporary or near contemporary sources available on the World Wide Web, whether from Project Gutenberg, Wikisource, the Internet Archive, Google Books, etc. Thankfully, many of these sources have long since fallen into the public domain, which permits me to use them freely. When this fails, I have used more modern sources and have cited them accordingly.

1816: A "Year Without A Summer" Classics Collection

Death-Bride

In the introduction to *Frankenstein*, Mary Shelley mentions the ghost story that inspired Lord Byron's game of ghost stories. The story she remembers being called 'The History of the Inconstant Lover', but is probably "La Morte Fiancée", written by Friedrich Laun. The 'Death-Bride' is one of eight German ghost stories included *Fantasmagoriana: Recueil d'histoires, d'apparitions, de spectres, revenans, fantômes, etc.; Traduit de l'allemand, par un Amateur*, published in 1813. The edition found in the library of the Villa Diodati was a French translation of the German ghost stories. Sarah Elizabeth Utterson translated the stories into English in her *Tales of the Dead*, also published in 1813. I have included this ghost story because it was the impetus for Lord Byron's game of ghost stories which gave a strange birth to Frankenstein.

The Burial: A Fragment of a Novel

Lord Byron's contribution to the game of ghost stories he proposed is *The Burial: A Fragment of a Novel*, an unfinished vampire horror novel. Along with Dr John Polidori's *The Vampyre*, *The Burial* is one of the earliest (if not the earliest) to explore vampire themes. He abandoned the tale to never be completed. Dr Polidori explained later 'that though the groundwork is certainly Lord Byron's, its development is mine'. Plagiarism surely be damned.

Christabel

'The Death-Bride' is not the only recitation of other authors' works that summer. Dr John Polidori records in his diary on June 18, 1816: 'My leg much worse. Shelley and party here. Mrs. S[helley] called me her brother (younger). Began my ghost-story after tea. Twelve o'clock, really began to talk ghostly. L[ord] B[yron] repeated some verses of Coleridge's *Christabel*, of the witch's breast; when silence ensued, and Shelley, suddenly shrieking and putting his hands to his head, ran out of the room with a candle. Threw water in his face, and after gave him ether. He was looking at Mrs. S[helley], and suddenly thought of a woman he had heard of who had eyes instead of nipples, which, taking hold of his mind, horrified him.'

Prometheus & Prometheus (Unbound)

Lord Bryon wrote and published 'Prometheus' in 1816. I am including it in this collection, not only because it was probably written during his stay at the Villa Diodati, but because Mary Shelley's alternate title to *Frankenstein* is *The Modern Prometheus*. It does not stretch credulity that the writing and recitation of Lord Byron's poem may have served as the inspiration for the alternate title of *Frankenstein*. Percy Bysshe Shelly also wrote and published a four-act lyrical drama based on the Greek myth, *Prometheus (Unbound)*, first published in 1820. There is no reason to believe that any of *Prometheus (Unbound)* was composed during the 'Year Without a Summer', but I have included the first lines because they fit the narrative.

Frankenstein

There is no question why I have included *Frankenstein; or The Modern Prometheus* in his collection of stories written during the 'Year Without a Summer'. It is by far the greatest contribution to Lord Byron's game of ghost stories. Lord Byron's own contribution is largely forgotten outside of Romantic circles. In Dr Polidori's own words, *The Vampyre* was not his contribution to the game, but instead was *Ernestus Berchtold; or The Modern Oedipus*, a most obscure work that is not readily available even on the Internet. Percy Bysshe Shelley seemingly contributed nothing to the game. But Mary's contribution gave birth to the modern concept of science-fiction. An eighteen-year-old girl is solely responsible for putting the 'science' in science-fiction. The work has never been out of print in the 200-plus years since its publication. While I have consider the 1818 text the best choice for this collection (being the most contemporary text to the 'Year Without Summer'), I have utilized certain passages from the 1831 edition when I feel they are the most appropriate.

The Prisoner of Chillon

This chapter includes a couple sources written in 1816. Lord Byron penned the poem, 'The Prisoner of Chillon' during a week-long excursion along Lake Geneva. There was a brief respite in the thunderstorms. His poem was inspired by a visit to the Château de Chillon, a medieval castle located on Lake Geneva, south of Veytaux. Percy Bysshe Shelley records this expedition in *History of a Six Weeks' Tour through a part of France, Switzerland, Germany, and Holland; with Letters Descriptive of a Sail Round the Lake of Geneva and of the Glaciers of Chamouni*, a collection of travelogues written by himself and Mary. I have included both the travelogue and the poem in this chapter.

Ernestus Berchtold

History records that Dr John Polidori's contribution to the game of ghost stories was *The Vampyre*, a blatant plagiarism of Lord Byron's *The Burial: A Fragment of a Novel*. But the doctor insists that the ghost story he began that summer was *Erenestus Berchtold; or a Modern Oedipus*. William Micheal Rossetti, the editor of *The Diary of Dr John William Polidori* comments, 'Polidori, after tea, began his ghost-story. This, according to Mrs. Shelley, was a tale about "a skull-headed lady, who was so punished for peeping through a keyhole—what to see, I forget; something very shocking and wrong, of course." So says Mrs. Shelley: but Polidori's own statement is that the tale which he at first began was the one published under the title of *Ernestus Berchtold*, which contains nothing about a skull-headed lady... Afterwards he took up the notion of a vampyre, when relinquished by Byron. The original story, *Ernestus Berchtold*, may possibly have been completed in 1816: at any rate it was completed at some time, and published in 1819, soon after *The Vampyre*.' Written in four parts, the story was influenced by Lord Byron's own incestuous relationship with his half-sister with whom he produced a child. I have chosen to include only the second part in the main text of my collection because of the length of the novella. Parts one, three, and four are included in the appendices for completionist's sake.

The Darkness

'The Darkness' was an apocalyptic poem written by Lord Byron during the 'Year Without a Summer'. It was, no doubt, inspired by the apocalyptic storms that assaulted Lake Geneva (and the rest of the world), which kept him and his friends sequestered in the Villa Diodoti. It was published in *The Prisoner of Chillon and Other Poems* in 1816.

The Vampyre

John William Polidori's *The Vampyre* was published in London's *New Monthly Magazine* on April 1, 1819 with Lord Byron's name as the author of the work. Incensed, Lord Byron sued for the reverse plagiarism. How dare this publisher, Henry Colburn, publish *The Vampyre* with *his* name when he did not write the story, but instead the publisher was trying to capitalize on Lord Byron's own fame to boost sales of the magazine. In the following issue, dated May 1, 1819, Polidori wrote a letter to the editor explaining 'that though the groundwork is certainly Lord Byron's, its development is mine'. Polidori himself admits to having written by story at the insistence of a 'lady', to whom he gave the only copy of the manuscript as a gift. Polidori never had any intention of publishing the story himself, but this mysterious 'lady' sought out publication of *The Vampyre*.

History of a Six Weeks' Tour

Mary Shelley and Percy Bysshe Shelley would publish a travelogue of two journeys, one across Europe in 1814 and the other, of most importance to this collection, one to Lake Geneva in 1816, the very save "year without summer". This collection's mission statement is to collect the writings made during this summer, whether they are stories, poems, letters, or even a travelogue. By including these letters and diary entries, I can flesh out the events prior to their arrival at the Villa Diodati.

Child Harold's Pilgrimage

The first two cantos of 'Child Harold's Pilgrimage' were published in 1812 at the insistence of John Murray, Lord Byron's friend and publisher. In 1816, while sequestered in the Villa Diodoti, he composed the third canto, with a fourth being written and published in 1818.

Memoir of Stamford Raffles

Prologues typically serve the purpose of establishing a element of the story that takes place before or separate from the novel's primary storyline. In my book, a specific selection from the *Memoir of the life and public services of Sir Thomas Stamford Raffles, F.R.S. &c., particularly in the government of Java 1811–1816, and of Bencoolen and its dependencies 1817–1824: with details of the commerce and resources of the eastern archipelago, and selections from his correspondence* serves this purpose to a 't'. The inciting incident of the 'Year Without a Summer' began a year before when Mount Tambora exploded (not merely erupted) in Indonesia. Raffles' contemporary reports from that time set the stage for weather disruptions that would trap Mary and Percy Shelley, Lord Byron, Dr Polidori, and Claire Clairmont in the Villa Diodati.

Mary Shelley, Lord Byron & Dr. Polidori Are

Playing a Game of

GhostStories

June 1816

June 1816

1

2

3

4

5

6

7

8

9

10

11

12

13

14

15
P. sprains his ankle.

16
Byron proposes the Game of Ghost Stories.

17
P. has dinner w/ Madame Odier's. Byron completes his fragment.

18
S. conniption over "Christabel". P. begins writing Ernestus. The Sun burns hot.

19
Teasing of Mary begins every morning.

20

21
P. & B. have their Spirited Debate. M. has her nightmare!

22
The Pale Student begins his tale of the Birth of the Creature.

23
Party leaves on eight-day tour of Lake Geneva.

24

25

26

27
B., M., P.S., & C. Visit Château de Chillon. B. writes "Prisoner" & presents at hotel.

28

29

30
Party returns from their tour of Lake Geneva.

Prologue[1]

Mr. Raffles gives the following account of the eruption from the Tomboro Mountain, in the Island of Sambawa, which took place at this time, (the 11th and 12th of April, 1815,) one of the most violent and extraordinary of such explosions yet known.

To preserve an authentic account of the violent and extraordinary eruption of the Tomboro Mountain on Sambawa, in April last, I required from the several Residents of districts on this Island a statement of the circumstances that occurred within their knowledge, and from their replies, the following narrative is collected; it is, perhaps, incomplete until some further accounts are received of the immediate effects upon the mountain itself; but the progress is sufficiently known to render interesting a present account of a phenomenon which exceeds any one of a similar description on record. The first explosions were heard on this Island in the evening of the 5th of April, they were noticed in every quarter, and continued at intervals until the following day. The noise was, in the first instance, almost universally attributed to distant cannon; so much so, that a detachment of troops were marched from *Djocjocarta*, in the expectation that a neighbouring post was attacked, and along the coast boats were in two instances dispatched in quest of a supposed ship in distress.

On the following morning, however, a slight fall of ashes removed all doubt as to the cause of the sound, and it is worthy of remark, that as the eruption continued, the sound appeared to be so close, that in each district it seemed near at hand; it was attributed to an emption from the Marapi, the Gunung Kloot or the Gunung Bromo.

From the 6th, the sun became obscured: it had every appearance of being enveloped in fog, the weather was sultry, and the atmosphere close and still; the sun seemed shorn of its rays, and the general stillness and pressure of the atmosphe0re foreboded an earthquake. This lasted several days, the explosions continued occasionally, but less violently, and less frequently than at first. Volcanic ashes also began to fall, but in small quantities; and so slightly as to be hardly perceptible in the western districts.

---

1 From the *Memoir of the life and public services of Sir Thomas Stamford Raffles, F.R.S. &c., particularly in the government of Java 1811–1816, and of Bencoolen and its dependencies 1817–1824: with details of the commerce and resources of the eastern archipelago, and selections from his correspondence* by his widow, Sophia (Hull) Raffles, published by John Murray, 1830

This appearance of the atmosphere remained with little variation, until the 10th of April, and till then it does not appear that the volcano attracted much observation, or was considered of greater importance than those which have occasionally burst forth in Java. But on the evening of the 10th, the emptions were heard more loud, and more frequent from Cheribon eastward; the air became darkened by the quantity of falling ashes, and in several situations, particularly at Solo and Rembang, many said that they felt a tremulous motion of the earth. It is universally remarked in the more eastern districts, that the explosions were tremendous, continuing frequently during the 11th, and of such violence as to shake the houses perceptibly; an unusually thick darkness was remarked all the following night, and the greater part of the next day. At Solo, on the 12th, at four P.M., objects were not visible at 300 yards distance. At Gresie, and other districts more eastward, it was dark as night the greater part of the 12th of April, and this saturated state of the atmosphere lessened as the cloud of ashes passed along and discharged itself on its way. Thus the ashes, which were eight inches deep at Banyuwangi, were but two in depth at Sumanap, and still less in Gresie; and the sun does not seem to have been actually obscured in any district westward of Samarang.

No description of mine, however, can so well express what happened, as the extracts from the reports at several places; the remarks there made are applicable also to all the other districts, only in a lesser degree, as the same became more distant from the cause of the phenomena.

Extract of a Letter from Gresie.

I woke on the morning of the 12th, after what seemed to be a very longnight, and taking my watch to the lamp, found it to be half-past eight o'clock; I immediately went out, and found a cloud of ashes descending; at nine o'clock no day-light; the layer of ashes on the terrace before my door at the Kradenan measures one line in thickness; ten A. INI. a faint glimmering of light can now be perceived over-head: half-past ten, can distinguish objects fifty yards distant; eleven, A.M. breakfasted by candle-light, the birds begin to chirrup as at the approach of day; half-past eleven, can discover the situation of the sun through a thick cloud of ashes; one, P.M. found the layer of ashes one line and a half thick, and measured in several places with the same results; three, P.M. the ashes have increased one-eighth of a line more; five, P.M. it is now lighter, but still I can neither read nor write without candle. In travelling through the district on the 13th, the appearances were described with very little variation from my account, and I am universally told that no one remembers, nor does their tradition record so tremendous an eruption. Some look upon it as typical of a change, of the re-establishment of the former government; others account for it in an easy way, by reference to the superstitious notions of their legendary tales, and say that the celebrated Nyai Loroh Kidul has been marrying one of her children, on which occasion she has been firing salutes from her supernatural artillery. They call the ashes the dregs of her ammunition.

Extract of a Letter from Sumanap.

On the evening of the 10th the explosions became very loud; one in particular shook the town, and they were excessively quick, resembling a heavy cannonade. Towards evening, next day, the atmosphere thickened so much, that by four o'clock it was necessary to light candles. At about seven, P.M., of the 11th, the tide being about ebb, a rush of water from the bay occasioned the river to rise four feet, and it subsided again in about forty minutes; the bay was much agitated about this time, and was illuminated from a northerly direction. On the Island of Sahotie, fire was seen distinctly at a short distance to the south-east. The uncommon darkness of this night did not break till ten and eleven, A.M. of the 12th, and it could hardly be called day-light all day. Volcanic ashes fell in abundance, and covered the earth about two inches thick, the trees also were loaded with them.'

Extract of a Letter from Banyuwangi.

At ten, P.M. of the first of April, we heard a noise resembling a cannonade, which lasted, at intervals, till nine o'clock next day; it continued at times loud, at others resembling distant thunder; but on the night of the 10th, the explosions became truly tremendous, frequently shaking the earth and sea violently. Towards morning they again slackened, and continued to lessen gradually till the 14th, when they ceased altogether. On the morning of the 3d of April, ashes began to fall like fine snow; and in the course of the day they were half-an-inch deep on the ground. From that time till the 11th the air was constantly impregnated with them to such a degree, that it was unpleasant to stir out of doors. On the morning of the 11th, the opposite shore of Bah was completely obscured in a dense cloud, which gradually approached the Java shore, and was dreary and terrific. By one, P.M. candles were necessary; by four, P.M. it was pitch-dark; and so it continued until two o'clock of the afternoon of the 12th, ashes continuing to fall abundantly: they were eight inches in depth at this time. After two o'clock it began to clear up; but the sun was not visible till the 14th, and during this time it was extremely cold. The ashes continued to fall, but less violently, and the greatest depth, on the 15th of April, was nine inches.

All reports concur in stating, that so violent and extensive an eruption has not happened within the memory of the oldest inhabitants, nor within tradition. They speak of similar effects in a lesser degree, when an eruption took place from the volcano of Carang Assum, in Bah, about seven years ago; and it was at first supposed that this mountain w^as the seat of eruption in the present instance. The Balinese attributed the event to a recent dispute between the two Rajahs of Bah Baliling, which terminated in the death of the younger Rajah, by order of his brother.

The haziness and heat of the atmosphere, and occasional fall of volcanic ashes, continued until the 14th, or, in some parts of the Island, until the 17th of April; they were cleared away universally by a heavy fall of rain, after which the atmosphere became clear and more cool; and it would seem that this seasonable relief prevented much injury to the crops, and removed an appearance of epidemic disease, which w'as beginning to prevail. This was especially the case at Batavia, where, for the two or three days preceding the rain, many persons where attacked with fever. As it was, however, no material injury was felt beyond the districts of Banjniw'angi. The cultivators every where took the precaution to shake off the ashes from the growing paddy as they fell, and the timely rain removed an apprehension very generally entertained, that insects would have been generated by the long continuance of the ashes at the root of the plant. At Rembang, where the rain did not fall till the 17th, and the ashes had been considerable, the crops were somewhat injured. In Gresie the injury was less; but in Banymvangi and the adjacent part of the Island, on which the cloud of ashes spent its force, the injury was more extensive: 126 horses and eighty-six head of cattle also perished, chiefly from want of forage during a month from the time of the eruption.

The local effects of this emption have been ascertained by Lieutenant Owen Phillips, who proceeded to Sumbawa for this purpose, and was charged to distribute to the sufferers a supply of rice, dispatched by this government on hearing of the extreme distress to which the inhabitants of Sumbawa had been reduced.

The Noquedah of a Malay prow from Timor had reported that on the 11th of April, while at sea, far distant from Sumbawa, he was in utter darkness; that on his passing the Tomboro mountain at a distance of five miles, the lower part of it was in flames, and the upper part covered with clouds; he went on shore for water, and found the ground covered with ashes to the depth of three feet, several large prows thrown on the land by a concussion of the sea, and many of the inhabitants dead from famine. On leaving Sumbawa, he experienced a strong current to the westward, and fell in with great quantities of cinders floating on the sea, through which he with difficulty forced his way; he was surrounded by them the whole of the night of the 12th, and says they formed a mass of two feet thick, and several miles in extent. This person states that the volcano of Carang Assam in Bali, was in commotion at the same time; and it appears from the several reports, that a greater rumbling than usual was heard in the mountains in the Rembang district, as well as in the Gunnug Gede in the Preanger Regencies, but after a strict enquiry, it does not appear that any simultaneous movement or connection could be traced on this occasion along the chain of Volcanic Mountains running east and west in Java.'

The Honourable Company's cruzier Benares, was at this time at Macasar, and the following official report, received from the Commander of this vessel, confirms the circumstances already related.

'On the 5th of April, a firing of cannon was heard at Macasar, continuing at intervals all the afternoon, and apparently coming from the southward: — towards sun-set the reports seemed to have approached much nearer, and sounded hke hea\y guns, with occasional slight reports between. Supposing it to be occasioned by pirates, a detachment of troops was embarked on board the Honourable Company's cruzier Benares, and sent in search of them, but after examining the neighbouring Islands, returned to Macasar on the 8th, without having found any cause of the alarm. During the night of the 11th, the firing was again heard, but much lower, and towards morning the reports were in quick succession, sometimes like three or four guns fired together, and so heavy that they shook the ship, as they did also the houses in Fort Rotterdam. Some of them seemed so near, that I sent people to the mast-heads to look out for the flashes, and weighed at day-dawn, proceeding to the southward to ascertain the cause. The morning of the 12th was extremely dark and lowering, particularly to the southward, and S.W., the wind light, and from the eastward. At eight A.M. it was apparent that some extraordinary occurrence had taken place; the face of the heavens to the southward and westward had assumed a dark aspect, and it was much darker than before the sun rose; as it came nearer it assumed a dusky red appearance, and spread fast over every part of the heavens; by ten it was so dark that a ship could hardly be seen a mile distant; by eleven the whole of the heavens were obscured, except a small space near the horizon to the eastward, the quarter from which the wind came. The ashes now began to fall in showers, and the appearance was altogether truly awful and alarming. By noon the light that had remained in the eastern part of the horizon disappeared, and complete darkness covered the face of day. This continued so profound during the remainder of the day, that I never saw any thing to equal it in the darkest night; it was impossible to see your hand when held up close to your eyes. The ashes fell without intermission throughout the night, and were so light and subtle, that not withstanding the precaution of spreading awnings fore and aft as much as possible, they pervaded every part of the ship.

'At six o'clock the next morning it continued as dark as ever, but began to clear about half-past seven; and about eight o'clock objects could be faintly discerned upon deck. From this time it began to get lighter very fast.

'The appearance of the ship when day-light returned was most singular; every part being covered with the falling matter: it had the appearance of calcined pumice stone, nearly the colour of wood-ashes; it lay in heaps of a foot in depth in many parts of the deck, and several tons weight of it must have been thrown overboard; for though an impalpable powder or dust when it fell, it was, when compressed, of considerable weight; a pint measure of it weighed twelve ounces and three-quarters, it was perfectly tasteless, and did not affect the eyes with painful sensation, had a faint burnt smell, but nothing like sulphur; when mixed with water it formed a tenacious mud difficult to be washed off.

'By noon of the 12th, the sun made his appearance again, hut very faintly, through the dusky atmosphere; the air being still charged with ashes, which continued to fall lightly all day.

'From the 12th to the 15th, the atmosphere remained thick and dusky, the rays of the sun scarce able to penetrate through it, with little or no wind the whole time.

'On the morning of the 13th left Macasar, and on the 18th made Sumbawa; on approaching the coast passed through great quantities of pumice-stone floating on the sea, which had at first strongly the appearance of shoals, so much so that I sent a boat to examine one, which, at the distance of less than a mile, I took for a dry sand-bank, upwards of three miles in length, with black rocks in several parts of it. It proved to be a complete mass of pumice-stone floating on the sea, some inches in depth, with great numbers of trees and logs, that appeared to be burnt and shivered as if by lightning. The boat had much difficulty in pulling through it, and until we reached the entrance of Bima Bay, the sea was literally covered with shoals of pumice and floating timber.

'On the 19th arrived in Bima Bay, in coming to an anchor grounded on the bank of Bima Town, shoaling suddenly from eight fathoms; hove off again as the tide was rising. The anchorage at Bima must have altered considerably, as where we grounded the Ternate cruizer lay at anchor in six fathoms a few months before. The shores of the bay had a most dreary appearance, being entirely covered with ashes.'

From the account of the Resident of Bima, it appears that the eruption proceeded from the Tomboro mountain, situated about forty miles to the westward of Bima. On the night of the 11th, the explosions he represents to have been most terrific, and compares them to the report of a heavy mortar close to his ear. The darkness commenced about seven in the morning, and continued twelve hours longer than it did at Macasar. The fall of ashes was so heavy as to break the Resident's house in many places, and render it uninhabitable, as well as many other houses in the town. The wind was still during the whole time, but the sea greatly agitated, its waves rolled in upon the shore, and filled the lower parts of the houses with water a foot deep. Every prow and boat was forced from the anchorage and driven on shore, and several large prows are now lying a considerable distance above high-water-mark.

'On the 22d, the Dispatch country ship arrived in the bay from Amboyna. It appears that this vessel had mistaken a bay to the westward, called Sampo or Sangin Bay, for Bima, and had gone into it; the Rajah of this place informed the officer that the whole of the country was entirely desolated, and the crops destroyed. The town of Sangin is situated about four or five leagues to the S. E. of the Tomboro mountain; the officer found great difficulty in landing in the bay, a considerable distance from the shore being completely filled up with pumice-stones, ashes, and logs of timber; the houses appeared beaten down and covered with ashes.

'Understanding that messengers had been sent into the interior, I waited till the evening of the 22d, and as they had not then returned, owing, as was supposed, to having found the country impassable, I left the bay at eleven o'clock that night, and the next day was off the Tomboro mountain; in passing it at the distance of six miles the summit was not visible, being enveloped in clouds of smoke and ashes. The sides were smoking in several places, apparently from lava which had flown down them not being cooled, several streams had reached the sea; a very considerable one to the N.N.W. of the mountain, the course of which was plainly discernible, both from the black colour of the lava contrasted with the ashes on each side of it, and the smoke arising from every part of it. The Tomboro Mountain in a direct line from Macasar is about 217 nautical miles distance.'

It has been ascertained that these eruptions of the Tomboro Mountain were heard through the whole chain of the Molucca Islands. The Honourable Company's cruizer Teignmouth was lying at anchor at Ternate on the 5th April; between six and eight, P.M., several very distinct reports like heavy cannon were heard in the S.W. quarter, which was supposed to be a ship in the offing, in consequence of which the Resident sent a boat round the Island to ascertain if it was so. The next morning, however, the boat returned without seeing any vessel in the offing, and the conclusion then drawn was that it might be occasioned by the bursting of some volcanic mountain in that quarter. Ternate Island 5° 0'N. 127° 30'E.

The easterly monsoon, however, had at this time distinctly set in, and consequently the sounds would not be heard so loudly and distinctly in the Moluccas, as from the relative distance would otherwise have happened. They extended, in the opposite direction, to Fort Marlbro', and several parts of Sumatra, as appears from the following extract from thence.

It is an extraordinary fact, that precisely the same noise (taken by all who heard it to be a cannonade) occurred at several stations along this coast at the same time, viz. the morning of the 11th April several gentlemen heard it in Marlbro', the people from the interior came down with accounts of it, and those from the higher Dusuns spoke of a kind of ash-dust which had covered the herbage and the leaves of the trees. Reports to the same effect, (not mentioning any fall of ashes however,) were received from Moco-moco, Laye, Salumah, Manna, Padang Guchee, Croee, and Semanka. From some of these stations the hill-people came down armed, to assist against attacks which they imagined might be made upon the head factories.'

It has not appeared that any noise of this kind was heard at Padang, or much further north than Moco-moco. I have since heard that the same noise was heard at Trumon in about 2'40'N. lat. and at Aver Bungi in about 0'15'N. lat. at aU on or about the 11th April last.

From Sumbawa to the port of Sumatra, where the sound was noticed, is about 970 geographical miles in a direct line; from Sumbawa to Ternate is a distance of 720 miles; and the existence of the S. E. monsoon at the time may account for the difference of distance to which the sound was heard in the westerly and easterly directions; the distance also, to which the cloud of ashes was carried, so thickly as to produce utter darkness, is clearly pointed out to have been the Island of Celebes, and the districts of Gresie on Java. The former is 217 nautical miles distant from the seat of the volcano — the latter in a direct line more than 300 geographical miles distant.

I shall conclude this account with an extract of a letter from Lieutenant Owen Phillips, written from Bima on the 23d ultimo. It has been mentioned in a former part, that on receiving intelligence of the extreme distress that had been occasioned by this extraordinary event, I dispatched a supply of rice to their relief, and Lieutenant Phillips was desired to proceed and adjust the delivery thereof, with instructions, at the same time, to ascertain, as nearly as possible, the local effects of the volcano. His report is as follows:

'On my trip towards the western part of the Island, I passed through nearly the whole of Dompo, and a considerable part of Bima. The extreme misery to which the inhabitants have been reduced, is shocking to behold; there were still on the road side the remains of several corjises, and the marks of where many others had been interred; the villages almost entirely deserted, and the houses fallen down, the surviving inhabitants having dispersed in search of food.

'In Dompo, the sole subsistence of the inhabitants for some time past has been the heads of the different species of palm, and the stalks of the papaya and plantain.

'Since the eruption, a violent diarrhoea has prevailed in Bima, Dompo, and Saugar, which has carried off a great number of people. It is supposed by the natives to have been caused by drinking water which has been impregnated with the ashes; and horses have also died, in great numbers, from a similar complaint.

'The Rajah of Saugar came to wait on me at Dompo on the 3d inst. The sufferings of the people there appear, from his account, to be still greater than in Dompo. The famine has been so severe, that even one of his own daughters died from hunger. I presented him with three coyangs of rice in your name, for which he appeared to be truly grateful.

'As the Rajah was himself a spectator of the late eruption, the following account which he gave me, is, perhaps, more to be depended upon than any other I can possibly obtain:

'About seven, P.M. on the 10th of April, three distinct columns of flame burst forth, near the top of Tomboro mountain, all of them apparently within the verge of the crater; and after ascending separately to a very great height, their tops united in the air in a troubled confused manner. In a short time the whole mountain next Saugar appeared like a body of liquid fire extending itself in every direction.

'The fire and columns of flame continued to rage with unabated fury, until the darkness caused by the quantity of falling matter obscured it at about eight, P.M. Stones at this time fell very thick at Saugar; some of them as large as two fists, but generally not larger than walnuts. Between nine and ten, P.M. ashes began to fall, and soon after a violent whirlwind ensued, which blew down nearly every house in the village

of Saugar, carrying the tops and high parts along with it. In the part of
Saugar adjoining Tomboro, its effects were much more violent, tearing
up by the roots the largest trees, and carrying them into the air, together
with men, houses, cattle, and whatever else came within its influence
(this will account for the immense number of floating trees seen at sea.)
The sea rose nearly twelve feet higher than it had ever been known to
be before, and completely spoiled the only small spots of rice-lands in
Saugar, sweeping away houses and every thing within its reach.

'The whirlwind lasted about an hour. No explosions were heard till
the whirlwind had ceased, at about eleven, A.M. From midnight till the
evening of the 11th, they continued without intermission; after that, their
violence moderated, and they were only heard at intervals; but the explosions did not cease entirely until the 15th of July. The mountain still
throws out immense volumes of smoke, and the natives are apprehensive of another eruption during the ensuing rainy season.

'Of the whole of the villages of Tomboro, Jempo, containing about
forty inhabitants, is the only one remaining. In Precate, no vestige of a
house is left. Twenty-six of the people who were at Sambawa at the time
are the whole of the population who have escaped.

'From the most particular inquiries I have been able to make, there
were certainly not fewer than 12,000 individuals in Tomboro and Precate
at the time of the eruption.

'The trees and herbage of every description along the whole of the
north and west sides of the Peninsula, have been completely destroyed,
with the exception of a high point of land near the spot where the village
of Tomboro stood; on it a few trees still remain. In the night of the eruption, two men and two women, I am informed, escaped to this point, and
were saved. I have sent in search of them, but have not yet been able to
get hold of them; no person has yet been along the eastern side of the
hill.

'A messenger who returned yesterday from Sambawa, relates that
the fall of ashes has been heavier at Sambawa than on this side the Gulf,
and that an immense number of people have been starved: they are now
parting with their horses and buffaloes for a half or quarter rupee's
worth of rice or corn. The distress has, however, I trust, been alleviated
by this time, as the brig, with sixty-three coyangs of rice, from Java, arrived there the day he was leaving it.'

—Batavia, September 28, 1815.

Second Prologue[2]

Letter 1.

Hôtel de Secheron, Geneva,
May 17, 1816.

We arrived at Paris on the 8th of this month, and were detained two days for the purpose of obtaining the various signatures necessary to our passports, the French government having become much more circumspect since the escape of Lavalette. We had no letters of introduction, or any friend in that city, and were therefore confined to our hotel, where we were obliged to hire apartments for the week, although when we first arrived we expected to be detained one night only; for in Paris there are no houses where you can be accommodated with apartments by the day.

The manners of the French are interesting, although less attractive, at least to Englishmen, than before the last invasion of the Allies: the discontent and sullenness of their minds perpetually betrays itself. Nor is it wonderful that they should regard the subjects of a government which fills their country with hostile garrisons, and sustains a detested dynasty on the throne, with an acrimony and indignation of which that government alone is the proper object. This feeling is honourable to the French, and encouraging to all those of every nation in Europe who have a fellow feeling with the oppressed, and who cherish an unconquerable hope that the cause of liberty must at length prevail.

Our route after Paris, as far as Troyes, lay through the same uninteresting tract of country which we had traversed on foot nearly two years before, but on quitting Troyes we left the road leading to Neufchâtel, to follow that which was to conduct us to Geneva. We entered Dijon on the third evening after our departure from Paris, and passing through Dôle, arrived at Poligny. This town is built at the foot of Jura, which rises abruptly from a plain of vast extent. The rocks of the mountain overhang the houses. Some difficulty in procuring horses detained us here until the evening closed in, when we proceeded, by the light of a stormy moon, to Champagnolles, a little village situated in the depth of the mountains. The road was serpentine and exceedingly steep, and was overhung on one side by half distinguished precipices, whilst the other was a gulph,

2 From *History of a Six Weeks Tour* by Mary Wollstonecraft Shelley and Percy Bysshe Shelley, published by
T Thomas Hookham, Jr. and Charles and James Ollier, 1817

filled by the darkness of the driving clouds. The dashing of the invisible mountain streams announced to us that we had quitted the plains of France, as we slowly ascended, amidst a violent storm of wind and rain, to Champagnolles, where we arrived at twelve o'clock, the fourth night after our departure from Paris.

The next morning we proceeded, still ascending among the ravines and vallies of the mountain. The scenery perpetually grows more wonderful and sublime: pine forests of impenetrable thickness, and untrodden, nay, inaccessible expanse spread on every side. Sometimes the dark woods descending, follow the route into the vallies, the distorted trees struggling with knotted roots between the most barren clefts; sometimes the road winds high into the regions of frost, and then the forests become scattered, and the branches of the trees are loaded with snow, and half of the enormous pines themselves buried in the wavy drifts. The spring, as the inhabitants informed us, was unusually late, and indeed the cold was excessive; as we ascended the mountains, the same clouds which rained on us in the vallies poured forth large flakes of snow thick and fast. The sun occasionally shone through these showers, and illuminated the magnificent ravines of the mountains, whose gigantic pines were some laden with snow, some wreathed round by the lines of scattered and lingering vapour; others darting their dark spires into the sunny sky, brilliantly clear and azure.

As the evening advanced, and we ascended higher, the snow, which we had beheld whitening the overhanging rocks, now encroached upon our road, and it snowed fast as we entered the village of Les Rousses, where we were threatened by the apparent necessity of passing the night in a bad inn and dirty beds. For from that place there are two roads to Geneva; one by Nion, in the Swiss territory, where the mountain route is shorter, and comparatively easy at that time of the year, when the road is for several leagues covered with snow of an enormous depth; the other road lay through Gex, and was too circuitous and dangerous to be attempted at so late an hour in the day. Our passport, however, was for Gex, and we were told that we could not change its destination; but all these police laws, so severe in themselves, are to be softened by bribery, and this difficulty was at length overcome. We hired four horses, and ten men to support the carriage, and departed from Les Rousses at six in the evening, when the sun had already far descended, and the snow pelting against the windows of our carriage, assisted the coming darkness to deprive us of the view of the lake of Geneva and the far distant Alps.

The prospect around, however, was sufficiently sublime to command our attention—never was scene more awfully desolate. The trees in these regions are incredibly large, and stand in scattered clumps over the white wilderness; the vast expanse of snow was chequered only by these gigantic pines, and the poles that marked our road: no river or rock-encircled lawn relieved the eye, by adding the picturesque to the sublime. The natural silence of that uninhabited desert contrasted strangely with the voices of the men who conducted us, who, with animated tones and gestures, called to one another in a patois composed of French and Italian, creating disturbance, where but for them, there was none.

To what a different scene are we now arrived! To the warm sunshine and to the humming of sun-loving insects. From the windows of our hotel we see the lovely lake, blue as the heavens which it reflects, and sparkling with golden beams. The opposite shore is sloping, and covered with vines, which however do not so early in the season add to the beauty of the prospect. Gentlemens' seats are scattered over these banks, behind which rise the various ridges of black mountains, and towering far above, in the midst of its snowy Alps, the majestic Mont Blanc, highest and queen of all. Such is the view reflected by the lake; it is a bright summer scene without any of that sacred solitude and deep seclusion that delighted us at Lucerne.

We have not yet found out any very agreeable walks, but you know our attachment to water excursions. We have hired a boat, and every evening at about six o'clock we sail on the lake, which is delightful, whether we glide over a glassy surface or are speeded along by a strong wind. The waves of this lake never afflict me with that sickness that deprives me of all enjoyment in a sea voyage; on the contrary, the tossing of our boat raises my spirits and inspires me with unusual hilarity. Twilight here is of short duration, but we at present enjoy the benefit of an increasing moon, and seldom return until ten o'clock, when, as we approach the shore, we are saluted by the delightful scent of flowers and new mown grass, and the chirp of the grasshoppers, and the song of the evening birds.

We do not enter into society here, yet our time passes swiftly and delightfully. We read Latin and Italian during the heats of noon, and when the sun declines we walk in the garden of the hotel, looking at the rabbits, relieving fallen cockchafers, and watching the motions of a myriad of lizards, who inhabit a southern wall of the garden. You know that we have just escaped from the gloom of winter and of London; and coming to this delightful spot during this divine weather, I feel as happy as a new-fledged bird, and hardly care what twig I fly to, so that I may try my new-found wings. A more experienced bird may be more difficult in its choice of a bower; but in my present temper of mind, the budding flowers, the fresh grass of spring, and the happy creatures about me that live and enjoy these pleasures, are quite enough to afford me exquisite delight, even though clouds should shut out Mont Blanc from my sight. Adieu!

M.

Letter II.

Campagne Chapuis near Coligny,
1st June.

You will perceive from my date that we have changed our residence since my last letter. We now inhabit a little cottage on the opposite shore of the lake, and have exchanged the view of Mont Blanc and her snowy aiguilles for the dark frowning Jura, behind whose range we every evening see the sun sink, and darkness approaches our valley from behind the Alps, which are then tinged by that glowing rose-like hue which is observed in England to attend on the clouds of an autumnal sky when day-light is almost gone. The lake is at our feet, and a little harbour contains our boat, in which we still enjoy our evening excursions on the water. Unfortunately we do not now enjoy those brilliant skies that hailed us on our first arrival to this country. An almost perpetual rain confines us principally to the house; but when the sun bursts forth it is with a splendour and heat unknown in England. The thunder storms that visit us are grander and more terrific than I have ever seen before. We watch them as they approach from the opposite side of the lake, observing the lightning play among the clouds in various parts of the heavens, and dart in jagged figures upon the piny heights of Jura, dark with the shadow of the overhanging cloud, while perhaps the sun is shining cheerily upon us. One night we enjoyed a finer storm than I had ever before beheld. The lake was lit up—the pines on Jura made visible, and all the scene illuminated for an instant, when a pitchy blackness succeeded, and the thunder came in frightful bursts over our heads amid the darkness.

But while I still dwell on the country around Geneva, you will expect me to say something of the town itself: there is nothing, however, in it that can repay you for the trouble of walking over its rough stones. The houses are high, the streets narrow, many of them on the ascent, and no public building of any beauty to attract your eye, or any architecture to gratify your taste. The town is surrounded by a wall, the three gates of which are shut exactly at ten o'clock, when no bribery (as in France) can open them. To the south of the town is the promenade of the Genevese, a grassy plain planted with a few trees, and called Plainpalais. Here a small obelisk is erected to the glory of Rousseau, and here (such is the mutability of human life) the magistrates, the successors of those who exiled him from his native country, were shot by the populace during that revolution, which his writings mainly contributed to mature, and which, notwithstanding the temporary bloodshed and injustice with which it was polluted, has produced enduring benefits to mankind, which all the chicanery of statesmen, nor even the great conspiracy of kings, can entirely render vain. From respect to the memory of their predecessors, none of the present magistrates ever walk in Plainpalais. Another Sunday recreation for the citizens is an excursion to the top of Mont Salève. This hill is within a league of the town, and rises perpendicularly from the cultivated plain. It is ascended on the other side, and I should judge from its situation that your toil is rewarded by a delightful view of the course of the Rhone and Arve, and of the shores of the lake. We have not yet visited it.

There is more equality of classes here than in England. This occasions a greater freedom and refinement of manners among the lower orders than we meet with in our own country. I fancy the haughty English ladies are greatly disgusted with this consequence of republican institutions, for the Genevese servants complain very much of their scolding, an exercise of the tongue, I believe, perfectly unknown here. The peasants of Switzerland may not however emulate the vivacity and grace of the French. They are more cleanly, but they are slow and inapt. I know a girl of twenty, who although she had lived all her life among vineyards, could not inform me during what month the vintage took place, and I discovered she was utterly ignorant of the order in which the months succeed to one another. She would not have been surprised if I had talked of the burning sun and delicious fruits of December, or of the frosts of July. Yet she is by no means deficient in understanding.

The Genevese are also much inclined to puritanism. It is true that from habit they dance on a Sunday, but as soon as the French government was abolished in the town, the magistrates ordered the theatre to be closed, and measures were taken to pull down the building.

We have latterly enjoyed fine weather, and nothing is more pleasant than to listen to the evening song of the vine-dressers. They are all women, and most of them have harmonious although masculine voices. The theme of their ballads consists of shepherds, love, flocks, and the sons of kings who fall in love with beautiful shepherdesses. Their tunes are monotonous, but it is sweet to hear them in the stillness of evening, while we are enjoying the sight of the setting sun, either from the hill behind our house or from the lake.

Such are our pleasures here, which would be greatly increased if the season had been more favourable, for they chiefly consist in such enjoyments as sunshine and gentle breezes bestow. We have not yet made any excursion in the environs of the town, but we have planned several, when you shall again hear of us; and we will endeavour, by the magic of words, to transport the ethereal part of you to the neighbourhood of the Alps, and mountain streams, and forests, which, while they clothe the former, darken the latter with their vast shadows. Adieu!

M.

Chapter One
An Introduction

Mary Wollstonecraft Godwin's Journal

29 August, in the Year of our Lord Eighteen-Hundred-and-Frozen-to-Death, Lake Geneva— Preparing to leave the most haunted Villa Diodoti and the company of Lord Byron after a long, cold, lightning-fuelled, and wintery summer on the shore of Lake Geneva. Despite the completeness of my journal over the course of the winter of 1816— correction, 'summer'— I'll allow myself to briefly summarize while the memories are fresh. The journey back to England and the prison of my father is long, but not nearly long enough.

At first we spent our pleasant hours on the lake, or wandering on its shores; and Lord Byron, who was writing the third canto of *Childe Harold*, was the first among us who put his thoughts upon paper. These, as he brought them successively to us, clothed in all the light and harmony of poetry, seemed to stamp as divine the glories of heaven and earth, whose influences we partook with him.

But it proved a wet, ungenial summer, and incessant rain often confined us for days to the house. Some volumes of ghost stories, translated from the German into French, fell into our hands. There was the *History of the Inconstant Lover*, who, when he thought to clasp the bride to whom he had pledged his vows, found himself in the arms of the pale ghost of her whom he had deserted. There was the tale of *The Sinful Founder of His Race*, whose miserable doom it was to bestow the kiss of death on all the younger sons of his fated house, just when they reached the age of promise. His gigantic, shadowy form, clothed like the ghost in *Hamlet*, in complete armour, but with the beaver up, was seen at midnight, by the moon's fitful beams, to advance slowly along the gloomy avenue. The shape was lost beneath the shadow of the castle walls; but soon a gate swung back, a step was heard, the door of the chamber opened, and he advanced to the couch of the blooming youths, cradled in healthy sleep. Eternal sorrow sat upon his face as he bent down and kissed the forehead of the boys, who from that hour withered like flowers snapt upon the stalk. I have not seen these stories since then; but their incidents are as fresh in my mind as if I had read them yesterday.

19

'We will each write a ghost story,' said Lord George Gordon Byron; and his proposition was acceded to. There were four of us. The noble author began a tale, a fragment. Shelley, more apt to embody ideas and sentiments in the radiance of brilliant imagery, commenced one founded on the experiences of his early life. Poor Polidori had some terrible idea about a modern OEdipus, a queer overblown ghost story, something very shocking and wrong of course; but overtly inspired by George's scandalous and incestuous relationship with Augusta Leigh, the daughter of John 'Mad Jack' Byron, his own disgraced father. Was Elizabeth Medora Leigh, born 15 April 1814, the lovechild of Lord Byron and his half-sister as gossiping hens suppose? Who knows! But clearly poor Polidori felt so inspired to quite queerly write his OEdipal ghost story. The illustrious poets also, annoyed by the platitude of prose, speedily relinquished the uncongenial task.

I busied myself to think of a story, — a story to rival those which had excited us to this task. One which would speak to the mysterious fears of our nature, and awaken thrilling horror— one to make the reader dread to look round, to curdle the blood, and quicken the beatings of the heart. If I did not accomplish these things, my ghost story would be unworthy of its name. I thought and pondered— vainly. I felt that blank incapability of invention which is the greatest misery of authorship, when dull Nothing replies to our anxious invocations. Have you thought of a story? I was asked each morning, and each morning I was forced to reply with a mortifying negative.

Every thing must have a beginning, to speak in Sanchean phrase; and that beginning must be linked to something that went before. The Hindoos give the world an elephant to support it, but they make the elephant stand upon a tortoise. Invention, it must be humbly admitted, does not consist in creating out of void, but out of chaos; the materials must, in the first place, be afforded: it can give form to dark, shapeless substances, but cannot bring into being the substance itself. In all matters of discovery and invention, even of those that appertain to the imagination, we are continually reminded of the story of Columbus and his egg. Invention consists in the capacity of seizing on the capabilities of a subject, and in the power of moulding and fashioning ideas suggested to it.

Many and long were the conversations between Lord Byron and Shelley, to which I was a devout but nearly silent listener. During one of these, various philosophical doctrines were discussed, and among others the nature of the principle of life, and whether there was any probability of its ever being discovered and communicated. They talked of the experiments of Dr Darwin, (I speak not of what the Doctor really did, or said that he did, but, as more to my purpose, of what was then spoken of as having been done by him,) who preserved a piece of vermicelli in a glass case, till by some extraordinary means it began to move with voluntary motion. Not thus, after all, would life be given. Perhaps a corpse would be re-animated; galvanism had given token of such things: perhaps the component parts of a creature might be manufactured, brought together, and endued with vital warmth.

Night waned upon this talk, and even the witching hour had gone by, before we retired to rest. When I placed my head on my pillow, I did not sleep, nor could I be said to think. My imagination, unbidden, possessed and guided me, gifting the successive images that arose in my mind with a vividness far beyond the usual bounds of reverie. I saw— with shut eyes, but acute mental vision, — I saw the pale student of unhallowed arts kneeling beside the thing he had put together. I saw the hideous phantasm of a man stretched out, and then, on the working of some powerful engine, show signs of life, and stir with an uneasy, half vital motion. Frightful must it be; for supremely frightful would be the effect of any human endeavour to mock the stupendous mechanism of the Creator of the world. His success would terrify the artist; he would rush away from his odious handywork, horror-stricken. He would hope that, left to itself, the slight spark of life which he had communicated would fade; that this thing, which had received such imperfect animation, would subside into dead matter; and he might sleep in the belief that the silence of the grave would quench for ever the transient existence of the hideous corpse which he had looked upon as the cradle of life. He sleeps; but he is awakened; he opens his eyes; behold the horrid thing stands at his bedside, opening his curtains, and looking on him with yellow, watery, but speculative eyes.

I opened mine in terror. The idea so possessed my mind, that a thrill of fear ran through me, and I wished to exchange the ghastly image of my fancy for the realities around. I see them still; the very room, the dark parquet, the closed shutters, with the moonlight struggling through, and the sense I had that the glassy lake and white high Alps were beyond. I could not so easily get rid of my hideous phantom; still it haunted me. I must try to think of something else. I recurred to my ghost story, my tiresome unlucky ghost story! O! if I could only contrive one which would frighten my reader as I myself had been frightened that night!

Swift as light and as cheering was the idea that broke in upon me. 'I have found it! What terrified me will terrify others; and I need only describe the spectre which had haunted my midnight pillow.' On the morrow I announced that I had thought of a story. I began that day with the words, It was on a dreary night of November, making only a transcript of the grim terrors of my waking dream.

At first I thought but of a few pages of a short tale; but my Beloved urged me to develope the idea at greater length. I certainly did not owe the suggestion of one incident, nor scarcely of one train of feeling, to my husband, and yet but for his incitement, it would never have taken the form in which it was presented. From this declaration I must except the preface. As far as I can recollect, it was entirely written by him.

And now, once again, I bid my hideous progeny go forth and prosper. I have an affection for it, for it was the offspring of happy days, when death and grief were but words, which found no true echo in my heart. Its several pages speak of many a walk, many a drive, and many a conversation, when I was not alone; and my companion was one who, in this world, I shall never see more. But this is for myself; my readers have nothing to do with these associations.[1]

ᙡᴏ-ᴀɴᴅ-ᴀ-ʜᴀʟᶠ ᴍᴏɴᴛʜs ᴇᴀʀʟɪᴇʀ

1O June. Lake Geneva— Lord Byron welcomed us to his villa with the warmest of welcomes despite— nay, in spite of— the frigid mixture of lightning filled thunderstorms and wintry squalls. If my upbringing had been any less atheistic and anarchistic, my mind may have turned to the small comforts of the apocalyptic. How would my intellect have been twisted and distorted if my father had been a devoutly religious man, a parson? Would he have seen the scripture in Daniel chapter eight, verse fourteen: *'Unto two thousand and three hundred days; then shall the sanctuary be cleansed'* as a warning that the End Times were nigh? Would Father, a student of mathematics, have calculated the end of our age having come two thousand and three hundred 'years of days' from 457 BC with the decree to rebuild Jerusalem by Artaxerxes I of Persia? Would Father have preached that this 'sanctuary' to be 'cleansed' as the Earth's purification in a hell-fiery Second Coming of Jesus the Christ? But Father is not a man of religious superstition but scientific supposition: therefore the answer is a simple, unequivocal no. Hell no!

But this weather we encountered on our travels across the channel, through France, and into the Swiss Alps certainly wasn't hell-fiery as is captured in the common imagination. But then Dante Alighieri viewed Judecca, the fourth division of Cocytus, so named for Judas Iscariot, as a glacial prison that bound the traitors to their lords and benefactors in a lake of ice.

---

1 From the Introduction to the 1831 Edition of *Frankenstein; or, The Modern Prometheus*, published by Henry Colburn & Richard Bentley.

When we were down within the darksome well,
Beneath the giant's feet, but lower far,
And I was scanning still the lofty wall,
I heard it said to me: "Look how thou steppest!
Take heed thou do not trample with thy feet
The heads of the tired, miserable brothers!"
Whereat I turned me round, and saw before me
And underfoot a lake, that from the frost
The semblance had of glass, and not of water.

What once perceived idyllic summer when we first set out from England were we to likely to experience trapped inside while lightning flashes, thunder crashes, and a blizzard clashes with very notion of summer? Purchasing a boat and rowing the mirror-glassed lake, while wasting away a pleasant summer, would likely prove impossible given the improbable reversal of the seasons. What was the source of Mother Nature's sudden and sullen retraction of that idyllic summer we dreamed of? My father, being atheistic and anarchistic, invited into our home a radical student of the weather for a rather formal lecture, as he is wont to do quite often, on both the meteorological and the historical significance of the volcanic eruption in the Dutch East Indies. The most probable solution, according to this student of science, and by extension by father, is seen through the lens of history, not the insinuations of superstition. There are no acts of God. The geological has proven much more likely to affect the meteorological than dances to the spirit-gods ever can. In certain circles, whether they be religious or scientific, this may either be blasphemy or pseudoscience. Remember, he reminded us, the Minoan eruption of Thera would be documented on the distant Egyptian Tempest Stele and in the far more distant Chinese Bamboo Annals as a volcanic winter of yellow skies and summer frost.

A network of travellers, whether they be merchants, pilgrims, or those on holiday, told us of tales of weather corruptions and crop destructions, and from the farthest corner of the world as far east as east goes came the reports from the Dutch East Indies as published in the newspapers. The hungered, we heard, had protested their dire straits in markets and in front of bakeries, having taken much affront at the inflation of prices of common necessaries. Would riots, arson, and looting swept utter and fiery destruction through the great cities of Europe only now beginning to recover from the Napoleonic wars? Sir Stamford Raffles, the Governor-General of the Dutch East Indies, when artillery fire was heard seemingly comings from the island of Java, Raffles scrambled the Royal Navy to rebuff an impending invasion to retake control of the Indies from the British. This artillery fire proved to be the rumblings of a volcanic eruption; but this first eruption on 5 April 1815 would prove to be mere musket shot compared to the thunderous cannon fire that would come in five days' time. A mountain named Tambora, on the island of Sumbawa, not known to the locals to be a volcano, indeed erupted with a volcanic fury only known in the far distance of ancient history.

> 'On my trip towards the western part of the island, I passed through nearly the whole of Dompo and a considerable part of Bima. The extreme misery to which the inhabitants have been reduced is shocking to behold. There were still on the road side the remains of several corpses, and the marks of where many others had been interred: the villages almost entirely deserted and the houses fallen down, the surviving inhabitants having dispersed in search of food... Since the eruption, a violent diarrhoea has prevailed in Bima, Dompo, and Sang'ir, which has carried off a great number of people. It is supposed by the natives to have been caused by drinking water which has been impregnated with ashes; and horses have also died, in great numbers, from a similar complaint.'
>
> — Lt. Philips, ordered by Raffles to go to Sumbawa.

The Villa Diodati, to which Lord Byron had rented for the anticipated idyllic summer, proved to be dourly grey, though quite handsome, remarkably square, but reasonably modern enough. My always operational writer's imagination invented a note written by the architect upon completion of the villa, 'North-east of the city limits of Geneva, along the southern shore of Lake Léman, extends the district of Cologny. In a superb location on the Cologny heights stands a modest, square, stucco house. From the balustraded balcony encircling its exterior on all but the south side (where the front entrance opens directly upon a small courtyard) a marvellous panorama of Nature lies visible. Beyond a foreground of vineyards and large trees, sloping steeply to the wooded bank, stretches both east and west a lake of crystalline blue; in the distance, across the water, rise the jagged, often snowcapped peaks of the magnificent Jura range.'[2] Why cannot I simply take in the splendour without such foolishness.

But the house would prove a pleasant place to waste away a summer in exile. My Beloved and I could no longer enjoy our privacy in London for the scandal set upon us because of love. I am no longer

---

2 From an essay 'Milton and the Villa Diodati' by William S. Clark.

content to be sent, by fatherly decree, here or there, wither and thither for protect his name. Our love was found in my father's home during many a dinner party and lecture. My Beloved says often my father enchanted him with his anarchistic politics and atheistic rationales; the ghost of my mother enchanted him with her feminist philosophies; and I enchanted him with my entire being. I come from good stock being the daughter of William Godwin and Mary Wollstonecraft. Therefore, we should take our flight due to an unfortunate lack of legal (and religious) marital contract.

But scandal would be content to follow us to the continent for we both fled away from it and toward it. If a woman were a nation-state, our own host would be more akin to Napoleon Bonaparte, exiled to Lake Geneva (instead of Elba) for having waged war with the entire continent of Europe. He is beset on all sides by scandal. How can a single man be so hated and loved, despised and admired, often in but a single breath? Including the breaths in our own party.

In his letter of invitation to Claire Clairemont, Lord Byron made it a point to reference John Milton having vacationed here in the summer of 1639. He proudly exclaimed in a letter written to sweetest Claire— one could audibly hear him while reading— that the landlord let slip a 'secret':

> '... while examining which place was best to lease, the landlord of the Villa Diodati let slip a secret. Giovanni Diodati, the original owner, who commissioned its construction, was the uncle of Charles Diodati. Sweetest Claire, you may be forgiven in asking, "Who?" because I most certainly had. The landlord explained he was a close and dear childhood friend to John Milton. Yes! That John Milton! had spent part of 1639 with said uncle during his "grand tour" of Europe at this very villa. What theorists and intellectuals guested with him for him to display his poetic mastery? What works of his were written within these walls? So, I purchased my lease without a moment's hesitation. If even the smallest fragment the ghost of John Milton still lingers in this villa— haunting it with such unbridled creativity— then what works could I write over course of the summer!'
> — Letter from Lord Byron to Claire Clairmont

But unfortunately for our overly and overtly romantic little Lord, Milton *may* never have vacationed in this house— physically. Not because of certain monetary concerns of the poet given the inherent familial relations, but the concerns of the temporal. Our carriage-driver, when my Beloved mentioned our hopes of being haunted by John Milton's spirit, chuckled. He regretted to inform us of an unfortunate truth. The villa had not been constructed until (in his words) 'the year of our Lord and Saviour 1710'. Slightly over seventy years is quite the temporal error one cannot easily dismiss as typographical. Why then is there a bronze plaque affixed to the wall of the caretaker's house proclaiming, '*John Milton, poéte anglaise, Secrétaire d'Etat d'Olivier Cromwell, auteur du* Paradis perdu, *vélcut ici l'hôte de Jean Diodati en 1639.*' Given Byron's anticipation for his own ceaseless creativity over the course of this summer, hopefully future generations of landlords will not set a bronze plaque declaring '*Lord Byron, poéte anglaise, auteur de* Child Harold, *habita la villa Diodati en* **1917**'. What else could explain such a wild discrepancy? My Beloved preferred this story, whether factual or not, because it amuses him and could precipitate an enjoyable argument with Lord Byron. As for me? I dismissed it as the idle-talking gossip of a layman. History— even such recent history— cannot possess a seven-decade discrepancy. Modern and enlightened theologians dispute the birth of Jesus in 1AD by a mere four to six years. Seventy-one? Amusing.

The Diary of Dr. John William Polidori

15June. Up late; began my letters. Fell madly, deeply, passionately in love with Mary Wollstonecraft Godwin. Percy Shelley presented her to us as his wife, though I believe she is merely his fiancée, or she is at worse a scarlet woman. If the situation is the former, then I must respect Percy's right to his wife; if she is the latter, then I am honour-bond to free Mary from such a strain... stain; if she is the centre, then I am free to woo for no marriage contract has been entered into either the registry of the state or the Church. George— Lord Byron to others— saw the restless fire of passion in my eyes when I look upon the fair Mary and mocked me relentlessly for my foolishness.

What is there not to love? Her porcelain skin; her straight nose; her high cheekbones; roselike lips; dainty hands; ink-stained, delicate fingers. The soft ringlets of her brunette hair. Her breasts supple with milk. Her hips shapely for childbearing. Her voice strong and sultry. Her laugh; her gorgeous laugh; a laugh at once joyous and vicious. Nightingales are jealous of that melodious song. If I but possessed a whit of wit, I could make that song ring out continuously. But her own eviscerating wit splits open my belly and spills my bowels upon my shined shoes. Her razor-sharp tongue is circumcising; she infantizes a professional, educated man back into being a snot-nosed boy toddling around his father's writing desk. If these barbs her tongue and lips willingly form, I wonder and ponder the dangers that creak under the floorboards in her haunted mind.

Or what of her pedigree? William Godwin, the renowned Utilitarianist and Anarchist, is a great stallion to be bred from. If I could expose the privileges of the aristocracy which are fuelled the abuses of power by a tyrannical and monarchist government with the skill of *Things as They Are; or The Adventures of Caleb Williams*, I could die a happy and justified author. My own prose is verbose compared to his skill with capturing the world in word. Oh! How can such vitriol and scorn fall upon the great man for his marriage to the overly loud (to the conflicting circles of society) and overtly proud (to all circles especially her own) advocate for women's rights, Mary Wollstonecraft? The marriage lasted but the length of a pregnancy! Mary Wollstonecraft Godwin's. Oh! How loss in childbirth haunts poor Mary to this very day. Her mother, the radical feminist author of *A Vindication of the Rights of Woman*, died mere days after young Mary's birth, leaving the child motherless. And then poor Mary lost her own unchristened and nameless daughter mere days after she gave birth, leaving the mother childless.'

But madly, deeply in love I found myself to be. And Lord Byron chose mockery and scorn over brotherly support. For days I withstood his pointed slings and arrows of derision at the passion that fuelled by heart and fired my blood, for the lovely Mary. But this morning, I believed he had turned another leaf as the idiom says. As lovely Mary came walking up the towards the Villa, George (I refuse to honour his Lordship in this entry for he lacks in all civility) proffered a quick lesson in chivalry that I should offer my arm to lovely Mary lest she fall on the dew-slicked stones that had turned to frost. His devilish tongue painted me, in with Arthurian analogies, as Tristan and Mary as Iseult. Leaping off the wall, I slipped on the dew-slicked frozen stones (for of course I did) and strained my left ankle (for of course I did). My spirits were suddenly fallen because my leap was certainly pratfallen. George, the lovely Mary, and the rivalrous Percy guffawed as if I were nothing more than a *zanni* in *commedia dell'arte*. Why cannot I be for once cast as a lover instead of a typecast the clown?

Shelley etc. came down in the evening. Lovely Mary presented herself to Lord Byron and myself in our parlour. She honoured me by not looking down upon me in my hobbled, wobbled state; she smiled a polite smile and took her seat by the fire. In spite of my tumble that same morning, there was precious little we could accomplish given the oxymoronic summer we all five were encountering at the shore of Lake

Geneva. They were as hobbled by the rained-in-weather as I was hobbled by my strained ankle. The antsy sought an activity to occupy the evening for our occupation of the Villa Diodati proved to be more a captivity. Lord Byron began to talk of my play, to which the Shelley etc. agreed to disguss by play— future readers of a future publication, this is not a clerical error— I will speak nothing of my play here for it is nothing to talk about. They entreated me to give them a one-man reading of a scene and I obliged them, though I should not have. Laughter during a dramatic reading is demeaning. How would The Bard have reacted to laughter during the readthrough of *Titus Andronicus*? Now I understand the emotions of an actor standing upon the stage when the audience pelts them with rotten tomatoes and cabbages. They did not pelt me with rotten corn or onions but scorn and derision. How could have I have written in the months previous this line, "Tis thus the got-er'd idiot of the Alps.' How could I have been so prescient to foresee my own strained ankle while on holiday on the shore of Lake Geneva. The French astrologer Nostradamus holds no candle to Dr John William Polidori. Is this evening an oxymoron? Or am I simply a moron?

Mary Wollstonecraft Godwin's Journal

15 June. Lord Bryon's Doctor presented us a scene from a play he had written, in which he possessed no title. This brief little scene, which could have been briefer and could have been littler, contained within it an unfortunate line, unfortunate in its timing, unfortunate that it elicited in his friends some laugher. There is not-a-thing so memorable in the work that I can transcribe (or remember) of the scene with the notable exception of the unfortunate line: "Tis thus the goter'd idiot of the Alps.' The Doctor sat in a comfortable chair with his unfortunate and uncomfortable script drifting down, like the snow sleeting down the windows, to his bandaged foot. A foot had been bandaged, not due to a foolish slip on the frozen stones, but due to a foolish passion for me. However, he possesses foolish fancies of even more foolish polyamorous love between the five of us. As if Percy, George, Clair, or I would ever be so foolish. We each love whom we love and do not love those whom we do not love, as unfortunate as this is for the scorned. The Doctor may scorn at such words as honest as they are, but this is why he is, by the very definition of the verb and noun, the 'scorned'.

Lord Byron attempted to comfort the suddenly sullen-tempera-mented Doctor that 'worse playscripts were often submitted to Drury Lane.' Our laughter had been unfortunate. This is the beauty, and in

the Doctor's case the horror, of the expression. One does not intention-
ally laugh. An intentional laugh is the height of condescension or perchance even condemnation. A clown whether on the stage or the street
may intend to evoke laughter, but he has no control over the evocation
of that laugh. If the joke is not humorous, then no laughter will be
evoked. But counter to this, the dramatic line, written to evoke tears,
gasps, or shrieks, may just evoke laugher. Both of his imaginings are
the worst horror a playwright can experience. To reiterate: our laughter
was not our intention. The Doctor's line: ''Tis thus the goter'd idiot of
the Alps,' when sitting with a bandaged foot— as if goitered— caused
such uproarious laugher as to make the clown envious. But no words
of support could draw the Doctor out of his being 'worth nothing'.
While he may have felt worth nothing, as he repeated to himself, his
unfortunate line has been forever imprinted on my mind that I cannot
stop saying over and over again: ''Tis thus the goter'd idiot of the Alps'.
Should these journals of mine be published, the line will be imprinted
on the mind of my reader. Is this not the wish of the playwright? To
have written a line memorable enough to last for time immemorial?

Chapter Two
The Death-Bride[3]

Mary Wollstonecraft Godwin's Journal

16 June.— Lord Byron had, in his brief residency at the Villa Diodati, found a peculiar French translation of German ghost stories absentmindedly left on a miscellaneous table in the parlour by a previous guest. The book had been titled, tantalizingly, *Fantasmagoriana, ou Recueil d'histoires, d'apparitions, de spectres, reve-nans, fantômes.* Was the ghost of John Milton playing games with us by presenting a scandalous book in the presence of a cabal of creatives as a present?

Lord Byron selected the second of the volumes and chose the first story in the table of contents (a most suitable selection given we know nothing of these tales other than their titles). What would we find reading the stories this anthology? Apparitions of spectres? Obviously. Revenants? Certainly. Phantoms? One can only hope. The story Byron chose was titled *La Morte Fiancée* in French, *Die Todtenbraut* in the original German, and *The Death-Bride* in the King's English.

Lord Byron began the evening's narration, '*L'été étoit superbe; aussi, de mémoire d'homme, jamais on n'avoit ru tant de monde aux caux. Mais les salons de réunion avoient beau se remplir, la gaité ne s'y trouvoit pas. La noblesse se tenoit à part, le militaire en faisoit autant, et la bour- geoisie médisoit de tous les deux. Tant de réunions partielles devoient nécessaire-ment obstacle à une réunion générale. Les bals publics même ne produ-isoient pas plus de rapprochement parmi les personnes du beau monde, parce que le propriétaire des eaux y paroissoit chamarré de cordons, et que cet éclat, joint à la roîdeur des manières de la famille de ce seigneur, et au grand nombre de laquai, vêtus de riches livrées, qui les suivoient, forçoit la plupart des personnes présentes a se renfermer silencieusement dans les bornes fixées par la diversité des rangs.*' Four us were fluent in French so to need no translation, with the exception of the Doctor, poor thing, who was familiar *enough* to understand and enjoy. Though I saw his brow furrow with the struggle of his mind's eye to promptly translate as

---

3 From *Fantasmagoriana, ou Recueil d'histoires, d'apparitions, de spectres, revenans, fantômes,* published by F. Schoell in 1812. 'The Death-Bride' was written by Friedrich Laun, translated into English by Sarah Elizabeth Utterson in *Tales of the Dead,* published in 1813 by White, Cochrane and Co.

Bryon hastily read. But for you dear Reader of my journal, rest assured here is the translation as I remember the story:

'The summer had been uncommonly fine,' a strange beginning for a ghost story. Byron stopped to note our own has been uncommonly awful. We all hear-heared. Then he continued the story, 'and the baths crowded with company beyond all comparison: but still the public rooms were scarce ever filled, and never gay. The nobility and military associated only with those of their own rank, and the citizens contented themselves by slandering both parties. So many partial divisions necessarily proved an obstacle to a general and united assembly.'

'Certainly a true statement in any nation or age,' my Beloved observed.

'Even the public balls did not draw the beau-monde together, because the proprietor of the baths appeared there bedizened with insignia of knighthood; and this glitter, added to the stiff manners of this great man's family, and the tribe of lackeys in splendid liveries who constantly attended him, compelled the greater part of the company assembled, silently to observe the rules prescribed to them according to their different ranks.'

'As true in England as anywhere else,' my Beloved bemoaned and he was not alone.

'For these reasons the balls became gradually less numerously attended. Private parties were formed, in which it was endeavoured to preserve the charms that were daily diminishing in the public assemblies.

'One of these societies met generally twice a week in a room which at that time was usually unoccupied. There they supped, and afterwards enjoyed, either in a walk abroad, or remaining in the room, the charms of unrestrained conversation.

'The members of this society were already acquainted, at least by name; but an Italian marquis, who had lately joined their party, was unknown to them, and indeed to every one assembled at the baths.

'The title of Italian marquis appeared the more singular, as his name, according to the entry of it in the general list, seemed to denote him of Northern extraction, and was composed of so great a number of consonants, that no one could pronounce it without difficulty.'

'I wonder and ponder if we will be provided his name, or will it prove too difficult for the author to transcribe,' my Beloved said.

'His physiognomy and manners likewise presented many singularities. His long and wan visage, his black eyes, his imperious look, had so little of attraction in them, that every one would certainly have avoided him, had he not possessed a fund of entertaining stories, the relation of which proved an excellent antidote to ennui: the only drawback against

them was, that in general they required rather too great a share of credulity on the part of his auditors.

The party had one day just risen from table, and found themselves
but ill inclined for gaiety. They were still too much fatigued from the ball
of the preceding evening to enjoy the recreation of walking, although invited so to do by the bright light of the moon. They were even unable to
keep up any conversation; therefore it is not to be wondered at, that they
were more than usually anxious for the marquis to arrive.

' "Where can he be?" exclaimed the countess in an impatient tone.

' "Doubtless still at the faro-table, to the no small grief of the bankers," replied Florentine. "This very morning, he has occasioned the sudden departure of two of these gentlemen."

' "No great loss," answered another.

' "To us— ," replied Florentine; "but it is to the proprietor of the
baths, who only prohibited gambling, that it might be pursued with
greater avidity."

' "The marquis ought to abstain from such achievements," said the
chevalier with an air of mystery. "Gamblers are revengeful, and have
generally advantageous connections. If what is whispered be correct,
that the marquis is unfortunately implicated in political affairs— ."

' "But," demanded the countess, "what then has the marquis done to
the bankers of the gaming-table?"

' "Nothing; except that he betted on cards which almost invariably
won. And what renders it rather singular, he scarcely derived any advantage from it himself, for he always adhered to the weakest party. But
the other punters were not so scrupulous; for they charged their cards
in such a manner that the bank broke before the deal had gone round."

' "Bankers"? "Punters"? Is he playing *Baccarat Banque*?'

'Aye, my sweet Claire,' poor Polidori answers, 'it is a ruinously
French game. A blight and a stain upon the psyche.'

The countess was on the point of asking other questions, when the
marquis coming in changed the conversation.

' "Here you are at last!" exclaimed several persons at the same moment.

' "We have," said the countess, "been most anxious for your society;
and just on this day you have been longer than usual absent."

' "I have projected an important expedition; and it has succeeded to
my wishes. I hope by to-morrow there will not be a single gaming-table
left here. I have been from one gambling-room to another; and there are
not sufficient post-horses to carry off the ruined bankers."

' "And cannot you," asked the countess, "teach us your wonderful art
of always winning?"

'Ha! Has no one ever studied the mathematics on such games of gambling? It is the ruin of many a good man,' Polidori protested.

' "It would be a difficult task, my fair lady; and in order to do it, one must ensure a fortunate hand, for without that nothing could be done."

'Sensible man, this marquis, to divert their attention and fortunes away from such a future,' my Beloved observed.

' "Nay," replied the chevalier, laughing, "never did I see so fortunate an one as yours."

' "As you are still very young, my dear chevalier, you have many novelties to witness."

'Saying these words, the marquis threw on the chevalier so piercing a look that the latter cried: "Will you then cast my nativity?"

' "Provided that it is not done to-day," said the countess; "for who knows whether your future destiny will afford us so amusing a history as that which the marquis two days since promised we should enjoy?"

' "I did not exactly say amusing."

' "But at least full of extraordinary events: and we require some such, to draw us from the lethargy which has overwhelmed us all day."

' "Most willingly: but first I am anxious to learn whether any of you know aught of the surprising things related of the Death-Bride."

'Ah! Ho-ho!', my Beloved exclaimed, 'The titular character comes anon!'

'No one remembered to have heard speak of her.

'The marquis appeared anxious to add something more by way of preface; but the countess and the rest of the party so openly manifested their impatience, that the marquis began his narration as follows:—

' "I had for a long time projected a visit to the count Lieppa, at his estates in Bohemia. We had met each other in almost every country in Europe: attracted hither by the frivolity of youth to partake of every pleasure which presented itself, but led thither when years of discretion had rendered us more sedate and steady.— At length, in our more advanced age, we ardently desired, ere the close of life, once again to enjoy, by the charms of recollection, the moments of delight which we had passed together. For my part, I was anxious to see the castle of my friend, which was, according to his description, in an extremely romantic district. It was built some hundred years back by his ancestors; and their successors had preserved it with so much care, that it still maintained its imposing appearance, at the same time it afforded a comfortable abode. The count generally passed the greater part of the year at it with his family, and only returned to the capital at the approach of winter. Being well acquainted with his movements, I did not think it needful to announce my visit; and I arrived at the castle one evening precisely at the time when I knew he would be there; and as I approached it, could not but admire the variety and beauty of the scenery which surrounded it.

' "The hearty welcome which I received could not, however, entirely conceal from my observation the secret grief depicted on the countenances of the count, his wife, and their daughter, the lovely Ida. In a short time, I discovered that they still mourned the loss of Ida's twin-sister, who had died about a year before. Ida and Hildegarde resembled each other so much, that they were only to be distinguished from each other by a slight mark of a strawberry visible on Hildegarde's neck. Her room, and every thing in it, was left precisely in the same state as when she was alive, and the family were in the habit of visiting it whenever they wished to indulge the sad satisfaction of meditating on the loss of this beloved child. The two sisters had but one heart, one mind: and the parents could not but apprehend that their separation would be but of short duration; they dreaded lest Ida should also be taken from them.' I cast my eyes down to my little William sleeping in his bassinet. My mind flashed back to my poor little nameless daughter lost to me. The very thought of losing an elder child proved to be as painful, if not more, than losing a mere babe in her crib, a child you loved but had yet to truly bond with.

' "I did everything in my power to amuse this excellent family, by entertaining them with laughable anecdotes of my younger days, and by directing their thoughts to less melancholy subjects than that which now wholly occupied them. I had the satisfaction of discovering that my efforts were not ineffectual. Sometimes we walked in the canton round the castle, which was decked with all the beauties of summer; at other times we took a survey of the different apartments of the castle, and were astonished at their wonderful state of preservation, whilst we amused ourselves by talking over the actions of the past generation, whose portraits hung in a long gallery.

' "One evening the count had been speaking to me in confidence, on the subject of his future plans: among other subjects he expressed his anxiety, that Ida (who had already, though only in her sixteenth year, refused several offers) should be happily married; when suddenly the gardener, quite out of breath, came to tell us he had seen the ghost (as he believed, the old chaplain belonging to the castle), who had appeared a century back. Several of the servants followed the gardener, and their pallid countenances confirmed the alarming tidings he had brought.

'A-ha!' my Beloved interrupted again, 'finally a ghost for this ghost story! I have experienced far too many words and far too few frights for a book threateningly called *Fantasmagoriana.*'

'Be patient, my Beloved,' I said, "Surely we will meet the titular "Death-Bride" as soon as the bathers do. It is the marquis' ghost story after all.'

'I'd have drowned in waters of the bathes waiting for the "Death-Bride' to appear,' my Beloved countered.

' "I believe you will shortly be afraid of your own shadow,' said the count to them. He then sent them off, desiring them not again to trouble him with the like fooleries.

' "It is really terrible,' said he to me, 'to see to what lengths superstition will carry persons of that rank of life; and it is impossible wholly to undeceive them. From one generation to another an absurd report has from time to time been spread abroad, of an old chaplain's ghost wandering in the environs of the castle; and that he says mass in the chapel, with other idle stories of a similar nature. This report has greatly died away since I came into possession of the castle; but it now appears to me, it will never be altogether forgotten.'

'I've always considered it queer,' the poor doctor said, 'that others in these ghost stories never tend to believe the superstitiously enchanted servants when they claim to have seen a ghost. Why must the practically arrogant nobility, in that moment, see with their own eyes the spectre and not heed the word of men who serve them well?'

'Would you believe me, Doctor,' my dearest sister said, 'if I claimed to see a spectre walking the halls of the Villa Diodati. Would you dismiss my observations as appearing when the lightning flashes and vanishing when the thunder crashes? Would you believe me if you hadn't seen its form. Would you disbelieve my account when you hadn't heard its chains and its moans. My dear Doctor, what if I was so afraid as to not leave my apartment out of perilous fear.'

'Claire,' Polidori cooed, 'I would stalk these very halls with you to find the spectre and drive it away from ever concerning you again.' He winked quickly in her direction so that I would not see, but I saw, and I kicked his chair. The doctor coughed and straightened his hair. He then turned his attention back to our little Lord who was not amused with the doctor's enthused flirtations. Claire, my sweet sister, was flattered by the doctor's flirtation solely because the object of her affection has continuously over the course of the dismal summer objected to her affections.

Lord Byron, irritated at these constant interrupts to his telling of this ghost story, huffed one long exhale that could have been mistaken for a rumbling thunderclap. Once he was satisfied with our silence, only then would he continue. ' "At this moment the duke de Marino was announced. The count did not recollect ever having heard of him.

' "I told him that I was tolerably well acquainted with his family; and that I had lately been present, in Venice, at the betrothing of a young man of that name.

' "The very same young man came in while I was speaking. I should have felt very glad at seeing him, had I not perceived that my presence caused him evident uneasiness.

' "'Ah,' said he in a tolerably gay tone, after the customary forms of politeness had passed between us; 'the finding you here, my dear marquis, explains to me an occurrence, which with shame I own caused me a sensation of fear. To my no small surprise, they knew my name in the adjacent district; and as I came up the hill which leads to the castle, I heard it pronounced three times in a voice wholly unknown to me: and in a still more audible tone this strange voice bade me welcome. I now, however, conclude it was yours.'

' "I assured him, (and with truth,) that till his name was announced the minute before, I was ignorant of his arrival, and that none of my servants knew him; for that the valet who accompanied me into Italy was not now with me.

' "'And above all,' added I, 'it would be impossible to discover any equipage, however well known to one, in so dark an evening.'

' "'That is what astonishes me,' exclaimed the duke, a little amazed.

' "The incredulous count very politely added, 'that the voice which had told the duke he was welcome, had at least expressed the sentiments of all the family.'

My Beloved said a single word, 'Curious!'

' "Marino, ere he said a word relative to the motive of his visit, asked a private audience of me; and confided in me, by telling me that he was come with the intention of obtaining the lovely Ida's hand; and that if he was able to procure her consent, he should demand her of her father.

' "'The countess Apollonia, your bride elect, is then no longer living?' asked I.

' "'We will talk on that subject hereafter,' answered he.

' "The deep sigh which accompanied these words led me to conclude that Apollonia had been guilty of infidelity or some other crime towards the duke; and consequently I thought that I ought to abstain from any further questions, which appeared to rend his heart, already so sensibly wounded.

' "Yet, as he begged me to become his mediator with the count, in order to obtain from him his consent to the match, I painted in glowing colours the danger of an alliance, which he had no other motive for contracting, than the wish to obliterate the remembrance of a dearly, and without doubt, still more tenderly, beloved object. But he assured me that he was far from thinking of the lovely Ida from so blameable a motive, and that he should be the happiest of men if she but proved propitious to his wishes.

' "His expressive and penetrating tone of voice, while he said this, lulled the uneasiness that I was beginning to feel; and I promised him I would prepare the count Lieppa to listen to his entreaties, and would give him the necessary information relative to the fortune and family of Marino. But I declared to him at the same time, that I should by no means hurry the conclusion of the affair by my advice, as I was not in the habit of taking upon myself so great a charge as the uncertain issue of a marriage.

' "The duke signified his satisfaction at what I said, and made me give (what then appeared to me of no consequence) a promise, that I would not make mention of the former marriage he was on the point of contracting, as it would necessarily bring on a train of unpleasant explanations.

' "The duke's views succeeded with a promptitude beyond his most sanguine hopes. His well-proportioned form and sparkling eyes smoothed the paths of love, and introduced him to the heart of Ida. His agreeable conversation promised to the mother an amiable son-in-law; and the knowledge in rural economy, which he evinced as occasions offered, made the count hope for an useful helpmate in his usual occupations; for since the first day of the duke's arrival he had been prevented from pursuing them.

' "Marino followed up these advantages with great ardour; and I was one evening much surprised by the intelligence of his being betrothed, as I did not dream of matters drawing so near a conclusion. They spoke at table of some bridal preparations of which I had made mention just before the duke's arrival at the castle; and the countess asked me whether that young Marino was a near relation of the one who was that very day betrothed to her daughter.'

' "'Near enough,' I answered, recollecting my promise.— Marino looked at me with an air of embarrassment.

' "'But, my dear duke,' continued I, 'tell me who mentioned the amiable Ida to you; or was it a portrait, or what else, which caused you to think of looking for a beauty, the selection of whom does so much honour to your taste, in this remote corner; for, if I am not mistaken, you said but yesterday that you had purposed travelling about for another six months; when all at once (I believe while in Paris) you changed your plan, and projected a journey wholly and solely to see the charming Ida?'

' "'Yes, it was at Paris,' replied the duke; 'you are very rightly informed. I went there to see and admire the superb gallery of pictures at the Museum; but I had scarcely entered it, when my eyes turned from the inanimate beauties, and were riveted on a lady whose incomparable features were heightened by an air of melancholy. With fear and trembling I approached her, and only ventured to follow without speaking to her. I still followed her after she quitted the gallery; and I drew her servant aside to learn the name of his mistress. He told it me: but when I expressed a wish to become acquainted with the father of this beauty, he said that was next to impossible while at Paris, as the family were on the point of quitting that city; nay, of quitting France altogether.

' "'Possibly, however,' said I, 'some opportunity may present itself.' And I looked everywhere for the lady: but she, probably imagining that her servant was following her closely, had continued to walk on, and was entirely out of sight. While I was looking around for her, the servant had likewise vanished from my view.'

' "'Who was this beautiful lady?' asked Ida, in a tone of astonishment.

' "'What! you really did not then perceive me in the gallery?'

' "'Me!'— — 'My daughter— — !' exclaimed at the same moment Ida and her parents.

' "'Yes, you yourself, mademoiselle. The servant, whom fortunately for me you left at Paris, and whom I met the same evening unexpectedly, as my guardian angel, informed me of all; so that after a short rest at home, I was able to come straight hither.'

' "'What a fable!' said the count to his daughter, who was mute with astonishment.

' "'Ida,' he added, turning to me, 'has never yet been out of her native country; and for myself, I have not been in Paris these seventeen years.'

' "The duke looked at the count and his daughter with similar marks of astonishment visible in their countenances; and conversation would have been entirely at an end, if I had not taken care to introduce other topics: but I had it nearly all to myself.

' "The repast was no sooner over, than the count took the duke into the recess of a window; and although I was at a considerable distance, and appeared wholly to fix my attention on a new chandelier, I overheard all their conversation.

' "'What motive,' demanded the count with a serious and dissatisfied air, 'could have induced you to invent that singular scene in the gallery of the Museum at Paris? for according to my judgment, it could in no way benefit you. Since you are anxious to conceal the cause which brought you to ask my daughter in marriage, at least you might have plainly said as much; and though possibly you might have felt repugnance at making such a declaration, there were a thousand ways of framing your answer, without its being needful thus to offend probability.'

'I have it. I have it,' Claire said, 'I know who the woman in the museum is!' As did we all, for the foreshadowing cast no shadow at all over the story. The title of the story and the twin-sisters cliché all but clinched the outcome of this plot. I'm sure the four of us writers prayed for a twist in this very predictable plot.

' "'Monsieur le comte,' replied the duke much piqued; 'I held my peace at table, thinking that possibly you had reasons for wishing to keep secret your and your daughter's journey to Paris. I was silent merely from motives of discretion; but the singularity of your reproaches compels me to maintain what I have said; and, notwithstanding your reluctance to believe the truth, to declare before all the world, that the capital of France was the spot where I first saw your daughter Ida.'

' "'But what if I prove to you, not only by the witness of my servants, but also by that of all my tenants, that my daughter has never quitted her native place?'—

' "'I shall still believe the evidence of my own eyes and ears, which have as great authority over me.'

' "'What you say is really enigmatical,' answered the count in a graver tone: 'your serious manner convinces me you have been the dupe of some illusion; and that you have seen some other person, whom you have taken for my daughter. Excuse me, therefore, for having taken up the thing so warmly.'

' "'Another person! What then, I not only mistook another person for your daughter; but the very servant of whom I made mention, and who gave me so exact a description of this castle, was, according to what you say, some other person!'

' "'My dear Marino, that servant was some cheat who knew this castle, and who, God only knows for what motive, spoke to you of my daughter as resembling the lady.'

' "''Tis certainly no wish of mine to contradict you; but Ida's features are precisely the same as those which made so deep an impression on me at Paris, and which my imagination has preserved with such scrupulous fidelity.'

' "The count shook his head; and Marino continued:—

' "'What is still more— (but pray pardon me for mentioning a little particularity, which nothing short of necessity would have drawn from me)— while in the gallery, I was standing behind the lady, and the handkerchief that covered her neck was a little disarranged, which occasioned me distinctly to perceive the mark of a small strawberry.'

' "'Another strange mystery!' exclaimed the count, turning pale: 'it appears you are determined to make me believe wonderful stories.'

' "'I have only one question to ask:— Has Ida such a mark on her neck?'

' "'No, monsieur,' replied the count, looking steadfastly at Marino.

' "'No!' exclaimed the latter, in the utmost astonishment.

' "'No, I tell you: but Ida's twin-sister, who resembled her in the most surprising manner, had the mark you mention on her neck, and a year since carried it with her into the grave.'

' "'And yet 'tis only within the last few months that I saw this person in Paris!'

' "At this moment the countess and Ida, who had kept aside, a prey to uneasiness, not knowing what to think of the conversation, which appeared of so very important a nature, approached; but the count in a commanding tone ordered them to retire immediately. He then led the duke entirely away into a retired corner of the window, and continued the conversation in so low a voice that I could hear nothing further.

' "My astonishment was extreme when, that very same evening, the count gave orders to have Hildegarde's tomb opened in his presence: but he beforehand related briefly what I have just told you, and proposed my assisting the duke and him in opening the grave. The duke excused himself, by saying that the very idea made him tremble with horror; for he could not overcome, especially at night, his fear of a corpse.

' "The count begged he would not mention the gallery scene to any one; and above all, to spare the extreme sensibility of the affianced bride from a recital of the conversation they had just had, even if she should request to be informed of it.

' "In the mean time the sexton arrived with his lantern. The count and I followed him.

' "'It is morally impossible,' said the count to me, as we walked together, 'that any trick can have been played respecting my daughter's death: the circumstances attendant thereon are but too well known to me. You may readily believe also, that the affection we bore our poor girl would prevent our running any risk of burying her too soon: but suppose even the possibility of that, and that the tomb had been opened by some avaricious persons, who found, on opening the coffin, that the body became re-animated; no one can believe for a moment that my daughter would not have instantly returned to her parents, who doted on her, rather than have fled to a distant country. This last circumstance puts the matter beyond doubt: for even should it be admitted as a truth, that she was carried by force to some distant part of the world, she would have found a thousand ways of returning. My eyes are, however, about to be convinced, that the sacred remains of my Hildegarde really repose in the grave.

' "'To convince myself!' cried he again, in a tone of voice so melancholy yet loud that the sexton turned his head.

' "This movement rendered the count more circumspect; and he continued in a lower tone of voice:

' "'How should I for a moment believe it possible that the slightest trace of my daughter's features should be still in existence, or that the destructive hand of time should have spared her beauty? Let us return, marquis; for who could tell, even were I to see the skeleton, that I should know it from that of an entire stranger, whom they may have placed in the tomb to fill her place?'

' "He was even about to give orders not to open the door of the chapel, (at which we were just arrived,) when I represented to him, that were I in his place I should have found it extremely difficult to determine on such a measure; but that having gone thus far, it was requisite to complete the task, by examining whether some of the jewels buried with Hildegarde's corpse were not wanting. I added, that judging by a number of well-known facts, all bodies were not destroyed equally soon.

' "My representations had the desired effect: the count squeezed my hand; and we followed the sexton, who, by his pallid countenance and trembling limbs, evidently shewed that he was unaccustomed to nocturnal employments of this nature.

' "I know not whether any of this present company were ever in a chapel at midnight, before the iron doors of a vault, about to examine the succession of leaden coffins enclosing the remains of an illustrious family. Certain it is, that at such a moment the noise of bolts and bars produces such a remarkable sensation, that one is led to dread the sound of the door grating on its hinges; and when the vault is opened, one cannot help hesitating for an instant to enter it.

'Oh, the sound of those doors opening,' Claire said, 'are sending bolts of lightning up my spine.'

' "The count was evidently seized with these sensations of terror, which I discovered by a stifled sigh; but he concealed his feelings: notwithstanding, I remarked that he dared not trust himself to look on any other coffin than the one containing his daughter's remains. He opened it himself.

' "'Did I not say so?' cried he, seeing that the features of the corpse bore a perfect resemblance to those of Ida. I was obliged to prevent the count, who was seized with astonishment, from kissing the forehead of the inanimate body.

' "'Do not,' I added, 'disturb the peace of those who repose in death.' And I used my utmost efforts to withdraw the count immediately from this dismal abode.

'So is she merely a ghost in this ghost story and not a revenant stolen from her grave?' Claire inquired.

'Naïve little girl,' Polidori said, 'this is a collection of ghost stories.'

'Oh, no little doctor,' I corrected him in defence of my dear sister. Having punctuated the *little*, Polidori's expression turned pained. 'Have you forgotten or are you ignorant of the subtitle to these volumes, "*Recueil d'histoires, d'apparitions, de spectres, revenans, fantômes, etc.*". Revenants, *little* doctor. Clearly Claire would be correct in assuming Ida's sister was a revenant.'

'Except for the fact,' Polidori countered, 'the body is still interred in the mausoleum! A revenant by its very definition is a reanimated corpse. Nothing in science can reanimate a corpse. This is left to the superstitions of the peasantry of the rural countryside. They cage gravesites and place blades over the necks of the corpse, lest it should arise in the night to stalk the bereaved families of the recently deceased. As a man of science, there is no cause to say that I have any fear of the reanimation of a corpse. For it is an impossibility, my sweet Mary. Nothing in the history of natural philosophy, the sciences, gives me cause to fear any corpse! And yes, by the subtitle, we can expect this poor girl to be a revenant, but having seen the corpse, she must be a ghost.'

'Can we,' Lord Byron said frustrated, 'Can we return to our ghost story?' To which we all acquiesced.

' "On our return to the castle, we found those persons whom we had left there, in an anxious state of suspense. The two ladies had closely questioned the duke on what had passed; and would not admit as a valid excuse, the promise he had made of secrecy. They entreated us also, but in vain, to satisfy their curiosity.

' "They succeeded better the following day with the sexton, whom they sent for privately, and who told them all he knew: but it only tended to excite their anxious wish to learn the subject of the conversation which had occasioned this nocturnal visit to the sepulchral vault.

' "As for myself, I dreamt the whole of the following night of the apparition Marino had seen at Paris; I conjectured many things which I did not think fit to communicate to the count, because he absolutely questioned the connection of a superior world with ours. At this juncture of affairs, I with pleasure saw that this singular circumstance, if not entirely forgotten, was at least but rarely and slightly mentioned.

' "But I now began to find another cause for anxious solicitude. The duke constantly persisted in refusing to explain himself on the subject of his previous engagement, even when we were alone: and the embarrassment he could not conceal, whenever I made mention of the good qualities that I believed his intended to have possessed, as well as several other little singularities, led me to conclude that Marino's attachment for Apollonia had been first shaken at the picture gallery, at sight of the lovely incognita; and that Apollonia had been forsaken, owing to his yielding to temptations; and that doubtless she could never have been guilty of breaking off an alliance so solemnly contracted.

'Foreseeing from this that the charming Ida could never hope to find much happiness in an union with Marino, and knowing that the wedding-day was nigh at hand, I resolved to unmask the perfidious deceiver as quickly as possible, and to make him repent his infidelity. An excellent occasion presented itself one day for me to accomplish my designs. Having finished supper, we were still sitting at table; and some one said that iniquity is frequently punished in this world: upon which I observed, that I myself had witnessed striking proofs of the truth of this remark;— when Ida and her mother entreated me to name one of these examples.

' "Under these circumstances, ladies,' answered I, 'permit me to relate a history to you, which, according to my opinion, will particularly interest you.'

' "Us!' they both exclaimed. At the same time I fixed my eyes on the duke, who for several days past had evidently distrusted me; and I saw that his conscience had rendered him pale.

' "That at least is my opinion,' replied I: 'But, my dear count, will you pardon me, if the supernatural is sometimes interwoven with my narration?'

' "Very willingly,' answered he smiling: 'and I will content myself with expressing my surprise at so many things of this sort having happened to you, as I have never experienced any of them myself.'

' "I plainly perceived that the duke made signs of approval at what he said: but I took no notice of it, and answered the count by saying,

' "That all the world have not probably the use of their eyes.

' "That may be,' replied he, still smiling.

' "But,' said I to him in a low and expressive voice, 'think you an uncorrupted body in the vault is a common phænomenon?'

' "He appeared staggered: and I thus continued in an under tone of voice:—

' "For that matter, 'tis very possible to account for it naturally, and therefore it would be useless to contest the subject with you.'

' "We are wandering from the point,' said the countess a little angrily; and she made me a sign to begin, which I accordingly did, in the following words:—

' "The scene of my anecdote lies in Venice.'

' "I possibly then may know something of it,' cried the duke, who entertained some suspicions.

' "'Possibly so,' replied I; 'but there were reasons for keeping the event secret: it happened somewhere about eighteen months since, at the period you first set out on your travels.

' "The son of an extremely wealthy nobleman, whom I shall designate by the name of Filippo, being attracted to Leghorn by the affairs consequent on his succession to an inheritance, had won the heart of an amiable and lovely girl, called Clara. He promised her, as well as her parents, that ere his return to Venice he would come back and marry her. The moment for his departure was preceded by certain ceremonies, which in their termination were terrible: for after the two lovers had exhausted every protestation of reciprocal affection, Filippo invoked the aid of the spirit of vengeance, in case of infidelity: they prayed even that whichever of the lovers should prove faithful might not be permitted to repose quietly in the grave, but should haunt the perjured one, and force the inconstant party to come amongst the dead, and to share in the grave those sentiments which on earth had been forgotten.'"

'This is a quite queerly constructed story,' said I, 'Lord Byron is telling us a story that begins with a story being told to a collection of bathers in a bathhouse and now continues with another story being told to the count and his family within the confines of the first story. This is a confounding Russian nesting doll! Inverted commas within inverted commas within inverted commas. The typesetter of this tale must have been driven mad!' My Beloved, Polidori, and Claire all hear-heared, but our little Lord continued reading this story unabated, as if he did not even see the unnatural levels of nesting as he read. But I'll see them in my nightmares!

' "The parents, who were seated by them at table, remembered their youthful days, and permitted the overheated and romantic imagination of the young people to take its free course. The lovers finished by making punctures in their arms, and letting their blood run into a glass filled with white champaigne.

' " "Our souls shall be inseparable as our blood!" exclaimed Filippo; and drinking half the contents of the glass, he gave the rest to Clara.

' "At this moment the duke experienced a violent degree of agitation, and from time to time darted such menacing looks at me, that I was led to conclude, that in his adventure some scene of a similar nature had taken place. I can however affirm, that I related the details respecting Filippo's departure, as they were represented in a letter written by the mother of Clara.

' "Who," continued I, "after so many demonstrations of such a violent passion, could have expected the denouement? Filippo's return to Venice happened precisely at the period at which a young beauty, hitherto educated in a distant convent, made her first appearance in the great world: she on a sudden exhibited herself as an angel whom a cloud had till then concealed, and excited universal admiration. Filippo's parents had heard frequent mention of Clara, and of the projected alliance between her and their son; but they thought that this alliance was like many others, contracted one day without the parties knowing why, and broken off the next with equal want of thought; and influenced by this idea, they presented their son to the parents of Camilla, (which was the name of the young beauty,) whose family were of the highest rank.

' "They represented to Filippo the great advantages he would obtain by an alliance with her. The Carnival happening just at this period completed the business, by affording him so many favourable opportunities of being with Camilla; and in the end, the remembrance of Leghorn held but very little place in his mind. His letters became colder and colder each succeeding day; and on Clara expressing how sensibly she felt the change, he ceased writing to her altogether, and did every thing in his power to hasten his union with Camilla, who was, without compare, much the handsomer and more wealthy. The agonies poor Clara endured were manifest in her illegible writing, and by the tears which were but too evidently shed over her letters: but neither the one nor the other had any more influence over the fickle heart of Filippo, than the prayers of the unfortunate girl. Even the menace of coming, according to their solemn agreement, from the tomb to haunt him, and carry him with her to that grave which threatened so soon to enclose her, had but little effect on his mind, which was entirely engrossed by the idea of the happiness he should enjoy in the arms of Camilla.

' "The father of the latter (who was my intimate friend) invited me before-hand to the wedding. And although numerous affairs detained him that summer in the city, so that he could not as usual enjoy the pleasures of the country, yet we sometimes went to his pretty villa, situated on the banks of the Brenta; where his daughter's marriage was to be celebrated with all possible splendour.

' "A particular circumstance, however, occasioned the ceremony to be deferred for some weeks. The parents of Camilla having been very happy in their own union, were anxious that the same priest who married them, should pronounce the nuptial benediction on their daughter. This priest, who, notwithstanding his great age, had the appearance of vigorous health, was seized with a slow fever which confined him to his bed: however, in time it abated, he became gradually better and better, and the wedding-day was at length fixed. But, as if some secret power was at work to prevent this union, the worthy priest was, on the very day destined for the celebration of their marriage, seized with a feverish shivering of so alarming a nature, that he dared not stir out of the house, and he strongly advised the young couple to select another priest to marry them.

' "The parents still persisted in their design of the nuptial benediction being given to their children by the respectable old man who had married them.— They would have certainly spared themselves a great deal of grief, if they had never swerved from their determination.— Very grand preparations had been made in honour of the day; and as they could no longer be deferred, it was decided that they should consider it as a ceremony of solemn affiance. At noon the bargemen attired in their splendid garb awaited the company's arrival on the banks of the canal: their joyous song was soon distinguished, while conducting to the villa, now decorated with flowers, the numerous gondolas containing parties of the best company.

' "During the dinner, which lasted till evening, the betrothed couple exchanged rings. At the very moment of their so doing, a piercing shriek was heard, which struck terror into the breasts of all the company, and absolutely struck Filippo with horror. Every one ran to the windows: for although it was becoming dark, each object was visible; but no one was to be seen."

' "Stop an instant," said the duke to me, with a fierce smile— His countenance, which had frequently changed colour during the recital, evinced strong marks of the torments of a wicked conscience. "I am also acquainted with that story, of a voice being heard in the air; it is borrowed from the 'Memoirs of Mademoiselle Clairon;' a deceased lover tormented her in this completely original manner. The shriek in her case was followed by a clapping of hands: I hope, *monsieur le marquis*, that you will not omit that particular in your story."

' "And why," replied I, "should you imagine that nothing of a similar nature could occur to any one besides that actress? Your incredulity appears to me so much the more extraordinary, as it seems to rest on facts which may lay claim to belief."

' "The countess made me a sign to continue; and I pursued my narrative as follows:

' "A short time after they had heard this inexplicable shriek, I begged Camilla, facing whom I was sitting, to permit me to look at her ring once more, the exquisite workmanship of which had already been much admired. But it was not on her finger: a general search was made, but not the slightest trace of the ring could be discovered. The company even rose from their seats to look for it, but all in vain.

' "Meanwhile, the time for the evening's amusements approached: fire-works were exhibited on the Brenta preceding the ball; the company were masked and got into the gondolas; but nothing was so striking as the silence which reigned during this fête; no one seemed inclined to open their mouth; and scarcely was heard a faint exclamation of Bravo, at sight of the fire-works.

' "The ball was one of the most brilliant I ever witnessed: the precious stones and jewels with which the ladies of the party were covered, reflected the lights in the chandeliers with redoubled lustre. The most splendidly attired of the whole was Camilla. Her father, who was fond of pomp, rejoiced in the idea that no one in the assembly was equal to his daughter in splendour or beauty.

' "Possibly to satisfy himself of this fact, he made a tour of the room; and returned loudly expressing his surprise, at having perceived on another lady precisely the same jewels which adorned Camilla. He was even weak enough to express a slight degree of chagrin. However, he consoled himself with the idea, that a bouquet of diamonds which was destined for Camilla to wear at supper, would alone in value be greater than all she then had on.

' "But as they were on the point of sitting down to table, and the anxious father again threw a look around him, he discovered that the same lady had also a bouquet which appeared to the full as valuable as Camilla's.

' "My friend's curiosity could no longer be restrained; he approached, and asked whether it would be too great a liberty to learn the name of the fair mask? But to his great surprise, the lady shook her head, and turned away from him.

' "At the same instant the steward came in, to ask whether since dinner there had been any addition to the party, as the covers were not sufficient.

' "His master answered, with rather a dissatisfied air, that there were only the same number, and accused his servants of negligence; but the steward still persisted in what he had said.

' "An additional cover was placed: the master counted them himself, and discovered that there really was one more in number than he had invited. As he had recently, on account of some inconsiderate expressions, had a dispute with government, he was apprehensive that some spy had contrived to slip in with the company: but as he had no reason to believe, that on such a day as that, any thing of a suspicious nature would be uttered, he resolved, in order to be satisfied respecting so indiscreet a procedure as the introduction of such a person in a family fête, to beg every one present to unmask; but in order to avoid the inconvenience likely to arise from such a request, he determined not to propose it till the very last thing.

' "'Every one present expressed their surprise at the luxuries and delicacies of the table, for it far surpassed every thing of the sort seen in that country, especially with respect to the wines. Still, however, the father of Camilla was not satisfied, and loudly lamented that an accident had happened to his capital red champaigne, which prevented his being able to offer his guests a single glass of it.

' "'The company seemed anxious to become gay, for the whole of the day nothing like gaiety had been visible among them; but no one around where I sat, partook of this inclination, for curiosity alone appeared to occupy their whole attention. I was sitting near the lady who was so splendidly attired; and I remarked that she neither ate nor drank any thing; that she neither addressed nor answered a word to her neighbours, and that she appeared to have her eyes constantly fixed on the affianced couple.

' "'The rumour of this singularity gradually spread round the room, and again disturbed the mirth which had become pretty general. Each whispered to the other a thousand conjectures on this mysterious personage. But the general opinion was, that some unhappy passion for Filippo was the cause of this extaordinary conduct. Those sitting next the unknown, were the first to rise from table, in order to find more cheerful associates, and their places were filled by others who hoped to discover some acquaintance in this silent lady, and obtain from her a more welcome reception; but their hopes were equally futile.

' "'At the time the champaigne was handed round, Filippo also brought a chair and sat by the unknown. She then became somewhat more animated, and turned towards Filippo, which was more than she had done to any one else; and she offered him her glass, as if wishing him to drink out of it.

' "'A violent trembling seized Filippo, when she looked at him steadfastly.

' "" 'The wine is red!" cried he, holding up the glass; "I thought there had been no red champaigne."

' "" 'Red!" said the father of Camilla, with an air of extreme surprise, approaching him from curiosity.

' "" 'Look at the lady's glass," replied Filippo.

' "" 'The wine in it is as white as all the rest," answered Camilla's father; and he called all present to witness it. They every one unanimously declared that the wine was white.

' "'Filippo drank it not, but quitted his seat; for a second look from his neighbour had caused him extreme agitation. He took the father of Camilla aside, and whispered something to him. The latter returned to the company, saying,

' "" "Ladies and gentlemen, I entreat you, for reasons which I will tell you presently, instantly to unmask."

' "'As in this request he but expressed in a degree the general wish, every one's mask was off as quick as thought, and each face uncovered, excepting that of the silent lady, on whom every look was fixed, and whose face they were the most anxious to see.

' "" "You alone keep on your mask," said Camilla's father to her, after a short silence: "May I hope you will also remove yours?"

' "'She obstinately persisted in her determination of remaining unknown.

' "'This strange conduct affected the father of Camilla the more sensibly, as he recognised in the others all those whom he had invited to the fête, and found beyond doubt that the mute lady was the one exceeding the number invited. He was, however, unwilling to force her to unmask; because the uncommon splendour of her dress did not permit him any longer to harbour the idea that this additional guest was a spy; and thinking her also a person of distinction, he did not wish to be deficient in good manners. He thought possibly she might be some friend of the family, who, not residing at Venice, but finding on her arrival in that city that he was to give this fête, had conceived this innocent frolic.

' "'It was thought right, however, at all events to obtain all the information that could be gained from the servants: but none of them knew any thing of this lady; there were no servants of hers there; and those belonging to Camilla's father did not recollect having seen any who appeared to appertain to her.

' "'What rendered this circumstance doubly strange was, that, as I before mentioned, this lady only put the magnificent bouquet into her bosom the instant previous to her sitting down to supper.

' "'The whispering, which had generally usurped the place of all conversation, gained each moment more and more ascendancy; when on a sudden the masked lady arose, and walking towards the door, beckoned Filippo to follow her; but Camilla hindered him from obeying her signal, for she had a long time observed with what fixed attention the mysterious lady looked at her intended husband; and she had also remarked, that the latter had quitted the stranger in violent agitation; and from all this she apprehended that love had caused him to be guilty of some folly or other. The master of the house, turning a deaf ear to all his daughter's remonstrances, and a prey to the most terrible fears, followed the unknown (at a distance, it is true); but she was no sooner out of the room than he returned. At this moment, the shriek which they had heard at noon was repeated, but seemed louder from the silence of night, and communicated anew affright to all present. By the time the father of

Camilla had returned from the first movement which his fear had occasioned him to make, the unknown was no where to be found.

' "The servants in waiting outside the house had no knowledge whatever of the masked lady. In every direction around there were crowds of persons; the river was lined with gondolas; and yet not an individual among them had seen the mysterious female.

' "All these circumstances had occasioned so much uneasiness to the whole party, that every one was anxious to return home; and the master of the house was obliged to permit the departure of the gondolas much earlier than he had intended.

' "The return home was, as might naturally be expected, very melancholy.

' "On the following day the betrothed couple were, however, pretty composed. Filippo had even adopted Camilla's idea of the unknown being some one whom love had deprived of reason; and as for the horrible shriek twice repeated, they were willing to attribute it to some people who were diverting themselves; and they decided, that inattention on the part of the servants was the sole cause of the unknown absenting herself without being perceived; and they even at last persuaded themselves, that the sudden disappearance of the ring, which they had not been able to find, was owing to the malice of some one of the servants who had pilfered it.

' "In a word, they banished every thing that could tend to weaken these explanations; and only one thing remained to harass them. The old priest, who was to bestow on them the nuptial benediction, had yielded up his last breath; and the friendship which had so intimately subsisted between him and the parents of Camilla, did not permit them in decency to think of marriage and amusements the week following his death.

' "The day this venerable priest was buried, Filippo's gaiety received a severe shock; for he learned, in a letter from Clara's mother, the death of that lovely girl. Sinking under the grief occasioned her by the infidelity of the man she had never ceased to love, she died: but to her latest hour she declared she should never rest quietly in her grave, until the perjured man had fulfilled the promise he had made to her."'

'He broke his engagement with Clara?' Claire said. 'The rogue. The scoundrel. The thief.'

' "This circumstance produced a stronger effect on him than all the imprecations of the unhappy mother; for he recollected that the first shriek (the cause of which they had never been able to ascertain) was heard at the precise moment of Clara's death; which convinced him that the unknown mask could only have been the spirit of Clara.

' "This idea deprived him at intervals of his senses.

' "He constantly carried this letter about him; and with an air of wandering would sometimes draw it from his pocket, in order to reconsider it attentively: even Camilla's presence did not deter him.

' "As it was natural to conclude this letter contained the cause of the extraordinary change which had taken place in Filippo, she one day gladly seized the opportunity of reading it, when in one of his absent fits he let it fall from his hands.

' "Filippo, struck by the death-like paleness and faintness which overcame Camilla, as she returned him the letter, knew instantly that she had read it. In the deepest affliction he threw himself at her feet, and conjured her to tell him how he must act.

' " "Love me with greater constancy than you did her,"— replied Camilla mournfully.

' "With transport he promised to do so. But his agitation became greater and greater, and increased to a most extraordinary pitch the morning of the day fixed for the wedding. As he was going to the house of Camilla's father before it became dark, (from whence he was to take his bride at dawn of day to the church, according to the custom of the country,) he fancied he saw Clara's spirit walking constantly at his side.

' "Never was seen a couple about to receive the nuptial benediction, with so mournful an aspect. I accompanied the parents of Camilla, who had requested me to be a witness: and the sequel has made an indelible impression on my mind of the events of that dismal morning.

' "We were proceeding silently to the church of the Salutation; when Filippo, in our way thither, frequently requested me to remove the stranger from Camilla's side, for she had evil designs against her.

' " "What stranger?" I asked him.

' " "In God's name, don't speak so loud," replied he; "for you cannot but see how anxious she is to force herself between Camilla and me."

' " "Mere chimera, my friend; there are none but yourself and Camilla."

' " "Would to Heaven my eyes did not deceive me!— Take care that she does not enter the church," added he, as we arrived at the door.

' " "She will not enter it, rest assured," said I: and to the great astonishment of Camilla's parents I made a motion as if to drive some one away.

' "We found Filippo's father already in the church; and as soon as his son perceived him, he took leave of him as if he was going to die. Camilla sobbed; and Filippo exclaimed:—

' " "There's the stranger; she has then got in."

' "The parents of Camilla doubted whether under such circumstances the marriage ceremony ought to be begun.

' "'But Camilla, entirely devoted to her love, cried:— 'These chimeras of fancy render my care and attention the more necessary.'

' "'They approached the altar. At that moment a sudden gust of wind blew out the wax-tapers. The priest appeared displeased at their not having shut the windows more securely; but Filippo exclaimed: 'The windows! See you not, then, that there is one here who blew out the wax-tapers purposely?'

' "'Every one looked astonished: and Filippo cried, as he hastily disengaged his hand from that of Camilla,— 'Don't you see, also, that she is tearing me away from my intended bride?'

' "'Camilla fell fainting into the arms of her parents; and the priest declared, that under such peculiar circumstances it was impossible to proceed with the ceremony.

' "'The parents of both attributed Filippo's state to mental derangement. They even supposed he had been poisoned; for an instant after, the unfortunate man expired in most violent convulsions. The surgeons who opened his body could not, however, discover any grounds for this suspicion.

' "'The parents, who as well as myself were informed by Camilla of the subject of these supposed horrors of Filippo, did every thing in their power to conceal this adventure: yet, on talking over all the circumstances, they could never satisfactorily explain the apparition of the mysterious mask at the time of the wedding fête. And what still appeared very surprising was, that the ring lost at the country villa was found amongst Camilla's other jewels, at the time of their return from church.'"

' "'This is, indeed, a wonderful history!' said the count. His wife uttered a deep sigh: and Ida exclaimed,—

' "'It has really made me shudder.'

'Are we in another nestling doll or has the previous doll been nested over us?' I inquired.

' "'That is precisely what every betrothed person ought to feel who listens to such recitals,' answered I, looking steadfastly at the duke, who, while I was talking, had risen and sat down again several times; and who, from his troubled look, plainly shewed that he feared I should counteract his wishes.

' "'A word with you!' he whispered me, as we were retiring to rest: and he accompanied me to my room. 'I plainly perceive your generous intentions; this history invented for the occasion— "

' "'Hold!' said I to him in an irritated tone of voice: 'I was eye-witness to what you have just heard. How then can you doubt its authenticity, without accusing a man of honour of uttering a falsehood?'

' "'We will talk on this subject presently,' replied he in a tone of raillery. 'But tell me truly from whence you learnt the anecdote relative to mixing the blood with wine?— I know the person from whose life you borrowed this idea.'

' "'I do assure you that I have taken it from no one's life but Filippo's; and yet there may be similar stories— as of the shriek, for instance. But even this singular manner of irrevocably affiancing themselves may have presented itself to any two lovers.'

' "'Perhaps so! Yet one could trace in your narration many traits resembling another history.'

' "'That is very possible: all love-stories are founded on the same stock, and cannot deny their parentage.'

' "'No matter,' replied Marino; 'but I desire that from henceforth you do not permit yourself to make any allusion to my past life; and still less that you relate certain anecdotes to the count. On these conditions, and only on these conditions, do I pardon your former very ingenious fiction.'

' "'Conditions!— — forgiveness!— — And do you dare thus to talk to me?— — This is rather too much. Now take my answer: To-morrow morning the count shall know that you have been already affianced, and what you now exact.'

' "'Marquis, if you dare— — '

' "'Oh! oh!— yes, I dare do it; and I owe it to an old friend. The impostor who dares accuse me of falsehood shall no longer wear his deceitful mask in this house.'

' "Passion had, spite of my endeavours, carried me so far, that a duel became inevitable. The duke challenged me. And we agreed, at parting, to meet the following morning in a neighbouring wood with pistols.

' "In effect, before day-light we each took our servant and went into the forest. Marino, remarking that I had not given any orders in case of my being killed, undertook to do so for me; and accordingly he told my servant what to do with my body, as if every thing was already decided. He again addressed me ere we shook hands;—

' "'For,' said he, 'the combat between us must be very unequal. I am young,' added he; 'but in many instances my hand has proved a steady one. I have not, it is true, absolutely killed any man; but I have invariably hit my adversary precisely on the part I intended. In this instance, however, I must, for the first time, kill my man, as it is the only effectual method of preventing your annoying me further; unless you will give me your word of honour not to discover any occurrences of my past life to the count, in which case I consent to consider the affair as terminated here.'

' "As you may naturally believe, I rejected his proposition.

' "'As it must be so,' replied he, 'recommend your soul to God.' We prepared accordingly.

' "'It is your first fire,' he said to me.

' "'I yield it to you,' answered I.

' "He refused to fire first. I then drew the trigger, and caused the pistol to drop from his hand. He appeared surprised: but his astonishment was great indeed, when, after taking up another pistol, he found he had missed me. He pretended to have aimed at my heart; and had not even the possibility of an excuse; for he could not but acknowledge that no sensation of fear on my part had induced me to move, and baulk his aim.

' "At his request I fired a second time; and again aimed at his pistol which he held in his left hand: and to his great astonishment it dropped also; but the ball had passed so near his hand, that it was a good deal bruised.

' "His second fire having passed me, I told him I would not fire again; but that, as it was possible the extreme agitation of his mind had occasioned him to miss me twice, I proposed adjusting matters.

' "Before he had time to refuse my offer, the count, who had suspicions that all was not right, was between us, with his daughter. He complained loudly of such conduct on the part of his guests; and demanded some explanation on the cause of our dispute. I then developed the whole business in presence of Marino, whose evident embarrassment convinced the count and Ida of the truth of the reproaches his conscience made him.

' "But the duke soon availed himself of Ida's affection, and created an entire change in the count's mind; who that very evening said to me,—

' "'You are right; I certainly ought to take some decided step, and send the duke from my house: but what could win the Apollonia whom he has abandoned, and whom he will never see again? Added to which, he is the only man for whom my daughter has ever felt a sincere attachment. Let us leave the young people to follow their own inclinations: the countess perfectly coincides in this opinion; and adds, that it would hurt her much were this handsome Venetian to be driven from our house. How many little infidelities and indiscretions are committed in the world and excused, owing to particular circumstances?'"

'Quite peculiar these particular circumstances,' my Beloved said, again bemused.

' "But it appears to me, that in the case in point, these particular circumstances are wanting,' answered I. However, finding the count persisted in his opinion, I said no more.

' "The marriage took place without any interruption: but still there was very little of gaiety at the feast, which usually on these occasions is of so splendid and jocund a nature. The ball in the evening was dull; and Marino alone danced with most extraordinary glee.

' "Fortunately, *monsieur le marquis*,' said he in my ear, quitting the dance for an instant and laughing aloud, "there are no ghosts or spirits here, as at your Venetian wedding.'

' "Don't,' I answered, putting up my finger to him, 'rejoice too soon: misery is slow in its operations; and often is not perceived by us blind mortals till it treads on our heels.'

' "Contrary to my intention, this conversation rendered him quite silent; and what convinced me the more strongly of the effect it had made on him, was, the redoubled vehemence with which the duke again began dancing.

' "The countess in vain entreated him to be careful of his health: and all Ida's supplications were able to obtain was, a few minutes' rest to take breath when he could no longer go on.

' "A few minutes after, I saw Ida in tears, which did not appear as if occasioned by joy; and she quitted the ball-room. I was standing as close to the door as I am to you at this moment; so that I could not for an instant doubt its being really Ida: but what appeared to me very strange was, that in a few seconds I saw her come in again with a countenance as calm as possible. I followed her, and remarked that she asked the duke to dance; and was so far from moderating his violence, that she partook of and even increased it by her own example. I also remarked, that as soon as the dance was over the duke took leave of the parents of Ida, and with her vanished through a small door leading to the nuptial apartment.

' "While I was endeavouring to account in my own mind how it was possible for Ida so suddenly to change her sentiments, a conference in an under tone took place at the door of the room, between the count and his valet.

' "The subject was evidently a very important one, as the greatly in-censed looks of the count towards his gardener evinced, while he con-firmed, as it appeared, what the valet had before said.

' "I drew near the trio, and heard, that at a particular time the church organ was heard to play, and that the whole edifice had been illuminated within, until twelve o'clock, which had just struck.

' "The count was very angry at their troubling him with so silly a tale, and asked why they did not sooner inform him of it. They answered, that every one was anxious to see how it would end. The gardener added, that the old chaplain had been seen again; and the peasantry who lived near the forest, even pretended that they had seen the summit of the moun-tain which overhung their valley illuminated, and spirits dance around it.

' "'Very well!' exclaimed the count with a gloomy air; 'so all the old idle trash is resumed: the Death-Bride is also, I hope, going to play her part.'

' "The valet having pushed aside the gardener, that he might not still further enrage the count, I put in my word; and said to the count, 'You might at least listen to what they have to say, and learn what it is they pretend to have seen.'

' "'What is said about the Death-Bride?' said I to the gardener.

' "He shrugged up his shoulders.

' "'Was I not right?' cried the count: 'here we are then, and must listen to this ridiculous tale. All these things are treasured in the memory of these people, and constantly afford subjects and phantoms to their imaginations.— — Is it permitted to ask under what form?'— —

' "'Pray pardon me,' replied the gardener; 'but it resembled the deceased mademoiselle Hildegarde. She passed close to me in the garden, and then came into the castle."

' "'O!' said the count to him, 'I beg, in future you will be a little more circumspect in your fancies, and leave my daughter to rest quietly in the tomb— — 'Tis well— '

' "He then made a signal to his servants, who went out.

' "'Well! my dear marquis!' said he to me.

' "'Well?'

' "'Your belief in stories will not, surely, carry you so far as to give credence to my Hildegarde's spirit appearing?'"

'The twin sister,' Claire squeeled.

' "'At least it may have appeared to the gardener only— — Do you recollect the adventure in the Museum at Paris?'

' "'You are right: that again was a pretty invention, which to this moment I cannot fathom. Believe me, I should sooner have refused my daughter to the duke for his having been the fabricator of so gross a story, than for his having forsaken his first love.'

' "'I see very plainly that we shall not easily accord on this point; for if my ready belief appears strange to you, your doubts seem to me incomprehensible.'

' "The company assembled at the castle, retired by degrees; and I alone was left with the count and his lady, when Ida came to the room-door, clothed in her ball-dress, and appeared astonished at finding the company had left.

' "'What can this mean?' demanded the countess. Her husband could not find words to express his astonishment.

' "'Where is Marino?' exclaimed Ida.

' "'Do you ask us where he is?' replied her mother; 'did we not see you go out with him through that small door?'

' "'That could not be;— you mistake.'

' "'No, no; my dear child! A very short time since you were dancing with singular vehemence; and then you both went out together.'

' "'Me! my mother?'

' "'Yes, my dear Ida: how is it possible you should have forgotten all this?'

' "'I have forgotten nothing, believe me.'

' "'Where then have you been all this time?'

' "'In my sister's chamber,' said Ida.

' "I remarked that at these words the count became somewhat pale; and his fearful eye caught mine: he however said nothing. The countess, fearing that her daughter was deceiving her, said to her in an afflicted tone of voice:—

' "'How could so singular a fancy possess you on a day like this?'

' "'I cannot account for it; and only know, that all on a sudden I felt an oppression at my heart, and fancied that all I wanted was Hildegarde. At the same time I felt a firm belief that I should find her in her room playing on her guitar; for which reason I crept thither softly.'

' "'And did you find her there?'

' "'Alas! no: but the eager desire that I felt to see her, added to the fatigue of dancing, so entirely overpowered me, that I seated myself on a chair, where I fell fast asleep.'

' "'How long since did you quit the room?'

' "'The clock in the tower struck the three-quarters past eleven just as I entered my sister's room.'

' "'What does all this mean?' said the countess to her husband in a low voice: 'she talks in a connected manner; and yet I know, that as the clock struck three-quarters past eleven, I entreated Ida on this very spot to dance more moderately.'

' "'And Marino?'— asked the count.

' "'I thought, as I before said, that I should find him here.'

' "'Good God!' exclaimed the mother, 'she raves: but the duke— Where is he then?'

' "'What then, my good mother?' said Ida with an air of great disquiet, while leaning on the countess.

' "Meanwhile the count took a wax-taper, and made a sign for me to follow him. A horrible spectacle awaited us in the bridal-chamber, whither he conducted me. We there found the duke extended on the floor. There did not appear the slightest signs of life in him; and his features were distorted in the most frightful manner.

' "Imagine the extreme affliction Ida endured when she heard this recital, and found that all the resources of the medical attendants were employed in vain.

' "The count and his family could not be roused from the deep consternation which threatened to overwhelm them. A short time after this event, some business of importance occasioned me to quit their castle; and certainly I was not sorry for the excuse to get away.

' "But ere I left that county, I did not fail to collect in the village every possible information relative to the Death-Bride; whose history unfortunately, in passing from one mouth to another, experienced many alterations. It appeared to me, however, upon the whole, that this affianced bride lived in this district, about the fourteenth or fifteenth century. She was a young lady of noble family, and she had conducted herself with so much perfidy and ingratitude towards her lover, that he died of grief; but afterwards, when she was about to marry, he appeared to her the night of her intended wedding, and she died in consequence. And it is said, that since that time, the spirit of this unfortunate creature wanders on earth in every possible shape; particularly in that of lovely females, to render their lovers inconstant.

' "As it was not permitted for her to appear in the form of any living being, she always chose amongst the dead those who the most strongly resembled them. It was for this reason she voluntarily frequented the galleries in which were hung family portraits. It is even reported that she has been seen in galleries of pictures open to public inspection. Finally, it is said, that, as a punishment for her perfidy, she will wander till she finds a man whom she will in vain endeavour to make swerve from his engagement; and it appears, they added, that as yet she had not succeeded.

' "Having inquired what connection subsisted between this spirit and the old chaplain (of whom also I had heard mention), they informed me, that the fate of the last depended on the young lady, because he had assisted her in her criminal conduct. But no one was able to give me any satisfactory information concerning the voice which had called the duke by his name, nor on the meaning of the church being illuminated at night; and why the grand mass was chanted. No one either knows how to account for the dance on the mountain's top in the forest.

' "For the rest," added the marquis, "you will own, that the traditions are admirably adapted to my story, and may, to a certain degree, serve to fill up the gaps; but I am not enabled to give a more satisfactory explanation. I reserve for another time a second history of this same Death-Bride; I only heard it a few weeks since: it appears to me interesting; but it is too late to begin to-day, and indeed, even now, I fear that I have intruded too long on the leisure of the company present by my narrative."

'He had just finished these words, and some of his auditors (though all thanked him for the trouble he had taken) were expressing their disbelief of the story, when a person of his acquaintance came into the room in a hurried manner, and whispered something in his ear. Nothing could be more striking than the contrast presented by the bustling and uneasy air of the newly arrived person while speaking to the marquis, and the calm air of the latter while listening to him.

' "Haste, I pray you," said the first (who appeared quite out of patience at the marquis's sang-froid): "In a few moments you will have cause to repent this delay."

' "I am obliged to you for your affecting solicitude," replied the marquis; who in taking up his hat, appeared more to do, as all the rest of the party were doing, in preparing to return home, than from any anxiety of hastening away.

' "You are lost," said the other, as he saw an officer enter the room at the head of a detachment of military, who inquired for the marquis. The latter instantly made himself known to him.

' "You are my prisoner," said the officer. The marquis followed him, after saying Adieu with a smiling air to all the party, and begging they would not feel any anxiety concerning him.

' "Not feel anxiety!" replied he whose advice he had neglected. "I must inform you, that they have discovered that the marquis has been detected in a connection with very suspicious characters; and his death-warrant may be considered as signed. I came in pity to warn him of his danger, for possibly he might then have escaped; but from his conduct since, I can scarely imagine he is in his proper senses."

The party, who were singularly affected by this event, were conjecturing a thousand things, when the officer returned, and again asked for the marquis.

' "He just now left the room with you," answered some one of the company.

' "But he came in again."

' "We have seen no one."

' "He has then disappeared," replied the officer, smiling: he searched every corner for the marquis, but in vain. The house was thoroughly examined, but without success; and the following day the officer quitted the baths with his soldiers, without his prisoner, and very much dissatisfied.'

The tale hangs in the air like the Death-Bride was present in this very room. I looked at Claire who was weeping. Polidoir seemed bored. My Beloved quite enjoyed the tale. And Lord Byron sat deep in thought. We remained in silence for a long while, as the lightning flashed and the thunder crashed in a collateral-damage cacophony of a natural-rage symphony. My mind did wander away from the tale of the Death-Bride to these unfortunates sitting in this parlour of the Villa Diodati, who have been forced by our circumstances to listen to a rather awful ghost story in a volume of, no doubt, further awful ghost stories. Is this our lot for the remaining days of the constantly raining days of summer?

We occupy this villa during this quite queer summer of rivers freezing, plains flooding, and dear personal friends plotting each other's murder. I plot to kill my Beloved as does Polidori, but for opposite reasons. There is the possibility one of us is going to murder all of the others in their sleep, then turn the pistol upon themselves. This act of passion the London newspapers would report as poets of Romance are wont to do; or we would prove the guests at the surrounding hotels correct of their rumourmongering of our Bohemian decadence by engaging in an ill-fated and ill-inducing orgy.

Who would be the first to take a pistol from the case, stalk the hallways of the Villa, entering into each bedchamber and with a feathered-pillow to muffle the sound snuffing out each life like our humanity was nothing more than a candle. The summer has transformed this pleasant lakeside mansion into a sanatorium. We are no longer free to jaunt on the lake or hike the rolling hills. We are imprisoned in the Villa Diodoti, and if we see not the sun warm our faces soon, we will continue to slip into madness. Though we are in great company, we are likewise ever so alone. Too much loneliness. Too much company. I love my Beloved as my lover; I love Claire as my sister; I love Lord Byron as our host; I even love Dr Polidori in a faint way, as shameful as that may sound. But they are slowly driving me slowly, ever so slowly, mad! And I am no doubt a cause of their own madness, because they each love me whether as family, as a friend, or as a lover. Love and madness are two sides of the same coin. When you look upon one face of the coin, you see only true love betwixt your lover and you, while those closest to you sees the other face and utter madness. And what of looking upon the face of the coin and you seeing utter madness, why then does the entire world believe this is surely a sign of true love? Love and madness? A paradox.

Or who would be the first to seduce one and then all in a free-love Bohemian orgy? The madlove of poor innocent Claire for Lord Byron could be the spark of the tinderbox that would light an orgy on fire; but one initiated by escape. Lord Byron would, no doubt, flee the childlike and childish advances of my young sister into the bedchamber shared by my Beloved and me. While I am not predisposed to sapphic love, I know by Beloved and the Lord have been tempted by strong callused hands and hard-pressing kisses. While that serpent of the garden of Eden is cursed to burrow into the crotch of Man to strike at the flower of a women with its bite and swell her belly with its milky venom to produce the rushing, gushing, putrid birth of birthwaters, like a festering boil bursting, Lucifer is not ashamed of borrowing in the dank and stank and rank sewers of the arse. Or perchance the impetus would be the unrequited love of Dr Polidori for me; he who pines away the hours with deep sighs and lusting eyes. Of his quickly diverting gaze, Noah Webster could easily assign such a look in his *A Compendious Dictionary of the English Language* under the definition of 'rape'. Would I contract a sickness as if his feverish love for me were typhoid? And would I fall ill and be so delirious with fever that my breath would be laboured and my brow would be sweating and my passions would be inflamed? Would I then in my delirium pass the fever to my Beloved with a kiss, a bite, the very act of love? Would our bedchamber be transformed into a ward in a hospital? Oh, but Lord Byron would consider it height of rudeness if we three then did not invite our host to join us in feverish decadence, if only to escape the lovesick Claire.

Murder and then suicide, or an orgy. These are the threads of fate that the Moirai weave: Clotho's feet rapidly pumping the treadle, spinning the drive wheel, and spinning together two distinct yarns this summer; which one will Lachesis select to weave into the tapestry of our lives; and which will Atropos snip and knot lest our mortal lives unravel? Murder and then suicide, or an orgy... or...

'Let us play a game. Not games of mine men's morris, troll-my-dames, Edward Shovel board, nor shall we a put each other on a wild-goose chase due to inclement weather, nor shall we implement a game of hoodman-blind. In-their-stead, I propose a game of ghost stories,' Lord Byron puts foward to his quieted and disquieted guests, 'We will each write a ghost story! There are five of us and in us five ghosts haunting the hallways and apartments of the Villa Diodati. Let the reading of this little volume be a séance that has lured lurid ghosts into haunting the Villa Diodoti. We will then under spells and signs force these ghosts, against their angered will, to tell us the story of their lives. Those trifles contained in his volume,' he said discarding and dismissing the book onto the floor, 'are a little too sleight in importance, while we five stand at the height of brilliance. These are at once too French in language and too German in origin. They do not arise above being fairy stories told by Irish servants to frighten the children of the households they serve. But we are not Irish servants bound by superstition and fear, but we are British gentry bound by reason and passion. If poets are not meant to commune with the ghosts of the dead, then why are the religious so fearful of our supposed Satanic rituals and rites. Why then not draw upon the wood of the flooring with a pentagram in human blood and place a lit candle at each point and intersection? We will then write the names of our ghosts in crude Hebrew; crude because none of us are possessed of the knowledge of that language and would write nothing but childish gibberish. For the demons of the Pit care not for reada-bility; they, like the angels of Heaven and perhaps God Himself, hear our very thoughts and intentions as if we are bellowing. Why must I confess my supposed sins to a priest when God is both omniscient and omnipotent. Nay, I say. God is impotent, but the lusts of the incubuses and succubae are potent!'

'Nay, faith, my Lord Byron,' Claire shrieks, 'if we partake in such a Satanic ritual and rite and tempt the spirit-world through the mocking of the dead with imagined ghost stories this wintry summer, we will be punished by the malevolent God of the Old Testament— not the benevolent God of the New Testament— for witchcraft! God does not suffer a witch to live! Will our men be cursed with short lives'— her wild eyes suddenly stand vacant, staring across the veil that separates the realms of Living and the Dead. What does she see? Ghosts of the Past? The Present? The Yet To Come? What journey has she under-taken to see that which should not be seen— 'due to bloodletting or drowning or suicide?!' I look upon the Lord; he appears pale. I look upon my Beloved; he appears blue. I look upon the Doctor; he appears green. What affliction has been set upon my eyes to see these men with tinted-and-tainted-glasses? Claire then shrieks again, 'Why should we women risk dead children?!'

This cut me like a rusted back-alley surgeon's scalpel. I glance at my little William cooing quietly in the corner of the parlour and I fear for this immortal soul. Will I be immoral for participating in the proposed game of ghost stories that have set fire to my mind in this weary, deary wintry summer? O! My memories of my lost little nameless daughter born two months premature flood my mind as tears well in my eye. I only had possession of her for nine days! O! how I wept and wailed and wrote to Thomas Jefferson Hogg, who had struck up a great friendship with my Beloved:

> 'My dearest Hogg my baby is dead— will you come to see me as soon as you can. I wish to see you— It was perfectly well when I went to bed— I awoke in the night to give it suck it appeared to be sleeping so quietly that I would not awake it. It was dead then, but we did not find that out till morning— from its appearance it evidently died of convulsions— Will you come— you are so calm

a creature & Shelley is afraid of a fever from the milk— for I am no longer a mother now.'[4]

Lord Byron rips me out of the painful memory and back into the present when he continues suddenly, having given Claire's warning of dancing too close to the spirit-world only the slightest hesitation, 'Therefore, my dear friends, I invite the fiends into haunting the Villa Diodoti this summer... winter... whatever.'

---

4 From a letter 6 March, 1815 to Thomas Jefferson Hogg

Chapter Three
The Burial: A Fragment of a Novel[5]
The Diary of Dr John William Polidori

17 June. Went into the town; dined with Shelley etc. here. Went after dinner to a ball at Madamn Oldier's. There I was introduced to Princess Something-or-other and Countess Gräfin Potocka. The countess belonged to the highest Polish nobility, grandniece of Stanislaus Augustus Poniatowski, who had been King of Poland up to 1798 when died of a stroke on 12 February 1798, while virtually imprisoned St. Petersburg's Marble Palace, there writing his memoirs. Another guest gossiped she was the daughter of Count Tyskiewicz, and married Count Potocki, and afterwards Count Wonsowicz. She was born in 1776, the same year the treasonous colonial Americans launched their 'revolutionary', but civil war against the crown of George III, but I digress. This strikingly handsome young woman, with dark eyes of singular brilliancy and sentiment gathered around herself a small confab of myself, Princess Something, and a couple of other hangers-on. Having danced (I should say *attempted* to dance; due to the horrid pain was forced to stop) and having glanced in her direction over the course of the evening, we all were soon entranced by Countess Potocka. There, in the centre of a ring of this confab, her beauteous voice would soon sing as she spun a most wonderous tapestry of a dinner with Napoleon, the failed Emperor of France himself:

'The emperor declared that, as there was to be no fighting, he wanted us to enjoy ourselves. The time was propitious, for the carnival had just begun. There was an impediment, however. The *liberators* were occupying all our houses; everywhere the proprietors were reduced, just like ourselves, to a few small rooms, where some sort of crowding in was possible, but where it was out of the question to think of entertaining.

'Prince Poniatowski, who alone could have invited a large company to the palace, was hampered by the presence of the emperor. After much discussion, it was decided to give the first ball at M. de Talleyrand's, Grand Chamberlain and Minister of Foreign Affairs.

'The emperor, as well as all the princes, were to be there. The assurance was given that there would be no more than fifty ladies, but such a

---

5 An unfinished 1819 vampire horror story written by Lord Byron, published under the title 'A Fragment' in the 1819 collection *Mazeppa: A Poem*, published by John Murray in London.

severe regulation could not hold out against the thousand and one little intrigues in vogue on similar occasions. It was certainly one of those parties which must not be missed for anything in the world.

'Everybody's vanity and curiosity were stretched to the ut-most. As for me, I was possessed of the liveliest desire to see the host at close quarters, who was reported to be the most affable and cleverest man of his time. To say the truth, he took little trouble to appear so to us. The intimates asserted that no one joined such dexterity to such brilliancy; but if I were to judge him according to the impression he then made upon me, I should say he was thoroughly satiated and bored with everything — greedy for fame and fortune, jealous of the favours of a master he detested, without either character or principles, and, in a word, as unhealthy in mind as in appearance.

'I can scarcely convey the surprise I experienced when I saw him advance laboriously to the middle of the drawing-room, a napkin folded under his arm, a gilt tray in his hand, and offer a glass of lemonade to the monarch whom he in private considered an upstart.

'In his youth M. de Talleyrand was said to have counted many successes among the ladies, and I have since seen him in the midst of his old seraglio. It was really very comical: all those dames, to whom he had in turn played lover, tyrant, or friend, vainly tried to amuse him. His rudeness defeated all their efforts. He yawned at one, was curt to another, and made fools of them all, maliciously recurring to reminiscences and dates.

'To return to the ball. It was one of the most remark-able that it was ever my privilege to attend. The emperor took part in a square dance, which paved the way for his affair with Madame Walewska.

' "How do you think I dance?" he asked me, smiling. "I suspect you have been laughing at me."

' "In truth, sire," I replied, "for a great man your dancing is perfect."

'A little before that Napoleon had seated himself between the future favourite and myself. After talking for a few minutes he asked me who his other neighbour was. As soon as I had mentioned her name, he turned to her as if no one knew more about her than he.

'We learnt afterward that M. de Talleyrand had extended his labours as far as managing this first interview and smoothing the preliminary obstacles. Napoleon, having expressed a wish to count a Pole among his conquests, one of the right kind was chosen — lovely and dull. Some pretended to have noticed that, after the quadrille, the emperor had shaken hands with her, which was equivalent, they said, to an appointment; and it did take place, in fact, the next evening. It was rumoured that a great dignitary had gone to fetch the fair one; quick and undeserved promotion for a good-for-nothing brother was spoken of, and a diamond ornament, which was said to have been refused. People said a great many things they perhaps did not know and invented at pleasure. They even went so far as to assert that Rustan, the Mameluke, had acted as lady's maid! What is certain, however, is that we were all distressed that a person admitted to society had shown such facility, and had defended herself as little as the fortress of Ulm.

'But time, which colours everything, gave this connection, so lightly contracted, a tinge of constancy and disinterestedness which partly effaced the irregularity of its origin, and ended in placing Madame Walewska among the notable personages of her period. Exquisitely pretty, she was a realization of Greuze's faces; her eyes, her mouth, and her teeth were beautiful. Her laugh was so fresh, her gaze so soft, her face so seductive, as a whole, that it was never apparent that anything was wanting to the complete regularity of her features.

'Married at sixteen to an octogenarian who never appeared in public, in society she had the position of a young widow. Her extreme youth, combined with such convenient circumstances, gave room to all sorts of surmises, and if Napoleon was her last lover, it was asserted that he had not been the first.

'After the emperor had made his choice the princes of the family wanted to follow suit. It was difficult, as there was more than glory involved in this audacious enterprise.

'One morning M. Janvier, Prince Murat's private secretary, was announced. He entered, a key in his hand, much embarrassed at his undertaking. Not knowing how to begin, he remained mute, and turned his key over and over without venturing to look at me, whilst I, on my side, racked my brain to guess what he wanted.

'In order that this anecdote may be understood, I must say a word about the arrangements of the palace. Between the story occupied by my mother-in-law and the ground floor, where the large apartment was situated which I had surrendered to Prince Murat, there were tiny mezzanine rooms, of which my mother-in-law never made use except in the coldest weather, because they communicated the heat thoroughly by way of a *secret staircase*.

'This charming retreat, furnished and decorated in Louis XV. style, was looked upon as a part of the large apartment. The key of it had been given to Prince Murat's servants when he had come to live in our house, and nobody had thought of it since. That was the key M. Janvier had been ordered to bring to me.

'Being a man of sense, he felt fully the impropriety of his mission, and was doubly confused when he perceived that I did not understand, and that I persisted in refusing the key as a useless object; because, inhabiting the same floor as my mother-in-law, her private stairs were all that concerned me. Seeing me utterly at a loss, he took the liberty to say, that His Highness, not caring to propose large parties, had thought I might perhaps be pleased to take tea occasionally in these charming nooks. I began to comprehend, and I got angry ! He must have read it in my eyes, for I thought he would fall from his chair. He rose, stumbling, and going to a bracket deposited there the miserable key, and made a profound bow, preparatory to his exit.

'I could scarce contain myself — indignation inspired me. Smiling as disdainfully as I was able, I begged M. Janvier to tell the prince that my mother-in-law would certainly be sensible to his attention, that at her age large parties were found objectionable, and that she might avail herself of His Highness' obliging offer; that, in any case, since he was leaving the key, I should hand it to my mother-in-law. And, bestowing my haughtiest salute on the poor secretary, who stood petrified by the door, I left the room.

'M. de Talleyrand's ball was followed by two others: one given by Prince Borghese, the other by Prince Murat. I was indisposed, and did not attend the first; it was my mother-in-law's opinion that I ought to be at the second, so as to sustain the part I had adopted towards M. Janvier, and not in any way change the relationship of frigid politeness existing between our guest and ourselves. The weather continuing to render the roads impassable, the emperor did not leave town, and his regular outings were limited to the parade which took place in Saxon Square. Although this was an almost daily drill, people flocked there in crowds whenever Napoleon showed himself. He was accompanied back to the palace with spontaneous shouts and hurrahs, which showed him how his fame and our hopes had endeared him to the nation. He did not seem in the least put out by these demonstrations, although sometimes the enthusiasm resulted in blocking his way.

'Besides the balls, there was a court reception once a week. The evening began with a splendid concert and ended with a game of whist. There was never any dancing at the palace.

'The emperor had a complete orchestra in his train, under the direction of the celebrated composer Paer. It was always Italian music. Napoleon seemed to be passionately devoted to it. He listened attentively, applauded with discrimination, and the sounds of harmony appeared to seize strongly upon his moral faculties. A proof was given us at one of the entertainments.

'He had just received information that General Victor, the bearer of a despatch of the highest importance, had allowed the Prussians to catch him! This piece of news put him beside himself. If not a case of treason

— so it was noised about — it was at least one of unpardonable care-lessness. Now, that very day a Dutch deputation, come to congratulate the emperor upon his victory at Jena, was to be admitted to audience immediately before the reception. It was near ten o'clock, we had been waiting a long time, and were beginning to suspect something extraordi-nary might be happening, when, the door being noisily thrown open, we saw the fat Dutchmen, in their scarlet clothes, roll rather than walk in. The emperor was prodding them, exclaiming in somewhat loud tones: "Go on ! Go on !"

'No doubt a number of people had accumulated at the door the mo-ment that Napoleon made his appearance, for he walked very quickly, as was his habit. The poor envoys lost their heads, and tumbled all over each other.

"At any other time this comical scene would have raised a laugh, but the master's voice and the expression of his face were not reassuring, and, to say truth, we should have preferred not to witness this episode. We were wrong. The music soothed the emperor quickly; towards the end of the concert he resumed his gracious smile, addressing pleasant words to the ladies he liked best, before sitting down to his whist table. The emperor always named the ladies in the morning who were to play with him in the evening. His choice habitually fell upon one of the oldest and two of the youngest. I was taught to play an indifferent game, and the first time the coveted distinction was mine I let slip a too hasty answer, which was apparently not taken amiss, seeing that from that day I was a fixture at the card table.

"At the moment when the cards were drawn, Napoleon, turning in my direction, inquired: 'What shall the stake be?'

' "Oh, sire,' I answered, 'some town, some province, some kingdom !"

'He laughed.

' "And supposing you should lose?" he asked, with a particularly sly look.

' "Your Majesty is in funds, and will perhaps deign to pay for me"

This speech won me favour which was never withdrawn. Whether in Poland or in Paris, Napoleon never failed to accord me a distinguished welcome, and to treat me with endless consideration.

'It was remarked that Madame Walewska never played cards, and this regard for propriety was universally commended.

'A really funny thing it was to see all the little German princes, who, under various pretexts remaining at headquarters, danced attendance at the emperor's game of cards. Among others there was the heir pre-sumptive to the throne of Bavaria, who respectfully kissed Napoleon's hand whenever he managed to get it. But he had the impudence to be in love with Madame Walewska! Napoleon's peace was not in the least disturbed by this rivalry, which was even supposed to amuse him. The prince, much maltreated by nature, was, besides, deaf and a stutterer.

'The foreign ministers apart and some of the high functionaries settled down at play, no one sat down in the emperor's presence, not even his brothers-in-law. This did not seem to displease Prince Murat, who did not lose the opportunity to pose, and to strike attitudes which he judged appropriate to show off the beauty of his figure. But little Borghese was enraged, and still had not the courage to sit down.

'After cards came supper. Napoleon never took a seat at table, but walked about, so as to chat with the ladies, diverting himself with asking a thousand questions, which sometimes were embarrassing, considering the extremely precise answers he exacted. He wanted to know what you did, what you read, what you thought about most, what you liked best.

'One day, or one evening rather, when, leaning on the back of my chair, he amused himself with examining me in this way as to my reading, he talked novels, and told me that of all which had come into his hands, the *'Comte de Comminges" had interested him by far the most. He had read it twice, and each time had been moved to tears.

'I did not know the book, and it may well be imagined that, no sooner had I reached home, I ransacked my fatherinlaw's library. Unfortunately, this novel was not there. Only a long time after that conversation did I succeed in getting a copy, and I too shed tears!

'My mother-in-law, being the only lady of Warsaw who had kept up a salon, found herself obliged to give drawingroom teas and dances. A host of strangers who had come with the diplomatic body asked nothing better than to be entertained. The princes, of the blood so-called, missed none of these parties, without, however, compromising their dignity, for they only danced at *court balls*!

'Prince Murat, little discountenanced by the failure of his absurd enterprise, seized this opportunity to talk to me, and overwhelmed me with insipid compliments. I scarcely made an effort to prevent his seeing how he wearied me. He finally, though somewhat late, did perceive it. Then, assuming a melodramatic air, he said this very ridiculous phrase — rendered more so by his Gascon accent — which has made my friends laugh so much: "Madame Alexandre! you are not ambitious; you do not care for princes!"

'At Paris I heard a companion anecdote. The day that Murat was proclaimed King of Naples, a fair one, touched by his greatness, accorded him a private interview. As the cares of his empire were not yet taking up much of his time, he arrived too early, and, impatient of waiting, he carried his hand to his forehead, exclaiming: "Was an unhappier monarch ever known?"

'When I reflect how petty and absurd all those princes of Napoleon's family seemed to us by the side of the colossus who overshadowed them, I repeat the maxim proved true by the ages, that in the eyes of mankind only a great character or great deeds can justify sudden elevation.'[6]

The party soon ended and the storms threatened, I retreated by to the Villa Diodati only to find the Shelleys, Lord Byron and Claire awaiting my arrival. Until I stepped foot over the threshold of the palour, I did not realize the importance of my absence. Lord Byron had completed his ghost-story. I quickly and silently took my seat, not entreating them to accept an apology I wasn't willing to offer. My absence, though an annoyance to them, was not inappropriate. I will not accept being a prisoner of the Villa Diodati.

Mary Wollstonecraft Godwin's Journal

18 June, the Small Hours.— Lord Byron, the first to complete his ghost-story with the fever of a dream, stood before us all, all before the fire. Even poor Polidori who arrived tardy, though he was unaware of the Lord's sudden abrupt invitation, sat at the ready to hear what ghost had possessed our little Lord in this most haunted of houses to write so feverishly throughout the night into the next day until now. He came not down to breakfast, nor for lunch or tea. But now with the backdrop of a roaring fire as the pouring freezing rain pelts the high windows, he stood with ink-stained hands. If I knew not the familiar stain, I may have mistaken the ink for blood. Given the slight gasp from Claire, she may have.

My.

Lord Byron began, 'In the year 17— , having for some time determined on a journey through countries not hitherto much frequented by travellers, I set out, accompanied by a friend, whom I shall designate by the name of Augustus Darvell. He was a few years my elder, and a man of considerable fortune and ancient family— advantages which an extensive capacity prevented him alike from undervaluing or overrating. Some peculiar circumstances in his private history had rendered him to me an object of attention, of interest, and even of regard, which neither the reserve of his manners, nor occasional indications of an inquietude at times nearly approaching to alienation of mind, could extinguish.

---

6 From *Memoirs of Countess Potocka*, edited by Casimir Stryienski, Authorized Translation by Lionel Strachey, published by Doubleday & McClure Co., 1901

'I was yet young in life, which I had begun early; but my intimacy with him was of a recent date: we had been educated at the same schools and university; but his progress through these had preceded mine, and he had been deeply initiated into what is called the world, while I was yet in my noviciate. While thus engaged, I had heard much both of his past and present life; and although in these accounts there were many and irreconcileable contradictions, I could still gather from the whole that he was a being of no common order, and one who, whatever pains he might take to avoid remark, would still be remarkable. I had cultivated his acquaintance subsequently, and endeavoured to obtain his friendship, but this last appeared to be unattainable; whatever affections he might have possessed seemed now, some to have been extinguished, and others to be concentred: that his feelings were acute, I had sufficient opportunities of observing; for, although he could control, he could not altogether disguise them: still he had a power of giving to one passion the appearance of another in such a manner that it was difficult to define the nature of what was working within him; and the expressions of his features would vary so rapidly, though slightly, that it was useless to trace them to their sources. It was evident that he was a prey to some cureless disquiet; but whether it arose from ambition, love, remorse, grief, from one or all of these, or merely from a morbid temperament akin to disease, I could not discover: there were circumstances alleged, which might have justified the application to each of these causes; but, as I have before said, these were so contradictory and contradicted, that none could be fixed upon with accuracy. Where there is mystery, it is generally supposed that there must also be evil: I know not how this may be, but in him there certainly was the one, though I could not ascertain the extent of the other— and felt loth, as far as regarded himself, to believe in its existence. My advances were received with sufficient coldness; but I was young, and not easily discouraged, and at length succeeded in obtaining, to a certain degree, that common-place intercourse and moderate confidence of common and every day concerns, created and cemented by similarity of pursuit and frequency of meeting, which is called intimacy, or friendship, according to the ideas of him who uses those words to express them.

'Darvell had already travelled extensively; and to him I had applied for information with regard to the conduct of my intended journey. It was my secret wish that he might be prevailed on to accompany me: it was also a probable hope, founded upon the shadowy restlessness which I had observed in him, and to which the animation which he appeared to feel on such subjects, and his apparent indifference to all by which he was more immediately surrounded, gave fresh strength. This wish I first hinted, and then expressed: his answer, though I had partly ex-

pected it, gave me all the pleasure of surprise— he consented; and, after
the requisite arrangements, we commenced our voyages. After journeying through various countries of the south of Europe, our attention was
turned towards the East, according to our original destination; and it was
in my progress through those regions that the incident occurred upon
which will turn what I may have to relate.

'The constitution of Darvell, which must from his appearance have
been in early life more than usually robust, had been for some time gradually giving way, without the intervention of any apparent disease: he had
neither cough nor hectic, yet he became daily more enfeebled: his habits
were temperate, and he neither declined nor complained of fatigue, yet
he was evidently wasting away: he became more and more silent and
sleepless, and at length so seriously altered, that my alarm grew proportionate to what I conceived to be his danger.

'We had determined, on our arrival at Smyrna, on an excursion to
the ruins of Ephesus and Sardis, from which I endeavoured to dissuade
him in his present state of indisposition— but in vain: there appeared
to be an oppression on his mind, and a solemnity in his manner, which
ill corresponded with his eagerness to proceed on what I regarded as a
mere party of pleasure, little suited to a valetudinarian; but I opposed him
no longer— and in a few days we set off together, accompanied only by a
serrugee and a single janizary.

'We had passed halfway towards the remains of Ephesus, leaving behind us the more fertile environs of Smyrna, and were entering upon that
wild and tenantless track through the marshes and defiles which lead to
the few huts yet lingering over the broken columns of Diana— the roof-
less walls of expelled Christianity, and the still more recent but complete
desolation of abandoned mosques— when the sudden and rapid illness
of my companion obliged us to halt at a Turkish cemetery, the turbaned
tombstones of which were the sole indication that human life had ever
been a sojourner in this wilderness. The only caravansera we had seen
was left some hours behind us, not a vestige of a town or even cottage
was within sight or hope, and this "city of the dead" appeared to be the
sole refuge for my unfortunate friend, who seemed on the verge of becoming the last of its inhabitants.

'In this situation, I looked round for a place where he might most
conveniently repose:— contrary to the usual aspect of Mahometan bur-
ial-grounds, the cypresses were in this few in number, and these thinly
scattered over its extent: the tombstones were mostly fallen, and worn
with age:— upon one of the most considerable of these, and beneath one
of the most spreading trees, Darvell supported himself, in a half-reclin-
ing posture, with great difficulty. He asked for water. I had some doubts

of our being able to find any, and prepared to go in search of it with hesitating despondency— but he desired me to remain; and turning to Suleiman, our janizary, who stood by us smoking with great tranquillity, he said, "Suleiman, verbana su," (i. e. bring some water,) and went on describing the spot where it was to be found with great minuteness, at a small well for camels, a few hundred yards to the right: the janizary obeyed. I said to Darvell, "How did you know this?"— He replied, "From our situation; you must perceive that this place was once inhabited, and could not have been so without springs: I have also been here before."

' "You have been here before!— How came you never to mention this to me? and what could you be doing in a place where no one would remain a moment longer than they could help it?"

'To this question I received no answer. In the mean time Suleiman returned with the water, leaving the serrugee and the horses at the fountain. The quenching of his thirst had the appearance of reviving him for a moment; and I conceived hopes of his being able to proceed, or at least to return, and I urged the attempt. He was silent— and appeared to be collecting his spirits for an effort to speak. He began.

' "This is the end of my journey, and of my life— I came here to die: but I have a request to make, a command— for such my last words must be— You will observe it?"

' "Most certainly; but have better hopes."

' "I have no hopes, nor wishes, but this— conceal my death from every human being."

' "I hope there will be no occasion; that you will recover, and— — "

' "Peace!— it must be so: promise this."

' "I do."

' "Swear it, by all that"— — He here dictated an oath of great solemnity.

' "There is no occasion for this— I will observe your request; and to doubt me is— — "

' "It cannot be helped,— you must swear."

'I took the oath: it appeared to relieve him. He removed a seal ring from his finger, on which were some Arabic characters, and presented it to me. He proceeded—

' "On the ninth day of the month, at noon precisely (what month you please, but this must be the day), you must fling this ring into the salt springs which run into the Bay of Eleusis: the day after, at the same hour, you must repair to the ruins of the temple of Ceres, and wait one hour."

' "Why?"

' "You will see."

' "The ninth day of the month, you say?"

' "The ninth."

'As I observed that the present was the ninth day of the month, his countenance changed, and he paused. As he sate, evidently becoming more feeble, a stork, with a snake in her beak, perched upon a tombstone near us; and, without devouring her prey, appeared to be stedfastly regarding us. I know not what impelled me to drive it away, but the attempt was useless; she made a few circles in the air, and returned exactly to the same spot. Darvell pointed to it, and smiled: he spoke— I know not whether to himself or to me— but the words were only, "'Tis well!"

' "What is well? what do you mean?"

' "No matter: you must bury me here this evening, and exactly where that bird is now perched. You know the rest of my injunctions."

'He then proceeded to give me several directions as to the manner in which his death might be best concealed. After these were finished, he exclaimed, "You perceive that bird?"

' "Certainly."

' "And the serpent writhing in her beak?"

' "Doubtless: there is nothing uncommon in it; it is her natural prey. But it is odd that she does not devour it."

'He smiled in a ghastly manner, and said, faintly, "It is not yet time!" As he spoke, the stork flew away. My eyes followed it for a moment, it could hardly be longer than ten might be counted. I felt Darvell's weight, as it were, increase upon my shoulder, and, turning to look upon his face, perceived that he was dead!

'I was shocked with the sudden certainty which could not be mistaken— his countenance in a few minutes became nearly black. I should have attributed so rapid a change to poison, had I not been aware that he had no opportunity of receiving it unperceived. The day was declining, the body was rapidly altering, and nothing remained but to fulfil his request. With the aid of Suleiman's ataghan and my own sabre, we scooped a shallow grave upon the spot which Darvell had indicated: the earth easily gave way, having already received some Mahometan tenant. We dug as deeply as the time permitted us, and throwing the dry earth upon all that remained of the singular being so lately departed, we cut a few sods of greener turf from the less withered soil around us, and laid them upon his sepulchre.

'Between astonishment and grief, I was tearless.'

The Diary of Dr John William Polidori

17 June.— The Shelleys and Claire had retired to their apartments to the night was waning fast. Lord Byron and myself as around the fire with fine glasses of absinthe, mixed in its accustomed fashion with a square of sugar and drops of laudanum, and our mood this evening had certainly not soured. Lord Byron was pained that this was only a fragment of a novel; one which he intended on finishing, but the spirit had for now passed from his mind. He had such a fever upon the brain having written this 'fragment' in only a day that he sat exhausted. He told me of the story he desired to tell: that Darvell would reappear, alive again, as a vampire! While the spirit may have passed from his mind, the spirit did not pass far beyond the walls of the Villa Diodati. In fact, the spirit did not even pass out of this very parlour before the fire. Abandoning Lord Bryon, the spirit possessed me!

Chapter Four
Christabel[7]

The Diary of Dr John William Polidori

18 June.— My leg grows much much worse. Why was I cursed by the barbed shaft of Eros to have fallen in love with the betrothed of Percy Shelley? If not for my chivalry, I would not be possessed a sprained ankle. Dispossessed of my mobility! The nobility of my profession is lost! The shame of doctor to be seen bandaged and wearing a splint for simply and foolishly jumping from a minor height is more akin to knight being stabbed by his own sword on the battlefield after tripping over a corpse.

Shelley and his party of sisters came down for breakfast. Mrs Shelley (though I know truly not if she is legally married, merely betrothed, or perhaps a scarlet woman) called me her brother (younger).

Again.

Began my ghost story after tea. I don't yet have a proper title for the work, but I have a brilliant subtitle: 'the Modern Oedipus'. Such a brilliant concept. Why haven't more caretakers of insane asylums studied one's desire to have sexual relations with one's mother while desiring to kill one's father? Not that I suppose one who possesses such desires is by very necessity insane, but that such specialized hospitals are more fertile grounds to study such subjects. Shame is not a hindrance when probing lunatics. This subject proved not to be a foreign concept in ancient times as scene in the legend of King Oedipus and the drama of the same name by Sophocles. Surely, it is not a foreign concept in the modern age. Taking the classical and exposing it as modern!

Now, I'll just have to write my story worthy of Sophocles.

Doable.

Twelve o'clock, the Five really began to talk ghostly again. This game of ghost stories has been quite fun, though I know not if there will truly be a winner awarded. Nor what the reward will be. The others were quite haughty and dismissive of my own contributions. They were so naughty! I was not born with a silver tongue like Lord Byron, nor the genius of Shelley, nor the beauty of Mary. The latter of these three has not shown herself to be quick with a pen, though her wit is quick

---

7 Extract from an unfinished long narrative ballad by Samuel Taylor Coleridge, published in a pamphlet in 1816, alongside *Kubla Khan* and *The Pains of Sleep*.

and her tongue sharp as a quill. I will continue to harangue her every morning until the time she produces her ghost story. Cut me? I'll fillet her, my love.

Lord Byron repeated some verses of Coleridge's *Christabel*, of the witch's breast, which would pleasant away the afternoon since jaunting around and about the lake is nigh impossible with the inclement weather. Why bother with our holiday if we're stuck inside reading rhymes and exchanging niceties. I could be stuck inside in equally dour weather in London. Yes, I admit my mood is foul. It is my mood and I'll possess it in any manner I so choose.

> *Tis the middle of night by the castle clock,*
> *And the owls have awakened the crowing cock;*
> *Tu— whit! Tu— whoo!*
> *And hark, again! the crowing cock,*
> *How drowsily it crew.*
> *Sir Leoline, the Baron rich,*
> *Hath a toothless mastiff bitch;*
> *From her kennel beneath the rock*
> *She maketh answer to the clock,*
> *Four for the quarters, and twelve for the hour;*
> *Ever and aye, by shine and shower,*
> *Sixteen short howls, not over loud;*
> *Some say, she sees my lady's shroud.*
>
> *Is the night chilly and dark?*
> *The night is chilly, but not dark.*
> *The thin gray cloud is spread on high,*
> *It covers but not hides the sky.*
> *The moon is behind, and at the full;*
> *And yet she looks both small and dull.*
> *The night is chill, the cloud is gray:*
> *'Tis a month before the month of May,*
> *And the Spring comes slowly up this way.*
>
> *The lovely lady, Christabel,*
> *Whom her father loves so well,*
> *What makes her in the wood so late,*
> *A furlong from the castle gate?*
> *She had dreams all yesternight*
> *Of her own betrothèd knight;*
> *And she in the midnight wood will pray*

For the weal of her lover that's far away.

She stole along, she nothing spoke,
The sighs she heaved were soft and low,
And naught was green upon the oak
But moss and rarest misletoe:
She kneels beneath the huge oak tree,
And in silence prayeth she.

The lady sprang up suddenly,
The lovely lady Christabel!
It moaned as near, as near can be,
But what it is she cannot tell.—
On the other side it seems to be,
Of the huge, broad-breasted, old oak tree.

The night is chill; the forest bare;
Is it the wind that moaneth bleak?
There is not wind enough in the air
To move away the ringlet curl
From the lovely lady's cheek—
There is not wind enough to twirl
The one red leaf, the last of its clan,
That dances as often as dance it can,
Hanging so light, and hanging so high,
On the topmost twig that looks up at the sky.

Hush, beating heart of Christabel!
Jesu, Maria, shield her well!
She folded her arms beneath her cloak,
And stole to the other side of the oak.
What sees she there?

There she sees a damsel bright,
Drest in a silken robe of white,
That shadowy in the moonlight shone:
The neck that made that white robe wan,
Her stately neck, and arms were bare;
Her blue-veined feet unsandl'd were,
And wildly glittered here and there
The gems entangled in her hair.
I guess, 'twas frightful there to see

A lady so richly clad as she—
Beautiful exceedingly!

Mary mother, save me now!
(Said Christabel) And who art thou?

The lady strange made answer meet,
And her voice was faint and sweet:—
Have pity on my sore distress,
I scarce can speak for weariness:
Stretch forth thy hand, and have no fear!
Said Christabel, How camest thou here?
And the lady, whose voice was faint and sweet,
Did thus pursue her answer meet:—

My sire is of a noble line,
And my name is Geraldine:
Five warriors seized me yestermorn,
Me, even me, a maid forlorn:
They choked my cries with force and fright,
And tied me on a palfrey white.
The palfrey was as fleet as wind,
And they rode furiously behind.
They spurred amain, their steeds were white:
And once we crossed the shade of night.
As sure as Heaven shall rescue me,
I have no thought what men they be;
Nor do I know how long it is
(For I have lain entranced I wis)
Since one, the tallest of the five,
Took me from the palfrey's back,
A weary woman, scarce alive.
Some muttered words his comrades spoke:
He placed me underneath this oak;
He swore they would return with haste;
Whither they went I cannot tell—
I thought I heard, some minutes past,
Sounds as of a castle bell.
Stretch forth thy hand (thus ended she).
And help a wretched maid to flee.

Then Christabel stretched forth her hand,

And comforted fair Geraldine:
O well, bright dame! may you command
The service of Sir Leoline;
And gladly our stout chivalry
Will he send forth and friends withal
To guide and guard you safe and free
Home to your noble father's hall.

She rose: and forth with steps they passed
That strove to be, and were not, fast.
Her gracious stars the lady blest,
And thus spake on sweet Christabel:
All our household are at rest,
The hall as silent as the cell;
Sir Leoline is weak in health,
And may not well awakened be,
But we will move as if in stealth,
And I beseech your courtesy,
This night, to share your couch with me.

They crossed the moat, and Christabel
Took the key that fitted well;
A little door she opened straight,
All in the middle of the gate;
The gate that was ironed within and without,
Where an army in battle array had marched out.
The lady sank, belike through pain,
And Christabel with might and main
Lifted her up, a weary weight,
Over the threshold of the gate:
Then the lady rose again,
And moved, as she were not in pain.

So free from danger, free from fear,
They crossed the court: right glad they were.
And Christabel devoutly cried
To the lady by her side,
Praise we the Virgin all divine
Who hath rescued thee from thy distress!
Alas, alas! said Geraldine,
I cannot speak for weariness.
So free from danger, free from fear,

They crossed the court: right glad they were.

Outside her kennel, the mastiff old
Lay fast asleep, in moonshine cold.
The mastiff old did not awake,
Yet she an angry moan did make!
And what can ail the mastiff bitch?
Never till now she uttered yell
Beneath the eye of Christabel.
Perhaps it is the owlet's scritch:
For what can ail the mastiff bitch?

They passed the hall, that echoes still,
Pass as lightly as you will!
The brands were flat, the brands were dying,
Amid their own white ashes lying;
But when the lady passed, there came
A tongue of light, a fit of flame;
And Christabel saw the lady's eye,
And nothing else saw she thereby,
Save the boss of the shield of Sir Leoline tall,
Which hung in a murky old niche in the wall.
O softly tread, said Christabel,
My father seldom sleepeth well.

Sweet Christabel her feet doth bare,
And jealous of the listening air
They steal their way from stair to stair,
Now in glimmer, and now in gloom,
And now they pass the Baron's room,
As still as death, with stifled breath!
And now have reached her chamber door;
And now doth Geraldine press down
The rushes of the chamber floor.

The moon shines dim in the open air,
And not a moonbeam enters here.
But they without its light can see
The chamber carved so curiously,
Carved with figures strange and sweet,
All made out of the carver's brain,
For a lady's chamber meet:

The lamp with twofold silver chain
Is fastened to an angel's feet.

The silver lamp burns dead and dim;
But Christabel the lamp will trim.
She trimmed the lamp, and made it bright,
And left it swinging to and fro,
While Geraldine, in wretched plight,
Sank down upon the floor below.

O weary lady, Geraldine,
I pray you, drink this cordial wine!
It is a wine of virtuous powers;
My mother made it of wild flowers.

And will your mother pity me,
Who am a maiden most forlorn?
Christabel answered— Woe is me!
She died the hour that I was born.
I have heard the grey-haired friar tell
How on her death-bed she did say,
That she should hear the castle-bell
Strike twelve upon my wedding-day.
O mother dear! that thou wert here!
I would, said Geraldine, she were!

But soon with altered voice, said she—
'Off, wandering mother! Peak and pine!
I have power to bid thee flee.'
Alas! what ails poor Geraldine?
Why stares she with unsettled eye?
Can she the bodiless dead espy?

And why with hollow voice cries she,
'Off, woman, off! this hour is mine—
Though thou her guardian spirit be,
Off, woman, off! 'tis given to me.'

Then Christabel knelt by the lady's side,
And raised to heaven her eyes so blue—
Alas! said she, this ghastly ride—
Dear lady! it hath wildered you!

The lady wiped her moist cold brow,
And faintly said, ' 'tis over now!'

Again the wild-flower wine she drank:
Her fair large eyes 'gan glitter bright,
And from the floor whereon she sank,
The lofty lady stood upright:
She was most beautiful to see,
Like a lady of a far countrèe.

And thus the lofty lady spake—
'All they who live in the upper sky,
Do love you, holy Christabel!
And you love them, and for their sake
And for the good which me befel,
Even I in my degree will try,
Fair maiden, to requite you well.
But now unrobe yourself; for I
Must pray, ere yet in bed I lie.'

Quoth Christabel, So let it be!
And as the lady bade, did she.
Her gentle limbs did she undress,
And lay down in her loveliness.

But through her brain of weal and woe
So many thoughts moved to and fro,
That vain it were her lids to close;
So half-way from the bed she rose,
And on her elbow did recline
To look at the lady Geraldine.

Beneath the lamp the lady bowed,
And slowly rolled her eyes around;
Then drawing in her breath aloud,
Like one that shuddered, she unbound
The cincture from beneath her breast:
Her silken robe, and inner vest,
Dropt to her feet, and full in view,
Behold! her bosom and half her side—
A sight to dream of, not to tell!
O shield her! shield sweet Christabel!

Lord Bryon paused to take a sip of water from the glass on the round table beside him, when a brief silence ensued. Shelley suddenly shrieked. We all turned to Shelley and found his eyes so white with fear that his iris and pupils were devoid of all colour. His hands clutched his head with such ferocity that he was squeezing his head with the intensity of a vice. Crimson stained his philtrum (the scientific name for that crease under your nose, for those reading this diary when published at a later date), dripping down onto his upper lip. His teeth then clenched in such fearfulness and with such ferociousness I feared his teeth would bite off his tongue or shatter. He ran out of the room wielding a candle as if it were a short sword. He swung the candle-sword so wildly that the flame was snuffed out by the passing breeze. Percy bolted into his room and attempted to bolt the door, but my poor ruined foot was caught between the door and the jamb. I screamed with the sharp pain like a birthing woman. Shelley shrieked again and again as he forced the door closed on my foot! We both shouted at the other to either close or open the door. Then Lord Byron threw his shoulder into stout wooden door, knocking Shelley off his feet. Having collapsed onto the ground, I removed my belt and forced in between his upper and lower sets of teeth so that he did not bite off his tongue. He struggled with the viciousness of a patient in need of, not science, but an exorcist. His hands clawed at me like raptor talons (and I wasn't fucking wearing my hawking gloves). Lovely Mary threw water in his face. Claire, without any instruction, ran into my apartment to retrieve my satchel that contained all my medical instruments. These tools were intended for use on Lord Byron, as I am his personal physician. But the Hippocratic oath, which I swore before the Christian God and not the pagan Olympians, required my intercession whether or not Shelley was a dear friend or not. I held a bottle of ether under his nose and in his fear, he inhaled deeply and soon peace washed over him. Why does a medical doctor need an exorcist when he possesses a bottle of ether to exorcise the possessed?

Shelley, as his breath smoothed, was looking of at Mrs Shelley confessed the cause of his sudden fright. He thought of a woman he had heard of from superstitious women who had eyes instead of nipples. In his mind's eye, he saw Christabel with such queer nipples. This remained me of the stories of the early explorers in the Americas believing manatees were mermaids, giants lived in South America, and headless men who possessed faces in their chests. Where had Percy heard such a tale that a woman had eyes instead of nipples. He apologized for the thought having taken hold of his mind and horrified his mind.

Although the reading of Coleridge had ended for the evening and was not taken up again for the remainder of our time at the Villa Diodati, for posterities sake, Diary, I will include the remainder of the poem.

> Yet Geraldine nor speaks nor stirs;
> Ah! what a stricken look was hers!
> Deep from within she seems half-way
> To lift some weight with sick assay,
> And eyes the maid and seeks delay;
> Then suddenly, as one defied,
> Collects herself in scorn and pride,
> And lay down by the Maiden's side!—
> And in her arms the maid she took,
> Ah wel-a-day!
> And with low voice and doleful look
> These words did say:
> 'In the touch of this bosom there worketh a spell,
> Which is lord of thy utterance, Christabel!
> Thou knowest to-night, and wilt know to-morrow,
> This mark of my shame, this seal of my sorrow;
> But vainly thou warrest,
> For this is alone in
> Thy power to declare,
> That in the dim forest
> Thou heard'st a low moaning,
> And found'st a bright lady, surpassingly fair;
> And didst bring her home with thee in love and in charity,
> To shield her and shelter her from the damp air.'

THE CONCLUSION TO PART I

> It was a lovely sight to see
> The lady Christabel, when she
> Was praying at the old oak tree.
> Amid the jaggèd shadows
> Of mossy leafless boughs,
> Kneeling in the moonlight,
> To make her gentle vows;
> Her slender palms together prest,
> Heaving sometimes on her breast;
> Her face resigned to bliss or bale—
> Her face, oh call it fair not pale,

And both blue eyes more bright than clear,
Each about to have a tear.

With open eyes (ah woe is me!)
Asleep, and dreaming fearfully,
Fearfully dreaming, yet, I wis,
Dreaming that alone, which is—
O sorrow and shame! Can this be she,
The lady, who knelt at the old oak tree?
And lo! the worker of these harms,
That holds the maiden in her arms,
Seems to slumber still and mild,
As a mother with her child.

A star hath set, a star hath risen,
O Geraldine! since arms of thine
Have been the lovely lady's prison.
O Geraldine! one hour was thine—
Thou'st had thy will! By tairn and rill,
The night-birds all that hour were still.
But now they are jubilant anew,
From cliff and tower, tu— whoo! tu— whoo!
Tu— whoo! tu— whoo! from wood and fell!

And see! the lady Christabel
Gathers herself from out her trance;
Her limbs relax, her countenance
Grows sad and soft; the smooth thin lids
Close o'er her eyes; and tears she sheds—
Large tears that leave the lashes bright!
And oft the while she seems to smile
As infants at a sudden light!

Yea, she doth smile, and she doth weep,
Like a youthful hermitess,
Beauteous in a wilderness,
Who, praying always, prays in sleep.
And, if she move unquietly,
Perchance, 'tis but the blood so free
Comes back and tingles in her feet.
No doubt, she hath a vision sweet.
What if her guardian spirit 'twere,

What if she knew her mother near?
But this she knows, in joys and woes,
That saints will aid if men will call:
For the blue sky bends over all!

The Diary of Dr John William Polidori

18 June.— My jealousy seethes. Lord Byron is a unbridged genius. Not because the societal ladies swoon over his poetry. Not like the gentlemen of society are jealous of wealth, his title, or striking looks. It is his creative soul that I am most jealous of. He plucked a charming and sophisticated vampyre to jaunt among society out of the alarming and superstitious vampryes that haunt the peasantry. Who can take a hungry, decaying revenant out of the rural legends and transubstantiate the vampyre into a suave, sophisticated resident of high society? How I wish to tell this story! Every fibre of my being needs to write this story. The unholy spirit that entered me yesternight counts itself amongst common thieves. As I breathe, I cannot betray my benefactor by plagiarising his vampire story, as much as the desire to complete his novel washes over me. Drowning me in a sea of despair! How I wish to come up for air! The very nature of plagiarism is vampiric, unholy, unnatural. It requires the drinking of the creative blood of another fellow passenger to the grave to give us unholy fame and unnatural wealth. This theft is as abnormal in modern society as it is unseemly. There is no lure enticing enough to cause me to invite this thieving spirit to possess my intellect again. The exorcising of this spirit proved to be soul rending. Though my intentions were pure— no! there is no defending my plagiaristic ambitions! Yesternight, the spirit had complete possession of my psyche! The fiend would not release my mind to peace without, at least, the intercession of a priest! The foul spirit whispered in my ear that no one, not even Lord Bryon, would ever be aware of my thievery. This was the knavery of the evil spirit! But through shear will and out of fear of ending my relationship with Lord Byron, I cast the demon out! Once I had finally sent the spirit descending to the pit of Hell everlasting, I sat in the parlour exhausted from my intellectual warfare with plagiarism.

As the lightning dances across the sky, I wish the architect of the Villa Diodati had installed eaves on this window to give me a moment of peace. But as I sit here before the fire, the thunder thankfully off in the distance, the spirit of a new story has possessed me and intoxicated my brain. Like the Pentecostals, will I pick up snakes and speak in tongues as commanded by the Christ? The tale boils in my brain.

The entire story, from first sentence ('Upon the left side of the lake of Thun lies the small village of Beatenberg, which, under the care of a simple pastor contains no individual above the rank of a peasant: it was in this village that I was born. Misfortune seemed to be anxious at my very birth to stamp me for its own.') to the very last words ("But you married; I dreamt of happiness, on Louisa's birth-day accompanied you to your room, and the demon's threat I found had indeed been fulfilled. Your mother's portrait was Matilda's. Olivieri had seduced, you married a daughter of Matilda, of Matilda's husband, and I was the murderer of her father.") have already fully formed in my skull. All I must do is transcribe the words written upon the dural folds of my brain down onto the page. My dearest friends will believe I have the fever upon my brain, that I may have eaten a bad bit of beef, a spoiled blot of mustard, a mouldy crumb of cheese, a fragment of underdone potato. But I am perfectly healthy, as healthy as author can be when so feverish with story. The only cure for this creative encephalitis is to begin writing my contribution to our game of ghost stories this very night!

Mary Wollstonecraft Godwin's Journal

19 June.— Dr Polidori came down to breakfast like a cock of the walk. There was an ungentlemanly strut to his gate; he truly was a rooster who believed he ruled the roost. He triumphantly boasted that he had found his ghost story. When he inquired if I had a ghost story of my own for Lord Byron's game of ghost stories, I was forced to admit I had not yet found my story. He began to roast me for my lack of creative spark. He proudly and quite loudly proclaimed that he not only had the first line to his ghost story and not only had the last line, but the entire story in between fully formed in his head. He even recited these lines which I will not disgrace my journal by including them here for posterity. As I hanged my head, he harangued me and taunted me, flaunting the fire of creativity that had set his psyche ablaze. The doctor has no shame to make me that object of ridicule in his game of mockery. My Beloved sat in stone-cold silence when he should have joined me in an alliance against the good doctor. I sat in defiance when Lord Byron joined Polidori in his cruel game. My two so-called friends were positively ghoulish wallowing in their cesspool of keen mockery. But I would not be their fool. I abandoned my breakfast and questioned my friendship!

20 June. The 'good' doctor came down to breakfast with a number of pages gripped in his covetous little hands. I sat with my head beginning to hang because I knew the harangue was eminent. These pages were, no doubt, the first pages written in Polidori's ghost story. He held them out reverently like a priest holding the Holy Writ during Easter Mass. He spoke of them like he had been God-breathed, that his ghost story had been *given to him by inspiration of God, and is profitable for doctrine, for reproof, for correction, for instruction in righteousness: that the man of God may be perfect, thoroughly furnished unto all good works*[8].His cruel ridicule continued for a second straight day. If I do not come up with a ghost story soon there will be no end to this keen mockery born. This very morning, I made it my sworn mission to find my ghost story that would trump anything that the 'good' doctor had composed, but I knew in the bottom of my heart— my very soul— that one simply does not order the Muses to provide me with such a story. Calliope will refuse to gift any epic poem or, in the modern day, any novel to a soul who dares command them. Their reprimand would be to utterly snuff out the creative spark. This silence is deafening. I seek their guidance to grant me the license to enter Lord Byron's game of ghost stories, but as of my writing this words into my journal, the Muses are still silent. Deafening!

21 June. I record these words in mourning because this very morning, my 'Beloved' joined the 'good' doctor and 'Lord' Byron in this game of cruel mockery. I have nothing but contempt for their attempts to shame me for having not written a single blessed word onto the page. My rage no longer knows any bounds. The productivity and prolificacy of the 'good' doctor is simultaneously astounding and confounding. Why has Calliope bequeathed unto the 'good' doctor this cornucopia of creativity. That for the second straight morning, he produces proof of his nightly conquest. I continue to request— nay! pray!— to the Muses to grant me the rewards at the end of the quest Lord Byron has set us out on. But the doctor continues to flout this drought in my creativity. Where is my ghost story?

22 June. Noon— There is no point in relating the cruel ridicule suffered by me at the hands of the good doctor, Lord Byron, and my Beloved this very morning for the third day in a row, they continue their scorn. I will no longer record for posterity any more keen mockery born from 'good' doctor, 'Lord' Byron, and my supposed 'Beloved'! The bell tolls midnight. To Hell with them all!

---

8 From 2 Timoth 3: 16-17 from the Authorized King James Bible.

22 June. Evening— Oh, how cruel this 'good' doctor is with is keen mockery. He is relentless and I am restless. Lord Byron and my Beloved have grown past this game with me, but the boy delights in toying with me. I will find a ghost to haunt me in the Villa Diodati this cruel year without a summer! And I will write that ghost's story down as part of our game of ghost stories. Shall I take dictation? Dedicatedly will I! I don't even care if my game story is born of my creativity, I will accept another's story, as long as I best Polidori in this game of ghost stories. If the Gospels and the Epistles could be written by mortal hands yet be inspired by a purely spiritual being in the Holy Ghost, then I will welcome such inspiration of God. Whether the ghost story is born out of my own perspiration or a markedly unholy ghost's inspiration, I will accept it. Am I tempted to offer my soul to Francis Dashwood's Order of the Friars of St. Francis of Wycombe; Beloved, am I willing to part with my very soul like Faust did before me?

23 June. Morning— Yesternight waned upon this talk, and even the witching hour had gone by, before we retired to rest. When I placed my head on my pillow, I did not sleep, nor could I be said to think. My imagination, unbidden, possessed and guided me, gifting the successive images that arose in my mind with a vividness far beyond the usual bounds of reverie. I saw— with shut eyes, but acute mental vision,— I saw the pale student of unhallowed arts kneeling beside the thing he had put together. I saw the hideous phantasm of a man stretched out, and then, on the working of some powerful engine, show signs of life, and stir with an uneasy, half vital motion. Frightful must it be; for supremely frightful would be the effect of any human endeavour to mock the stupendous mechanism of the Creator of the world. His success would terrify the artist; he would rush away from his odious handywork, horror-stricken. He would hope that, left to itself, the slight spark of life which he had communicated would fade; that this thing, which had received such imperfect animation, would subside into dead matter; and he might sleep in the belief that the silence of the grave would quench for ever the transient existence of the hideous corpse which he had looked upon as the cradle of life. He sleeps; but he is awakened; he opens his eyes; behold the horrid thing stands at his bedside, opening his curtains, and looking on him with yellow, watery, but speculative eyes.

I opened mine in terror. The idea so possessed my mind, that a thrill of fear ran through me, and I wished to exchange the ghastly image of my fancy for the realities around. I see them still; the very room, the dark parquet, the closed shutters, with the moonlight struggling through, and the sense I had that the glassy lake and white high Alps were beyond.

I could not so easily get rid of my hideous phantom; still it haunted me. I must try to think of something else. I recurred to my ghost story,— my tiresome unlucky ghost story! O! if I could only contrive one which would frighten my reader as I myself had been frightened that night!

Swift as light and as cheering was the idea that broke in upon me. 'I have found it! What terrified me will terrify others; and I need only describe the spectre which had haunted my midnight pillow.' On the morrow I announced that I had thought of a story. I began that day with the words, *It was on a dreary night of November*, making only a transcript of the grim terrors of my waking dream.[9]

23 June, Evening— I had burst into the kitchen this morning, exclaiming, 'I have found it!' My Beloved, poor Polidori, and our little Lord already sat for breakfast, with my helping of bacon and sausage still sizzling in the iron pan. 'Found what, my dove,' my love inquired. 'I found my ghost story!' I beamed. Then the doctor said, 'About time.' I nearly screamed in frustration. How I have grown tired of this man! My hands desired to wring his neck, for every morning for days he inquired if I had found my ghost story yet; every morning for days I had *not* found my ghost story yet; yet on the day that I find my ghost story, I find him unimpressed.

---

9 From the Introduction to the 1831 Edition of *Frankenstein; or, The Modern Prometheus,* published by Henry Colburn & Richard Bentley.

Chapter Five
A Galvanising Debate[10]

Mary Wollstonecraft Godwin's Journal

21 June. Lake Geneva— Many and long are the conversations between Lord Byron and Shelley, to which I am a devout but nearly silent listener. During one of these, various philosophical doctrines are discussed, and among others the nature of the principle of life, and whether there was any probability of its ever being discovered and communicated. They talk of the experiments of Dr Darwin, (I speak not of what the Doctor really did, or said that he did, but, as more to my purpose, of what was then spoken of as having been done by him,) who preserved a piece of vermicelli in a glass case, till by some extraordinary means it began to move with voluntary motion. Not thus, after all, would life be given. Perhaps a corpse would be re-animated; galvanism had given token of such things: perhaps the component parts of a creature might be manufactured, brought together, and endued with vital warmth.[11]

'I myself am a student of Luigi Galvani, the discoverer of the natural philosophy of animal electricity,' my Beloved boasted to Lord Byron who sits in the armchair opposite him by the hearth. Lord Byron heard the boast but, feared the cold seeping through the edges in the window-panes of glass more, fed the flames an extra log from the metal basket. A heavenly battle waged as violent as any battlefield in the Napoleonic wars. Lightning incessantly flashed. Thunder violently crashed. Rain torrentially dashed any hope of expeditions outside the villa. Trapped in our opulent prison, my Beloved Percy and Lord Byron sought to make a game not of ghost stories, but of natural philosophical debate.

---

10 'All of the other chapters of this book (and its sequel) are myopically focused on collecting all the creative works written during, shortly after, or at very least inspired by the "Year Without Summer". This chapter on the other hand is a debate between Percy Shelley, Byron, and Polidori (with Mary and Claire as voyeurs) as it concerns the science of galvanism. This is THE VERY debate that precipitated Mary's "waking dream" which would inspire her novel *Frankenstein*. This is such a key scene, the penultimate scene. Therefore, I am drawing on quotations from contemporary scientific sources (or near contemporary) that Shelley, Bryon, and Polidori often literally and liberally quote to prove this point or that point in their debate, giving the fertile material to feed Mary' Shelley's dream.'— R.D.B.

11 From the Introduction to the 1831 Edition of *Frankenstein; or, The Modern Prometheus*, published by Henry Colburn & Richard Bentley.

'A student? Before the age of ten?' Lord Byron said mocking his friend. 'My. You were quite learned as a youth to be studying at the teat of the founder of galvanism.'

'Correction then. Perhaps I was more inspired by the experiments of Giovanni Aldini, his nephew, who continued Galvani's great work in animal electricity after his death.'

'Speak precisely then if you have any hope of winning our debate.'

'Very well. It is Galvani, professor of anatomy in Bologna, who in 1780 discovered the new electrical phenomena. By chance he noticed that a recently killed frog, put near an electric machine, produced lively contractions when sparks were drawn from the machine. It was a simple phenomenon. It was nothing else than the effect of a return shock, and a physicist would have given no importance to it.

'Unfortunately, Galvani,' Lord Byron countered, 'a clever anatomist, was poorly versed in electric knowledge.'

'Oh, no, Lord Byron! He varied his experiments in thousands of ways to find out the explanation of the phenomenon. Eventually, looking for what a physicist would have not have deemed worthy of investigation, he made one of those discoveries which—'

'— As properly said' Lord Byron said, 'come from a shaking ignorance than from a resting knowledge.'

'One day,' my Beloved electrically exclaimed, 'he saw a dead frog suspended from a copper hook on the railings of a balcony, and noticed violent muscular contractions whenever the wind blew the lower extremities again the iron bards of the balcony. This was a strange, inexplicable fact, because there was no intervention of any external electricity, with no electric machine or return stroke.'[12]

'So, I purchased the prerequisite equipment from a laboratory. I paid a young chap to catch some frogs and bring them to me. Why had I sent the urchin to the Thames (that dark and dismal river, the dirty one, and a river that smells to heaven) for merely catching frogs for a measly experiment? Towering warehouses, devouring factories, and glowering apartments built by the preposterously prosperous upon one shore and ramshackle shacks and embattled shanties housing the impoverished upon the demolished other. Into stinking back eddies, he dove sinking knee deep in the muck and mire; all to earn my shillings, he stroved... strived,' my Beloved quickly corrected himself. 'With a sack of leaping frogs, he returned and in turn I paid him his shillings.

'I was not alone in my desire to repeat Galvani's experiment. In the later years of the 18th century the poor little froggies in their ponds and pools must have believe the Biblical Apocalypse had been trumpeted.

12 From *Cours de Physique* by Adolphe Ganot, published by Chex, l'auteur in 1859.

The experiment was easily set up and easily replicated. Having cut off the frog's head, I suspended the hind half of the body in a copper hook passed between the back bone and the nerve filaments s which run on each side of it; then holding a small plate of zinc in one hand, I brought one end of it in contact with the copper stem that holds the hook, then touch the legs of the frog with the other end. At every contact I saw the legs bending and shaking, thus reproducing all the motion of life. To account for this phenomenon, Galvani assumed the existence of an electricity proper to the animal tissues, which, passing from the nerves to the muscle through the metals through the metallic arc, produced the contracts. Under the phrase *animal electricity* or *vital fluid* this theory was adopted especially by physicians and physiologists, who supposed that the secret of life had been discovered.[13] Lord Byron, I witnessed with my mortal eyes the spark of life causing the frog's legs to dance. Instantly, I had been handed the primordial fire from Prometheus himself.'

'I have no doubt, my friend, you felt so inspired to compare yourself with Prometheus. Hubris is not a common trait amongst our company, but I must contest that by developing his contact theory Volta went on to invent that wonderful instrument which won him an immortal fame, known also nowadays as the *pile of Volta*. Wishes to multiply the contacts and sum up together the electricity produced by every one of them, the celebrated physicist contrived to put together one above the other, a zinc disk, a copper disk, and afterwards a small piece of cloth moistened with acidulated water; and again a zinc disk, a copper disk, and a small piece of cloth, and again in the same way, with the caution of never inverting the order. What could be expected from such an arrangement. Indeed one should not hesitate in saying it, this apparently inert stuff, this *pile* so many different metallic couples separated by a tiny liquid, is, as far as the effects are concerned, the most wonderful instrument ever invented with no exception, not even that of the steam engine and the telescope.'[14]

'Oh ho!' my Beloved bellowed quite mellowly, 'how by chance Volta invents the battery! Out of pure spite to prove the experiments of Galvani insufficient.'

'Chance? Chance, you say? Why did Galvani possess the jumping frogs?' Lord Byron protested, 'It certainly was not premeditated to investigate the role of electricity in violent muscular contractions. Oh! no! Perchance Giovani or his servant or a waitress acquired the frog to prepare as a delicacy to stimulate— no pun intended my dear friend, at least not entirely— his beloved wife, Lucia's, appetite, who was of a frail constitution. Was it merely to be prepared as a *bouillon* or perhaps

---

13 Ibid.
14 Ibid.

a more delicate preparation of *Cuisses de Grenouille à la Provençale?'*
History never recorded the answer, because the frog gave birth to an
entire new natural philosophy a science of animal electricity!

'As did an apple falling upon the head of natural *philosopher* Sir
Isaac Newton,' my Beloved says, 'Your argument is faulty at its core.
How many discoveries were made by mere chance? Many more than
those sought by hypothesis and subsequent experimentation. Did not
Archimedes of Syracuse, an original natural *philosopher*, exclaim, "Eureka! Eureka!", when sitting down to bath and perceived the water level
rise and attributed this rise to the displacement of water equal to the
volume of the submerged portion of his body? Chance, my dear little
Lord, is in the very definition of a eureka moment, which I argue the
nascent natural *philosopher* Galvani experienced first-hand.'

'Might I interject a brief tangent?' Dr Polidori said.

'Of course, doctor,' my Beloved said acquiescing his point momentarily.

'The tendency of the sciences has long been an increasing proclivi-
ty to separation and dismemberment ...The mathematician turns away
from the chemist; the chemist from the naturalist; the mathematician,
left to himself, divides himself into a pure mathematician and a mixed
mathematician, who soon part company; the chemist is perhaps a chemist of electro-chemistry; if so, he leaves common chemical analysis to
others; between the mathematician and the chemist is to be interpolat-
ed a *"physician"* (we have no English name for him), who studies heat,
moisture, and the like. And thus science, even mere physical science,
loses all traces of unity. A curious illustration of this result may be observed in the want of any name by which we can designate the students
of the knowledge of the material world collectively. We are informed that
this difficulty was felt very oppressively by the members of the British
Association for the Advancement of Science, in their meetings at York,
Oxford, and Cambridge, in the last three summers. There was no general term by which these gentlemen could describe themselves with reference to their pursuits. *Philosophers* was felt to be too wide and too lofty
a term, and was very properly forbidden them by Mr Coleridge, both in
his capacity of philologer and metaphysician; *savans* was rather assuming, besides being French instead of English; some ingenious gentleman
[apparently William Whewell himself] proposed that, by analogy with
artist, they might form *scientist*, and added that there could be no scruple
in making free with this termination when we have such words as *sciolist*,
economist and *atheist*— but this was not generally palatable. Perhaps we
should use the new coinage, lest the term fall out of fashion.[15]

---

15 From an unsigned book review authored by William Whewell in *The Quarterly Review*, vol. 51 (March

'Of course, Doctor, from this point hence we will say *scientist*,' my Beloved says and Lord Byron, with a slight nod, agreed. Dr Polidori smiled, pleased with himself. My Beloved then continued his argument, 'What was the point I was arguing before the doctor's etymological tangent?' he paused to collect his thoughts, 'Ah! Yes! I have it. Luigi Galvani was both revered in certain scientific circles for his revolutionary experiments on the frogs and rivalled in a quite specific circle much to his reputation's detriment and never did these sets intersect with commonality. Scientists, to use the doctor's coinage, delight in thumbing their academic noses at the religious by claiming the sciences are uniquely adaptable to new evidences while the religious are stagnant in their archaic beliefs. The scientist, they claim, embraces new evidences while the religious dismiss the new evidences holding firm to spurious superstitions. But, I argue, scientists often find themselves mired in their own scientific dogmas when new evidences present themselves. In this stagnant swamp of scientific progress, one Alessandro Volta finds himself so mired. But I am not quite ready to debate concerning him yet. Luigi Galvani is where this debate begins, and I shall begin with his beginning.'

'Then hurry along, my dear friend,' Lord Byron said, needling his friend. 'The night wanes fast and our audience of young women may grow weary of our galvanising debate.' I take umbrage at the little Lord's insinuation. I find myself as enraptured by my three companions as I was as a child dropping eaves on my father's parlour! Why should my age or my gender play any part in my audience? How my mother would loathe this little Lord for his ignorance and my father would chastise him for his insult.

'Let us back up a bit in time. Did not the Joseph Priestly, an esteemed naturalist and a great populariser of science conclude that electrical experiments are, of all other, the cleanest and most elegant that the compass of philosophy exhibits. They are performed with the least trouble, there is an amazing variety in them, they furnish the most pleasing and surprising appearances from the entertainment of one's friends, and the expense of instruments may well be supplied, by a proportional deduction from the purchase of books, which are generally read and laid aside, without yielding half the entertainment.[16]

'Was not the society of the Enlightenment enraptured with great fascination over this new field of the scientific study and discovery of electricity? One can easily conclude that if we only consider what it is in objects that makes them capable of exciting the pleasing astonishment,

---

& June, 1834), pp. 58-59
16 From *History and Present State of Electricity* by Joseph Priestly

which has such charms for all mankind, we shall not wonder at the eagerness with which persons of both sexes, and of every age and condition, run to see electrical experiments. Here we see the course of nature, to all appearance, entirely reversed, in its most fundamental laws, and by causes seemingly the slightest imaginable. And not only are the greatest effects, and by causes which seem to be inconsiderable, but by those with which they seem to have no connection. Here, contrary to the principle of gravitation, we see bodies attracted, repelled, and held suspended by others, which are seen to have acquired that power by nothing but a very slight friction; while another body, with the very same friction, reverses all its effects. Here we see a piece of cold metal, or even water, or ice emitting strong sparks of fire, so as to kindle many inflammable substances, and *in vacuo* its light is prodigiously diffused and copious, so as exactly to resemble what is really is, the lightning of heaven.[17]

'Do you not, Lord Byron, question what can seem more miraculous than to find, that a common glass phial or jar, should, after a littler preparation (which, however, leaves no visible effect, whereby it can be distinguished from other phials or jars) be capable of giving a person such a violent sensation as nothing else in nature can give, and even of destroying animal life; and this shock attended with an explosion like thunder, and a flash like that of lightning?[18]

And then as if on the cue of the stage manager at the Dreary Lane Theatre, the divine sound effects hand rattled a thinned sheet of metal and flashed limelight to signal to the audience in attendance that thunder and lightning could be produced outside of inclement weather and inside a building made of brick and mortar. But outside the parlour's window, the divine sound effects hand was the Creator of the Natural World, and the thinned sheet of metal was the ominous darkened clouds that hung low over the lake and the flashes of limelight were electricity. The crash of thunder and the clash of lightning accentuated my Beloved's argument as if the Creator concurred.

Lord Byron countered with affirmation of my Beloved's argument, though from a different point-of-view. 'It could easily be said that the further experiments and discoveries in electricity— of which Newton had seen only the principle— seem to reinforce the great Philosopher's doubts. The speed with which the electrical vapour moves, changes direction, stops and races forth again seem consistent with the speed and changes in animal sensations and motions. The single ease of its travel— in general, through electrical bodies by communication, and in particular, through the nervous and muscular parts of animals— is consistent

17 Ibid
18 Ibid

with the ease with which the mutations induced in organ by various objects are conveyed to the seat of sentience; it is also consistent with the agility with which other motions correspondingly ensue in the body. And the contractions and dilatations caused in the muscles by an electrical spark or electrical shock are arguments, perhaps, even decisive ones, for the above-mentioned conjecture.'[19]

Poor Polidori, itching with anticipation to enter into the argument between my Beloved and our little Lord, blurted out as soon as Lord Byron's final syllable was uttered, 'Was it not high time for John Welsh to acquaint Benjamin Franklin with the result of my experiments on the Isle de Ré and he must do it in a word if he mean to use in a letter. The vigour of the fresh-taken torpedoes there was not able to force the Torpedinal fluid across the most minute tract of air, not from one link of a small chain to another, not even thro' a separation made by the edge of a knife in a slip of tinfoil pasted on sealing wax. The spark therefore and snapping noise attending it were denied to all their attempts, either in the light or complete darkness. Walsh observed to Franklin in his last the singularity of the Torpedo being able when insulated to give to an insulated person a great number of successive shocks: In this circumstance he has taken no less than fifty shocks from him in the space of a minute and half. All their experiments confirmed that the Torpedinal fluid was concentrated in the very instant of it's explosion by a sudden energy of the animal; and as there was no gradual accumulation and retention of this elastick fluid as in the case of charged glass, it is not surprizing that there should be no effect on Canton's Balls of attraction or repulsion. In short, the Torpedinal shock appears to arise from a compressed elastick fluid restoring itself to its former state by the same conductors as the elastick fluid compressed in charged glass. The skin of the animal, bad conductor as it is, appears to be a better conductor of the Torpedinal elastick fluid than the least tract of the likewise elastick fluid air. Notwithstanding the weak spring of the Torpedinal fluid Walsh was able to convey it in the publick exhibitions at La Rochelle thro' two brass wires of twelve feet each and thro' four to eight persons, at different times, the wires and persons communicating with each other by the medium of water, in basins placed between each. The Torpedo laid on a wet napkin was placed on a table six feet distant from the table on which the basins stood. One end of one of the wires was wrapt in the wet napkin and the other end went into the first basin in which the first gentleman put a finger of one hand, with a finger of the other hand in the next Basin. The circuit was in this manner continued to the last basin. One end of the other wire was put into this last basin and with the other end he just touched the back of

---

19 From *Of Artificial and Natural Electricity* by Giambatista Beccaria, published in 1753.

the fish, when all the persons in the circuit were affected, but Walsh, the toucher, being out of it felt nothing. The effect in air, on many repeated experiments, is about four times as strong as it is in water.'[20]

The hyperbolic statement hung in the air like a balloon made of lead.

Polidori then barrelled on bloviating about some letter from one Sieur Seignette, Mayor of la Rochelle, and second perpetual Secretary of the Academy of that City, to the publisher of the *French Gazette.* He had written, "In the Gazette of the 14th August, the publisher mentioned the discovery made by Mr. Walsh, Member of the parliament of England, and of the Royal Society of London. The experiment, of which I am going to give you an account, was made in the presence of the Academy of this city. A live Torpedo was placed on a table. Round another table stood five persons insulated. Two brass wires, each thirteen feet long, were suspended to the ceiling by silken strings. One of these wires rested by one end on the wet napkin on which the fish lay; the other end was immersed in a basin full of water placed on the second table, on which stood four other basins likewise full of water. The first person put a finger of one hand in the basin in which the wire was immersed, and a finger of the other hand in the second basin. The second person put a finger of one hand in this last basin, and a finger of the other hand in the third; and so on successively, till the five persons communicated with one another by the water in the basins. In the last basin one end of the second wire was immersed; and with the other end Mr. Walsh touched the back of the Torpedo, when the five persons felt a commotion which differed in nothing from that of the Leyden experiment, except in the degree of force. Mr. Walsh, who was not in the circle of conduction, received no shock. This experiment was repeated several times, even with eight persons; and always with the same success. The action of the Torpedo is communicated by the same mediums as that of the electric fluid. The bodies which intercept the action of the one, intercept likewise the action of the other. The effects produced by the Torpedo resemble in every respect a weak electricity.'"[21]

AND!

'Did not Sir Isaac Newton write in his *Principia*: In experimental philosophy, propositions collected from the phenomena of induction, are deemed (notwithstanding contrary hypotheses) either exactly or very nearly true, till other phenomena occur by which they may be rendered either more accurate, or liable to exception?[22] Because! Even

20 From a letter to Benjamin Franklin from John Walsh, 27 August 1772.
21 Extract of a Letter from the Sieur Seignette, Mayor of la Rochelle, and second perpetual Secretary of the Academy of that City, to the publisher of the French Gazette
22 From *The Mathematical Principles of Natural Philosophy* by Isaac Newton, published in 1726.

Felice Fontana, the strongest and most ardent disciple in the discipline of Albrecht von Haller, who was himself the fiercest of opponents to the conception of the electrical nature of animal spirits, changed his mind. Did Fontana not concur that in short, not only the mechanism of muscle motion is unknown, but we cannot even image anything capable of accounting for it? It seems that we are forced to make recourse to some other principle, perhaps to something analogous to electricity, if not to ordinary electricity itself. The electric Gymnotus and the torpedo make the thing at least possible, if not probable. One could believe that this principle follows the most ordinary laws of electricity. It might be even more modified in nerves than it is in the torpedo and the Gymnoti. Nerves would be the organs devoted to conducting his fluid, and possibly also to exciting it. But all remains to be done.'[23] 'We must first assure ourselves by firm experiments, whether the electrical principle has really its site in the contracting muscles; we must determine the laws that this fluid observes in the animal body; and after all it remains to be known what excites this principle and who it is excited.' [24]

Pleased with his contribution to the debate, poor Polidori sat back again; he had been on sitting, quite literally, on the edge of his seat, hunched over his haunches.

'True. True,' my Beloved said complimenting Dr Polidori. He then continued his argument from the point-of-view of Galvani. 'As several anatomists have thought that the electric fluid either enters into the composition of that very subtle fluid which is considered, and not without reason, to flow through the nerves, or it is that same nervous fluid, so he decided to carry out some experiments on the nerves with the electric fluid, in the hope that they could disclose the truth or at least contribute to throw some light on the obscurity of the phenomena of nerves.[25] Giovani prepared his frogs in the usual way: 'The frogs being cut transversally below the upper limbs, skinned and disembowelled, he flet only their inferior limbs joined together, with their long crural nerves inserted. These latter were wither left loose and free, or attached to the spinal cord, which in turn was either left intact in its vertebral canal or artificially extracted from it and partly or wholly separated. The phenomena he describe occurred only if the animals had been prepared for experimentation in the manner I have mentioned above; otherwise the contractions failed to take place.' [26]

---

23 From *Treatise on viper venom, on American poison, on cherry laurel, and on some other vegetable poisons* by Felice Fontana, published in 1781.
24 Ibid
25 From an unpublished draft by Luigi Galvani
26 Ibid

Then Lord Byron chimed in with his own critique, 'Did not Marcellow Malpighi know that the way our souls use the body in operating is ineffable. Yet it is certain that in the operations of growth, sensation, and motion the soul is forced to act in conformity with the machine on which it is acting. Just as a clock or a mill is moved in the same way be a pendulum of lead or stone, or by an animal, or a man; indeed, if an angel moved it, he would produce the same motion with changes of position as the animals or other agents do. Hence, even though he did not know how the angel operates, if on the other hand he did know the precise structure of the mill, he would understand this motion and action, and if the mill were out of order,he would try to repair the wheels or the damage to their structure without bothering to investigate how the angel moving them operated.'[27]

'How an angel operates?' my Beloved countered with slight mockery, 'Galvani himself formulated a handful of laws that function outside of how an angel operates. Law 1: The muscular contraction produced by nerve irritation is proportional both to the minimum parts of the nerve moved by the stimulus and to the force by which they are moved. Law 2: Independently on the irritating cause, the irritation is almost uniquely local, that is, it spreads very poorly— if any— beyond the place of application. Law 3: The communication, as well as the propagation to the muscle, of either the action of the nervous force or of the induced motion is dependent only on the nerve.[28] He would observe what could be considered a fourth law, though he did not state it thus, in Galvani's words, very little electric fluid which is far from giving any electric sign, is able to excite the contractions.

Dr Polidori piped in, 'Was not Galvani to have said, to be sure, that a direct proportion seemed to him to be maintained in the contractions, but only within certain limits. It has been found, for example, that if, after fixing a certain length of a nerve-conductor which is sufficient to bring about contractions, you shorten it, then the contractions do not diminish, but disappear. If, however, you lengthen it, the contractions in fact grow strong, but only up to a certain point, beyond which— however far you extend the nerve-conductor— the contractions are augmented imperceptibly, if at all. The same can be said about the other elements of the proportion I have set forth.'[29]

And with these words, this chapter of their Galvanising debate closed.

---

27 From Response of Doctor Marcellow Malpighi to the Letter by Mercello Malpighi, published posthumously.

28 From Luigi Galvani's manuscripts kept in the archives of the Academy of Sciences of Bologna.

29 From De viribus elecricitatis in motu musculari commentaries by Luigi Galvani.

* * *

Only to reopen again after the briefest of intermissions to pour new brandy.

Dr Polidori continued his liberal quoting, 'Was not Priestly to have seen abundant reason, since the publication of his former volume of *Observations on different kinds of air,* to applaud himself for the little delay he made in putting it to press; the consequences having been that, instead of the experiments being prosecuted by himself only, or a few other, the subject had now gained almost universal attention among philosophers, in every part of Europe,' poor Polidori paused to breathe, 'and this branch of science, of which nothing, in a manner was known till very lately indeed, now bids fair to be farther advanced than any other in the whole compass of natural philosophy.'[30]

'Ah, yes,' Lord Byron said, 'Was it not then possible to isolate "inflammable air" or hydrogen, "phlogisticated air" or nitrogen, "fixed air" otherwise now known as carbon dioxide, "swamp air" or methane" and "dephlogisticated air" or the wonderous oxygen? Is it not queer that remarkable advancements of scientists would rival the poets and philosophizers in the understanding of our world. No longer are we restricted to the laughably mythological Scriptures of the Jews and Christians.'

'Yes! Yes,' Dr Polidori exclaimed, continuing his argument, 'In the meantime, did not Galvani among others, diligently examine the above mentioned principles [i.e. the various airs] with the aim of finding their quality and quantity in the various fluid and solid parts of animals, an examination— as far as they would know— that nobody has done before.[31] Did not Galvani find that inflammable air was to be found present in all animal parts– both the solid and the fluid— and in particular the nerves? Was not this in flammable principle wholly or partly that fluid in the nerves called nervous fluid or animal spirits, which is the author of sense and motion? For either the nerves are of an idioelectric [i.e. non-conductive] nature, as many affirm, and for this reason they could not function as conductors, or else they are conductive; and how can it then happen that they retain the animal electric fluid within them so that it is not diffused and spread to adjacent parts, with, undoubtedly, a great diminution of muscular contractions? On the other hand this idoelectric substance of the nerves, which seems to have the function of preventing the electric nerve fluid from being dispersed with great consequent damage. Will not prevent this fluid coursing through the inner conducting

---

30 From *History and Present State of Electricity* by Joseph Priestly.
31 From Luigi Galvani's manuscripts kept in the archives of the Academy of Sciences of Bologna.

substance of the nerves, from leaving these same nerves when needed to produce contractions.'[32]

My Beloved asserted his own argument on the pedanticness of these arguments, 'We are trudging through the weeds too greatly. Let us dine on the meat of the argument we are having this evening by debating the war of not only words, but philosophies between Luigi Galvani and Alessandro Volta. I choose to speak for Galvani.'

'And I'll speak for Volta,' Lord Byron said, effectively cutting poor Polidori out of any further debate. But knowing the doctor as well as I do, only having known him less than a fortnight, silencing him will be a task of Herculean efforts rivalling the cleaning out of the Aegean stables. 'Do we know if Galvani and Volta ever have any direct interactions before or during or after the controversy?' Dr Polidori inquired, the Herculean task already falling defeated. My Beloved and our Little Lord and I knew the intent of his inquiry. He was putting either my Beloved's or Byron's feet to the proverbial flame.

'Well, dearest doctor,' my Beloved said, 'Volta tarried a few days in Bologna, where he visited the Institute of Sciences. Did not Sebastiano Canterzani, the secretary of the Academy of Sciences, remember the visit in a letter dated September 20, 1780, and addressed to Carlo Bianconi, the secretary of the Academy of Milan?'

'Perchance he did,' Dr Polidori said, truly doubting such a letter ever existed.

Then my Beloved quoted it in part, 'I am most obliged to You, illustrious Sir, for giving me the possibility of personally meeting Mr Alessandro Volta, whose celebrated name I knew before for his great discoveries in physics! The special esteem provided for similar people renders their company most satisfactory, in particular when they possess such a likable character and exquisite manners Don Alessandro. But he stayed in Bologna very briefly, only two days. I went with him to the Institute, where he spent several hours, and I introduced him to Mr Monti, Veratti, Metteucci, and some others of our professors.'[33]

Defeated, Poor Polidori, slumped back in his chair. Now, the adults in the room would continue their Galvanising debate.

'First off,' Lord Byron said, 'it must be stated first before any argument— or disagreement— can be made concerning the debate before Volta and Galavani that the former hailed Galvani's discovery of animal electricity as "one of those great and brilliant discoveries, which deserves to be considered defining an ear in the field of physical and

---

32 From *De viribus elecricitatis in motu musculari commentaries* by Luigi Galvani.
33 From a letter from S Canterzani to C Bianconi, Bologna, September 20, 1780.

medical science."[34] Is this not a comparison with Franklin's discovery of the electrical nature of lightning?' Did not Volta esteem and appreciate "his very fine experience" or for "the many nice experiment he made", even when Volta disagreed. Vehemently. This could not and should not be the nature of electricity that the Bolognese doctor "obsintately" called "animal".'

'It is the height of scientific rigor and method,' my Beloved added, 'that for every argument raised and for every answer submitted, they returned, time and time again, to experimentation to get the necessary elements to refute the other's criticisms. Did not Galvania write, in clear reference to Volta, "However I do not want to base my claims only on analogy arguments, and, as Mr Volta uses experiments to prove the truth of his theory and the falsity of mind, so it is fair that I purse a similar path".'[35]

'But first,' Lord Byron said, 'Galvani was charged with resurrected Tommaso Laghi's discredited neuro-electric hypothesis. Galvani must first, the argument held, overcome the objections raised some decades previous by Felice Fontana and Leopoldo Caldani, whom we have mentioned during our Galvanising debate.'

'Oh! Ho! Galvani would indeed argue in these objections are contradicted by the example and existence of tourmaline and of electric fish, which produce electricity even when completely immersed in water. Remember, Lord Byron, that water is in itself a conducting liquid. And Galvani argued that his own experiments, as well as Volta's, proved that "animal humidity does not prevent electrical excitation; on the contrary, it makes an easy way for electricity to obey the soul and, on its command, to move toward various places in order to put muscles in motion."[36] I would argue, Lord Byron, as Aldini and Galvani did before me, that the Hallerian theory of irritability is "not a well known" principle as Haller himself conceded, I challenge you to prove its existence within the framework of "established laws" as Galvani as so proven for animal electricity! Prove it or abandon your theory in favour of Galvani's!'

Lord Byron sat silent.

But then protested, 'Did not Volta's criticize the crucial experiments on muscular contractions without the use of metals gave doubtful and inconstant results?'

Oh! Ho!,' my Beloved answered, 'Galvani himself answered this criticism, "I can assure that I obtained the motions of the frog's legs not

---

34 From *Le opere di Alessandro Volta. Edizione nazionale sotto gli auspice della Reale Accademia dei Licnei e el Reale Istituto Lambardo di Scinze e Lettere* by Alessandro Volta
35 From *De viribus elecricitatis in motu musculari commentaries* by Luigi Galvani.
36 From *Memorie ed esperimenti inedita* by Luigi Galvani.

a few times, as Volta claims, but in many, many experience, so that in a hundred times the effect had not happened just once; and these experiments have been recently replicated in our Institute of Sciences in the presence of many learned scholars, and other people well, versed in this sort of things, and they never failed.' AND! 'To confirm the truth, I succeeded in obtaining the kind attention and assistance of several illustrious friends to my experiments; among them I think it suffices to cite the most learned secretary of our academy, Sebastiano Canterzani, to whom I never omitted to show any of my experiments, and to communicate any of my contjectures before publishing; but more than any other I could quote, You"— meaning Lazzaro Spallanzani— "who are such an excellent and absolute master in every scientific field, as in the difficult art of experiment, and who, for my good fortune, have been only a witness to this experiment, but an approving judge."'[37]

Lord Byron then challenged Galvani on his overuse of a literary style in his scientific works, which my Beloved countered by quoting them freely from the book that had rested upon his lap, "If a frog is held by one leg with the fingers so that the hook fastened in the spinal cord touches a silver plate and if the other leg calls down freely on the same plate, the muscles are immediately contracted at the instant that this leg makes contact with the plate. There upon the leg is raised and lifted up, but soon, however, it spontaneously relaxes and again falls down on the plate. As soon as contact is made, the leg is again lifted for the same reason and thus it continues alternately to be raised and lowered so that the great astonishment and pleasure of the observer, the leg seems to function like an electric pendulum."[38]

Lord Byron altered the argument back to Volta. 'I acknowledge that Volta had repeated some of Galvani's experiments but I argue that Volta himself had stated "the existence of a real and true animal electricity is evidently proved in the third part of the work you hold in your hands, dearest Percy, with many well combined and accurately described experiments." He acknowledged Galvani having "all the merit and paternity of this great and stupendous discovery!"[39] But this love affair with Galvani's experiments and scientific concludes would be short lived. There was no animal electricity, instead he introduced a new concept into physics: the electromotive power of metals!'

'In fact, Volta's criticism goes well beyond Galvani's first experiment. The criticism encompasses the very foundation of Galvani's theory of animal electricity, namely the analogy between the neuromuscular

---

37 From *Memorie sulla electricita... al celebre abate Lazzaro Spallanzani* by Luigy Galvani, published in 1797.
38 From *De viribus electricitatis in motu musculari commenarius* by Luigi Galvani, published in 1791.
39 From *Le opere di Alessandro Volta. Edizione nazionale sotto gli auspice della Reale Accademia dei Licnei e el Reale Istituto Lambardo di Scinze e Lettere* by Alessandro Volta.

system and the Leyden jar: "The most plausible and fascinating explanations, which seem in agreement with the fist general appearances, are
rarely confirmed by a more rigorous examination of particular phenomenon; and when we try to extend a nice discovery, which has presented
us, to great and magnificent consequences, we are often obliged to make
a step backward and to renounce to great part of our conceived plans."[40]

'In a letter to Giovanni Aldini, whom we know to be Galvani's
nephew, Volta argued he believed that: "It is on the nerves, and solely
on them that electricity acts, both in the case of a mild artificial electricity
and of animal electricity; it is not at all necessary that the electric fluid
flows through the nerves to the muscles; even less so that there follows
any discharge between nerve and muscle, or between the internal and
external surface of the latter: in sum, the electric fluid is not the immediate cause, even if as a stimulus,.., of muscular motions, but only mediate,
occasional and remote cause, as his proper action consists in stimulating
and exciting the nerves."[41]

'But,' my Beloved countered, 'while Volta may have rejected Galvani's explanation of muscle motion, based on the analogy between the
muscle and the Leyden jar, Volta, who however still acknowledge Galvani with the great merit of having opened a new and important path:
"There remain the materials of Galvani's edifice, namely the beautiful
outcomes of his original experiments and the discoveries that followed;
oh yes, there remain such precious materials for another fabric, more
solid if not finer, which may be raised."'[42]

'But!' Lord Byron argued, 'Did not an esteemed publication, that
had previously reviewed Galvani's work, report the news that "the most
illustrious Prof Volta, by continuing the experiments on animal electricity— a subject which can now be considered his own— makes new discoveries everyday"?'

Poor Polidori, sitting on his hands, interjected, 'What was the path
that led Volta in a few months to change his opinion from an enthusiastic acceptance of Galvani's theory of animal electricity to the rejection
of the analogy between the muscle and the Leyden jar, and to the denial
of the existence of animal electricity?'

Lord Byron offered an answer, 'In his but first letter to Tiberio Cav-
allo, Volta wrote, "I do not know whether Galvani has carried out other
experiments, but hose which he has made public in his work are restricted in an excessively narrow circle; every time they consist in uncovering
and isolating the nerves, and in establishing a communication between

40 Ibid
41 Ibid
42 Ibid

these nerves and the depending muscles through electrical conducting bodies. However, by varying this sort of experiences in multiple ways, I showed that both these conditions, to uncover and isolate the nerves and to simultaneously touch these and the muscles in order to produce the pretended discharge, are not at all necessary."[43]

Eagerly biding his time and biting his lip, My Beloved launched into his counter argument: 'Galvani needed to understand the role of a conducting arc in the phenomena of contractions, it was necessary, first of all, to assess the "natural muscular force" of the animal. If, indeed, the same type of ace produced contractions in one animal but not another, that could depend not on the characteristics of the arc, but on the "varying strength of the animals". Likewise, and that was the case pointed out by Volta, the variable efficacy of different arcs applied to the same animal could be due to the variation in the strength of the animal, and not to the difference in the arc.'

Lord Byron argued, 'Did not Galvani distinguish three degrees of "animal force"— maximum, medium, and minimum—?' Did he not say, 'It is not convenient to perform the experiments, especially those implying comparisons, in the third degree, that is the minimum degree of the said force, as the re-occurring of contractions through a new type of arc in this case may be not the effect of this arc; so that the conclusions of a more powerful activity of the given arc could be erroneous.'[44] Erroneous! Percy, erroneous!

My Beloved laughed, 'Here Galvani is clearly referring to Volta's experiments in which the special efficacy of bimetal arcs was particularly evident! But it is the choice of the type of animal, on which Galvini insisted, was one of the fundamental criteria of the experimental method developed by Lazzaro Spallanzani. Spallanzani, for example, in his research on blood circulation carried out in the 1770s, had used "preferably the water newt, as it seems very apt to manifest and clear up those phenomena thanks to the easy preparation of its vases, their great transparency, and the most vivid purple-red colour of its blood. The choice of this animal, like that of the frog by Galvani, had been particularly felicitous, so much so that Spallanzani commented: "In truth, from the examination of the newt I acquired so much physiological knowledge, that I doubt whether a different animal had conceded the same to another observer after the discovery of circulation"

'Volta did in fact attribute great importance to experimental conditions. He considered, for example the variability of the action exerted

---

43 Ibid
44 From *Dell'uo e dell'attivita dell'arco conduttore nelle contrazioni dei muscoli* by Luigi Galvani, publishing in 1794

by external stimuli on animal preparations, as Volta would write: "as this action depends on the varying strength and disposition of the same animal on it being more of less well prepared, recently or less recently on ambient temperature, etc." Moreover he distinguished, on the basis of his observations on the animals "electric vitality," "four degrees of stages of death." About the contractions obtained in a "living and intact" animal, Volta wrote: "As to the animal preparation, these experiments are easier to perform than those carried out in Mr Galvani's way, as no dissection of the animal is needed: and they much finer and more pleasant.[45]""

My Beloved laughed again as Lord Byron was contributing to his own side of the argument, 'Surely, Volta was surprised when he noticed the contractions could be excited in animals where were alive and prepared, or "lacerated" in various ways, and his surprise was followed by the felling that this was indeed an original observation, a discovery of his own. It was similar to what had happened to Galvani when he placed the conducting arc between the nervle and muscle of the prepared from "in the unusual manner"; Volta placed the bitmetal arc on the skin of the "alive and intact" animal, often armed with thin metal "shirts" or "dresses" and this because the ideal point of reference for interpreting the electrical phenomenon included in neuromuscular physiology.'

'What Galvani needed' my Beloved argued, 'was an general interpretation that could account for all the experiments and phenomena observed up to that point. The new theoretical conception proposed by Galvani in his *Trattato* did not just off a coherent explanation of the special efficacy of bimetal arcs in the production of muscular contractions but accounted for a number of observations that were difficult to explain on the basis of the initial model of the animal Leyden jar developed in *De viribus*.

'He proposed the following "small machine": "Let's take a glass jar in the form of a flask, which is more convenient to build, and armed [i.e., covered with a metal coating] both internally and externally as usual; a conductor connected to the internal surface must exit from the flask's neck as long as one like, then it must be all plastered with some insulating matter like wax and be put into conact with the external armature. Let's now make little holes in different points of the plastering which relates to the conductor and then pour water or another conducting fluid on all the plastering so that the fluid enters the holes and gets into direct contact with the conductor. In this way it is sure that there is communi-

---

45 From *Le opere di Alessandro Volta. Edizione nazionale sotto gli auspice della Reale Accademia dei Licnei e el Reale Istituto Lambardo di Scinze e Lettere* by Alessandro Volta.

cation between the internal and external surfaces of the jar through the fluid."

'This "small machine", a perfected version of the animal Leyden jar could artificially reproduce the normal conditions of the electric flow within the nerve-muscle system. The flask represented the muscle fibre, while the conductor communicating with its internal and external surfaces presented the nerve, which was covered by an insulating but perforated sheath that allowed a moderate passage of electric fluid from the interior to the exterior of the muscle. This mechanism was designed to keep an electrical disequilibrium in the system, at the same time avoiding an excessive accumulation of electricity, which could produce "a serious danger of lesion and alteration" of both nerves and muscles.'

Eagerly biding his time and biting his lip, My Beloved launched into his counter argument: 'Galvani's further experiments allowed him to respond to Volta's objections also from a methodological point of view: "In truth, as it is firm and proved by many facts that the arc applied from the nerve to the muscle elicits the contractions, before admitting a new and equally efficient one which is applied to other parts or to the same part, namely to the same nerve, it seems necessary– in view of prudent laws of philosophising– that this new arc cannot refer to the fire one, i.e., that it cannot ever communicate with the muscles through any conducting body: but in this case it is certain that this communication is established through the humidity which extends itself from the nerve to the muscle; therefore to suppose that the above mentioned contractions are excited by the mere arc applied form one nerve to another, or from a part of the nerve to another part of the same nerve is contrary to the right law of philosophising."[46]

'These "right laws of philosophising"', My Beloved argued, 'implied that one should not invoke a new cause to explain new phenomena that culd be explained by known causes, were often referred to by both Galvani and Volta during their controversy on animal electricity.'

'With the publication of the *Tratto* and its *Supplemento* Galvani believed he had answered Volta's objections again this theory of animal electricity and refuted his opponent's ideas. Reversing the meaning of one of Volta's judgments, he thus claimed: "If things are as I said, if such electricity is truly and completely proper to the animal, and not common and external to it, what will it be of Mr Volta's opinion, who on the basis of the alleged experiments has pretended to completely exclude animal

---

46 From *Dell'uo e dell'attivita dell'arco conduttore nelle contrazioni dei muscoli* by Luigi Galvani, publishing in 1794.

electricity, and to limit Galvani's discovery to the mere invention of the most exquisite electrometer in the animal?[47]"'

"Oh! Ho! My dearest Shelley,' Lord Byron crowed, 'the debate was far from over.'

My Beloved added to the argument, 'In publishing the *Tratto dell'arco coduttore*, Galvani hoped that "the experiments and arguments" he was adducing were such as to convince everybody of the existence of "an electricity proper to animal,' as he expressed himself in a letter addressed to Lazzaro Spallanzani. The choice of Spallanzani as an interlocutor was made with intent. First, he was one of my most found scientific scholars of the period. He had been studying a great vvariety of phenomena, from volcanoes to sea animals, from geological conformation of the territory to the "sense" of bats. Moreover, since 1769, he had been professor of natural history in Pavia, the University where Volta also works, where the criticism to Galvani and Volta's theory of metallic electricity were well received.

'I can site a comment Spallanzani made in a letter of October 1797 as evidence of the areful and objective view he held with regard to Galvani's work. Spallanzani remarked that the experiments on spark production in the torpedo referred to by the Bolognese doctor had indeed been carried out exclusively in the "electric gymnotus". In his response, he praised the "new pamphlet" and its author. Thess words would have sounded very sweet to Galvani's ears because in a letter dated August 1, 1794, he answered in this way:

"I give thanks to Your very Illustrious Lordship for the letter you sent me, which could not be more courteous and appreciated. Concerning the controversies and doubts on animal electricity, this letter produces a fulsome calmness in my soul, which was indeed rather restless. I was very much concerned that, with the possibility of many opposing opinions, this new branch of animal physics would remain without some of those advantages that hopefully sometimes it could produce. In hearing now your judgment, a judgement of complete certitude and authoritativeness, as favourable to the afore-said animal electricity, and to the expressed laws, I no longer have any doubt about the truth of the thing and of the usefulness that is desired for it."

Lord Byron countered, 'Galvani (together with Spallanzani and various of their colleaues) *may have* convinced *themselves* that the *Trattato dell'arco conduttore* would solve all doubts and put an end to any controversy, clarifying the problem of the existence of animal electricity and the mechanism of muscle contraction. This was not, however a

---

47 Ibid

unanimous opinion. Volta was quick to read the *Tratto* and used it to restate his views on the arguments raised by Galvani. Volta did that by inserting his comments in a letter sent to Piedmontese abbot Anton Maria Vassalli, perpetual secretary of the Turin Academy of Sciences. Galvani sometimes shows that he has not fully understood the meaning of Volta's theory of the electromotive powers of metals. For instance, in once passage he negates the possibility of an electric disequilibrium between heterogenous metals. This is because "being metal conductive bodies, the electricity of one part of the arc should necessarily be in a condition of equilibrium with the electricity of the other part.'

'Oh! Ho!' my Beloved answered, 'On the other hand, Volta did not fully apricate the new model of animal electric developed by Galvani in the *Tratto*. In the third letter to Vassalli, Volta opposes his concept of "circulation, i.e., of a continuous flow of electric fluid" between different conductors, to Galvani's theory based on the concept of "charge or un-balance, and consequent discharge in animal organisms!"'

'Oh! Ho!' Lord Byron countered, 'Far from admitting the need of an animal type of electricity in the circumstances of direct muscle-nerve contact, what Volta actually did was modify and extend his conception the electromotive power of metals. It sufficed to assume that electricity could be moved by contact of two dissimilar bodies, without them needed to be metals. "In this way the principle is generalized, that any time two different conductors are connected, an action arises, which pushes more or less the electric fluid: in such a way that, as far as the circuit is closed between three of them, whatever they are, with the proviso that they are different from each other, some current is constantly excited , either modest, or week or very weak."[48] In other words, a current could be produced not only by connecting tother different metals, between them or with the Galvanian frog, but also by the contact of all "humid" conductive bodies of different natures! The new theory of Volta appeared to be at the same time simple and comprehensive: with a single principle, it sufficed to account for all phenomena put on the stage by the various protagonists of the controversy of animal electricity.'

'I will admit' my Beloved said 'In their researches, both Galvani and Volta had become progressively aware of the importance of coating (or "arming") both nerves and muscles with laminas of different metals. This experimental arragment proved to be particularly important with weak frog preparations, that is, with preparations that did not show any contractions when tested in the ordinary way.'

---

48 From *Le opere di Alessandro Volta. Edizione nazionale sotto gli auspice della Reale Accademia dei Licnei e el Reale Istituto Lambardo di Scinze e Lettere* by Alessandro Volta.

'Volta made his victor lap,' Lord Bryon added, 'in a fourth letter to Vassalli: "There could perhaps be a possibility to straighten up this pretended animal electricity, that I declare as nonexistent, and that with many experiments I think to have knock down; I have substitutes it with the other principle that I have contrived, of a purely artificial electricity, i.e., a form of electricity moved by an extrinsic cause. It would be necessary that adversaries show the appearance of convulsions in frogs etc, with the making of conductor, all of the same species, by no way dissimilar the one from the other; this they would never be able to do so."[49]

'In then unpublished letters which are of great importance for the complete picture,' Lord Byron said, 'Volta wrote to Fransico Mocchetti, a doctor who had been a student at University: "This discovery makes it clear that the course of electric fluid in nerves most favourable to the excitation of motion in muscles is that made in the same direction in which the power of will acts and manifests itself on the muscles under its control. That is, by going down from head or trunk toward the branks. This could induce us to conjecture that the electric fluid is the one used by the soul in order to produce motions in Voluntary muscles" And! "To put an end, if the electric fluid has an influence on animal movements, it does have it under the domain of will. The will commands to the electric fluid, which is stationary in all bodies and in all the parts of the living animal, and particularly in the nerves of voluntary motion, which are perhaps more conductive than other parts. On the other hand, in dead animals, or in the excised parts, in which the action of will is cased, electric fluid remains equilibrated and quiet, as in any other Conductor whatsoever." AND! "What I have mentioned here suffices to make it clear that I do no exclude all forms of *Animal electricity*; on the contrary I ascribe to it the most noble part in the Economy, whereas I show to be inexistent the one put on the stage by Galvani, and supported by his adherents; one based on the supposed unbalance of electric fluid between nerves and muscles, or between interior and the exterior of muscles"[50]

Believing he had won the argument and the debate, Lord Byron stood and bowed. Repeatedly bowed. Obscenely bowed.

'While Galvani may have gone silent as a friar, he was not inactive!' My Beloved argued. 'Had he not gone in August 1795 "for leisure, together with some honest friends, to the beaches of the Adriatic Seas" first in Senigallia and afterward in Rimini? But Galvani would publish the results of these experiments in *Memorie sulla electrrcita animale* addressed to Sapallanzani. Oh! The horror to know when one shall die!

49 Ibid
50 Ibid

This was his last public document! For in one year, he would be dead. The legacy of this fundamental document cannot be underrepresented or underappreciated!

'Spallanzani judgment is my own! "For his novelty, for the importance of its doctrines, for the nobility and delicacy of its experiments, for the subtle analysis and the solid criterion accompanying them, for the felicity of the explanations of the most complex and abstruse phenomena, for the clarity and brilliance with which it is written, this work appears to me as one of the most beautiful and valuable of the eighteenth century Physics."[51]

'Galvani *sought* to remove the problem of mechanical stimulation in an experimental setup based on the use of small pieces of muscles tissues excised from the animal. One of those pieces was placed in contact with the nerve and the other with muscle of the leg remaining in situ. When the circuit was completed by manipulating with a small glass rod a third piece of muscle (or even a small piece of frog skin), contractions were produced despite the absence of any movement in the preparation. He concluded by saying: "Everybody sees therefore that the arc is here made up exclusively of animal substances. He sees, moreover, that any uncertainty or doubt is removed, together with any suspicion of mechanical stimulus, and, finally, proved at once that the circulation of electricity depends exclusively on the animal machine that is thus active."[52]

'Are you implying that,' Lord Byron said, 'with these experiments Galvani seems to answer Volta's objections purposefully and with the force of experiments?

'In these particular circumstances he was addressing the challenge contained in a note added by Volta to the second letter to Vassalli, where the physicist of Pavia claimed that a mechanical artifact could not be excluded even when Galvani did his nerve-muscle experiments with the greatest care, bringing the two tissues to a delicate contact rather than to a hit: "Let us conclude then that these experiments do not prove anything, because they leave the suspicion of a mechanical stimulus. In order to exclude a suspicion of this type, one should come to experiments in which the frog nerves and muscles do rest quietly, and are not touched or pressed in any other possible way."'[53]

'Galvani's answer to Volta's initial objection against the experiment of the contact between nerve and muscle can be undoubtedly be considered detailed and timely. Galvani himself describes his new experi-

51 From a letter by L. Spallanzani to L. Galvani, Scandinao, October 25, 1797.

52 From *Memorie sulla electricita... al celebre abate Lazzaro Spallanzani* by Luigy Galvani, published in 1797.

53 From *Le opere di Alessandro Volta. Edizione nazionale sotto gli auspice della Reale Accademia dei Licnei e el Reale Istituto Lambardo di Scinze e Lettere* by Alessandro Volta.

ment thusly,' my Beloved said, lifting the books that had been resting open-faced on his lap, "I prepared the animal in the usual way; then I cut the one and the other of the sciatic nerves near their exit from the vertebral canal; afterwards, I divided, and separated a leg from the other, in such a way that any of them would remain with its corresponding nerve; in the following I bent the nerve of one in the shape of a small bow, and after that having lifted with the usual small glass rod the nerve of the other leg. I let its fall, the nerve should touch in two points the other nerve bent as a bow; and moreover, that the small mouth of the first nerve is one of the two points. I saw then the moving of the leg corresponding t the nerve that I let fall onto the nerve of the other; sometimes even both legs. The experiment succeeds while the two preparations are totally isolated one from the other, and have no reciprocal relation, except for the touching of the nerves."[54]

'Did,' my Beloved asked Lord Byron, 'did either Volta or the other adversaries of animal electricity propose any substantial objection capable of undermining the evidential value of the experiment as support of an electricity intrinsic to the animal? Volta could not even invoke the agency of mechanical artifact at the moment the circuit between the nerves was closed. The counterargument was expressed by Galvani himself, who anticipated this kind of objection, with these words: "But why then by hitting one of the same nerves on an arc much hard and rougher made of non-conductive materials, as those made up of sulphur of glass contractions are not produced? And still in this case the stimulus originating from the hitting should be much stronger?[55]

'Galvani,' my Beloved crowed, 'summarized his theory in a series of points:

I.   That the electricity which induces muscle contractions is already singularly gathered and cumulated in muscle... in a condition of imbalance.
II.   That this imbalance is the basis for the circulation of the electricity in the muscle itself.
III. That this circulation consists of electricity leaving the muscle and returning to the same muscle by an inviolable law.
IV.   That this circulation occurs in the following way: The electricity leaves the muscle by the way of the nerve; it rushes to the place of that nerve to which it is attracted by the force of the armature, and arc; its comes out from the nerve in this same place, being drawn by the same forces; then it enters into the

---

54 From *Memorie sulla electricita... al celebre abate Lazzaro Spallanzani* by Luigy Galvani, published in 1797.
55 Ibid

arc and by means of it returns eventually with all the power of the muscle from which it left.

V.   That because of this tendency, and of the effort that electricity uses in order to come back to the muscle, it chooses always the shortest route to arrive there.

VI. That nerves are the natural and specific conductors of that electricity.

VII. Finally, that the nerves exert this duty with their intimate and medullar substance."[56]

'Concerning the nature of the principle of life,' the doctor blurted out. Poor Polidori had been sitting on his hands, listening to this Galvanising debate between two equals. He sought to add to the argument in the spirit of debate between my Beloved and our little Lord, 'Dr Erasmus Darwin, who we all esteem, would record, "If two particles of iron lie near each other without motion, and afterwards approach each other; it is reasonable to conclude that something besides the iron particles is the cause of their approximation; this invisible something is termed magnetism. The contraction of a muscular fibre may be compared to the following electric experiment, which is here mentioned not as a philosophical analogy, but as an illustration or simile to facilitate the conception of a difficult subject.

' "The attractions of electricity or of magnetism do not apply philosophically to the illustration of the contraction of animal fibres, since the force of those attractions increases in some proportion inversely as the distance, but in muscular motion there appears no difference in velocity or strength during the beginning or end of the contraction, but what may be clearly ascribed to the varying mechanic advantage in the approximation of one bone to another. Nor can muscular motion be assimilated with greater plausibility to the attraction of cohesion or elasticity; for in bending a steel spring, as a small sword, a less force is required to bend it the first inch than the second; and the second than the third; the particles of steel on the convex side of the bent spring endeavouring to restore themselves more powerfully the further they are drawn from each other."

Poor Polidori beamed. He seemed absolutely delighted to be participating in the game of debate with my Beloved and our little Lord. He continued, 'The esteemed Dr Darwin, was no doubt aware that this may be explained another way, because he wrote, "By supposing the elasticity of the spring to depend more on the compression of the particles on the concave side than on the extension of them on the convex side; and by supposing the elasticity of the elastic gum to depend more

---

56 Ibid

on the resistance to the lateral compression of its particles than to the longitudinal extension of them. Nevertheless in muscular contraction, as above observed, there appears no difference in the velocity or force of it at its commencement or at its termination; from whence we must conclude that animal contraction is governed by laws of its own, and not by those of mechanics, chemistry, magnetism, or electricity.

' "On these accounts I do not think the experiments conclusive, which were lately published by Galvani, Volta, and others, to shew a similitude between the spirit of animation, which contracts the muscular fibres, and the electric fluid. Since the electric fluid may act only as a more potent stimulus exciting the muscular fibres into action, and not by supplying them with a new quantity of the spirit of life. Thus in a recent hemiplegia I have frequently observed, when the patient yawned and stretched himself, that the paralytic limbs moved also, though they were totally disobedient to the will. And when he was electrified by passing shocks from the affected hand to the affected foot, a motion of the paralytic limbs was also produced. Now as in the act of yawning the muscles of the paralytic limbs were excited into action by the stimulus of the irksomeness of a continued posture, and not by any additional quantity of the spirit of life; so we may conclude, that the passage of the electric fluid, which produced a similar effect, acted only as a stimulus, and not by supplying any addition of sensorial power.

' "If nevertheless this theory should ever become established, a stimulus must be called an eductor of vital ether; which stimulus may consist of sensation or volition, as in the electric eel, as well as in the appulses of external bodies; and by drawing off the charges of vital fluid may occasion the contraction or motions of the muscular fibres, and organs of sense.

' "For nothing can act, where it does not exist; for to act includes to exist; and therefore the particles of the muscular fibre (which in its state of relaxation are supposed not to touch) cannot affect each other without the influence of some intermediate agent; this agent is here termed the spirit of animation, or sensorial power, but may with equal propriety be termed the power, which causes contraction; or may be called by any other name, which the reader may choose to affix to it.

' "Thus in the common experiments, where the vitreous or resinous ether is accumulated by art, metallic bodies have been esteemed the best conductors, and next to these water, and all other moist bodies; but it was lately discovered, that dry charcoal, recently burnt, was a more perfect conductor than metals; and it appears from the experiments discovered by Galvani, which have thence the name of Galvanism, that animal flesh, and particularly perhaps the nerves of animals, both which are composed of much carbon and water, are the most perfect conductors yet discovered; that is, that they give the least resistance to the junction of the spontaneous electric atmospheres, which exist round metallic bodies, and which differ very little in respect to the proportions of their vitreous and resinous ingredients.'

Lord Byron interrupted his personal physician, 'O! my lovely companion, even Dr Darwin's own experiments preclude the need for electricity in simple creatures whom naturally reanimate. As the doctor himself wrote, "Some of the microscopic animals are said to remain dead for many days or weeks, when the fluid in which they existed is dried up, and quickly to recover life and motion by the fresh addition of water and warmth. Thus the chaos redivivum of Linnæus dwells in vinegar and in bookbinders paste: it revives by water after having been dried for years, and is both oviparous and viviparous. Thus the vermicelli'— (why did I hear and get stuck in my mind 'vermicelli'? I struggled to reconcile this error. There is no doubt in my mind that he said something-anything other than 'vermicelli'. While it may be true that *vermicelli* in Italian translates as 'little worm', I obviously misheard. As I sit in my bedchamber recording this debate into my journal, I ponder the origin of this mishearing and I believe I have found it![57])— 'or wheel animal, which is found in rain water that has stood some days in leaden gutters, or in hollows of lead on the tops of houses, or in the slime or sediment left by such water, though it discovers no sign of life except when in the water, yet it is capable of continuing alive for many months though kept in a dry state. In this state it is of a globulous shape, exceeds not the bigness of a grain of sand, and no signs of life appear; but being put into water, in the space of half an hour a languid motion begins, the globule turns itself about, lengthens itself by slow degrees, assumes the form of a lively maggot, and most commonly in a few minutes afterwards puts out its wheels, swimming vigorously through the water as if in search of food; or else, fixing itself by the tail, works the wheels in such a manner as to bring its food to its mouth." Therefore, my friend, natural reanimation is common, at least in less complex creatures.'

My Beloved interjected himself between the Lord and the Doctor pressing his own argument, 'Ho-ho! You strike down your own argu-

---

57 Dr Darwin writes, 'These microscopic animals are believed to possess a power of generating others like themselves by solitary reproduction without sex; and these gradually enlarging and improving for innumerable successive generations. Mr Ellis gives drawings of six kinds of *animalcula infusoria*, which increase by dividing across the middle into two distinct animals. Thus in PASTE COMPOSED OF FLOUR AND WATER, which has been suffered to become acescent, the animalcules called eels, *vibrio anguillula*, are seen in great abundance; their motions are rapid and strong; they are viviparous, and produce at intervals a numerous progeny: animals similar to these are also found in vinegar. These eels were probably at first as minute as other microscopic animalcules; but by frequent, perhaps hourly reproduction, have gradually become the large animals above described, possessing wonderful strength and activity.'

ment. I concede to you your facts, but! natural reanimation is *not* common in the *more* complex creature! I will give you points for mentioning "vermicelli" (again! with this error! My Beloved and I are so often in synchronization that we finish sentences and make similar errors!) What of reptilians or of mammalians?' I return you to John's argument of Dr Darwin who wrote, "Would it be too bold to imagine, that all warm-blooded animals have arisen from one living filament, which THE GREAT FIRST CAUSE endued with animality, with the power of acquiring new parts, attended with new propensities, directed by irritations, sensations, volitions, and associations; and thus possessing the faculty of continuing to improve by its own inherent activity, and of delivering down those improvements by generation to its posterity, world without end!"[58]

'THE FIRST GREAT CAUSE? Are you going to skew our argument into the Aquinasian? Shame! Shame! Here we are debating the philosophers Galvani and Volta and Darwin, esteemed natural philosophers and yet you, by-the-way-of Dr Darwin, bring in Thomas Aquinas into our purely scientific conversation. Surely, I will not allow the Five Ways of St. Thomas Aquinas to taint our electric debate, pun quite intended. If we are to continue our lines of argument, let me further the point of reanimation in more complex creations.'

'Did you not just argue "natural reanimation is common, at least in *less* complex creatures?"' my Beloved countered, 'and now you wish to argue natural reanimation in *more* complex creatures? My head is spinning with this turnabout.'

'Oh! no! my dearest Percy, you misunderstand me. My only desire to not to descend into religiosity. Our debate concerns the natural philosophers— nay! scientists— Luigi Galvani and Alessandro Volta and Erasmus Darwin and hopefully Galvani's nephew Giovanni Aldini.'

'Giovanni Aldini!' both my Beloved and poor Polidori parroted simultaneously.

'Quite. We need to bring our debate to the subject of George Foster if it is to continue at all. This is of the utmost importance!'

'Point well taken. Please, continue.'

'Thank you,' Lord Byron said, bowing is head slightly in acknowledgement of the permission, 'It is one thing to experiment on frog's legs or cattle heads, but certainly another when the subject of experimentation is a man. Man is far too complex and noble a creature for reanimation. Despite the scientific air we breathe in our modern age, there are certain natural philosophies that go a step too far. The British

---

58 From *Zoonomia; or The Laws of Organic Life. Vol. 1* and *The Temple of Nature; or, The Origin of Society* by Erasmus Darwin. M.D. F.R.S.

Parliament erred when they instituted the Murder Act of 1751, pro-claiming it is "an act for better preventing the horrid crime of murder that some further terror and peculiar mark of infamy be added to the punishment of death. It shall be in the power of any such judge or justice to appoint the body of any such criminal to be hung in chains: but that in no case whatsoever the body of any murderer shall be suffered to be buried; unless after such body shall have been dissected and anatomized as aforesaid." O! the indignity of dissection even on those executed for murder! The sanctity of the body and the sanctity of the grave is a nec-essary even for the condemned.

'George Forster in some accounts; George Foster in this one' the Lord read from his personal copy of the *Newgate Calendar* (subtitled *The Malefactors' Bloody Register*) which he, no doubt, travelled with, 'The conviction of this wretched man was founded entirely upon circum-stantial evidence. He was indicted on the 14th January, 1803, at the Old Bailey, for the wilful murder of his wife and child.'

Why is it said by the respectable that every respectable English household should possess a copy of the King James' Bible, Foxe's *Book of Martyrs*, the *Pilgrim's Progress*, and an edition of the *Newgate Cal-endar*? Why would its editors steadfastly compose a ghastly nursery rhyme encouraging devoted mothers to gift their cherished children a copy of the *Newgate Calendar* and be nourished at bedtime by reading the horrid and sordid accounts of perished criminals and their crimes?

> *'The anxious Mother with a Parents Care,*
> *Presents our Labours to her future Heir*
> *"The Wise, the Brave, the temperate and the Just,*
> *Who love their neighbour, and in God who trust*
> *Safe through the Dang'rous paths of Life may Steer,*
> *Nor dread those Evils we exhibit Here".'*

The Lord's eyes darted over the horry backstory concerning the crimes committed by George Foster, the chimes of testimonies from witnesses, and the rhymes and reasonings of the prosecutors regarding the execution of the sentence. His eyes landed on the moment he wish-es to relate in his debate with my Beloved Percy and continues, 'This un-fortunate malefactor was executed pursuant to his sentence, January 18, 1803. At three minutes after eight he appeared on the platform before the debtor's door in the Old Bailey, and after passing a short time in prayer with Dr Ford, the ordinary of Newgate, the cap was pulled over his eyes, when the stage falling from under him, he was launched into eternity.

'When he ascended the platform his air was dejected in the extreme; and the sorrow manifested in his countenance depicted the inward workings of a heart conscious of the heinous crime be had committed, and the justness of his sentence.

'From the time of his condemnation to the moment of his dissolution, he had scarcely taken the smallest nourishment; which, operating with a tortured conscience, had so enfeebled him, that he was obliged to be supported from the prison to the gallows, being wholly incapable of ascending the staircase with out assistance. Previous to his decease, he fully confessed his having perpetrated the horrible crime for which he suffered: confessed that he had unhappily conceived a most inveterate hatred for his wife, that nothing could conquer, and determined to rid himself and the world of a being he loathed: acknowledged also, that he had taken her twice before to the Paddington canal, with the wicked intent of drowning her, but that his resolution had failed him, and she had returned unhurt; and even at the awful moment of his confession, and the assurance of his approaching dissolution, he seemed to regret more the loss of his infant, than the destruction of the woman he had sworn to cherish and protect. He was questioned, as far as decency would permit, if jealousy had worked him to the horrid act; but be made no reply, except saying, that 'he ought to die'; and dropped into a settled and fixed melancholy, which accompanied him to his last moments. He was a decent looking young man, and wore a brown great coat, buttoned over a red waistcoat, the same in which be was tried.

'He died very easy; and, after hanging the usual time, his body was cut down and conveyed to a house not far distant, where it was subjected to the galvanic process by Professor Aldini, under the inspection of Mr Keate, Mr Carpue and several other professional gentlemen. M. Aldini, who is the nephew of the discoverer of this most interesting science, showed the eminent and superior powers of galvanism to be far beyond any other stimulant in nature. On the first application of the process to the face, the jaws of the deceased criminal began to quiver, and the adjoining muscles were horribly contorted, and one eye was actually opened. In the subsequent part of the process the right hand was raised and clenched, and the legs and thighs were set in motion. Mr Pass, the beadle of the Surgeons' Company, who was officially present during this experiment, was so alarmed that he died of fright soon after his return home.

'Some of the uninformed bystanders thought that the wretched man was on the eve of being restored to life. This, however, was impossible, as several of his friends, who were under the scaffold, had violently pulled his legs, in order to put a more speedy termination to his sufferings. The experiment, in fact, was of a better use and tendency. Its object was to show the excitability of the human frame when this animal electricity was duly applied. In cases of drowning or suffocation it promised to be of the utmost use, by reviving the action of the lungs, and thereby rekindling the expiring spark of vitality. In cases of apoplexy, or disorders of the head, it offered also most encouraging prospects for the benefit of mankind.

'The professor, we understand, had made use of galvanism also in several cases of insanity, and with complete success. It was the opinion of the first medical men that this discovery, if rightly managed and duly prosecuted, could not fail to be of great, and perhaps as yet unforeseen, utility.'[59]

My mind's eye travelled back through time to a memory of when I was five. I stood in my childhood home, peaking around the corner of a doorframe. Behind me was the hallway leading to my bedchamber on the left and the apartment of my father on the right. In front of me was the grand parlour of William Godwin. How ladies and their gentlemen cherished invitations to Godwin's home on a Saturday. My father hosted many literary, scientific, and philosophical salons. Dinner was served promptly at eight, usually of four courses, but sometimes of seven, and rarely of anything more. These evenings were not intended for nourishment or merriment, but for enlightenment, though guests often left with all three. Esteemed and interesting persons were brought in to speak on any subject that struck my father's fancy this week or that week. Many critics would accuse my father of atheism, anarchism, anti-monarchism, feminism, utilitarianism, and radicalism inspired by the revolutionaries of France. My father was nothing if not outspoken.

This night, when I was five, my father had invited one Anthony Carlisle to speak. This student of the natural arts had eyewitnessed the very experiment Lord Byron spoke of in 1816. But in 1803, Mr Carlisle had presented himself to my father, William Godwin, with all of the pomp and pageantry these cocktail parties warranted. He wore his hair wild, his muttonchops long, his ascot neat, his suit pressed, and his shoes shined. To the guests assembled to hear him, in particular, speak, he told his harrowing tale: 'George Foster,' Mr Carlisle paused not for effect, but as unaccustomed to public speaking as he was, he required a moment to find the beginning which was at the end of poor George Foster's life, 'Galvanism is every day offering so many new objects to our research, that we have no hesitation in pronouncing it the most curious subject of inquiry that is now engaging the attention of the lovers of natural philosophy. The experiments lately performed in this town by

---

59 From an edition of *The Newgate Calendar*.

Professor Aldini, must be fresh in the memory of those who were gratified with a sight of these infinitely interesting phenomena; and by those
who were not so fortunate, this short narration will be perused with interest, and may suggest a variety of new and untried objects of inquiry.
The subject of the experiments was a malefactor executed at Newgate,
on the morning of the 17th of January last. The body was exposed a
whole hour, in a temperature of about 30°, after which it was delivered to
the College of Surgeons, in pursuance of the usual sentence of the law,
and was transferred to Professor Aldini, who with the assistance of Mr
Keate, Mr Carpue, Mr Hutchins, Mr Cuthbertson, and other able men,
subjected it to the following experiments, the galvanic power being in
all of them supplied by three troughs, combined together, each of which
contained forty plates of zinc, and as many of copper; the interposed fluid
was diluted muriatic acid.

'1. One arc being applied to the mouth and another to the ear (wetted
with a solution of common salt) the jaw immediately began to quiver,
the adjoining muscles were horribly contorted, and the left eye actually
opened.

2. On applying the arc to both ears, a motion of the head was manifested, all the muscles of the face became convulsed, and the lips and
eye lids were evidently affected. The action was increased by making
one extremity of the arc to communicate with the nostrils and the other
with the ear.

'3. On applying the conductors to the ear and to the rectum, such
violent muscular contractions were excited, as almost to give the appearance of re animation.

'4. Volatile alkali was first applied to the nostrils and mouth, but without the least sensible effect; but galvanism immediately excited violent
action. This, however, was still more increased by uniting both of these
stimuli; and applying them together.

'5. The fibres of the biceps flexor cubiti were laid bare, and one arc
was applied to them, whilst the other remained in the ear. This produced
violent convulsions of all the muscles of the arm.

'6. One arc remaining in the ear, and the other being applied to an
incision in the wrist, among the small filaments of the nerves and cellular
membrane, a very strong action of the muscles of the forearm and hand
was perceived. In these two last experiments, the natural moisture of the
part was sufficient to conduct the galvanic influence without the intervention of salt water.

'7. The short muscles of the thumb were dissected, and on applying
the conductor to them, a forcible effort to clench the hand was induced.

'8. The effect of other powerful stimulants, caustic ammonia, concentrated sulphuric acid, and the mechanical stimulus of pricking the fibres with the point of the scalpel, were tried by way of comparison with galvanism, but without producing the smallest effect.

'9. The thorax and pericardium being opened, and the heart exposed *in situ*, the conducting are was applied to the ventricles, first upon its surface then in the substance of its fibres, then upon the carneæ columnæ, and the septum ventriculorum; and, lastly, in the course of the nerves by the coronary arteries, but without being followed by the slightest contraction or muscular motion.

'10. The arc was then conveyed to the right auricle and the appendix auricularis, and considerable contraction was immediately produced, even without the intervention of salt water. In the left auricle, however, scarcely any motion was excited.

'11. Conductors being applied from the spinal marrow to the fibres of the biceps flexor cubiti, the gluteus maximus, and the gastrocnemius, separately, no considerable action in the muscles of the arm and leg was produced.

'12. One of the conducting arcs being applied to the spinal marrow, and the other to the sciatic nerve, (which was exposed between the great trochanter and the tuberosity of the ischium, and dissected out from its sheath) no contraction whatever ensued in the muscles. But the conductor being removed from the nerve to the adjacent muscular fibres and cellular membrane, as strong an action was manifested as in the former experiments.

'13. By making the arc to communicate with the sciatic nerve, and the gastrocnemius muscle, a very great action was produced in the latter.

'14. Conductors being applied from the sciatic to the peroneal nerve, scarcely any motion was excited in the muscle.

'15. The sciatic nerve being divided about the middle of the thigh, and conductors being applied from the biceps flexor auris to the gastrocnemius, there ensued a violent contraction of both.

'Mr Carpue, giving account of the appearances on dissection, observes that the blood in the head was not extravasated, but several vessels were prodigiously swelled, and the lungs were entirely deprived of air; he also saw that there was a great inflammation of the intestines, and that the bladder was fully distended with urine.

'These are the principal circumstances of the interesting experiments which are here related; and the reader will readily concur in the leading inference which Professor Aldini deduces from them; namely, that the power of galvanism, as a stimulant, is stronger than any mechanical action whatever, and that hence it affords very powerful means of resuscitation in cases of suspended animation under common circumstances, perhaps superior to any that are usually employed. This consideration may serve to give this study additional interest to those who are not satisfied with any object of philosophical pursuit, without discovering n it an immediate prospect of benefit to mankind. The physiologist, however, will not fail to perceive the variety of curious questions for future inquiry, involved in the singular unsusceptibility of the ventricles of the heart to a stimulus which powerfully affects every other muscle with this influence, compared with that of nerve and medulla spinalis.

'From the circumstance of the rapid exhaustion of the power of the troughs, and the extent of active metallic surface requisite to produce the galvanic action in sufficient intensity to exhibit the above phenomena, the author infers the probability that the method of coating nerves with metallic surface, as first practised by Galvani, (on frogs and cold blooded animals) serves merely to conduct the fluid pre existent in the animal system; whereas, with Volta's galvanic batteries, the muscles are excited to action by the influence of the apparatus itself.'[60]

As I dropped my eaves on this (not quite a bedtime) story, I witnessed respectable women faint and distinguished men become green with nausea. My father found enthusiasm for this particular peculiar salon immediately extinguished. With *sal volatile,* Mr Carlisle revived many those reviled by the recitation of his eyewitness account. The witless found their mind's cloudy as they exited out of my family's front door into the streets to awaiting carriages. No a one would publicly disparage my father's literary, scientific, and philosophical salons lest a future invitation be rescinded.

Suddenly my grasp on this scene in my father's salon wrenched free from memory. My eyes slowly opened to find myself back in the parlour at the Villa Diodati dropping eaves on the previous scene of the electric debate between Lord Byron and my Beloved, but after my brief interlude in the past, the scene had continued on without my being conscious of the passage of time. My Beloved now stood before the fire where Lord Byron had told a mere fragment of a story and where Dr Polidori would no doubt soon tell own his substantial one. He held a handful of pages handwritten in this often-smudged scrawl. Was he at last contributing to Lord Byron's game of ghost stories.

---

60 From the Appendix in *General Views on the Application of Galvanism to Medical Purposes* by John Aldini, published by J. Callow, Princes-Street, and Burgess and Mill, Great Windmil-Street, 1819.

Chapter Six
Prometheus (Unbound)

Mary Wollstonecraft Godwin's Journal

21 June. Witching hour— 'I'm afraid this is not my contribution to the game of ghost stories, my Beloved said dashing my hopes upon the rocks of the sea. 'My mind has not been inspired by the ghostly and the ghastly, but the mythological. Upon these shelves,' he says indicating the bookshelves, 'I have found, not a French translation of German ghost stories, but a playscript written in its original Greek. The Greek tragic writers, in selecting as their subject any portion of their national history or mythology, employed in their treatment of it a certain arbitrary discretion. They by no means conceived themselves bound to adhere to the common interpretation or to imitate in story as in title their rivals and predecessors. Such a system would have amounted to a resignation of those claims to preference over their competitors which incited the composition. The Agamemnonian story was exhibited on the Athenian theatre with as many variations as dramas.

'I have presumed to employ a similar license. The "Prometheus Unbound" of Æschylus supposed the reconciliation of Jupiter with his victim as the price of the disclosure of the danger threatened to his empire by the consummation of his marriage with Thetis. Thetis, according to this view of the subject, was given in marriage to Peleus, and Prometheus, by the permission of Jupiter, delivered from his captivity by Hercules. Had I framed my story on this model, I should have done no more than have attempted to restore the lost drama of Æschylus; an ambition which, if my preference to this mode of treating the subject had incited me to cherish, the recollection of the high comparison such an attempt would challenge might well abate. But, in truth, I was averse from a catastrophe so feeble as that of reconciling the Champion with the Oppressor of mankind. The moral interest of the fable, which is so powerfully sustained by the sufferings and endurance of Prometheus, would be annihilated if we could conceive of him as unsaying his high language and quailing before his successful and perfidious adversary. The only imaginary being, resembling in any degree Prometheus, is Satan; and Prometheus is, in my judgment, a more poetical character than Satan, because, in addition to courage, and majesty, and firm and patient opposition to omnipotent force, he is susceptible of being described as exempt from the taints of ambition, envy, revenge, and a desire for personal aggrandisement, which, in the hero of Paradise Lost, interfere with the interest. The character of Satan engenders in the mind a pernicious casuistry which leads us to weigh his faults with his wrongs, and to excuse the former because the latter exceed all measure. In the minds of those who consider that magnificent fiction with a religious feeling it engenders something worse. But Prometheus is, as it were, the type of the highest perfection of moral and intellectual nature, impelled by the purest and the truest motives to the best and noblest ends.[61] Permit me the pleasure, if you have the leisure, to read of the few lines thus far written. First the character of Prometheus:'

> *Monarch of Gods and Dœmons, and all Spirits*
> *But One, who throng those bright and rolling worlds*
> *Which Thou and I alone of living things*
> *Behold with sleepless eyes! regard this Earth*
> *Made multitudinous with thy slaves, whom thou*
> *Requitest for knee-worship, prayer, and praise,*
> *And toil, and hecatombs of broken hearts,*
> *With fear and self-contempt and barren hope.*
> *Whilst me, who am thy foe, eyeless in hate,*
> *Hast thou made reign and triumph, to thy scorn,*
> *O'er mine own misery and thy vain revenge.*
> *Three thousand years of sleep-unsheltered hours,*
> *And moments aye divided by keen pangs*
> *Till they seemed years, torture and solitude,*
> *Scorn and despair,— these are mine empire:*
> *More glorious far than that which thou surveyest*
> *From thine unenvied throne, O, Mighty God!*
> *Almighty, had I deigned to share the shame*
> *Of thine ill tyranny, and hung not here*
> *Nailed to this wall of eagle-baffling mountain,*
> *Black, wintry, dead, unmeasured; without herb,*
> *Insect, or beast, or shape or sound of life.*
> *Ah me! alas, pain, pain ever, for ever!*
>
> *No change, no pause, no hope! Yet I endure.*
> *I ask the Earth, have not the mountains felt?*
> *I ask yon Heaven, the all-beholding Sun,*

---

61 From the preface to *Prometheus Unbound* by Percy Bysshe Shelley, published by C and Jo Ollier, 1820.

Has it not seen? The Sea, in storm or calm,
Heaven's ever-changing Shadow, spread below,
Have its deaf waves not heard my agony?
Ah me! alas, pain, pain ever, for ever!

The crawling glaciers pierce me with the spears
Of their moon-freezing crystals; the bright chains
Eat with their burning cold into my bones.
Heaven's winged hound, polluting from thy lips
His beak in poison not his own, tears up
My heart; and shapeless sights come wandering by,
The ghastly people of the realm of dream,
Mocking me: and the Earthquake-fiends are charged
To wrench the rivets from my quivering wounds
When the rocks split and close again behind:
While from their loud abysses howling throng
The genii of the storm, urging the rage
Of whirlwind, and afflict me with keen hail.
And yet to me welcome is day and night,
Whether one breaks the hoar-frost of the morn,
Or starry, dim, and slow, the other climbs
The leaden-colored east; for then they lead
The wingless, crawling hours, one among whom
— As some dark Priest hales the reluctant victim—
Shall drag thee, cruel King, to kiss the blood
From these pale feet, which then might trample thee
If they disdained not such a prostrate slave.
Disdain! Ah, no! I pity thee. What ruin
Will hunt thee undefended thro' the wide Heaven!
How will thy soul, cloven to its depth with terror,
Gape like a hell within! I speak in grief,
Not exultation, for I hate no more,
As then ere misery made me wise. The curse
Once breathed on thee I would recall. Ye Mountains,
Whose many-voiced Echoes, through the mist
Of cataracts, flung the thunder of that spell!
Ye icy Springs, stagnant with wrinkling frost,
Which vibrated to hear me, and then crept
Shuddering thro' India! Thou serenest Air
Thro' which the Sun walks burning without beams!
And ye swift Whirlwinds, who on poisèd wings
Hung mute and moveless o'er yon hushed abyss,

As thunder, louder than your own, made rock
The orbèd world! If then my words had power,
Though I am changed so that aught evil wish
Is dead within; although no memory be
Of what is hate, let them not lose it now!
What was that curse? for ye all heard me speak.[62]

Our little Lord guffawed mightily and slapped his knee in excitement and exaltation and said, 'O! Muse sing, O! Goddess sing of the spontaneous plagiarism of Mad Jack Byron's son George and his son's dearest friend Percy Bysshe Shelley, whom in midst of these swirling storms and swelling waters of Lake Geneva are both inspired by Calliope, the mother of Orpheus and Linus from the loins of King Oeagrus of Thrace, to produce works based upon Prometheus? The gifter of fire to mankind stands before us this dark and stormy night as a phantasm summoned by our interwoven minds.' He laughed again and shapped his knee again and stood to grasp my Beloved in a hearty and heathy embrace. 'How is it possible that we two friends find ourselves this very night holdings pages composed yesternight with no foreknowledge of the other's composition! If we were in the separate homes back in merry ol' England, warring poets might accuse the other of outright thievery and seek to murder the other professionally... or perchance personally. But how queer is the ghost of an idea that we both saw floating in the ether possessing the premise of poetic Prometheus. This literary ghost mingles with literal ghosts on the edge of human perception. But only a poet's eye can see these ghosts of ideas, so the layman is blind to such spectres. Our ghost, no doubt, floated through the Villia Diodati praying that one of the four of us writers would see it out of our peripheral vision and seize upon it. If none of us did, the idea would slip through the walls of his villa and continue on until another poetic soul saw it and recognized it for what it was: inspiration. And! we both saw that phantom and seized it independently of the other.

'Give me space. Give me space, dearest Percy,' and my Beloved yielded the floor to Lord Byron, 'and listen to my own interpretation of that literary ghost of an idea!'

Titan! to whose immortal eyes
The sufferings of mortality,
Seen in their sad reality,

---

62 From *Prometheus Unbound* by Percy Bysshe Shelley, published by C and Jo Ollier, 1820. "This is the only work not actually begun during the stay at the Villa Diodati in1816, though it is certainly conceivable the closet play had been conceived then. The first to describe its writing is Mary in a letter on 5 September 1818." – R.D.B.

Were not as things that gods despise;
What was thy pity's recompense?
A silent suffering, and intense;
The rock, the vulture, and the chain,
All that the proud can feel of pain,
The agony they do not show,
The suffocating sense of woe,
Which speaks but in its loneliness,
And then is jealous lest the sky
Should have a listener, nor will sigh
Until its voice is echoless.

Titan! to thee the strife was given
Between the suffering and the will,
Which torture where they cannot kill;
And the inexorable Heaven,
And the deaf tyranny of Fate,
The ruling principle of Hate,
Which for its pleasure doth create
The things it may annihilate,
Refused thee even the boon to die:
The wretched gift Eternity
Was thine— and thou hast borne it well.
All that the Thunderer wrung from thee
Was but the menace which flung back
On him the torments of thy rack;
The fate thou didst so well foresee,
But would not to appease him tell;
And in thy Silence was his Sentence,
And in his Soul a vain repentance,
And evil dread so ill dissembled,
That in his hand the lightnings trembled.

Thy Godlike crime was to be kind,
To render with thy precepts less
The sum of human wretchedness,
And strengthen Man with his own mind;
But baffled as thou wert from high,
Still in thy patient energy,
In the endurance, and repulse
Of thine impenetrable Spirit,
Which Earth and Heaven could not convulse,

A mighty lesson we inherit:
Thou art a symbol and a sign
To Mortals of their fate and force;
Like thee, Man is in part divine,
A troubled stream from a pure source;
And Man in portions can foresee
His own funereal destiny;
His wretchedness, and his resistance,
And his sad unallied existence:
To which his Spirit may oppose
Itself— an equal to all woes—
And a firm will, and a deep sense,
Which even in torture can descry
Its own concentered recompense,
Triumphant where it dares defy,
And making Death a Victory.[63]

23 June. Morning— Yesternight waned upon this talk, and even the witching hour had gone by, before we retired to rest. When I placed my head on my pillow, I did not sleep, nor could I be said to think. My imagination, unbidden, possessed and guided me, gifting the successive images that arose in my mind with a vividness far beyond the usual bounds of reverie. I saw— with shut eyes, but acute mental vision,— I saw the pale student of unhallowed arts kneeling beside the thing he had put together. I saw the hideous phantasm of a man stretched out, and then, on the working of some powerful engine, show signs of life, and stir with an uneasy, half vital motion. Frightful must it be; for supremely frightful would be the effect of any human endeavour to mock the stupendous mechanism of the Creator of the world. His success would terrify the artist; he would rush away from his odious handywork, horror-stricken. He would hope that, left to itself, the slight spark of life which he had communicated would fade; that this thing, which had received such imperfect animation, would subside into dead matter; and he might sleep in the belief that the silence of the grave would quench for ever the transient existence of the hideous corpse which he had looked upon as the cradle of life. He sleeps; but he is awakened; he opens his eyes; behold the horrid thing stands at his bedside, opening his curtains, and looking on him with yellow, watery, but speculative eyes.

I opened mine in terror. The idea so possessed my mind, that a thrill of fear ran through me, and I wished to exchange the ghastly image of

---

63 From *Prisoner of Chillon, and Other Poems* by Lord Byron, published by John Murray, 1816

my fancy for the realities around. I see them still; the very room, the dark parquet, the closed shutters, with the moonlight struggling through, and the sense I had that the glassy lake and white high Alps were beyond. I could not so easily get rid of my hideous phantom; still it haunted me. I must try to think of something else. I recurred to my ghost story,— my tiresome unlucky ghost story! O! if I could only contrive one which would frighten my reader as I myself had been frightened that night!

Swift as light and as cheering was the idea that broke in upon me. 'I have found it! What terrified me will terrify others; and I need only describe the spectre which had haunted my midnight pillow.' On the morrow I announced that I had *thought of a story*. I began that day with the words, It was on a dreary night of November, making only a transcript of the grim terrors of my waking dream.

I opened mine in terror. The idea so possessed my mind, that a thrill of fear ran through me, and I wished to exchange the ghastly image of my fancy for the realities around. I see them still; the very room, the dark parquet, the closed shutters, with the moonlight struggling through, and the sense I had that the glassy lake and white high Alps were beyond. I could not so easily get rid of my hideous phantom; still it haunted me. I must try to think of something else. I recurred to my ghost story,— my tiresome unlucky ghost story! O! if I could only contrive one which would frighten my reader as I myself had been frightened that night!

Swift as light and as cheering was the idea that broke in upon me. "I have found it! What terrified me will terrify others; and I need only describe the spectre which had haunted my midnight pillow." On the morrow I announced that I had thought of a story. I began that day with the words, *It was on a dreary night of November*, making only a transcript of the grim terrors of my waking dream.

At first I thought but of a few pages— of a short tale; but Shelley urged me to develope the idea at greater length. I certainly did not owe the suggestion of one incident, nor scarcely of one train of feeling, to my husband, and yet but for his incitement, it would never have taken the form in which it was presented to the world.[64]

---

64 From the Introduction to the 1831 Edition of *Frankenstein; or, The Modern Prometheus*, published by Henry Colburn & Richard Bentley.

Chapter Seven
Frankenstein[65]
(The Birth of the Creature)

P.B. Shelley Writing In Mary Wollstonecraft Godwin's Journal

28 August. Lake Geneva— The event on which this fiction (which Mary has been chronicling in a second journal) is founded has been supposed, by Dr Darwin, and some of the physiological writers of Germany, as not of impossible occurrence. I shall not be supposed as according the remotest degree of serious faith to such an imagination; yet, in assuming it as the basis of a work of fancy, I have not considered myself as merely weaving a series of supernatural terrors. The event on which the interest of the story depends is exempt from the disadvantages of a mere tale of spectres or enchantment. It was recommended by the novelty of the situations which it developes; and, however impossible as a physical fact, affords a point of view to the imagination for the delineating of human passions more comprehensive and commanding than any which the ordinary relations of existing events can yield.

I have thus endeavoured to preserve the truth of the elementary principles of human nature, while I have not scrupled to innovate upon their combinations. The *Iliad*, the tragic poetry of Greece,— Shakespeare, in the *Tempest* and *Midsummer Night's Dream*,— and most especially Milton, in *Paradise Lost*, conform to this rule; and the most humble novelist, who seeks to confer or receive amusement from his labours, may, without presumption, apply to prose fiction a licence, or rather a rule, from the adoption of which so many exquisite combinations of human feeling have resulted in the highest specimens of poetry.

The circumstance on which my story rests was suggested in casual conversation. It was commenced, partly as a source of amusement, and partly as an expedient for exercising any untried resources of mind. Other motives were mingled with these, as the work proceeded. I am by no means indifferent to the manner in which whatever moral tendencies exist in the sentiments or characters it contains shall affect the reader; yet my chief concern in this respect has been limited to the avoiding of the

---

65 From *Frankenstein; or the Modern Prometheus* by Mary Wollstonecraft Shelley, published by Lackington, Hughes, Harding, Mavor & Jones, 1818

enervating effects of the novels of the present day, and to the exhibitions of the amiableness of domestic affection, and the excellence of universal virtue. The opinions which naturally spring from the character and situation of the hero are by no means to be conceived as existing always in my own conviction; nor is any inference justly to be drawn from the following pages as prejudicing any philosophical doctrine of whatever kind.

It is a subject also of additional interest to the author, that this story was begun in the majestic region where the scene is principally laid, and in society which cannot cease to be regretted. I passed the summer of 1816 in the environs of Geneva. The season was cold and rainy, and in the evenings we crowded around a blazing wood fire, and occasionally amused ourselves with some German stories of ghosts, which happened to fall into our hands. These tales excited in us a playful desire of imitation. Two other friends (a tale from the pen of one of whom would be far more acceptable to the public than any thing I can ever hope to produce) and myself agreed to write each a story, founded on some supernatural occurrence.

The weather, however, suddenly became serene; and my two friends left me on a journey among the Alps, and lost, in the magnificent scenes which they present, all memory of their ghostly visions. The following tale is the only one which has been completed.[66]

TWO MONTHS EARLIER!

Mary Wollstonecraft Godwin's Journal

Chapter I

22 June. Small hours— I awoke from the dead of sleep. Curious phrase. Do the dead sleep in a dreamless slumber? Or do they dream of the Resurrection of the dead? Do Christians not believe we believe that *Jesus died and rose again, even so them also which sleep in Jesus will God bring with him*? I believe St. Austin said of this very passage, 'That the Scripture saith of those that are dead, that they are but asleep, because of the certain hope of a Resurrection, by which they shall speedily be awakened from the sleep of death, and raised out of their Sepulchres as out of their beds.' But I awoke to find myself not dead, but in the curious state of a women longing for the return of her lover having been parted.

I felt the weight of my Beloved next to me in bed, the candle on his side having long been snuffed out and his book having fallen to the

---

66 From the Introduction to the 1818 Edition of *Frankenstein; or, The Modern Prometheus,* published by Lackinton, Hughes, Harding, Mavor, and Jones, London.

floor. But in the corner of the bedchamber, sitting in an armchair was a nameless human-shaped form. Briefly— quite briefly— I thought maybe this was my Beloved having awoke in the night and now sits in the armchair. But then I remembered the weight of my Beloved next to me and came to the sudden realization that someone else... something else sat across from me in the darkness. Was this the poor doctor having violated the sanctity of my Beloved's bedchamber? The fire of my ire quickly lit, and I prepared myself to chastise him for his impudence. Then lightning flashed and I saw the hollowed face of the pale student of the unhallowed arts. In the brief moment my eyes captured his image, he looked forlorn.

I hurried to the hearth, the final embers slowly dying. Retrieving a spill from its holder, I lit it on an ember and immediately relit the candles on the mantle and on my bedside table. The form was my pale student of the unhallowed arts, but he was dressed not for scientific experimentation as if did ereyesterday, but for a gentleman's morning ride. He wore a smart, charcoal cutaway morning coat, a grey vest over a high stand collared shirt, and a puff tie. A governor's cane propped against his ankle high dress boot with the head resting on one knee, and his top hat sat upon the small table beside the chair. His shoulder-length blonde hair, having lost all its lustre, appeared flustered as if by a blustery day. His lips were thin, so thin as to be expressionless. His sharp cheekbones were shrunken; his sunken eyes brightened tolerably in the candlelight, that forlorn expression slowly melting away like candlewax. He was handsome, looking like he could have been a long-lost Shelley, the brother of my Beloved.

My pale student quietly— so quietly in fact that he uttered not a word— asked me to sit at the writing desk opposite him in the adjacent corner of the room. I did as he bid. I found my journal sitting where I left off with 'It was on a dreary night of November, making only a transcript of the grim terrors of my waking dream.' I had failed to record how I had burst into the kitchen the next morning, exclaiming, 'I have found it!'. My Beloved, poor Polidori, and our little Lord already sat for breakfast, with my helping of bacon and sausage still sizzling in the iron pan. 'Found what, my dove,' my love inquired. 'I found my ghost story!' I beamed. Then the doctor said, 'About time.' I nearly screamed in frustration. How I have grown tired of this supposedly grown man! My hands desired to wring his neck, for every morning for days he inquired if I had found my ghost story yet; every morning for days I had *not* found my ghost story yet; yet on the day that I find my ghost story, I find him unimpressed. Since that morning of exaltation, I have, in my exhaustion, been in mourning. How I longed for my pale student to be returned to me. But his voice had been eerily quiet— so eerily quiet that I had not yet written a single word in my journal. Back in the present, I opened my journal to an empty page. This queer clairvoyance did not in any way strike me as odd, but quite natural. Had I been of right mind, with the effects of sleep still not having worn off, I would have been frightened by this preternatural experience, but instead, I readied myself to transcribe the tale which he was to begin:

'I am by birth a Genevese,' my pale student said. He certainly had not travelled far to visit me at the Villa Diodati, itself positioned on the shore of Lake Geneva. I wonder where the estate lies. 'And my family is one of the most distinguished of that republic. My ancestors had been for many years counsellors and syndics; and my father had filled several public situations with honour and reputation. He was respected by all who knew him for his integrity and indefatigable attention to public business. He passed his younger days perpetually occupied by the affairs of his country; and it was not until the decline of life that he thought of marrying, and bestowing on the state sons who might carry his virtues and his name down to posterity.

'As the circumstances of his marriage illustrate his character, I cannot refrain from relating them. One of his most intimate friends was a merchant, who, from a flourishing state, fell, through numerous mischances, into poverty. This man, whose name was Beaumont, was of a proud and unbending disposition, and could not bear to live in poverty and oblivion in the same country where he had formerly been distinguished for his rank and magnificence. Having paid his debts, therefore, in the most honourable manner, he retreated with his daughter to the town of Lucerne, where he lived unknown and in wretchedness. My father loved Beaumont with the truest friendship, and was deeply grieved by his retreat in these unfortunate circumstances. He grieved also for the loss of his society, and resolved to seek him out and endeavour to persuade him to begin the world again through his credit and assistance.

'Beaumont had taken effectual measures to conceal himself; and it was ten months before my father discovered his abode. Overjoyed at this discovery, he hastened to the house, which was situated in a mean street, near the Reuss. But when he entered, misery and despair alone welcomed him. Beaumont had saved but a very small sum of money from the wreck of his fortunes; but it was sufficient to provide him with sustenance for some months, and in the mean time he hoped to procure some respectable employment in a merchant's house. The interval was consequently spent in inaction; his grief only became more deep and rankling, when he had leisure for reflection; and at length it took so fast hold of his mind, that at the end of three months he lay on a bed of sickness, incapable of any exertion.

'His daughter attended him with the greatest tenderness; but she saw with despair that their little fund was rapidly decreasing, and that there was no other prospect of support. But Caroline Beaumont possessed a mind of an uncommon mould; and her courage rose to support her in her adversity. She procured plain work; she plaited straw; and by various means contrived to earn a pittance scarcely sufficient to support life.

'Several months passed in this manner. Her father grew worse; her time was more entirely occupied in attending him; her means of subsistence decreased; and in the tenth month her father died in her arms, leaving her an orphan and a beggar. This last blow overcame her; and she knelt by Beaumont's coffin, weeping bitterly, when my father entered the chamber. He came like a protecting spirit to the poor girl, who committed herself to his care, and after the interment of his friend he conducted her to Geneva, and placed her under the protection of a relation. Two years after this event Caroline became his wife.

'When my father became a husband and a parent, he found his time so occupied by the duties of his new situation, that he relinquished many of his public employments, and devoted himself to the education of his children. Of these I was the eldest, and the destined successor to all his labours and utility. No creature could have more tender parents than mine. My improvement and health were their constant care, especially as I remained for several years their only child. But before I continue my narrative, I must record an incident which took place when I was four years of age.'

The tenor of my pale student of the unhallowed arts' voice was a baritone, low and weighty, bearing the sins of a lifetime on his timbre. His accent was proper though foreign, his diction clean, and his language educated. The weight of his grievous sin also hunched his shoulders. What sin could he have committed in the short span of his young life to create this darkness haunting his eyes? Was his mortal sin that of creating the hideous phantasm of a man I had seen stretched out, and then, on the working of some powerful engine, shown signs of life and stirred with an uneasy, half vital motion? Is the guilt-ridden story he had just begun a confession of this very sin? Is his penance before God to repent of his sin to me in a Rite of Reconciliation? I am a laywoman, not a priest who can bestow the assurance of pardon and the grace of absolution. Is this phantasm the ghost of a real student of the unhallowed arts having committed a very real sin of the resurrection of the dead; or is he a mere figment of an overactive imagination longing for the ghost story to share?

I should halt this expositional digression and allow him his own story in his own time.

'My father had a sister, whom he tenderly loved, and who had married early in life an Italian gentleman. Soon after her marriage, she had accompanied her husband into his native country, and for some years my father had very little communication with her. About the time I mentioned she died; and a few months afterwards he received a letter from her husband, acquainting him with his intention of marrying an Italian lady, and requesting my father to take charge of the infant Elizabeth, the only child of his deceased sister. "It is my wish," he said, "that you should consider her as your own daughter, and educate her thus. Her mother's fortune is secured to her, the documents of which I will commit to your keeping. Reflect upon this proposition; and decide whether you would prefer educating your niece yourself to her being brought up by a stepmother."

'My father did not hesitate, and immediately went to Italy, that he might accompany the little Elizabeth to her future home. I have often heard my mother say, that she was at that time the most beautiful child she had ever seen, and shewed signs even then of a gentle and affectionate disposition. These indications, and a desire to bind as closely as possible the ties of domestic love, determined my mother to consider Elizabeth as my future wife; a design which she never found reason to repent.

'From this time Elizabeth Lavenza became my playfellow, and, as we grew older, my friend. She was docile and good tempered, yet gay and playful as a summer insect. Although she was lively and animated, her feelings were strong and deep, and her disposition uncommonly affectionate. No one could better enjoy liberty, yet no one could submit with more grace than she did to constraint and caprice. Her imagination was luxuriant, yet her capability of application was great. Her person was the image of her mind; her hazel eyes, although as lively as a bird's, possessed an attractive softness. Her figure was light and airy; and, though capable of enduring great fatigue, she appeared the most fragile creature in the world. While I admired her understanding and fancy, I loved to tend on her, as I should on a favourite animal; and I never saw so much grace both of person and mind united to so little pretension.

'Every one adored Elizabeth.' As do I already! 'If the servants had any request to make, it was always through her intercession. We were strangers to any species of disunion and dispute; for although there was a great dissimilitude in our characters, there was an harmony in that very dissimilitude. I was more calm and philosophical than my companion; yet my temper was not so yielding. My application was of longer endurance;

but it was not so severe whilst it endured. I delighted in investigating the facts relative to the actual world; she busied herself in following the aërial creations of the poets. The world was to me a secret, which I desired to discover; to her it was a vacancy, which she sought to people with imaginations of her own.

'My brothers were considerably younger than myself; but I had a friend in one of my schoolfellows, who compensated for this deficiency. Henry Clerval was the son of a merchant of Geneva, an intimate friend of my father. He was a boy of singular talent and fancy. I remember, when he was nine years old, he wrote a fairy tale, which was the delight and amazement of all his companions. His favourite study consisted in books of chivalry and romance; and when very young, I can remember, that we used to act plays composed by him out of these favourite books, the principal characters of which were Orlando, Robin Hood, Amadis, and St. George.

'No youth could have passed more happily than mine. My parents were indulgent, and my companions amiable. Our studies were never forced; and by some means we always had an end placed in view, which excited us to ardour in the prosecution of them. It was by this method, and not by emulation, that we were urged to application.' Oh, how I can hear my father's own words: Refer them to reading, to conversation, to meditation; but teach them neither creeds nor catechisms, either moral or political... Speak the language of truth and reason to your child, and be under no apprehension for the result. Show him that what you recommend is valuable and desirable, and fear not but he will desire it. Convince his understanding, and enlist all his powers animal and intellectual in your service.[67]

'Elizabeth was not incited to apply herself to drawing, that her companions might not outstrip her; but through the desire of pleasing her aunt, by the representation of some favourite scene done by her own hand. We learned Latin and English, that we might read the writings in those languages; and so far from study being made odious to us through punishment, we loved application, and our amusements would have been the labours of other children. Perhaps we did not read so many books, or learn languages so quickly, as those who are disciplined according to the ordinary methods; but what we learned was impressed the more deeply on our memories.

'In this description of our domestic circle I include Henry Clerval; for he was constantly with us. He went to school with me, and generally passed the afternoon at our house; for being an only child, and destitute of companions at home, his father was well pleased that he should find

---

67 From *Political Justice* by William Godwin.

associates at our house; and we were never completely happy when Clerval was absent.

'I feel pleasure in dwelling on the recollections of childhood, before misfortune had tainted my mind, and changed its bright visions of extensive usefulness into gloomy and narrow reflections upon self. But, in drawing the picture of my early days, I must not omit to record those events which led, by insensible steps to my after tale of misery: for when I would account to myself for the birth of that passion, which afterwards ruled my destiny, I find it arise, like a mountain river, from ignoble and almost forgotten sources; but, swelling as it proceeded, it became the torrent which, in its course, has swept away all my hopes and joys.

'Natural philosophy is the genius that has regulated my fate; I desire therefore, in this narration, to state those facts which led to my predilection for that science. When I was thirteen years of age, we all went on a party of pleasure to the baths near Thonon: the inclemency of the weather obliged us to remain a day confined to the inn. In this house I chanced to find a volume of the works of Cornelius Agrippa.' Ah! No doubt, the magician-alchemist and philosopher's *De Oculta Philosophlia libri III!* I hope and pray that my pale student recites no incantations said to invoke demonic beings. Being haunted by my pale student is certainly enough. 'I opened it with apathy; the theory which he attempts to demonstrate, and the wonderful facts which he relates, soon changed this feeling into enthusiasm. A new light seemed to dawn upon my mind; and, bounding with joy, I communicated my discovery to my father. I cannot help remarking here the many opportunities instructors possess of directing the attention of their pupils to useful knowledge, which they utterly neglect. My father looked carelessly at the title-page of my book, and said, "Ah! Cornelius Agrippa! My dear Victor, do not waste your time upon this; it is sad trash." Which is certainly is.

'If, instead of this remark, my father had taken the pains, to explain to me, that the principles of Agrippa had been entirely exploded, and that a modern system of science had been introduced, which possessed much greater powers than the ancient, because the powers of the latter were chimerical, while those of the former were real and practical; under such circumstances, I should certainly have thrown Agrippa aside, and, with my imagination warmed as it was, should probably have applied myself to the more rational theory of chemistry which has resulted from modern discoveries. It is even possible, that the train of my ideas would never have received the fatal impulse that led to my ruin.' Oh, how he suffers. Fatal impulses? Ruin? How I desire to be a comfort to the pale student, but he is as transient as a phantasm. 'But the cursory glance my father had taken of my volume by no means assured me that he was acquainted with its contents; and I continued to read with the greatest avidity.' Such oedipal hostility towards his father.

'When I returned home, my first care was to procure the whole works of this author, and afterwards of Paracelsus'–curious– 'and Albertus Magnus.' –Curiouser– While the teachings of these magician-alchemists may have been overthrown in the modern age, they have their place in natural philosophic history for their stress on experimentation and observation. 'I read and studied the wild fancies of these writers with delight; they appeared to me treasures known to few beside myself; and although I often wished to communicate these secret stores of knowledge to my father, yet his definite censure of my favourite Agrippa always withheld me. I disclosed my discoveries to Elizabeth, therefore, under a promise of strict secrecy; but she did not interest herself in the subject, and I was left by her to pursue my studies alone.

'It may appear very strange, that a disciple of Albertus Magnus should arise in the eighteenth century; but our family was not scientifical, and I had not attended any of the lectures given at the schools of Geneva. My dreams were therefore undisturbed by reality; and I entered with the greatest diligence into the search of the philosopher's stone and the elixir of life.'

What draws an man born into modernity to pursue such anachronisms. If my Beloved had overheard the pale student utter such absurdities, he would be readily dismissed out of hand... with the wave of a hand. But I am one to dismiss anyone of their studies, no matter how overthrown they may have been. How wondrous would it be to discover the 'alkahest,' that universal solvent known in great secrecy to dissolve anything or transmute lead into gold. Did not Eirenæus Philathese write, 'It is a Catholic and Universal Menstruum, and in a word, may be called *(Ignis-Aqua)* a firery water, an uncompounded and immortal *ens,,* which is penetrative, resolving all things into their first Liquid Matter, nor can anything resist its power, for it acteth without any reaction from the patient, nor doth it suffer from anything but its equal, by which it is brought into subjection; but after it hath dissolved all other things, it remaineth in its former nature, and is of the same virtue after a thousand operations as at the first'?[68] Did not *Encyclopædia Britanica* observe that 'the third method of making gold is by transmutation, or by turning all metals readily into pure gold, by melting them in fire, and calling a little quantity of a certain preparation into the fushed matter; upon which the feces retire, are volatized and burnt, and carried off, and the rest of the mass is turned into pure gold. That which works this change in the metals is called the philosopher's stone... Whether this third meth-

---

68 From *The Secret of the Immortal Liquor Called Alkahest, or Ignis-aqua* by Eirenæus Philalethes.

od is possible or not, it is difficult to say. We have so many testimonies of it from persons who on all other occasions speak truth that it is hard to say they are guilty of direct falsehood, even when they say that they have been masters of the secret.'[69] While my pale student's father would readily dismiss this encyclopædic entry as hogwash, did not Isaac Newton, the author of *Philosophiæ Naturalis Principia Mathematica*, also pursue the philosopher's stone and the elixir of life? How could my pale student be faulted for following in the alchemical footsteps of Isaac Newton? I do not!

'But the latter obtained my most undivided attention: wealth was an inferior object; but what glory would attend the discovery, if I could banish disease from the human frame, and render man invulnerable to any but a violent death!

'Nor were these my only visions. The raising of ghosts or devils was a promise liberally accorded by my favourite authors, the fulfilment of which I most eagerly sought; and if my incantations were always unsuccessful, I attributed the failure rather to my own inexperience and mistake, than to a want of skill or fidelity in my instructors.

'The natural phænomena that take place every day before our eyes did not escape my examinations. Distillation, and the wonderful effects of steam, processes of which my favourite authors were utterly ignorant, excited my astonishment; but my utmost wonder was engaged by some experiments on an air-pump, which I saw employed by a gentleman whom we were in the habit of visiting.

'The ignorance of the early philosophers on these and several other points served to decrease their credit with me: but I could not entirely throw them aside, before some other system should occupy their place in my mind.

'When I was about fifteen years old, we had retired to our house near Belrive,' –that is only a few miles removed for the Villa Diodati. How short a distance has my pale student journeyed to educate me– 'when we witnessed a most violent and terrible thunder-storm.' How I know this feeling intimately. Does a violent and terrible thunder-storm not rage outside my bedchamber's windows as my pale student visits me. 'It advanced from behind the mountains of Jura; and the thunder burst at once with frightful loudness from various quarters of the heavens. I remained, while the storm lasted, watching its progress with curiosity and delight. As I stood at the door, on a sudden I beheld a stream of fire issue from an old and beautiful oak, which stood about twenty yards from our house; and so soon as the dazzling light vanished, the oak had disappeared, and nothing remained but a blasted stump. When we visited

---

69 From 1797 *Encyclopædia Britannica* (Vol. 14)

it the next morning, we found the tree shattered in a singular manner. It was not splintered by the shock, but entirely reduced to thin ribbands of wood. I never beheld any thing so utterly destroyed.

'The catastrophe of this tree excited my extreme astonishment; and I eagerly inquired of my father the nature and origin of thunder and lightning. He replied, "Electricity;" describing at the same time the various effects of that power.' As my Beloved and our little Lord discussed electricity exciting frog's legs a few short days ago, they have made their debates of many subjects. I have heard John Abernethy's famous lecture oft quoted to me through obstinate opposition, because our friend and my Beloved's physician William Lawrence so publicly opposed this belief: The phaenomena of electricity and of life correspond. Electricity may be attached to, or inhere, in a wife; it may be suddenly dissipated, or have its powers annulled, or it may be removed by degrees or in portions, and the wire may remain less and less strongly electrified, in proportion as it is abstracte. So life inheres in vegetables and animals; it may sometimes be suddenly dissipated, or have its powers abolished, though in general it is lost by degrees, without any apparent change taking place in the structure; and in either case purification begins when life terminates.[70] 'He constructed a small electrical machine, and exhibited a few experiments; he made also a kite, with a wire and string, which drew down that fluid from the clouds.

'This last stroke completed the overthrow of Cornelius Agrippa, Albertus Magnus, and Paracelsus, who had so long reigned the lords of my imagination. But by some fatality I did not feel inclined to commence the study of any modern system; and this disinclination was influenced by the following circumstance.

'My father expressed a wish that I should attend a course of lectures upon natural philosophy, to which I cheerfully consented. Some accident prevented my attending these lectures until the course was nearly finished. The lecture, being therefore one of the last, was entirely incomprehensible to me. The professor discoursed with the greatest fluency of potassium and boron, of sulphates and oxyds, terms to which I could affix no idea.' How is my pale student so keenly aware of the contents of my travelling library? I am currently (no pun intended) reading Sir Humphry Davy's *A Discourse, Introductory to A Course of Lectures on Chemistry*? I too share my pale student of the unhallowed arts' optimism! 'And I became disgusted with the science of natural philosophy, although I still read Pliny and Buffon with delight, authors, in my estimation, of nearly equal interest and utility.

---

70 From "An Enquiry into the Probability and Rationality of Mr. Hunter's Theory of Life", a lecture by John Abernethy.

'My occupations at this age were principally the mathematics, and most of the branches of study appertaining to that science. I was busily employed in learning languages; Latin was already familiar to me, and I began to read some of the easiest Greek authors without the help of a lexicon. I also perfectly understood English and German. This is the list of my accomplishments at the age of seventeen; and you may conceive that my hours were fully employed in acquiring and maintaining a knowledge of this various literature.

'Another task also devolved upon me, when I became the instructor of my brothers. Ernest was six years younger than myself, and was my principal pupil. He had been afflicted with ill health from his infancy, through which Elizabeth and I had been his constant nurses: his disposition was gentle, but he was incapable of any severe application. William, the youngest of our family, was yet an infant, and the most beautiful little fellow in the world; his lively blue eyes, dimpled cheeks, and endearing manners, inspired the tenderest affection.

'Such was our domestic circle, from which care and pain seemed for ever banished. My father directed our studies, and my mother partook of our enjoyments. Neither of us possessed the slightest pre-eminence over the other; the voice of command was never heard amongst us; but mutual affection engaged us all to comply with and obey the slightest desire of each other.)

Chapter II

When I had attained the age of seventeen, my parents resolved that I should become a student at the university of Ingolstadt. I had hitherto attended the schools of Geneva; but my father thought it necessary, for the completion of my education, that I should be made acquainted with other customs than those of my native country. My departure was therefore fixed at an early date; but, before the day resolved upon could arrive, the first misfortune of my life occurred— an omen, as it were, of my future misery.' Oh! No! His story has only just begun, and he is already suffering misfortune. Omens? Future misery? If this was but the first, surely there will be a second misfortune of his life! And what a third? Or a fourth? What future misery was to come? I know of both misery and misfortune! With the birth of my dear boy, William, I struggled through the first nine days of his life despondent; I lived in constant fear that he too would succumb to a death in infancy as my first child had. But my William is alive! He thrives into infancy sleeping peacefully in this very room! The death of my firstborn was not, however, the first misfortune of my life; the death of my mother as a result of my own birth was the first misfortune of my life. I was only eleven days old when she succumbed to childbed fever and septic shock.

> 'My Dear Friend. The passage in your last kind letter that related to the subject of self-reproach was rather out of season. It has dwelt upon my mind ever since. My wife is now dead. She died this morning at eight o'clock. She grew worse before your letter arrived. Nobody has a greater call to reproach himself, except for want of kindness and attention in which I hope I have not been very deficient, than I have. But reproach would answer no good purpose, and I will not harbour it. I firmly believe that there does not exist her equal in the world. I know from experience we were formed to make each other happy. I have not the least expectation that I can now ever know happiness again. When you come to town, look at me, and talk to me, but do not-if you can help it-exhort me, or console me.
>
> —My father, William Godwin, to Thomas Holcroft

How could an all-loving God in Heaven insult me so?! He left a suckling babe motherless. But I digress. My pale student is telling me the story of the first misfortune in his life; my own is in this moment immaterial.

'Elizabeth had caught the scarlet fever' Oh no! Scarlatina? Oh! Would Hippocrates be surprised to know how many of the diseases he described still threaten humanity after two thousand years? He would have mourned that superstition and religiosity and ignorance have yet to fully acquiesce to the sciences. How many countless children and adults have been lost to such diseases as scarlatina? 'Her illness was *not* severe, and she quickly recovered.' Thank God! I was afeared she was in the greatest danger. But Victor's emphasis on the severity of the Elizabeth's illness gives a particular and peculiar weight to both pain and blame. What of Elizabeth's illness still haunts him so so many years later? 'During her confinement, many arguments had been urged to persuade my mother to refrain from attending upon her. She had, at first, yielded to our entreaties; but when she heard that her favourite was recovering, she could no longer debar herself from her society, and entered her chamber long before the danger of infection was past.' As any good mother would do her part to tend the health of this girl. A mother's instincts are primal (even towards a niece), an urge so deep seeded into the very soil of her being that it supersedes the most basic of instincts: her own survival. She thinks not of the consequences, though... 'The consequences of this imprudence were fatal. On the third day my mother sickened; her fever was very malignant, and the looks of her attendants prognosticated the worst event. On her death-bed the fortitude and benignity of this admirable woman did not desert her. She joined the hands of Elizabeth and myself:' As any good mother would share her heart to them. She joins the hands of the child of her flesh and the child of her choice, not to mourn but to rejoice! "'My children," she said, "my firmest hopes of future happiness were placed on the prospect of your union. This expectation will now be the consolation of your father. Elizabeth, my love, you must supply my place to your younger cousins. Alas! I regret that I am taken from you; and, happy and beloved as I have been, is it not hard to quit you all? But these are not thoughts befitting me; I will endeavour to resign myself cheerfully to death, and will indulge a hope of meeting you in another world.'" As any good mother should depart this world. Where had Victor dug up these words? I am not naïve of the fact that this Victor Frankenstein is doubtless a figment of my overactive imagination and not a haunting incorporeal entity nor a daunting corporeal reality relating his life's story to me. Is Victor reaching back through my own memories into the past immemorial to retrieve the final words of my mother, Mary Wollstonecraft? I would be delighted if this were true. To know as an adult what an eleven-day-old babe was told by her dying mother. Did my dying mother possess the strength to hold me swaddled her in arms? Was my father present to catch me should her strength fail her, and I should fall? Oh, philosophers from the ancient to the modern surely have pondered why is it that adults remember nothing of the first few years of our lives. Perhaps our minds are so immature in our grasp of language and grammar that we as adults could never decipher the memories of what was spoken to us as children. I cannot imagine that an eleven-day-old has enough knowledge of their parent's language to remember the words accurately; the memory of my mother's final words would be as incomprehensible as a babbling child.

'She died calmly; and her countenance expressed affection even in death. I need not describe the feelings of those whose dearest ties are rent by that most irreparable evil, the void that presents itself to the soul, and the despair that is exhibited on the countenance. It is so long before the mind can persuade itself that she, whom we saw every day, and whose very existence appeared a part of our own, can have departed for ever— that the brightness of a beloved eye can have been extinguished, and the sound of a voice so familiar, and dear to the ear, can be hushed, never more to be heard. These are the reflections of the first days; but when the lapse of time proves the reality of the evil, then the actual bitterness of grief commences. Yet from whom has not that rude hand rent away some dear connexion; and why should I describe a sorrow which all have felt, and must feel? The time at length arrives, when grief is rather an indulgence than a necessity; and the smile that plays upon the lips, although it may be deemed a sacrilege, is not banished. My mother was dead, but we had still duties which we ought to perform; we must continue our course with the rest, and learn to think ourselves fortunate, whilst one remains whom the spoiler has not seized.' The death of a parent is an irreparable evil only surpassed by the death of a child. To lose a parent at the age of seventeen is a difficult struggle that leaves one's life in utter rubble. To know the deceased parent will never hold their grandchild in their loving arm; nor will they ever spoil that bugger rotten as every grandparent is wont to do. To lose a child as I had at age of seventeen is a unique endeavour that haunts one's life forever. My daughter haunted me with visons! Nightmares may scare; but visions of a dead child were incisions in my eyes! How I loathed waking because I the daughter I had cradled in my arms, suckling at my own breast, slowly evaporated into the ether of waking's reality. Sitting upright in bed, I would only hold her tearstained and empty swaddling clothes. The only solace I found was finding myself pregnant so soon again! I listened acutely for William to breathe or sigh in his sleep. Once I heard the cherished sound, I returned my focus back to my pale student.

'My journey to Ingolstadt, which had been deferred by these events, was now again determined upon. I obtained from my father a respite of some weeks. This period was spent sadly; my mother's death, and my speedy departure, depressed our spirits; but Elizabeth endeavoured to renew the spirit of cheerfulness in our little society. Since the death of her aunt, her mind had acquired new firmness and vigour. She determined to fulfil her duties with the greatest exactness; and she felt that that most imperious duty, of rendering her uncle and cousins happy, had devolved upon her. She consoled me, amused her uncle, instructed my brothers; and I never beheld her so enchanting as at this time, when she was continually endeavouring to contribute to the happiness of others, entirely forgetful of herself.' How Elizabeth has not only become a woman at such a tender age, but also a surrogate mother. Women are often called upon to rear the children of widowers, whose wives so often die in childbirth. Was not my own step-mother, Mary Jane Clairmont, called upon by marital vows to rear me after her marriage to my father? But my father's new wife was certainly not up to the task! I wrote my Beloved in a letter:

> 'I detest Mrs. Godwin; she plagues my father out of his life; and
> these— —Well, no matter. Why will Godwin not follow the obvi-
> ous bent of his affections, and be reconciled to us? No; his prej-

udices, the world, and she— all these forbid it. What am I to do? trust to time, of course, for what else can I do. Good-night, my love; to-morrow I will seal this blessing on your lips. Press me, your own Mary, to your heart. Perhaps she will one day have a father; till then be everything to me, love; and, indeed, I will be a good girl, and never vex you. I will learn Greek and— — but when shall we meet when I may tell you all this, and you will so sweetly reward me? But good-night; I am wofully tired, and so sleepy. One kiss—well, that is enough— to-morrow!'[71]

'The day of my departure at length arrived. I had taken leave of all my friends, excepting Clerval, who spent the last evening with us. He bitterly lamented that he was unable to accompany me: but his father could not be persuaded to part with him, intending that he should become a partner with him in business, in compliance with his favourite theory, that learning was superfluous in the commerce of ordinary life. Henry had a refined mind; he had no desire to be idle, and was well pleased to become his father's partner, but he believed that a man might be a very good trader, and yet possess a cultivated understanding.' Fathers and their steely will! Do not the desires of education, enlightenment, and love not factor into decisions when it concerns their offspring? Of course not. Even into adulthood, they treat us as children.

'We sat late, listening to his complaints, and making many little arrangements for the future. The next morning early I departed. Tears gushed from the eyes of Elizabeth; they proceeded partly from sorrow at my departure, and partly because she reflected that the same journey was to have taken place three months before, when a mother's blessing would have accompanied me.

'I threw myself into the chaise that was to convey me away, and indulged in the most melancholy reflections. I, who had ever been surrounded by amiable companions, continually engaged in endeavouring to bestow mutual pleasure, I was now alone. In the university, whither I was going, I must form my own friends, and be my own protector. My life had hitherto been remarkably secluded and domestic; and this had given me invincible repugnance to new countenances. I loved my brothers, Elizabeth, and Clerval; these were "old familiar faces;"' Oh! I know this poem. *Where are they gone, the old familiar faces?/ I had a mother, but she died, and left me,/ Died prematurely in a day of horrors—/ All, all are gone, the old familiar faces!*[72] Victor continued, 'But I believed myself totally unfitted for the company of strangers. Such were my reflections as I commenced my journey; but as I proceeded, my spirits and hopes

---

71 From a letter from Mary Wollstonecraft Godwin to Percy Bysshe Shelley on 25 October 1814.
72 From the June 1798 poem, 'The Old Familiar Faces' by Charles Lamb.

rose. I ardently desired the acquisition of knowledge. I had often, when at home, thought it hard to remain during my youth cooped up in one place, and had longed to enter the world, and take my station among other human beings. Now my desires were complied with, and it would, indeed, have been folly to repent.

'I had sufficient leisure for these and many other reflections during my journey to Ingolstadt, which was long and fatiguing. At length the high white steeple of the town met my eyes. I alighted, and was conducted to my solitary apartment, to spend the evening as I pleased.

'The next morning I delivered my letters of introduction, and paid a visit to some of the principal professors, and among others to Mr Krempe, professor of natural philosophy. He received me with politeness, and asked me several questions concerning my progress in the different branches of science appertaining to natural philosophy. I mentioned, it is true, with fear and trembling, the only authors I had ever read upon those subjects.' Oh no! My dearest Victor do not mention them! Had you not learned from your father how the modern world had abandoned them. Albertus Magnus! Paracelsus! You will be run out of town by a mob of professors and undergraduants carrying torches and pitchforks. 'The professor stared: "Have you," he said, "really spent your time in studying such nonsense?"' Oh!

'I replied in the affirmative. "Every minute," continued Mr Krempe with warmth, "every instant that you have wasted on those books is utterly and entirely lost. You have burdened your memory with exploded systems, and useless names. Good God! in what desert land have you lived, where no one was kind enough to inform you that these fancies, which you have so greedily imbibed, are a thousand years old, and as musty as they are ancient? I little expected in this enlightened and scientific age to find a disciple of Albertus Magnus and Paracelsus. My dear Sir, you must begin your studies entirely anew."

'So saying, he stept aside, and wrote down a list of several books treating of natural philosophy, which he desired me to procure, and dismissed me, after mentioning that in the beginning of the following week he intended to commence a course of lectures upon natural philosophy in its general relations, and that Mr Waldman, a fellow-professor, would lecture upon chemistry the alternate days that he missed.'

'I returned home, not disappointed, for I had long considered those authors useless whom the professor had so strongly reprobated; but I did not feel much inclined to study the books which I procured at his recommendation.' Oh, no, my dearest, Victor. No! The joy of a new venture in education of immeasurable. Getting a new bibliography to explore is a wondrous adventure. Even the scribes of the Bible can write wisdom the Apostle Paul advices: *When I was a child, I spake as a child, I understood as a child, I thought as a child: but when I became a man, I put away childish things.*[73] Mr Krempe was a little squat man, with a gruff voice and repulsive countenance.' Oh, for shame, Victor! Do not fall into the pseudoscience of physiognomy. First alchemy. Now physiognomy! Your studies have been as useless as Mr Krempe has adviced. Do not believe that there is so intimate a relation between the dispositions of the mind and the features of the countenance is a fact which cannot be questioned.[74] 'The teacher, therefore, did not prepossess me in favour of his doctrine. Besides, I had a contempt for the uses of modern natural philosophy. It was very different, when the masters of the science sought immortality and power; such views, although futile, were grand: but now the scene was changed. The ambition of the inquirer seemed to limit itself to the annihilation of those visions on which my interest in science was chiefly founded. I was required to exchange chimeras of boundless grandeur for realities of little worth.

'Such were my reflections during the first two or three days spent almost in solitude. But as the ensuing week commenced, I thought of the information which Mr Krempe had given me concerning the lectures. And although I could not consent to go and hear that little conceited fellow deliver sentences out of a pulpit, I recollected what he had said of Mr Waldman, whom I had never seen, as he had hitherto been out of town.

'Partly from curiosity, and partly from idleness, I went into the lecturing room, which Mr Waldman entered shortly after. This professor was very unlike his colleague. He appeared about fifty years of age, but with an aspect expressive of the greatest benevolence; a few gray hairs covered his temples, but those at the back of his head were nearly black. His person was short, but remarkably erect; and his voice the sweetest I had ever heard. ' Not physiognomy again! I am growly weary of your wary intellect. Let us hope that your schooling widens your mind. 'He began his lecture by a recapitulation of the history of chemistry and the various improvements made by different men of learning, pronouncing with fervour the names of the most distinguished discoverers. He then took a cursory view of the present state of the science, and explained many of its elementary terms. After having made a few preparatory experiments, he concluded with a panegyric upon modern chemistry, the terms of which I shall never forget:—

' "The ancient teachers of this science," said he, "promised impossibilities, and performed nothing. The modern masters promise very little; they know that metals cannot be transmuted, and that the elixir of life is

---

73 From 1 Corinthians 13:11
74 From the 1797 Encyclopædia Britanica.

a chimera. But these philosophers, whose hands seem only made to dabble in dirt, and their eyes to pour over the microscope or crucible, have indeed performed miracles. They penetrate into the recesses of nature, and shew how she works in her hiding places. They ascend into the heavens; they have discovered how the blood circulates, and the nature of the air we breathe. They have acquired new and almost unlimited powers; they can command the thunders of heaven, mimic the earthquake, and even mock the invisible world with its own shadows."'

I would have adored this Mr Waldman as would my father and my Beloved. Was not the grand parlour of William Godwin a bastion of learning? How ladies and their gentlemen cherished invitations to Godwin's home on a Saturday. My father hosted many literary, scientific, and philosophical salons. Dinner was served promptly at eight, usually of four courses, but sometimes of seven, and rarely of anything more. These evenings were not intended for nourishment or merriment, but for enlightenment, though guests often left with all three. Esteemed and interesting persons were brought in to speak on any subject that struck my father's fancy this week or that week. Many critics would accuse my father of atheism, anarchism, anti-monarchism, feminism, utilitarianism, and radicalism inspired by the revolutionaries of France. My father was nothing if not outspoken. And my Beloved as well. He devoured the lectures held in my father's parlour and scoured the globe for papers and letters on this new discovery or this new discovery. Did not my Beloved and our little Lord spend a fateful evening debating galvanism? And if not for this singular debate my pale student of the unhallowed arts would not have visited me.

'I departed highly pleased with the professor and his lecture, and paid him a visit the same evening. His manners in private were even more mild and attractive than in public; for there was a certain dignity in his mien during his lecture, which in his own house was replaced by the greatest affability and kindness. He heard with attention my little narration concerning my studies, and smiled at the names of Cornelius Agrippa, and Paracelsus, but without the contempt that Mr Krempe had exhibited.' Curious! 'He said, that "these were men to whose indefatigable zeal modern philosophers were indebted for most of the foundations of their knowledge. They had left to us, as an easier task, to give new names, and arrange in connected classifications, the facts which they in a great degree had been the instruments of bringing to light. The labours of men of genius, however erroneously directed, scarcely ever fail in ultimately turning to the solid advantage of mankind." Curiouser! 'I listened to his statement, which was delivered without any presumption or affectation; and then added, that his lecture had removed my prejudices against modern chemists; and I, at the same time, requested his advice concerning the books I ought to procure.

' "I am happy," said Mr Waldman, "to have gained a disciple; and if your application equals your ability, I have no doubt of your success. Chemistry is that branch of natural philosophy in which the greatest improvements have been and may be made; it is on that account that I have made it my peculiar study; but at the same time I have not neglected the other branches of science. A man would make but a very sorry chemist, if he attended to that department of human knowledge alone. If your wish is to become really a man of science, and not merely a petty experimentalist, I should advise you to apply to every branch of natural philosophy, including mathematics."

'He then took me into his laboratory, and explained to me the uses of his various machines; instructing me as to what I ought to procure, and promising me the use of his own, when I should have advanced far enough in the science not to derange their mechanism. He also gave me the list of books which I had requested; and I took my leave.

'Thus ended a day memorable to me; it decided my future destiny.

Chapter III

From this day natural philosophy, and particularly chemistry, in the most comprehensive sense of the term, became nearly my sole occupation. I read with ardour those works, so full of genius and discrimination, which modern inquirers have written on these subjects. I attended the lectures, and cultivated the acquaintance, of the men of science of the university.' Good! Wondrous is learning. How often did I stand in my childhood home, peaking around the corner of a doorframe. Behind me was the hallway leading to my bedchamber on the left and the apartment of my father on the right. In front of me was the grand parlour of William Godwin, where many a lecture was made after a glorious dinner party. I was, more often than not, shooed away to bed because the lecture would be to advanced or heady for a child. But, more often than not, I crept from my bed to witness and absorb these lectures. My father knew, of course he did, that I was dropping eaves, but seeing that I was not shooed away a second or even third time implies his acceptance of my disobedience. 'And I found even in Mr Krempe a great deal of sound sense and real information, combined, it is true, with a repulsive physiognomy and manners, but not on that account the less valuable. In Mr Waldman I found a true friend. His gentleness was never tinged by dogmatism; and his instructions were given with an air of frankness and good nature, that banished every idea of pedantry. It was, perhaps, the amiable character of this man that inclined me more to that branch of natural philosophy which he professed, than an intrinsic love for the science itself. But this state of mind had place only in the first steps towards knowledge: the more fully I entered into the science, the more exclusively I pursued it for its own sake. That application, which at first had been a matter of duty and resolution, now became so ardent and eager, that the stars often disappeared in the light of morning whilst I was yet engaged in my laboratory.

'As I applied so closely, it may be easily conceived that I improved rapidly. My ardour was indeed the astonishment of the students; and my proficiency, that of the masters. Professor Krempe often asked me, with a sly smile, how Cornelius Agrippa went on? whilst Mr Waldman expressed the most heart-felt exultation in my progress.'

A sly smile. Mr Krempe would have concerned me more if his digs were genuine. I have encountered too many professors, lecturers, and supposed experts in their field, who dismissed alternate views of their dogmatic believes as blasphemous. And their dismissal of women was as pointed as clergymen. Where is it written in any of scientific words of Nicolaus Copernicus, Galileo Galilei, Johannes Kepler, René Descartes, William Harvey, Isaac Newton, Tycho Brahe, Andreas Vesalius, Robert Boyle, Antonie van Leeuwenhoek, and Evangelista Torricelli: *Let your women keep silence: for it is not permitted unto them to speak; but they are commanded to be under obedience, as also saith the law.*[75] No! Only in the words of religious scripture do you find such decrees. Yet, too often, women are summarily dismissed for the crime of being born without a penis. Sorry for this digression. Let us return to my pale student.

'Two years passed in this manner, during which I paid no visit to Geneva, but was engaged, heart and soul, in the pursuit of some discoveries, which I hoped to make. None but those who have experienced them can conceive of the enticements of science. In other studies you go as far as others have gone before you, and there is nothing more to know; but in a scientific pursuit there is continual food for discovery and wonder. A mind of moderate capacity, which closely pursues one study, must infallibly arrive at great proficiency in that study; and I, who continually sought the attainment of one object of pursuit, and was solely wrapt up in this, improved so rapidly, that, at the end of two years, I made some discoveries in the improvement of some chemical instruments, which procured me great esteem and admiration at the university.'

Hear! Hear! I could not have written it better myself. But perchance I have written it myself. I am not foolish enough to believe that my phantasm is nothing more than my eager imagination made

---

75 From 1 Corinthians 14:34

manifest. How weary had I grown of poor Polidori's relentless teasing *every* morning when I did not have a ghost story to enter into Lord Byron's game. For far too long I tried far too hard to conceive of a ghost story, but the spark of inspiration did not come. Only when I was too weary from a long evening of debate between my Beloved and our little Lord and poor Polidori on galvanism, was my mind finally primed to conceive of a ghost story to enter into our little game. While it is far too early to tell this story to my fellow prisoners in the Villa Diodati, Polidori has shifted his teasing from when would I get an idea for a ghost story to when would I share my ghost idea. He is an infuriating small man.

'When I had arrived at this point, and had become as well acquainted with the theory and practice of natural philosophy as depended on the lessons of any of the professors at Ingolstadt, my residence there being no longer conducive to my improvements, I thought of returning to my friends and my native town, when an incident happened that protracted my stay.

'One of the phænonema which had peculiarly attracted my attention was the structure of the human frame, and, indeed, any animal endued with life. Whence, I often asked myself, did the principle of life proceed? It was a bold question, and one which has ever been considered as a mystery.' This word. This confounded word. When the clergyman encountered a question that their particular translation of the Holy Bible or their peculiar variation of Christianity cannot answer, they answer with this word and the conversation is ended. Natural philosophers, at the very least, seek an answer, but when one cannot be readily found, they likewise answer with this word and the conversation is ended. Infuriating!

'Yet with how many things are we upon the brink of becoming acquainted, if cowardice or carelessness did not restrain our inquiries. I revolved these circumstances in my mind, and determined thenceforth to apply myself more particularly to those branches of natural philosophy which relate to physiology. Unless I had been animated by an almost supernatural enthusiasm, my application to this study would have been irksome, and almost intolerable. To examine the causes of life, we must first have recourse to death. I became acquainted with the science of anatomy: but this was not sufficient; I must also observe the natural decay and corruption of the human body. In my education my father had taken the greatest precautions that my mind should be impressed with no supernatural horrors.' Alphonse Frankenstein sounds very similar to William Godwin. Which he would, of course, seeing that William Godwin is my father and Victor Frankenstein is me, at least while immersed in this harrowing tale. As a writer, our protagonist is ourselves, no matter the deviation from ourselves. If the deviation is slight, we will trumpet the similarity. If the deviation is too great, we will dismiss the character as a mere creation and not anything like ourselves. As Thomas, Duke of Norfolk opined to Thomas Cromwell: 'a man cannot have his cake and eat his cake.' But to date, Victor is very much me. I cannot wait to see when he deviates from my own psyche.

'I do not ever remember to have trembled at a tale of superstition, or to have feared the apparition of a spirit. Darkness had no effect upon my fancy; and a church-yard was to me merely the receptacle of bodies deprived of life, which, from being the seat of beauty and strength, had become food for the worm. Now I was led to examine the cause and progress of this decay, and forced to spend days and nights in vaults and charnel houses. My attention was fixed upon every object the most insupportable to the delicacy of the human feelings. I saw how the fine form of man was degraded and wasted; I beheld the corruption of death succeed to the blooming cheek of life; I saw how the worm inherited the wonders of the eye and brain. I paused, examining and analysing all the minutiæ of causation, as exemplified in the change from life to death, and death to life, until from the midst of this darkness a sudden light broke in upon me— a light so brilliant and wondrous, yet so simple, that while I became dizzy with the immensity of the prospect which it illustrated, I was surprised that among so many men of genius, who had directed their inquiries towards the same science, that I alone should be reserved to discover so astonishing a secret.' My pale student makes me long to stalk the cemeteries, vaults, and charnel houses too. How would William Godwin or my Beloved react if a mere woman examined the dead as my dear Victor did? How will Lord Byron or poor Polidori react when I write read these very words as part of our little game of ghost stories? How unseemly it would be for a woman to have written these words. This will be seen as an 'aggravation of that which is the prevailing fault of the novel; but if our authoress can forget the gentleness of her sex, it is no reason why we should; and we shall therefore dismiss the novel without further comment.'[76]

'Remember, I am not recording the vision of a madman. The sun does not more certainly shine in the heavens, than that which I now affirm is true. Some miracle might have produced it, yet the stages of the discovery were distinct and probable. After days and nights of incredible labour and fatigue, I succeeded in discovering the cause of generation and life; nay, more, I became myself capable of bestowing animation upon lifeless matter.'

---

76 From *The British Critic. New Series.* 9: 432–438. April 1818

'The astonishment which I had at first experienced on this discovery soon gave place to delight and rapture. After so much time spent in painful labour, to arrive at once at the summit of my desires, was the most gratifying consummation of my toils. But this discovery was so great and overwhelming, that all the steps by which I had been progressively led to it were obliterated, and I beheld only the result. What had been the study and desire of the wisest men since the creation of the world, was now within my grasp. Not that, like a magic scene, it all opened upon me at once: the information I had obtained was of a nature rather to direct my endeavours so soon as I should point them towards the object of my search, than to exhibit that object already accomplished. I was like the Arabian who had been buried with the dead, and found a passage to life aided only by one glimmering, and seemingly ineffectual light.' No! Do not dismiss Elizabeth so! I know this tale from *One Thousand and One Nights* well. You are not trapped by a *dead wife*! Elizabeth has not died like Sinbad's on the island of pepper-growers. She still lives! You are not bound to their most vile, lewd custom that if the wife dies first, to bury the husband alive with her and in like manner the wife, if the husband dies first; so that neither may enjoy life after losing his or her mate. You must not cry out:

> ' "Almighty Allah never made it lawful to bury the quick with the dead! I am a stranger, not one of your kind; and I cannot abear your custom, and had I known it I never would have wedded among you!" They heard me not and paid no heed to my words, but laying hold of me, bound me by force and let me down into the cavern, with a large gugglet of sweet water and seven cakes of bread, according to their custom... When they left me in the cavern with my dead wife and, closing the mouth of the pit, went their ways, I looked about me and found myself in a vast cave full of dead bodies, that exhaled a fulsome and loathsome smell and the air was heavy with the groans of the dying.'[77]

My pales student unfazed by my silent cry continued, 'I see by your eagerness and the wonder and hope which your eyes express, my dearest Mary, that you expect to be informed of the secret with which I am acquainted; that cannot be. Listen patiently until the end of my story, and you will easily perceive why I am reserved upon that subject. I will not lead you on, unguarded and ardent as I then was, to your destruction and infallible misery. Learn from me, if not by my precepts, at least by my example, how dangerous is the acquirement of knowledge, and how

---

77 From *One Thousand and One Nights*, translated by Richard F. Burton, 1885

much happier that man is who believes his native town to be the world, than he who aspires to become greater than his nature will allow.' My greatest fear was that my pale student would take this secret to his own grave. But it is best for the writer of fictional works to keep this knowledge 'secret', therefore withholding it from the reader, lest the science one day be disproven, or God forbid, the reader seeks to recreate our fictional science, no matter how thorough our research may have been. I would greatly fear newspaper headlines screaming that readers of my novel were inspired to stalk cemeteries, vaults, and charnel houses and to purchase the requisite equipment from laboratories and attempt a recreation of Victor's experiments. So, he keeps the secret from me so I can withhold the secret from my readers.

'When I found so astonishing a power placed within my hands, I hesitated a long time concerning the manner in which I should employ it. Although I possessed the capacity of bestowing animation, yet to prepare a frame for the reception of it, with all its intricacies of fibres, muscles, and veins, still remained a work of inconceivable difficulty and labour. I doubted at first whether I should attempt the creation of a being like myself or one of simpler organization; but my imagination was too much exalted by my first success to permit me to doubt of my ability to give life to an animal as complex and wonderful as man. The materials at present within my command hardly appeared adequate to so arduous an undertaking; but I doubted not that I should ultimately succeed. I prepared myself for a multitude of reverses; my operations might be incessantly baffled, and at last my work be imperfect: yet, when I considered the improvement which every day takes place in science and mechanics, I was encouraged to hope my present attempts would at least lay the foundations of future success. Nor could I consider the magnitude and complexity of my plan as any argument of its impracticability. It was with these feelings that I began the creation of a human being. As the minuteness of the parts formed a great hindrance to my speed, I resolved, contrary to my first intention, to make the being of a gigantic stature; that is to say, about eight feet in height, and proportionably large.' My! How would he find bones of such proportion in the vaults and charnel houses around the vicinity of Ingolstadt. Surely the men of that region are similarly proportioned to the men of Britian where the average height of an English solider being five foot five. How could he assemble such height in such a creature! Oh! Victor would not limit himself to human cadavers! Will he seek out the slaughterhouses for meat and bones of cattle and horses? What of the exotic species of rhinoceroses and elephants and the great cats of the zoos! What manner of abomination does Victor desire to as his creation? After having formed this determination, and having spent some months in successfully collecting and arranging my materials, I began.' Surely, he must have had difficulty in finding the requisite human parts for the experiment. Did not resurrectionist, those grotesque body snatchers who stole corpses from graveyards, not struggle in the finding the bodies to supply the market? Where would students of human anatomy find the cadavers required for their studies. The fashionable decline in capital punishment, which is a great advancement of the modern age, likewise contributed to the scarcity of human cadavers.

'No one can conceive the variety of feelings which bore me onwards, like a hurricane, in the first enthusiasm of success. Life and death appeared to me ideal bounds, which I should first break through, and pour a torrent of light into our dark world. A new species would bless me as its creator and source; many happy and excellent natures would owe their being to me. No father could claim the gratitude of his child so completely as I should deserve their's. Pursuing these reflections, I thought, that if I could bestow animation upon lifeless matter, I might in process of time (although I now found it impossible) renew life where death had apparently devoted the body to corruption.' I desired to cry out to my pale student as he relates his story to me concerning his foolishness and hubris. 'A new species?' We are not living in Ancient Greece where natural creatures were an amalgamation of man and beast: the minotaur of man and bull, the centaur of man and horse, the griffon of lion and eagle, the chimera of lion and goat and snake, the pegasus of horse and bird, the sphynx of woman and lion and eagle, the harpies of woman and bird, *etc. ad nauseum.* This 'new species' is a comedy of errors!

'These thoughts supported my spirits, while I pursued my undertaking with unremitting ardour. My cheek had grown pale with study, and my person had become emaciated with confinement. Sometimes, on the very brink of certainty, I failed; yet still I clung to the hope which the next day or the next hour might realize. One secret which I alone possessed was the hope to which I had dedicated myself; and the moon gazed on my midnight labours, while, with unrelaxed and breathless eagerness, I pursued nature to her hiding places. Who shall conceive the horrors of my secret toil, as I dabbled among the unhallowed damps of the grave, or tortured the living animal to animate the lifeless clay?'

Oho, my dear Victor. There is your hubris. The Jewish magicians who created Golems saw Adam as but the first: With regard to Adam the first man, his torso was fashioned from clay taken from Babylonia, and his head was fashioned from clay taken from Eretz Yisrael, the most important land, and his limbs were fashioned from clay taken from the rest of the lands in the world. With regard to his buttocks, Rav Aha says: They were fashioned from clay taken from Akra De'agma, on the outskirts of

Babylonia.[78] And here my dearest Victor is plotting and planning to create a new Adam, not created in the likeness of the Judaeo-Christian God, but himself! You are taking pieces from this vault and that charnel house, this farm and that slaughterhouse in cruel blasphemy of the creation of the first man.

'My limbs now tremble, and my eyes swim with the remembrance; but then a resistless, and almost frantic impulse, urged me forward; I seemed to have lost all soul or sensation but for this one pursuit. It was indeed but a passing trance, that only made me feel with renewed acuteness so soon as, the unnatural stimulus ceasing to operate, I had returned to my old habits. I collected bones from charnel houses; and disturbed, with profane fingers, the tremendous secrets of the human frame. In a solitary chamber, or rather cell, at the top of the house, and separated from all the other apartments by a gallery and staircase, I kept my workshop of filthy creation; my eyeballs were starting from their sockets in attending to the details of my employment. The dissecting room and the slaughter-house furnished many of my materials; and often did my human nature turn with loathing from my occupation, whilst, still urged on by an eagerness which perpetually increased, I brought my work near to a conclusion.

'The summer months passed while I was thus engaged, heart and soul, in one pursuit. It was a most beautiful season; never did the fields bestow a more plentiful harvest, or the vines yield a more luxuriant vintage: but my eyes were insensible to the charms of nature. And the same feelings which made me neglect the scenes around me caused me also to forget those friends who were so many miles absent, and whom I had not seen for so long a time. I knew my silence disquieted them; and I well remembered the words of my father: "I know that while you are pleased with yourself, you will think of us with affection, and we shall hear regularly from you. You must pardon me, if I regard any interruption in your correspondence as a proof that your other duties are equally neglected."

'I knew well therefore what would be my father's feelings; but I could not tear my thoughts from my employment, loathsome in itself, but which had taken an irresistible hold of my imagination. I wished, as it were, to procrastinate all that related to my feelings of affection until the great object, which swallowed up every habit of my nature, should be completed.

'I then thought that my father would be unjust if he ascribed my neglect to vice, or faultiness on my part; but I am now convinced that he was justified in conceiving that I should not be altogether free from blame. A human being in perfection ought always to preserve a calm

---

78 From Sanhedrin 38b, one of ten tractates of Seder Nezikin (a section of the Talmud that deals with damages, i.e. civil and criminal proceedings)

and peaceful mind, and never to allow passion or a transitory desire to disturb his tranquillity. I do not think that the pursuit of knowledge is an exception to this rule. If the study to which you apply yourself has a tendency to weaken your affections, and to destroy your taste for those simple pleasures in which no alloy can possibly mix, then that study is certainly unlawful, that is to say, not befitting the human mind. If this rule were always observed; if no man allowed any pursuit whatsoever to interfere with the tranquillity of his domestic affections, Greece had not been enslaved.' 'Cæsar would have spared his country; America would have been discovered more gradually; and the empires of Mexico and Peru had not been destroyed.' Oh, how the words of Lord Byron linger in my mind. He recently complete is third canto in his 'Child Harold's Pilgrimage', but in his second he lamented the Greeks' *trembling beneath the scourge of Turkish hand/ From birth till death enslaved; in word, in deed, unmanned.*

'But I forget that I am moralizing in the most interesting part of my tale; and your looks remind me to proceed.

'My father made no reproach in his letters; and only took notice of my silence by inquiring into my occupations more particularly than before. Winter, spring, and summer, passed away during my labours; but I did not watch the blossom or the expanding leaves— sights which before always yielded me supreme delight, so deeply was I engrossed in my occupation. The leaves of that year had withered before my work drew near to a close; and now every day shewed me more plainly how well I had succeeded. But my enthusiasm was checked by my anxiety, and I appeared rather like one doomed by slavery to toil in the mines, or any other unwholesome trade, than an artist occupied by his favourite employment. Every night I was oppressed by a slow fever, and I became nervous to a most painful degree.' I longed to add my own words to his but could not bring myself to speak: 'the fall of a leaf startled me, and I shunned my fellow-creatures as if I had been guilty of a crime. Sometimes I grew alarmed at the wreck I perceived that I had become; the energy of my purpose alone sustained me: my labours would soon end, and I believed that exercise and amusement would then drive away incipient disease'. In my silence, my pale student continued, 'A disease that I regretted the more because I had hitherto enjoyed most excellent health, and had always boasted of the firmness of my nerves. But I believed that exercise and amusement would soon drive away such symptoms; and I promised myself both of these, when my creation should be complete.'

Chapter IV

I awakened when a thundercrack thundered and cracked so violent my first fear was Napoleon had returned to wage war on Lake Geneva. Had he not been defeated by Duke Wellington at Waterloo? Had he not been a second time exiled, this time on the island of Saint Helena? Did he escape Saint Helena as easily as he had his first exile on Elba? Oh! The thunder shook walls of the Villa Diodati as if rained on by cannon fire. Droplets of rain struck the windowpanes as if rained on by musket fire. I shook. My Beloved slept. I almost wept.

I found the door to our chamber was ajar. Had my pale student of the unhallowed arts abandoned our nightly conversation in fear of sheer violence of the storm? I wrapped my robe securely and fastened around the waist and crept out of the chamber so not to disturb my slumbering Beloved. When I stepped into the hallway, I found myself no longer in hallways of the Villa Diodati. I did not see Lord Byron's apartment, nor the doctor's, nor Claire's where they should be found. Did I find myself in a dream? Can one have consciousness of being in a dream? Seldom if ever do I come to the realisation I am in a dream. And if so, what recourse does one have but to allow the dream to continue. Does one fight the dream? Does one allow the dream to overwhelm them? Does one not control the dream? Or does one fight to awake? My conversation with my pale student was quite lucid. I could not have possibly dreamt them; my pale student could not be merely a dream, because the transcriptions are in my journal in each morning. And! This night I had awoken so clearly and experienced the thunderstorm so severely, that I could not possibly be dreaming.

I found myself not in the Villa Diodati, but a castle I had visited briefly while on our six weeks' tour through a part of France, Switzerland, Germany, and Holland with my Beloved and my dearest Claire. I had encountered the dark haunted forests and narrow valleys surrounding the castle that were as much shrouded in legendary mystery as they were a darkness that hung like London fog. Was this where my pale student of the unhallowed arts had acquired his name? Were my inner thoughts and memories affecting our conversations?

My Beloved wished to tarry at the castle because he personally knew several members of the '*Kreis der Empfindsamen*', a literary circle from Darmstadt, who used the castle for their readings. Did they believe they were a Hellfire Club reciting their poems as if spells to summon the Great Dragon himself, that old serpent, called the Devil, and Satan, who deceives the whole world? At the Castle Frankenstein, we encountered students from the University of Strasbourg, of which Johann Konrad Dippel was an infamous alumnus. We learned from them of Dippel's discovery of the 'Elixir of Life', as evidenced by his *Maladies and Remedies of the Life of the Flesh*. He made this dark, viscous, tar-like, and putrid oil through the destructive distillation of bones. How could rotting death ever be an 'elixir of life'? The students spoke quiet highly of the Pietist theologian, physician, and alchemist, though they admitted that one Emanuel Swedenborg, both once a devoted disciple and then staunch critic had dismissed him as 'bound to no principles, but was in general opposed to all, whoever they may be, of whatever principle or faith ... becoming angry with any one for contradicting him.' How Swedenborg had fallen from once being enamoured to then being repulsed by 'a most vile devil... who attempted wicked things.' But the students hailed the glorious alchemist (though locals remembered him as notorious graverobber), who experimented in anatomy and supposedly transferred the souls from one cadaver to another with a funnel, as an exorcist and a saint! Did he not, they claimed, create an alchemic potion concocted from boiled animal bones and their flesh to supplant the *Rituale Romanum*, and therefore the Vatican, in the exorcising of demons?

After the mysterious, almost dreamlike transition of stepping foot over the threshold of the hold, I went from being in my bedchamber at the Villa Diodati to the halls of the castle Frankenstein. The walls of the medieval castle did little protect from the thunderous storm raging outside. If it had been daylight, I could have peered out one of the windows, over the sheer cliff, and down into the hauntingly forested valley far below. I made my way upwards toward the tower that had been so utterly collapsed that it was exposed to the elements. Not alchemical elements mind you, but the natural elements. The students who had two years previous pointed up towards this very tower, telling us of nitro-glycerine experiments that destroyed it; though my Beloved doubted whether or not it was an anachronism. When nitro-glycerine was first discovered, we could not deduce; surely this discovery was not made by Johann Konrad Dippel! In the ruins of the tower, I found my pale student of the unhallowed arts sitting in an armchair near an extinguished fireplace with a ruined chimney. Behind him stood the very same powerful engine I saw in my awaking dream but now fully destroyed; the metal spilt open from explosions within. The walls of the tower had been charred black by a raging inferno. I did not see the hideous phantasm of a man stretched out as I had seen before. Oh! The violence of the thunderstorm that had awaken me from a dreamless slumber was so much more explosive above the ruined tower. The rain-drops buffeted our shoulders; the wind whipped against our faces like painful slaps. Even though the torrential rain drenched us in a deluge not seen by man since the days of Noah, the pale student offered me a chair opposite it. I took out my journal fearful that the previous conversation with my pale student would be obliterated by the weather, but the rain did not wet the pages nor ruin the ink. *Thanks be to God!* Where did this come from? I could not have possibly heard it during the Roman Mass. I shook off the saying as my nervous shivering shook off the rain.

Victor continued his tale: 'It was on a dreary night of November, that I beheld the accomplishment of my toils.' November! Did my pale student not say that winter, spring, and summer had passed away during his 'labours'! March. April. May. June. July. August. September. October. And now November have passed away. Oh! 'Labours!' This is the word my pale student chose! He gestated on his 'labours' for nine months! This is most telling.

'With an anxiety that almost amounted to agony, I collected the instruments of life around me, that I might infuse a spark of being'— Curious phrase this. Reminds me of the phrase *flavilla viae*, or when translated literally into English, 'the spark of vitality. Of course, Erasmus Darwin was describing the passing of vitality from parent to offspring in plants. But 'spark of being' is quite the interesting turn of phrase.— 'into the lifeless thing that lay at my feet. It was already one in the morning; the rain pattered dismally against the panes, and my candle was nearly burnt out, when, by the glimmer of the half-extinguished light, I saw the dull yellow eye of the creature open; it breathed hard, and a convulsive motion agitated its limbs.' The poor creature is jaundiced. Dear God! Curse God! I remember intimately giving birth at only six months gestation. I was not ready. I was not prepared. The yellow pallor of my daughter who was too live only nine short days is so vivid in my memory that I wish to cry out again:

> 'My dearest Hogg my baby is dead— will you come to see me as soon as you can. I wish to see you— It was perfectly well when I went to bed— I awoke in the night to give it suck it appeared to be sleeping so quietly that I would not awake it. It was dead then, but we did not find that out till morning— from its appearance it evidently died of convulsions— Will you come— you are so calm a creature & Shelley is afraid of a fever from the milk— for I am no longer a mother now.'[79]

'How can I describe my emotions at this catastrophe, or how delineate the wretch whom with such infinite pains and care I had endeavoured

---

79 From a letter 6 March, 1815 to Thomas Jefferson Hogg

to form? His limbs were in proportion, and I had selected his features as beautiful. Beautiful!— Great God! His yellow skin scarcely covered the work of muscles and arteries beneath; his hair was of a lustrous black, and flowing; his teeth of a pearly whiteness; but these luxuriances only formed a more horrid contrast with his watery eyes, that seemed almost of the same colour as the dun white sockets in which they were set, his shrivelled complexion, and straight black lips.'

Beautiful and repulsive all in one Creation. Can a mother look down at her child newly born, twisted and distorted by a malignant pregnancy and not feel even a sliver of maternal love for her child? Does she not desire to put the abomination to her breast to suckle the life-giving nourishment of her breast? The father, who did not carry the growing child in his own body, feeding it nourishment through the afterbirth as the womb grows bone and knits the fibres of the foetal flesh, will seek to snatch the child away from its mother's breast to cast the deformed newborn off a cliff into the battering waves of the sea. Having lost my own sickly jaundiced child at only nine days, this is beyond my comprehension.

'The different accidents of life are not so changeable as the feelings of human nature. I had worked hard for nearly two years, for the sole purpose of infusing life into an inanimate body. For this I had deprived myself of rest and health. I had desired it with an ardour that far exceeded moderation; but now that I had finished, the beauty of the dream vanished, and breathless horror and disgust filled my heart.'

My pale student has created an offspring without the contribution of a woman! Now unnatural is this phenomenon. He has sewn disparate parts from the bodies he desperately stole from the grave, bought from the laboratories, and acquired from the slaughterhouses. And yet my pale student is disgusted by its unnatural appearance. So typical of men. He did not carry this creation in his womb feeling the kicks of the foetus and seeing his belly grow with each passing day. He did not experience the discomfort the child causes, disrupting sleep and disturbing common everyday activities. And yet the mother caresses her belly with eager anticipation of the birth and the coming years of rearing the child into adulthood. The father is physically disconnected from the pregnancy. True, he may rest his head on the growing belly to feel the child kick and therefore feel some connection to the child, but this feeling is fleeting. His own eager preparations for the coming of the child are purely financial. He wants the best possible future for his child, but a father's mind is preoccupied with how he will provide for the child, and this involves money and perchance the growing of his station in life. The nurturing of the growing baby and the education of

the child is left into the service of the mother, or if the family is affluent enough, a nurse. If a man experiences an unnatural growing in his
body is not the result cancerous? Such swelling is nearly always fatal.
My pale student did not grow his Creation his womb, but assembled
it on a slab.

'Unable to endure the aspect of the being I had created, I rushed out
of the room, and continued a long time traversing my bed-chamber, unable to compose my mind to sleep. At length lassitude succeeded to the tumult I had before endured; and I threw myself on the bed in my clothes,
endeavouring to seek a few moments of forgetfulness. But it was in vain:
I slept indeed, but I was disturbed by the wildest dreams. I thought I saw
Elizabeth, in the bloom of health, walking in the streets of Ingolstadt. Delighted and surprised, I embraced her; but as I imprinted the first kiss on
her lips, they became lurid with the hue of death; her features appeared
to change, and I thought that I held the corpse of my dead mother in my
arms; a shroud enveloped her form, and I saw the grave-worms crawling
in the folds of the flannel.'

Shall I attempt to analyse this dream or if this even be a dream?
Ancient man saw dreams as messages from the gods, but did not Aristotle believe them merely a psychosomatic phenomenon? Given the
absence of external sensory stimulation, our eyes are closed and unable
to see, he posits that sleep is akin to hallucinations, 'that the faculty
by which, in waking hours, we are subject to illusion when affected by
disease, is identical with that which produces illusory effects in sleep.'[80]
This dream– nay! hallucination– may rest the blame for the death of his
mother at the hands of Elizabeth. Did not the disease first come into
the Frankenstein home through his cousin! On her death-bed, Caroline decreed that Elizabeth must supply Caroline's place to her younger
cousins. Did Victor believe that Elizabeth, his mother's 'favourite', presumed to replace his mother or did he believe his mother was forcing
him into an incestuous marriage with his own cousin? These abomina-
tions of marriages were reserved for royalty! Or did Victor believe— fie!
It would be folly to continue further down the rabbit-hole of dream
interpretation. We could awaken any number of interpretations and
drown ourselves in speculation. It is best to leave the sleeping world to
the sleeping.

'I started from my sleep with horror; a cold dew covered my forehead, my teeth chattered, and every limb became convulsed; when, by
the dim and yellow light of the moon, as it forced its way through the
window-shutters, I beheld the wretch— the miserable monster whom I
had created. He held up the curtain of the bed; and his eyes, if eyes they

---

80 From *On Dreams* by Aristotle, translated by J. I. Beare

may be called, were fixed on me. His jaws opened, and he muttered some inarticulate sounds, while a grin wrinkled his cheeks. He might have spoken, but I did not hear; one hand was stretched out, seemingly to detain me, but I escaped, and rushed down stairs.' No! My dear Victor! No! Your Creation is but a babbling babe reaching out for a parent's love. He may not purse his lips longing to nurse upon his mother's breast, but he longs for the connection that any child desires of a parent. You see his height and his weight, and see a man, but no man is this. His speech is inarticulate because he is an infant. Any other parent would delight if a grin wrinkled the cheeks of their child. But Victor is not just any parent. 'I took refuge in the court-yard belonging to the house which I inhabited; where I remained during the rest of the night, walking up and down in the greatest agitation, listening attentively, catching and fearing each sound as if it were to announce the approach of the demoniacal corpse to which I had so miserably given life.' The endless hubris of a man. This is why men were not gifted by the gods to grow life within their bellies. A man is an external creature with his sexual organs hanging limp and flaccid on the outside of his body; only when the fires of desire stir within a man does that serpentine organ show signs of life. A woman in an internal creature, the workings of her body a mystery. A man concerns himself with the external world while a woman concerns herself with her children she has grown internally. This is the natural order. One that my pale student of the unhallowed arts has torn assunder.

At this moment, I know not why I endeavoured to gain from Frankenstein the particulars of his creatures formation: but on this point he was impenetrable.

'Are you mad, my dear?' said Victor; 'or whither does your senseless curiosity lead you? Would you also create for yourself and the world a demoniacal enemy? Peace, peace! learn my miseries, and do not seek to increase your own.' He then continued his tale as if I had not interrupted nor irritated him so greatly.

'Oh! no mortal could support the horror of that countenance. A mummy again endued with animation could not be so hideous as that wretch. I had gazed on him while unfinished; he was ugly then; but when those muscles and joints were rendered capable of motion, it became a thing such as even Dante could not have conceived.

'I passed the night wretchedly. Sometimes my pulse beat so quickly and hardly, that I felt the palpitation of every artery; at others, I nearly sank to the ground through languor and extreme weakness. Mingled with this horror, I felt the bitterness of disappointment: dreams that had been my food and pleasant rest for so long a space, were now become a hell to me; and the change was so rapid, the overthrow so complete!

'Morning, dismal and wet, at length dawned, and discovered to my sleepless and aching eyes the church of Ingolstadt, its white steeple and clock, which indicated the sixth hour.' Victor is speaking as if he is not in Castle Frankenstein, but in Ingolsdtadt. Are these surroundings I see around me a dreamlike illusion? Victor did not create his creation here in the ruined castle, but in his private apartment in Ingolstadt. ' The porter opened the gates of the court, which had that night been my asylum, and I issued into the streets, pacing them with quick steps, as if I sought to avoid the wretch whom I feared every turning of the street would present to my view. I did not dare return to the apartment which I inhabited, but felt impelled to hurry on, although wetted by the rain, which poured from a black and comfortless sky.

'I continued walking in this manner for some time, endeavouring, by bodily exercise, to ease the load that weighed upon my mind. I traversed the streets, without any clear conception of where I was, or what I was doing. My heart palpitated in the sickness of fear; and I hurried on with irregular steps, not daring to look about me:

> 'Like one who, on a lonely road,
>   Doth walk in fear and dread,
>   And, having once turn'd round, walks on,
>   And turns no more his head;
> Because he knows a frightful fiend
>   Doth close behind him tread.

'Continuing thus, I came at length opposite to the inn at which the various diligences and carriages usually stopped. Here I paused, I knew not why; but I remained some minutes with my eyes fixed on a coach that was coming towards me from the other end of the street. As it drew nearer, I observed that it was the Swiss diligence: it stopped just where I was standing; and, on the door being opened, I perceived Henry Clerval, who, on seeing me, instantly sprung out. "My dear Frankenstein,"— ah! The pale student finally utters his family name but has put the words onto the lips of her most cherished friend. And it is the very name of the castle which I and my Beloved visited during our six weeks tour through a part of France, Switzerland, Germany, and Holland. It is most curious that I would envisage my surroundings as the Castle Frankenstein despite never hearing his family name spoken aloud until this very moment. Curious and curiouser— 'exclaimed he, "how glad I am to see you! how fortunate that you should be here at the very moment of my alighting!"

'Nothing could equal my delight on seeing Clerval; his presence brought back to my thoughts my father, Elizabeth, and all those scenes of home so dear to my recollection. I grasped his hand, and in a moment forgot my horror and misfortune; I felt suddenly, and for the first time during many months, calm and serene joy. I welcomed my friend, therefore, in the most cordial manner, and we walked towards my college. Clerval continued talking for some time about our mutual friends, and his own good fortune in being permitted to come to Ingolstadt. "You may easily believe," said he, "how great was the difficulty to persuade my father that it was not absolutely necessary for a merchant not to understand any thing except book-keeping; and, indeed, I believe I left him incredulous to the last, for his constant answer to my unwearied entreaties was the same as that of the Dutch schoolmaster in the *Vicar of Wakefield*: 'You see me, young man; I never learned Greek, and I don't find that I ever missed it. I have had a Doctor's cap and gown without Greek: I have ten thousand florins a year without Greek, I eat heartily without Greek In short, I don't know Greek, and I do not believe there is any use in it.' But his affection for me at length overcame his dislike of learning, and he has permitted me to undertake a voyage of discovery to the land of knowledge."

' "It gives me the greatest delight to see you; but tell me how you left my father, brothers, and Elizabeth."

' "Very well, and very happy, only a little uneasy that they hear from you so seldom. By the bye, I mean to lecture you a little upon their account myself.— But, my dear Frankenstein," continued he, stopping short, and gazing full in my face, "I did not before remark how very ill you appear; so thin and pale; you look as if you had been watching for several nights."

' "You have guessed right; I have lately been so deeply engaged in one occupation, that I have not allowed myself sufficient rest, as you see: but I hope, I sincerely hope, that all these employments are now at an end, and that I am at length free."

'I trembled excessively; I could not endure to think of, and far less to allude to the occurrences of the preceding night. I walked with a quick pace, and we soon arrived at my college. I then reflected, and the thought made me shiver, that the creature whom I had left in my apartment might still be there, alive, and walking about. I dreaded to behold this monster; but I feared still more that Henry should see him. Entreating him therefore to remain a few minutes at the bottom of the stairs, I darted up towards my own room. My hand was already on the lock of the door before

I recollected myself. I then paused; and a cold shivering came over me. I threw the door forcibly open, as children are accustomed to do when they expect a spectre to stand in waiting for them on the other side; but nothing appeared. I stepped fearfully in: the apartment was empty; and my bedroom was also freed from its hideous guest. I could hardly believe that so great a good-fortune could have befallen me; but when I became assured that my enemy had indeed fled, I clapped my hands for joy, and ran down to Clerval.

'We ascended into my room, and the servant presently brought breakfast; but I was unable to contain myself. It was not joy only that possessed me; I felt my flesh tingle with excess of sensitiveness, and my pulse beat rapidly. I was unable to remain for a single instant in the same place; I jumped over the chairs, clapped my hands, and laughed aloud. Clerval at first attributed my unusual spirits to joy on his arrival; but when he observed me more attentively, he saw a wildness in my eyes for which he could not account; and my loud, unrestrained, heartless laughter, frightened and astonished him.

' "My dear Victor," cried he, "what, for God's sake, is the matter? Do not laugh in that manner. How ill you are! What is the cause of all this?"

' "Do not ask me," cried I, putting my hands before my eyes, for I thought I saw the dreaded spectre glide into the room; "*he* can tell.— Oh, save me! save me!" I imagined that the monster seized me; I struggled furiously, and fell down in a fit.

'Poor Clerval! what must have been his feelings? A meeting, which he anticipated with such joy, so strangely turned to bitterness. But I was not the witness of his grief; for I was lifeless, and did not recover my senses for a long, long time.

'This was the commencement of a nervous fever, which confined me for several months. During all that time Henry was my only nurse. I afterwards learned that, knowing my father's advanced age, and unfitness for so long a journey, and how wretched my sickness would make Elizabeth, he spared them this grief by concealing the extent of my disorder. He knew that I could not have a more kind and attentive nurse than himself; and, firm in the hope he felt of my recovery, he did not doubt that, instead of doing harm, he performed the kindest action that he could towards them.

'But I was in reality very ill; and surely nothing but the unbounded and unremitting attentions of my friend could have restored me to life. The form of the monster on whom I had bestowed existence was for ever before my eyes, and I raved incessantly concerning him. Doubtless my words surprised Henry: he at first believed them to be the wanderings of my disturbed imagination; but the pertinacity with which I continually recurred to the same subject persuaded him that my disorder indeed owed its origin to some uncommon and terrible event.

'By very slow degrees, and with frequent relapses, that alarmed and grieved my friend, I recovered. I remember the first time I became capable of observing outward objects with any kind of pleasure, I perceived that the fallen leaves had disappeared, and that the young buds were shooting forth from the trees that shaded my window. It was a divine spring; and the season contributed greatly to my convalescence. I felt also sentiments of joy and affection revive in my bosom; my gloom disappeared, and in a short time I became as cheerful as before I was attacked by the fatal passion.

' "Dearest Clerval," exclaimed I, "how kind, how very good you are to me. This whole winter, instead of being spent in study, as you promised yourself, has been consumed in my sick room. How shall I ever repay you? I feel the greatest remorse for the disappointment of which I have been the occasion; but you will forgive me."

' "You will repay me entirely, if you do not discompose yourself, but get well as fast as you can; and since you appear in such good spirits, I may speak to you on one subject, may I not?"

'I trembled. One subject! what could it be? Could he allude to an object on whom I dared not even think?

' "Compose yourself," said Clerval, who observed my change of colour, "I will not mention it, if it agitates you; but your father and cousin would be very happy if they received a letter from you in your own hand-writing. They hardly know how ill you have been, and are uneasy at your long silence."

' "Is that all? my dear Henry. How could you suppose that my first thought would not fly towards those dear, dear friends whom I love, and who are so deserving of my love."

' "If this is your present temper, my friend, you will perhaps be glad to see a letter that has been lying here some days for you: it is from your cousin, I believe."

When I awoke the next morning, I found myself wearing yesternight's clothes. Yesternight's clothing, my hair, and myside of the bed were drenched as if I had in reality been in that deluge at the ruined tower of Castle Frankenstein. My rational mind struggled to dismiss the sogginess as night sweats... of a Biblical magnitude.

Chapter Eight
The Prisoner of Chillon[81]

P.B. Shelley Writing a Letter to Thomas Love Peacock

Montalègre, near Colgoni,
July 12

It is nearly a fortnight since I have returned from Vevai. This journey has been on every account delightful, but most especially, because then I first knew the divine beauty of Rousseau's imagination, as it exhibits itself in Julie. It is inconceivable what an enchantment the scene itself lends to those delineations, from which its own most touching charm arises. But I will give you an abstract of our voyage, which lasted eight days, and if you have a map of Switzerland, you can follow me.

G.G.B., M., C., and I[82] left Montalègre at half past two on the 23d of June. J. disappeared for the first of twice this summer. Perhaps with Countess P. or Princess Something. No one knows; no one cares. The care we did have was the sullenly wet, ungenial summer gave such a strange birth to a suddenly pleasant, genial week; one in which us four all escaped our prison at the Villa Diodati. The lake was calm, and after three hours of rowing we arrived at Hermance, a beautiful little village, containing a ruined tower, built, the villagers say, by Julius Cæsar. There were three other towers similar to it, which the Genevese destroyed for their own fortifications in 1560. We got into the tower by a kind of window. The walls are immensely solid, and the stone of which it is built so hard, that it yet retained the mark of chisels. The boatmen said, that this tower was once three times higher than it is now. There are two staircases in the thickness of the walls, one of which is entirely demolished, and the other half ruined, and only accessible by a ladder. The town itself, now an inconsiderable village inhabited by a few fishermen, was built by a Queen of Burgundy, and reduced to its present state by the inhabitants of Berne, who burnt and ravaged every thing they could find.

Leaving Hermance, we arrived at sunset at the village of Nerni. After looking at our lodgings, which were gloomy and dirty, we walked out by the side of the lake. It was beautiful to see the vast expanse of these purple and misty waters broken by the craggy islets near to its slant and "beached margin." There were many fish sporting in the lake, and multi-

---

81 From *Prisoner of Chillon, and Other Poems* by Lord Byron, published by John Murray, 1816
82 George Gordin Byron, Lord; Mary Wollstonecraft Godwin; Claire Clairmont

tudes were collected close to the rocks to catch the flies which inhabited them.

On returning to the village, we sat on a wall beside the lake, looking at some children who were playing at a game like ninepins. The children here appeared in an extraordinary way deformed and diseased. Most of them were crooked, and with enlarged throats; but one little boy had such exquisite grace in his mien and motions, as I never before saw equalled in a child. His countenance was beautiful for the expression with which it overflowed. There was a mixture of pride and gentleness in his eyes and lips, the indications of sensibility, which his education will probably pervert to misery or seduce to crime; but there was more of gentleness than of pride, and it seemed that the pride was tamed from its original wildness by the habitual exercise of milder feelings. My companion gave him a piece of money, which he took without speaking, with a sweet smile of easy thankfulness, and then with an unembarrassed air turned to his play. All this might scarcely be; but the imagination surely could not forbear to breathe into the most inanimate forms some likeness of its own visions, on such a serene and glowing evening, in this remote and romantic village, beside the calm lake that bore us hither.

On returning to our inn, we found that the servant had arranged our rooms, and deprived them of the greater portion of their former disconsolate appearance. They reminded my companion of Greece: it was five years, he said, since he had slept in such beds. The influence of the recollections excited by this circumstance on our conversation gradually faded, and I retired to rest with no unpleasant sensations, thinking of our journey tomorrow, and of the pleasure of recounting the little adventures of it when we return.

The next morning we passed Yvoire, a scattered village with an ancient castle, whose houses are interspersed with trees, and which stands at a little distance from Nerni, on the promontory which bounds a deep bay, some miles in extent. So soon as we arrived at this promontory, the lake began to assume an aspect of wilder magnificence. The mountains of Savoy, whose summits were bright with snow, descended in broken slopes to the lake: on high, the rocks were dark with pine forests, which become deeper and more immense, until the ice and snow mingle with the points of naked rock that pierce the blue air; but below, groves of walnut, chesnut, and oak, with openings of lawny fields, attested the milder climate.

As soon as we had passed the opposite promontory, we saw the river Drance, which descends from between a chasm in the mountains, and makes a plain near the lake, intersected by its divided streams. Thousands of besolets, beautiful water-birds, like sea-gulls, but smaller, with purple on their backs, take their station on the shallows, where its waters mingle with the lake. As we approached Evian, the mountains descended more precipitously to the lake, and masses of intermingled wood and rock overhung its shining spire.

We arrived at this town about seven o'clock, after a day which involved more rapid changes of atmosphere than I ever recollect to have observed before. The morning was cold and wet; then an easterly wind, and the clouds hard and high; then thunder showers, and wind shifting to every quarter; then a warm blast from the south, and summer clouds hanging over the peaks, with bright blue sky between. About half an hour after we had arrived at Evian, a few flashes of lightning came from a dark cloud, directly over head, and continued after the cloud had dispersed. '*Diespiter, per pura tonantes egit equos:*' a phenomenon which certainly had no influence on me, corresponding with that which it produced on Horace.

The appearance of the inhabitants of Evian is more wretched, diseased and poor, than I ever recollect to have seen. The contrast indeed between the subjects of the King of Sardinia and the citizens of the independent republics of Switzerland, affords a powerful illustration of the blighting mischiefs of despotism, within the space of a few miles. They have mineral waters here, eaux savonneuses, they call them. In the evening we had some difficulty about our passports, but so soon as the syndic heard my companion's rank and name, he apologized for the circumstance. The inn was good. During our voyage, on the distant height of a hill, covered with pine-forests, we saw a ruined castle, which reminded me of those on the Rhine.

We left Evian on the following morning, with a wind of such violence as to permit but one sail to be carried. The waves also were exceedingly high, and our boat so heavily laden, that there appeared to be some danger. We arrived however safe at Mellerie, after passing with great speed mighty forests which overhung the lake, and lawns of exquisite verdure, and mountains with bare and icy points, which rose immediately from the summit of the rocks, whose bases were echoing to the waves.

We here heard that the Empress Maria Louisa had slept at Mellerie, before the present inn was built, and when the accommodations were those of the most wretched village, in remembrance of St. Preux. How beautiful it is to find that the common sentiments of human nature can attach themselves to those who are the most removed from its duties and its enjoyments, when Genius pleads for their admission at the gate of Power. To own them was becoming in the Empress, and confirms the affectionate praise contained in the regret of a great and enlightened nation. A Bourbon dared not even to have remembered Rousseau. She owed this power to that democracy which her husband's dynasty outraged, and of which it was however in some sort the representative among the nations of the earth. This little incident shews at once how unfit and how impossible it is for the ancient system of opinions, or for any power built upon a conspiracy to revive them, permanently to subsist among mankind. We dined there, and had some honey, the best I have ever tasted, the very essence of the mountain flowers, and as fragrant. Probably the village derives its name from this production. Mellerie is the well known scene of St. Preux's visionary exile; but Mellerie is indeed inchanted ground, were Rousseau no magician. Groves of pine, chesnut, and walnut overshadow it; magnificent and unbounded forests to which England affords no parallel. In the midst of these woods are dells of lawny expanse, inconceivably verdant, adorned with a thousand of the rarest flowers and odorous with thyme.

The lake appeared somewhat calmer as we left Mellerie, sailing close to the banks, whose magnificence augmented with the turn of every promontory. But we congratulated ourselves too soon: the wind gradually increased in violence, until it blew tremendously; and as it came from the remotest extremity of the lake, produced waves of a frightful height, and covered the whole surface with a chaos of foam. One of our boatmen, who was a dreadfully stupid fellow, persisted in holding the sail at a time when the boat was on the point of being driven under water by the hurricane. On discovering his error, he let it entirely go, and the boat for a moment refused to obey the helm; in addition, the rudder was so broken as to render the management of it very difficult; one wave fell in, and then another. My companion, an excellent swimmer, took off his coat, I did the same, and we sat with our arms crossed, every instant expecting to be swamped. The sail was however again held, the boat obeyed the helm, and still in imminent peril from the immensity of the waves, we arrived in a few minutes at a sheltered port, in the village of St. Gingoux.

I felt in this near prospect of death a mixture of sensations, among which terror entered, though but subordinately. My feelings would have been less painful had I been alone; but I know that my companion would have attempted to save me, and I was overcome with humiliation, when I thought that his life might have been risked to preserve mine. When we arrived at St. Gingoux, the inhabitants, who stood on the shore, unaccustomed to see a vessel as frail as ours, and fearing to venture at all on such a sea, exchanged looks of wonder and congratulation with our boatmen, who, as well as ourselves, were well pleased to set foot on shore.

St. Gingoux is even more beautiful than Mellerie; the mountains are higher, and their loftiest points of elevation descend more abruptly to the lake. On high, the aerial summits still cherish great depths of snow in their ravines, and in the paths of their unseen torrents. One of the highest of these is called Roche de St. Julien, beneath whose pinnacles the forests become deeper and more extensive; the chesnut gives a peculiarity to the scene, which is most beautiful, and will make a picture in my memory, distinct from all other mountain scenes which I have ever before visited.

As we arrived here early, we took a voiture to visit the mouth of the Rhone. We went between the mountains and the lake, under groves of mighty chesnut trees, beside perpetual streams, which are nourished by the snows above, and form stalactites on the rocks, over which they fall. We saw an immense chesnut tree, which had been overthrown by the hurricane of the morning. The place where the Rhone joins the lake was marked by a line of tremendous breakers; the river is as rapid as when it leaves the lake, but is muddy and dark. We went about a league farther on the road to La Valais, and stopped at a castle called La Tour de Bouverie, which seems to be the frontier of Switzerland and Savoy, as we were asked for our passports, on the supposition of our proceeding to Italy.

On one side of the road was the immense Roche de St. Julien, which overhung it; through the gateway of the castle we saw the snowy mountains of La Valais, clothed in clouds, and on the other side was the willowy plain of the Rhone, in a character of striking contrast with the rest of the scene, bounded by the dark mountains that overhang Clarens, Vevai, and the lake that rolls between. In the midst of the plain rises a little isolated hill, on which the white spire of a church peeps from among the tufted chesnut woods. We returned to St. Gingoux before sunset, and I passed the evening in reading Julie.

As my companion rises late, I had time before breakfast, on the ensuing morning, to hunt the waterfalls of the river that fall into the lake at St. Gingoux. The stream is indeed, from the declivity over which it falls, only a succession of waterfalls, which roar over the rocks with a perpetual sound, and suspend their unceasing spray on the leaves and flowers that overhang and adorn its savage banks. The path that conducted along this river sometimes avoided the precipices of its shores, by leading through meadows; sometimes threaded the base of the perpendicular and caverned rocks. I gathered in these meadows a nosegay of such flowers as I never saw in England, and which I thought more beautiful for that rarity.

On my return, after breakfast, we sailed for Clarens, determining first to see the three mouths of the Rhone, and then the castle of Chillon; the day was fine, and the water calm. We passed from the blue waters of the lake over the stream of the Rhone, which is rapid even at a great distance from its confluence with the lake; the turbid waters mixed with those of the lake, but mixed with them unwillingly. I read Julie all day; an overflowing, as it now seems, surrounded by the scenes which it has so wonderfully peopled, of sublimest genius, and more than human sensibility. Mellerie, the Castle of Chillon, Clarens, the mountains of La Valais and Savoy, present themselves to the imagination as monuments of things that were once familiar, and of beings that were once dear to it. They were created indeed by one mind, but a mind so powerfully bright as to cast a shade of falsehood on the records that are called reality.

We passed on to the Castle of Chillon, and visited its dungeons and towers. These prisons are excavated below the lake; the principal dungeon is supported by seven columns, whose branching capitals support the roof. Close to the very walls, the lake is 800 feet deep; iron rings are fastened to these columns, and on them were engraven a multitude of names, partly those of visitors, and partly doubtless of the prisoners, of whom now no memory remains, and who thus beguiled a solitude which they have long ceased to feel. One date was as ancient as 1670. At the commencement of the Reformation, and indeed long after that period, this dungeon was the receptacle of those who shook, or who denied the system of idolatry, from the effects of which mankind is even now slowly emerging.

Close to this long and lofty dungeon was a narrow cell, and beyond it one larger and far more lofty and dark, supported upon two unornamented arches. Across one of these arches was a beam, now black and rotten, on which prisoners were hung in secret. I never saw a monument more terrible of that cold and inhuman tyranny, which it has been the delight of man to exercise over man. It was indeed one of those many tremendous fulfilments which render the *"pernicies humani generis"* of the great Tacitus, so solemn and irrefragable a prophecy. The gendarme, who conducted us over this castle, told us that there was an opening to the lake, by means of a secret spring, connected with which the whole dungeon might be filled with water before the prisoners could possibly escape![83]

But what was the story of their most famous prisoner? The gendarme, a little old man, his eyes wise, his hair wild, his back hunched, served as the custodian of the castle and its guide. He launched into his spiel as soon as we dropped coins into his outstretched, withered hand, which snapped shut like a steal-trap. His tour had grown a little long in the tooth for me, as I wished to continue our tour of the lake, but G.G.B. was enthused by the old man's stories of the castle, of whom I was only barely amused. The gendarme waxed historical and philosophical on the Prisoner of Chillon. Afterwords, when the words and

83 From the *History of a Six Weeks Tour Through a Part of France, Germany, Switzerland, and Holland* by Mary Shelley, published by T. Hookham, Jun. Old Bond Street, and C. and J. Ollier, Welback Street, 1817

the words and – oh God!– the words were uttered, we ascended from the dungeon having had this story bludgeoned into our skulls like a war-mallet. My brains oozed from my ears from the pummelling of such verbosity. But my companion on the other hand seemed moved by this news. So enthused was he that was already writing a new poem in his head:

> *Eternal Spirit of the chainless Mind!*
> *Brightest in dungeons, Liberty! thou art:*
> *For there thy habitation is the heart—*
> *The heart which love of thee alone can bind;*
> *And when thy sons to fetters are consigned—*
> *To fetters, and the damp vault's dayless gloom,*
> *Their country conquers with their martyrdom,*
> *And Freedom's fame finds wings on every wind.*
> *Chillon! thy prison is a holy place,*
> *And thy sad floor an altar— for 'twas trod,*
> *Until his very steps have left a trace*
> *Worn, as if thy cold pavement were a sod,*
> *By Bonnivard!— May none those marks efface!*
> *For they appeal from tyranny to God.*

We proceeded with a contrary wind to Clarens, against a heavy swell. I never felt more strongly than on landing at Clarens, that the spirit of old times had deserted its once cherished habitation. A thousand times, thought I, have Julia and St. Preux walked on this terraced road, looking towards these mountains which I now behold; nay, treading on the ground where I now tread. From the window of our lodging our landlady pointed out "le bosquet de Julie." At least the inhabitants of this village are impressed with an idea, that the persons of that romance had actual existence. In the evening we walked thither. It is indeed Julia's wood. The hay was making under the trees; the trees themselves were aged, but vigorous, and interspersed with younger ones, which are destined to be their successors, and in future years, when we are dead, to afford a shade to future worshippers of nature, who love the memory of that tenderness and peace of which this was the imaginary abode. We walked forward among the vineyards, whose narrow terraces overlook this affecting scene. Why did the cold maxims of the world compel me at this moment to repress the tears of melancholy transport which it would have been so sweet to indulge, immeasurably, even until the darkness of night had swallowed up the objects which excited them?

I forgot to remark, what indeed my companion remarked to me, that our danger from the storm took place precisely in the spot where Julie and her lover were nearly overset, and where St. Preux was tempted to plunge with her into the lake.

On the following day we went to see the castle of Clarens, a square strong house, with very few windows, surrounded by a double terrace that overlooks the valley, or rather the plain of Clarens. The road which conducted to it wound up the steep ascent through woods of walnut and chesnut. We gathered roses on the terrace, in the feeling that they might be the posterity of some planted by Julia's hand. We sent their dead and withered leaves to the absent.

We went again to "the bosquet de Julie," and found that the precise spot was now utterly obliterated, and a heap of stones marked the place where the little chapel had once stood. Whilst we were execrating the author of this brutal folly, our guide informed us that the land belonged to the convent of St. Bernard, and that this outrage had been committed by their orders. I knew before, that if avarice could harden the hearts of men, a system of prescriptive religion has an influence far more inimical to natural sensibility. I know that an isolated man is sometimes restrained by shame from outraging the venerable feelings arising out of the memory of genius, which once made nature even lovelier than itself; but associated man holds it as the very sacrament of his union to forswear all delicacy, all benevolence, all remorse, all that is true, or tender, or sublime.

We sailed from Clarens to Vevai. Vevai is a town more beautiful in its simplicity than any I have ever seen. Its market-place, a spacious square interspersed with trees, looks directly upon the mountains of Savoy and La Valais, the lake, and the valley of the Rhone. It was at Vevai that Rousseau conceived the design of Julie.

From Vevai we came to Ouchy, a village near Lausanne. The coasts of the Pays de Vaud, though full of villages and vineyards, present an aspect of tranquillity and peculiar beauty which well compensates for the solitude which I am accustomed to admire. The hills are very high and rocky, crowned and interspersed with woods. Water-falls echo from the cliffs, and shine afar. In one place we saw the traces of two rocks of immense size, which had fallen from the mountain behind. One of these lodged in a room where a young woman was sleeping, without injuring her. The vineyards were utterly destroyed in its path, and the earth torn up.

The rain detained us two days at Ouchy. We however visited Lausanne, and saw Gibbon's house. We were shewn the decayed summer-house where he finished his History, and the old acacias on the terrace, from which he saw Mont Blanc, after having written the last sentence. There is something grand and even touching in the regret which he expresses at the completion of his task. It was conceived amid the ruins of the Capitol. The sudden departure of his cherished and accustomed toil must have left him, like the death of a dear friend, sad and solitary.

My companion gathered some acacia leaves to preserve in remembrance of him. I refrained from doing so, fearing to outrage the greater and more sacred name of Rousseau; the contemplation of whose imperishable creations had left no vacancy in my heart for mortal things. Gibbon had a cold and unimpassioned spirit. I never felt more inclination to rail at the prejudices which cling to such a thing, than now that Julie and Clarens, Lausanne and the Roman Empire, compelled me to a contrast between Rousseau and Gibbon.

When we returned, in the only interval of sunshine during the day, I walked on the pier which the lake was lashing with its waves. A rainbow spanned the lake, or rather rested one extremity of its arch upon the water, and the other at the foot of the mountains of Savoy. Some white houses, I know not if they were those of Mellerie, shone through the yellow fire.

On Saturday the 30th of June we quitted Ouchy, and after two days of pleasant sailing arrived on Sunday evening at Montalègre.[84]

Mary Wollstonecraft Godwin's Journal

2 July. Lake Geneva— Lord Byron presents 'The Prisoner of Chillon' to the group.

> *My hair is grey, but not with years,*
> *Nor grew it white*
> *In a single night,*
> *As men's have grown from sudden fears:*
> *My limbs are bowed, though not with toil,*
> *But rusted with a vile repose,*
> *For they have been a dungeon's spoil,*
> *And mine has been the fate of those*
> *To whom the goodly earth and air*
> *Are banned,* and barred—forbidden *fare;*
> *But this was for my father's faith*
> *I suffered chains and courted death*
> *That father perished at the stake*
> *For tenets he would not forsake;*

84 From the *History of a Six Weeks Tour Through a Part of France, Germany, Switzerland, and Holland* by Mary Shelley, published by T. Hookham, Jun. Old Bond Street, and C. and J. Ollier, Welback Street, 1817

And for the same his lineal race
In darkness found a dwelling place;
We were seven—who now are one,
Six in youth, and one in age,
Finished as they had begun,
Proud of Persecution's rage;
One in fire, and two in field,
Their belief with blood have sealed,
Dying as their father died,
For the God their foes denied;—
Three were in a dungeon cast,
Of whom this wreck is left the last.

II.

There are seven pillars of Gothic mould,
In Chillon's dungeons deep and old,
There are seven columns, massy and grey,
Dim with a dull imprisoned ray,
A sunbeam which hath lost its way,
And through the crevice and the cleft
Of the thick wall is fallen and left;
Creeping o'er the floor so damp,
Like a marsh's meteor lamp:
And in each pillar there is a ring,
And in each ring there is a chain;
That iron is a cankering thing,
For in these limbs its teeth remain,
With marks that will not wear away,
Till I have done with this new day,
Which now is painful to these eyes,
Which have not seen the sun so rise
For years—I cannot count them o'er,
I lost their long and heavy score
When my last brother drooped and died,
And I lay living by his side.

III.

They chained us each to a column stone,
And we were three—yet, each alone;
We could not move a single pace,
We could not see each other's face,
But with that pale and livid light

That made us strangers in our sight:
And thus together—yet apart,
Fettered in hand, but joined in heart,
'Twas still some solace in the dearth
Of the pure elements of earth,
To hearken to each other's speech,
And each turn comforter to each
With some new hope, or legend old,
Or song heroically bold;
But even these at length grew cold.
Our voices took a dreary tone,
An echo of the dungeon stone,
A grating sound, not full and free,
As they of yore were wont to be:
It might be fancy—but to me
They never sounded like our own.

IV.

I was the eldest of the three,
And to uphold and cheer the rest
I ought to do—and did my best—
And each did well in his degree.
The youngest, whom my father loved,
Because our mother's brow was given
To him, with eyes as blue as heaven—
For him my soul was sorely moved:
And truly might it be distressed
To see such bird in such a nest;
For he was beautiful as day—
(When day was beautiful to me
As to young eagles, being free)—
A polar day, which will not see
A sunset till its summer's gone,
Its sleepless summer of long light,
The snow-clad offspring of the sun:
And thus he was as pure and bright,
And in his natural spirit gay,
With tears for nought but others' ills,
And then they flowed like mountain rills,
Unless he could assuage the woe
Which he abhorred to view below.

V.

The other was as pure of mind,
But formed to combat with his kind;
Strong in his frame, and of a mood
Which 'gainst the world in war had stood,
And perished in the foremost rank
With joy:—but not in chains to pine:
His spirit withered with their clank,
I saw it silently decline—
And so perchance in sooth did mine:
But yet I forced it on to cheer
Those relics of a home so dear.
He was a hunter of the hills,
Had followed there the deer and wolf;
To him this dungeon was a gulf,
And fettered feet the worst of ills.

VI.

Lake Leman lies by Chillon's walls:
A thousand feet in depth below
Its massy waters meet and flow;
Thus much the fathom-line was sent
From Chillon's snow-white battlement,
Which round about the wave inthralls:
A double dungeon wall and wave
Have made—and like a living grave.
Below the surface of the lake
The dark vault lies wherein we lay:
We heard it ripple night and day;
Sounding o'er our heads it knocked;
And I have felt the winter's spray
Wash through the bars when winds were high
And wanton in the happy sky;
And then the very rock hath rocked,
And I have felt it shake, unshocked,
Because I could have smiled to see
The death that would have set me free.

VII.

I said my nearer brother pined,
I said his mighty heart declined,
He loathed and put away his food;

It was not that 'twas coarse and rude,
For we were used to hunter's fare,
And for the like had little care:
The milk drawn from the mountain goat
Was changed for water from the moat,
Our bread was such as captives' tears
Have moistened many a thousand years,
Since man first pent his fellow men
Like brutes within an iron den;
But what were these to us or him?
These wasted not his heart or limb;
My brother's soul was of that mould
Which in a palace had grown cold,
Had his free breathing been denied
The range of the steep mountain's side;
But why delay the truth?—he died.
I saw, and could not hold his head,
Nor reach his dying hand—nor dead,—
Though hard I strove, but strove in vain,
To rend and gnash my bonds in twain.
He died—and they unlocked his chain,
And scooped for him a shallow grave
Even from the cold earth of our cave.
I begged them, as a boon, to lay
His corse in dust whereon the day
Might shine—it was a foolish thought,
But then within my brain it wrought,
That even in death his freeborn breast
In such a dungeon could not rest.
I might have spared my idle prayer—
They coldly laughed—and laid him there:
The flat and turfless earth above
The being we so much did love;
His empty chain above it leant,
Such Murder's fitting monument!

VIII.

But he, the favourite and the flower,
Most cherished since his natal hour,
His mother's image in fair face,
The infant love of all his race,
His martyred father's dearest thought,

My latest care, for whom I sought
To hoard my life, that his might be
Less wretched now, and one day free;
He, too, who yet had held untired
A spirit natural or inspired—
He, too, was struck, and day by day
Was withered on the stalk away.
Oh, God! it is a fearful thing
To see the human soul take wing
In any shape, in any mood:
I've seen it rushing forth in blood,
I've seen it on the breaking ocean
Strive with a swoln convulsive motion,
I've seen the sick and ghastly bed
Of Sin delirious with its dread:
But these were horrors—this was woe
Unmixed with such—but sure and slow:
He faded, and so calm and meek,
So softly worn, so sweetly weak,
So tearless, yet so tender—kind,
And grieved for those he left behind;
With all the while a cheek whose bloom
Was as a mockery of the tomb,
Whose tints as gently sunk away
As a departing rainbow's ray;
An eye of most transparent light,
That almost made the dungeon bright;
And not a word of murmur—not
A groan o'er his untimely lot,—
A little talk of better days,
A little hope my own to raise,
For I was sunk in silence—lost
In this last loss, of all the most;
And then the sighs he would suppress
Of fainting Nature's feebleness,
More slowly drawn, grew less and less:
I listened, but I could not hear;
I called, for I was wild with fear;
I knew 'twas hopeless, but my dread
Would not be thus admonished;
I called, and thought I heard a sound—
I burst my chain with one strong bound,

And rushed to him:—I found him not,
I only stirred in this black spot,
I only lived, I only drew
The accursed breath of dungeon-dew;
The last, the sole, the dearest link
Between me and the eternal brink,
Which bound me to my failing race,
Was broken in this fatal place.
One on the earth, and one beneath—
My brothers—both had ceased to breathe:
I took that hand which lay so still,
Alas! my own was full as chill;
I had not strength to stir, or strive,
But felt that I was still alive—
A frantic feeling, when we know
That what we love shall ne'er be so.
I know not why
I could not die,
I had no earthly hope—but faith,
And that forbade a selfish death.

IX.

What next befell me then and there
I know not well—I never knew—
First came the loss of light, and air,
And then of darkness too:
I had no thought, no feeling—none—
Among the stones I stood a stone,
And was, scarce conscious what I wist,
As shrubless crags within the mist;
For all was blank, and bleak, and grey;
It was not night—it was not day;
It was not even the dungeon-light,
So hateful to my heavy sight,
But vacancy absorbing space,
And fixedness—without a place;
There were no stars—no earth—no time—
No check—no change—no good—no crime—
But silence, and a stirless breath
Which neither was of life nor death;
A sea of stagnant idleness,
Blind, boundless, mute, and motionless!

X.

A light broke in upon my brain,—
It was the carol of a bird;
It ceased, and then it came again,
The sweetest song ear ever heard,
And mine was thankful till my eyes
Ran over with the glad surprise,
And they that moment could not see
I was the mate of misery;
But then by dull degrees came back
My senses to their wonted track;
I saw the dungeon walls and floor
Close slowly round me as before,
I saw the glimmer of the sun
Creeping as it before had done,
But through the crevice where it came
That bird was perched, as fond and tame,
And tamer than upon the tree;
A lovely bird, with azure wings,
And song that said a thousand things,
And seemed to say them all for me!
I never saw its like before,
I ne'er shall see its likeness more:
It seemed like me to want a mate,
But was not half so desolate,
And it was come to love me when
None lived to love me so again,
And cheering from my dungeon's brink,
Had brought me back to feel and think.
I know not if it late were free,
Or broke its cage to perch on mine,
But knowing well captivity,
Sweet bird! I could not wish for thine!
Or if it were, in wingéd guise,
A visitant from Paradise;
For—Heaven forgive that thought! the while
Which made me both to weep and smile—
I sometimes deemed that it might be
My brother's soul come down to me;
But then at last away it flew,
And then 'twas mortal well I knew,
For he would never thus have flown—

And left me twice so doubly lone,—
Lone—as the corse within its shroud,
Lone—as a solitary cloud,
A single cloud on a sunny day,
While all the rest of heaven is clear,
A frown upon the atmosphere,
That hath no business to appear
When skies are blue, and earth is gay.

XI.

A kind of change came in my fate,
My keepers grew compassionate;
I know not what had made them so,
They were inured to sights of woe,
But so it was:—my broken chain
With links unfastened did remain,
And it was liberty to stride
Along my cell from side to side,
And up and down, and then athwart,
And tread it over every part;
And round the pillars one by one,
Returning where my walk begun,
Avoiding only, as I trod,
My brothers' graves without a sod;
For if I thought with heedless tread
My step profaned their lowly bed,
My breath came gaspingly and thick,
And my crushed heart felt blind and sick.

XII.

I made a footing in the wall,
It was not therefrom to escape,
For I had buried one and all,
Who loved me in a human shape;
And the whole earth would henceforth be
A wider prison unto me:
No child—no sire—no kin had I,
No partner in my misery;
I thought of this, and I was glad,
For thought of them had made me mad;
But I was curious to ascend
To my barred windows, and to bend

Once more, upon the mountains high,
The quiet of a loving eye.

XIII.

I saw them—and they were the same,
They were not changed like me in frame;
I saw their thousand years of snow
On high—their wide long lake below,
And the blue Rhone in fullest flow;
I heard the torrents leap and gush
O'er channelled rock and broken bush;
I saw the white-walled distant town,
And whiter sails go skimming down;
And then there was a little isle,
Which in my very face did smile,
The only one in view;
A small green isle, it seemed no more,
Scarce broader than my dungeon floor,
But in it there were three tall trees,
And o'er it blew the mountain breeze,
And by it there were waters flowing,
And on it there were young flowers growing,
Of gentle breath and hue.
The fish swam by the castle wall,
And they seemed joyous each and all;
The eagle rode the rising blast,
Methought he never flew so fast
As then to me he seemed to fly;
And then new tears came in my eye,
And I felt troubled—and would fain
I had not left my recent chain;
And when I did descend again,
The darkness of my dim abode
Fell on me as a heavy load;
It was as is a new-dug grave,
Closing o'er one we sought to save,—
And yet my glance, too much opprest,
Had almost need of such a rest.

XIV.

It might be months, or years, or days—
I kept no count, I took no note—

I had no hope my eyes to raise,
And clear them of their dreary mote;
At last men came to set me free;
I asked not why, and recked not where;
It was at length the same to me,
Fettered or fetterless to be,
I learned to love despair.
And thus when they appeared at last,
And all my bonds aside were cast,
These heavy walls to me had grown
A hermitage—and all my own!
And half I felt as they were come
To tear me from a second home:
With spiders I had friendship made,
And watched them in their sullen trade,
Had seen the mice by moonlight play,
And why should I feel less than they?
We were all inmates of one place,
And I, the monarch of each race,
Had power to kill—yet, strange to tell!
In quiet we had learned to dwell;
My very chains and I grew friends,
So much a long communion tends
To make us what we are:—even I
Regained my freedom with a sigh.

Chapter Nine
Ernestus Berchtold;
or, The Modern Oedipus — Part Two[85]

Dr. Polidor's Letter to His Publisher' 1819

The tale here presented to the public is the one I began at Coligny, when *Frankenstein* was planned, and when a noble author having determined to descend from his lofty range, gave up a few hours to a tale of terror, and wrote the fragment published at the end of Mazeppa. Though I cannot boast of the horrible imagination of the one, or the elegant classical style of the latter, still I hope the reader will not throw mine away, because it is not equal to these. Whether the use I have made of supernatural agency, and the colouring I have given to the mind of *Ernestus Berchtold*, are original or not, I leave to the more erudite in novels and romances to declare. I am not conscious of having seen any where a prototype of either; yet I fear that whatever is original, is not always pleasing. Nor is this my only apprehension. A tale that rests upon improbabilities, must generally disgust a rational mind; I am therefore afraid that, though I have thrown the superior agency into the back ground as much as was in my power, still, that many readers will think the same moral, and the same colouring, might have been given to characters acting under the ordinary agencies of life; I believe it, but I had agreed to write a supernatural tale, and that does not allow of a completely every-day narrative.[86]

Mary Wollstonecraft Godwin's Journal

1 July. — Lord Byron's personal physician and my personal annoyance stood before the four of us in earnest with pages of his manuscript in hand. Sweat dripped from his brow as his clammy hands grip the pages with a surprisingly light touch. Torrential rain buffeted and violent lightning flashed through the high windows and apocalyptic thunder crashed in a fearsome overture preluding the doctor's

---

85 Published by John William Polidori as *Ernestus Berchtold; or, The Modern Oedipus: A Tale* in 1819, publisher unknown.'Parts one, three, and four are included in the appendix located by the end of this book. I feel part two is the most self-contained section to include in the main text. I feel it would too greatly detract from the 'Playing a Game of Ghost Stories' to include the entire novella-length work here.' – R.D.B.
86 From the Introduction to *Ernestus Berchtold; or, The Modern Oedipus: A Tale*.

ghost story. Winds whipped across the panes of glass, rattling not only the panes but also the doctor's nerves. Poor Polidori, his hands trembled first with tremors, then with shakes, and finally and fatefully with quakes. The pages of his manuscript fell from his quivering hands just as a tree branch breaks through a pane in the window. Shards and slivers of glass rained onto the stone tiles. The storm twirled into a whirlwind that scattered the pages of poor Polidori's contribution to Lord Byron's game. Suddenly and sullenly panicked, John dropped to his knees, quite in distress, to collect the pages. Many were lost under chairs and tables and the piano, some slid under the door into the hallway beyond. An unknown number burnt to cinder having being blown into the hearth. Poor Polidori lunged towards the hearth and plunged his hands into the flames hoping beyond all hope to rescue the burning pages before they curl into ash. The doctor saw and seized a fateful stack that appeared the most intact. Were the pages collected into his still shaking and quaking hands the beginning of his tale or the end or somewhere in the middle? I'm afraid the poor Polidori didn't even know.

I cast a glance at Lord Byron perchance he was thinking of heckling poor Polidori, but the expression of the Lord's face gave me the impression that no such improper commentary would issue force from his lips. I was thankful for this small mercy afforded to poor Polidori by Lord Byron. One night, after being engaged in marital sport, as we lay in bed, I admonished my Beloved not to make a scene when it came to Dr Polidori's reading of his 'feverishly' written work (not my words, but John's). I, myself, possessed no desire in my heart to fluster the Doctor during the recitation of his story. I could see his heart fluttering in his throat, his temples damp, and his throat parched. He sipped on a glass of wine sitting on the table nearest the hearth. Wine slapped over the rim of the glass, so violent were his shaking— nay! quaking— Then in earnest, Dr Polidori began reading from *Ernestus Berchtold*, his contribution to Lord Byron's game of ghost stories:

'You have visited our alpine scenes and have undoubtedly been witness to the approach of one of those dreadful visitations of angry nature, which sometimes occur in the pent-up valleys.' By the pained expression on poor Polidori's face, this place in his story did not mark the beginning. Was its placement somewhere in the middle or was this at the end? I'm afraid only the doctor could answer the question. But he soldiered on. 'The black speck gathers upon the mountain's brow; amidst the silence and dead stillness of the air, it seems as if all were resting, in hopes of gaining strength to resist the desolating fury of the powers let loose against them. Only the lowing of the cattle, which, with its hollow lengthened sound, seems to give unheeded notice of the dread storm's approach, echoes upon the air, awed by the very stillness. Yet the sun shines brilliantly on the scene, doubled in the unrippled surface of the lake that seems proudly to bear the beauteous image, as if it were conscious how soon that smiling scene would be changed.— So passed the years, in which day succeeded day in unperceived succession, in which I lived under the same roof, partook innocently of the same joys and sorrows as Louisa. There was yet a weight upon my heart I could not explain; my dreams always terminated unhappily, and sleep, that refuge common to all misery, was to me like the waking hours of others. Immediately after our arrival, my sister was visited with a threatening appeal from our mother, who bade her depart with me once more to our native wilds, and never return. We could not understand the decrees of fate, lulled by the peace and apparent happiness around us, we were unconscious of what was in future,— we remained,— and I am what you see— a spectre amongst the living.

'Encouraged by Louisa, I again returned to my studies. All the morning engaged in the library of my benefactor, I followed them under his direction, chiefly reading the modern poets and historians, with whom I had little acquaintance. Louisa would often come, and, sitting by my side, read the same passages, and discuss the merits of a particular image, often directing my taste, and pointing out many beauties I had not before perceived, even in my favourite authors. You see those volumes; they are those we read together; they now form my whole library, but you cannot know the pleasure there is contained in a single one of those pages. I read them, and every word again sounds upon my ear, as if she spoke it. I turn round and am undeceived, Louisa is not by my side, though her voice seems speaking as when we were innocent.

'In the evening we assembled in the saloon of the palace. Doni was distinguished from his countrymen by a state of affluence, which was apparently boundless, but which was the more extraordinary in this respect, that it did not excite the envy of his neighbours. His riches indeed seemed less for his own use than for that of his friends. He was of a noble family, but being the offspring of a younger branch, he had been early inured to hardships. Disdaining the mean idle life he was obliged to lead, in subservience to the will of a proud relation, he had left Milan at an early age, and had travelled into the East. He never, however, spoke of his journey, and always seemed anxious to direct the conversation into another channel, whenever it turned upon subjects in any manner connected with it. He had returned rich, no one knew whence; but there were whisperings abroad, that he had not gained his riches by commerce; though no one could trace where his riches lay; yet as his gold was poured forth with so liberal a hand, his wealth was deemed almost infinite. He had been strikingly handsome, and was extremely intelligent; but grief had weighed down his energies, and sorrow had broken his faculties. After his return he had married. Beauty was the mere casket, the riches were within; his wife was described as having possessed a mind, that without laying aside all that appealing delicacy and weakness, which binds woman to man; had all those powers and accomplishments, which unfortunately in her sex have generally been the panders to vice; but which, with her, were the handmaids to virtue. Her presence was commanding, but her voice was persuasive; its tones struck the heart and produced those emotions, which all remember, none can express, the feeling, as if we had been always virtuous, and were worthy of listening to the voice of a being superior to ourselves. The poor followed her steps, not with their usual boisterous cry for charity, but in silence; they seemed to watch the glance of her eye, as if the sympathy which shone there, had made them even forget their ragged miseries. Louisa was her counterpart, when I heard any one describing what her mother had been, it seemed that I could read the whole upon her daughter's face, and methought I could often perceive the speaker reading on the same page. Doni had loved her; nay more, had adored her, but she had married him by the persuasion of her parents, while her heart was engaged to another far away; he had returned, they saw one another, and fled together; Doni pursued them, fired at the carriage which was escaping and blood fell upon the road;— they did not stop. Doni then entirely lost all command of himself, he fell in the road, calling for mercy and relief from that curse, which had already begun to blast him. He had never recovered the shock; had retired from all those gaieties in which he had been once engaged, and devoted himself to the education of his children. For their sake he had, however, again entered into society, but in a very different style from his former magnificence. These are the circumstances which I heard of his history, from those friends with whom I spoke in the course of the two first years of my stay at Milan; besides this, I also found the reports of his supernatural powers to be believed: and whenever I enquired concerning them, the speaker always looked round the room, before he ventured to speak, and would then only answer in whispers.

'I have mentioned our evening assembly in the saloon of the palace; thither all distinguished by rank or science came— all visitors were alike welcome. There, no ceremony, which is but the vain-pointing of selfishness to its sacrifices, incommoded those, who, invited by the society they found there, chose to take a chair in this circle. Louisa's father always held the reins of conversation in his own hands, and instead of letting it fall upon the common place subjects of fashion, he turned the minds of

his company to disquisitions that gave to each an opportunity of showing his information or judgement. At times, the existence and powers of
the Deity were canvassed,— at times, the reality of beings intermediate
between God and man; their qualities, and the facts related concerning
them, came under consideration. Other evenings heard discussions upon
the nature of virtue, whether it really were definite and felt, as is beauty,
in every breast, or whether it were not merely an object of policy and
self-convenience. The father and son generally took opposite sides, and
under one or the other, each individual of the company enlisted himself,
accordingly as it happened that he were either in a humour to be pleased
with the general dispensation of providence throughout the day to himself, or was smarting under what he conceived to be an undeserved infliction of the evil spirit.

'Olivieri made it a point to bewilder every one. He was a little older
than myself; his head, though not perfect, had much beauty; a fine forehead, black hair, a dark, though small eye, united to a Grecian contour,
formed, if not a pleasing, a striking physiognomy. I soon found that he
had read much. His body also had been exercised; though not graceful, he was active, and hardly any excelled him in a certain quickness of
adaptation, both of mind and body, to any thing required. His opinions
were paradoxical and singular. In religion he outwardly professed Catholicism, and strongly opposed those scribbling philosophers, who by
sarcasm, attempt to overturn the religion of ages, though at the same
time he allowed the absurdity and falsehood of the prevailing doctrines.
This did not appear to arise from a spirit of opposition, but, if the motives
he gave were true, from a chain of thought that did honour to his heart,
not head. He asserted that Catholicism was the only religion affording to
the poor and to the sick of heart, a balm for their evils. Calvinism, deism
and atheism, were by him called the professions of the northern nations,
cold as their native rocks. Professions to which enthusiasm, and the feeling of a certain refuge, so heart-soothing in Catholicism, were unknown.
He maintained that it was not for individuals, who had the advantage
of education and imagination, to shelter them from the overwhelming
force of mental miseries, and unlooked for misfortunes, to attempt under
a real, though vain pretence of the love of truth, to deprive the poor and
uneducated millions forming the mass of mankind, of the consolation always offered by this religion, which instead of shunning the poor, gladly
seeks their miserable hovel, in the hope of administering present comfort and future hope. Indeed he was inconsistent in his principles. He had
not mingled much in general life, but while at Padua, where he had been
sent to study, he had sought the acquaintance of all. From the knowledge
of man he had there acquired, whether it were that he had constant-

ly met with mean and weak companions, or that conscious of his own bad qualities, he had thence estimated the value of man's professions, he always seemed to view the human character in a darker hue than was warranted by truth, and to have formed his mind into a general contempt for mankind as a mass, and a determination, if ever an occasion offered, of rising at their expence, considering them but as tools to work with. His manners were at first always engaging, and rather pleasing, but this seemed irksome to him, and he gave way to an imperious, assuming air in conversation, which soon disgusted his friends. His ideas of a life after death seemed strangely childish, he did not believe in an immortality, yet he had so strong a love of fame, that there was no reputation he did not covet. He sometimes formed visions of a throne raised upon the blood of his countrymen spilt in civil war; at times, of the fame of a benefactor to debtors and galley slaves. He sought at the same time for the applause of the philosophers and the drunkard, the divine, and the libertine. Things, of which, even at the moment of action he was ashamed, were often done by him in the view of proving himself capable of excelling even in vice. It was hard to say, whether he owed a certain frankness and easiness of attachment, to his weakness, or to seeds sown in his breast by nature. But whether it were from his incapability of constantly acting up to his system, or to the overpowering force of nature, it was strange to hear him express himself a follower of a doctrine that has proved the leech of human blood, and at the same time refuse to tread upon a worm. The evil was, his riches induced the young to pander for him, the old to flatter him, on account of his specious talents and handsome appearance. He was a student, a gambler, and a libertine.

This man became my companion, his father often pointed me out to him, as the model for his conduct, and when he had to reproach him for the losses at the Ridotto, or when Olivieri sought an excuse in the plea of youth, for the ruin his libertinism had brought on many families, he would speak of me as an example of strength, resisting all the temptations of vice. I was a reed when the storm came, Olivieri had watched me at the meetings in the saloon, I was generally a mere listener, but my curiosity was alive, though silent; my mind had an insatiable thirst for knowledge. I was a catholic, Berchtold had educated me in doctrines, without teaching me the foundation upon which they were built; he thought it impiety to question them. The conversation to which I was now present, seemed to rest upon the entire conviction, that all I believed was false. Yet this was not satisfactory. I heard arguments adduced in support of one assertion which seemed irresistible; but what was my surprise, on another evening to hear the same person adduce more than plausibilities in favour of the contrary hypothesis. I at last was bewildered, I was unwilling to believe the human mind incapable of truth, the more I examined, the more difficulty I found in the attainment of it. I heard the deist and the atheist contend; following but one of the chains of argument, I was convinced; looking at them together, I saw the lustre of truth equally on both; I knew not which to choose. I was a sceptic in fact, not in name. Night after night upon my sleepless couch, I called upon the God, whose existence I doubted, to visit me, as if God heeded the belief of an individual, as if the happiness of an infinite being like him depended on a man's faith in his existence. Olivieri perceived the state of my mind, I asked his assistance, he laughed at my attempt at knowledge, and bewildered me still more; I was restless, and seemed at length to be deprived of all motive for action. No superior being to smile upon our efforts, to whom we may show our gratitude, and whose approbation we may obtain; no virtue, but artificial trammels set up under its name, to lure the unwary into the toils of the wittiest knave. I wished I had never left those mountains, amidst which, I had thought, I felt the breath of a superior being, though he was clothed by my imagination in terrors. Nothing above man, and that man the sport of chance, of his own caprice. Yet within my breast it seemed as if aspirings dwelt which seemed to have been born with me. Were they but a mockery? I grew melancholy, whole days confined to my room, I meditated till my brain became a wilderness of various thoughts so entangled I knew not how to extricate myself.

'My sister, fearing I was ill, would often sit by me, would bring Louisa, and they would together listen to my doubts. Julia seemed to be as much affected by them as myself, she listened with avidity, and echoed my own ideas. Not so Louisa, she talked of revelation, of a beneficent Deity, who had for a while left man in ignorance, to prove to him his own weakness, but had at last revealed himself, and announced a better state. While she spoke, she seemed like the first vision of the Wengern Alp destined again to save me, and set me free from these bewilderings, the first step towards vice. She soothed my mind, her lips quelled doubt into the peaceful certainty attendant upon Christianity. I no more paid any attention to the conversation of the evening, but set myself down by Louisa, and listened to her, while she was engaged in some work, which, though it employs the hands, leaves the mind at liberty. I sat by her, asking for some errand, some office, in doing which I might do her bidding; she was evidently gratified by my attentions, she would blush at my approach and smile; she would make room for me by her side. Oftentimes I gazed in silence upon her, and often our eyes met. Her breath at moments played upon my cheek, and sometimes her hand by accident touched mine. She would bid me read poetry to her, and often love was the subject of the poet's lay; my voice trembled, I dared not look upon her, for fear she should perceive the emotion upon my face. I loved her, but it was not a common love. I did not rest upon the hope of gaining her, she appeared a being superior to myself, of whom I was unworthy, yet it seemed, as if her smile were necessary to induce me to exert myself, and was a reward sufficient for the greatest deeds. She would sing to me, she would walk with me in the garden; but you must imagine, I cannot paint the charm, the magic, in her conversation. I have not described her person, for I could not, her mind was more heavenly than her eye, its expressions more delicately varying than the bloom on her cheek; there was meekness attendant upon power, softness upon strength.

'If she had not left me for a moment, I might have been spared much guilt; but the sickness of a near relation was a call she could not resist. I had often followed her, when masked, she attended upon the sick in the hospitals. It is an Italian custom: often have I, disguised in the covering gown of the Misericordia, stood by her, whom it was impossible not to recognize. The dying called for her, though they knew her not; they soon distinguished her powerful tones which pierced through the bond of grief around the most withered heart, and poured upon it those precious consolations afforded by her religion. Her manner, her voice, her gestures, seemed at such moments to be those of a being who was conscious of the truth of what it announced; not from the testimony of man, but from having witnessed the presence of the very Deity. The loud groan, the stifled sigh, were silenced in her presence; pain seemed to have no power; conscience no sting. She left me to visit her relation. For some days I felt lost; I knew not to whom to apply; my sister seemed always occupied; she spoke with me; but I was sorry to find she had imbibed those doctrines so easily eradicated, as I thought, from my own mind. I observed Olivieri paid her particular attention, and often conversed with her. He at last perceived how restless I was; he seized the opportunity, determined to gain an object, which I did not think him capable of attempting. During my stay at Milan, I had hardly ever been out in the evening, for, as it is not customary for unmarried females to go into society, I should have lost the pleasure of sitting by Louisa. Now I had no inducement to remain at home. Olivieri persuaded me to accompany him to the theatre of La Scala. I was induced by the splendour of the scenery, the beautiful dancers, the exquisite singing, to return. I was led into the boxes of our friends, and behind the scenes. I found my companion was every where well received. The dancers and actresses crowded around him: their conversation was lively and various. Gradually, the freedom in their discourse, which had at first disgusted me, grew indifferent; then pleasing by the wit sometimes shown even upon such subjects. One of these women, to whom Olivieri introduced me, was a mistress in her art, and well understood the artifices by which the young and unwary are misled: she was beautiful, and though her eye was never free from a certain look of confidence, the characteristic of this class, she could soften its expression, and cause it, in the presence of him she intended to inveigle, to send forth such glances as it was impossible to resist. By Olivieri's desire she attached herself to me, and I gradually took pleasure in her company; I saw her neglect the attentions of the first nobles in Milan to gain mine; in the midst of the rapturous applause of the whole theatre, she would turn her eye upon me to see if I approved; she seemed to sacrifice herself for me. When the opera was over, she would take my arm and lead me to the saloon of the theatre, where all were engaged in gambling. Sitting at a window, she drew me into conversation, gradually she approached the table; we at first stood merely as spectators; at last she tempted me to try my fortune: I consented, laid down my stake, it was soon increased to an enormous amount, for I was successful: I threw it into her lap, and we parted. For several nights I was equally fortunate; but at length I lost. I was so profusely supplied with money by the kind friend who called me son, that I did not at first heed my losses. I had given all I gained to the syren, who still urged me on: I lost every franc I had. She then supplied me; I was ashamed to take it of her, though it was what I myself had gained; but I hoped my luck would change; I lost the whole. She then began to exert her more baneful powers, she led me from folly to vice, in search of what she assured me was an antidote to memory; I joined the libertine and the desperate. I was ashamed of letting Doni know that he, whom he had pointed out as a model of virtue to his son, had sunk into the lowest debauchery. Louisa's image often— often was before me; but how dare I name her in conjunction with my vices. She had thrice been a ministering angel, guiding my steps, but then I was innocent. I dared not now rest upon the thought; and often I threw myself deeper into the sinks of vice, in hopes that such reflections would not pursue me thither.

The syren, instigated by Olivieri, led me into every excess; while he plied me again with insinuations against religion, and sneers upon my credulous conscience that pictured a future state. I was now glad to seek refuge in unbelief; and I strove to lose myself in those thoughts which I had before fled, and from which I had been saved by my protecting angel. He also excited me to gamble, lent me money himself when I had none, and gathered round me every incentive to vice. He had been mortified at his father's holding me up as a pattern of strength against temptation; he was revenged, he exposed my weakness. I had hardly resisted the first approaches of vice, and had, in a short time, sunk below the lowest frequenters of its haunts.

'One night I was desperate, every thing of value that I had was gone. Olivieri himself had been unsuccessful; and I knew not where to seek for the money I wanted to satisfy my creditors. I rushed out from the house, and found myself in the Piazza del Duomo. My brain was hot, my hair dishevelled; I rushed along, not knowing what I was about. I knew not where to apply. To destroy at once Doni's opinion of my virtue by telling him my situation, seemed worse than my present feeling. I stood still holding my head with my hand; I lifted my eyes from the ground on which they had been fixed. It was night, there was no light save from the glimmering stars and the newly risen moon, upon the dark canopy of heaven. The white façade of the Duomo raised its huge mass in contrast with the night; shining even upon its dark veil, it seemed to awe the mind by its indistinct mass, which, weighing on the earth, forced itself upon the eye when all else was lost in the shading darkness. All was still and sunk to rest; I alone seemed waking midst sleep; in anguish, midst repose. I stood, I know not why, for some time gazing upon the marble statues and forms which gained a certain charm from the moon's silvering light. The mats, spread like a curtain before the doors, being raised by the dying breeze, struck with a measured impulse the wall: unconsciously I entered. Save where the light of the moon fell upon the heavy columns, vesting them with the faint hues of the coloured glass that adorned the windows, it was all darkness that seemed sensible to the touch. I walked towards the high altar. There is a subterranean chapel dedicated to St. Borromeo, which receives its light through the flooring of the dome. The silver lamps, hung over the shrine, sent up a column of light to the very roof. I descended the stairs, and found myself within the chapel. The lamps were almost failing, and the silver walls darkened by the torch of the devotees absorbed the little light they emitted. I approached the shrine; the dried corpse of the saint, arrayed in his pontificals, seemed, by its repose, to invite me to seek peace where he possessed it. His eye, which once might also have known anguish, was now sunk in the socket, and presented but a mass of blackened mould in the corner of its former throne. I gazed upon it until I thought I saw it move; methought there was a smile upon its lips, as if it mocked my thoughts of peace. I repose with him, a benefactor to the poor, a saint! A laugh was almost playing upon my lips, when the words, half stifled with emotion, "intercede my patron, intercede for Berchtold," sounded on my ear.— I turned; a female figure, I had not observed, was kneeling near the wall in earnest prayer. I approached, "who prays for Berchtold? your prayer is mocked." Alarmed, she raised her head; it was— you know whom I would say— it was Louisa. She looked upon my face convulsed with the violence of my emotions, upon my dishevelled hair. "Is it you? Ernestus," she said, rising, "are you come to pray; heaven has then heard even me, and has not left you. Break not my heart." I could not utter more. She took my arm, we passed through the long nave; I dared not look around, methought some other form would burst upon my eyes in spite of the circling darkness, and blast me. A carriage was waiting at a little distance; she had left the gay dance to pray for me. I had handed her into her carriage, and was going; "Berchtold," she said, "will you leave me?" She wished me, the wretch, to be still near her. I jumped into the carriage, and blessed the darkness that hid my face; we spoke no more. Every one had retired at Doni's. She took my hand when leaving me, and pressing it in her's, whilst she gazed upon my face; she bade me think— she would have said more; a tear fell from her unwilling eye, and she hastily turned away.

'I returned to my room, I had not entered it for many days. Louisa knew my guilt; sleep would not refresh me, my thoughts revelled in a maddening breast. Whither could I turn for refuge from their power? Religion I had cast from me, as a foul fiend's mock; Louisa! rest upon purity, I dared not; then my native mountains rushed upon my sight, I seemed bounding along the crags, Berchtold smiled upon my innocence, I laughed aloud— innocence? it was but the want of temptation. I threw myself upon my bed, and though not asleep, I became so stupified by the very excess of pain, that even the phantoms of conscience no longer passed with distinctness before me. The night seemed to hang suspended over my head, as if in pity it would hide me from the day, so slow was its progress; morning at last returned, but with it were the same thoughts as had visited me during the night.

'It was hardly day before I heard some one at my door, I opened it, it was Doni. I turned away my head ashamed to look upon him, he did not reproach me, telling me that he knew my present way of life needed a more abundant supply of money, than he had given me, he bade me to apply to him for any sum I wanted. I could not speak, I had expected he would have attempted to show me my vices in all their native horror; he pressed his offer upon me; ashamed to tell him the whole amount of my folly, I at last named a sum not half sufficient to satisfy my creditors, but I thought it would stop the mouths of the most clamorous, and that in the mean time, by economizing my allowance, I might clear the rest. He asked me repeatedly, if it was the entire sum I owed; I answered yes; he left me, and in a few minutes returned, with gold to the amount required; "take it" he said, "it is no loss to me, but your wonted happiness I see is fled, that grieves me. Believe one who is older than yourself, Vice is not the path of happiness." I was silent. I intended immediately to pay my debts as far as I could, and at once to free myself from the life of a gambler, and a libertine.

'My sister came to see me in my room, for I was ashamed of appearing at the breakfast table. I observed that the colour in her cheeks was gone, that she no longer was the open-hearted girl I remembered; attributing this however to the effect of my own follies upon her mind, I said nothing. She remained with me some time, but I no longer felt that pleasure I had always known in her company upon former occasions. We seemed both afraid of touching upon any thing relating to ourselves, and both evidently with minds deeply occupied about other important objects, talked of the most trivial circumstances.

'When night came, I issued forth, determined to pay my debts, as far as was in my power; I entered the saloon of the theatre; there were only the banker and the punters arrived; they had arranged every thing for the faro table, and immediately they saw me, they began talking of the various successes of the last night. They told me how Olivieri had regained every thing at the very close of the evening. One or two gradually stepped in; amongst them was my friend, he was in high spirits; I took him aside, and told him that I was weary of this kind of life, and was determined to pay every one as far as I had it in my power. He would not let me finish, he laughed at my intentions, and told me, that as our good luck was now returned, it would be a folly to throw it away, that as I acknowledged myself incapable of paying the whole, it would be as well to owe a greater as a lesser sum.

'His companions soon perceived the subject of our conversation, and joined us. They all ridiculed my intention, and I was persuaded to venture once more. I at first lost, but suddenly the rouleaus poured upon me; one more stake, and I had regained even all my enormous losses; it was soon too late to retire, I almost lost all I had that morning received from Doni. It was now quite useless to think of retreating, I fell again into my former life, with more than double energy. I was at times surprised to find that great sums were paid to several of my creditors, I could not learn by whom; I imagined it was by Olivieri's father; this did not stop me. My vicissitudes were great, but I could never entirely extricate myself, so that I was always either lured by hope or urged by despair.

'I need not describe to you the progress of my other vices; debauched women, men of whom one is ashamed, and wine, are generally the attendants upon gambling. I could not seek the house of Doni, nor of virtue; I threw myself into every haunt of desperate characters like myself, and learnt to boast alike of the smile of the prostitute, or of the tear of the debauched virgin; when losing, I stupified my mind with wine, and was glad to fall from my chair, provided memory failed with my senses. Noted cheats, and men proscribed from society for their low dissoluteness, often seized upon my arm on the Corso, as if I were one of their equals, and I dared not repel their familiarity, for I was in their power. Once Louisa saw me in this situation, she never again rode out on the Corso; I had the maddened impudence to bow to her. I at last became mad, and once, was induced to aid in depriving a young novice of all his wealth, by means of false dice. I could not however stand by and see his horrible despair, he had beggared a wife and two lovely babes. I had just then been lucky, I confessed my participation to him, and gave him the whole amount of his loss; it became known, and I was laughed at; but for once I could withstand ridicule.

'At the Doni palace in the mean time, the same outward appearance was preserved; there were still the same evening assemblies, but they were less frequented, for Olivieri was almost always with me. He was apparently afraid I should escape him; he was constantly stifling all thoughts that arose in my breast, tending towards a return to virtue. He never left me but when I was deeply engaged in play or debauch; then he constantly went I knew not whither. I have since found it out, and that discovery has not been the least of those pangs my guilt has brought upon me. I entered so little into society, that I heard nothing of what was passing there. I was, however, one day standing on the Corso with Olivieri, speaking to some ladies who had drawn up their carriage close to a shop, when the conversation turning upon the number of foreigners, who were moving about in consequence of the peace which had just been concluded, a lady turning, asked me if I had seen the stranger who excited so much the curiosity of all circles. Upon my saying I had not, she began expatiating upon his singular character, rested upon his powers of fascination, and told me that all the ladies were in love with him. I did not pay much attention to this, thinking it but the foolish prattle of a young girl. She however continued; she wondered that I had not seen him, as he was a constant attendant upon Louisa, she having engrossed the whole of his attention, much to the mortification of all Milan.

'Now I was roused. I let go Olivieri's arm, and wandered about alone. I dared not hope that Louisa could resist one whom all seemed to admire. The whole weight of my guilt fell heavily upon my recollection, and one after another all my vices presented themselves, arrayed against me. I did not return that day to any of my usual haunts. Towards evening, I found myself, fatigued with wandering, at the gate of the Doni palace. I know not what inspired me, it seemed as if I wished to gain the certainty of my fate. My steps, which till now had been slow and measured, suddenly quickened. I found myself at the entrance of the saloon; all was silent; the red purple glare of sunset pierced the windows. I stood for a moment still; a sigh burst upon my ear— I entered— Louisa was sitting looking upon the setting sun. It was her sigh. She did not turn: "Is it you, my father?" I did not speak, she turned her head, her face was pale, but a blush mantled her cheek at the sight of me; her eyes were sunk and dim, but they brightened at my presence. She spoke my name, she rose, and with faultering steps attempted to reach a door leading to her apartments. I murmured audibly, but with a stifled voice: "She flies, she flies, she hates me!" She turned. "Oh no: I do not Ernestus, do no believe it." She fell upon the floor; approached, knelt by her side, but dared not touch her. I attempted it, my hand retreated; there seemed to be pollution in my touch; I dared not. The cool air played upon her face, and the chill of the marble floor gradually recovered her; she opened her eyes; I was not near her; I could see the marks of a suffering mind upon her face; her cheek now had no colour, save that reflected from the red light of the illumined west. Her tresses were disordered and neglected; her eyes sunk deep in their socket, how changed from the vision of the Wengern Alp! Her subdued voice could hardly articulate when she again assured me with earnestness that she did not hate me, that she forgave me. Tears flowed down my cheeks, and I did not try to stop them. She looked upon me: "It is too late," she said, smiling with the smile of a broken heart; "it is too late, Berchtold; I wish that I could weep, but my eyes are dried up." The sounds of approaching footsteps were heard; she rose with difficult; trembling, I offered my arm, she took it. I thought she would have spurned it. I could hardly support my own weight. I saw her to her door, and threw myself upon the staircase hear it; but I soon heard strange voices in the saloon; the thought of its being his voice, who, I had heard, was my rival, at once made me start. I rose, retired for a moment to my room, and then entered.

The apartment was now lit up. The company were in greater numbers than I have ever seem before. My rival, I said to myself, is them so attractive. No one observed my entry; they all seemed engaged around one man. It was my rival; I never saw so singular a figure. His bust and head here handsome, and bore the sings of strength. His black hair was in ringlets; his face was pale with a blueish tint that diminished even the colour of a naturally pale eye. His hands were joined with their palms tuned towards the ground; his eyelids almost covered his eyes, which turned upon the floor, while his head erect, bore in its general expression the marks of contempt. He was speaking with elegance upon the fallen glories of some sunken nation; when he had ended, and the conversation had became more general, he raised his eyes, and affecting surprize, he seemed ashamed of having attracted so much notice, though he did not blush, for the hue of his features seemed invariable. He retreated to a corner of the room, left vacant by the pressure of the company towards the sport he had just occupied. He there bent down his head, as if abstracted in thought; but looking under his eye-brows, he was evidently engaged in remarking the effect he had made upon the company. He again gradually go a circle round him, and again was apparently carried away by the great powers of his mind, and held forth upon some subject, and then once more retreated. I was tired of watching such acting, and look round for my sister. She was at that moment entering; she immediately addressed Doni, who seemed alarmed, and wet out. I approached— Louisa was il and could not appear. Julia looked upon me as if she knew it had been my presence which had thus affected her friend; I could not bear that look: "Do not reproach me, I feed all the shame of my crimes." "I reproach you!" she answered, "You mock me, I! it is not for one like me to do it." She turned away, I did not understand her; I asked her why she rested upon one like her. "Oh! do not ask me, my shame must not be spoken." The noble stranger approached, and broke off our conversation by asking after Louisa. I could not stand by him, but joined some of my former acquaintances; for though my heart was breaking, I dared not leave the room, determined to watch minutely every action of him I fancied my rival.

'I entered into conversation, and forced myself to enquire about this stranger, who thus engaged the attention of all. There was a certain affectation of mystery about hi, which induced all to seek him, in hopes of penetrating the veil he threw round his actions/ I met with one who had know him intimately in his own country. From whom I learnt several traits of his character; it appeared that this German was much distinguished amongst his countrymen for his talents,— that he was generally esteemed a hater of all the vanities of the world, but that he passed many hours at his toilette; that he was deemed broken-hearted from having been cross in love; but that he was incapable of feeling that passion, being wrapt in selfishness, that made his sacrifice every thing around him to the whim of the moment: that he was deemed irresistible, and that no woman upon whom he fixed his eye could withstand the fascination of his tongue, but that he had never dared to tempt any woman, who was not the most abandoned character; that even they were never addressed with boldness, but were always made to compromise themselves by some folly with him in public, before he would give them the least marked sign of attention; that in fine he was a confirmed coward with women. In society he was playing off a strange coquetry with the whole world, affecting to be modest and diffident, whilst he protruded himself into notice. He was, however, rich, handsome, and noble by birth, I was an orphan dependent upon charity. He was every where received with great attention, no where with greater than in Doni's palace.

'Perceiving that Louisa's father did not return, I became alarmed, and anxious to gain some information, I sought for him. He was walking with hasty steps before her door. Upon seeing me, he was turning away, but moved by my broken voice, he stopped looked upon me, and addressed me, "You saved my son, Berchtold, but my daughter, my beloved daughter dies; it is however, useless to speak to you, leave me, go to you room, Louisa's better" Every thing seemed confused to me, I could not believe that I was the cause of Louisa's illness, I could not believe that she could love such an outcast as myself. I was several times in the course of the night by her door, listening for some sound that should assure me of her existence. I fell asleep at last upon the sofa in my room, and I saw her in my dream as when she first appeared before me, glowing in health, buoyant with spirits; suddenly I thought she ran towards me, but ere she reached me, she faded like a flower, and fell to the ground. I awoke, all was still, but my heart beat violently. I seemed as if this were the fulfilment of my former drams, my vices were the evils, the warning voice of my mother commanded my sister to fly, for thy were doomed to be the death of all I loved.

'Morning came, my first enquires were concerning Louisa; she was very ill, and in a state of great weakness. Doni was not yet rise, and was apparently quite overcome. During the whole day, I was not one moment at rest; I wandered from one room to another, and sent every instant to enquire concerning my protector's daughter. I stood by the door watching all who came from her room, and begged them to tell me every change they observed. Towards evening a packet was put into my hands; it contained receipts from every one of my creditors. There was no explanatory paper. Imagining it to be the gift of Doni, I determined to thank him; I went to his room; I found him lying upon his couch very much fatigued and exhausted; he was courting repose, but it was in vain; anxiety was painted upon his face, and grief seemed to stamp him with its chilling furrows. My first question was concerning his daughter. I then showed him the packet, and had begun to thank him, when he interrupted me. "Young man, thank not one, who wished that you should first have paid the price of your vices before he freed you from your embarrassments. I had resistered my daughter's entreaties, till last night, she offered to give up her allowance, every thing, to free you; I refused, but I could no long do so, to a child I thought dying." I was thunderstruck, the packet fell from my hand; I thought I should have fallen through shame; but he spoke again, "Would that your apparent shame were the least security against your follies, but I believe you to be incurable." He motioned me away; I fell at his feet, and called Heaven to witness that I would never again partake of vicious pleasure. He raised me from the ground, pressed me to his bosom, and with a blessing told me, that if I kept this promise, he might yet be happy; he bade me leave him to his hopes, again embraced me, and I left him.

'For the first time during the last many weary months, I felt something like repose in my mind. I seemed as if the vow I had made to heaven might be relied on, and as if I again might know the consolation of a conscience at rest. That night I slept quietly and soundly, for Louisa was announced to be much better, and my heart felt a little repose. I was but to give me strength to bear worse than I had yet endured.

'Next morning Louisa saw me, she was upon the bed of sickness, but she had partly recovered the show my abrupt entry had caused her. I shall never forget the moment I entered. I had expected she would have received me with marks of horror; she smiled; oh, no! she did not hate me. I sat by her, she allowed me to take her thin cold hand within my own; it chilled my heart with its touch. There was a clear whiteness that overspread her face, where it was not tinged by the hectic flush, her eye shone with a glassy brilliancy that seemed not mortal, it was the glance of death mocking my senses thought a beauteous vizour, for there were the seeds of death sown deep through broken heart. She spoke but a little, what she did utter, however, were words of kindness, and they were all her weakness allowed her to say. She often turned her brilliant eyes upon me, and the soft smile upon her lip, I thought was excited by the gentle whisperings of hope, that I was snatch for ever from vice. The latter part of the morning was passed near her in a silence that was not mute, for there is a language which, though no addressed to the ear, still speaks the thought within. Her physician came and advised me to retire. I bade her farewell; an anxious look accompanied the words, "where are you going?" but when intimated my determination of staying at home, I cannot describe to you the joy expressed upon her face as she repeated my farewell.

'I had been so little at home, that I knew nothing of what had lately happened. I was, therefore, much surprised, when, upon desiring a servant, towards night, to see if Doni was in his apartment, he refused, saying he had not courage. Upon making enquiries, I found that their mater's supernatural powers had been much talked of lately amongst the servants; for during the latter days unusual noises had been heard in his room, and every morning, all his things had been found in a strange confusion while he was apparently so exhausted, that it was evident had had no rest during the night. Thinking of all the very explicable from the state of anxiety in which he had been kept, I tried to convince the servant, he appeared firm in his belief, and refused to carry my message.

'Louisa seemed rapidly to recover strength. As we were in the very middle of summer it was thought proper by her physicians that she should be removed to a cooler situation than the neighbourhood of a great city. We accordingly retired to the banks of the Lago Maggiore. The palace close to the lake weas refreshed by the cooling breeze that passed over the water's vast expanse, and the playful fountains that sported with their noisy showers in the apartments towards the land, promised to shield the invalid from the noxious effects of an Italian sun; while the magnificent scenery of the varying basin before our view, seemed to promise relaxation to the mind. We arrived late at night, and immediately retired to our beds. I arose betimes, and issuing forth ascended the numerous terraces, which, one above another, seemed like the work of some enchanter. When viewed from the water's edge, garden seemed to be hanging above garden, as if man had acquired the power of piling nature's gift even into the air. I did not heed this, for my native mountains were in sight; I did not gaze upon the rich islands, which seemed dwellings springing from the lake; I gazed upon Monte Rosa, which, high above the neighbouring hills, asserted the glory of its alpine birth. Though all around seemed burnt by the sun's ray, it marked his power and bore its unvarying white vest, in defiance of his frown, upon its aged limbs. While yet engaged looking upon its high summit, with all the crowded images of infancy offered by my memory, my sister passed me. She seemed lately to have lost all of her spirits, she did not appear to be attracted by the beautiful scene near us, or the sublimity of the alpine ridge beyond. She was gazing upon the ground, I joined her, she started, and with a trembling voice asked me, "Why I was come?" I answered here; at that moment I saw Olivieri turn the corner of the alley and approach; but immediately he saw me he retired, and I at the same time perceived that my sister was violently agitated. I looked at her, and begged of her to tell me what I was to imagine; she hastily replied, "Nothing, nothing;" and her colour, which had deserted her at the sight of Olivieri returned with greater rapidity than it had fled the moment before. I insisted upon an explanation; she said she was unwell, weak, and made other excuses of the same nature. I now remembered her agitation a few evenings before, when we were interrupted by the Count Wilhelm. I threatened, if she would not satisfy me, to seek an explanation from Olivieri. She fell upon her knees before me, begged me not, assured me that it concerning a third person. I was moved, I had the weakness to promise that I would seek no farther.

'I had not seen my friend till this moment, since the payment of my debts; he had never been home, and I had not sought him. He had not accompanied us, and I had not been aware that he was expected. I re-entered the house, hoping to find him; but no one had seen him, and he did not appear at breakfast.

'Louisa made her appearance at that meal. You may imagine my pleasure at again seeing her out of her sick chamber. She made room for me by her side. I accompanied her into the orange-walk near the house while she enjoyed the beauty of the scene. She looked at the Alps, then at me, it seemed as if the recollection of our first meeting passed though the minds of both. Involuntarily I opened the bosom of my vest and showed her the scarf, which I had constantly worn since that day. She smiled. "I did not think of this at that time" she said, "I did not know your name, but when the fame of Berchtold, Ernestus Berchtold, was echoed by the wild rocks to the voice of every peasant, I sighed and wished he might be the chamois hunter of the Wengern Alp. It was I set the saviour of my brother's life to battle. I sent the hero to aid in the rescue of his country; it was in vain, yet I was conscious of a feeling of pride whenever I thought of it." She spoke of my former life, and passed in silence over that part, when every moment had been spent in shame. I cannot describe my sensations to you. The feeling of how little I deserved such praise, mingling with the pleasure of hearing it from Louisa's lips, embittered what else would have been the proudest moment of my life. Her father joined us, and seemed pleased at seeing us together; he seated himself upon the other side of his daughter, and we spent the whole morning together in conversation, till the sun becoming too powerful, Louisa was obliged to retire for shelter and repose, and we separated.

'Day passed after day, and Louisa's health seemed rapidly to recover; but my sister evidently became more and more restless. She generally avoided, and very seldom sought our society. I knew not what to understand; determined however to force her to an explanation, I one evening, finding her alone, induced to her to walk out with me. We wandered, without perceiving it, into the garden. She seemed determined upon silence. Wrapt in thought, the sun's red disk fast sinking in the west, the bird's evening carol, the varied light of the heavens reflected from the soft silky cloudes over the purling surface of the late, the cooling breeze which played upon her feverish cheek, were all unnoticed. Yet she was wont, in all that feeling of nature's charms which accompanies youth, to gaze upon that orb, and figuring it as the image of that Providence she adored, and all was unheeded. There was a seat upon the river's side, which, shaded by the plants that crept entangled round the branches of a noble chestnut, formed a bower, whence all the beauties of the rich nature round could be view. I attempted in vain to enter upon the subject of what was causing this apparent misery in her breast; she was abstracted, and answered merely by monosyllables. I at last ceased to press her, and we both sunk into silence.

'The spreading clematis of the bower hid us completely from the path near us, while its open leaves allowed us to see distinctly all that passed in the avenue. There was a wall of cypress which ran along one side of the gravel walk, fully exposed at his moment to the sun's rays. I saw at last approaching from the bottom, the Count our protector; he seemed in earnest conversation with some one, but I could perceive no one near him; yet his lips and hands certainly moved as if he spoke. As he gradually approached, I could even distinguish sounds. I motioned Julia to observe him; she did so and soon pointed to the hedge. I could not at first see to what she directed my attention; but at last I perceived the outline of a figure, through the shape of whose body the very leaves were visible; something in the manner that I have seen in the summer, a current of heated air, accurately defined by the wavering outline of the things between which and our sight it stands., only that this was even more sensible to vision. I could not distinguish its voice, but I at last caught some of the words of Doni. I had hardly time to make these observations, when the Count seemed to start, and the figure vapour went.

'We did not move; we for some time seemed rooted to our seats; at last Doni disappeared amidst the trees, and we looked at each other. It was then true that we heard at the lake of Thun, our protector had communication with a spirit. My sister seized the subject of conversation with avidity. We related to one another several slight circumstances, which had come to our knowledge, many incidents which we could not explain. The reluctance of the servants to approach the chambers of the Count all pressed upon our minds. The immense wealth, which seemed inexhaustible, must, it appeared to us, be connected with this untenanting spirit. We resolved not to mention the circumstance we had just witnessed to any one. But it was not effaced from our own memory. We returned to the house and saw our protector there as usual, but his face was, or I imagined it to be, pale; his eyes wandered, and then seemed to fix their angry glance at times upon us; but whether there were imagination or reality, I could not decide. I went to bed, but not to sleep, the thoughts of having seen an unembodied being, the tales of my foster-mother, of power, of wealth, arising from the communication with beings of another world, arose before me. Obtaining such a power, it seemed as if I might learn things hidden in the earth's deepest recesses, the ocean's depth; I even thought, that by such a power, I might tear away the veil which the first Cause had thrown over itself. Nor did these visions disappear with the morning's light, they were as distinct in the sun's brightness, as in the night's obscurity. I arose determined to speak on the subject with the

Count. He met me with an affectionate embrace; I took his hand, had the words upon my lips, when, meeting his eye, I saw expressed therein such anxious fear, such meaning, that the words fell into inarticulate sounds; instantly his eye was as usuals; nothing but brilliancy was there. We went to felth Louisa from her apartment, and descended to the breakfast table.

'Louisa seemed to take a great pleasure in my society, and sought in every way to bring me near her; she seemed afraid of trusting me to myself in my first steps towards retracing the paths of virtue. She again resumed the subject which had formed the topic of conversation, before her fatal departure to visit her sick relation. She painted to me the charms of religion, which taught us to look up to the infinite power above us, not as to an object of terror and fear, but of love and hope. Her mind, without losing the least of that delicacy which is the magic charm that spreads its influence round the footsteps of woman, was energetic and clear. Her simplicity was not misled by the winding, intricate sophisms of the deist and unbeliever; her belief was built upon persuasion, which though it had at first depended upon faith, had not scorned the bulwarks of reason. The earnestness with which she spoke, did not make her appear bold or presuming; for the mild look in her dark eye seemed looking to heaven to beg for inspiration from him, whose cause her lips were pleading. She would often lead me towards the chapel, and without affectation, would kneel down by my side motioning me to imitate her, and bending devoutly before her maker, would pray for me. I did not think myself; but gazing upon that veiled eye, which did not seem to think itself worthy of looking towards the throne of God, while petitioning for strength against mortal weakness, a prayer would involuntarily rise from my heart for her. I did not feel the time long when near her, though it was even spent in prayer; to have communication with the Almighty in union with her, seemed to be an additional bond against those numberless ties which bound me to her. From the first moment that I had seen her, she seemed to visit this earth as my protecting angel; now it appeared as if such a being had led me to the throne of him of whose commands she was the bearer. I did not notice the lapse of months; and autumn had already vested the scene around with its checquered hues, ere this happiness was interrupted; I had even forgotten all my imaginations concerning the being attendant upon Doni. It seemed as if misfortune could no longer visit me; such is human foresight.

'I have already mentioned to you the singularity of my sister's conduct; it grew more and more remarkable. She never came down in the morning, but, confined to her room, she spent the hours in solitude: when she did appear, it was to retire to a corner, where, enveloping herself in her shawl, she apparently brooded over some thoughts that destroyed her peace. Her appearance was completely changed; her auburn hair, which once floated in ringlets of soft varying light upon her shoulders, was now entangled and neglected; her cheeks, on which was wont to play a hue more delicate than that of the white rose, were pale and sickly; her eyes no longer shone with sparkling lustre, they were now heavy and inflamed from the want of sleep. I often saw the silent tears fall from her eye; but it was in vain to question her; she wept bitterly at every enquiry I made, and seemed agitated to the most violent excess whenever Olivieri's name was mentioned. I was bewildered by the enquiries of Doni and Louisa, who constantly expressed their anxiety concerning her.

'We were assembled together at the breakfast table as usual one morning, and were conversing about Julia, who had made her appearance the evening before at the supper table, which she had not done for a long time, when a servant came to tell us that her maid had applied several times in the course of the last hour for admission to her room, but that she could obtain no answer. Louisa offered to see if she could obtain admission; in vain, we went together; all, all was silent. We burst open the door, there was no one, every thing seemed in disorder, the bed had not been slept in the last night; upon the floor there were many pieces of paper torn into fragments; and upon the table there was a note addressed to myself. I took it trembling, I was afraid she had committed some desperate act. I could not open it, but gave it into Doni's hands; he read it:

'My shame can no longer be hidden; I fly then to hide myself; curse not your sister, my own feelings are sufficiently bitter to satisfy even the injured honour of Berchtold.— Your degraded Julia.

'I sunk upon the bed; Olivieri immediately pressed himself to my mind as the seducer of y sister. I could not speak, and my friends were silent, they looked upon me with pity. I dared not inform them of my suspicions, they would bring the old man's grey hairs to their grave, and would cut off the feeble thread of life with Louisa. She bore up against the shock; and while the tear trembled in her eye, she sat down by me, and strove to sooth, no console me, for that she knew was impossible.

'Servants were sent in every direction. I searched all the neighbourhood. I determined instantly to go to Milan, and make enquiries directly to Olivieri, concerning the fate of my sister. I made a plausible excuse for my departure, and soon reached the Corso, Doni' palace. The servants had no seen him for some time. I forced himself to seek him in the laces which had been my former resort. My late companions hailed my approach; but I turned from them in disgust. Olivieri had no where been heard of lately. Distracted by my suspicions, which now seemed to wear the semblance of certainty, after several days spent in the vain search, I returned to the Lake.

'We soon fixed ourself again at Milan. It was now impossible to keep his son's absence a secret from Doni. He learnt it, but did not seem to imagine any connection between the flight of my sister and his son's conduct. Perceiving this, I did not intimate to him my horrible doubts, but left him in entire ignorance. In the mean time I made the most minute enquiries concerning both; but could learn nothing;

'Louisa's health in the mean time gradually recovered; but she never lost the hectic flush upon her cheek; she gained strength, but the seeds of death were hidden, not destroyed. During her gradual recovery, I was always with her; and if you can picture the happy hours of one sitting by a being he loves— adores, at the same time, that his imagination paints her to him as a spirit of heaven, you may imagine my happiness, when sitting by Louisa, whose smile, whose glance told me she loved. She had gained me fame; had saved my life, my honour; had restored to me the hopes of a future state, the belief in a kind God. I know no your belief, your principles; you may sneer at the feeling which dictates my ranking the two last with the former; but, young man! Believe one who has experienced the whole of fate's wanton inflictions;— he who can still rest upon futurity, confident in the goodness of his maker, may find a refuge in the greatest misery; he who cannot, may indeed despair, he has but the present, and that may indeed be dreadful.

'Louisa's image was always with me. I loved her, but so did every one; I could not for that reason hope to gain her. I was an orphan, how often has the thought of that sunk my buoyant hope, which still would revive. I had no rank. Count Wilhelm had again renewed his addresses. It seemed dishonourable in me to continue any long near her, endeavouring to gain her affections; it seemed as if the debt of gratitude I owed to Doni forbade my attempting to gain his daughter. The count had rank and wealth. I could no hope that her father should prefer me, degraded by vice, my birth perhaps tainted with dishonour, to one whose name was a spell upon all Europe. I had determined to leave Milan, and to please the necessity of further enquiries for my sister. Doni approved of my intentions, and in a few days I was set off. I had been preparing for my departure, and had been talking to the servant about the trifles necessary for a solitary journey; it was not yet the hour for the company to assemble, and lost in sorrow I was slowly approaching the saloon, when those notes which had sung hope to me in prison, sounded on the air. They were falling upon the breeze broken, and in a melancholy tone; though the air was lively, it seemed as if Louisa was sought to sing of hope, while her heart could not echo back the strain. I had not heard the song since I sunk into vice. The sound was silences, I entered; Louisa was leaning upon her harp, the head was fallen upon her hand. There was no light, and the lowering clouds hid the little daylight that might have been afforded by the setting sun. I could just distinguish her form, almost lost in the obscurity, suddenly she moved, struck her harp in wild notes, and sung the words of a broken heart. I could not hear more; Louisa's name feel from my lips; "Sing not so, Louisa, if you have not happiness, who shall possess it?" she sunk upon a chair, and I approached. "You leave me to morrow," she said, "I shall no longer have any one to cheer me, any one, whom I can"— She stopped and hesitated. I stood breathless by her side. "I shall, I will return." "You will find me a corpse, I feel no power of life within me, it seems as if my soul still clung to life that it might converse with you, when you are gone." I took her hand; I bade her, if she loved me, not to speak in words that pierced my heart. "Love you," she answered, "you cannot know what I feel towards you, I am myself ashamed that any can divide my heart with God, but you— " I fell upon my knees. I will not go, I cannot, Louisa has confessed her love, she loves the orphan Berchtold, if that words could express the least part of what I feel, I would speak. I love you, let my silence speak the rest. I felt her feeble hand press mine, she had fainted, her weak health had not given her strength to listen. We had not heard the storm which had burst over our heads, I had not seen the flashes of heaven's anger, which had unobserved spread its lurid light around us. I lifted her in my arms, carried her to her chamber, and observed her to her maid. She recovered.

'I was alone; the thunders echoed still in the distance, and the horizon was lit by the forked lightning. But in my breast the convulsions were no subsiding. At the first moment it seemed as if happiness indeed were mine; but Doni's imagine came quickly across my mind, and all I owed him seemed to be imagined as so many reproaches for my having stolen the affections of my benefactor's daughter. The company assembled, but I could not joie them. The tumult in my breast was too powerful to allow me to participate in the light frivolity of a drawing room. I retired to my chamber, and was soon lost in mediation upon that fatality, which made the very circumstance on which I had rested as the bourne of all my hopes, a cause of anguish and reproach. I determined to see the Count immediately after the company had retired. No malefactor, who is listening in expectation of hearing the lengthened toll, warning him of the executioner's approach, ever counted the moments with greater anxiety than mine. The clock stuck, and each brazen sound seemed to vibrate thought my body, as if it bore grief upon its sound. At last the carriages began to depart, and I entered the apartment of my friend. I had never dared to call him father, it seemed to my mind too sacred a title to be profaned by me; he was Louisa's father.

'I had been some time in his apartment before he entered. He came, his face was full of anxiety. "My daughter," he said "I fear is going to relapse, something has agitated her strongly, and she will not tell even her father what it is. Berchtold," he continued, "you have never before seen a father in the agony that I endure, my daughter's life sinks visibly before me, and I cannot discover the cause. You have therefore no conception of the pain it brings." I knew not what to say. "Olivieri too is I know not where, perchance in the haunt of the lowest vice, perhaps acting again the hero, as when with you. You are not my child, yet you now form my only comfort, my only hope." I could not hear more;— he praise me! Who had, like the snake stinging the child enchanted by the beauty of its scales, robbed him of his treasure, insidiously won his daughter's love; I interrupted him. "I am a wretch, not worthy of your affection, your daughter love me. I have dared to tell her she was my only hope; spurn me from you, I expect it; but do not blame her." I fell upon my knees. "Do not blame her for loving such a wretch as me, she pitied me and my daring devotion changed pity into love." My head was hid within my ahdns, I expected to be cursed by him I looked up to as a father. He raised me from the ground, "Ernestus, this is nobly spoken, I will not reproach you with your former vices, Louisa shall be security to me, that you will always prove what you now show yourself." I was amazed; I embraced him, but could not speak. Louisa was to be mine,— my guide, my wife. At that moment of happiness seemed to be descending from heaven to be our handmaid, while in fact despair and horror seemed to be preparing their flight from the lowest abyss to wait upon our nuptials.

'Next morning I was admitted to Louisa's chamger; I told her that her father had consent to our union. A gleam of Joy cross her pale face, she said she was happy, but those words were in a broken and weak voice. I heeded it not, so great was my joy, I sat with her, she listened to my plans of happiness, and smiled; it seemed as if she were conscious of their being but to be imagined. I was at last called away by my own servant, who putting a letter in my hand, told me that he had found it thrown in at the door. It was my sister's hand writing; fearful of agitating Louisa, I hastily put it into my bosom, and making an excuse left her. When in my chamber, I opened the note. The lines were few:

' "A mother appeals for her child to your charity, she has but a short time to live, but her child has not a break heart. Julia."

'Berchhold had been written, but a tear had effaced the characters. There was the name of an obscure street in the most retired part of Milan.

'I immediately repaired thither, and soon found myself in an abode of misery I cannot describe. It was upon the highest story, the roof in several parts let in the hot ray of the sun, and the window was not glazed, but stuffed with dirty rags. It could not be called a shelter, for the floor bore on its black soft texture the marks of every cloud that had passed over it. In one corner there was a bedstead, over which was spread a blanket, that seemed not to have been removed for many years, it was no black and thick with dirt. A broken dish and rags, which I but too well recognized as the remnants of my sister's dress, were the only things upon the floor. I heard a difficult breathing, which proceeded from the bed. I approached, and found my sister. She was pale and squalid, her hair entangled and loose, covered her face and bosom, and her clasped hands hung from the bed. She was apparently asleep, and her child was grasping her breast with its little hand, trying in vain to obtain sustenance from its fevered mother. I stood for some time gazing upon her; finding she slept soundly, I descended the creaking stairs, and sending some person of the house for clothes and food, I waited till they returned and carried them up with me. The noise I made awakened her, she shrunk from me; "I did not call you for myself, but this child's cry pierced my heart,— do, do not therefore curse me, if I have even brought you to witness your sister's infamy. I could not die and leave my child sinking unaided upon my putrid corpse." I spoke findly to her, she looked upon me and said, "Ernestus", with an incredulous voice, and burst into tears. I soothed her, spoke to her of her child, induced her to take a little nourishment, and saw her feed her little bade. She looked at its eager eye and face will feeding, at moments hugged it to her bosom, while a stifled laugh escaped her; she did not seem to notice me, and I spoke not. At last she fell exhausted upon the bed. I gave her the clothes I had brought, she did not heed m.e

'I hastened to Doni, related what I had seen; he ordered every thing to be got ready at he palace, and procuring a litter he accompanied me to the abode of my wretched Julia. At sight of him, she hid her face, and would not speak. I had her conveyed to the little with her child, and we arrived at the palace. The physician of the family being sent for, announced to us, that from the state of exhaustion, into which she had fallen, there were but a few hours remaining of her life. I watched by her all night, she did not speak; I took Louisa for my model, and spoke to her of those hopes which had seemed on her lips to have the power of soothing sickness, and to still the fears of death. She was moved by what I said, for her cold hand pressed mine. I put questions to her with regard to her seducer; she was silent; but a convulsive motion seemed to seize her whole features. I urged her no more. She seemed to revive a little in the morning; auguring well from it, I began to speak to her of her child, talked to her of its health, said it should be named Ernestus, and promised that I would be its father. She raised her fallen head, and looking with tears in her eyes, blessed me, but hardly had the words fallen from her lips, when shuddering, she said, "my blessing! That, that's a curse." I took her to my breast, she shrunk from me, "you know not whom you embrace." "It is my sister whom I hold in my hands," I cried, she burst into loud sobs, and fell again, upon her pillow. "You shall hear," she replied, "what a sister!" She prepared to relate to me the whole of her late history; I advised her to repose awhile first. "Well, well, I shall have the less time to feel the blush of shame, and to hear your reproaches. 'Tis better so. She fell asleep after uttering these words, but she was restless, her face was convulsed, and the twitching of her arms began to give the signs of the rapid approach death.

'I seized this moment of apparent rest to enquire for Louisa. She was much better; we had kept our discovery of Julia a secret, fearful of agitating her too much; I determined therefore to see her, lest, making some enquiry concerning me, she might hear now I was engaged. I entered her room, and staid with her for some time; she spoke of her love, and added, that all that she thought wanting was the presence of her brother and Julia. I could not answer, but rose, and again went to my unconscious sister. She was disturbed in her sleep, and was calling upon Louisa's name; she seemed to reproach her for not seeing her; but then she appeared to meditate and said; "true, true, I am an outcast". She awoke, looked wildly around, met my eye. She was lost some time in thought, and then addressed me; "I know what you are waiting for but ere I unfold the whole of my shame, give me your solemn promise that you will grant your sister her last dying request." I gave it her. "You will then never mention to either of my former friends what I narrate, and you will let me die, certain that you will never injure him that ruined me, for still, still I love him." I assured her, that I would leave it to heave to punish hi, for I was conscious it was Olivieri, Louisa's brother. It was him, the account that I had given of his bravery in the Swiss war, the description I had made of his daring feats had gained an entire possession of her imagination. When, therefore, she met him at Milan, his beauty, his specious manner and apparent knowledge had completed her fascination. I myself, when bewildered by doubts, had sapped the foundation of her religious principles; and Olivieri, who was not blind to her partiality, had fanned the spark of scepticism, till he had destroyed all belief in virtue and a future state. I lost myself at the gambling table; and my conduct was but an additional proof in her mind, that the present was all that belong to man. Before we left Milan, the seducer accomplished his criminal purpose. Though however, she had become a convert to his theories, she could not divest herself of all feeling of shame, much less could she entirely drive from her heart those doctrines which Berchtold had instilled at that age when the first impressions become part of our very nature; they hung around her, and haunted her day and night; she had sought for courage to apply to Louisa or myself in her difficulties, but had not dared.

'Her mind being in this state, she described the effect upon it, at the sight of that being almost lost amidst the ambient air in conversation with Doni, as wonderful. Her mind had immediately recovered its elasticity, for she hoped, if she could obtain communication with such a being, to be able to find some certainty amidst the horrid doubts that revelled in her mind, and to procure the means of hiding her shame, or daring to face the day, but means of its power. Determined to learn the spell which could raise a transparent, all pervading being, she resolved to watch without remission, the conduction of the Count; she learnt nothing for some time. He apparently differed in no habit from the others around. But the impression in her mind was not effaced: at last it appeared to her that upon certain days, the Count never touched animal food, and she found by observation that this happened on every combination of seven in the days of the month. Upon enquiry amongst the servants, she found that upon the morning of those days, the room of Doni was always in the greatest confusion, and she herself remarked, that upon the evening proceeding, he seemed always more anxious, and the day after more fatigued than usual.

'Julia resolved to watch the Count upon the next seventh night; she found that it was possible to look into his room through the wainscot of a closet for wood that opened into the passage leading to his apartment. The night name, meat had been avoided, all were gone to their rooms, only the footsteps of the domestics arranging every thing for rest, sounded on her ear; she described herself, as having listened apparently for hours; though only minutes elapsed, while these sounds continued. At last, all was silent; she said, that not even the vine leaves overspreading her casement were heard to rustle; for every breeze was hushed, all was so quiet, that the ear seemed to feel as it were the silence. She was awed, her heart beat quick, she held her breath; at that moment she thought a slow step sounded along the corridor; alarmed she knew not why, she seized her lamp, and was upon the point of rushing out, when the door slowly opened, and a figure clad in a white robe entered; its dark black eye was fixed; its grey locks seemed as if no breath of air could move their weight; no sign of life, save the moving feet belonged to it, for the face was pale, the lips blueish. It approached with an unvarying step; it was Doni! Its hand took her's within its cold grasp, its eye shone, as if a tear had passed over it, its lips quivered as if it wished to speak, or thought it spoke. She stood still, motionless; while it approached, it seemed as if she had strength for any thing, but when it turned to go, the lamp fell from her hand, and she fell upon the floor. It was morn, ere her wildered senses returned, it was too late. Doni never noticed in any way the event of that night. She was bewildered, she knew not what to think, it seemed from his unchanged conduct towards her, that he was unconscious of the event. Yet she asserted that she could not have mistaken the features of him who had visited her in that awful manner; her imagination laboured, her judgment laid down the balance and became as dead. Her phantasy painted to her mind pictures of splendour and of power, more brilliant than those of the Arab tale-teller, or God creating Bramin. But more than all, it represented to her the means of ensuring Olivieri's love, which she could no longer flatter herself she possessed it; he had not seen her, but for a moment, since she had left Milan dishonoured, and then it was but to laugh at her fears, which she was but too conscious were not in vain.

'Day followed day towards the seventh. At times she caught Doni's eye fixed upon her, as if it sought to read her mind; but she thought this might be imagination, yet it seemed to her if her intentions were divined, and that from some cause or other, they could not be opposed, else why all this silence? That fatal night came. Julia, determined to brace very thing, went down that evening, which she had not lately done to supper. Her agitation was great, but she forced herself to conceal it. She was conscious of the Count's eyes were fixed upon her's, yet she dared not to look up and meet his. She rose to depart, he came to her room; she determined, frightened by the awful silence of her protection, to give up her intentions. She threw herself upon her bed, but sleep abandoned her, or if it for the moment came, it presented such brilliant visions to her eyes, that nothing mortal was to be compared to it, She seemed to have spirits instead of pages to attend her, genii instead of servants. It seemed as if at their bidding the very earth would heave and show within its entrails, all its richest treasures. Olivieri appeared joined with her in this state of power. She roused herself. The clock with its solemn peal seemed trembling to intrude upon the solemn night. One might have thought nature was dead, for not even the owl shrieked, and the darkness and nocturnal sleep that weighed on the earth, seemed no longer the type of the eternal rest of the world, but its fulfilment, all appeared sunk into such undisturbed repose. Julia alone seemed living, she looked in the creation like the Arab in the sandy plain, animate amidst inanimation, organized amidst unorganized matter. Even she must have appeared as if she were some sort of spirit of another more restless sphere, for her hurrying glance, the fearful resolution breathing in her face, must have made her bear the stamp of something more than mortality. She seized her lamp, started, then advanced, and laughed with that laugh that plays upon the lips, when the heart ceases to beat through violence of feeling.

'At least she reached the gallery of her protector's room; she opened with a trembling hand, the door of the adjoining closet, and entered. The dread silence still continued, it was only broken by the loud breathing of her heaving bosom. She sat down upon the pile of wood in the corner of the closet. She could not find courage to pursue her undertaking; at last a deep groan made her start; terrified she leant against the wall; as she gradually recovered herself, she raised her eyes, and looked through the crevice that opened to her sight the Count's room. I could not learn what she saw, she however informed me that she discovered the means of raising a superior being; but that startled at his appearance, she sunk to the ground. She found herself, when recovered, upon her bed, but no one was near her. She determined to put her power into effect the ensuing night. She would not join the family at breakfast, but remained in her all day. She did attempt to raise a spirit, but what was her horror, when the walls of her apartment echoed but scoffs and mockings, they seemed to say that she needed not a greater price than the gratification of her passions, and that they would not give her more; that she was theirs already, and that to command them could only be obtained by one not already damned. Unappalled she repeated her call, but it was in vain, all sunk to quiet. Desperate, for her shame could no longer be hidden, she formed at once the resolution of leaving the house and seeking her seducer. She got out, and entering a boat, managed by skulking along the banks of the lake throughout the day, ot arrive in the night at Sesto Calende; she thence easily obtained a conveyance, and reached Milan.

'She had sought refuge at a small in, and sending to Olivieri, he came to her, but it was only make fully known to her the horrors of the situation. It appears he treated her with brutality, thought she did not say so. He staid with her but a few minutes, and left her for ever. He offered her no assistance, seemed seven to have implied that if unwilling to return to her brother, she might live by exposing her shame to all, and boldly seeking whom she might inveigle. He left her with only the small sum remaining from what she had taken with her, and immediately left Milan to go she knew not where. She had thence retired to the room where I had found her, and had there managed to support life, and was delivered of her child. Her money however failed her, and at least, her poor neighbours, tireds of assisting her who could no longer pay them, having refused to aide her any more, she had struggled with the pains of hunger for two days in solitude, hoping for relief from death. But her milk had failed, and her child's voice had pierced its mother's heart; she could nor resist such an appeal; she arose, wrote a few lines to me, and stagger-

ing, in the morning, while all were at rest, to the gate of the palace, had
thrown them under the gate. Form thence she had hardly found strength
sufficient to reach her miserable couch, when fatigued, she sunk into a
kind of stupor from which my approach had roused her.

'This is the substance of what my sister told me. Her narration was
broken, and many were the pauses she was forced to make to recover
strength. Her feeble breathe hardly seemed sufficient to allow her to end
her tale. Night came, and she was delirious. She screamed for Olivieri,
called on him to come and see her die. She held my hands, and looking
on my asked me my name, denied it could be men, for I could not be
more kind than Olivieri; but why rest upon such a scene? She died in the
morning without a return of reason, but still calling, in the last moment,
upon her lover.

'My sister was dead. Her tale had unfolded to me the causes whence
her misconduct arose. I was the source of all, my colouring of Olivieri's
good qualities, my exposing her to the sources of doubt int those doctrines our sainted foster-father had taught us, my example in the career
of vice were the causes of her fault— her death. It was yet but the second
victim to my fate; there were two others waiting; I sat by the dead body
reflecting upon the horrible fatality that had caused my virtues and my
vices to prove alike mortal to the two beings who for many years had
been my only companions I possessed in nature, the only sympathizers
in my joys and sorrows. If the pangs of conscience could be depicted, I
would, for your sake, young man, painting its truest colours, the horror I
then felt, the pangs I now feel; but the attempt would be vain. I had loved
my sister will all my affection two isolated beings naturally feel towards
each other. She had been to me as the darker part of myself, which always needed protection and defence. To me she had been the holder of
all my secrets, the partaker of all my sorrows; when an outcast, she had
received me; when a wretch, she had not spurned me.

'No one was with me when she died. The servant of Louisa found
me many hours after her decease, extended upon her corpse. She came
from her mistress to seek me. I rose; I knew not how to conceal my anguish of my mind. Louisa soon discovered it, and obtained from me the
knowledge of my sister's illness and death. She did not enquire further;
she perceived I was not willing she should know the rest, and was silent.
I was astonished to see how firmly she bore the shock, she exerted herself to find some means of allaying my grief, but she did not know that it
was conscience that work within. I left her, and her pretended strength
was gone. She had forced herself to assume an apparent calm to assuage
my grief, but could not command her own.

'My sister was interred privately. Doni and myself, were the only mourners, and a tablet, with merely the name of Julie Berchtold, marked the spot where my sister lay. Her child was put to nurse. I gave him his mother's and my own name, that I might still have a bond between us. Every day I went to see the little orphan, and taking him from the fearful nurse, I gaze upon his infantile face, while a bitter tear fell from the eye of him who had been the cause of his birth being loaded with infamy and shame. While I looked upon him he would smile, but that smile brought to my mind my sister's, it was melancholy playing of the lips, that seemed to mock at the pleasure that excited it; the eyes was not lit up with the same feeling, but still appeared absorbed in its continued grief.'

We cheered poor Polidori and we hear-heared. For a writer to put words to the page is an act of bravery. The blank page staring at all writers when we begin a story or poem is the most frightening beast of all. Many would rather undertake Hercules' Nine Labours than write a story or God-forbid a poem. What are we trying to say? Where does one begin? When does one begin? How does one begin? Why does one begin? Who are we to begin? All writers put ourselves into our work so completely that any criticism of our story is an evisceration of our very bowels. To criticize a writer's story is a cruelty akin to complaining about a child to his parent. We desire constructive criticism not destructive cynicism. If an author asks of her reader, whether family, friend, or a fellow traveller on this journey of creativity, we will bloody the pages with constructive criticism. For the author who wielded the quill of creativity and the friend who wields the quill of criticism both desire the work to be the best it can be. This early criticism must murder the story so that author can resurrect the story into its final glorious form. If Dr Polidori requests and requires such criticism, I will freely give it in the spirit of the Muses who inspire us all. Now, do not misunderstand me, we all have our opinions, some sharper than others. I'm convinced Lord Byron itched to criticize the verbose prose of his personal physician; the Lord, no doubt, wondered if the ink was laid on the page has heavy handed as the words, but his lips were sewn shut. I knew by the looks on each of faces of our party, having heard Dr Polidori's recitation of his 'Modern Oedipus' that our opinions of this work would be taken to our graves. And you, Constant Reader, your opinions are you own.

Chapter Ten
Frankenstein[87]
(The Abandonment of the Creature)

Chapter 1

1 July. Back at Lake Geneva.— After a hearty breakfast, I lounged in the parlour deliriously rereading my transcriptions from my encounter with my pale student of the unhallowed arts in Castle Frankenstein. After our eight-day tour of Lake Geneva, our party had returned to the Villa Diodati just as the inclement weather also returns from its eight-day tour of who knows where. But last night and into the morning, the storms promised not only rain, but in the small hours threatened snow. The date is the first of July in the Year of Our Lord Eighteen Hundred and Sixteen and the first snowfall is cascading large fluffy snowflakes past the parlour window. The fire is roaring in the hearty to such a degree that I feel immersed in Dante's Inferno. Hellfire and brimstone from the hearth and only a few feet away outside the window, I feel the promise of Lake Geneva freezing over into a crude imitation of Cocytus, the Ninth Circle of Hell. Will I and my Beloved and our Little Lord and poor Polidori and dearest Claire become trapped in the frozen lake like the traitors. How I remember the words of the Florentine poet:

> *"Vexilla Regis prodeunt Inferni'*
> *Towards us; therefore look in front of thee,"*
> *My Master said, "if thou discernest him."*
>
> *As, when there breathes a heavy fog, or when*
> *Our hemisphere is darkening into night,*
> *Appears far off a mill the wind is turning,*
>
> *Methought that such a building then I saw;*
> *And, for the wind, I drew myself behind*
> *My Guide, because there was no other shelter.*

---

87 From *Frankenstein; or the Modern Prometheus* by Mary Wollstonecraft Shelley, published by Lackington, Hughes, Harding, Mavor & Jones, 1818

Now was I, and with fear in verse I put it,
There where the shades were wholly covered up,
And glimmered through like unto straws in glass.

Some prone are lying, others stand erect,
This with the head, and that one with the soles;
Another, bow-like, face to feet inverts.

When in advance so far we had proceeded,
That it my Master pleased to show to me
The creature who once had the beauteous semblance,

He from before me moved and made me stop,
Saying: "Behold Dis, and behold the place
Where thou with fortitude must arm thyself."[88]

I turned away from poetic digressions and the coming wintry squall to my journal. The effects of my reading of the experiences of the Creation of the Creature and my pale student's subsequent abandonment of his very Creation lingered more as a memory of clear waking than a memory of a mere dream. I can still hear the thunder; I can still feel the rumble; I can still see the lightning burned into my eyes when I blink; I can still taste and smell the electricity in the air. My hair is still damp. My nerves shivered. Then there can a clear rapping upon the entry door. Claire called out that she would answer; then moments later she appeared in parlour holding two envelopes having arrived by post. 'Strange', Claire said, 'these letters must have addressed to be previous guest of the Villa Diodati; or perhaps posted in anticipation of a future guest?' I inquired to whom the letters were addressed, and Claire answered, '*To* V. Frankenstein.' I leapt from my chair like a Burmese tiger pouncing upon its prey and snatched the envelope from poor little Claire's dainty hand. Startled, she cowered, then threatened to bolt from the parlour as if I had been a Burmese tiger raring to strike. I tore the envelope open with a fury of claws. The letters were indeed addressed to my pale student of the unhallowed arts. They were written by his cousin, Elizabeth and his father, Alphonse. Curious that my psychosomatic phantasm would choose to communication his tale through physical letters. But having seen inspiration strike my Beloved and our little Lord in queer ways, I will trust my pale student to tell his tell in any manner he so choses. I read the letter out loud in the quiet of

---

88 From *The Divine Comedy – The Inferno* (Canto XXXIV) by Dante Alighieri, translated by Henry Wadsworth Longfellow

the parlour as if my pale student was sitting by the hearth surrounded by books.

To V. Frankenstein

My Dear Cousin,

I cannot describe to you the uneasiness we have all felt concerning your health. We cannot help imagining that your friend Clerval conceals the extent of your disorder: for it is now several months since we have seen your hand-writing; and all this time you have been obliged to dictate your letters to Henry. Surely, Victor, you must have been exceedingly ill; and this makes us all very wretched, as much so nearly as after the death of your dear mother. My uncle was almost persuaded that you were indeed dangerously ill, and could hardly be restrained from undertaking a journey to Ingolstadt. Clerval always writes that you are getting better; I eagerly hope that you will confirm this intelligence soon in your own hand-writing; for indeed, indeed, Victor, we are all very miserable on this account. Relieve us from this fear, and we shall be the happiest creatures in the world. Your father's health is now so vigorous, that he appears ten years younger since last winter. Ernest also is so much improved, that you would hardly know him: he is now nearly sixteen, and has lost that sickly appearance which he had some years ago; he is grown quite robust and active.

My uncle and I conversed a long time last night about what profession Ernest should follow. His constant illness when young has deprived him of the habits of application; and now that he enjoys good health, he is continually in the open air, climbing the hills, or rowing on the lake. I therefore proposed that he should be a farmer; which you know, Cousin, is a favourite scheme of mine. A farmer's is a very healthy happy life; and the least hurtful, or rather the most beneficial profession of any. My uncle had an idea of his being educated as an advocate, that through his interest he might become a judge. But, besides that he is not at all fitted for such an occupation, it is certainly more creditable to cultivate the earth for the sustenance of man, than to be the confidant, and sometimes the accomplice, of his vices; which is the profession of a lawyer. I said, that the employments of a prosperous farmer, if they were not a more honourable, they were at least a happier species of occupation than that of a judge, whose misfortune it was always to meddle with the dark side of human nature. My uncle smiled, and said, that I ought to be an advocate myself, which put an end to the conversation on that subject.

And now I must tell you a little story that will please, and perhaps amuse you. Do you not remember Justine Martin? Probably you do not; I will relate her history, therefore, in a few words. Madame Martin, her mother, was a widow with four children, of whom Justine was the third. This girl had always been the favourite of her father; but, through a strange perversity, her mother could not endure her, and, after the death of Monsieur Martin, treated her very ill. My aunt observed this; and, when Justine was twelve years of age, prevailed on her mother to allow her to live at her house. The republican institutions of our country have produced simpler and happier manners than those which prevail in the great monarchies that surround it. Hence there is less distinction between the several classes of its inhabitants; and the lower orders being neither so poor nor so despised, their manners are more refined and moral. A servant in Geneva does not mean the same thing as a servant in France and England.

This is the same sentiment as my Beloved. My Beloved observed in a letter dated June 1, 1816, merely a month ago while on our journey to visit Lord Byron at the Villa Diodati, where we would hopefully spent our summer lounging, hiking, and touring the lake by boat, that 'There is more equality of classes here than in England. This occasions a great-er freedom and refinement of manners among the lower orders than we meet with in our own country. I fancy the haughty English ladies are greatly disgusted with this consequence of republican institutions, for the Genevese servants complain very much of their scolding, an exercise of the tongue, I believe, perfectly unknown here. The peasants of Switzerland may not however emulate the vivacity and grace of the French. They are more cleanly, but they are slow and inapt. I know a girl of twenty, who although she had lived all her life among vineyards, could not inform me during what month the vintage took place, and I discovered she was utterly ignorant of the order in which the months succeed to one another. She would not have been surprised if I had talked of the burning sun and delicious fruits of December, or of the frosts of July. Yet she is by no means deficient in understanding.'[89] Are own memories are creeping into Victor's tale– nay! Elizabeth's letter– again?

Justine, thus received in our family, learned the duties of a servant; a condition which, in our fortunate country, does not include the idea of ignorance, and a sacrifice of the dignity of a human being.

After what I have said, I dare say you well remember the heroine of my little tale: for Justine was a great favourite of your's; and I recollect you once remarked, that if you were in an ill-humour, one glance from Justine could dissipate it, for the same reason that Ariosto gives concern-ing the beauty of Angelica— she looked so frank-hearted and happy. My

---

89 From the *History of a Six Weeks Tour Through a Part of France, Germany, Switzerland, and Holland* by Mary Shelley, published by T. Hookham, Jun. Old Bond Street, and C. and J. Ollier, Welback Street, 1817

aunt conceived a great attachment for her, by which she was induced to give her an education superior to that which she had at first intended. This benefit was fully repaid; Justine was the most grateful little creature in the world: I do not mean that she made any professions, I never heard one pass her lips; but you could see by her eyes that she almost adored her protectress. Although her disposition was gay, and in many respects inconsiderate, yet she paid the greatest attention to every gesture of my aunt. She thought her the model of all excellence, and endeavoured to imitate her phraseology and manners, so that even now she often reminds me of her.

When my dearest aunt died, every one was too much occupied in their own grief to notice poor Justine, who had attended her during her illness with the most anxious affection. Poor Justine was very ill; but other trials were reserved for her.

One by one, her brothers and sister died; and her mother, with the exception of her neglected daughter, was left childless. The conscience of the woman was troubled; she began to think that the deaths of her favourites was a judgment from heaven to chastise her partiality. She was a Roman Catholic; and I believe her confessor confirmed the idea which she had conceived. Accordingly, a few months after your departure for Ingolstadt, Justine was called home by her repentant mother. Poor girl! she wept when she quitted our house: she was much altered since the death of my aunt; grief had given softness and a winning mildness to her manners, which had before been remarkable for vivacity. Nor was her residence at her mother's house of a nature to restore her gaiety. The poor woman was very vacillating in her repentance. She sometimes begged Justine to forgive her unkindness, but much oftener accused her of having caused the deaths of her brothers and sister. Perpetual fretting at length threw Madame Martin into a decline, which at first increased her irritability, but she is now at peace for ever. She died on the first approach of cold weather, at the beginning of this last winter. Justine has returned to us; and I assure you I love her tenderly. She is very clever and gentle, and extremely pretty; as I mentioned before, her mien and her expressions continually remind me of my dear aunt.

I must say also a few words to you, my dear cousin, of little darling William. I wish you could see him; he is very tall of his age, with sweet laughing blue eyes, dark eye-lashes, and curling hair. When he smiles, two little dimples appear on each cheek, which are rosy with health. He has already had one or two little *wives*, but Louisa Biron is his favourite, a pretty little girl of five years of age.

My! How William Frankenstein reminds me of my own William, my babbling little 'Willmouse'. Again and again and again my own life creeps into Victor's tale. My own William is a mere six months old, but how I can imagine him having one or two little wives when he reaches the age of schooling. How delightful. I cannot help but to think that the name 'Louisa Biron' could be prescient, a form of prophecy, that my own William will encounter a girl named 'Louisa Biron' at some point in his schooling. Would this girl be his first childhood 'wife' or perchance this is the name of a woman he will encounter at university. I hope I look back on the journal with found remembering. Maybe I will gift these pages, torn from my journal, to the young woman on their wedding day!

Now, dear Victor, I dare say you wish to be indulged in a little gossip concerning the good people of Geneva. The pretty Miss Mansfield has already received the congratulatory visits on her approaching marriage with a young Englishman, John Melbourne, Esq. Her ugly sister, Manon, married Mr Duvillard, the rich banker, last autumn. Your favourite schoolfellow, Louis Manoir, has suffered several misfortunes since the departure of Clerval from Geneva. But he has already recovered his spirits, and is reported to be on the point of marrying a very lively pretty Frenchwoman, Madame Tavernier. She is a widow, and much older than Manoir; but she is very much admired, and a favourite with every body.

I have written myself into good spirits, dear cousin; yet I cannot conclude without again anxiously inquiring concerning your health. Dear Victor, if you are not very ill, write yourself, and make your father and all of us happy; or— — I cannot bear to think of the other side of the question; my tears already flow. Adieu, my dearest cousin.

Elizabeth Lavenza
Geneva, March 19th 1795

Having read the letter, I looked up and the thunderclouds must have grown so dark and dreary that noon now appeared midnight. The thunderstorm raged as violently as those I experienced above the Castle Frankenstein yesterweek. In the armchair set next to the hearth, where my Beloved preferred to sit, including during his galvanising debate with Lord Byron, sat not my Beloved, but the pale student of the unhallowed arts. Had he heard my reading of the letter under my breath? Perhaps, I read a little too loudly for the reading had caught his attention. I apologized most furiously for having betrayed him by reading a letter clearly addressed to him. I recognized in myself that I still believed the pale student to be a figment of my overactive imagination and not a person. But here and now he appeared more a person than a dream. He exclaimed when I read her letter:

' "Dear, dear Elizabeth! I will write instantly, and relieve them from the anxiety they must feel." I wrote, and this exertion greatly fatigued me; but my convalescence had commenced, and proceeded regularly. In another fortnight I was able to leave my chamber.' I wonder how much time has passed since that 'deary night in November' when his Creation was born without the necessity of a womb. Four months? Perhaps five? And still he makes little reference to his Creation. Does he ponder his Creation's hereabouts or his happenings. Four months is a long time for a creature with the mentality of a child to experience this cruel world created by an equally cruel God. And speak of the cruel world, did not Marcion of Sinope, an early Church Father turned Heretic, believe that the God of the Old Testament, the Demiurge, was far too severely just with all His precise and preposterous Laws written through the Torah of Moses? Did he not believe that Jesus the Christ was the Son of the Good God and not as Christians suppose the Son of the God of the Old Testament? Victor is behaving like the Demiurge with no concern for his Creation. Does not the God of the Old Testament command: *Remember, O Lord, the children of Edom in the day of Jerusalem; who said, Rase it, rase it, even to the foundation thereof. O daughter of Babylon, who art to be destroyed; happy shall he be, that rewardeth thee as thou hast served us. Happy shall he be, that taketh and dasheth thy little ones against the stones.*[90] I am growing in dislike and distrust and disgust for my pale student when it concerns his Creation created by the unhallowed arts!

'One of my first duties on my recovery was to introduce Clerval to the several professors of the university. In doing this, I underwent a kind of rough usage, ill befitting the wounds that my mind had sustained. Ever since the fatal night, the end of my labours, and the beginning of my misfortunes, I had conceived a violent antipathy even to the name of natural philosophy. When I was otherwise quite restored to health, the sight of a chemical instrument would renew all the agony of my nervous symptoms. Henry saw this, and had removed all my apparatus from my view.'

Curious and curiouser. In my waking dream of the laboratory at Castle Frankenstein where he breathed life into his Creation through unrelatable means, I did not think to imagine what his apartment in Ingolstadt with its queer apparatuses collected by a desperate student from disparate laboratories around Ingolstadt and the bloody and rotting and now putrid body parts collected from charnel houses and slaughterhouses. My pale student makes little mention having repaired his apartment to a natural state before falling deep into his coma. If his dearest Henry saw nothing out of the ordinary, can the readiest explanation be that all of this the product of a deeply disturbed imagination?

---

90 From Psalm 137:7-9

Or did he choose to omit this fact from his telling. And if he did choose to omit this fact, what else is he withholding from me!

'He had also changed my apartment; for he perceived that I had acquired a dislike for the room which had previously been my laboratory. But these cares of Clerval were made of no avail when I visited the professors. Mr Waldman inflicted torture when he praised, with kindness and warmth, the astonishing progress I had made in the sciences. He soon perceived that I disliked the subject; but, not guessing the real cause, he attributed my feelings to modesty, and changed the subject from my improvement to the science itself, with a desire, as I evidently saw, of drawing me out. What could I do? He meant to please, and he tormented me. I felt as if he had placed carefully, one by one, in my view those instruments which were to be afterwards used in putting me to a slow and cruel death. I writhed under his words, yet dared not exhibit the pain I felt. Clerval, whose eyes and feelings were always quick in discerning the sensations of others, declined the subject, alleging, in excuse, his total ignorance; and the conversation took a more general turn. I thanked my friend from my heart, but I did not speak. I saw plainly that he was surprised, but he never attempted to draw my secret from me; and although I loved him with a mixture of affection and reverence that knew no bounds, yet I could never persuade myself to confide to him that event which was so often present to my recollection, but which I feared the detail to another would only impress more deeply.

'Mr Krempe was not equally docile; and in my condition at that time, of almost insupportable sensitiveness, his harsh blunt encomiums gave me even more pain than the benevolent approbation of Mr Waldman. "Damn the fellow!" cried he; "why, Mr Clerval, I assure you he has outstript us all. Aye, stare if you please; but it is nevertheless true. A youngster who, but a few years ago, believed Cornelius Agrippa as firmly as the gospel, has now set himself at the head of the university; and if he is not soon pulled down, we shall all be out of countenance.— Aye, aye," continued he, observing my face expressive of suffering, "Mr Frankenstein is modest; an excellent quality in a young man. Young men should be diffident of themselves, you know, Mr Clerval; I was myself when young: but that wears out in a very short time."

'Mr Krempe had now commenced an eulogy on himself, which happily turned the conversation from a subject that was so annoying to me.

'Clerval was no natural philosopher. His imagination was too vivid for the minutiæ of science. Languages were his principal study; and he sought, by acquiring their elements, to open a field for self-instruction on his return to Geneva. Persian, Arabic, and Hebrew, gained his attention, after he had made himself perfectly master of Greek and Latin. For my own part, idleness had ever been irksome to me; and now that I wished to fly from reflection, and hated my former studies, I felt great relief in being the fellow-pupil with my friend, and found not only instruction but consolation in the works of the orientalists. Their melancholy is soothing, and their joy elevating to a degree I never experienced in studying the authors of any other country. When you read their writings, life appears to consist in a warm sun and garden of roses,— in the smiles and frowns of a fair enemy, and the fire that consumes your own heart. How different from the manly and heroical poetry of Greece and Rome.

'Summer passed away in these occupations, and my return to Geneva was fixed for the latter end of autumn; but being delayed by several accidents, winter and snow arrived, the roads were deemed impassable, and my journey was retarded until the ensuing spring. I felt this delay very bitterly; for I longed to see my native town, and my beloved friends. My return had only been delayed so long from an unwillingness to leave Clerval in a strange place, before he had become acquainted with any of its inhabitants. The winter, however, was spent cheerfully; and although the spring was uncommonly late, when it came, its beauty compensated for its dilatoriness.

'The month of May had already commenced.' Damn this Victor Frankenstein straight to Hell. I no longer wish to be haunted by him. How long has his Creation wandered alone through the cruel world without a parent to guide his education. Not a single thought is given. This abandonment of his Creation has my intestines twisted into knots. The pain I feel for his Creation is a mother's pain. But a father? Ha! A father often cares not for his offspring. Lord Byron has abandoned all children: The Honourable Augusta Ada Bryon, his only legitimate child, and Elizabeth Medora Leigh, born of an incestuous relation with his half-sister. His daughters know not the love of a father. And of that child growing in the womb of my dearest sister Claire, he cares nothing, and it is not yet born. He is greatly inconvenienced by the mere presence of dearest Claire. Lord Byron only concerns himself physical aspects of the intimate acts and nothing for its consequences. And Victor has taken up our little Lord's mantle.

'And I expected the letter daily which was to fix the date of my departure, when Henry proposed a pedestrian tour in the environs of Ingolstadt that I might bid a personal farewell to the country I had so long inhabited. I acceded with pleasure to this proposition: I was fond of exercise, and Clerval had always been my favourite companion in the rambles of this nature that I had taken among the scenes of my native country.

'We passed a fortnight in these perambulations: my health and spirits had long been restored, and they gained additional strength from the salubrious air I breathed, the natural incidents of our progress, and the conversation of my friend. Study had before secluded me from the intercourse of my fellow-creatures, and rendered me unsocial; but Clerval called forth the better feelings of my heart; he again taught me to love the aspect of nature, and the cheerful faces of children. Excellent friend! how sincerely did you love me, and endeavour to elevate my mind, until it was on a level with your own. A selfish pursuit had cramped and narrowed me, until your gentleness and affection warmed and opened my senses; I became the same happy creature who, a few years ago, loving and beloved by all, had no sorrow or care. When happy, inanimate nature had the power of bestowing on me the most delightful sensations. A serene sky and verdant fields filled me with ecstacy. The present season was indeed divine; the flowers of spring bloomed in the hedges, while those of summer were already in bud: I was undisturbed by thoughts which during the preceding year had pressed upon me, notwithstanding my endeavours to throw them off, with an invincible burden.

'Henry rejoiced in my gaiety, and sincerely sympathized in my feelings: he exerted himself to amuse me, while he expressed the sensations that filled his soul. The resources of his mind on this occasion were truly astonishing: his conversation was full of imagination; and very often, in imitation of the Persian and Arabic writers, he invented tales of wonderful fancy and passion. At other times he repeated my favourite poems, or drew me out into arguments, which he supported with great ingenuity.

'We returned to our college on a Sunday afternoon: the peasants were dancing, and every one we met appeared gay and happy. My own spirits were high, and I bounded along with feelings of unbridled joy and hilarity.'

The pale student looked down at his hands and then up at me. He requested of me; he required of me to read the second letter. I observed the address '*To* V. Frankenstein' was written in a man's handwriting and Victor exclaimed that it must be from his father! I pealed open the envelope and revealed the letter that had, in fact, been written by his father! I prepared to hand him the letter, but he waved his hand away, so I read it aloud it aloud to him as I had the first:

Chapter II

'My Dear Victor,

You have probably waited impatiently for a letter to fix the date of your return to us; and I was at first tempted to write only a few lines, merely mentioning the day on which I should expect you. But that would be a cruel kindness, and I dare not do it. What would be your surprise, my son, when you expected a happy and gay welcome, to behold, on the contrary, tears and wretchedness? And how, Victor, can I relate our misfortune? Absence cannot have rendered you callous to our joys and griefs; and how shall I inflict pain on an absent child? I wish to prepare you for the woeful news, but I know it is impossible; even now your eye skims over the page, to seek the words which are to convey to you the horrible tidings.

'William is dead!— that sweet child, whose smiles delighted and warmed my heart, who was so gentle, yet so gay! Victor, he is murdered!'

I burst into tears when I read the words, weeping wildly. In the moment, I failed to connect my own unchristened daughter's infantile death to these very words and my sudden sullen sadness. But now writing these words into my journal, I do realize that not only am I weeping for my own unchristened daughter, but as a daughter having lost my mother due to my own childbirth. If my own birth had not been so laboured and difficult, the placenta that nourished me for nine months would have been discharged intact, but the afterbirth did not discharge intact. The childbed fever caused by my birth took my mother's life. How cursed are the Wollstonecrafts?

How cursed are the Frankensteins? I wept for Victor; I wept for his father, I wept for William. I struggled to look up for the page, becoming stained with my teardrops. Oh! no! I cannot allow the ink to become smudged. If this letter is ruined, then how will Victor know the conclusion? In a moment of sheer will, I looked over at Victor to see all life go out of my pale student. If he had been pale of complexion due to the burden of his creation of the Creature, now he was pale due to pain of having lost his younger brother. But what of Alphonse Frankenstein's own pain? He has lost a son! There is no pain equal to this! No man or woman becomes a father or mother and looks down at their child, believing they will outlive their own creation. But I do not intend to dismiss Victor's own pain, for now news comes by post that your cherished brother is murdered. Victor's legs weakened and his arm went wimp. His head rolled back onto his spine. He laboured to take a breath and when he exhaled the breath was nothing more than a wheeze. After several long moments for me and an eternity for him, he begged me to continue, and I did:

'I will not attempt to console you; but will simply relate the circumstances of the transaction.' Nor will I attempt to console my pale student. I too can only relate the circumstances of the transaction as written in his father's letter. How can this father, the patriarch of the Frankensteins, steel himself to relate the 'circumstances of the transaction' of his own son's murder in a mere letter to his surviving son? Were the tearstains and smudged ink of my cause or the father's in the penning of the letter? I did not attempt to answer my own question because I steeled myself to continue reading to my poor pale student:

'Last Thursday (May 7th) I, my niece, and your two brothers, went to walk in Plainpalais.' I know this location and the incident that occurred there well! My Beloved and I learned of the 'incident' during our *Six Weeks' Tour*:

> To the south of the town of Gevena is the promenade of the Genevese, a grassy plain planted with a few trees, and called Plainpalais. Here a small obelisk is erected to the glory of Rousseau, and here (such is the mutability of human life) the magistrates, the successors of those who exiled him from his native country, were shot by the populace during that revolution, which his writings mainly contributed to mature, and which, notwithstanding the temporary bloodshed and injustice with which it was polluted, has produced enduring benefits to mankind, which all the chicanery of statesmen, nor even the great conspiracy of kings, can entirely render vain. From respect to the memory of their predecessors, none of the present magistrates ever walk in Plainpalais.[91]

'The evening was warm and serene, and we prolonged our walk farther than usual. It was already dusk before we thought of returning; and then we discovered that William and Ernest, who had gone on before, were not to be found. We accordingly rested on a seat until they should return. Presently Ernest came, and inquired if we had seen his brother: he said, that they had been playing together, that William had run away to hide himself, and that he vainly sought for him, and afterwards waited for him a long time, but that he did not return.

'This account rather alarmed us, and we continued to search for him until night fell, when Elizabeth conjectured that he might have returned to the house. He was not there. We returned again, with torches; for I could not rest, when I thought that my sweet boy had lost himself, and was exposed to all the damps and dews of night: Elizabeth also suffered extreme anguish. About five in the morning I discovered my lovely boy, whom the night before I had seen blooming and active in health, stretched on the grass livid and motionless: the print of the murderer's finger was on his neck.' To lose a small child to illness is one nightmare for a parent, but to lose a small child to murder is an unwakeable nightmare! I look to my own William sleeping peacefully in his bassinette

---

91 From the *History of a Six Weeks Tour Through a Part of France, Germany, Switzerland, and Holland* by Mary Shelley, published by T. Hookham, Jun. Old Bond Street, and C. and J. Ollier, Welback Street, 1817

and my nerves are aflame with shudders. Gooseflesh prickles on my arms. Tear threaten to overwhelm my eyes. I cannot stomach to look upon my pale student and I continue my recitation of the letter:

'He was conveyed home, and the anguish that was visible in my countenance betrayed the secret to Elizabeth. She was very earnest to see the corpse. At first I attempted to prevent her; but she persisted, and entering the room where it lay, hastily examined the neck of the victim, and clasping her hands exclaimed, 'O God! I have murdered my darling infant!'

'She fainted, and was restored with extreme difficulty. When she again lived, it was only to weep and sigh. She told me, that that same evening William had teazed her to let him wear a very valuable miniature that she possessed of your mother. This picture is gone, and was doubtless the temptation which urged the murderer to the deed. We have no trace of him at present, although our exertions to discover him are unremitted; but they will not restore my beloved William.

'Come, dearest Victor; you alone can console Elizabeth. She weeps continually, and accuses herself unjustly as the cause of his death; her words pierce my heart. We are all unhappy; but will not that be an additional motive for you, my son, to return and be our comforter? Your dear mother! Alas, Victor! I now say, Thank God she did not live to witness the cruel, miserable death of her youngest darling!

'Come, Victor; not brooding thoughts of vengeance against the assassin, but with feelings of peace and gentleness, that will heal, instead of festering the wounds of our minds. Enter the house of mourning, my friend, but with kindness and affection for those who love you, and not with hatred for your enemies.

Your affectionate and afflicted father,
'Alphonse Frankenstein
'Geneva, May 12th, 1795'

I, who had watched Victor's countenance as I read this letter, was surprised to observe the despair that succeed to the joy he at first expressed on receiving news from his friends. I threw the letter on the table, and he covered his face with his hands.

'My dear Frankenstein,' exclaimed Henry, when he perceived him weep with bitterness. I heard this Henry Clerval speak audibly as he addressed his dear friend, though I saw him not. Was he standing in the parlour of the Villa Diodati with Victor and me, or his own study of oriental languages? Or both? I found myself no longer merely being a transcriber of the tale Victor was telling me; I was now a voyeur as this very scene played out. I tried desperately to force my eyes to capture

Henry's ghostly visage but could not. He was an invisible phantasm. 'Are you always to be unhappy? My dear friend, what has happened?' Was Henry's disembodied voice a mere figment of my overactive imagination? Or do authors of great fiction often hear the voices of imaginary characters speaking quite audibly? I heard Henry quite clearly; I heard and saw Victor with even more reality! Should I commit myself to in Bethlem Royal Hospital upon my return to London? I do not know!

My pale student motioned to Henry to take up the letter, while he walked up and down the parlour in the Villa Diodati in the extremest agitation. Tears no doubt gushed from their eyes as they all had heard the account of his misfortune.

'I can offer you no consolation, my friend,' said Henry again most audibly to my ears; 'your disaster is irreparable. What do you intend to do?'

'To go instantly to Geneva: come with me, Henry, to order the horses.'

'Poor William!' Clerval said clearly endeavouring to raise Victor's spirits; he did not do this by common topics of consolation, but by exhibiting the truest sympathy, 'that dear child; he now sleeps with his angel mother. His friends mourn and weep, but he is at rest: he does not now feel the murderer's grasp; a sod covers his gentle form, and he knows no pain. He can no longer be a fit subject for pity; the survivors are the greatest sufferers, and for them time is the only consolation. Those maxims of the Stoics, that death was no evil, and that the mind of man ought to be superior to despair on the eternal absence of a beloved object, ought not to be urged. Even Cato wept over the dead body of his brother.'

My pale student took back his armchair. My voyeurship of this all too brief scene ended abruptly as it had played to its conclusion. Victor resumed his tale as he had before my quite queer recitation of the mysterious letters upended our routine. I picked up my pen again to continue my transcription of this harrowing, horrifying tale: 'Soon we hurried through the streets; the words impressed themselves on my mind, and I remembered them afterwards in solitude. But now, as soon as the horses arrived, I hurried into a cabriole, and bade farewell to my friend.

'My journey, dearest Mary, was very melancholy. At first I wished to hurry on, for I longed to console and sympathize with my loved and sorrowing friends; but when I drew near my native town, I slackened my progress. I could hardly sustain the multitude of feelings that crowded into my mind. I passed through scenes familiar to my youth, but which I had not seen for nearly six years. How altered every thing might be during that time? One sudden and desolating change had taken place; but a thousand little circumstances might have by degrees worked other alterations which, although they were done more tranquilly, might not be the less decisive. Fear overcame me; I dared not advance, dreading a thousand nameless evils that made me tremble, although I was unable to define them.

'I remained two days at Lausanne, in this painful state of mind. I contemplated the lake: the waters were placid; all around was calm, and the snowy mountains, "the palaces of nature," were not changed. By degrees the calm and heavenly scene restored me, and I continued my journey towards Geneva.'

'The palaces of Nature.' Such a curious turn of phrase for my pale student to utter. On our eight-day excursion across the lake, Lord Byron confided to me in private, he did not wish Percy to know, that he was composing a third canto to 'Childe Harold's Pilgrimage'. I was delighted to know that he had picked up the poem having gestated for four long years since the publication of the first and second. The poem had not yet been completed and therefore not ready for recitation in the parlour of the Villa Diodati, but he handed me some pages, not the first and not the last, but somewhere in the middle, and asked me to give him my criticism. Not that there would be much to criticize, but an author is overeager to hear constructive feedback of his labours. Amongst the stanzas gifted to me that night was this particular one:

> But these recede. Above me are the Alps,
> The palaces of Nature, whose vast walls
> Have pinnacled in clouds their snowy scalps,
> And throned Eternity in icy halls
> Of cold sublimity, where forms and falls
> The avalanche—the thunderbolt of snow!
> All that expands the spirit, yet appals,
> Gathers around these summits, as to show
> How Earth may pierce to Heaven,
> Yet leave vain man below.[92]

'The road ran by the side of the lake, which became narrower as I approached my native town. I discovered more distinctly the black sides of Jura, and the bright summit of Mont Blânc; I wept like a child: "Dear mountains! my own beautiful lake! how do you welcome your wanderer? Your summits are clear; the sky and lake are blue and placid. Is this to prognosticate peace, or to mock at my unhappiness?"

'I fear, dearest Mary, that I shall render myself tedious by dwelling on these preliminary circumstances; but they were days of comparative

---

92 From *Childe Harold's Pilgrimage, a Romaunt* by Lord Byron, published by John Murray, 1816

happiness, and I think of them with pleasure. My country, my beloved country! who but a native can tell the delight I took in again beholding thy streams, thy mountains, and, more than all, thy lovely lake.

'Yet, as I drew nearer home, grief and fear again overcame me. Night also closed around; and when I could hardly see the dark mountains, I felt still more gloomily. The picture appeared a vast and dim scene of evil, and I foresaw obscurely that I was destined to become the most wretched of human beings. Alas! I prophesied truly, and failed only in one single circumstance, that in all the misery I imagined and dreaded, I did not conceive the hundredth part of the anguish I was destined to endure.

'It was completely dark when I arrived in the environs of Geneva; the gates of the town were already shut; and I was obliged to pass the night at Secheron, a village half a league to the east of the city.' I and my Beloved and dearest Claire encountered a similar encounter. On the first of June, as we neared beginning our summer with Lord Byron, we learned too 'that he town is surrounded by a wall, the three gates of which are shut exactly at ten o'clock, when no bribery (as in France) can open them.'[93] My pale student continued, while I was scribbling my digression, 'The sky was serene; and, as I was unable to rest, I resolved to visit the spot where my poor William had been murdered. As I could not pass through the town, I was obliged to cross the lake in a boat to arrive at Plainpalais. During this short voyage I saw the lightnings playing on the summit of Mont Blânc in the most beautiful figures. The storm appeared to approach rapidly; and, on landing, I ascended a low hill, that I might observe its progress. It advanced; the heavens were clouded, and I soon felt the rain coming slowly in large drops, but its violence quickly increased.

'I quitted my seat, and walked on, although the darkness and storm increased every minute, and the thunder burst with a terrific crash over my head. It was echoed from Salêve, the Juras, and the Alps of Savoy; vivid flashes of lightning dazzled my eyes, illuminating the lake, making it appear like a vast sheet of fire; then for an instant every thing seemed of a pitchy darkness, until the eye recovered itself from the preceding flash.' And if, like an actor waiting offstage for the hearing of their cue, a thunderstorm burst over Lake Geneva and buffeted the windows with wind and rain. 'The storm, as is often the case in Switzerland, appeared at once in various parts of the heavens. The most violent storm hung exactly north of the town, over that part of the lake which lies between the promontory of Belrive and the village of Copêt. Another storm en-

---

93 From the *History of a Six Weeks Tour Through a Part of France, Germany, Switzerland, and Holland* by Mary Shelley, published by T. Hookham, Jun. Old Bond Street, and C. and J. Ollier, Welback Street, 1817

lightened Jura with faint flashes; and another darkened and sometimes disclosed the Môle, a peaked mountain to the east of the lake.

'While I watched the storm, so beautiful yet terrific, I wandered on with a hasty step. This noble war in the sky elevated my spirits; I clasped my hands, and exclaimed aloud, "William, dear angel! this is thy funeral, this thy dirge!" As I said these words, I perceived in the gloom a figure which stole from behind a clump of trees near me; I stood fixed, gazing intently: I could not be mistaken. A flash of lightning illuminated the object, and discovered its shape plainly to me; its gigantic stature, and the deformity of its aspect, more hideous than belongs to humanity, instantly informed me that it was the wretch, the filthy dæmon to whom I had given life.' His Creation has returned. What wondrous news! 'What did he there? Could he be (I shuddered at the conception) the murderer of my brother? No sooner did that idea cross my imagination, than I became convinced of its truth; my teeth chattered, and I was forced to lean against a tree for support.'

'No! How can you be so certain', I said out loud. For the first time, I interrupted my pale student to the unhallowed arts, the very unhallowed arts that created his Creation, what he calls his Creature. 'The letter from your father was dated and posted on May the Twelfth and no doubt took a handful of days to reach your apartment in Ingolstadt. And! You yourself said that you tarried a tid bit on your journey home. Had your Creation lingered in the vicinity of the Plainpalais for all this time? No murderer no matter how mad lingers for so long. True, a murderer may linger awhile to bear witness to the aftermath of his deeds, but to linger, exposed to the elements for so long reeks of a lunatic or the innocent. Do you so dismiss your Creation as a lunatic? You assembled him. You breathed life into its amalgamation of body parts from charnel houses and slaughterhouses. And yet, you are so quick to lay the blame on your own Creation. Is it not just as logical that your Creation had learned of the murder, heard the child's surname, and sought the location out in hopes of finding you? His Creator.'

Dismissing my words as if I never uttered them, he continued, 'The figure passed me quickly, and I lost it in the gloom. Nothing in human shape could have destroyed that fair child. *He* was the murderer! I could not doubt it. The mere presence of the idea was an irresistible proof of the fact. I thought of pursuing the devil; but it would have been in vain, for another flash discovered him to me hanging among the rocks of the nearly perpendicular ascent of Mont Salêve, a hill that bounds Plainpalais on the south. He soon reached the summit, and disappeared.

'I remained motionless. The thunder ceased; but the rain still continued, and the scene was enveloped in an impenetrable darkness. I revolved in my mind the events which I had until now sought to forget: the whole train of my progress towards the creation; the appearance of the work of my own hands alive at my bed side; its departure. Two years had now nearly elapsed since the night on which he first received life; and was this his first crime?'

Did his Creation linger all this time in the vicinity of Ingolstadt? Where had his Creation been in the interim? Did his Creation learn of his Creator's surname? Did his Creation discover the homeland of his Creator? Question upon questions upon questions stir in my mind. A walk from Ingolstadt to Geneva would be perhaps a month in length, depending on the weather and weariness. Victor admitted he tarried a day here or there on his own carriage journey. Or is Victor correct? And his Creation had learned his surname and his homeland and sought to murder a cherished loved one. No! I cannot bear to think these thoughts. True, his Creation had been abandoned by his Creator mere moments after awaking, but nothing my pale student has said in the telling of this tale will lead me to the conclusion that his Creation murdered William Frankenstein in the coldest of blood. Does not a human heart beat within his chest, or did Victor implant the heart of a bull in his massive chest?

'Alas! I had turned loose into the world a depraved wretch, whose delight was in carnage and misery; had he not murdered my brother?

'No one can conceive the anguish I suffered during the remainder of the night, which I spent, cold and wet, in the open air. But I did not feel the inconvenience of the weather; my imagination was busy in scenes of evil and despair. I considered the being whom I had cast among mankind, and endowed with the will and power to effect purposes of horror, such as the deed which he had now done, nearly in the light of my own vampire, my own spirit let loose from the grave, and forced to destroy all that was dear to me.

'Day dawned; and I directed my steps towards the town. The gates were open; and I hastened to my father's house. My first thought was to discover what I knew of the murderer, and cause instant pursuit to be made. But I paused when I reflected on the story that I had to tell. A being whom I myself had formed, and endued with life, had met me at midnight among the precipices of an inaccessible mountain. I remembered also the nervous fever with which I had been seized just at the time that I dated my creation, and which would give an air of delirium to a tale otherwise so utterly improbable. I well knew that if any other had communicated such a relation to me, I should have looked upon it as the ravings of insanity. Besides, the strange nature of the animal would elude all pursuit, even if I were so far credited as to persuade my relatives to commence it. Besides, of what use would be pursuit? Who could arrest a creature capable of scaling the overhanging sides of Mont Salêve? These reflections determined me, and I resolved to remain silent.

'It was about five in the morning when I entered my father's house. I told the servants not to disturb the family, and went into the library to attend their usual hour of rising.

'Six years had elapsed, passed as a dream but for one indelible trace, and I stood in the same place where I had last embraced my father before my departure for Ingolstadt. Beloved and respectable parent! He still remained to me. I gazed on the picture of my mother, which stood over the mantle-piece. It was an historical subject, painted at my father's desire, and represented Caroline Beaumont in an agony of despair, kneeling by the coffin of her dead father.

'Her garb was rustic, and her cheek pale; but there was an air of dignity and beauty, that hardly permitted the sentiment of pity. Below this picture was a miniature of William; and my tears flowed when I looked upon it. While I was thus engaged, Ernest entered: he had heard me arrive, and hastened to welcome me. He expressed a sorrowful delight to see me: "Welcome, my dearest Victor," said he. "Ah! I wish you had come three months ago, and then you would have found us all joyous and delighted. But we are now unhappy; and, I am afraid, tears instead of smiles will be your welcome. Our father looks so sorrowful: this dreadful event seems to have revived in his mind his grief on the death of Mamma. Poor Elizabeth also is quite inconsolable." Ernest began to weep as he said these words.' As do I. The scene in which my pale student paints, like the painting of his dear, sweet Mother kneeling beside the coffin her dead father, is likewise inconsolable. I am also in the agony of despair.

' "Do not," said I, "welcome me thus; try to be more calm, that I may not be absolutely miserable the moment I enter my father's house after so long an absence. But, tell me, how does my father support his misfortunes? and how is my poor Elizabeth?"

' "She indeed requires consolation; she accused herself of having caused the death of my brother, and that made her very wretched. But since the murderer has been discovered—" Wait! What? The murderer discovered! Good God! How can that be?

Then Victor repeated my own words, ' "The murderer discovered! Good God! how can that be? who could attempt to pursue him? It is impossible; one might as well try to overtake the winds, or confine a mountain-stream with a straw."

' "I do not know what you mean; but we were all very unhappy when she was discovered. No one would believe it at first; and even now Elizabeth will not be convinced, notwithstanding all the evidence. Indeed, who would credit that Justine Martin, who was so amiable, and fond of all the family, could all at once become so extremely wicked?"

I know little of this poor girl, other than the brief words my pale student has spoken of her in his telling of his tale. Victor, of course he does, knows this girl more intimately as she has served his family for many years. As I know nothing of her, I can pass no judgments until I learn more of her situation.

' "Justine Martin! Poor, poor girl, is she the accused? But it is wrong-fully; every one knows that; no one believes it, surely, Ernest?"

' "No one did at first; but several circumstances came out, that have almost forced conviction upon us: and her own behaviour has been so confused, as to add to the evidence of facts a weight that, I fear, leaves no hope for doubt. But she will be tried to-day, and you will then hear all."

'He related that, the morning on which the murder of poor William had been discovered, Justine had been taken ill, and confined to her bed; and, after several days, one of the servants, happening to examine the apparel she had worn on the night of the murder, had discovered in her pocket the picture of my mother, which had been judged to be the temp-tation of the murderer. The servant instantly shewed it to one of the oth-ers, who, without saying a word to any of the family, went to a magistrate; and, upon their deposition, Justine was apprehended. On being charged with the fact, the poor girl confirmed the suspicion in a great measure by her extreme confusion of manner.

'This was a strange tale, but it did not shake my faith; and I replied earnestly, "You are all mistaken; I know the murderer. Justine, poor, good Justine, is innocent."'

My pale student exposes his own prejudices against his Creation, the very Creation he abandoned mere moments after gifting it with life. It took mankind's Creator far longer to abandon His Creation. The Holy Scripture does not provide a perceptible timeline from Ad-am's creation from the dust of the earth and Eve's creation from his rib to their consuming of the fruit of the Tree of the Knowledge of Good and Evil. But God's abandonment of man did not come in mere mo-ments after Adam's creation, but perhaps many years. And why was man cast out of the Garden of Eden? Not being he was evil, but merely because he now possessed the knowledge of *both* Good *and* Evil. My pale student of the unhallowed is so ready to dismiss his Creation as inherently evil. Why does he not see any good in his Creation. Here he is presented with evidence that jurisprudence finds accepting and he is completely dismissive of it.

'At that instant my father entered. I saw unhappiness deeply im-pressed on his countenance, but he endeavoured to welcome me cheerfully; and, after we had exchanged our mournful greeting, would have introduced some other topic than that of our disaster, had not Ernest exclaimed, "Good God, Papa! Victor says that he knows who was the murderer of poor William."

' "We do also, unfortunately," replied my father; "for indeed I had rather have been for ever ignorant than have discovered so much depravity and ingratitude in one I valued so highly."

' "My dear father, you are mistaken; Justine is innocent."

' "If she is, God forbid that she should suffer as guilty. She is to be tried to-day, and I hope, I sincerely hope, that she will be acquitted."

'This speech calmed me. I was firmly convinced in my own mind that Justine, and indeed every human being, was guiltless of this murder.' All humankind is guiltless of this murder? Oh, Victor. It is quite telling that you do not count your Creation among humankind? You sought to be the Creator of your own race of men but now cannot bear having created his own race of men. Your hubris knows no bounds. 'I had no fear, therefore, that any circumstantial evidence could be brought forward strong enough to convict her; and, in this assurance, I calmed myself, expecting the trial with eagerness, but without prognosticating an evil result.

'We were soon joined by Elizabeth. Time had made great alterations in her form since I had last beheld her. Six years before she had been a pretty, good-humoured girl, whom every one loved and caressed. She was now a woman in stature and expression of countenance, which was uncommonly lovely. An open and capacious forehead gave indications of a good understanding, joined to great frankness of disposition. Her eyes were hazel, and expressive of mildness, now through recent affliction allied to sadness. Her hair was of a rich, dark auburn, her complexion fair, and her figure slight and graceful. She welcomed me with the greatest affection. "Your arrival, my dear cousin," said she, "fills me with hope. You perhaps will find some means to justify my poor guiltless Justine.'

Elizabeth believes in the innocence of her servant and friend because of the nature of the feminine creature. Victor believes in the guilt of his Creation due to nature of the masculine creature. I do not regret the choosing of my words here. If the Christianity can lay the blame of Original Sin upon a single woman, Eve, then I can be afforded the same luxury by laying the hubris of mankind upon a single man, Victor Frankenstein!

'Alas! who is safe, if she be convicted of crime? I rely on her innocence as certainly as I do upon my own. Our misfortune is doubly hard to us; we have not only lost that lovely darling boy, but this poor girl, whom I sincerely love, is to be torn away by even a worse fate. If she is condemned, I never shall know joy more. But she will not, I am sure she will not; and then I shall be happy again, even after the sad death of my little William."

' "She is innocent, my Elizabeth," said I, "and that shall be proved; fear nothing, but let your spirits be cheered by the assurance of her acquittal."

' "How kind you are! every one else believes in her guilt, and that made me wretched; for I knew that it was impossible: and to see every one else prejudiced in so deadly a manner, rendered me hopeless and despairing." She wept.

' "Sweet niece," said my father, "dry your tears. If she is, as you believe, innocent, rely on the justice of our judges, and the activity with which I shall prevent the slightest shadow of partiality."'

Chapter III

2 July. Morning— 'We passed a few sad hours, until eleven o'clock, when the trial was to commence. My father and the rest of the family being obliged to attend as witnesses, I accompanied them to the court. During the whole of this wretched mockery of justice, I suffered living torture. It was to be decided, whether the result of my curiosity and lawless devices would cause the death of two of my fellow-beings: one a smiling babe, full of innocence and joy; the other far more dreadfully murdered, with every aggravation of infamy that could make the murder memorable in horror. Justine also was a girl of merit, and possessed qualities which promised to render her life happy: now all was to be obliterated in an ignominious grave; and I the cause! A thousand times rather would I have confessed myself guilty of the crime ascribed to Justine; but I was absent when it was committed, and such a declaration would have been considered as the ravings of a madman, and would not have exculpated her who suffered through me.'

What is the source of this guilt? The innerworkings of the mind remain a mystery to the natural philosophers. Confined to terms like mad and lunacy, these words do not capture the true depth and breadth of the mind that exists below consciousness. This is where Victor's guilt lies, under layers upon layers of the conscious mind. I believe the Creation is the source of this guilt. If Victor had not be playing God in his laboratory and was instead at home with his family, none of this horror would have occurred. And there is a part of the innerworkings of my mind that cannot shake the shocking belief that Victor's Creation has a part to play is this sadness.

The appearance of Justine was calm. She was dressed in mourning; and her countenance, always engaging, was rendered, by the solemnity

of her feelings, exquisitely beautiful. Yet she appeared confident in innocence, and did not tremble, although gazed on and execrated by thousands; for all the kindness which her beauty might otherwise have excited, was obliterated in the minds of the spectators by the imagination of
the enormity she was supposed to have committed. She was tranquil, yet
her tranquillity was evidently constrained; and as her confusion had before been adduced as a proof of her guilt, she worked up her mind to an
appearance of courage. When she entered the court, she threw her eyes
round it, and quickly discovered where we were seated. A tear seemed
to dim her eye when she saw us; but she quickly recovered herself, and a
look of sorrowful affection seemed to attest her utter guiltlessness.

'The trial began; and after the advocate against her had stated the
charge, several witnesses were called. Several strange facts combined
against her, which might have staggered any one who had not such proof
of her innocence as I had. She had been out the whole of the night on
which the murder had been committed, and towards morning had been
perceived by a market-woman not far from the spot where the body of
the murdered child had been afterwards found. The woman asked her
what she did there; but she looked very strangely, and only returned
a confused and unintelligible answer. She returned to the house about
eight o'clock; and when one inquired where she had passed the night,
she replied, that she had been looking for the child, and demanded earnestly, if any thing had been heard concerning him. When shewn the
body, she fell into violent hysterics, and kept her bed for several days.
The picture was then produced, which the servant had found in her
pocket; and when Elizabeth, in a faltering voice, proved that it was the
same which, an hour before the child had been missed, she had placed
round his neck, a murmur of horror and indignation filled the court.

'Justine was called on for her defence. As the trial had proceeded,
her countenance had altered. Surprise, horror, and misery, were strongly expressed. Sometimes she struggled with her tears; but when she was
desired to plead, she collected her powers, and spoke in an audible although variable voice:—

' "God knows," she said, "how entirely I am innocent. But I do not
pretend that my protestations should acquit me: I rest my innocence
on a plain and simple explanation of the facts which have been adduced
against me; and I hope the character I have always borne will incline my
judges to a favourable interpretation, where any circumstance appears
doubtful or suspicious."

'She then related that, by the permission of Elizabeth, she had passed
the evening of the night on which the murder had been committed, at
the house of an aunt at Chêne, a village situated at about a league from

Geneva. On her return, at about nine o'clock, she met a man, who asked her if she had seen any thing of the child who was lost. She was alarmed by this account, and passed several hours in looking for him, when the gates of Geneva were shut, and she was forced to remain several hours of the night in a barn belonging to a cottage, being unwilling to call up the inhabitants, to whom she was well known. Unable to rest or sleep, she quitted her asylum early, that she might again endeavour to find my brother.' — why, oh, why do I wish her to have said, 'Most of the night she spent here watching; towards morning she believed that she slept for a few minutes; some steps disturbed her, and she awoke. It was dawn, and she quitted her asylum, that she might again endeavour to find my brother.' What a difference a few words make in her defence to aid in her acquittal— 'If she had gone near the spot where his body lay, it was without her knowledge. That she had been bewildered when questioned by the market-woman, was not surprising, since she had passed a sleepless night, and the fate of poor William was yet uncertain. Concerning the picture she could give no account.

' "I know," continued the unhappy victim, "how heavily and fatally this one circumstance weighs against me, but I have no power of explaining it; and when I have expressed my utter ignorance, I am only left to conjecture concerning the probabilities by which it might have been placed in my pocket. But here also I am checked. I believe that I have no enemy on earth, and none surely would have been so wicked as to destroy me wantonly. Did the murderer place it there? I know of no opportunity afforded him for so doing; or if I had, why should he have stolen the jewel, to part with it again so soon?'

Why am I seeing a scene and hearing words in my mind that are not the scene that Victor's words are relating? I hear a deep, rumbling, unnatural voice in my head say, 'While I was overcome by these feelings, I left the spot where I had committed the murder, and was seeking a more secluded hiding-place, when I perceived a woman passing near me. She was young, not indeed so beautiful as her whose portrait I held, but of an agreeable aspect, and blooming in the loveliness of youth and health. Here, I thought, is one of those whose smiles are bestowed on all but me; she shall not escape: thanks to the lessons of Felix, and the sanguinary laws of man, I have learned how to work mischief. I approached her unperceived, and placed the portrait securely in one of the folds of her dress.' Who... or what is the source of this voice speaking within the layers and layers of my conscious mind?

' "I commit my cause to the justice of my judges, yet I see no room for hope. I beg permission to have a few witnesses examined concerning my character; and if their testimony shall not overweigh my supposed guilt, I must be condemned, although I would pledge my salvation on my innocence."

'Several witnesses were called, who had known her for many years, and they spoke well of her; but fear, and hatred of the crime of which they supposed her guilty, rendered them timorous, and unwilling to come forward. Elizabeth saw even this last resource, her excellent dispositions and irreproachable conduct, about to fail the accused, when, although violently agitated, she desired permission to address the court.'

How infuriating that she must ask permission of the court to address the court! Women are not allowed to testify in the western countries whose source of jurisprudence is based on the Ancient Greeks and Romans. My own mother, Mary Wollstonecraft, fought this quite legal silencing of women throughout her far too brief life! We must no longer suffer this silencing in silence. The suffrage movement just succeed!

' "I am," said she, "the cousin of the unhappy child who was murdered, or rather his sister, for I was educated by and have lived with his parents ever since and even long before his birth. It may therefore be judged indecent in me to come forward on this occasion; but when I see a fellow-creature about to perish through the cowardice of her pretended friends, I wish to be allowed to speak, that I may say what I know of her character. I am well acquainted with the accused. I have lived in the same house with her, at one time for five, and at another for nearly two years. During all that period she appeared to me the most amiable and benevolent of human creatures. She nursed Madame Frankenstein, my aunt, in her last illness with the greatest affection and care; and afterwards attended her own mother during a tedious illness, in a manner that excited the admiration of all who knew her. After which she again lived in my uncle's house, where she was beloved by all the family. She was warmly attached to the child who is now dead, and acted towards him like a most affectionate mother. For my own part, I do not hesitate to say, that, notwithstanding all the evidence produced against her, I believe and rely on her perfect innocence. She had no temptation for such an action: as to the bauble on which the chief proof rests, if she had earnestly desired it, I should have willingly given it to her; so much do I esteem and value her."

Why am I obsessing on choice words? '*My* aunt'? '*My* uncle?' Is there a deep oedipal connect between Elizabeth and Alphonse that fuels her antipathy towards Justine? Get out of your own head, Mary. Get out of your own way!

'Excellent Elizabeth! A murmur of approbation was heard; but it was excited by her generous interference, and not in favour of poor Justine, on whom the public indignation was turned with renewed violence, charging her with the blackest ingratitude. She herself wept as Elizabeth spoke, but she did not answer. My own agitation and anguish was extreme during the whole trial. I believed in her innocence; I knew it. Could the dæmon, who had (I did not for a minute doubt) murdered my brother, also in his hellish sport have betrayed the innocent to death and ignominy.' Victor has had the same premonition that I have had! Has he heard the low, haunting voice of his Creation, too? 'I could not sustain the horror of my situation; and when I perceived that the popular voice, and the countenances of the judges, had already condemned my unhappy victim, I rushed out of the court in agony. The tortures of the accused did not equal mine; she was sustained by innocence, but the fangs of remorse tore my bosom, and would not forego their hold.

'I passed a night of unmingled wretchedness. In the morning I went to the court; my lips and throat were parched. I dared not ask the fatal question; but I was known, and the officer guessed the cause of my visit. The ballots had been thrown; they were all black, and Justine was condemned.

'I cannot pretend to describe what I then felt. I had before experienced sensations of horror; and I have endeavoured to bestow upon them adequate expressions, but words cannot convey an idea of the heart-sickening despair that I then endured. The person to whom I addressed myself added, that Justine had already confessed her guilt. "That evidence," he observed, "was hardly required in so glaring a case, but I am glad of it; and, indeed, none of our judges like to condemn a criminal upon circumstantial evidence, be it ever so decisive."

'When I returned home, Elizabeth eagerly demanded the result.

' "My cousin," replied I, "it is decided as you may have expected; all judges had rather that ten innocent should suffer, than that one guilty should escape."' — what is this nonsense that Victor speaks? Did not Benjiman Franklin, the American statesman say concerning Blackstone's Ratio, 'it is better one-hundred guilty Persons should escape than that one innocent Person should suffer'? Did not the French revolutionize the legal system proclaiming 'As every man is presumed innocent until he has been declared guilty, if it should be considered necessary to arrest him, any undue harshness that is not required to secure his person must be severely curbed by law'[94] — ' "But she has confessed."

This was a dire blow to poor Elizabeth, who had relied with firmness upon Justine's innocence. "Alas!" said she, "how shall I ever again believe in human benevolence? Justine, whom I loved and esteemed as my sister, how could she put on those smiles of innocence only to betray; her mild

---

94 From Article IX of the Declaration of the Rings of Man and of the Citizen, written in 1789.

eyes seemed incapable of any severity or ill-humour, and yet she has committed a murder."

'Soon after we heard that the poor victim had expressed a wish to see my cousin. My father wished her not to go; but said, that he left it to her own judgment and feelings to decide. "Yes," said Elizabeth, "I will go, although she is guilty; and you, Victor, shall accompany me: I cannot go alone." The idea of this visit was torture to me, yet I could not refuse.

'We entered the gloomy prison-chamber, and beheld Justine sitting on some straw at the further end; her hands were manacled, and her head rested on her knees. She rose on seeing us enter; and when we were left alone with her, she threw herself at the feet of Elizabeth, weeping bitterly. My cousin wept also.

' "Oh, Justine!" said she, "why did you rob me of my last consolation. I relied on your innocence; and although I was then very wretched, I was not so miserable as I am now."

' "And do you also believe that I am so very, very wicked? Do you also join with my enemies to crush me?" Her voice was suffocated with sobs.

' "Rise, my poor girl," said Elizabeth, "why do you kneel, if you are innocent? I am not one of your enemies; I believed you guiltless, notwithstanding every evidence, until I heard that you had yourself declared your guilt. That report, you say, is false; and be assured, dear Justine, that nothing can shake my confidence in you for a moment, but your own confession."

' "I did confess; but I confessed a lie. I confessed, that I might obtain absolution; but now that falsehood lies heavier at my heart than all my other sins. The God of heaven forgive me! Ever since I was condemned, my confessor has besieged me; he threatened and menaced, until I almost began to think that I was the monster that he said I was. He threatened excommunication and hell fire in my last moments, if I continued obdurate.'

How I loathe the Catholic Church that this sword of Damocles they hang over heads of their sycophants called excommunication. To be denied Communion with the Lord is its very construction! And Catholics still cleave to the cannibalistic intent of the Transubstantiation of bread and wine into the literal Body and Blood of Jesus the Christ. The natural philosophies will never prove this religoius fallacy to be true on a molecular level based on John Dalton's atomic theory. Transubstantiation may be found true on a superstitious level! There is no doubt in my mind, but the sciences will ultimately prevail over superstition!

' "Dear lady, I had none to support me; all looked on me as a wretch doomed to ignominy and perdition. What could I do? In an evil hour I subscribed to a lie; and now only am I truly miserable."

'She paused, weeping, and then continued— "I thought with horror, my sweet lady, that you should believe your Justine, whom your blessed aunt had so highly honoured, and whom you loved, was a creature capable of a crime which none but the devil himself could have perpetrated. Dear William! dearest blessed child! I soon shall see you again in heaven, where we shall all be happy; and that consoles me, going as I am to suffer ignominy and death."

' "Oh, Justine! forgive me for having for one moment distrusted you. Why did you confess? But do not mourn, my dear girl; I will every where proclaim your innocence, and force belief. Yet you must die; you, my playfellow, my companion, my more than sister. I never can survive so horrible a misfortune."

' "Dear, sweet Elizabeth, do not weep. You ought to raise me with thoughts of a better life, and elevate me from the petty cares of this world of injustice and strife. Do not you, excellent friend, drive me to despair."

' "I will try to comfort you; but this, I fear, is an evil too deep and poignant to admit of consolation, for there is no hope. Yet heaven bless thee, my dearest Justine, with resignation, and a confidence elevated beyond this world. Oh! how I hate its shews and mockeries! when one creature is murdered, another is immediately deprived of life in a slow torturing manner; then the executioners, their hands yet reeking with the blood of innocence, believe that they have done a great deed. They call this *retribution*."'

Why do the words of Cesare Beccaria ring in my ears? 'The war of a nation against a citizen ... It appears absurd to me that the laws, which are the expression of the public will and which detest and punish homicide, commit murder themselves, and in order to dissuade citizens from assassination, commit public assassination.'[95] Why do the words of Jean-Jacques Rouseeau likewise ring in my ears? 'There is no man so bad that he cannot be made good for something. No man should be put to death, even as an example, if he can be left to live without danger to society.'[96]

' "Hateful name! When that word is pronounced, I know greater and more horrid punishments are going to be inflicted than the gloomiest tyrant has ever invented to satiate his utmost revenge. Yet this is not consolation for you, my Justine, unless indeed that you may glory in escaping from so miserable a den. Alas! I would I were in peace with my aunt and

---

95 From *On Crimes and Punishments* by Cesare Beccaria, published in 1764.
96 From *The Social Contract* by Jean-Jacques Rousseau, published in 1762.

my lovely William, escaped from a world which is hateful to me, and the visages of men which I abhor."

'Justine smiled languidly. "This, dear lady, is despair, and not resignation. I must not learn the lesson that you would teach me. Talk of something else, something that will bring peace, and not increase of misery."

'During this conversation I had retired to a corner of the prison-room, where I could conceal the horrid anguish that possessed me. Despair! Who dared talk of that? The poor victim, who on the morrow was to pass the dreary boundary between life and death, felt not as I did, such deep and bitter agony. I gnashed my teeth, and ground them together, uttering a groan that came from my inmost soul. Justine started. When she saw who it was, she approached me, and said, "Dear Sir, you are very kind to visit me; you, I hope, do not believe that I am guilty."

'I could not answer. "No, Justine," said Elizabeth; "he is more convinced of your innocence than I was; for even when he heard that you had confessed, he did not credit it."

' "I truly thank him. In these last moments I feel the sincerest gratitude towards those who think of me with kindness. How sweet is the affection of others to such a wretch as I am! It removes more than half my misfortune; and I feel as if I could die in peace, now that my innocence is acknowledged by you, dear lady, and your cousin."

'Thus the poor sufferer tried to comfort others and herself. She indeed gained the resignation she desired. But I, the true murderer, felt the never-dying worm alive in my bosom, which allowed of no hope or consolation. Elizabeth also wept, and was unhappy; but her's also was the misery of innocence, which, like a cloud that passes over the fair moon, for a while hides, but cannot tarnish its brightness. Anguish and despair had penetrated into the core of my heart; I bore a hell within me, which nothing could extinguish. We staid several hours with Justine; and it was with great difficulty that Elizabeth could tear herself away. "I wish," cried she, "that I were to die with you; I cannot live in this world of misery."

'Justine assumed an air of cheerfulness, while she with difficulty repressed her bitter tears. She embraced Elizabeth, and said, in a voice of half-suppressed emotion, "Farewell, sweet lady, dearest Elizabeth, my beloved and only friend; may heaven in its bounty bless and preserve you; may this be the last misfortune that you will ever suffer. Live, and be happy, and make others so."

My mind heard the next words that Victor spoke, but my own mind revised the words into something else... something more. I needed the consolation that this revision brought to my mind, lest the suffering of Justine be insufferable to me.

'And on the morrow Justine died. Elizabeth's heart-rending eloquence failed to move the judges from their settled conviction in the criminality of the saintly sufferer. My passionate and indignant appeals were lost upon them. And when I received their cold answers, and heard the harsh unfeeling reasoning of these men, my purposed avowal died away on my lips. Thus I might proclaim myself a madman, but not revoke the sentence passed upon my wretched victim. She perished on the scaffold as a murderess!

'From the tortures of my own heart, I turned to contemplate the deep and voiceless grief of my Elizabeth. This also was my doing! And my father's woe, and the desolation of that late so smiling home—all was the work of my thrice-accursed hands! Ye weep, unhappy ones; but these are not your last tears! Again shall you raise the funeral wail, and the sound of your lamentations shall again and again be heard! Frankenstein, your son, your kinsman, your early, much-loved friend; he who would spend each vital drop of blood for your sakes—who has no thought nor sense of joy, except as it is mirrored also in your dear countenances—who would fill the air with blessings, and spend his life in serving you—he bids you weep—to shed countless tears; happy beyond his hopes, if thus inexorable fate be satisfied, and if the destruction pause before the peace of the grave have succeeded to your sad torments!

'Thus spoke my prophetic soul, as, torn by remorse, horror, and despair, I beheld those I loved spend vain sorrow upon the graves of William and Justine, the first hapless victims to my unhallowed arts.'

Chapter IV

Nothing is more painful to the human mind, than, after the feelings have been worked up by a quick succession of events, the dead calmness of inaction and certainty which follows, and deprives the soul both of hope and fear. Justine died; she rested; and I was alive. The blood flowed freely in my veins, but a weight of despair and remorse pressed on my heart, which nothing could remove. Sleep fled from my eyes; I wandered like an evil spirit, for I had committed deeds of mischief beyond description horrible, and more, much more, (I persuaded myself) was yet behind. Yet my heart overflowed with kindness, and the love of virtue. I had begun life with benevolent intentions, and thirsted for the moment when I should put them in practice, and make myself useful to my fellow-beings. Now all was blasted: instead of that serenity of conscience, which allowed me to look back upon the past with self-satisfaction, and from thence to gather promise of new hopes, I was seized by remorse and the sense of guilt, which hurried me away to a hell of intense tortures, such as no language can describe.

'This state of mind preyed upon my health, which had entirely re-covered from the first shock it had sustained. I shunned the face of man; all sound of joy or complacency was torture to me; solitude was my only consolation— deep, dark, death-like solitude.

'My father observed with pain the alteration perceptible in my dis-position and habits, and endeavoured to reason with me on the folly of giving way to immoderate grief. "Do you think, Victor," said he, "that I do not suffer also? No one could love a child more than I loved your brother;" (tears came into his eyes as he spoke); "but is it not a duty to the survivors, that we should refrain from augmenting their unhappiness by an appearance of immoderate grief? It is also a duty owed to yourself; for excessive sorrow prevents improvement or enjoyment, or even the discharge of daily usefulness, without which no man is fit for society."

'This advice, although good, was totally inapplicable to my case; I should have been the first to hide my grief, and console my friends, if remorse had not mingled its bitterness with my other sensations. Now I could only answer my father with a look of despair, and endeavour to hide myself from his view.

'About this time we retired to our house at Belrive. This change was particularly agreeable to me. The shutting of the gates regularly at ten o'clock, and the impossibility of remaining on the lake after that hour, had rendered our residence within the walls of Geneva very irksome to me. I was now free. Often, after the rest of the family had retired for the night, I took the boat, and passed many hours upon the water. Some-times, with my sails set, I was carried by the wind; and sometimes, after rowing into the middle of the lake, I left the boat to pursue its own course, and gave way to my own miserable reflections. I was often tempted, when all was at peace around me, and I the only unquiet thing that wandered restless in a scene so beautiful and heavenly, if I except some bat, or the frogs, whose harsh and interrupted croaking was heard only when I ap-proached the shore— often, I say, I was tempted to plunge into the silent lake, that the waters might close over me and my calamities for ever.'

No! Victor! That is the solution permanent to a problem tempo-rary. I know better than most the loss of a child! While Victor did carry the life of his brother in his heart, he did not carry the life of his brother in his womb as I had my nameless, unbaptized daughter. There is a certain pain, a longing that aches in my belly like an amputated solider who still feels the unscratchable tickle of an itch in the phantom limb. I still feel the ghostly kicks of my daughter in my belly and her phantom suckling at my breast! It is a pain that will prove to be eternal.

'But I was restrained, when I thought of the heroic and suffering Elizabeth, whom I tenderly loved, and whose existence was bound up in mine. I thought also of my father, and surviving brother: should I by my base desertion leave them exposed and unprotected to the malice of the fiend whom I had let loose among them?'

But the pain that I do not possess is the pain that your Creation may be the cause of death. I cast a glance at my sweet William sleeping in his bassinette and I wonder and ponder what I would do, if at some point during his life I sit in a courtroom with my child accused of murder... or worse. To know that that evil had grown in my womb; that I had nourished that evil with my own blood and milk would be a torture unimaginable! And if this Creation is guilty as Victor believes? Inconsolable would I be.

'At these moments I wept bitterly, and wished that peace would revisit my mind only that I might afford them consolation and happiness. But that could not be. Remorse extinguished every hope. I had been the author of unalterable evils; and I lived in daily fear, lest the monster whom I had created should perpetrate some new wickedness. I had an obscure feeling that all was not over, and that he would still commit some signal crime, which by its enormity should almost efface the recollection of the past. There was always scope for fear, so long as any thing I loved remained behind. My abhorrence of this fiend cannot be conceived. When I thought of him, I gnashed my teeth, my eyes became inflamed, and I ardently wished to extinguish that life which I had so thoughtlessly bestowed. When I reflected on his crimes and malice, my hatred and revenge burst all bounds of moderation. I would have made a pilgrimage to the highest peak of the Andes, could I, when there, have precipitated him to their base. I wished to see him again, that I might wreak the utmost extent of anger on his head, and avenge the deaths of William and Justine.

'Our house was the house of mourning. My father's health was deeply shaken by the horror of the recent events. Elizabeth was sad and desponding; she no longer took delight in her ordinary occupations; all pleasure seemed to her sacrilege toward the dead; eternal woe and tears she then thought was the just tribute she should pay to innocence so blasted and destroyed. She was no longer that happy creature, who in earlier youth wandered with me on the banks of the lake, and talked with ecstacy of our future prospects. She had become grave, and often conversed of the inconstancy of fortune, and the instability of human life.

' "When I reflect, my dear cousin," said she, "on the miserable death of Justine Martin, I no longer see the world and its works as they before appeared to me. Before, I looked upon the accounts of vice and injustice, that I read in books or heard from others, as tales of ancient days, or imaginary evils; at least they were remote, and more familiar to reason than to the imagination; but now misery has come home, and men appear to me as monsters thirsting for each other's blood. Yet I am certainly unjust. Every body believed that poor girl to be guilty; and if she could have committed the crime for which she suffered, assuredly she would have been the most depraved of human creatures. For the sake of a few jewels, to have murdered the son of her benefactor and friend, a child whom she had nursed from its birth, and appeared to love as if it had been her own! I could not consent to the death of any human being; but certainly I should have thought such a creature unfit to remain in the society of men. Yet she was innocent. I know, I feel she was innocent; you are of the same opinion, and that confirms me. Alas! Victor, when falsehood can look so like the truth, who can assure themselves of certain happiness? I feel as if I were walking on the edge of a precipice, towards which thousands are crowding, and endeavouring to plunge me into the abyss. William and Justine were assassinated, and the murderer escapes; he walks about the world free, and perhaps respected. But even if I were condemned to suffer on the scaffold for the same crimes, I would not change places with such a wretch."

'I listened to this discourse with the extremest agony.' As did I, my pale student of the unhallowed arts, ' I, not in deed, but in effect, was the true murderer. Elizabeth read my anguish in my countenance, and kindly taking my hand said, "My dearest cousin, you must calm yourself. These events have affected me, God knows how deeply; but I am not so wretched as you are. There is an expression of despair, and sometimes of revenge, in your countenance, that makes me tremble. Be calm, my dear Victor; I would sacrifice my life to your peace. We surely shall be happy: quiet in our native country, and not mingling in the world, what can disturb our tranquillity?"

'She shed tears as she said this'— as did I, my pale student of the unhallowed arts — 'distrusting the very solace that she gave; but at the same time she smiled, that she might chase away the fiend that lurked in my heart. My father, who saw in the unhappiness that was painted in my face only an exaggeration of that sorrow which I might naturally feel, thought that an amusement suited to my taste would be the best means of restoring to me my wonted serenity. It was from this cause that he had removed to the country; and, induced by the same motive, he now proposed that we should all make an excursion to the valley of Chamounix.'

Would I read, in another lifetime, in a handbook for travellers stern warnings that 'these retired wilds, amidst the most sublime scenery in nature. And at the foot of the loftiest mountain of Europe, where thousands have made their pilgrimage. Unlike other places, merely fashionable, and crowded by idlers, no extent of participation can lessen the sublime emotions and impressions made by the scenery of the vale of

Chamouny. The route form Geneva is so much frequented by strangers in this season, that it is beset by all sorts of vagabonds, who plant themselves in the way openly as beggars, or covertly as dealers in mineral specimens, guides to thing which do not require their aid, dealers in echoes, by firing small cannon where its reverberation may be heard two or three times. These idle nuisances should be discountenanced.'[97]

'I had been there before, but Elizabeth and Ernest never had; and both had often expressed an earnest desire to see the scenery of this place, which had been described to them as so wonderful and sublime. Accordingly we departed from Geneva on this tour about the middle of the month of August, nearly two months after the death of Justine.

'The weather was uncommonly fine; and if mine had been a sorrow to be chased away by any fleeting circumstance, this excursion would certainly have had the effect intended by my father. As it was, I was somewhat interested in the scene; it sometimes lulled, although it could not extinguish my grief.

'During the first day we travelled in a carriage. In the morning we had seen the mountains at a distance, towards which we gradually advanced. We perceived that the valley through which we wound, and which was formed by the river Arve, whose course we followed, closed in upon us by degrees; and when the sun had set, we beheld immense mountains and precipices overhanging us on every side, and heard the sound of the river raging among rocks, and the dashing of water-falls around.

'The next day we pursued our journey upon mules. And as we ascended still higher, the valley assumed a more magnificent and astonishing character. Ruined castles hanging on the precipices of piny mountains; the impetuous Arve, and cottages every here and there peeping forth from among the trees, formed a scene of singular beauty. But it was augmented and rendered sublime by the mighty Alps, whose white and shining pyramids and domes towered above all, as belonging to another earth, the habitations of another race of beings.

'We passed the bridge of Pelissier, where the ravine, which the river forms, opened before us, and we began to ascend the mountain that overhangs it.'

Again, I recall observations mad during a residence in Switzerland and Auvergne that I have not myself made of the Pont Pelissier, a bridge over the Arve 'crosses this river a little below the sot where it issues from one of the most striking chasms or gorges in the Alps. On the eastern side are slate rocks of amazing height, nearly perpendicular, their summits, and feet ornaments with pine-trees; and, on the western side, there is a granitic mountain over which, the road is carried. The river Arve, a

---

97 From *Handbook for Travellers in Switzerland* by John Murray, published in 1838.

large and impetuous torrent, rushes between these two ranges of rocks, and towering over the whole, the snows of Mount Blânc are seen in dazzling whiteness, which, contrasted with the dark blue of the sky, almost overpowers the sight.'[98]

'Soon after we entered the valley of Chamounix. This valley is more wonderful and sublime, but not so beautiful and picturesque as that of Servox, through which we had just passed. The high and snowy mountains were its immediate boundaries; but we saw no more ruined castles and fertile fields. Immense glaciers approached the road; we heard the rumbling thunder of the falling avalanche, and marked the smoke of its passage. Mont Blânc, the supreme and magnificent Mont Blânc, raised itself from the surrounding *aiguilles*, and its tremendous *dome* overlooked the valley.

'During this journey, I sometimes joined Elizabeth, and exerted myself to point out to her the various beauties of the scene. I often suffered my mule to lag behind, and indulged in the misery of reflection. At other times I spurred on the animal before my companions, that I might forget them, the world, and, more than all, myself. When at a distance, I alighted, and threw myself on the grass, weighed down by horror and despair. At eight in the evening I arrived at Chamounix. My father and Elizabeth were very much fatigued; Ernest, who accompanied us, was delighted, and in high spirits: the only circumstance that detracted from his pleasure was the south wind, and the rain it seemed to promise for the next day.

'We retired early to our apartments, but not to sleep; at least I did not. I remained many hours at the window, watching the pallid lightning that played above Mont Blânc, and listening to the rushing of the Arve, which ran below my window.'

Chapter V

The next day, contrary to the prognostications of our guides, was fine, although clouded. We visited the source of the Arveiron, and rode about the valley until evening. These sublime and magnificent scenes afforded me the greatest consolation that I was capable of receiving. They elevated me from all littleness of feeling; and although they did not remove my grief, they subdued and tranquillized it. In some degree, also, they diverted my mind from the thoughts over which it had brooded for the last month. I returned in the evening, fatigued, but less unhappy, and conversed with my family with more cheerfulness than

---

98 From *Travels, Comprising Observations Made During a Residence in the Tarentaise and Various Parts of the Grecians and Pennine Alps, and in Switzerland and Auvergne, in the years 1820, 1821, and 1822* by Robert Bakewell, published in 1823.

had been my custom for some time. My father was pleased, and Elizabeth overjoyed. "My dear cousin," said she, "you see what happiness you diffuse when you are happy; do not relapse again!"

'The following morning the rain poured down in torrents, and thick mists hid the summits of the mountains. I rose early, but felt unusually melancholy. The rain depressed me; my old feelings recurred, and I was miserable. I knew how disappointed my father would be at this sudden change, and I wished to avoid him until I had recovered myself so far as to be enabled to conceal those feelings that overpowered me. I knew that they would remain that day at the inn; and as I had ever inured myself to rain, moisture, and cold, I resolved to go alone to the summit of Montanvert.'

My mind returned to travelogues, which are all the rage in modern literature (I should know, I and my Beloved wish to publish one: 'On the other side of the valley of the Arveiron rises the immense glacier of Montanvert, fifty miles in extent, occupying a chasm among mountains of inconceivable heigh, and of forms so point and abrupt that they seem to piece the sky. From this glacier we saw as we sat on a rock, close to one of the streams of the Arveiron, Masses of ice detach themselves from on high, and rush with a loud dull noise into the vale. The violence of their fall turned them into powder, which flowed over the rocks in imitation of waterfalls, whose ravines they usurped and filled.'[99]

'I remembered the effect that the view of the tremendous and ever-moving glacier had produced upon my mind when I first saw it. It had then filled me with a sublime ecstacy that gave wings to the soul, and allowed it to soar from the obscure world to light and joy. The sight of the awful and majestic in nature had indeed always the effect of solemnizing my mind, and causing me to forget the passing cares of life. I determined to go alone, for I was well acquainted with the path, and the presence of another would destroy the solitary grandeur of the scene.'

How I wish to see Montanvert with my own eyes! I must endeavour to persuade my Beloved to undertake an excursion to the glacier! The journey will prove excellent material for our own travelogue.

'The ascent is precipitous, but the path is cut into continual and short windings, which enable you to surmount the perpendicularity of the mountain. It is a scene terrifically desolate. In a thousand spots the traces of the winter avalanche may be perceived, where trees lie broken and strewed on the ground; some entirely destroyed, others bent, leaning upon the jutting rocks of the mountain, or transversely upon other trees. The path, as you ascend higher, is intersected by ravines of snow, down which stones continually roll from above; one of them is particu-

---

99 From *Handbook for Travellers in Switzerland* by John Murray, published in 1838.

larly dangerous, as the slightest sound, such as even speaking in a loud voice, produces a concussion of air sufficient to draw destruction upon the head of the speaker. The pines are not tall or luxuriant, but they are sombre, and add an air of severity to the scene. I looked on the valley beneath; vast mists were rising from the rivers which ran through it, and curling in thick wreaths around the opposite mountains, whose summits were hid in the uniform clouds, while rain poured from the dark sky, and added to the melancholy impression I received from the objects around me.'

Curious how my pale student of the unhallowed arts describes this setting to me in such exquisite detail, when I, the source of his existence, have not yet laid my eyes upon the sights! Curiouser and curiouer!

'Alas! why does man boast of sensibilities superior to those apparent in the brute; it only renders them more necessary beings. If our impulses were confined to hunger, thirst, and desire, we might be nearly free; but now we are moved by every wind that blows, and a chance word or scene that that word may convey to us.

> *We rest; a dream has power to poison sleep.*
> *We rise; one wand'ring thought pollutes the day.*
> *We feel, conceive, or reason; laugh, or weep,*
> *Embrace fond woe, or cast our cares away;*
> *It is the same: for, be it joy or sorrow,*
> *The path of its departure still is free.*
> *Man's yesterday may ne'er be like his morrow;*

Nought may endure but mutability!'

Where have I heard these words spoken by my dearest Victor? I know the source! But I know not how Victor comes to possess the knowledge of these words? They come from the most innermost recesses of my own mind. These words are words that I heard upon their composition by my Beloved and only published by Baldwin, Cradock, and Joy in London this very year. Curiously, they have found themselves on the lips of a phantasm relating events that take their place decades previous to my own. My dearest, Journal, shall I reprint the poem in its entirety? For posterity's sake, I shall.

> *We are as clouds that veil the midnight moon;*
> *How restlessly they speed, and gleam, and quiver,*
> *Streaking the darkness radiantly!—yet soon*
> *Night closes round, and they are lost forever:*

Or like forgotten lyres, whose dissonant strings
Give various response to each varying blast,
To whose frail frame no second motion brings
One mood or modulation like the last.

We rest.—A dream has power to poison sleep;
We rise.—One wandering thought pollutes the day;
We feel, conceive or reason, laugh or weep;
Embrace fond woe, or cast our cares away:

It is the same!—For, be it joy or sorrow,
The path of its departure still is free:
Man's yesterday may ne'er be like his morrow;
Nought may endure but mutability![100]

'It was nearly noon when I arrived at the top of the ascent. For some time I sat upon the rock that overlooks the sea of ice. A mist covered both that and the surrounding mountains. Presently a breeze dissipated the cloud, and I descended upon the glacier. The surface is very uneven, rising like the waves of a troubled sea, descending low, and interspersed by rifts that sink deep. The field of ice is almost a league in width, but I spent nearly two hours in crossing it. The opposite mountain is a bare perpendicular rock. From the side where I now stood Montanvert was exactly opposite, at the distance of a league; and above it rose Mont Blânc, in awful majesty. I remained in a recess of the rock, gazing on this wonderful and stupendous scene. The sea, or rather the vast river of ice, wound among its dependent mountains, whose aërial summits hung over its recesses. Their icy and glittering peaks shone in the sunlight over the clouds. My heart, which was before sorrowful, now swelled with something like joy; I exclaimed— "Wandering spirits, if indeed ye wander, and do not rest in your narrow beds, allow me this faint happiness, or take me, as your companion, away from the joys of life."

'As I said this, I suddenly beheld the figure of a man, at some distance, advancing towards me with superhuman speed. He bounded over the crevices in the ice, among which I had walked with caution; his stature also, as he approached, seemed to exceed that of man. I was troubled: a mist came over my eyes, and I felt a faintness seize me; but I was quickly restored by the cold gale of the mountains. I perceived, as the shape came nearer, (sight tremendous and abhorred!) that it was the wretch whom I had created. I trembled with rage and horror, resolving to wait his approach, and then close with him in mortal combat.

100 From *Alastor, or The Spirit of Solitude: And Other Poems* by Percy Bysshe Shelley in 1816.

He approached; his countenance bespoke bitter anguish, combined with disdain and malignity, while its unearthly ugliness rendered it almost too horrible for human eyes. But I scarcely observed this; anger— nay! rage— and hatred had at first deprived me of utterance, and I recovered only to overwhelm him with words expressive of furious detestation and contempt.

' "Devil!" I exclaimed, "do you dare approach me? and do not you fear the fierce vengeance of my arm wreaked on your miserable head? Begone, vile insect! or rather stay, that I may trample you to dust! and, oh, that I could, with the extinction of your miserable existence, restore those victims whom you have so diabolically murdered!"

' "I expected this reception," said the dæmon. "All men hate the wretched; how then must I be hated, who am miserable beyond all living things! Yet you, my creator, detest and spurn me, thy creature, to whom thou art bound by ties only dissoluble by the annihilation of one of us. You purpose to kill me. How dare you sport thus with life? Do your duty towards me, and I will do mine towards you and the rest of mankind. If you will comply with my conditions, I will leave them and you at peace; but if you refuse, I will glut the maw of death, until it be satiated with the blood of your remaining friends."

' "Abhorred monster! fiend that thou art! the tortures of hell are too mild a vengeance for thy crimes. Wretched devil! you reproach me with your creation; come on then, that I may extinguish the spark which I so negligently bestowed."

'My rage was without bounds; I sprang on him, impelled by all the feelings which can arm one being against the existence of another.

'He easily eluded me, and said,

' "Be calm! I entreat you to hear me, before you give vent to your hatred on my devoted head. Have I not suffered enough, that you seek to increase my misery? Life, although it may only be an accumulation of anguish, is dear to me, and I will defend it. Remember, thou hast made me more powerful than thyself; my height is superior to thine; my joints more supple. But I will not be tempted to set myself in opposition to thee. I am thy creature, and I will be even mild and docile to my natural lord and king, if thou wilt also perform thy part, the which thou owest me. Oh, Frankenstein, be not equitable to every other, and trample upon me alone, to whom thy justice, and even thy clemency and affection, is most due. Remember, that I am thy creature: I ought to be thy Adam; but I am rather the fallen angel, whom thou drivest from joy for no misdeed. Every where I see bliss, from which I alone am irrevocably excluded. I was benevolent and good; misery made me a fiend. Make me happy, and I shall again be virtuous."'

How and by what source did this Creation come to be so articulate? By what means did a creature born from a deceased— and perchance diseased— brain retain or regain its intellect! Curiouser and curiouser. I feel myself physically and literally leaning into this tale of Victor's. I can only hope and pray that I can hear the Creation's own tale.

‘ "Begone! I will not hear you. There can be no community between you and me; we are enemies. Begone, or let us try our strength in a fight, in which one must fall."

‘ "How can I move thee? Will no entreaties cause thee to turn a favourable eye upon thy creature, who implores thy goodness and compassion? Believe me, Frankenstein: I was benevolent; my soul glowed with love and humanity: but am I not alone, miserably alone? You, my creator, abhor me; what hope can I gather from your fellow-creatures, who owe me nothing? they spurn and hate me. The desert mountains and dreary glaciers are my refuge. I have wandered here many days; the caves of ice, which I only do not fear, are a dwelling to me, and the only one which man does not grudge. These bleak skies I hail, for they are kinder to me than your fellow-beings. If the multitude of mankind knew of my existence, they would do as you do, and arm themselves for my destruction. Shall I not then hate them who abhor me? I will keep no terms with my enemies. I am miserable, and they shall share my wretchedness. Yet it is in your power to recompense me, and deliver them from an evil which it only remains for you to make so great, that not only you and your family, but thousands of others, shall be swallowed up in the whirlwinds of its rage. Let your compassion be moved, and do not disdain me. Listen to my tale.'

Hazzah! My hopes and prayers have been answered so quickly. But how will Victor relate the tale of his Creation to me? Will it be a tale within a tale? Or perchance I can hope and pray again that the Creation itself visits me in as equal a phantasmagorical conversation as I may presently having with my pale student of the unhallowed arts. Hopes and prayers.

'When you have heard that, abandon or commiserate me, as you shall judge that I deserve. But hear me. The guilty are allowed, by human laws, bloody as they may be, to speak in their own defence before they are condemned. Listen to me, Frankenstein. You accuse me of murder; and yet you would, with a satisfied conscience, destroy your own creature. Oh, praise the eternal justice of man! Yet I ask you not to spare me: listen to me; and then, if you can, and if you will, destroy the work of your hands."

‘ "Why do you call to my remembrance circumstances of which I shudder to reflect, that I have been the miserable origin and author?

Cursed be the day, abhorred devil, in which you first saw light! Cursed (although I curse myself) be the hands that formed you! You have made me wretched beyond expression. You have left me no power to consider whether I am just to you, or not. Begone! relieve me from the sight of your detested form."

' "Thus I relieve thee, my creator," he said, and placed his hated hands before my eyes, which I flung from me with violence; "thus I take from thee a sight which you abhor. Still thou canst listen to me, and grant me thy compassion. By the virtues that I once possessed, I demand this from you. Hear my tale; it is long and strange, and the temperature of this place is not fitting to your fine sensations; come to the hut upon the mountain. The sun is yet high in the heavens; before it descends to hide itself behind yon snowy precipices, and illuminate another world, you will have heard my story, and can decide. On you it rests, whether I quit for ever the neighbourhood of man, and lead a harmless life, or become the scourge of your fellow-creatures, and the author of your own speedy ruin."

'As he said this, he led the way across the ice: I followed. My heart was full, and I did not answer him; but, as I proceeded, I weighed the various arguments that he had used, and determined at least to listen to his tale. I was partly urged by curiosity, and compassion confirmed my resolution. I had hitherto supposed him to be the murderer of my brother, and I eagerly sought a confirmation or denial of this opinion. For the first time, also, I felt what the duties of a creator towards his creature were, and that I ought to render him happy before I complained of his wickedness. These motives urged me to comply with his demand. We crossed the ice, therefore, and ascended the opposite rock. The air was cold, and the rain again began to descend: we entered the hut, the fiend with an air of exultation, I with a heavy heart, and depressed spirits.'

I no longer wish to be haunted by my pale student of the unhallowed arts. I am done with him! His soul is as rotten and worm infested as an apple left on the windowsill to fester in the sun. My pale student of the unhallowed arts, whom I longed to know more about from our first chance encounter during that thunderstorm-and-lightning-fuelled nightmare after a spirited and galvanising debate, was shown to me to be nothing more than failed student with a hollow heart.

But I do wish to know what the story of his Creation is. How did he become so esteemingly articulate and so seemingly wise? What manner of education did this Creation have? Was he 'born' with the innate knowledge of language which having survived death was born again in this new form through the alchemical and forbidden processes created by my pale student of the unhallowed arts.

THESE ARE ANSWERS I MUST KNOW!

How a Game of Ghost Stories Gives Birth To A Strange Birth To Frankenstein

July–August 1816

1 — P. presents 1st part of "feverishly" written "Modern Oedipus."

2 — The pale student returns to tells of his Abandonment of the Creature.

3

4

5

6

7 — The Creation visits M. to tell of his Education

8 — E. arrives. Begins haunting P.

9 — E. begins haunting B., convincing him that P. is a plagiarist.

10 — E. continues haunting both P. & B. manipulating them.

11 — P. disappears for the weekend with the Countess Erzsébet.

12 — P. begins writing The Vampyre at her request in the morning.

13

14 — P. completes The Vampyre. Pale student is silent.

15 — E. arrives back & gives the manuscript of The Vampyre to B.

16 — B. writes his Monody on the Death of the R.B. Sheridan

17

18 — B. reads "The Darkness" the day an Italian astronomer said the sun dies.

19

20 — P. is forced at gunpoint to read his plagiarism: "The Vampyre!"

21 — The Shelleys set out for the glacier.

22

23 — M. receives the "Letters" from the Arctic.

24

25

26

27 — The Shelleys return from the glacier.

29 — B. presents Child Harold's Pilgrimage (3rd Canto)

30

31

Aug. 29 — The Shelleys & C. set off to return to London.

Chapter Eleven
Frankenstein[1]
(The Education of the Creature)

Mary Wollstonecraft Godwin's Journal

7 July. After First Sleep— The nightmare was formed like rolling, ominous dark storm clouds of recollection, but not my own memories, but those of my pale student of the unhallowed arts. In the dream, I saw his world through his own eyes: The moon gazed on my midnight labours, while, with unrelaxed and breathless eagerness, I pursued nature to her hiding places. Who shall conceive the horrors of my secret toil, as I dabbled among the unhallowed damps of the grave, or tortured the living animal to animate the lifeless clay? My limbs now tremble, and my eyes swim with the remembrance; but then a resistless, and almost frantic impulse, urged me forward; I seemed to have lost all soul or sensation but for this one pursuit. It was indeed but a passing trance, that only made me feel with renewed acuteness so soon as, the unnatural stimulus ceasing to operate, I had returned to my old habits. I collected bones from charnel houses; and disturbed, with profane fingers, the tremendous secrets of the human frame.

In a solitary chamber, or rather cell, at the top of the house, and separated from all the other apartments by a gallery and staircase, I kept my workshop of filthy creation; my eyeballs were starting from their sockets in attending to the details of my employment. The dissecting room and the slaughter-house furnished many of my materials; and often did my human nature turn with loathing from my occupation, whilst, still urged on by an eagerness which perpetually increased, I brought my work near to a conclusion.

It was on a dreary night of November, that I beheld the accomplishment of my toils. With an anxiety that almost amounted to agony, I collected the instruments of life around me, that I might infuse a spark of being into the lifeless thing that lay at my feet. It was already one in the morning; the rain pattered dismally against the panes, and my can-

---

1 From *Frankenstein; or the Modern Prometheus* by Mary Wollstonecraft Shelley, published by Lackington, Hughes, Harding, Mavor & Jones, 1818

dle was nearly burnt out, when, by the glimmer of the half-extinguished light, I saw the dull yellow eye of the creature open; it breathed hard, and a convulsive motion agitated its limbs.

How can I describe my emotions at this catastrophe, or how delineate the wretch whom with such infinite pains and care I had endeavoured to form? His limbs were in proportion, and I had selected his features as beautiful. Beautiful!—Great God! His yellow skin scarcely covered the work of muscles and arteries beneath; his hair was of a lustrous black, and flowing; his teeth of a pearly whiteness; but these luxuriances only formed a more horrid contrast with his watery eyes, that seemed almost of the same colour as the dun white sockets in which they were set, his shrivelled complexion, and straight black lips.

The different accidents of life are not so changeable as the feelings of human nature. I had worked hard for nearly two years, for the sole purpose of infusing life into an inanimate body. For this I had deprived myself of rest and health. I had desired it with an ardour that far exceeded moderation; but now that I had finished, the beauty of the dream vanished, and breathless horror and disgust filled my heart. Unable to endure the aspect of the being I had created, I rushed out of the room, and continued a long time traversing my bed-chamber, unable to compose my mind to sleep. At length lassitude succeeded to the tumult I had before endured; and I threw myself on the bed in my clothes, endeavouring to seek a few moments of forgetfulness. But it was in vain: I slept indeed, but I was disturbed by the wildest dreams. I thought I saw Elizabeth, in the bloom of health, walking in the streets of Ingolstadt. Delighted and surprised, I embraced her; but as I imprinted the first kiss on her lips, they became livid with the hue of death; her features appeared to change, and I thought that I held the corpse of my dead mother in my arms; a shroud enveloped her form, and I saw the grave-worms crawling in the folds of the flannel. I started from my sleep with horror; a cold dew covered my forehead, my teeth chattered, and every limb became convulsed; when, by the dim and yellow light of the moon, as it forced its way through the window-shutters, I beheld the wretch—the miserable monster whom I had created. He held up the curtain of the bed; and his eyes, if eyes they may be called, were fixed on me. His jaws opened, and he muttered some inarticulate sounds, while a grin wrinkled his cheeks. He might have spoken, but I did not hear; one hand was stretched out, seemingly to detain me, but I escaped, and rushed down stairs. I took refuge in the court-yard belonging to the house which I inhabited; where I remained during the rest of the night, walking up and down in the greatest agitation, listening attentively, catching and fearing each sound as if it were to announce the approach of the demoniacal corpse to which I had so miserably given life.

Oh! no mortal could support the horror of that countenance. A mummy again endued with animation could not be so hideous as that wretch. I had gazed on him while unfinished; he was ugly then; but when those muscles and joints were rendered capable of motion, it became a thing such as even Dante could not have conceived.

I awoke with a start. Bolt upright in bed, sweat staining my sheets, however cliché that scene is in the modern day. I had fallen asleep but for a handful of minutes. Curious to experience days turned into weeks turned into months all in less time than it takes to prepare a small meal.

7 July. The Small Hours— As the witching hour approached, I saw not my pale student of the unhallowed arts. Why does he continue to continuously fail to appear unto me as a phantasm as he had over those two long, cold, evenings: one a week ago and the other a fortnight prior to this. I do not wish him to go missing. I have cajoled my Beloved plotting and planning an expedition to the glacier at Mer de Glace. I wish to visit the very place my pale student met his Creation. It is all that I speak of. In but a fortnight shalt we begin our expedition, and I will see the ice fields myself! It is my own fault that my pale student had grown as silence as the grave. I and my Beloved and our silent Little Lord and dearest Claire made our eight-day tour just as he was beginning his tale. But the tour was a necessity due to the briefest of respites from the thunderous storms that had imprisoned myself and my friends in our palatial prison called the Villa Diodati. My pale student two days whence we made our return returned to tell me of his abandonment of his Creation. Such a harrowing and horrifying tale. But for a week, he has unable to visit me. I require his conversation as I need to draw breath; I require the transcription of his tale as I need my heart to pulse blood through my veins. I pray he is unable to visit me due to the unwritten and unknowable requirements of being a phantasm, but not by his free will. Why did he leave off on such a tremendous ending, which was no ending at all. He tale could not have been completed. I forbid it!

I tossed and turned in fitful slumber. I could not bring myself to look into his corner where his armchair remained unmoved and unmovable. My Beloved once moved the chair to be closer to the fire and I chastised him greatly. He sulkingly returned to the chair to his previous location. Why was I being so hysterical? I buried my face into the down pillow unable and unwilling to cast my eyes upon an empty chair. I silently wept.

Then I heard the chair move.

My pale student had returned! I bolted upright in bed and turned towards the chair seated in the corner of the bedchamber to see not my pale student, but his Creation! My pale student continued to abandon me! But why had his Creation taken his place in the chair? I dared not speak. The Creation dared not to speak either.

My pale student's description from his pales in comparison to the reality. Where he described having selected his features 'beautiful', the features are in reality 'grotesque'. True his yellow skin scarcely covers the work of muscles and arteries beneath; his hair is of a lustrous black and flowing; his teeth of a pearly whiteness. True, his watery eyes, that seemed almost of the same colour as the dun white sockets in which they were set, his shrivelled complexion and straight black lips. But my pale student proved to be a most accomplished unreliable narrator. Victor had minimized the extent slaugher-houses were the source of his flesh and bones.

In the regions surrounding Ingolstadt, even counting for his wandering far and wide, he would have encountered few human cadavers suffering from gigantism, let alone the multitude required to form his Creation from the requisite parts. Did he saw and assemble multiple *femurs* to create a single one with the proper proportions he sought? Did he do the same with the *tibias* and *fibulas*, the *humeri* and the *ulnas* and *radii*? How many *vertebrae* are in his Creation? Surely more than the human thirty-three. How was the rib cage fashioned?

Seeing his Creation in the flesh, or as a phantasm as the case may be, I saw Victor's fullest utilization of slaughter-houses. True, the right side of the Creations face appears remarkably human, probably sourced from a cadaver suffering from *macrocephaly*, or an enlarged head. But the macrocephalic skull may not have been complete, perhaps having been damaged through violence in life, so Victor was forced to substitute half of the frontal and the left parietal bone, orbital socket, and zygomatic bone with those from a bull. The eye itself appears human sourced, but the bones are clearly bovine. Victor has sawn the horn off to give this Creation a much more human silhouette. The jawbone appears, at first glance, to be from an orangutan, but the teeth are much more human in appearance. Perhaps, Victor took the time for post-mortem dental work. As for the limbs and rib cage, I believe that, while *bovines* could have been the source, I believe Victor sourced equines. The bones of the horse are the most humanlike between the two desperate species. The hands were the hands of a mountain gorilla, though through Victor's surgical skills refined for human dexterity.

Except for the brain, the internal organs of his Creation will be forever a mystery to me. I wonder if they were too as veraciously drawn from the slaugher-houses. Along with the bovine and equine, he could have sourced the ovine and the caprine and the swine. But as for the, no doubt, human brain, even one sourced from a non-macrocephalic skull, could have been utilized with minimal alteration. Perhaps Victor packed additional fat into the brainbox.

The clothing that his Creation wore, very modern and fashionable, was a patchwork of the stitching of several men's shirts, vests, jackets, and trousers together to clothe his massive frame. The stitchwork of his clothing eerily mirrored the Victor's stitchwork of his flesh. His shoes, monstrous in size, seemed cobbled together (no pun intended) likewise from several men's shoes and boots.

My mind continued to imagine and theorize the manner of his creation until I realized that his Creation wished to relate *his* tale to me. It would have been the height of impropriety for my pale student to relate the tale of the Creation to me. That tale would have been hearsay and although I trusted my pale student of the unhallowed arts, he may have proven himself to be an unreliable narrator. Not that he would have outright lied to me to blatant falsehoods, but he may subconsciously smoothed over the rougher edges of his Creation's tale. His Creation could not look me in the eye, instead keeping his head hung low, with his chin laying upon his chest. Without speaking a word, I consented to listen; and, seating myself by the fire which my odious companion had lighted, he thus began his tale.

Chapter 7

7 July. Before Second Sleep— 'It is with considerable difficulty that I remember the original æra of my being: all the events of that period appear confused and indistinct.' Victor's Creation speaks with an eloquence that is betrayed by his appearance. How did he learn to speak with such articulation? Is there some remembrance from his brain's past life in another man's skull? Or was his Creation a blank slate having been wiped clean by the hand of death and decay? If the previous owner's soul has transcended this mortal sphere, then perchance there was not-a-thing still possessed by the crude matter that now thinks and seemingly feels!

'A strange multiplicity of sensations seized me, and I saw, felt, heard, and smelt, at the same time; and it was, indeed, a long time before I learned to distinguish between the operations of my various senses. By degrees, I remember, a stronger light pressed upon my nerves, so that I was obliged to shut my eyes. Darkness then came over me, and troubled me; but hardly had I felt this, when, by opening my eyes, as I now suppose, the light poured in upon me again. I walked, and, I believe, descended; but I presently found a great alteration in my sensations. Before, dark and opaque bodies had surrounded me, impervious to my touch or sight; but I now found that I could wander on at liberty, with no obstacles which I could not either surmount or avoid. The light became more and more oppressive to me; and, the heat wearying me as I walked, I sought a place where I could receive shade. This was the forest near Ingolstadt; and here I lay by the side of a brook resting from my fatigue, until I felt tormented by hunger and thirst. This roused me from my nearly dormant state, and I ate some berries which I found hanging on the trees, or lying on the ground. I slaked my thirst at the brook; and then lying down, was overcome by sleep.'

Such horror what the crude matter experiences when experiencing such sensations anew! I glance over to my little William sleeping in his bassinette and I cast my mind back when he was newly born. Is this what the infantile brain experiences in its first waking moments but its voice cannot articulate. But lo! Perchance, the babes are communicating this unspeakable horror through their cries, but as mother's we dismiss their terror as hunger by putting them to our breast! Our children have swum in the warm darkness of our wombs, and now they are assaulted by sensations they know not the cause of their pain nor hide from! If my child possessed the mental or physical properties to speak at such an infantile age, would he describe his world any less eloquently as this Creation did just now?

'It was dark when I awoke; I felt cold also, and half-frightened as it were instinctively, finding myself so desolate. Before I had quitted Victor's apartment, on a sensation of cold, I had covered myself with some clothes; but these were insufficient to secure me from the dews of night. I was a poor, helpless, miserable wretch; I knew, and could distinguish, nothing; but, feeling pain invade me on all sides, I sat down and wept.' As did I. How could I not at such a harrowing tale?

'Soon a gentle light stole over the heavens, and gave me a sensation of pleasure. I started up, and beheld a radiant form rise from among the trees. I gazed with a kind of wonder. It moved slowly, but it enlightened my path; and I again went out in search of berries. I was still cold, when under one of the trees I found a huge cloak, with which I covered myself, and sat down upon the ground. No distinct ideas occupied my mind; all was confused. I felt light, and hunger, and thirst, and darkness; innumerable sounds rung in my ears, and on all sides various scents saluted me: the only object that I could distinguish was the bright moon, and I fixed my eyes on that with pleasure.'

My own mind is just as assaulted as this poor Creation's had been. I felt the sting of the light and pangs of hunger and assault thirst and the oppression of darkness and the ringing of innumerable sounds in my ears anew for the first time since I was a mere babe in the cradle. I cast another glance at my dearest William. I wondered and I pondered once more.

'Several changes of day and night passed, and the orb of night had greatly lessened when I began to distinguish my sensations from each other. I gradually saw plainly the clear stream that supplied me with drink, and the trees that shaded me with their foliage. I was delighted when I first discovered that a pleasant sound, which often saluted my ears, proceeded from the throats of the little winged animals who had often intercepted the light from my eyes. I began also to observe, with greater accuracy, the forms that surrounded me, and to perceive the boundaries of the radiant roof of light which canopied me. Sometimes I tried to imitate the pleasant songs of the birds, but was unable. Sometimes I wished to express my sensations in my own mode, but the uncouth and inarticulate sounds which broke from me frightened me into silence again.

'The moon had disappeared from the night, and again, with a lessened form, shewed itself, while I still remained in the forest. My sensations had, by this time, become distinct, and my mind received every day additional ideas. My eyes became accustomed to the light, and to perceive objects in their right forms; I distinguished the insect from the herb, and, by degrees, one herb from another. I found that the sparrow uttered none but harsh notes, whilst those of the blackbird and thrush were sweet and enticing.'

Did not Jean-Jacques Rousseau hypothesize similar experiences to those of this Creation? Did he not write so eloquently in *Emile*, 'Suppose a child born with the size and strength of manhood, entering upon life full grown like Pallas from the brain of Jupiter; such a child-man would be a perfect idiot, an automaton, a statue without motion and almost without feeling; he would see and hear nothing, he would recognise no one, he could not turn his eyes towards what he wanted to see; not only would he perceive no external object, he would not even be aware of sensation through the several sense-organs. His eye would not perceive colour, his ear sounds, his body would be unaware of contact with neighbouring bodies, he would not even know he had a body, what his hands handled would be in his brain alone; all his sensations would be united in one place, they would exist only in the common "sensorium," he would have only one idea, that of self, to which he would refer all his sensations; and this idea, or rather this feeling, would be the only thing in which he excelled an ordinary child. This man, full grown at birth, would also be unable to stand on his feet, he would need a long time to learn how to keep his balance; perhaps he would not even be able to try to do it, and you would see the big strong body left in one place like a stone, or creeping and crawling like a young puppy.

'He would feel the discomfort of bodily needs without knowing what was the matter and without knowing how to provide for these needs. There is no immediate connection between the muscles of the stomach and those of the arms and legs to make him take a step towards food, or stretch a hand to seize it, even were he surrounded with it; and as his body would be full grown and his limbs well developed he would be without the perpetual restlessness and movement of childhood, so that he might die of hunger without stirring to seek food. However little you may have thought about the order and development of our knowledge, you cannot deny that such a one would be in the state of almost primitive ignorance and stupidity natural to man before he has learnt anything from experience or from his fellows.'[2]

Rousseau imagines the man/child as an imbecile, an automaton, an immobile and almost insensible statue, who would learn to stand, if he attempted it at all, with the greatest difficult and would not connect hunger with food, while Victor's Creation gains motor control almost at once and instinctively slakes his hunger with berries.[3]

Despite my brief lapse in focus to wander along a digressive path, the Creation continued with his tale. 'One day, when I was oppressed by cold, I found a fire which had been left by some wandering beggars, and was overcome with delight at the warmth I experienced from it. In my joy I thrust my hand into the live embers, but quickly drew it out again with a cry of pain. How strange, I thought, that the same cause should produce such opposite effects! I examined the materials of the fire, and to my joy found it to be composed of wood. I quickly collected some branches; but they were wet, and would not burn. I was pained at this, and sat still watching the operation of the fire. The wet wood which I had placed near the heat dried, and itself became inflamed. I reflected on this; and, by touching the various branches, I discovered the cause, and busied myself in collecting a great quantity of wood, that I might dry it, and have a plentiful supply of fire. When night came on, and brought sleep with it, I was in the greatest fear lest my fire should be extinguished. I covered it carefully with dry wood and leaves, and placed wet branches upon it; and then, spreading my cloak, I lay on the ground, and sunk into sleep.

2 From *Emile, or On Education* by Jean-Jacques Rousseau, published in English in 1763.

3 From "From *Emile* to *Frankenstein*: The education of Monsters", *European Romantic Review* 1, no. 2 [1991]: 147-62.

'It was morning when I awoke, and my first care was to visit the fire. I uncovered it, and a gentle breeze quickly fanned it into a flame. I observed this also, and contrived a fan of branches, which roused the embers when they were nearly extinguished. When night came again, I found, with pleasure, that the fire gave light as well as heat; and that the discovery of this element was useful to me in my food; for I found some of the offals that the travellers had left had been roasted, and tasted much more savoury than the berries I gathered from the trees. I tried, therefore, to dress my food in the same manner, placing it on the live embers. I found that the berries were spoiled by this operation, and the nuts and roots much improved.

'Food, however, became scarce; and I often spent the whole day searching in vain for a few acorns to assuage the pangs of hunger. When I found this, I resolved to quit the place that I had hitherto inhabited, to seek for one where the few wants I experienced would be more easily satisfied. In this emigration, I exceedingly lamented the loss of the fire which I had obtained through accident, and knew not how to re-produce it. I gave several hours to the serious consideration of this difficulty; but I was obliged to relinquish all attempt to supply it; and, wrapping myself up in my cloak, I struck across the wood towards the setting sun. I passed three days in these rambles, and at length discovered the open country. A great fall of snow had taken place the night before, and the fields were of one uniform white; the appearance was disconsolate, and I found my feet chilled by the cold damp substance that covered the ground.

'It was about seven in the morning, and I longed to obtain food and shelter; at length I perceived a small hut, on a rising ground, which had doubtless been built for the convenience of some shepherd. This was a new sight to me; and I examined the structure with great curiosity. Finding the door open, I entered. An old man sat in it, near a fire, over which he was preparing his breakfast. He turned on hearing a noise; and, perceiving me, shrieked loudly, and, quitting the hut, ran across the fields with a speed of which his debilitated form hardly appeared capable. His appearance, different from any I had ever before seen, and his flight, somewhat surprised me. But I was enchanted by the appearance of the hut: here the snow and rain could not penetrate; the ground was dry; and it presented to me then as exquisite and divine a retreat as Pandæmonium appeared to the dæmons of hell after their sufferings in the lake of fire.' Curiouser and curiouser! From whence did this Creation learn of John Milton? Perhaps there is a chance this knowledge of Paradises lost will be related in his tale to me. One can only hope and dream. 'I greedily devoured the remnants of the shepherd's breakfast, which consisted of bread, cheese, milk, and wine; the latter, however, I did not like. Then overcome by fatigue, I lay down among some straw, and fell asleep.

'It was noon when I awoke; and, allured by the warmth of the sun, which shone brightly on the white ground, I determined to recommence my travels; and, depositing the remains of the peasant's breakfast in a wallet I found, I proceeded across the fields for several hours, until at sunset I arrived at a village. How miraculous did this appear! the huts, the neater cottages, and stately houses, engaged my admiration by turns. The vegetables in the gardens, the milk and cheese that I saw placed at the windows of some of the cottages, allured my appetite. One of the best of these I entered; but I had hardly placed my foot within the door, before the children shrieked, and one of the women fainted. The whole village was roused; some fled, some attacked me, until, grievously bruised by stones and many other kinds of missile weapons,' Oh! The horror of humanity's penchant for violence! This poor Creation is an alien to these villagers as a man from Mars would be stepping foot on the green grasses Earth, so foreign from the red dirt of his native world. Would these villagers believe that our world was being watched keenly and closely by intelligences greater than man's and yet as mortal as his own; that as men busied themselves about their various concerns they were scrutinised and studied, perhaps almost as narrowly as a man with a microscope might scrutinise the transient creatures that swarm and multiply in a drop of water. With infinite complacency men went to and fro over this globe about their little affairs, serene in their assurance of their empire over matter. To them it is possible that the infusoria under the microscope do the same. No one gave a thought to the older worlds of space as sources of human danger, or thought of them only to dismiss the idea of life upon them as impossible or improbable. It is curious to recall some of the mental habits of those departed days. At most terrestrial men fancied there might be other men upon Mars, perhaps inferior to themselves and ready to welcome a missionary enterprise. Yet across the gulf of space, minds that are to our minds as ours are to those of the beasts that perish, intellects vast and cool and unsympathetic, regarded this earth with envious eyes, and slowly and surely drew their plans against us.[4] These would be the villagers and the city dwellers reaction to an otherworldly or unnatural threat which Victor's Creation surely was.

'I escaped to the open country, and fearfully took refuge in a low hovel, quite bare, and making a wretched appearance after the palaces I had beheld in the village. This hovel, however, joined a cottage of a neat and pleasant appearance; but, after my late dearly-bought experience, I dared

---

4 From *The War of the Worlds* by H.G. Welles, serialised in *Pearson's Magazine* in 1897.

not enter it. My place of refuge was constructed of wood, but so low, that I could with difficulty sit upright in it. No wood, however, was placed on the earth, which formed the floor, but it was dry; and although the wind entered it by innumerable chinks, I found it an agreeable asylum from the snow and rain.

'Here then I retreated, and lay down, happy to have found a shelter, however miserable, from the inclemency of the season, and still more from the barbarity of man.

'As soon as morning dawned, I crept from my kennel, that I might view the adjacent cottage, and discover if I could remain in the habitation I had found. It was situated against the back of the cottage, and surrounded on the sides which were exposed by a pig-stye and a clear pool of water. One part was open, and by that I had crept in; but now I covered every crevice by which I might be perceived with stones and wood, yet in such a manner that I might move them on occasion to pass out: all the light I enjoyed came through the stye, and that was sufficient for me.

'Having thus arranged my dwelling, and carpeted it with clean straw, I retired; for I saw the figure of a man at a distance, and I remembered too well my treatment the night before, to trust myself in his power. I had first, however, provided for my sustenance for that day, by a loaf of coarse bread, which I purloined, and a cup with which I could drink, more conveniently than from my hand, of the pure water which flowed by my retreat. The floor was a little raised, so that it was kept perfectly dry, and by its vicinity to the chimney of the cottage it was tolerably warm.

'Being thus provided, I resolved to reside in this hovel, until something should occur which might alter my determination. It was indeed a paradise, compared to the bleak forest, my former residence, the rain-dropping branches, and dank earth. I ate my breakfast with pleasure, and was about to remove a plank to procure myself a little water, when I heard a step, and, looking through a small chink, I beheld a young creature, with a pail on her head, passing before my hovel. The girl was young and of gentle demeanour, unlike what I have since found cottagers and farm-house servants to be. Yet she was meanly dressed, a coarse blue petticoat and a linen jacket being her only garb; her fair hair was plaited, but not adorned; she looked patient, yet sad. I lost sight of her; and in about a quarter of an hour she returned, bearing the pail, which was now partly filled with milk. As she walked along, seemingly incommoded by the burden, a young man met her, whose countenance expressed a deeper despondence. Uttering a few sounds with an air of melancholy, he took the pail from her head, and bore it to the cottage himself. She followed, and they disappeared. Presently I saw the young man again, with some tools in his hand, cross the field behind the cottage; and the girl was also busied, sometimes in the house, and sometimes in the yard.

'On examining my dwelling, I found that one of the windows of the cottage had formerly occupied a part of it, but the panes had been filled up with wood. In one of these was a small and almost imperceptible chink, through which the eye could just penetrate. Through this crevice, a small room was visible, white-washed and clean, but very bare of furniture. In one corner, near a small fire, sat an old man, leaning his head on his hands in a disconsolate attitude. The young girl was occupied in arranging the cottage; but presently she took something out of a drawer, which employed her hands, and she sat down beside the old man, who, taking up an instrument, began to play, and to produce sounds, sweeter than the voice of the thrush or the nightingale. It was a lovely sight, even to me, poor wretch! who had never beheld aught beautiful before. The silver hair and benevolent countenance of the aged cottager, won my reverence; while the gentle manners of the girl enticed my love. He played a sweet mournful air, which I perceived drew tears from the eyes of his amiable companion, of which the old man took no notice, until she sobbed audibly; he then pronounced a few sounds, and the fair creature, leaving her work, knelt at his feet. He raised her, and smiled with such kindness and affection, that I felt sensations of a peculiar and over-powering nature: they were a mixture of pain and pleasure, such as I had never before experienced, either from hunger or cold, warmth or food; and I withdrew from the window, unable to bear these emotions.

'Soon after this the young man returned, bearing on his shoulders a load of wood. The girl met him at the door, helped to relieve him of his burden, and, taking some of the fuel into the cottage, placed it on the fire; then she and the youth went apart into a nook of the cottage, and he shewed her a large loaf and a piece of cheese. She seemed pleased; and went into the garden for some roots and plants, which she placed in water, and then upon the fire. She afterwards continued her work, whilst the young man went into the garden, and appeared busily employed in digging and pulling up roots. After he had been employed thus about an hour, the young woman joined him, and they entered the cottage together.

'The old man had, in the mean time, been pensive; but, on the appearance of his companions, he assumed a more cheerful air, and they sat down to eat. The meal was quickly dispatched. The young woman was again occupied in arranging the cottage; the old man walked before the cottage in the sun for a few minutes, leaning on the arm of the youth. Nothing could exceed in beauty the contrast between these two excellent creatures. One was old, with silver hairs and a countenance beaming with benevolence and love: the younger was slight and graceful in his figure, and his features were moulded with the finest symmetry; yet his eyes and attitude expressed the utmost sadness and despondency. The old man returned to the cottage; and the youth, with tools different from those he had used in the morning, directed his steps across the fields.

'Night quickly shut in; but, to my extreme wonder, I found that the cottagers had a means of prolonging light, by the use of tapers, and was delighted to find, that the setting of the sun did not put an end to the pleasure I experienced in watching my human neighbours. In the evening, the young girl and her companion were employed in various oc-cupations which I did not understand; and the old man again took up the instrument, which produced the divine sounds that had enchanted me in the morning. So soon as he had finished, the youth began, not to play, but to utter sounds that were monotonous, and neither resembling the harmony of the old man's instrument or the songs of the birds; I since found that he read aloud, but at that time I knew nothing of the science of words or letters.

'The family, after having been thus occupied for a short time, extin-guished their lights, and retired, as I conjectured, to rest.' I too, briefly, thought of the lateness of the hour and the stalking exhaustion that the Creation's story kept at bay like firelight does wolves. But the Creation continued his tale with only the merest of pauses.

Chapter II

I lay on my straw, but I could not sleep. I thought of the occurrences of the day. What chiefly struck me was the gentle manners of these people; and I longed to join them, but dared not. I remembered too well the treatment I had suffered the night before from the barbarous vil-lagers, and resolved, whatever course of conduct I might hereafter think it right to pursue, that for the present I would remain quietly in my hovel, watching, and endeavouring to discover the motives which influenced their actions.

'The cottagers arose the next morning before the sun. The young woman arranged the cottage, and prepared the food; and the youth de-parted after the first meal.

'This day was passed in the same routine as that which preceded it. The young man was constantly employed out of doors, and the girl in var-ious laborious occupations within. The old man, whom I soon perceived to be blind, employed his leisure hours on his instrument, or in contem-plation. Nothing could exceed the love and respect which the younger cottagers exhibited towards their venerable companion. They performed towards him every little office of affection and duty with gentleness; and he rewarded them by his benevolent smiles.

They were not entirely happy. The young man and his companion often went apart, and appeared to weep. I saw no cause for their unhappiness; but I was deeply affected by it. If such lovely creatures were miserable, it was less strange that I, an imperfect and solitary being, should be wretched. Yet why were these gentle beings unhappy? They possessed a delightful house (for such it was in my eyes), and every luxury; they had a fire to warm them when chill, and delicious viands when hungry; they were dressed in excellent clothes; and, still more, they enjoyed one another's company and speech, interchanging each day looks of affection and kindness. What did their tears imply? Did they really express pain? I was at first unable to solve these questions; but perpetual attention, and time, explained to me many appearances which were at first enigmatic.

'A considerable period elapsed before I discovered one of the causes of the uneasiness of this amiable family; it was poverty: and they suffered that evil in a very distressing degree. Their nourishment consisted entirely of the vegetables of their garden, and the milk of one cow, who gave very little during the winter, when its masters could scarcely procure food to support it. They often, I believe, suffered the pangs of hunger very poignantly, especially the two younger cottagers; for several times they placed food before the old man, when they reserved none for themselves.

This trait of kindness moved me sensibly. I had been accustomed, during the night, to steal a part of their store for my own consumption; but when I found that in doing this I inflicted pain on the cottagers, I abstained, and satisfied myself with berries, nuts, and roots, which I gathered from a neighbouring wood.'

Did the David the Psalmist sing, *Out of the mouth of babes and sucklings hast thou ordained strength because of thine enemie?* How did this Creation, only days old, come to this knowledge when the vastness of humanity with the vastness of human experiences cannot? Surely our biases are learnt from our parents and our teachers and our priests, and not born innate in the human condition. True, the religious will teach and preach that we are all born with Original Sin. It was this act of consuming the fruit of the Tree of the Knowledge of Good and Evil that has condemned all of mankind to the pain and suffering found outside of Eden. When I look at my dearest William slumbering quietly, breathing in and exhaling out so minutely, that a parent, even one who has not lost a child to death, listens intently to see if their child still lives, I cannot believe he possesses even one iota of sin. Original or otherwise. The religious be damned!

'I discovered also another means through which I was enabled to assist their labours. I found that the youth spent a great part of each day in collecting wood for the family fire; and, during the night, I often took his tools, the use of which I quickly discovered, and brought home firing sufficient for the consumption of several days.

'I remember, the first time that I did this, the young woman, when she opened the door in the morning, appeared greatly astonished on seeing a great pile of wood on the outside. She uttered some words in a loud voice, and the youth joined her, who also expressed surprise. I observed, with pleasure, that he did not go to the forest that day, but spent it in repairing the cottage, and cultivating the garden.

'By degrees I made a discovery of still greater moment. I found that these people possessed a method of communicating their experience and feelings to one another by articulate sounds. I perceived that the words they spoke sometimes produced pleasure or pain, smiles or sadness, in the minds and countenances of the hearers. This was indeed a godlike science, and I ardently desired to become acquainted with it. But I was baffled in every attempt I made for this purpose. Their pronunciation was quick; and the words they uttered, not having any apparent connexion with visible objects, I was unable to discover any clue by which I could unravel the mystery of their reference. By great application, however, and after having remained during the space of several revolutions of the moon in my hovel, I discovered the names that were given to some of the most familiar objects of discourse: I learned and applied the words *fire*, *milk*, *bread*, and *wood*. I learned also the names of the cottagers themselves. The youth and his companion had each of them several names, but the old man had only one, which was *father*. The girl was called *sister*, or *Agatha*; and the youth *Felix*, *brother*, or *son*. I cannot describe the delight I felt when I learned the ideas appropriated to each of these sounds, and was able to pronounce them. I distinguished several other words, without being able as yet to understand or apply them; such as *good, dearest, unhappy*.'

Again and again this poor Creation articulates the experiences of the infantile in the language of an adult. Again and again, I glance at my dearest William becoming full of the knowledge of his own experiences as he grows from infant to toddler. Even when he is toddling around my Beloved's writing desk, would he be able to communicate his infantile experiences as articulately as this Creation.

'I spent the winter in this manner.' What year was this? If his 'birth' had been in November of 1793, this would imply that the Creation is describing the spring of 1794. I will strive to keep these dates recorded on the calendar in my mind. 'The gentle manners and beauty of the cottagers greatly endeared them to me: when they were unhappy, I felt depressed; when they rejoiced, I sympathized in their joys. I saw few human beings beside them; and if any other happened to enter the cottage, their harsh manners and rude gait only enhanced to me the superior accomplishments of my friends. The old man, I could perceive, often endeavoured to encourage his children, as sometimes I found that he called them, to cast off their melancholy. He would talk in a cheerful accent, with an expression of goodness that bestowed pleasure even upon me. Agatha listened with respect, her eyes sometimes filled with tears, which she endeavoured to wipe away unperceived; but I generally found that her countenance and tone were more cheerful after having listened to the exhortations of her father. It was not thus with Felix. He was always the saddest of the groupe; and, even to my unpractised senses, he appeared to have suffered more deeply than his friends. But if his countenance was more sorrowful, his voice was more cheerful than that of his sister, especially when he addressed the old man.

'I could mention innumerable instances, which, although slight, marked the dispositions of these amiable cottagers. In the midst of poverty and want, Felix carried with pleasure to his sister the first little white flower that peeped out from beneath the snowy ground. Early in the morning before she had risen, he cleared away the snow that obstructed her path to the milk-house, drew water from the well, and brought the wood from the out-house, where, to his perpetual astonishment, he found his store always replenished by an invisible hand. In the day, I believe, he worked sometimes for a neighbouring farmer, because he often went forth, and did not return until dinner, yet brought no wood with him. At other times he worked in the garden; but, as there was little to do in the frosty season, he read to the old man and Agatha.

'This reading had puzzled me extremely at first; but, by degrees, I discovered that he uttered many of the same sounds when he read as when he talked. I conjectured, therefore, that he found on the paper signs for speech which he understood, and I ardently longed to comprehend these also; but how was that possible, when I did not even understand the sounds for which they stood as signs? I improved, however, sensibly in this science, but not sufficiently to follow up any kind of conversation, although I applied my whole mind to the endeavour: for I easily perceived that, although I eagerly longed to discover myself to the cottagers, I ought not to make the attempt until I had first become master of their language; which knowledge might enable me to make them overlook the deformity of my figure; for with this also the contrast perpetually presented to my eyes had made me acquainted.

'I had admired the perfect forms of my cottagers— their grace, beauty, and delicate complexions: but how was I terrified, when I viewed myself in a transparent pool! At first I started back, unable to believe that it was indeed I who was reflected in the mirror; and when I became fully convinced that I was in reality the monster that I am, I was filled with the bitterest sensations of despondence and mortification. Alas! I did not yet entirely know the fatal effects of this miserable deformity.'

Oh! My sweet Creation, how did you come to his regrettable knowledge that you are deformed? True, Victor fled from you in the moments after your creation. True, the villagers stoned you for the sin of being different. But! How did you come to his regrettable knowledge? Are you as blank a slate as I perceive you to be. Or! Is there some semblance of memory that survived the death of the previous possessor of your brain?

'As the sun became warmer, and the light of day longer, the snow vanished, and I beheld the bare trees and the black earth. From this time Felix was more employed; and the heart-moving indications of impending famine disappeared. Their food, as I afterwards found, was coarse, but it was wholesome; and they procured a sufficiency of it. Several new kinds of plants sprung up in the garden, which they dressed; and these signs of comfort increased daily as the season advanced.

'The old man, leaning on his son, walked each day at noon, when it did not rain, as I found it was called when the heavens poured forth its waters. This frequently took place; but a high wind quickly dried the earth, and the season became far more pleasant than it had been.

'My mode of life in my hovel was uniform. During the morning I attended the motions of the cottagers; and when they were dispersed in various occupations, I slept: the remainder of the day was spent in observing my friends. When they had retired to rest, if there was any moon, or the night was star-light, I went into the woods, and collected my own food and fuel for the cottage. When I returned, as often as it was necessary, I cleared their path from the snow, and performed those offices that I had seen done by Felix. I afterwards found that these labours, performed by an invisible hand, greatly astonished them; and once or twice I heard them, on these occasions, utter the words *good spirit*, *wonderful*; but I did not then understand the signification of these terms.

'My thoughts now became more active, and I longed to discover the motives and feelings of these lovely creatures; I was inquisitive to know why Felix appeared so miserable, and Agatha so sad. I thought (foolish wretch!) that it might be in my power to restore happiness to these deserving people. When I slept, or was absent, the forms of the venerable blind father, the gentle Agatha, and the excellent Felix, flitted before me.

I looked upon them as superior beings, who would be the arbiters of my future destiny. I formed in my imagination a thousand pictures of presenting myself to them, and their reception of me. I imagined that they would be disgusted, until, by my gentle demeanour and conciliating words, I should first win their favour, and afterwards their love.

'These thoughts exhilarated me, and led me to apply with fresh ardour to the acquiring the art of language. My organs were indeed harsh, but supple; and although my voice was very unlike the soft music of their tones, yet I pronounced such words as I understood with tolerable ease. It was as the ass and the lap-dog; yet surely the gentle ass, whose intentions were affectionate, although his manners were rude, deserved better treatment than blows and execration.'

Oh! The Ass and the Lapdog! Such a wonderful table by Aesop. Shall I relate it to you, my Journal? It is but a trifle of a digression: 'A MAN had an Ass, and a Maltese Lapdog, a very great beauty. The Ass was left in a stable and had plenty of oats and hay to eat, just as any other Ass would. The Lapdog knew many tricks and was a great favorite with his master, who often fondled him and seldom went out to dine without bringing him home some tidbit to eat. The Ass, on the contrary, had much work to do in grinding the corn-mill and in carrying wood from the forest or burdens from the farm. He often lamented his own hard fate and contrasted it with the luxury and idleness of the Lapdog, till at last one day he broke his cords and halter, and galloped into his master's house, kicking up his heels without measure, and frisking and fawning as well as he could. He next tried to jump about his master as he had seen the Lapdog do, but he broke the table and smashed all the dishes upon it to atoms. He then attempted to lick his master, and jumped upon his back. The servants, hearing the strange hubbub and perceiving the danger of their master, quickly relieved him, and drove out the Ass to his stable with kicks and clubs and cuffs. The Ass, as he returned to his stall beaten nearly to death, thus lamented: 'I have brought it all on myself! Why could I not have been contented to labor with my companions, and not wish to be idle all the day like that useless little Lapdog!'"[5]

'The pleasant showers and genial warmth of spring greatly altered the aspect of the earth. Men, who before this change seemed to have been hid in caves, dispersed themselves, and were employed in various arts of cultivation. The birds sang in more cheerful notes, and the leaves began to bud forth on the trees. Happy, happy earth! fit habitation for gods, which, so short a time before, was bleak, damp, and unwholesome. My spirits were elevated by the enchanting appearance of nature; the

---

5 From *Aesop's Fables,* a translation by George Fyler Townsend, published in 1887.

past was blotted from my memory, the present was tranquil, and the future gilded by bright rays of hope, and anticipations of joy."

Chapter III

I now hasten to the more moving part of my story. I shall relate events that impressed me with feelings which, from what I was, have made me what I am.'

Yes, Creation, please do!

'Spring advanced rapidly; the weather became fine, and the skies cloudless. It surprised me, that what before was desert and gloomy should now bloom with the most beautiful flowers and verdure. My senses were gratified and refreshed by a thousand scents of delight, and a thousand sights of beauty.

'It was on one of these days, when my cottagers periodically rested from labour— the old man played on his guitar, and the children listened to him— I observed that the countenance of Felix was melancholy beyond expression: he sighed frequently; and once his father paused in his music, and I conjectured by his manner that he inquired the cause of his son's sorrow. Felix replied in a cheerful accent, and the old man was recommencing his music, when some one tapped at the door.

'It was a lady on horseback, accompanied by a countryman as a guide. The lady was dressed in a dark suit, and covered with a thick black veil. Agatha asked a question; to which the stranger only replied by pronouncing, in a sweet accent, the name of Felix. Her voice was musical, but unlike that of either of my friends. On hearing this word, Felix came up hastily to the lady; who, when she saw him, threw up her veil, and I beheld a countenance of angelic beauty and expression. Her hair of a shining raven black, and curiously braided; her eyes were dark, but gentle, although animated; her features of a regular proportion, and her complexion wondrously fair, each cheek tinged with a lovely pink.

'Felix seemed ravished with delight when he saw her, every trait of sorrow vanished from his face, and it instantly expressed a degree of ecstatic joy, of which I could hardly have believed it capable; his eyes sparkled, as his cheek flushed with pleasure; and at that moment I thought him as beautiful as the stranger. She appeared affected by different feelings; wiping a few tears from her lovely eyes, she held out her hand to Felix, who kissed it rapturously, and called her, as well as I could distinguish, his sweet Arabian.' Arabian? So delightful and curious. 'She did not appear to understand him, but smiled. He assisted her to dismount, and, dismissing her guide, conducted her into the cottage. Some conversation took place between him and his father; and the young stranger knelt at the old man's feet, and would have kissed his hand, but he raised her, and embraced her affectionately.

'I soon perceived, that although the stranger uttered articulate sounds, and appeared to have a language of her own, she was neither understood by, or herself understood, the cottagers. They made many signs which I did not comprehend; but I saw that her presence diffused gladness through the cottage, dispelling their sorrow as the sun dissipates the morning mists. Felix seemed peculiarly happy, and with smiles of delight welcomed his Arabian. Agatha, the ever-gentle Agatha, kissed the hands of the lovely stranger; and, pointing to her brother, made signs which appeared to me to mean that he had been sorrowful until she came. Some hours passed thus, while they, by their countenances, expressed joy, the cause of which I did not comprehend. Presently I found, by the frequent recurrence of one sound which the stranger repeated after them, that she was endeavouring to learn their language; and the idea instantly occurred to me, that I should make use of the same instructions to the same end. The stranger learned about twenty words at the first lesson, most of them indeed were those which I had before understood, but I profited by the others.

'As night came on, Agatha and the Arabian retired early. When they separated, Felix kissed the hand of the stranger, and said, 'Good night, sweet Safie.' He sat up much longer, conversing with his father; and, by the frequent repetition of her name, I conjectured that their lovely guest was the subject of their conversation. I ardently desired to understand them, and bent every faculty towards that purpose, but found it utterly impossible.

'The next morning Felix went out to his work; and, after the usual occupations of Agatha were finished, the Arabian sat at the feet of the old man, and, taking his guitar, played some airs so entrancingly beautiful, that they at once drew tears of sorrow and delight from my eyes. She sang, and her voice flowed in a rich cadence, swelling or dying away, like a nightingale of the woods.

'When she had finished, she gave the guitar to Agatha, who at first declined it. She played a simple air, and her voice accompanied it in sweet accents, but unlike the wondrous strain of the stranger. The old man appeared enraptured, and said some words, which Agatha endeavoured to explain to Safie, and by which he appeared to wish to express that she bestowed on him the greatest delight by her music.

'The days now passed as peaceably as before, with the sole alteration, that joy had taken place of sadness in the countenances of my friends. Safie was always gay and happy; she and I improved rapidly in the knowledge of language, so that in two months I began to comprehend most of the words uttered by my protectors.

'In the meanwhile also the black ground was covered with herbage, and the green banks interspersed with innumerable flowers, sweet to the scent and the eyes, stars of pale radiance among the moonlight woods; the sun became warmer, the nights clear and balmy; and my nocturnal rambles were an extreme pleasure to me, although they were considerably shortened by the late setting and early rising of the sun; for I never ventured abroad during daylight, fearful of meeting with the same treatment as I had formerly endured in the first village which I entered.

'My days were spent in close attention, that I might more speedily master the language; and I may boast that I improved more rapidly than the Arabian, who understood very little, and conversed in broken accents, whilst I comprehended and could imitate almost every word that was spoken.'

Again, not as blank a slate as I would have first perceived!

'While I improved in speech, I also learned the science of letters, as it was taught to the stranger; and this opened before me a wide field for wonder and delight.

Again and again, not as blank a slate as I would have first perceived! It is certainly not possible or, at the very least, plausible. That he should have not only learned to speak, but to read, and for aught we know, to write... by listening through a hole in a wall, seems as unlikely as that he should have acquired, in the same way, the problems of Euclid, or the art of bookkeeping, by single and double entry.[6]

'The book from which Felix instructed Safie was Volney's *Ruins of Empires*. I should not have understood the purport of this book, had not Felix, in reading it, given very minute explanations. He had chosen this work, he said, because the declamatory style was framed in imitation of the eastern authors. Through this work I obtained a cursory knowledge of history, and a view of the several empires at present existing in the world; it gave me an insight into the manners, governments, and religions of the different nations of the earth. I heard of the slothful Asiatics; of the stupendous genius and mental activity of the Grecians; of the wars and wonderful virtue of the early Romans— of their subsequent degeneration— of the decline of that mighty empire; of chivalry, Christianity, and kings. I heard of the discovery of the American hemisphere, and wept with Safie over the hapless fate of its original inhabitants.

'These wonderful narrations inspired me with strange feelings. Was man, indeed, at once so powerful, so virtuous, and magnificent, yet so vicious and base? He appeared at one time a mere scion of the evil prin-

---

6 From an 1818 review by Walter Scott of *Frankenstein* for *Blackwood's Edinburgh Magazine*.

ciple, and at another as all that can be conceived of noble and godlike. To be a great and virtuous man appeared the highest honour that can befall a sensitive being; to be base and vicious, as many on record have been, appeared the lowest degradation, a condition more abject than that of the blind mole or harmless worm. For a long time I could not conceive how one man could go forth to murder his fellow, or even why there were laws and governments; but when I heard details of vice and bloodshed, my wonder ceased, and I turned away with disgust and loathing.'

Again and again, the wisdom of Victor's Creation! Will it take this Creation standing in the great halls of Parliament to fully communicate this observation of Mankind? Does it take the unnatural creation of this Creation to finally convince man of not only the folly of man but his greatness? Surely, Victor's Creation will burn either by torch or pyre or in Hellfire for this quite human observation.

'Every conversation of the cottagers now opened new wonders to me. While I listened to the instructions which Felix bestowed upon the Arabian, the strange system of human society was explained to me. I heard of the division of property, of immense wealth and squalid poverty; of rank, descent, and noble blood.

'The words induced me to turn towards myself. I learned that the possessions most esteemed by your fellow-creatures were, high and un-sullied descent united with riches. A man might be respected with only one of these acquisitions; but without either he was considered, except in very rare instances, as a vagabond and a slave, doomed to waste his powers for the profit of the chosen few. And what was I? Of my creation and creator I was absolutely ignorant; but I knew that I possessed no money, no friends, no kind of property. I was, besides, endowed with a figure hideously deformed and loathsome; I was not even of the same na-ture as man. I was more agile than they, and could subsist upon coarser diet; I bore the extremes of heat and cold with less injury to my frame; my stature far exceeded their's. When I looked around, I saw and heard of none like me. Was I then a monster, a blot upon the earth, from which all men fled, and whom all men disowned?'

I wept openly and without shame, but the Creation continued his tale unabated.

'I cannot describe to you the agony that these reflections inflicted upon me; I tried to dispel them, but sorrow only increased with knowl-edge. Oh, that I had for ever remained in my native wood, nor known or felt beyond the sensations of hunger, thirst, and heat!

'Of what a strange nature is knowledge! It clings to the mind, when it has once seized on it, like a lichen on the rock. I wished sometimes to shake off all thought and feeling; but I learned that there was but one means to overcome the sensation of pain, and that was death— a state which I feared yet did not understand. I admired virtue and good feelings, and loved the gentle manners and amiable qualities of my cottagers; but I was shut out from intercourse with them, except through means which I obtained by stealth, when I was unseen and unknown, and which rather increased than satisfied the desire I had of becoming one among my fellows. The gentle words of Agatha, and the animated smiles of the charming Arabian, were not for me. The mild exhortations of the old man, and the lively conversation of the loved Felix, were not for me. Miserable, unhappy wretch!

'Other lessons were impressed upon me even more deeply. I heard of the difference of sexes; of the birth and growth of children; how the father doated on the smiles of the infant, and the lively sallies of the older child; how all the life and cares of the mother were wrapt up in the precious charge; how the mind of youth expanded and gained knowledge; of brother, sister, and all the various relationships which bind one human being to another in mutual bonds.

'But where were my friends and relations? No father had watched my infant days, no mother had blessed me with smiles and caresses; or if they had, all my past life was now a blot, a blind vacancy in which I distinguished nothing. From my earliest remembrance I had been as I then was in height and proportion. I had never yet seen a being resembling me, or who claimed any intercourse with me. What was I? The question again recurred, to be answered only with groans.'

Again and again, I wept openly. Will these tears never cease?

And then, in an instant, he was no longer relating his story to me but instead directly addressing me: 'I will soon explain to what these feelings tended.' And then just as quickly, he returned to his tale, 'But allow me now to return to the cottagers, whose story excited in me such various feelings of indignation, delight, and wonder, but which all terminated in additional love and reverence for my protectors (for so I loved, in an innocent, half painful self-deceit, to call them).'"

I wept.

Chapter IV

Some time elapsed before I learned the history of my friends. It was one which could not fail to impress itself deeply on my mind, unfolding as it did a number of circumstances each interesting and wonderful to one so utterly inexperienced as I was.

'The name of the old man was De Lacey. He was descended from a good family in France, where he had lived for many years in affluence, respected by his superiors, and beloved by his equals. His son was bred in the service of his country; and Agatha had ranked with ladies of the highest distinction. A few months before my arrival, they had lived in a large and luxurious city, called Paris, surrounded by friends, and possessed of every enjoyment which virtue, refinement of intellect, or taste, accompanied by a moderate fortune, could afford.

'The father of Safie had been the cause of their ruin. He was a Turkish merchant, and had inhabited Paris for many years, when, for some reason which I could not learn, he became obnoxious to the government.' Oh! No doubt the merchant sold goods to the aristocracy and then got caught up in the mass arrests of the royalists that seized a revolutionary France and cost the royalists their heads. Literally. And liberally was the guillotine utilized. 'He was seized and cast into prison the very day that Safie arrived from Constantinople to join him. He was tried, and condemned to death. The injustice of his sentence was very flagrant; all Paris was indignant; and it was judged that his religion and wealth, rather than the crime alleged against him, had been the cause of his condemnation.' The revolutionaries cared not if your noble blood was French or foreign. The condemnation was the same throughout the nation. Off with their heads!

'Felix had been present at the trial; his horror and indignation were uncontrollable, when he heard the decision of the court. He made, at that moment, a solemn vow to deliver him, and then looked around for the means. After many fruitless attempts to gain admittance to the prison, he found a strongly grated window in an unguarded part of the building, which lighted the dungeon of the unfortunate Mahometan; who, loaded with chains, waited in despair the execution of the barbarous sentence. Felix visited the grate at night, and made known to the prisoner his intentions in his favour. The Turk, amazed and delighted, endeavoured to kindle the zeal of his deliverer by promises of reward and wealth. Felix rejected his offers with contempt; yet when he saw the lovely Safie, who was allowed to visit her father, and who, by her gestures, expressed her lively gratitude, the youth could not help owning to his own mind, that the captive possessed a treasure which would fully reward his toil and hazard.' The foolishness and folly of youth.

'The Turk quickly perceived the impression that his daughter had made on the heart of Felix, and endeavoured to secure him more entirely in his interests by the promise of her hand in marriage, so soon as he should be conveyed to a place of safety. Felix was too delicate to accept this offer; yet he looked forward to the probability of that event as to the consummation of his happiness.

'During the ensuing days, while the preparations were going forward for the escape of the merchant, the zeal of Felix was warmed by several letters that he received from this lovely girl, who found means to express her thoughts in the language of her lover by the aid of an old man, a servant of her father's, who understood French. She thanked him in the most ardent terms for his intended services towards her father; and at the same time she gently deplored her own fate.

'I have copies of these letters; for I found means, during my residence in the hovel, to procure the implements of writing; and the letters were often in the hands of Felix or Agatha. Before I depart, I will give them to you, they will prove the truth of my tale; but at present, as the sun is already far declined, I shall only have time to repeat the substance of them to you.' Was the Creation addressing me or Victor Frankenstein at this moment? There is no means by which I could take possession of phantasmagorical letters. But if this Creation was addressing Victor while they both sit beside a roaring fire in a cave fashioned in ice? Either audience could easily be being addressed by Victor's Creation.

'Safie related, that her mother was a Christian Arab.' A *jizyah*. I whispered under my breath. I know not where the word came from, for I know not Arabic, excepting my dropping of eaves during the dinners my father. Perhaps. Perhaps not. 'Seized and made a slave by the Turks; recommended by her beauty, she had won the heart of the father of Safie, who married her. The young girl spoke in high and enthusiastic terms of her mother, who, born in freedom spurned the bondage to which she was now reduced. She instructed her daughter in the tenets of her religion, and taught her to aspire to higher powers of intellect, and an independence of spirit, forbidden to the female followers of Mahomet.'

The Quran is not alone in its condemnation of the education of women. Does not Paul the Apostle instruct thus, *Let the woman learn in silence with all subjection. And I do not permit a woman to teach or to have authority over a man, but to be in silence. For Adam was first formed, then Eve. And Adam was not deceived, but the woman being deceived was in the transgression. Notwithstanding she shall be saved in childbearing, if they continue in faith and charity and holiness with sobriety.* AND! *Let your women keep silence in the churches: for it is not permitted unto them to speak; but they are commanded to be under obedience as also saith the law. And if they will learn any thing, let them ask their husbands at home: for it is a shame for women to speak in the church.* AND! *Wives, submit yourselves unto your own husbands, as unto the Lord. For the husband is the head of the wife, even as Christ is the head of the church: and he is the saviour of the body. Therefore as the church is subject unto Christ, so let the wives be to their own husbands in every thing.*

How my mother loathed these scriptures!

'This lady died; but her lessons were indelibly impressed on the mind of Safie, who sickened at the prospect of again returning to Asia, and the being immured within the walls of a harem, allowed only to occupy herself with puerile amusements, ill suited to the temper of her soul, now accustomed to grand ideas and a noble emulation for virtue. The prospect of marrying a Christian, and remaining in a country where women were allowed to take a rank in society, was enchanting to her.

'The day for the execution of the Turk was fixed; but, on the night previous to it, he had quitted prison, and before morning was distant many leagues from Paris. Felix had procured passports in the name of his father, sister, and himself. He had previously communicated his plan to the former, who aided the deceit by quitting his house, under the pretence of a journey, and concealed himself, with his daughter, in an obscure part of Paris.

'Felix conducted the fugitives through France to Lyons, and across Mont Cenis to Leghorn, where the merchant had decided to wait a favourable opportunity of passing into some part of the Turkish dominions.

'Safie resolved to remain with her father until the moment of his departure, before which time the Turk renewed his promise that she should be united to his deliverer; and Felix remained with them in expectation of that event; and in the mean time he enjoyed the society of the Arabian, who exhibited towards him the simplest and tenderest affection. They conversed with one another through the means of an interpreter, and sometimes with the interpretation of looks; and Safie sang to him the divine airs of her native country.

'The Turk allowed this intimacy to take place, and encouraged the hopes of the youthful lovers, while in his heart he had formed far other plans. He loathed the idea that his daughter should be united to a Christian; but he feared the resentment of Felix if he should appear lukewarm; for he knew that he was still in the power of his deliverer, if he should choose to betray him to the Italian state which they inhabited. He revolved a thousand plans by which he should be enabled to prolong the deceit until it might be no longer necessary, and secretly to take his daughter with him when he departed. His plans were greatly facilitated by the news which arrived from Paris.

'The government of France were greatly enraged at the escape of their victim, and spared no pains to detect and punish his deliverer. The plot of Felix was quickly discovered, and De Lacey and Agatha were thrown into prison. The news reached Felix, and roused him from his dream of pleasure. His blind and aged father, and his gentle sister, lay in a noisome dungeon, while he enjoyed the free air, and the society of her whom he loved. This idea was torture to him. He quickly arranged with the Turk, that if the latter should find a favourable opportunity for escape before Felix could return to Italy, Safie should remain as a boarder at a convent at Leghorn; and then, quitting the lovely Arabian, he hastened to Paris, and delivered himself up to the vengeance of the law, hoping to free De Lacey and Agatha by this proceeding.

'He did not succeed. They remained confined for five months before the trial took place; the result of which deprived them of their fortune, and condemned them to a perpetual exile from their native country.

'They found a miserable asylum in the cottage in Germany, where I discovered them. Felix soon learned that the treacherous Turk, for whom he and his family endured such unheard-of oppression, on discovering that his deliverer was thus reduced to poverty and impotence, became a traitor to good feeling and honour, and had quitted Italy with his daughter, insultingly sending Felix a pittance of money to aid him, as he said, in some plan of future maintenance.

'Such were the events that preyed on the heart of Felix, and rendered him, when I first saw him, the most miserable of his family. He could have endured poverty, and when this distress had been the meed of his virtue, he would have gloried in it: but the ingratitude of the Turk, and the loss of his beloved Safie, were misfortunes more bitter and irreparable. The arrival of the Arabian now infused new life into his soul.

'When the news reached Leghorn, that Felix was deprived of his wealth and rank, the merchant commanded his daughter to think no more of her lover, but to prepare to return with him to her native country. The generous nature of Safie was outraged by this command; she attempted to expostulate with her father, but he left her angrily, reiterating his tyrannical mandate.

'A few days after, the Turk entered his daughter's apartment, and told her hastily, that he had reason to believe that his residence at Leghorn had been divulged, and that he should speedily be delivered up to the French government; he had, consequently, hired a vessel to convey him to Constantinople, for which city he should sail in a few hours. He intended to leave his daughter under the care of a confidential servant, to follow at her leisure with the greater part of his property, which had not yet arrived at Leghorn.

'When alone, Safie resolved in her own mind the plan of conduct that it would become her to pursue in this emergency. A residence in Turkey was abhorrent to her; her religion and feelings were alike adverse to it. By some papers of her father's, which fell into her hands, she heard of the exile of her lover, and learnt the name of the spot where he then resided. She hesitated some time, but at length she formed her determination. Taking with her some jewels that belonged to her, and a small sum of money, she quitted Italy, with an attendant, a native of Leghorn, but who understood the common language of Turkey, and departed for Germany.

'She arrived in safety at a town about twenty leagues from the cottage of De Lacey, when her attendant fell dangerously ill. Safie nursed her with the most devoted affection; but the poor girl died, and the Arabian was left alone, unacquainted with the language of the country, and utterly ignorant of the customs of the world. She fell, however, into good hands. The Italian had mentioned the name of the spot for which they were bound; and, after her death, the woman of the house in which they had lived took care that Safie should arrive in safety at the cottage of her lover."

Again and again the foolishness and folly of youth! But this is a foolishness and folly I am all to accustomed to. My soul has been ascribed with this very foolishness and folly to have followed my Beloved from the rightful grip of my father into flight from our marital plight across France into the Villa Diodati. But the wrath of my father— nay! the wrath of the Eternal Father— has descended upon us with thunderous dark and violent storm clouds.

Chapter V

Such was the history of my beloved cottagers. It impressed me deeply. I learned, from the views of social life which it developed, to admire their virtues, and to deprecate the vices of mankind.

'As yet I looked upon crime as a distant evil; benevolence and generosity were ever present before me, inciting within me a desire to become an actor in the busy scene where so many admirable qualities were called forth and displayed. But, in giving an account of the progress of my intellect, I must not omit a circumstance which occurred in the beginning of the month of August of the same year.' This must be 1795. Or is it? I'm getting lost in the whirlwind of my own mind.

'One night, during my accustomed visit to the neighbouring wood, where I collected my own food, and brought home firing for my protectors, I found on the ground a leathern portmanteau, containing several articles of dress and some books. I eagerly seized the prize, and returned with it to my hovel. Fortunately the books were written in the language the elements of which I had acquired at the cottage; they consisted of *Paradise Lost*, a volume of *Plutarch's Lives*, and the *Sorrows of Werter.*' Oh! to read Milton in French would prove to be such an abomination. I have no doubt that Nicolas-François Dupré de Saint-Maur's translation is estimable, but something must be lost in the translation! Jacques Amyot's translation of Plutarch is in itself estimable, but only because it is the source of Sir Thomas North's own English translation. A translation of a translation? The horror! While I have yet to read Goethe in his original German, Baron Karl Siemund von Seckendorff's French translation is no doubt serviceable. 'The possession of these treasures gave me extreme delight; I now continually studied and exercised my mind upon these histories, whilst my friends were employed in their ordinary occupations.'

His delight at discovering the joys and wonders of the written word upon the page delights me so! The joy of reading the histories, the epics, the dramas, the philosophies, the sciences is only surpassed by the joy of writing. To create entire characters and worlds out of the ether is a form of creation that is only rivalled by the growing of a child in your womb. And just as the mother knows not the destiny of the child growing in her womb, the author knows not the fate of her characters. It is the strangest of paradoxes when a character created by your own mind turns on its author by exclaiming, 'No! this is my story now. I shall relate it the way I wish!' Sometimes, this happens on the very first page of the ink-stained manuscript! And curiously, I am feeling this queer experience at this very moment listening to Victor's Creation relate his story unto me!

'I can hardly describe to you the effect of these books. They produced in me an infinity of new images and feelings, that sometimes raised me to ecstacy, but more frequently sunk me into the lowest dejection. In the *Sorrows of Werter*, besides the interest of its simple and affecting story, so many opinions are canvassed, and so many lights thrown upon what had hitherto been to me obscure subjects, that I found in it a never-ending source of speculation and astonishment. The gentle and domestic manners it described, combined with lofty sentiments and feelings, which had for their object something out of self, accorded well with my experience among my protectors, and with the wants which were for ever alive in my own bosom. But I thought Werter himself a more divine being than I had ever beheld or imagined; his character contained no pretension, but it sunk deep. The disquisitions upon death and suicide were calculated to fill me with wonder. I did not pretend to enter into the merits of the case, yet I inclined towards the opinions of the hero, whose extinction I wept, without precisely understanding it.

'As I read, however, I applied much personally to my own feelings and condition. I found myself similar, yet at the same time strangely unlike the beings concerning whom I read, and to whose conversation I was a listener. I sympathized with, and partly understood them, but I was unformed in mind; I was dependent on none, and related to none. 'The path of my departure was free.' How Victor's Creation has stolen into my own mind to steal the words of my Beloved! It is impossible for the Creation to have read published this very year! Shall I share again the original words composed by my Beloved, my dearest Journal?

We are as clouds that veil the midnight moon;
        How restlessly they speed, and gleam, and quiver,
Streaking the darkness radiantly!—yet soon
        Night closes round, and they are lost forever:

Or like forgotten lyres, whose dissonant strings
        Give various response to each varying blast,
To whose frail frame no second motion brings
        One mood or modulation like the last.

We rest.—A dream has power to poison sleep;
        We rise.—One wandering thought pollutes the day;
We feel, conceive or reason, laugh or weep;
        Embrace fond woe, or cast our cares away:

It is the same!—For, be it joy or sorrow,
        The path of its departure still is free:
Man's yesterday may ne'er be like his morrow;
        Nought may endure but mutability![7]

'And there was none to lament my annihilation. My person was hideous, and my stature gigantic: what did this mean? Who was I? What was I? Whence did I come? What was my destination? These questions continually recurred, but I was unable to solve them.'

But solve them you shall. Solve them you must!

'The volume of *Plutarch's Lives* which I possessed, contained the histories of the first founders of the ancient republics. This book had a far different effect upon me from the *Sorrows of Werter*. I learned from Werter's imaginations despondency and gloom: but Plutarch taught me high thoughts; he elevated me above the wretched sphere of my own reflections, to admire and love the heroes of past ages. Many things I read surpassed my understanding and experience. I had a very confused knowledge of kingdoms, wide extents of country, mighty rivers, and boundless seas. But I was perfectly unacquainted with towns, and large assemblages of men. The cottage of my protectors had been the only school in which I had studied human nature; but this book developed

---

7 From *Alastor, or The Spirit of Solitude: And Other Poems* by Percy Bysshe Shelley in 1816.

new and mightier scenes of action. I read of men concerned in public affairs governing or massacring their species. I felt the greatest ardour for virtue rise within me, and abhorrence for vice, as far as I understood the signification of those terms, relative as they were, as I applied them, to pleasure and pain alone. Induced by these feelings, I was of course led to admire peaceable law-givers,'— which he named his favourites— 'Numa, Solon, and Lycurgus, in preference to Romulus and Theseus.'

Of Numa, whom Plutarch wrote, 'It is true, indeed, of all just and good men, that they are praised more after they have left the world than before, since envy does not long survive them, and some even see it die before them; but in Numa's case the misfortunes of the kings who followed him made his fame shine all the brighter.'[8]

Of Solon, whom Plutarch wrote, 'Thus he represents the multitude and men of low degree as speaking of him. However, though he rejected the tyranny, he did not administer affairs in the mildest possible manner, nor in the enactment of his laws did he show a feeble spirit, nor make concessions to the powerful, nor consult the pleasure of his electors. Nay, where a condition was as good as it could well be, he applied no remedy, and introduced no innovation, fearing lest, after utterly confusing and confounding the city, he should be too weak to establish it again and recompose it for the best. But those things wherein he hoped to find them open to persuasion or submissive to compulsion, these he did, "Combining both force and justice together," as he says himself. Therefore when he was afterwards asked if he had enacted the best laws for the Athenians, he replied, "The best they would receive."[9]

Of Lycurgus, whom Plutarch wrote, 'Concerning Lycurgus the lawgiver, in general, nothing can be said which is not disputed, since indeed there are different accounts of his birth, his travels, his death, and above all, of his work as lawmaker and statesman; and there is least agreement among historians as to the times in which the man lived.'[10]

Of Romulus, whom Plutarch wrote, 'From whom, and for what reason the great name of Rome, so famous among mankind, was given to that city, writers are not agreed. Some say it was Roma, a daughter of the Trojan woman I have mentioned, who was wedded to Latinus the son of Telemachus and bore him Romulus; others that Aemilia, the daughter of Aeneas and Lavinia, bore him to Mars; and others still rehearse what is altogether fabulous concerning his origin. For instance, they say that Tarchetius, king of the Albans, who was most lawless and cruel, was vis-

---

8 From *Plutarch's Lives*, 'The Life of Numa', as translated by Bernadotte Perrin.

9 From *Plutarch's Lives*, 'The Life of Solon', as translated by Bernadotte Perrin.

10 From *Plutarch's Lives*, 'The Life of Lyrcurgus', as translated by Bernadotte Perrin.

ited with a strange phantom in his house, namely, a phallus rising out of the hearth and remaining there many days.'[11]

Of Theseus, whom Plutarch wrote, 'But after publishing my account of Lycurgus the lawgiver and Numa the king, I thought I might not unreasonably go back still farther to Romulus, now that my history had brought me near his times. And as I asked myself, "With such a warrior" (as Aeschylus says) "who will dare to fight?" "Whom shall I set against him? Who is competent?" it seemed to me that I must make the founder of lovely and famous Athens the counterpart and parallel to the father of invincible and glorious Rome. May I therefore succeed in purifying Fable, making her submit to reason and take on the semblance of History. But where she obstinately disdains to make herself credible, and refuses to admit any element of probability, I shall pray for kindly readers, and such as receive with indulgence the tales of antiquity.'[12]

Despite, or in spite of, my mind's rapid digressions onto the bookshelves of the library of human memory where Plutarhc's *Lives of the Noble Greek and Romans* is currently shelved, Victor's Creation continued on with his tale unabetted, 'The patriarchal lives of my protectors caused these impressions to take a firm hold on my mind; perhaps, if my first introduction to humanity had been made by a young soldier, burning for glory and slaughter, I should have been imbued with different sensations.

'But *Paradise Lost* excited different and far deeper emotions. I read it, as I had read the other volumes which had fallen into my hands, as a true history. It moved every feeling of wonder and awe, that the picture of an omnipotent God warring with his creatures was capable of exciting. I often referred the several situations, as their similarity struck me, to my own. Like Adam, I was created apparently united by no link to any other being in existence; but his state was far different from mine in every other respect. He had come forth from the hands of God a perfect creature, happy and prosperous, guarded by the especial care of his Creator; he was allowed to converse with, and acquire knowledge from beings of a superior nature: but I was wretched, helpless, and alone. Many times I considered Satan as the fitter emblem of my condition; for often, like him, when I viewed the bliss of my protectors, the bitter gall of envy rose within me.'

Oh! No! Dearest Creation of Victor's! Take not this lesson from Milton! But I cannot and will not make any defence of Satan! I shall allow my Beloved to make his own defence: 'The distorted notions of invisible things which Dante and his rival Milton have idealized are merely

---

11 From *Plutarch's Lives*, 'The Life of Romulus', as translated by Bernadotte Perrin.
12 From *Plutarch's Lives*, 'The Life of Theseus', as translated by Bernadotte Perrin.

the mask and the mantle in which these great poets walk through eternity enveloped and disguised. It is a difficult question to determine how far they were conscious of the distinction which must have subsisted in their minds between their own creeds and that of the people. Dante at least appears to wish to mark the full extent of it by placing Riphæus, whom Virgil calls *justissimus unus,* in Paradise, and observing a most heretical caprice in his distribution of rewards and punishments. And Milton's poem contains within itself a philosophical refutation of that system of which, by a strange and natural antithesis, it has been a chief popular support. Nothing can exceed the energy and magnificence of the character of Satan as expressed in Paradise Lost. It is a mistake to suppose that he could ever have been intended for the popular personification of evil. Implacable hate, patient cunning, and a sleepless refinement of device to inflict the extremest anguish on an enemy, these things are evil; and although venial in a slave are not to be forgiven in a tyrant; although redeemed by much that ennobles his defeat in one subdued, are marked by all that dishonours his conquest in the victor. Milton's Devil as a moral being is as far superior to his God as one who perseveres in some purpose which he has conceived to be excellent in spite of adversity and torture, is to one who in the cold security of undoubted triumph inflicts the most horrible revenge upon his enemy, not from any mistaken notion of inducing him to repent of a perseverance in enmity, but with the alleged design of exasperating him to deserve new torments. Milton has so far violated the popular creed (if this shall be judged a violation) as to have alleged no superiority of moral virtue to his God over his Devil. And this bold neglect of a direct moral purpose is the most decisive proof of Milton's genius. He mingled as it were the elements of human nature, as colours upon a single pallet, and arranged them into the composition of his great picture according to the laws of epic truth; that is, according to the laws of that principle by which a series of actions of the external universe and of intelligent and ethical beings is calculated to excite the sympathy of succeeding generations of mankind.'[13]

Again and again, my mind's incessant digressions distract from the tale being related by this Creation, 'Another circumstance strengthened and confirmed these feelings. Soon after my arrival in the hovel, I discovered some papers in the pocket of the dress which I had taken from *your* laboratory.' Was the Creation addressing me in the moment, or Victor? I possessed no laboratory. I possessed no papers secreted in the pocket of a dress. 'At first I had neglected them; but now that I was able to decypher the characters in which they were written, I began to study

---

13 From an unfinished essay by Percy Bysshe Shelley written in February and March of 1821, though it is conceivable he composed it as early as 1816.

them with diligence. It was your journal of the four months that preceded my creation. You minutely described in these papers every step you took in the progress of your work; this history was mingled with accounts of domestic occurrences. You, doubtless, recollect these papers. Here they are. Every thing is related in them which bears reference to my accursed origin; the whole detail of that series of disgusting circumstances which produced it is set in view; the minutest description of my odious and loathsome person is given, in language which painted your own horrors, and rendered mine ineffaceable. I sickened as I read. "Hateful day when I received life!" I exclaimed in agony. "Cursed creator! Why did you form a monster so hideous that even you turned from me in disgust? God in pity made man beautiful and alluring, after his own image; but my form is a filthy type of your's, more horrid from its very resemblance. Satan had his companions, fellow-devils, to admire and encourage him; but I am solitary and detested.'"

Oh! No! Dearest Creation, think not this thought of your Creation!

'These were the reflections of my hours of despondency and solitude; but when I contemplated the virtues of the cottagers, their amiable and benevolent dispositions, I persuaded myself that when they should become acquainted with my admiration of their virtues, they would compassionate me, and overlook my personal deformity. Could they turn from their door one, however monstrous, who solicited their compassion and friendship? I resolved, at least, not to despair, but in every way to fit myself for an interview with them which would decide my fate.' I shutter with terrified anticipation of this moment. 'I postponed this attempt for some months longer; for the importance attached to its success inspired me with a dread lest I should fail. Besides, I found that my understanding improved so much with every day's experience, that I was unwilling to commence this undertaking until a few more months should have added to my wisdom.

'Several changes, in the mean time, took place in the cottage. The presence of Safie diffused happiness among its inhabitants; and I also found that a greater degree of plenty reigned there. Felix and Agatha spent more time in amusement and conversation, and were assisted in their labours by servants. They did not appear rich, but they were contented and happy; their feelings were serene and peaceful, while mine became every day more tumultuous. Increase of knowledge only discovered to me more clearly what a wretched outcast I was. I cherished hope, it is true; but it vanished, when I beheld my person reflected in water, or my shadow in the moon-shine, even as that frail image and that inconstant shade.

'I endeavoured to crush these fears, and to fortify myself for the trial which in a few months I resolved to undergo; and sometimes I allowed my thoughts, unchecked by reason, to ramble in the fields of Paradise, and dared to fancy amiable and lovely creatures sympathizing with my feelings and cheering my gloom; their angelic countenances breathed smiles of consolation. But it was all a dream: no Eve soothed my sorrows, or shared my thoughts; I was alone. I remembered Adam's supplication to his Creator; but where was mine? he had abandoned me, and, in the bitterness of my heart, I cursed him.

'Autumn passed thus. I saw, with surprise and grief, the leaves decay and fall, and nature again assume the barren and bleak appearance it had worn when I first beheld the woods and the lovely moon. Yet I did not heed the bleakness of the weather; I was better fitted by my conforma- tion for the endurance of cold than heat. But my chief delights were the sight of the flowers, the birds, and all the gay apparel of summer; when those deserted me, I turned with more attention towards the cottagers. Their happiness was not decreased by the absence of summer. They loved, and sympathized with one another; and their joys, depending on each other, were not interrupted by the casualties that took place around them. The more I saw of them, the greater became my desire to claim their protection and kindness; my heart yearned to be known and loved by these amiable creatures: to see their sweet looks turned towards me with affection, was the utmost limit of my ambition. I dared not think that they would turn them from me with disdain and horror. The poor that stopped at their door were never driven away. I asked, it is true, for great- er treasures than a little food or rest; I required kindness and sympathy; but I did not believe myself utterly unworthy of it.

'The winter advanced, and an entire revolution of the seasons had taken place since I awoke into life. My attention, at this time, was solely directed towards my plan of introducing myself into the cottage of my protectors. I revolved many projects; but that on which I finally fixed was, to enter the dwelling when the blind old man should be alone. I had sagacity enough to discover, that the unnatural hideousness of my person was the chief object of horror with those who had formerly be- held me. My voice, although harsh, had nothing terrible in it; I thought, therefore, that if, in the absence of his children, I could gain the good-will and mediation of the old De Lacy, I might, by his means, be tolerated by my younger protectors.

'One day, when the sun shone on the red leaves that strewed the ground, and diffused cheerfulness, although it denied warmth, Safie, Agatha, and Felix, departed on a long country walk, and the old man, at his own desire, was left alone in the cottage. When his children had departed, he took up his guitar, and played several mournful, but sweet airs, more sweet and mournful than I had ever heard him play before. At first his countenance was illuminated with pleasure, but, as he continued, thoughtfulness and sadness succeeded; at length, laying aside the instrument, he sat absorbed in reflection.

'My heart beat quick.'

As does mine, dearest Creation!

'This was the hour and moment of trial, which would decide my hopes, or realize my fears. The servants were gone to a neighbouring fair. All was silent in and around the cottage: it was an excellent opportunity; yet, when I proceeded to execute my plan, my limbs failed me, and I sunk to the ground. Again I rose; and, exerting all the firmness of which I was master, removed the planks which I had placed before my hovel to conceal my retreat. The fresh air revived me, and, with renewed determination, I approached the door of their cottage.

'I knocked. "Who is there?" said the old man— "Come in."

'I entered; "Pardon this intrusion," said I, "I am a traveller in want of a little rest; you would greatly oblige me, if you would allow me to remain a few minutes before the fire."

' "Enter," said De Lacy; "and I will try in what manner I can relieve your wants; but, unfortunately, my children are from home, and, as I am blind, I am afraid I shall find it difficult to procure food for you."

' "Do not trouble yourself, my kind host, I have food; it is warmth and rest only that I need."

'I sat down, and a silence ensued. I knew that every minute was precious to me, yet I remained irresolute in what manner to commence the interview; when the old man addressed me—

' "By your language, stranger, I suppose you are my countryman;— are you French?'

' "No; but I was educated by a French family, and understand that language only. I am now going to claim the protection of some friends, whom I sincerely love, and of whose favour I have some hopes."

' "Are these Germans?"

' "No, they are French. But let us change the subject. I am an unfortunate and deserted creature; I look around, and I have no relation or friend upon earth. These amiable people to whom I go have never seen me, and know little of me. I am full of fears; for if I fail there, I am an outcast in the world for ever.'

' "Do not despair. To be friendless is indeed to be unfortunate; but the hearts of men, when unprejudiced by any obvious self-interest, are full of brotherly love and charity. Rely, therefore, on your hopes; and if these friends are good and amiable, do not despair."

' "They are kind— they are the most excellent creatures in the world; but, unfortunately, they are prejudiced against me. I have good dispositions; my life has been hitherto harmless, and, in some degree, beneficial; but a fatal prejudice clouds their eyes, and where they ought to see a feeling and kind friend, they behold only a detestable monster."

' "That is indeed unfortunate; but if you are really blameless, cannot you undeceive them?"

' "I am about to undertake that task; and it is on that account that I feel so many overwhelming terrors. I tenderly love these friends; I have, unknown to them, been for many months in the habits of daily kindness towards them; but they believe that I wish to injure them, and it is that prejudice which I wish to overcome."

' "Where do these friends reside?"

' "Near this spot."

'The old man paused, and then continued, "If you will unreservedly confide to me the particulars of your tale, I perhaps may be of use in undeceiving them. I am blind, and cannot judge of your countenance, but there is something in your words which persuades me that you are sincere. I am poor, and an exile; but it will afford me true pleasure to be in any way serviceable to a human creature."

' "Excellent man! I thank you, and accept your generous offer. You raise me from the dust by this kindness; and I trust that, by your aid, I shall not be driven from the society and sympathy of your fellow-creatures."

' "Heaven forbid! even if you were really criminal; for that can only drive you to desperation, and not instigate you to virtue. I also am unfortunate; I and my family have been condemned, although innocent: judge, therefore, if I do not feel for your misfortunes."

' "How can I thank you, my best and only benefactor? from your lips first have I heard the voice of kindness directed towards me; I shall be for ever grateful; and your present humanity assures me of success with those friends whom I am on the point of meeting."

' "May I know the names and residence of those friends?"

'I paused. This, I thought, was the moment of decision, which was to rob me of, or bestow happiness on me for ever. I struggled vainly for firmness sufficient to answer him, but the effort destroyed all my remaining strength; I sank on the chair, and sobbed aloud. At that moment I heard the steps of my younger protectors. I had not a moment to lose; but, seizing the hand of the old man, I cried, "Now is the time!— save and protect me! You and your family are the friends whom I seek. Do not you desert me in the hour of trial!"

' "Great God!" exclaimed the old man, "who are you?"

'At that instant the cottage door was opened, and Felix, Safie, and Agatha entered. Who can describe their horror and consternation on beholding me? Agatha fainted; and Safie, unable to attend to her friend, rushed out of the cottage. Felix darted forward, and with supernatural force tore me from his father, to whose knees I clung: in a transport of fury, he dashed me to the ground, and struck me violently with a stick. I could have torn him limb from limb, as the lion rends the antelope. But my heart sunk within me as with bitter sickness, and I refrained. I saw him on the point of repeating his blow, when, overcome by pain and anguish, I quitted the cottage, and in the general tumult escaped unperceived to my hovel.'

I too, like Agatha, fainted upon hearing of exchange between the De Lacys and Victor's Creation. I awoke, in my bed within my apartment at the Villa Diodati with my Beloved by my side still peacefully slumbering. The Creation had moved from his chair beside the fire and held my hand in his. My hand appeared swallowed by his own as if my hand was Jonah and his was the whale. I felt its enormity and also its tenderness. A salty wetness threatened to overwell his eyes; eyes that shown with human kindness. His voiced soothed me with cooing warmth and gentleness. Once the Creation had been assured of my wellbeing, he sat again in the chair beside the fire and continued his tale... full of wrath and rage!

Chapter VI

Sing, O goddess, the wrath of Achilles, son of Peleus, that brought countless ills upon the Achaeans, just as I believe Victor's Creation shall be countless ills upon his Creator!

'Cursed, cursed creator! Why did I live? Why, in that instant, did I not extinguish the spark of existence which you had so wantonly bestowed? I know not; despair had not yet taken possession of me; my feelings were those of rage and revenge. I could with pleasure have destroyed the cottage and its inhabitants, and have glutted myself with their shrieks and misery.'

Victor's mangled Creation reminds me of God's magnificent Creation, Satan. Where Adam and Eve are often seen by the JudeoChristian as perfect creations, their fall from Eden by eating of the fruit of the Tree of the Knowledge of Good and Evil speaks to their imperfection. And were not the angels created perfect and yet their Fall likewise speaks to their imperfections. Victor's Creation is seen by not only his Creator but by the Creation itself as imperfect. Did not Victor's Creation say only mere moments ago, 'Many times I considered Satan as the fitter emblem of my condition; for often, like him, when I viewed the bliss of my protectors, the bitter gall of envy rose within me.' And thus Satan's opening soliloquy against God by Milton speaks volumes:

> *'Is this the Region, this the Soil, the Clime',*
> *Said then the lost Arch Angel, 'this the seat*
> *That we must change for Heav'n, this mournful gloom*
> *For that celestial light? Be it so, since he*
> *Who now is Sovran can dispose and bid*
> *What shall be right: farthest from him is best*
> *Whom reason hath equalled, force hath made supreme*
> *Above his equals. Farewell happy Fields*
> *Where Joy for ever dwells: Hail horrors, hail*
> *Infernal world, and thou profoundest Hell*
> *Receive thy new Possessor: One who brings*
> *A mind not to be chang'd by Place or Time.*
> *The mind is its own place, and in it self*
> *Can make a Heav'n of Hell, a Hell of Heav'n.*
> *What matter where, if I be still the same,*
> *And what I should be, all but less then he*
> *Whom Thunder hath made greater? Here at least*
> *We shall be free; th' Almighty hath not built*
> *Here for his envy, will not drive us hence:*
> *Here we may reign secure, and in my choice*
> *To reign is worth ambition though in Hell:*
> *Better to reign in Hell, then serve in Heav'n.*
> *But wherefore let we then our faithful friends,*
> *Th' associates and copartners of our loss*
> *Lye thus astonished on th' oblivious Pool,*
> *And call them not to share with us their part*
> *In this unhappy Mansion, or once more*
> *With rallied Arms to try what may be yet*
> *Regained in Heav'n, or what more lost in Hell?'*[14]

'When night came, I quitted my retreat, and wandered in the wood; and now, no longer restrained by the fear of discovery, I gave vent to my anguish in fearful howlings. I was like a wild beast that had broken the toils; destroying the objects that obstructed me, and ranging through the wood with a stag-like swiftness. Oh! what a miserable night I passed! the cold stars shone in mockery, and the bare trees waved their branches above me: now and then the sweet voice of a bird burst forth amidst the universal stillness. All, save I, were at rest or in enjoyment: I, like the arch

---

14 From Book I of *Paradise Lost* by John Milton.

fiend, bore a hell within me; and, finding myself unsympathized with, wished to tear up the trees, spread havoc and destruction around me, and then to have sat down and enjoyed the ruin.

'But this was a luxury of sensation that could not endure; I became fatigued with excess of bodily exertion, and sank on the damp grass in the sick impotence of despair. There was none among the myriads of men that existed who would pity or assist me; and should I feel kindness towards my enemies? No: from that moment I declared everlasting war against the species, and, more than all, against him who had formed me, and sent me forth to this insupportable misery.'

> *'O Sun, to tell thee how I hate thy beams*
> *That bring to my remembrance from what state*
> *I fell, how glorious once above thy Sphere;*
> *Till Pride and worse Ambition threw me down*
> *Warring in Heav'n against Heav'ns matchless King:*
> *Ah wherefore! he deserved no such return*
> *From me, whom he created what I was*
> *In that bright eminence, and with his good*
> *Upbraided none; nor was his service hard.*
> *What could be less then to afford him praise,*
> *The easiest recompense, and pay him thanks,*
> *How due! yet all his good prov'd ill in me,*
> *And wrought but malice; lifted up so high*
> *I sdeined subjection, and thought one step higher*
> *Would set me highest, and in a moment quit*
> *The debt immense of endless gratitude,*
> *So burthensome, still paying, still to owe;*
> *Forgetful what from him I still received,*
> *And understood not that a grateful mind*
> *By owing owes not, but still pays, at once*
> *Indebted and discharged; what burden then?*
> *O had his powerful Destiny ordained*
> *Me some inferior Angel, I had stood*
> *Then happy; no unbounded hope had rais'd*
> *Ambition. Yet why not? some other Power*
> *As great might have aspir'd, and me though mean*
> *Drawn to his part; but other Powers as great*
> *Fell not, but stand unshak'n, from within*
> *Or from without, to all temptations arm'd.*
> *Hadst thou the same free Will and Power to stand?*
> *Thou hadst: whom hast thou then or what to accuse,*

But Heav'ns free Love dealt equally to all?
Be then his Love accurst, since love or hate,
To me alike, it deals eternal woe.
Nay curs'd be thou; since against his thy will
Chose freely what it now so justly rues.
Me miserable! which way shall I fly
Infinite wrath, and infinite despair?
Which way I fly is Hell; my self am Hell;
And in the lowest deep a lower deep
Still threatening to devour me opens wide,
To which the Hell I suffer seems a Heav'n.[15]

'The sun rose; I heard the voices of men, and knew that it was impossible to return to my retreat during that day. Accordingly I hid myself in some thick underwood, determining to devote the ensuing hours to reflection on my situation.

'The pleasant sunshine, and the pure air of day, restored me to some degree of tranquillity; and when I considered what had passed at the cottage, I could not help believing that I had been too hasty in my conclusions. I had certainly acted imprudently. It was apparent that my conversation had interested the father in my behalf, and I was a fool in having exposed my person to the horror of his children. I ought to have familiarized the old De Lacy to me, and by degrees have discovered myself to the rest of his family, when they should have been prepared for my approach. But I did not believe my errors to be irretrievable; and, after much consideration, I resolved to return to the cottage, seek the old man, and by my representations win him to my party.

'These thoughts calmed me, and in the afternoon I sank into a profound sleep; but the fever of my blood did not allow me to be visited by peaceful dreams. The horrible scene of the preceding day was for ever acting before my eyes; the females were flying, and the enraged Felix tearing me from his father's feet. I awoke exhausted; and, finding that it was already night, I crept forth from my hiding-place, and went in search of food.

'When my hunger was appeased, I directed my steps towards the well-known path that conducted to the cottage. All there was at peace. I crept into my hovel, and remained in silent expectation of the accustomed hour when the family arose. That hour past, the sun mounted high in the heavens, but the cottagers did not appear. I trembled violently, apprehending some dreadful misfortune. The inside of the cottage

---

15 From Book IV of *Paradise Lost* by John Milton.

was dark, and I heard no motion; I cannot describe the agony of this suspence.'

I feel it too. Deeply.

'Presently two countrymen passed by; but, pausing near the cottage, they entered into conversation, using violent gesticulations; but I did not understand what they said, as they spoke the language of the country, which differed from that of my protectors. Soon after, however, Felix approached with another man: I was surprised, as I knew that he had not quitted the cottage that morning, and waited anxiously to discover, from his discourse, the meaning of these unusual appearances.

"Do you consider,' said his companion to him, 'that you will be obliged to pay three months' rent, and to lose the produce of your garden? I do not wish to take any unfair advantage, and I beg therefore that you will take some days to consider of your determination.'

"It is utterly useless,' replied Felix, 'we can never again inhabit your cottage. The life of my father is in the greatest danger, owing to the dreadful circumstance that I have related. My wife and my sister will never recover their horror. I entreat you not to reason with me any more. Take possession of your tenement, and let me fly from this place.'

'Felix trembled violently as he said this. He and his companion entered the cottage, in which they remained for a few minutes, and then departed. I never saw any of the family of De Lacy more.

'I continued for the remainder of the day in my hovel in a state of utter and stupid despair. My protectors had departed, and had broken the only link that held me to the world. For the first time the feelings of revenge and hatred filled my bosom, and I did not strive to controul them; but, allowing myself to be borne away by the stream, I bent my mind towards injury and death. When I thought of my friends, of the mild voice of De Lacy, the gentle eyes of Agatha, and the exquisite beauty of the Arabian, these thoughts vanished, and a gush of tears somewhat soothed me. But again, when I reflected that they had spurned and deserted me, anger returned, a rage of anger; and, unable to injure any thing human, I turned my fury towards inanimate objects. As night advanced, I placed a variety of combustibles around the cottage; and, after having destroyed every vestige of cultivation in the garden, I waited with forced impatience until the moon had sunk to commence my operations.'

No! Give not into anger and despair!

'As the night advanced, a fierce wind arose from the woods, and quickly dispersed the clouds that had loitered in the heavens: the blast tore along like a mighty avalanche, and produced a kind of insanity in my spirits, that burst all bounds of reason and reflection. I lighted the dry branch of a tree, and danced with fury around the devoted cottage, my eyes still fixed on the western horizon, the edge of which the moon nearly touched. A part of its orb was at length hid, and I waved my brand; it sunk, and, with a loud scream, I fired the straw, and heath, and bushes, which I had collected. The wind fanned the fire, and the cottage was quickly enveloped by the flames, which clung to it, and licked it with their forked and destroying tongues.

'As soon as I was convinced that no assistance could save any part of the habitation, I quitted the scene, and sought for refuge in the woods.

'And now, with the world before me, whither should I bend my steps? I resolved to fly far from the scene of my misfortunes; but to me, hated and despised, every country must be equally horrible. At length the thought of you crossed my mind.' Me? Oh! He is addressing Victor again! Does he see me as a substitute for his Creator or *as* his Creator being born of a figment of my imagination? 'I learned from your papers that you were my father, my creator; and to whom could I apply with more fitness than to him who had given me life?' Oh! it is true. He sees me as only his Creator from that figment of my imagination born from the galvanizing debate between my Beloved and our little Lord, but his father as well. All his pain and suffering are caused by the decisions I have made as the author of his life. Just as Jesus the Son of God is considered by the Christian to be the Author of Life, I, like God the Father, am the omnipotent third-person creator of their very European world. And I saw that it was good! Far too little does the author care for the fate of our creations. Only the advancement of the story!

'Among the lessons that Felix had bestowed upon Safie geography had not been omitted: I had learned from these the relative situations of the different countries of the earth. You had mentioned Geneva as the name of your native town; and towards this place I resolved to proceed.

'But how was I to direct myself? I knew that I must travel in a south-westerly direction to reach my destination; but the sun was my only guide. I did not know the names of the towns that I was to pass through, nor could I ask information from a single human being; but I did not despair. From you only could I hope for succour, although towards you I felt no sentiment but that of hatred. Unfeeling, heartless creator! you had endowed me with perceptions and passions, and then cast me abroad an object for the scorn and horror of mankind. But on you only had I any claim for pity and redress, and from you I determined to seek that justice which I vainly attempted to gain from any other being that wore the human form.

'My travels were long, and the sufferings I endured intense. It was late in autumn when I quitted the district where I had so long resided. I travelled only at night, fearful of encountering the visage of a human being. Nature decayed around me, and the sun became heatless; rain and snow poured around me; mighty rivers were frozen; the surface of the earth was hard, and chill, and bare, and I found no shelter. Oh, earth! how often did I imprecate curses on the cause of my being! The mildness of my nature had fled, and all within me was turned to gall and bitterness. The nearer I approached to your habitation, the more deeply did I feel the spirit of revenge enkindled in my heart. Snow fell, and the waters were hardened, but I rested not. A few incidents now and then directed me, and I possessed a map of the country; but I often wandered wide from my path. The agony of my feelings allowed me no respite: no incident occurred from which my rage and misery could not extract its food; but a circumstance that happened when I arrived on the confines of Switzerland, when the sun had recovered its warmth, and the earth again began to look green, confirmed in an especial manner the bitterness and horror of my feelings.

'I generally rested during the day, and travelled only when I was secured by night from the view of man. One morning, however, finding that my path lay through a deep wood, I ventured to continue my journey after the sun had risen; the day, which was one of the first of spring,'— Ah! It must be 1795 now— 'cheered even me by the loveliness of its sunshine and the balminess of the air. I felt emotions of gentleness and pleasure, that had long appeared dead, revive within me. Half surprised by the novelty of these sensations, I allowed myself to be borne away by them; and, forgetting my solitude and deformity, dared to be happy. Soft tears again bedewed my cheeks, and I even raised my humid eyes with thankfulness towards the blessed sun which bestowed such joy upon me.

'I continued to wind among the paths of the wood, until I came to its boundary, which was skirted by a deep and rapid river, into which many of the trees bent their branches, now budding with the fresh spring. Here I paused, not exactly knowing what path to pursue, when I heard the sound of voices, that induced me to conceal myself under the shade of a cypress. I was scarcely hid, when a young girl came running towards the spot where I was concealed, laughing as if she ran from some one in sport. She continued her course along the precipitous sides of the river, when suddenly her foot slipt, and she fell into the rapid stream.' No! You must save her, Creation! 'I rushed from my hiding-place, and, with extreme labour from the force of the current, saved her, and dragged her to shore. She was senseless; and I endeavoured, by every means in my power, to restore animation, when I was suddenly interrupted by the approach of a rustic, who was probably the person from whom she had playfully fled. On seeing me, he darted towards me, and, tearing the girl from my arms, hastened towards the deeper parts of the wood. I followed speedily, I hardly knew why; but when the man saw me draw near, he aimed a gun, which he carried, at my body, and fired. I sunk to the ground, and my injurer, with increased swiftness, escaped into the wood.'

No! This is the reward then for his benevolence?

'This was then the reward of my benevolence! I had saved a human being from destruction, and, as a recompense, I now writhed under the miserable pain of a wound, which shattered the flesh and bone. The feelings of kindness and gentleness, which I had entertained but a few moments before, gave place to hellish rage and gnashing of teeth. Inflamed by pain, I vowed eternal hatred and vengeance to all mankind. But the agony of my wound overcame me; my pulses paused, and I fainted.'

As do I threaten to swoon again!

'For some weeks I led a miserable life in the woods, endeavouring to cure the wound which I had received. The ball had entered my shoulder, and I knew not whether it had remained there or passed through; at any rate I had no means of extracting it. My sufferings were augmented also by the oppressive sense of the injustice and ingratitude of their infliction. My daily vows rose for revenge— a deep and deadly revenge, such as would alone compensate for the outrages and anguish I had endured.

'After some weeks my wound healed, and I continued my journey. The labours I endured were no longer to be alleviated by the bright sun or gentle breezes of spring; all joy was but a mockery, which insulted my desolate state, and made me feel more painfully that I was not made for the enjoyment of pleasure.

'But my toils now drew near a close; and, two months from this time, I reached the environs of Geneva.

'It was evening when I arrived, and I retired to a hiding-place among the fields that surround it, to meditate in what manner I should apply to you. I was oppressed by fatigue and hunger, and far too unhappy to enjoy the gentle breezes of evening, or the prospect of the sun setting behind the stupendous mountains of Jura.

'At this time a slight sleep relieved me from the pain of reflection, which was disturbed by the approach of a beautiful child, who came running into the recess I had chosen with all the sportiveness of infancy. Suddenly, as I gazed on him, an idea seized me, that this little creature was unprejudiced, and had lived too short a time to have imbibed a horror of deformity. If, therefore, I could seize him, and educate him as my companion and friend, I should not be so desolate in this peopled earth.

'Urged by this impulse, I seized on the boy as he passed, and drew him towards me. As soon as he beheld my form, he placed his hands before his eyes, and uttered a shrill scream: I drew his hand forcibly from his face, and said, 'Child, what is the meaning of this? I do not intend to hurt you; listen to me.'

'He struggled violently; 'Let me go,' he cried; 'monster! ugly wretch! you wish to eat me, and tear me to pieces— You are an ogre— Let me go, or I will tell my papa.'

"Boy, you will never see your father again; you must come with me.'

"Hideous monster! let me go; My papa is a Syndic— he is Mr Frankenstein— he would punish you. You dare not keep me.'

"Frankenstein! you belong then to my enemy— to him towards whom I have sworn eternal revenge; you shall be my first victim.'

'The child still struggled, and loaded me with epithets which carried despair to my heart: I grasped his throat to silence him, and in a moment he lay dead at my feet.'

No! You are the source of pain that found me in the second of the two letters delivered into my hands by my dearest Claire. Had not Claire called out that she would answer the door; then moments later had she not appeared in parlour holding two envelopes having arrived by post? 'Strange', Claire had said, 'these letters must have addressed to be previous guest of the Villa Diodati; or perhaps posted in anticipation of a future guest?' I had inquired to whom the letters were addressed, and Claire answered, '*To* V. Frankenstein.' I had leapt from my chair like a Burmese tiger pouncing upon its prey and snatched the envelope from poor little Claire's dainty hand. Startled, she had cowered, then threatened to bolt from the parlour as if I had been a Burmese tiger raring to strike. I had torn the envelope open with a fury of claws. The letters had been indeed addressed to my pale student of the unhallowed arts. They were written by his cousin, Elizabeth and his father, Alphonse. Curious that my psychosomatic phantasm had chosen to communication his tale through physical letters. But having had seen inspiration strike my Beloved and our little Lord in queer ways, I had to trust my pale student to tell his tell in any manner he so choses.

'I gazed on my victim, and my heart swelled with exultation and hellish triumph: clapping my hands, I exclaimed, 'I, too, can create desolation; my enemy is not impregnable; this death will carry despair to him, and a thousand other miseries shall torment and destroy him.'

'As I fixed my eyes on the child, I saw something glittering on his breast. I took it; it was a portrait of a most lovely woman. In spite of my malignity, it softened and attracted me. For a few moments I gazed with delight on her dark eyes, fringed by deep lashes, and her lovely lips; but presently my rage returned: I remembered that I was for ever deprived of the delights that such beautiful creatures could bestow; and that she whose resemblance I contemplated would, in regarding me, have changed that air of divine benignity to one expressive of disgust and affright.

'Can you wonder that such thoughts transported me with rage? I only wonder that at that moment, instead of venting my sensations in exclamations and agony, I did not rush among mankind, and perish in the attempt to destroy them.

'While I was overcome by these feelings, I left the spot where I had committed the murder, and was seeking a more secluded hiding-place...' No! I know what Victor's Creation intends to say, but I must revise the words before he even utters them. He is not intent on murder but fearing the mistreatment that is his longsuffering! 'I entered a barn which had appeared to me to be empty. A woman was sleeping on some straw; she was young: not indeed so beautiful as her whose portrait I held; but of an agreeable aspect, and blooming in the loveliness of youth and health. Here, I thought, is one of those whose joy-imparting smiles are bestowed on all but me. And then I bent over her, and whispered 'Awake, fairest, thy lover is near—he who would give his life but to obtain one look of affection from thine eyes: my beloved, awake!'

'The sleeper stirred; a thrill of terror ran through me. Should she indeed awake, and see me, and curse me, and denounce the murderer? Thus would she assuredly act, if her darkened eyes opened, and she beheld me. The thought was madness; it stirred the fiend within me—not I, but she shall suffer: the murder I have committed because I am for ever robbed of all that she could give me, she shall atone. The crime had its source in her: be hers the punishment! Thanks to the lessons of Felix and the sanguinary laws of man, I had learned now to work mischief. I bent over her, and placed the portrait securely in one of the folds of her dress. She moved again, and I fled.'

Despicable, loathsome Creature! I regret ever having given birth to you! How is my intellect capable of forming you from my own experiences? You are insufferable in your suffering! And unexplainable in your explaintions!

'For some days I haunted the spot where these scenes had taken place; sometimes wishing to see you, sometimes resolved to quit the world and its miseries for ever. At length I wandered towards these mountains, and have ranged through their immense recesses, consumed by a burning passion which you alone can gratify. We may not part until you have promised to comply with my requisition. I am alone, and miserable; man will not associate with me; but one as deformed and horrible as myself would not deny herself to me. My companion must be of the same species, and have the same defects. This being you must create.'

The Creature finished speaking, and fixed his looks upon me in expectation of a replay. But I was bewildered, perplexed, and unable to arrange my ideas sufficiently to understand the full extent of his proposition. Then he slowly faded before my eyes and the chair positioned beside the fire sat empty of its previous occupant. And my vision itself began to fade as my eyes, heavy with sleep, closed. I struggled to record this tale of Victor's Creature onto my memory so that when I awoke the next morning, I would be able to record it and having written these words into my journal, I have been successful.

Chapter Twelve
Monody on the Death of the
Right Honourable R.B. Sheridan

The Diary of Dr John William Polidori

18 July. Lord Byron, Claire (herself deep in the malignancy of her pregnancy), and I sat in the library as the incessant rain and insistent wind battered the windowpanes. The story of our summer. Claire sits at Lord Byron's knee holding a letter that had arrived in the post, she read it aloud, again:

My dear Byron,

D. L. Theatre closed for the Season on the 29th June, and poor Sheridan's eyes for ever the day before yesterday – I have not classed these events in the order in which they will interest you or even his less-admiring Friends – The object of this letter being purely theatrical, I shall rush in medias res – It has occurred to me, & G. Lamb strongly favors the idea, of our opening the Theatre on the 7th Sept next with a monody or address on poor Sheridan – to be spoken by Mrs Davison as the Comic Muse in Mourning – such address or monody to be written by you – and this we should follow, by playing all his pieces in succession – I trust you will not refuse – The subject is not unworthy <u>your</u> Pen.

It has struck me that a sort of Temple or other Structure should be represented on the Stage, & large pictures around representing the best Scene of each of his best pieces –

If you chose to point out these particular scenes, & meant to allude to it in the lines, we will set Greenwood to work – Pray give this your earliest & earnest attention, for I really think you can bring us both honor & profit – Will not the very titles of his three best pieces suggest Stage-points? There is one other subject I implore you to satisfy me upon – when shall I receive a Tragedy from you – Never was there a moment when you could try it on the stage with such a certainty of the author being unknown – you will of course have read & heard how pertinaciously one half of the public believe you to be the conceal'd author of Bertram – I have ever treated the question mysteriously with a view to the power it wd afford you of producing a play with the certainty of your name being conceal'd – No one but myself need know the secret – & I would be rogue enough to have it believ'd to be Maturin's who is known to be employ'd about another – If you wish'd it, I should not hesitate to come to Geneva to receive your directions about it in Person; when it is done – Pray, pray, pray finish what you have written begun –

Miss Somerville, who made her debut in Bertram, is too tall for a Juliet, but is after Miss O'Neill unquestionably the most interesting Tragic actress – She really is very good where energy is required –

I shall open your reply to this with the utmost agitation – for your refusal to either of these requests will damp half the ardour with which I shall re-commence the Campaign –

Kean finish'd the Season with the utmost success –

He is to play Timon – & King John –

Adieu, My dear Byron –

P.S. The effect of the Monody might be heighten'd by a previous music –

Your's ever faithfully
Douglas Kinnaird

'You should write it, George,' she cooed. 'Douglas Kinnaird is a dear friend of yours and the request has travelled some distance to meet you here at Campagne Diodati. It is to be read at Drury Land Theatre in London! If you dictate it, I will transcribe your words.'

Byron paused in thought. He sought a Muse. Of the nine specific daughters of Zeus tasked with the inspiration of literature, the sciences, and the arts, is it Erato– or perchance is it Calliope– who must fight the fury of the flurry of thunderstorms to reach the Villa Diodati? I could see is eyes dance as the words slowly formed in his brain. This is a most curious process, the creation a poem, or monody in this particular case. Writing is the closest to being the Christian God that Man will ever attain. The creation of something out of nothing. We breathe life into our characters– our creations. Every writer has experienced the queer sensation of our characters taking on a life of their own. The reader may find it strange that our characters possess a Free Will. To the writer, they are as tangible as humanity is to God Himself. Creation and Creator. Is not Jesus the Christ called the 'Author of Life' for a reason? Did not the Creator form the world with words, not deeds? *Let there be Light!* And there was light! It is true that Byron's monody was without form, and void; and darkness was upon the face of the deep. And the Spirit of God moved upon the face of the waters.

I know I am committing a grave error mixing my mythologies. The Christians would not care for their Creator to be associated with the pagan Muses, but an author, often suffering extended bouts of writer's block, is not fickle to whom we pray. We will take inspiration from whatever pantheon offers productive communion. Even the Devil. Just ask Faust.

'At the request of a friend,' he mused, and then he began reciting the following:

> When the last sunshine of expiring day
> In summer's twilight weeps itself away,
> Who hath not felt the softness of the hour
> Sink on the heart, as dew along the flower?
> With a pure feeling which absorbs and awes
> While Nature makes that melancholy pause,
> Her breathing moment on the bridge where Time
> Of light and darkness forms an arch sublime,
> Who hath not shared that calm, so still and deep,
> The voiceless thought which would not speak but weep,
> A holy concord, and a bright regret,
> A glorious sympathy with suns that set?
> 'Tis not harsh sorrow, but a tenderer woe,
> Nameless, but dear to gentle hearts below,
> Felt without bitterness, but full and clear,
> A sweet dejection, a transparent tear,
> Unmix'd with worldly grief or selfish stain,
> Shed without shame, and secret without pain.
>
> Even as the tenderness that hour instils
> When Summer's day declines along the hills.
> So feels the fulness of our heart and eyes
> When all of Genius which can perish dies.
> A mighty Spirit is eclipsed – a Power
> Hath pass'd from day to darkness – to whose hour
> Of light no likeness is bequeath'd – no name,
> Focus at once of all the rays of Fame!
> The flash of Wit, the bright Intelligence,
> The beam of Song, the blaze of Eloquence,
> Set with their Sun, but still have left behind

The enduring produce of immortal Mind;
Fruits of a genial morn, and glorious noon,
A deathless part of him who died too soon.
But small that portion of the wondrous whole,
These sparkling segments of that circling soul,
Which all embraced, and lighten'd over all,
To cheer, to pierce, to please, or to appal.
From the charm'd council to the festive board,
Of human feelings the unbounded lord;
In whose acclaim the loftiest voices vied,
The praised, the proud, who made his praise their pride.
When the loud cry of trampled Hindostan
Arose to Heaven in her appeal from man,
His was the thunder, his the avenging rod,
The wrath – the delegated voice of God!
Which shook the nations through his lips, and blazed
Till vanquish 'd senates trembled as they praised.

And here, oh! here, where yet all young and warm,
The gay creations of is spirit charm,
The matchless dialogue, the deathless wit,
Which knew not what it was to intermit;
The glowing portraits, fresh from life, that bring
Home to our hearts the truth from which they spring;
These wondrous beings of his fancy, wrought
To fulness by the fiat of his thought,
Here in their first abode you still may meet,
Bright with the hues of his Promethean heat;
A halo of the light of other days,
Which still the splendour of its orb betrays.

But should there be to whom the fatal blight
Of failing Wisdom yields a base delight,
Men who exult when minds of heavenly tone
Jar in the music which was born their own,
Still let them pause – ah! little do they know
That what to them seem'd Vice might be but Woo.
Hard is his fate on whom the public gaze
Is fix'd for ever to detract or praise;
Repose denies her requiem to his name,
And Folly loves the martyrdom of Fame.

The secret enemy whose sleepless eye
Stands sentinel, accuser, judge, and spy,
The foe, the fool, the jealous, and the vain,
The envious who but breathe in others' pain,
Behold the host! delighting to deprave,
Who track the steps of Glory to the grave,
Watch every fault that daring Genius owes
Half to the ardour which its birth bestows,
Distort the troth, accumulate the lie,
And pile the pyramid of Calumny!
These are his portion – but if join'd to these
Gaunt Poverty should league with deep Disease,
If the high Spirit must forget to soar,
And stoop to strive with Misery at the door,
To soothe Indignity – and face to face
Meet sordid Rage, and wrestle with Disgrace,
To find in Hope but the renew'd caress,
The serpent-fold of further Faithlessness:-
If such may be the ills which men assail,
What marvel if at last the mightiest fail?
Breasts to whom all the strength of feeling given
Bear hearts electric–charged with fire from Heaven,
Black with the rude collision inly torn,
By clouds surrounded, and on whirlwinds borne,
Driven o'er the lowering atmosphere that nurst
Thoughts which have turn'd to thunderscorch, and burst.

But far from us and from our mimic scene
Such things should be – if such have ever been
Ours be the gentler wish, the kinder task,
To give the tribute Glory need not ask,
To mourn the vanish'd beam, and add our mite
Of praise in payment of a long delight.
Ye Orators! whom yet our councils yield,
Mourn for the veteran Hero of your field!
The worthy rival of the wondrous Three!
Whose words were sparks of Immortality!
Ye Bards! to whom the Drama's muse is dear,
He was your Master-emulate him her!
Ye men of wit and social eloquence!
He was your brother – bear his ashes hence!

While Powers of mind almost of boundless range,
Complete in kind, as various in their change,
While Eloquence, Wit, Poesy, and Mirth,
That humbler Harmonist of care on Earth,
Survive within our souls – while lives our sense
Of pride in Merit's proud preeminence,
Long shall we seek his likeness, long in vain,
And turn to all of him which may remain,
Sighing that nature form'd but one such man,
And broke the die – in moulding Sheridan!

Letter From Bryon To Kinnaird

Diodati – Geneva – July 20th. 1816

Dear Kinnaird,

I send you – not what you want – but all I can give – and such as it is I give it with good will. – – It may be too long & if so – whatever may be cut in speaking – at least let it be published entire – as it is written so as not very well to condone curtailment without the sense suffering also. – Let Miss Somerville – (& none else) deliver it – if she has energy – that's the woman I want – I mean for spouting. – I protest against Mrs Davison – I protest against the temple – or anything but an Urn on the scene – and above all I protest against the "Comic Muse in Mourning." –

If she is Comic – she should not be in Mourning – if she is in mourning – she ought not to be in Mourning – but should she be comic & in mourning too – the verses & Sheridan's memory (for that occasion at least) will go to the devil together. – – –

No – I say an Urn (not a tea Urn) and Miss Somerville with a little teaching as to "Energy" I have spiced it with Cayenne all through – except a small infusion of the pathetic at starting. – I send the lines (118 in Number) in a separate sheet by the post – & will send a duplicate in a day or two – for fear of your not receiving this copy in time. –

Tragedy – I have none, – an act – a first act of one – I had nearly finished some time before my departure from England – when events occurred which furnished me with so many real passions for time to come – that I had no attention for fictitious ones: – – The scenes I had scrawled are thrown with other papers & sketches into one of my trunks now in England – but into which I know not – nor care not – except that I should have been glad to have done anything you wished in my power, – but I have no power nor will to recommence – & surely – Maturin is your man – not I: – of what has passed in England I know but little – & have no desire to know more – except that you & any other friends are well.

I have written a third Canto of Childe Harold (of 118 Stanzas) and a short (not long) poem on the Castle of Chillon – both of which I mean to send to England soon for publication – of during which I could wish to ask you to correct the proofs and arrange with Murray for me: – I merely wait a good opportunity to convey these to your care – if you can afford leisure & patience – perhaps G. Lamb – or some other good natured fellow would halve it with you – though I have hardly the conscience to ask either them or you. – – I have now answered you and arrived at my Sheets' end – with my best remembrances to Mrs K – (whose silk kerchief is as precious as Othello's) believe me ever yrs.

Letter From Kinnaird To Bryon

Liverpool August 8th. 1816

My dear Byron,

I have just receiv'd your two letters & Packets – I cannot express how very very much I admire your Lines – I defy any one to hear them & not recognize you in them – There is no one but you could have written them – They are exquisite – No pains shall be spared to make Miss Somerville speak them well – I most sincerely agree with all your ideas about the urn – & submit implicitly, to your ideas about the Comic Muse – But I should have preferr'd Mrs Davison speaking the Lines to Miss Somerville – The scene shall discover Miss S. leaning over the urn – The date of my letter requires an explanation, & I give it the more readily as I am sure you will be gratified to read it –

I came here a week ago incog to witness the debut of Miss Keppel in Rosetta in Love in a village – She played that character, on Monday the 5th inst. to the delight & astonishment of every body – She played Polly last night with double effect – I never saw a better piece of acting on the stage by any body – Her singing is admirable – In short she has far outrun the expectations of her warmest friends & admirers – She is announc'd as Mr Weichsel's Pupil – & is currently believ'd to be Mrs Billington's daughter –

She is exceedingly flatter'd by your care of the handkerchief – If you don't return, She may meet you in Italy next Summer – for Weichsel declares she shall be a second Billington on the Italian Stage – I shall write to you again on my return to London – For God's sake do not persist in your anti-tragical (I do not mean comical) humour – on Davis' return pray allow me to rummage in the Trunks – Maturin is writing – I heard from him yesterday – The visitation is over – & he has not had his gown stripp'd over his shoulders – the honor you do me in committing the correction of the press to my hands I cannot too highly prize – nor shall assiduity or anxiety to do it correctly be wanting – nothing but the sense of my incompetency would induce me to share the task with any one else – But I have no doubt Lamb will be very much flatter'd in joining me –

Adieu my dear B.

Believe me ever
Your faithful friend

Chapter Thirteen
The Darkness[16]

The Diary of Dr John William Polidori

18 June.— The day had proved long and hot for the unagreeable summer had given us a respite from the gloom and doom of torrential rains, sensational lightning, exponential thunder, calamitous flooding, and cataclysmal hail. The sun shined with an intensity not seen since the previous summer. The Shelleys, including Claire, rented one boat, while I and Lord Byron rented another. My foot was often troubled in new normal dampness of summer. Now, in the unnatural heat of the glaring sun, my foot itched to such a degree that I thought perchance my foot has turned gangrenous under the sweat-soaked wrappings. Yet, I ventured forth with Byron for a tour of the lake with my satchel tucked under my seat lest anything untoward happen to my patient. With the sun as high overhead as astronomically possible given our latitude, we thought that our eyes deceived us. The sun seemed quite aberrant. I ruffled through my satchel for a particular and peculiar pair of spectacles, and I found them! Popping the coloured protective lens out of their frames, I instructed Byron to use lenses to protect our eyes. Peering through the amber colour we could see a great black bile that danced and pranced on the surface of the sun. If either Byron or myself had been of the superstitious lot, we would have believe the sun was about to be snuffed out like a candle on the bedside table; eight minutes later, the earth would cool to a wintery degree only for life to quickly freeze to death.

I could see the trouble on the face of Lord Byron. I assured him that the summers of 1718 and 1719 had been the hottest on record like this very day and that sunspots were quite active over those two years. And did not the summer of 1816 possess no recorded sunspots? And was not the weather tempestuous and the crops disastrous? He proved not impressed by my reasoning and was instead became incensed beyond all reason. Had I not heard of an anonymous Italian astronomer out of Bologna who said that the world would end on July 18th 1816 when

---

16 From *Prisoner of Chillon, and Other Poems* by Lord Byron, published by John Murray, 1816

the sun was burnt out and the earth would be plunged into a darkness never before seen by man? Of course, I had not heard such claptrap, and if I had I would not have listened. I scoffed at him with a cacophonous gawfaw. I explainded that the large spots which may now be seen upon the sun's disk have given rise to ridiculous apprehensions and absurd predications. These spots are said to be the cause of the remarkable and wet weather we have had this Summer; and the increase of these spots is represented to announce a general removal of heat from the glove, the extension of nature and the end of the world.[17] I continued my mockery, scoffing at the superstitious anxiety excited at present among the vulgar, and even among people who would be offended at being so classed, by the great news of spots on the Sun.'[18] In recent years, Christian ministers like Christopher Love, Mary Bateman, and Joanna Southcott all claimed to know when the end of the world would come, and the end of the world would not come, nor would it in our lifetimes or our children's or the many descendant generations whom would come. Ms. Southcott, an elderly self-proclaimed prophetess, claimed her barren womb bore fruit with the Christ-child Himself, whom would be born again into a body of mortal flesh on October 9th 1814; this is such a rather queer date of a second Christmas. She died (of course, she did), then an autopsy concluded she was not pregnant (of course, she was not) and the world did not end on October 9th (of course, it did not). But because this End of the World prophecy came from an Italian astronomer, not from a Christian madman— I mean, minster— but from an astronomer, Lord Byron had mistaken prophecy in the guise of scientific prediction. What had caused this superstitious predilection in my dear friend? Why had this unexpected visitation from Heaven, added to the severe distress to which the country is otherwise reduced, for it has infused into the minds of the people generally the greatest apprehension and alarm?[19] Hoe! Their superstition is extravagant. A gossip's story has travelled all the way from Bolonga according to which the world is to be at an end on the 18th of July.[20]

But Byron continued his protestations. 'According to the calculations of an astronomer of Bologna, who has latterly published some observations on the subject, on the 18th of July a great solar catastrophe is to put an end to the world by confragration.— The sings of these are the spots to be remarked at present on the sun's disk.' Then he complained that the Government, thinking it improper to suffer the circulation of

---

17 From the unsigned article 'The Spots on the Sun', publishing in the *London Chronicle* and the *Examiner*.
18 From a French newspaper.
19 From the *Times*
20 From the *New British Lady's Magazine*

such predictions has put the astronomer under arrest![21] Was this not the most unnatural summer without an actual summer? The inclement weather was incessant with the rains and thunder coming every day without end. We seldom enjoyed a tour of the lake. Twice in the last week and thrice since our arrival on the shore of Geneva, he calculated. Did not the sunsets look jaundiced and sulphurous? Were not my spectacles modest? And did we not see the great sunspots through them with our naked eyes, without the need for a telescope, spyglass, or other instruments? Modest glass, he bellowed!

I explained away the silly report that the world is to be at an end on 18th of July has been circulated at Paris as well as at London and every other part of the Continent. The report had its origin in the appearance of the sun at present having some sport upon its disk. Lord Byron countered with the spots announced the speedy extinction of this luminary, and consequently the end of the world![22]

I schooled my benefactor that all prophecies, whether religious or scientific in nature, are routinely postponed when the prophecy does not come to pass. I asked had not the Italian mountebanks who in the course of their erratic lectures circulated this report... had in general fixed the grand catastrophe for the 25th of May, but afterwards postponed it to the 18th of July! Because of course they did. And July 18th would come and pass without the end of the world. My mockery proved a bit too keen for I composed a poem on the spot— sun spots?— to both cruelty and jest:

> *Pray, what do the spots in the sun' mean?*
> *Can nobody tell me about 'em?*
> *My neighbours and I have our fears—*
> *And who has a right, Sirs to doubt 'em?*
> *Pray, will 'the world be at an end?'*
> *If not, then what else will take place?*
> *What do these strange matters portend?*
> *Nay, answer— and don't' hide your face—*
> *I know you're afraid like myself!*[23]

So convinced had Lord Byron that this nameless Italian astronomer was a latter-day Nostradamus or St. John the Divine, that Lord Byron offered a wager of such an ungodly sum (one I will not note in this diary) that the sun would snuff out in exactly one month's time. I laughed

---

21 From the June 21 edition of the *Morning Chronicle*

22 From the London Chronicle

23 From *Napoleon and the Spots in the Sun; or, The Regents Waltz* by "Syntax Sidrophel, 1816

at him! Again! If the sun is indeed snuffed out, then what good would winning the wager be to him, since all of earth would be dead. And if the sun was indeed not snuffed out, then winning this wager would end our friendship. Nay! I told him. I would not make any such wager. But I would sit with him on the shores of the lake and await the end of the world and if the sun rose again the next day, I would remain his friend without any mockery nor jocularity.

Speaking of mockery and jocularity, I suddenly realized my current state in the boat upon the lake of Geneva proved to be improper. At my urging, we left the subject of prophecies to the wayside and enjoyed our tour until the we saw the clouds coming over the mountaintops again threatening another storm.

18 July. I returned to the Villa Diodati, from my brief holiday with Countess Erzsébet, a Hungarian noblewoman and acquaintance of Lord Byron whom he encountered on his Grand Tour of the Mediterranean, just as the sun was cresting over the Alps. Her withered old carriage-driver deposited my luggage in the foyer with a disagreeable *thud*, then he disagreeably disappeared back into the night hence we came. Though I painfully missed my dear countess, I was thankful to be finally rid of her withered old footman. I abandoned my luggage and lumbered towards my apartment. As my body fell virtually lifeless onto my bed into a dreamless slumber. Not even the smell of bacon frying in the morning was enough to rouse my weary body out of its deep sleep. Lunch came and went as did teatime. But when I finally shambled into the parlour at our given time, I was greeted with Lord Byron standing before the fire. He held a page of paper in his hand and his hands were stained with ink. His trademark. George had prepared something new and wonderful! Having heard its recitation, I have no doubt no work will ever eclipse the Darkness of this poem, considering I have had the ill-fortune to hear with my own ears a poem that will haunt the rest of my remaining my years.

> *I had a dream, which was not all a dream.*
> *The bright sun was extinguish'd, and the stars*
> *Did wander darkling in the eternal space,*
> *Rayless, and pathless, and the icy earth*
> *Swung blind and blackening in the moonless air;*

Little did I realize how literally the Lord would take our conversation, debate, argument, whatever it was. Was the source of this poem the sunspots we observed through the amber of spectacle glass? Was it the anonymous prophecy of the End of the World? Or were his paranoias given birth on June 9th or 10th (I can't require recall the exact date) when a solar eclipse shrouded Europe in an ever so brief darkness. To the superstitious of European society, the poor, the uneducated, the blindly religious, the sun appeared to be slowly eaten as if it were a biscuit at teatime. Panic gripped society; there were brief riots in the major cities, only for the sun to reappear from behind the moon. The educated did not panic because we were possessed the knowledge of the root cause of solar eclipses: the moon's orbit merely came between the Earth and the sun, casting a mere shadow upon the earth. Perchance, my benefactor is more superstitious than I'd care to admit to myself.

> *Morn came and went— and came, and brought no day,*
> *And men forgot their passions in the dread*
> *Of this their desolation; and all hearts*
> *Were chill'd into a selfish prayer for light:*
> *And they did live by watchfires— and the thrones,*
> *The palaces of crowned kings— the huts,*
> *The habitations of all things which dwell,*
> *Were burnt for beacons; cities were consum'd,*

Oh, my! Lord Byron may have hit the nail with the hammer here and missed the nail entirely. While he hit the nail by stating that in such a calamitous event of the sun dying, not even the 'palaces of crown kings' would fall just as quickly as 'the huts, the habitations of all things wich dwell' on the Earth. But he missed the nail as well. Light from that burning orb in the sky takes eight minutes to reach the earth in its orbit. If the sun had been extinguished by a supernova, then the violence that would overtake the earth when bombarded by star matter would extinguish life on this globe almost instantaneously. Would the burning light of the sun burn off our atmosphere? Or would the star matter rain down upon the earth rending it asunder? The human race would not have the time to burn the thrones, the palaces, the cities to ash. But if the death of the sun came from being extinguished by being snuffed out like a candle on the bedside table, then perhaps this is how the world would end. Truly horrifying.

> *And men were gather'd round their blazing homes*
> *To look once more into each other's face;*
> *Happy were those who dwelt within the eye*
> *Of the volcanos, and their mountain-torch:*
> *A fearful hope was all the world contain'd;*

> *Forests were set on fire— but hour by hour*
> *They fell and faded— and the crackling trunks*
> *Extinguish'd with a crash— and all was black.*

Is this what Lord Byron believes will happen in July should the anonymous Italian astronomer's prediction comes to pass? I cannot accept that Lord Byron, the romantic poet extraordinaire, my benefactor, truly believes that the End of the World is nigh. Has his mind been so gripped with panic that he has written what he believes upon the page. St. Paul wrote that *All scripture is God-breathed, given by inspiration of God, and is profitable for doctrine, for reproof, for correction, for instruction in righteousness: That the man of God may be perfect, thoroughly furnished unto all good works* (Timothy 3:16-17). Is Lord Byron breathing in the breath of God to write such beautiful and yet harrowing prophecy? Is Lord Byron joining St. John the Divine in recording his own Apocalyptic poetry?

> *The brows of men by the despairing light*
> *Wore an unearthly aspect, as by fits*
> *The flashes fell upon them; some lay down*
> *And hid their eyes and wept; and some did rest*
> *Their chins upon their clenched hands, and smil'd;*
> *And others hurried to and fro, and fed*
> *Their funeral piles with fuel, and look'd up*
> *With mad disquietude on the dull sky,*
> *The pall of a past world; and then again*
> *With curses cast them down upon the dust,*
> *And gnash'd their teeth and howl'd:*

Why must a man of medicine quote the scripture of the religious? Because End of the World thoughts and fears tend to be Apocalyptic and ornately religious. Why should I, an Atheist, not be permitted to quote the words of Jesus of Nazareth, whether or not he is actually the Christ? Even if Jesus of Nazereth were a wholly (and not holy) mortal man or a figment of the gospel writers, Matthew, Mark, Luke, and John, or the creation of Paul the Apostle, do the words attributed to Jesus not ring true? Would a Christians faith be rent asunder if Jesus were not the Christ? Indubitably! But an Atheist's acceptance of the teachings of Jesus of Nazareth requires no faith, as does believing in the teachings of Aristotle or Plato. I can quote Jesus' teaching, chapter and verse, and feel no faith. Jesus (presumably) said: *That many shall come from the east and west, and shall sit down with Abraham, and Isaac, and*

Jacob, in the kingdom of heaven. But the children of the kingdom shall be cast out into outer darkness: there shall be weeping and gnashing of teeth (Matthew 8:11-12).

> *And gnash'd their teeth and howl'd: the wild birds shriek'd*
> *And, terrified, did flutter on the ground,*
> *And flap their useless wings; the wildest brutes*
> *Came tame and tremulous; and vipers crawl'd*
> *And twin'd themselves among the multitude,*
> *Hissing, but stingless— they were slain for food.*

The collapse of society is frightening but the collapse of nature is all the more harrowing. If ever have I feared the End of the World, my thoughts always turned to the fate of humanity, never have I considered the fate of the natural world. This is the blindness that has struck the human race to believe we alone are suffering. Over the course of this unnatural summer, I have been consumed with my own suffering. Why can we not tour the lake or hike the hills? Never have I ever considered the suffering of the wildlife, the beasts of the land, the fowls of the air, and the fish in the sea. Humanity's hubris unmatched in the history of the natural world. Did not the scripture record our stewardship of the earth when *God blessed Noah and his sons, and said unto them, Be fruitful, and multiply, and replenish the earth. And the fear of you and the dread of you shall be upon every beast of the earth, and upon every fowl of the air, upon all that moveth upon the earth, and upon all the fishes of the sea; into your hand are they delivered* (Genesis 9:1-2). It is the arrogance of mankind to believe that our sudden industrialization that has gripped Europe will not, in the end, destroy the planet. And when the earth in unnaturally warming from the black pollution we spew into the air, from our factories, the religious will not heed our own stewardship of the earth, believing instead that the fate of the planet is in God's hands. God has given us the stewardship. The fate of the world is in our hands. And I fear that the future generations will experience unimaginable heat, unprecedented storms, and unending famine. Dear God, how is this poem affecting my mind? It is as if this poem of Lord Byron's has stirred a hurricane of harrowing in my mind.

I must note that the prophetic books of the Holy Writ, whether written by St. John or Isaiah or Daniel, talk of the 'kingdom of God' being a place where even the animals are at peace. I give you the words of the prophet Isaiah, from my dusty and musty copy: *The wolf also shall dwell with the lamb, and the leopard shall lie down with the kid; and the calf and the young lion and the fatling together; and a little child shall lead them. And the cow and the bear shall feed; their young ones shall lie down together: and the lion shall eat straw like the ox. And the sucking child shall play on the hole of the asp, and the weaned child shall put his hand on the cockatrice' den. They shall not hurt nor destroy in all my holy mountain: for the earth shall be full of the knowledge of the Lord, as the waters cover the sea* (Isaiah 11:6-9). Where God promises an Apocalypse of peace everlasting, Lord Byron rightly forewarns an End of the World accurately!

> *And War, which for a moment was no more,*
> *Did glut himself again: a meal was bought*
> *With blood, and each sate sullenly apart*
> *Gorging himself in gloom: no love was left;*
> *All earth was but one thought— and that was death*
> *Immediate and inglorious; and the pang*
> *Of famine fed upon all entrails— men*
> *Died, and their bones were tombless as their flesh;*
> *The meagre by the meagre were devour'd,*

When the religious speak of God ending all war when the Parousia of Jesus the Christ is fulfilled, they mean all war. There prophet Isaiah deceitfully promises a wondrous end to all war: *man shall beat their swords into plowshares, and their spears into pruninghooks: nation shall not lift up sword against nation, neither shall they learn war any more* (Isaiah 2:5). Lord Byron mentioned War (presumably the Roman god Mars) was, for the moment, no more. This would be in lockstep with the Parousia, but since the beginning of civilization, we speak of war as religious or political warfare. Now a global war for survival would be waged. Would nation fight nation or family fight family as the famine raged? Byron also spoke of the horrid reality of cannibalism. Neighbour would devour neighbour and family would devour their own when this dreadful reality is sown.

> *Even dogs assail'd their masters, all save one,*
> *And he was faithful to a corse, and kept*
> *The birds and beasts and famish'd men at bay,*
> *Till hunger clung them, or the dropping dead*
> *Lur'd their lank jaws; himself sought out no food,*
> *But with a piteous and perpetual moan,*
> *And a quick desolate cry, licking the hand*
> *Which answer'd not with a caress— he died.*

A single tear welled up, then overflowed my eye.

> *The crowd was famish'd by degrees; but two*
> *Of an enormous city did survive,*
> *And they were enemies: they met beside*
> *The dying embers of an altar-place*
> *Where had been heap'd a mass of holy things*
> *For an unholy usage; they rak'd up,*
> *And shivering scrap'd with their cold skeleton hands*
> *The feeble ashes, and their feeble breath*
> *Blew for a little life, and made a flame*
> *Which was a mockery; then they lifted up*
> *Their eyes as it grew lighter, and beheld*
> *Each other's aspects— saw, and shriek'd, and died—*
> *Even of their mutual hideousness they died,*
> *Unknowing who he was upon whose brow*
> *Famine had written Fiend.*

'Tis the fate of mankind.

> *Famine had written Fiend. The world was void,*
> *The populous and the powerful was a lump,*
> *Seasonless, herbless, treeless, manless, lifeless—*
> *A lump of death— a chaos of hard clay.*
> *The rivers, lakes and ocean all stood still,*
> *And nothing stirr'd within their silent depths;*
> *Ships sailorless lay rotting on the sea,*
> *And their masts fell down piecemeal: as they dropp'd*
> *They slept on the abyss without a surge—*
> *The waves were dead; the tides were in their grave,*
> *The moon, their mistress, had expir'd before;*
> *The winds were wither'd in the stagnant air,*
> *And the clouds perish'd; Darkness had no need*
> *Of aid from them— She was the Universe.*

'Tis the fate of the world!

I cannot contain the horror I have experienced by merely listening to the recitation of a poem. Claire is a weeping, snotty mess. Her limbs are all shaking— nay quaking— with the violence of the earth slipping under the geological faults. My sweet Mary is more composed than her sister, yet still crying, her cheeks stained with red lines. Percy Shelley so troubled he has become momentary dumb; his eyes blank and staring off into the distance. I pray his mind is not irrevocably broken. Gooseflesh has prickled on my arms and lightning repeatedly strikes my spine. My mind, not rendered dumb like poor Shelley, is filled with electricity. My thoughts are out of control with fear, with terror, with harrowing. How could the language of Shakespeare, the iambic pentameter of this poem, which begins with the first line and endures until the last, render such horror? The survival of the meter is most impressive, but not as impressive as the yarn that he spins. This unholy, unnatural tapestry Lord Byron has woven now hangs on the walls of the parlour of my mind. Never shalt I allow the servants in my psyche to take this tapestry down, although the more religious priests within my consciousness want the tapestry torn down from the walls and burnt on the pyre of forgetfulness. If the beauty and horror of this poem has been born of the anonymous ramblings of an Italian astronomer, than can such madness truly be dismissed as superstitious claptrap? I am struck fearful of going to sleep, lest the sun burn out and I never again wake.

18 July. Morning. The bright sun was extinguis'd!
Nay! Faith! I cannot tell a lie. The day the sun was to be extinguised came and went without the sun having been extinguished (the horror!) as the anonymous Italian astronomer prophesied. I will honour the charlatan with the more scientific 'predicted', because there was little to no science to his prophecy. Observable sunspots could be utilized by an astronomer for natural philosophy utilizing scientific instruments; but observable sunspots can also be claimed at astrologers to portend because Jupiter is ascending or Mercury in retrograde or Orion is flatulent that the end of the world is nigh!

Chapter Fourteen
The Vampyre[24]

Extract of a Letter by Dr Polidori

I breathe freely in the neighbourhood of this lake; the ground upon which I tread has been subdued from the earliest ages; the principal objects which immediately strike my eye, bring to my recollection scenes, in which man acted the hero and was the chief object of interest. Not to look back to earlier times of battles and sieges, here is the bust of Rousseau—here is a house with an inscription denoting that the Genevan philosopher first drew breath under its roof. A little out of the town is Ferney, the residence of Voltaire; where that wonderful, though certainly in many respects contemptible, character, received, like the hermits of old, the visits of pilgrims, not only from his own nation, but from the farthest boundaries of Europe. Here too is Bonnet's abode, and, a few steps beyond, the house of that astonishing woman Madame de Stael: perhaps the first of her sex, who has really proved its often claimed equality with the nobler man. We have before had women who have written interesting novels and poems, in which their tact at observing drawing-room characters has availed them; but never since the days of Heloise have those faculties which are peculiar to man, been developed as the possible inheritance of woman. Though even here, as in the case of Heloise, our sex have not been backward in alledging the existence of an Abeilard in the person of Mr Schlegel as the inspirer of her works. But to proceed: upon the same side of the lake, Gibbon, Bonnivard, Bradshaw, and others mark, as it were, the stages for our progress; whilst upon the other side there is one house, built by Diodati, the friend of Milton, which has contained within its walls, for several months, that poet whom we have so often read together, and who—if human passions remain the same, and human feelings, like chords, on being swept by nature's impulses shall vibrate as before—will be placed by posterity in the first rank of our English Poets. You must have heard, or the Third Canto of *Childe Harold* will have informed you, that Lord Byron resided many months in this neighbourhood. I went with some friends a few days ago, after having seen Ferney, to view this mansion. I trod the floors with the same

24 From a short work of prose fiction written in 1819 by John William Polidori taken from the story Lord Byron, published by Sherwood, Neely, and Jones, London. 'Though not explicitly written during the summer of 1816, this story was obviously inspired by the fragment of the vampire story written by Lord Byron this particular volcanic winter' – R.D.B.

feelings of awe and respect as we did, together, those of Shakspeare's dwelling at Stratford. I sat down in a chair of the saloon, and satisfied myself that I was resting on what he had made his constant seat. I found a servant there who had lived with him; she, however, gave me but little information. She pointed out his bed-chamber upon the same level as the saloon and dining-room, and informed me that he retired to rest at three, got up at two, and employed himself a long time over his toilette; that he never went to sleep without a pair of pistols and a dagger by his side, and that he never eat animal food. He apparently spent some part of every day upon the lake in an English boat. There is a balcony from the saloon which looks upon the lake and the mountain Jura; and I imagine, that it must have been hence he contemplated the storm so magnificently described in the Third Canto; for you have from here a most extensive view of all the points he has therein depicted. I can fancy him like the scathed pine, whilst all around was sunk to repose, still waking to observe, what gave but a weak image of the storms which had desolated his own breast.

> *The sky is changed!—and such a change; Oh, night!*
> *And storm and darkness, ye are wond'rous strong,*
> *Yet lovely in your strength, as is the light*
> *Of a dark eye in woman! Far along*
> *From peak to peak, the rattling crags among,*
> *Leaps the live thunder! Not from one lone cloud,*
> *But every mountain now hath found a tongue,*
> *And Jura answers thro' her misty shroud,*
> *Back to the joyous Alps who call to her aloud!*
>
> *And this is in the night:—Most glorious night!*
> *Thou wer't not sent for slumber! let me be*
> *A sharer in thy far and fierce delight,—*
> *A portion of the tempest and of me!*
> *How the lit lake shines a phosphoric sea,*
> *And the big rain comes dancing to the earth!*
> *And now again 'tis black,—and now the glee*
> *Of the loud hills shakes with its mountain mirth,*
> *As if they did rejoice o'er a young earthquake's birth,*
>
> *Now where the swift Rhine cleaves his way between*
> *Heights which appear, as lovers who have parted*
> *In haste, whose mining depths so intervene,*
> *That they can meet no more, tho' broken hearted;*
> *Tho' in their souls which thus each other thwarted,*

Love was the very root of the fond rage
Which blighted their life's bloom, and then departed—
Itself expired, but leaving them an age
Of years all winter—war within themselves to wage.

I went down to the little port, if I may use the expression, wherein his vessel used to lay, and conversed with the cottager, who had the care of it. You may smile, but I have my pleasure in thus helping my personification of the individual I admire, by attaining to the knowledge of those circumstances which were daily around him. I have made numerous enquiries in the town concerning him, but can learn nothing. He only went into society there once, when Mr Pictet took him to the house of a lady to spend the evening. They say he is a very singular man, and seem to think him very uncivil. Amongst other things they relate, that having invited Mr Pictet and Bonstetten to dinner, he went on the lake to Chillon, leaving a gentleman who travelled with him to receive them and make his apologies. Another evening, being invited to the house of Lady D. H., he promised to attend, but upon approaching the windows of her ladyship's villa, and perceiving the room to be full of company, he set down his friend, desiring him to plead his excuse, and immediately returned home. This will serve as a contradiction to the report which you tell me is current in England, of his having been avoided by his countrymen on the continent. The case happens to be directly the reverse, as he has been generally sought by them, though on most occasions, apparently without success. It is said, indeed, that upon paying his first visit at Coppet, following the servant who had announced his name, he was surprised to meet a lady carried out fainting; but before he had been seated many minutes, the same lady, who had been so affected at the sound of his name, returned and conversed with him a considerable time— such is female curiosity and affectation! He visited Coppet frequently, and of course associated there with several of his countrymen, who evinced no reluctance to meet him whom his enemies alone would represent as an outcast.

Though I have been so unsuccessful in this town, I have been more fortunate in my enquiries elsewhere. There is a society three or four miles from Geneva, the centre of which is the Countess of Breuss, a Russian lady, well acquainted with the agrémens de la Société, and who has collected them round herself at her mansion. It was chiefly here, I find, that the gentleman who travelled with Lord Byron, as physician, sought for society. He used almost every day to cross the lake by himself, in one of their flat-bottomed boats, and return after passing the evening with his friends, about eleven or twelve at night, often whilst the storms were raging in the circling summits of the mountains around. As he became intimate, from long acquaintance, with several of the families in this neighbourhood, I have gathered from their accounts some excellent traits of his lordship's character, which I will relate to you at some future opportunity.

Among other particulars mentioned, was the outline of a ghost story by Lord Byron. It appears that one evening Lord Byron, Mr Percy Bysshe Shelly, two ladies and the gentleman before alluded to, after having perused a German work, entitled *Phantasmagoriana*, began relating ghost stories; when his lordship having recited the beginning of Christabel, then unpublished, the whole took so strong a hold of Mr Shelly's mind, that he suddenly started up and ran out of the room. The physician and Lord Byron followed, and discovered him leaning against a mantle-piece, with cold drops of perspiration trickling down his face. After having given him something to refresh him, upon enquiring into the cause of his alarm, they found that his wild imagination having pictured to him the bosom of one of the ladies with eyes (which was reported of a lady in the neighbourhood where he lived) he was obliged to leave the room in order to destroy the impression. It was afterwards proposed, in the course of conversation, that each of the company present should write a tale depending upon some supernatural agency, which was undertaken by Lord B., the physician, and one of the ladies before mentioned. I obtained the outline of each of these stories as a great favour, and herewith forward them to you, as I was assured you would feel as much curiosity as myself, to peruse the ebauches of so great a genius, and those immediately under his influence.[25]

The Diary of Dr John William Polidori

8 July. The Game of Ghost Stories that had kept the five of us awake until the small hours for three harrowing weeks has slowly petered out with only lovely Mary continuing to write her dreadfull contribution (not dreadful, mind you, howbeit her story fills me so full of dread!) George and I alone have offered our ghost stories (his vampyre still haunts both my waking and dreaming minds); Shelley gracefully declined the Lord's invitation to play his game (of course he did); Claire refuses to share hers (I doubt she played the game at all); and lovely Mary is being haunted by this mysterious 'student of the unhallowed arts'. I am left alone in the parlour absentmindedly leafing through the book of ghost stories that served as the impetus for our little game (although I am affably fluent in the language of France, I am regretta-

---

25 From an extract of a letter from Geneva printed in *The Vampyre* by John William Polidori, published by Sherwood, Neely, and Jones, London.

bly illiterate). The 'Shelleys' have already retired for the evening to the privacy of their bedchamber, no doubt playing Aphrodite's favourite game, and George seeks to escape the needful Claire by imprisoning himself within his own apartment, with her secluded to her own.

Night fell at its usual hour for the day and month of our modern calendar; though the weather with its dour grey skies and chilled winds gave both the appearance and sensations of winter, the sun has stayed in its rightful course through the sky throughout this summer. The flames of the candles flickered, and the curtains fluttered with a sudden gust of wintry winds slipping through the windowpanes; the chill prickled gooseflesh upon my arms. A withered, almost haunted voice floated in from the foyer begging my pardon. I burst from the parlour brandishing a poker like a samurai warrior. Rain sleeted in through the open front doorway as a second mysterious figure fled into the protective embrace of the foyer from the cloud-shrouded moonless night. The withered old man soon returned; he set down two heavy suitcases and then disappeared back into darkness. The second figure stood as a woman out of time and of country: she reeked of English opulence, wore an Italian reticella lace ruff that has been out of style for centuries, adorned in Polish ornamentation, with a French farthingale. I might have questioned the rigidity of Spanish severity for travel; but a cultured woman cannot be so easily relieved of her culture. Her French gown was soaked from the sleet, while her kirtle and petticoat strained to keep her warm. She wore a safeguard to protect her while on travel, and a mantle of marten wrapped around her dainty shoulders. The withered, ancient man returned with a trunk– far too stout for his far too frail frame– but carried it with relative ease, setting it down daintily with an audible *thunk*. Without another word, he closed thick wooden door with a *thud* and vanished from both sight and memory.

'Georgie-poo,' the mysterious woman called out, her feminine voice echoing through the hallways of the Villa Diodati. 'Georgie-poo,' she calls out again as the echo returns, the reverb resounding. Her accent foreign hung thick in the air like London's fog. 'I have arrived as requested at Cologny.' This latter phrase died upon speaking, but her 'Georgie-poo' continued to ring out as if caught by the ghosts who sang out in a Gregorian chant. Lightning flashed through the narrow windows around the door seemingly striking the base of my spine; the electricity sparking through my veins, prickling gooseflesh once again. Now, I am the one begging her pardon, but Georgie-poo— I mean, Lord Byron— had retired early for the evening. She stood there incredulous that her 'Georgie-poo' would lay down to sleep at such an *unnatural* hour; the twelve tolls of midnight just come to pass. I invited her into the parlour to sit before the fire to have a warm. She sloughed off the sleet onto the rug in the entry, not like a serpent shedding its skin, but like a belly dancer alluring the eyes of me...— I mean, men— Then she joined me before the hearth.

Her name is Countess Erzsébet, a Hungarian noblewoman and acquaintance of Lord Byron whom he encountered on his Grand Tour of the Mediterranean a few years past, and she comes to stay with us in Cologny this night. Though I suspect she had seen at least a half-century of birthdays, she has the stature and appearance of an ingénue in a Russian ballet. Her skin is porcelain white, as if she had bathed in the blood of virgins. I chuckle at the morbid thought; the troubling image presents in my mind's eye, of her immersed in the deep crimson blood with her bare breasts barely submerged, was quite arousing— embarrassingly arousing. I had to shift a leg to discretely conceal the proof of my male arousal. Then my doctor's intellect stole back my attention from my primitive reptilian brain. A petite young virgin has, at most, a gallon of blood coursing through her veins. I could easily calculate the number of virgins that bathing in a ball-and-claw-footed white coated cast iron tub filled with human blood would necessitate the exsanguinating of at thirty. Quite the body count even for the promise of eternal youth. Perchance the countess blood-letted the virgin into a porcelain basin and then sponge-bathed herself by dipping a dainty toe into the crimson gore. Ha! This proved to my doctor's pedigree the most economical and certainly less homicidal method of bathing in virginal blood. Her Irishesque hair seemed perpetually stained by such bathing. Her wide eyes shone like emeralds, an unnatural fire in such Slavic stock. Everything about her struck me as unnatural, like she had been touched by the preternatural. Something... undead.

I chuckled again; my spine tingled again.

Erzsébet regaled me, 'My squalid, tempestuous journey through squalls and tempests,' (as English is not her native tongue, her use of these adjectives with the particular and peculiar roots alter their definitions both poetically and appropriately). I make my home at the foot of the Little Carpathian Mountains in the castle ⬛achtice, which lords over the lands and villages surrounding my prison, which were purchased as a bridal gift from the Nádasdy's family upon my wedding night to their son, Ferenc.' Since she sat enjoying a warm before the fire, I presume she speaks not of a literal prison but is taking literary license with her story to me. 'I received my invitation from Georgie-poo... I mean...' she corrected herself politely, the tone of her pleasant voice took on aristocratic formality, 'George Gordon Byron, 6th Baron Byron, to sojourn for the summer at the Villa Diodati on the shore of Lake Geneva in the esteemed company of his personal physician John William Polidori, the poet Percy Bysshe Shelley and the two sisters in his companionship.' She then returned to her natural playful lilt, 'My journey south would be brief because at the foot of the Little Carpathians lies Pressburg nestled between the Rivers Danube and Morava. A sharp turn to the west my carriage followed the bluest, yet queerestly frozen Danube to Vienna at the northeasternmost foothills of the alps, then further west into Munich which straddles the River Isar to the north of the alps. And then onto Bern surrounded on all sides by the River Aare like a God-ordained moat.' During this briefest of travelogues, my mind's pictured each as if I had seen them with my own eyes. It was if she had telepathically— preternaturally— inserted the pictures into my brain! 'Oh! my dear doctor,' she sighed, and she swooned with the back her his dainty hand resting upon her forehead, 'the roads were so long and so cruel. I would briefly and for a mere night rest in each of these jewels of Europe due to the hospitality my rank and station and coin still afford me. But woe! my dear doctor,' she cried, and she crooned, 'I feared the reproach of the suffering citizens because famine and diseased gripped every city, village, and hamlet I dared approach with such finery and such wares. The miserable wretches could at any moment mimic the revolutionaries of France and take my head from my shoulders. I was forced by necessity to put aside all signs of my aristocracy to travel as a commoner until this, the final leg of my journey. Oh! my dear doctor,' she sighed again, and she swooned again, 'on my ghoulish travels, my carriage passed failed crop-fields and unnaturally frozen rivers, drove through mirky woods, and over snow-laden mountain passes, to finally and fatefully this very summer night deliver me here where I can enjoy a warm around your hearth at our Lord's rented villa on the shore of Lake Geneva. I have fulfilled my obligation having accepted his gracious invitation.'

'Do you not desire to retire to a bedchamber? Surely you must be fatigued from your harrowing journey across the breadth of Europe?'

'At this natural hour? No,' she countered. 'What intrigue have I missed due to the lateness of my arrival?'

I would never dismiss a countess of such beauty, so I recounted, 'When Lord Byron and I set out from England on a Grand Tour towards our destination of Greece, we anticipated daily tours of the serene lake by rented boat and hiking through the scenic hills, but we have been plagued fast-flashing lightning and harsh-crashing thunder. We have suffered our imprisonment in the Villa Diodati like French aristocracy in the Bastille due such revolutionary weather. Lovely Mary once observed (and how I acquired this forbidden knowledge from her hidden journal must be required hereafter to remain a mystery): "An almost perpetual rain confines us principally to the house; but when the sun bursts forth it is with a splendour and cold even unknown in England. The thunder storms that visit us are grander and more terrific than I have ever seen before. We watch them as they approach from the opposite side of the lake, observing the lightning play among the clouds in various parts of the heavens, and dart in jagged figures upon the piny heights of Jura, dark with the shadow of the overhanging cloud, while perhaps the sun is shining cheerily upon us. One night we enjoyed a finer storm than I had ever before beheld. The lake was lit up— the pines on Jura made visible, and all the scene illuminated for an instant, when a pitchy blackness succeeded, and the thunder came in frightful bursts over our heads amid the darkness."[26]

'Your dear Georgie-poo,' I paused, casting my eyes to the rug fearful that I had just mocked her, 'My apologies, countess— Lord Byron given our state of agitation due to our immurement in these stately walls and irritation with each other in our rapprochement proposed a game of ghost stories. Having found a needless volume of a French translation of German ghost stories as our inspiration, Lord Byron leads us to seek out a literary haunting in our own corners of the Villa Diodati. The tale I presented to my friends is the one I began here at Coligny, when Frankenstein was planned, and when a noble author having determined to descend from his lofty rang, gave up a few hours to a tale of terror, and wrote a fragment. Though I cannot boast of the horrible imagination of the one, or the elegant classical style of the latter, still I hoped they would not throw mine away, because it is not equal to these.' The countess laid her dainty hand upon mine having leaned over the brief gulf between us. 'Whether the use I have made of supernatural agency, and the colouring I have given to the mind of Ernestus Berchtold, are original or not, I leave to the more erudite in novels and romances to declare I am not conscious of having seen any where a prototype of either; yet I fear that whatever is original, is not always pleasing. Nor is this my only apprehension. A tale that rests upon improbabilities, must generally disgust a rational mind; I am therefore afraid that, though I have thrown the superior agency into the back ground as much as was in my power, still, that many readers will think the same moral, and the same colouring, might have been given to characters acting under the ordinary agencies of life; I believe it, but I had agreed to write a supernatural tale, and that does not allow a completely every-day narrative.'[27] The countess, her

---

26 From the *History of a Six Weeks Tour Through a Part of France, Germany, Switzerland, and Holland* by Mary Shelley, published by T. Hookham, Jun. Old Bond Street, and C. and J. Ollier, Welbeck Street, 1817
27 From the Introduction by the author to *Ernestus Berchtold; or, The Modern Oedipus: A Tale* in 1819,

hand still resting on mine having descended from her chair to fall upon her knees at my feet, gave a precious squeeze.

'If mine was by far the worst, Lord Byron produced the first. Two friends were to travel from England into Greece (not unlike Lord Byron and myself); while there, one of them should die, but before his death, should obtain from his friend an oath of secrecy with regard to his disease. Some short time after, the remaining traveller returning to his native country, should be startled at perceiving his former companion moving about in society, and should be horrified at finding that he made love to his former friend's sister.[28]

'Oh! Oh!' the countess said, delicately agitated, 'Georgie-poo sent me a poem once that reeks of this viral vampirism! I still have it memorized! Shall I recite to you the relevant lines featuring the revenant, Doctor?' I simply nodded for I desired to hear the poem spoken in her lovely exotic accent.

> *A supposition alluded to in the "Giaour."*
> *'But first on earth, as Vampyre sent,*
> *Thy corse shall from its tomb be rent;*
> *Then ghastly haunt the native place,*
> *And suck the blood of all thy race;*
> *There from thy daughter, sister, wife,*
> *At midnight drain the stream of life;*
> Yet loathe the banquet which perforce
> *Must feed thy livid living corse,*
> *Thy victims, ere they yet expire,*
> *Shall know the demon for their sire;*
> *As cursing thee, thou cursing them,*
> *Thy flowers are withered on the stem.*
> *But one that for* thy crime must fall,
> *The youngest, best beloved of all,*
> *Shall bless thee with a* father's name—
> *That word shall wrap thy heart in flame!*
> *Yet thou must end thy task and mark*
> *Her cheek's last tinge—her eye's last spark,*
> *And the last glassy glance must view*
> *Which freezes o'er its lifeless blue;*
> *Then with unhallowed hand shall tear*
> *The tresses of her yellow hair,*

---

publisher unknown.
28 From a footnote to the Introduction by the author to *Ernestus Berchtold; or, The Modern Oedipus: A Tale* in 1819, publisher unknown.

Of which, in life a lock when shorn
Affection's fondest pledge was worn—
But now is borne away by thee
Memorial of thine agony!
Yet with thine own best blood shall drip;
Thy gnashing tooth, and haggard lip;
Then stalking to thy sullen grave,
Go— and with Gouls and Afrits rave,
Till these in horror shrink away
From spectre more accursed than they.[29]

'But... my dear doctor,' the countess continued, 'I deny the possibility of such a ground-work forming the outline of a tale which should bear the slightest appearance of probability. This is the reason my Georgie-poo abandoned the concept as a mere fragment. There is not-a-thing more to this story other than the brief pages he wrote.'

The creative, non-caporal voice that lives in the heads of all poets and novelists protested loudly, not only in the confines of my skull, but out of my mouth as well. 'Upon this foundation is a great story! Even if Lord Byron chose to leave it unfinished, it is certainly not an unfinishable story. Where he chose to begin and to end his intentional fragment leaves open the possibility of its completion by another.

'That's plagiarism,' the countess protested. 'The story is not yours to finish. It is my Georgie-poo's to do with or do without as he chooses.'

'Was not the Bard William Shakespeare himself an unrepentant plagiarist?' I countered, '*Romeo and Juliet* was stolen from an Arthur Brooke's English translation of Pierre Boaistuau's French translation of Matteo Bandello Italian *Giuletta e Romeo*. His theft of Raphael Holinshed's *Chronicles* proved to be obscene: nearly every one of the historical plays, including both Richards and all the Henrys, and Kings Lear and John, along with the framework of *MacBeth*, were stolen. Thief! Thief!' I exclaimed as if I were a merchant in an Arabian bizarre demanding Shakespeare's hand be cut off by city guards for his thievery! 'Did he take literary liberties with all of sources making them his own? Emphatically. Did he steal nearly every line from one or two of the Henrys word-for-word, line-for-line from Holinshed? Indubitably! We should, no doubt, retire the epithet 'The Bard' and substitute 'The Plagiarist'. 'Tis a more fitting title.'

'If it is possible, which it is not, then pluck the abandoned fragment from our little Lord's dustbin and complete the fragment,' she said

---

29 From *The Giaour* a poem by Lord Byron, published by T. Davison, Whitefriars, for John Murray, Albemarle-Street, 1813.

smacking me across the cheek with her dainty hand as if she clutched a metaphorical duellist's glove.' She lifted herself to her feet, straightened her skirt, courteously curtsied, and requested my services to deliver her baggage to her bedchamber given the sudden lateness of the hour. Our conversation had stolen away the night. Standing in the door-frame to her apartment, I wished her a good night, kissing the back of her dainty hand, then returned to the warm of the hearth to stew as if boiling in a cooking pot.

I reached down before the hearth to pick up the metaphorical duellist's glove she left lying invisible upon the rug, folded it nicely, then pocketed it, and said quite audibly and quite audaciously, 'I will complete the fragment.'

July 9. I awoke the next morning to join the Shelleys and Claire for breakfast. They knew not about the countess' arrival the night previous for she did not come out of the privacy of her bedchamber for breakfast nor lunch nor tea nor dinner. When she spoke yesternight of the late evening being a 'natural hour' for her I did not take her so literally, but given her absence during the waking hours, she proved to be as nocturnal as the vampire I planned to steal from Lord Byron.

Lord Byron's Diary

9 July 1816. I sought my escape from Claire's obsession for yet another night innumerable, but this prison in the form of the Villa Diodati keeps me enclosed to close to her! As I hide yet another night in my apartment, the words I had written in a letter to my dearest sister Augusta ring in my ears. Shall I repeat them, Diary? Hells-bells! Why not!

> Now don't scold; but what could I do?–a foolish girl, in spite of all I could say or do, would come after me, or rather went before--for I found her here–and I have had all the plague possible to persuade her to go back again; but at last she went. Now, dearest, I do most truly tell thee that I could not help this, that I did all I could to prevent it, and have at last put an end to it. I was not in love, nor have any love left for any; but I could not exactly play the Stoic with a woman who had scrambled eight hundred miles to unphilosophise me. Besides, I had been regaled of late with so many 'two courses and a desert' (Alas!) of aversion, that I was fain to take a little love (if pressed particularly) by way of novelty.
> —Letter from Lord Byron to Augusta Leigh

How I wish to sit up late with my dear Percy and debate galvanism again or another natural philosophy or the lack of natural philosophy in the religious or religion in the religious or the lack of religion in the irreligious, Percy's own kind. Howbeit, Claire, by her unwanted and wanton attention towards me, has immured me in my apartment. What crime have I committed to be so imprisoned within my own rented villa? Her pregnancy, you say? Until a natural philosopher can determine through some study of my semen in his laboratory to be the source of Claire's pregnancy, I say 'Balderdash!' to the paternity of her unborn. How would a comparison of my semen and the amniotic waters her unborn bathes in even be possible? Perchance, Percy and I can debate whether or not there is chance residual traces of semen can be found lingering the woman's womb or the child's body days, weeks, months, or even years removed from the sexual act. And I'd debate the following argument in Claire's presence surely out of spite: whether a kind-loving God would never permit such a comparison be made by the sciences and should paternity be proven only by the acceptance of the born in a man's heart. There can be no other proof of fatherhood other than in a man's heart because women can be such deceitful, despiteful creatures as it concerns their liaisons with men... innumerable.

And in my heart, her unborn is no progeny of mine!

Suddenly there came a tapping of someone excitedly rapping on my chamber door! Here I should be pleasantly napping instead of obsessing on Claire's obsession, trapping me in her womb with her unborn child. Was Claire so clairvoyant to hear my thoughts and came to assail me again? I crept to the stout wood separating me from my nocturnal assailant. Silence! I placed my ear to my chamber door hoping to hear something... anything... a moment, a long moment... there was nothing! Then there came another tapping of someone excitedly rapping on my chamber door. So close to a dreary midnight, I flung open the door and to my shock and surprise I laid my weak and weary eyes on Countess Erzsébet! How had she come to be at the Villa Diodati? No invitations had been sent, so no obligations needed to be spent on such a long and cruel journey to Lake Geneva. I embraced her with a ferocity that would chase away lesser maidens. We danced to the symphony of atmospheric timpani drums sounding and rain pounding out a rhythm on the windowpanes.

'Georgie-poo,' my sweetest Erzsébet cooed.

'Countess,' I said with a voice expressing both bewilderment and amazement. 'How did you find me here at a rented house on the shore of Lake Geneva? I sent no invitation to join our company at the Villa Diodati. And if I had, you would have been under no obligation to holiday the duration of this dreary, weary summer on the shores of a lake we cannot often tour. How are you here in my arms this evening?

'Georgie-poo, do you believe that the expanse of land and gulf of time that separated us could not be navigated to bring me to you?' she said, resting her delicate head upon my shoulder.

'How?'

'Do you question how a pigeon finds its way in delivering a message?'

'No.'

'Do you question how the butterflies migrate an unfathomable stretch from continent to continent?'

'No.'

'Do you question how the salmon find their birth waters to spawn a new generation, swimming naturally upstream to memories of a pool as remote as a dream?'

'No, but...'

'Then rest your troubled mind and do not question how it is I am snuggled in your arms this night having been smuggled across the breadth of Europe. Except the reality that needs no causality. The road was both long and cruel. Your unusual physician entertained me yesternight with a wonderful story of a game you and your company played thunderstorm-bound this queer winter,' she said with a sly wink.'

'Oh! It was such a wonderful game!'

'And what of your contribution to the game?'

'Oh, that fragment of a... thing,' I complained, 'It is not-a-thing to worry yourself about. A trifle. Speaking of trifles! Why should I tell you of that... nothing... when I can shower you with bracelets of my hair, rings, gawds, conceits, knacks, trifles, nosegays, sweetmeats, messengers of strong prevailment in unharden'd youth', I wooed stealing liberally and literally from Shakespeare.

'Oh! Georgie-poo, you woo far too liberally and literally from Shakespeare. Shame! Poets do not steal from one and another,' she said as I hung my head melodramatically. She lifted my chin with her dainty, white long-gloved hand, 'They do not.'

'No! Countess,' I counted in mock protest, 'a poet of high esteem could easily say something akin to, "Immature poets imitate; mature poets steal; bad poets deface what they take, and good poets make it into something better, or at least something different. The good poet welds his theft into a whole of feeling which is unique, utterly different from that from which it was torn."'

'I do not accept such a radical concept. Please, Georgie-poo, let us return to this game you played. Let us not speak of thieves and thievery when there is the excitement of the Creation of creativity!'

'What more can I tell you of the game we played? It was an unholy creature born of the cursed womb of this villa. We gestated in these confines for days, for weeks, and probably for the months to come. How we wished to be born with the sun on our faces, but in a season preternaturally cold thunderstorms, we poets all took up our quills to pen our own ghost stories. I will tell you how an awful French translation of even more awful German stories set us off on this course. I will not speak of mine, however, but I will tell you of theirs. My dearest doctor, whom you have had chance to encounter, contributed a most foul work, bloated, like a stinking corpse washed up upon the shore, with words. He knows no editor! My beloved Percy, a friend of mine from England, who is visiting with his fiancée and her sister, has chosen to not participate in my little game. The scoundrel. But of his fiancée, her contribution is magnificent in its horror! She has blended science with fiction! Who but lovely Mary would create a ghost of flesh and blood! Her creature is harrowing! As for my contribution, I have forgotten mine already.'

'Oh! your fine physician remembers it acutely and fondly. Please, forgive him, but he told me all about it.'

'Then why do I need to speak on it more? The fragmentary pages lie in a drawer in the owner of his villa's desk. If I had a stronger constitution, I would turn those pages into my crumpled globe and pitch it in an apocalyptic fire and watch its world burn. I should never have plucked vampirism out of folklore.'

'What is a vampire?' she said, continuing to coo, but I would choose not to woo her with my creative spark. Her desire is to light the fire of poet's heart. 'I know not this creature you speak of.'

'Oh, you are far too demure to demur too greatly. You know as well as I know, vampires were the reanimated corpses of persons newly buried, which were supposed to suck the blood and suck out the life of their selected victims. The marks by which a vampire corpse was recognized were the apparent non-putrefaction of the body and effusion of blood from the lips. A suspected vampire was exhumed, and if the marks were perceived or imagined to be present, a stake was driven through the heart, and the body was burned. This, if Southey's authorities may be believed, "laid" the vampire, and the community might sleep in peace. The Vampire superstition is still general in the Levant. Honest Tournefort tells a long story about these *"Vroucolachas"*, as he calls them. The Romaic term is *"Vardoulacha"*. I recollect a whole family being terrified by the scream of a child, which they imagined must proceed from such a visitation. The Greeks never mention the word without horror. I find that "*Broucolokas*" is an old legitimate Hellenic appellation— the moderns, however, use the word I mention. The stories told in Hungary and Greece of these foul feeders are singular, and some of them most incredibly attested.[30] These are your ancestorial lands I speak of. Your nursery stories, I have no doubt, spoke of rumours and the rumours of rumours of the risen dead. Superstitions! Are you too haughty from the height of your castle to listen to the folk tales of the common people. *Vroucolachas*! *Vardoulacha*! *Gouls*! *Broucolokas*!'

The Countess slapped me across the cheek; I felt the all too familiar sting. 'How dare you mock me! I may be born of aristocratic stock, but my roots are in the land and its people. I know intimately the stories of the beloved dead crawling from their graves to menace the begrieved. I have witnessed once virile men so fearful of rising from their consecrated graves and assailing their grieving wives and weeping children that on their deathbeds they ask— they plead— they bribe the undertaker's man to be buried with a blade resting across their necks. If the dead can raise their heads to sit up, the dead can then crawl through the moist earth to return to their families turn their beloveds into *Vroucolachas*! *Vardoulacha*! *Gouls*! *Broucolokas*! like themselves. I have had to console the begrieved, who've had yet another in their family fall fatally ill by an assault from the recently deceased. The family begs me for the release from vampirism. They beg me to order to the undertaker to exhume to corpse to observe any signs of life, as you so expertly detailed. My order! And by my order a stake is driven into the heart of the dead. I give this order over and over again— not so dead will no longer rise from the grave, according to the absurd superstition, but for the peace of mind of the living! Until you, my little Lord, are forced by your nobility to order the desecration of a corpse while priests pray and families wail, hold your bitter tongue!'

'My apologies, Countess!' I bent my head in not only genuflection, but affection— and submission. I offered my confession. I apologized for my clumsy tongue.

'Stubborn tongue,' the countess countered. 'Your native tongue may not be my own, but if we were in my country, I could rightfully and righteously have your slanderous tongue cut out for your mockery and insolence. Speak to me thus never again!'

I knew she was not truly angry with me. We, the denizens of the Villa Diodati, may have played a game of ghost stories this summer, but this game that the countess I engaged in is played with barbed tongues.

---

30 From the notes *The Giaour* by Lord Bryon, published by John Murray, Albemarle Street, 1813.

The sharper the better. A keen edge of the tongue that can eviscerate, slicing open our rival's belly and spilling their entrails upon their shoes. Such a wicked game to play.

The Diary of Dr John William Polidori

11 July. I woke in the morning before the sun had even risen, Lord Byron, the Shelleys, and Ms. Clairemont would not be up for breakfast, but I could no longer sleep my mind preoccupied with sizzling bacon and sausage and a few eggs scrabbled. Strange! As soon as I open by bedchamber door, there sat some luggage at my feet, small and made ready for travel. Curious, I picked of the luggage and made my way to the foyer, in preparation for what? I knew not. There stood Countess Erzsébet dressed for travel, dressed as she had been when she had arrived at the Villa Diodati just Monday evening. Concerned that she was cutting her visit to the villa short, I inquired if she was retiring back to Hungary. She shook her head slowly to the left and then to the right, returning to the proper centre for a gentlewoman. I then required of her the knowledge of her presence in the foyer and the small luggage she obviously had packed and curiously left at my bedchamber door.

Oh! we were going on a brief holiday.

Outside the villa stood her carriage and her mysterious elderly carriage-driver who had seemingly disappeared into the ether just a few days before. The sun had not yet risen over the Alps, but there was the merest hint of light painting the sky behind the mountaintops. Soon dawn would be upon us. I helped the countess into the carriage, as any good gentlemen would and off we set for a destination unknown. Her forthrightness in planning a cryptic holiday had thrown me for a loop. Why was I alone invited and not Lord Byron, nor the Shelleys, nor Ms. Clairemont. The Shelleys and Claire not receiving an invitation at the very least was explainable, but Lord Byron not sitting in this carriage with the countess and me, was truly perplexing and quite vexing. My curiosity had grown more and more as the villa and Lake Geneva shrank in distance behind us. She now shown an unpredictability that was as alluring as it was alarming.

The carriage curiously had the windows painted black, so the interior was as pitch as midnight with the moon obscured by the clouds or in its newness. The rhythmic motion of the carriage immediately lulled both the countess and I into a quaint and quite queer dreamless slumber. I awoke startled at the sudden halt of the carriage. The elderly driver opened the door on my side of the carriage. I was greeted by the presence of a hotel of surprising opulence in a metropolis I could not readily identify. The hotel was completely and gloriously lit by gas-light! Night had already fallen? How far and for how long had we travelled while we both slept so soundly that we may have been counted amongst the dead? This was a profoundly serious question. Curiouser and curiouser!

Our room rented for the weekend was fit for a king, or at the very least a countess of a distant land. The walls were gilded quite obscenely and the bed itself was quilted quite cleanly with the rarest of silk panels. The curtains were of the thickest wool, no doubt sheered from golden-woolled, winged ram, Chrysomallos! (But I digress into preposterous pedanticness) The paintings hung on all the walls were all unrecognized by me, but by their quality, were no doubt created by prized Renascence masters. The museums of London would be envious of the paintings and the sculptures housed in a mere hotel room. Oh! the pretentiousness! Oh! the licentiousness! How this room's very culture made me feel like an imposter instead of a proper guest in this hotel!

As I gawked at the room, there came a knock on the locked hotel room door. When I opened the door, there stood a porter who would not have been out of place as a valet at Buckingham Palace. He was dressed to impress king, emperors, and perhaps even the Pope, whom stands above all in the pantheon of European royalty. He handed me an ornate box, which I peered down at and when I returned my gaze to the page to thank him, perchance to tip him, he had vanished like a fart in a whirlwind. The countess motioned for me to sit at a no less ornate desk positioned against the gilded walls. I sat in its chair inspired by a particular French king, and opened the box. Slowly. As it was once owned by Pandora. What would I find inside? Hope? 'A kingly gift fit for an author of such singing prose!' Erzsébet squealed as the interior was revealed in the candlelight. I found a journal bound in the finest leather, its edges gilded in gold leaf as real as the gold in this room, along with a quill from a blackest swan and pot with the purest India ink.

The Countess and I sat at dinner in, not in the hotel's restaurant of the finest European culinary fare, but a backwater kitchen hidden among filth strewn streets of the peasantry. Where we would find the truest, purest example of this land's cuisine. My plate, when delivered to me, proved so exotic and foreign that I was momentarily repulsed. But I would not insult my host who did the ordering nor the chef who did the preparation. My father had gone to great lengths in instruct me in the manners of a gentleman. You ate whatever was placed on the plate. No gentleman would attend a gallery presentation of an artist, only to request and require the art to make alterations to the painting

before you would purchase it; a gentleman simply does not enter a restaurant and request and require the chef to make alterations to his dish.
Like the painter or sculpture dedicated their lives to their art, the chef
has spent a lifetime mastering flavours and textures to produce his own
work of art. And if you do not desire this ingredient or that ingredient,
then my father would admonish me, do not order that dish. And if
there is not-a-thing on the menu that strikes your stomach's fancy, you
do not eat!

And I did eat.

During our small talk, the Countess Erzsébet inquired what did I
knew of vampires! Unfettered by her doubts and intent on flouting my
own knowledge and experience in all things, I waxed, 'The superstition
is very general in the East. Among the Arabians it appears to be common: it did not, however, extend itself to the Greeks until after the estab-
lishment of Christianity; and it has only assumed its present form since
the division of the Latin and Greek churches; at which time, the idea
becoming prevalent, that a Latin body could not corrupt if buried in their
territory, it gradually increased, and formed the subject of many wonderful stories, still extant, of the dead rising from their graves, and feeding
upon the blood of the young and beautiful. In the West it spread, with
some slight variation, all over Hungary, Poland, Austria, and Lorraine,
where the belief existed, that vampyres nightly imbibed a certain portion
of the blood of their victims, who became emaciated, lost their strength,
and speedily died of consumptions; whilst these human blood-suckers
fattened—and their veins became distended to such a state of repletion,
as to cause the blood to flow from all the passages of their bodies, and
even from the very pores of their skins.

'In the London Journal, of March 1732, is a curious, and, of
course, credible account of a particular case of vampyrism, which is
stated to have occurred at Madreyga, in Hungary. It appears, that upon
an examination of the commander-in-chief and magistrates of the place,
they positively and unanimously affirmed, that, about five years before,
a certain Heyduke, named Arnold Paul, had been heard to say, that, at
Cassovia, on the frontiers of the Turkish Servia, he had been tormented
by a vampyre, but had found a way to rid himself of the evil, by eating
some of the earth out of the vampyre's grave, and rubbing himself with
his blood. This precaution, however, did not prevent him from becoming
a vampyre himself; for, about twenty or thirty days after his death
and burial, many persons complained of having been tormented by him, and a deposition was made, that four persons had
been deprived of life by his attacks. To prevent further mischief,
the inhabitants having consulted their Hadagni, took up the body,

and found it (as is supposed to be usual in cases of vampyrism) fresh, and entirely free from corruption, and emitting at the mouth, nose, and ears, pure and florid blood. Proof having been thus obtained, they resorted to the accustomed remedy. A stake was driven entirely through the heart and body of Arnold Paul, at which he is reported to have cried out as dreadfully as if he had been alive. This done, they cut off his head, burned his body, and threw the ashes into his grave. The same measures were adopted with the corses of those persons who had previously died from vampyrism, lest they should, in their turn, become agents upon others who survived them.

'This monstrous <u>rodomontade</u> is here related, because it seems better adapted to illustrate the subject of the present observations than any other instance which could be adduced. In many parts of Greece it is considered as a sort of punishment after death, for some heinous crime committed whilst in existence, that the deceased is not only doomed to vampyrise, but compelled to confine his infernal visitations solely to those beings he loved most while upon earth—those to whom he was bound by ties of kindred and affection.— A supposition alluded to in the "Giaour" as you recited to me upon our first meeting!

'Mr Southey has also introduced in his wild but beautiful poem of "Thalaba," the vampyre corse of the Arabian maid Oneiza, who is represented as having returned from the grave for the purpose of tormenting him she best loved whilst in existence. But this cannot be supposed to have resulted from the sinfulness of her life, she being pourtrayed throughout the whole of the tale as a complete type of purity and innocence. The veracious Tournefort gives a long account in his travels of several astonishing cases of vampyrism, to which he pretends to have been an eye-witness; and Calmet, in his great work upon this subject, besides a variety of anecdotes, and traditionary narratives illustrative of its effects, has put forth some learned dissertations, tending to prove it to be a classical, as well as barbarian error.

'Many curious and interesting notices on this singularly horrible superstition might be added; though the present may suffice for the limits of a note, necessarily devoted to explanation, and which may now be concluded by merely remarking, that though the term Vampyre is the one in most general acceptation, there are several others synonimous with it, made use of in various parts of the world: as *Vroucolocha, Vardoulacha, Goul, Broucoloka,* &c.'[31]

When I spoke these foreign terms used for what the English call a vampyre, I saw the muscles in her face twitch. She winced, ever so

---

31 From the Introduction to *The Vampyre* by John William Polidori, published by Sherwood, Neely, and Jones, London.

slightly, ever so politely. Had someone somewhere in her past use these words offensively towards her. The words could have been used offensively to deeply hurt her; the words could have been used offensively to aggressively attack her. Now, being offensive, in either manner, is the shame of any gentlemen worth his salt. I did not intend to slur her or her people with terms that may be, in her language, slurs. To me these are merely words that would be translated in 'vamypre', but with the word 'vampyre' in English is inoffensive. Instead it is seductive, not suggestive. *Vroucolocha, Vardoulacha, Goul, Broucoloka* could carry within themselves the very offence I did not intend. And if she had taken offence, then as gentleman I would gladly accept her long glove across the cheek. A single tear, overflowed her eye and with my finger, I wiped it away and apologized. My beliefs on what a vampyre is are coloured by being British, while hers are stained with the blood of her countrymen. I would not stand on a colonial soapbox to scold her for her beliefs. The bright light of modernity cannot always— and perhaps should not— pierce the darkness of superstition. The gaslights of modern London expose what lurks in our civilized shadows to be mere foolishness. What lurks in their rural shadows may be truly ghoulishness.

Back in our room, surrounding by the opulence of the aristocratic class, Erzsébet cajoled me, not with sweet words to inspire an author's creativity, but with cruel words: 'I do not believe such a story could be told. Vampyres are hideous, odious creatures risen from the grave where they continue to rot. They cannot walk in the society of men. Even if they had been learned in life, that learning has decayed into mindlessness. This Lord Ruthven, whom you speak of, cannot be a suave and sophisticated English nobleman. Ha!' she laughed in my face. 'Even if a Count from my own homeland had risen as a vampyre, he would retain none of the aristocratic gifts. He may attempt to mimic them, but they would be a pale shade of his former self. This story cannot be written.'

And with that, I seized pen in hand and would write my story!

Lord Byron's Diary

11 July 1816. My beloved Erzsébet came down from her apartment in the attic (she did not complain of her placement there but instead insisted because there were few windows to disturb her slumber during the bright light of the day) just as the sun was setting over the mountains to the west of the lake. Sleep had always does wonders for her complexion. A proper Englishwoman would moisturize and condition her skill with cold creams, rose water, glycerin and cucumber in queer mysterious feminine beauty rituals; women tend to

keep their beauty secrets not unlike a secret society from which most men are excluded. As for me, women tend to tell me their deepest, darkest secrets without ever meaning to or realizing they have, because they do not see me as a threat. Is it because we share the same taste in men? Perhaps! As for the countess, I know not what mysterious foreign products Erzsébet uses to keep her skin so porcelain white and so rosy of cheek and so crimson lipped. The countess' regimen for beauty is unmatched in all the Continent. But I am too afraid of her sharp tongue to ever inquire, lest that tongue cut me to the bone.

Mary and Percy had retired to their apartment early, far too early for them, for Mary had woken in the morning deathly pale and in desperate need of red wine and redder meat, even for breakfast. We had been mourning (my sarcasm is positively dripping) the sudden disappearance of Dr Pollydolly. Over the past month, he often spoke of the Countess Gräfin Potocka and often pondered her whereabouts. Like a besotted schoolboy. Perhaps, he received a letter from her and jaunted off on some tour of the region with her. I know no clue and no desire to know his whereabouts. And as for Claire, she was holed up in her own apartment. Perhaps she too had come down with a foul sickness. Namely pregnancy! Thankfully, the evening at the Villa Diodati was now reserved for Erzsébet and me.

Erzsébet seemed to exist only in my presence for when she appeared she is my companion, but must have encountered Dr Pollydolly during her brief stay. This night she speaks endlessly of theft and thievery. 'It is a curious link between *The Tempest*, *Love's Labour's Lost*, and *A Midsummer Night's Dream* that these are the three plays, out of thirty-nine, where Shakespeare does not follow a primary source. Even *The Merry Wives of Windsor*, which has no definite source, takes a clear starting point from Ovid. The Tempest is essentially plotless, and almost nothing happens in *Love's Labour's Lost*, but Shakespeare uniquely took pains to work out a fairly elaborate and outrageous plot for *A Midsummer Night's Dream*. Inventing plot was not a Shakespearean gift; it was the one dramatic talent that nature had denied him.[32]'

She was goading me into an argument. The Bard is held sacrosanct amongst English poets, whom I count myself a member, and the Drury Lane Theatre, of which I am a board member. William Shakespeare is held in the highest regard by not only thespians but poets as well. Every actor would give his eye teeth to play Romeo as a youth, Hamlet as a man, and King Lear when aged. Just as every poet strives to have their poetry resonate with the ferocity with words now two centuries old!

---

32 From *Shakespeare: The Invention of the Human* by Harold Bloom, published by Riverhead Books, 1998

Will my own poems be remembered, read, and recited at the turn of the millennium? A poet only can hope.

'Need I speak of his endless theft and thievery of Raphael Holinshed's *Chronicles*?', she continued.

Oh ho! Oh no!

I. Will. Not. Be. Goaded. Into. An. Argument.

19 July 1816. I write these words in the small hours, confused and confounded. I hold in my hands pages written by my personal physician, Dr Pollydolly, their having been in my possession for a week. They were exquisite, gilded stationary torn from a journal. How did a poor physician come into possession of such finery? The pages have been wrinkled by my firm raging grip. My dearest Erzsébet, upon her escape from the prison, which is the Villa Diodati, handed me the hand-written pages. I recognized the handwriting instantly from its physician scrawl. Dr Pollydolly had written her something. A love letter? A confession? Worse! Was this the plagiarizing she spoke of? While John was off on his weekend-long jaunt, she whispered paranoias of plagiarism in my ear! And now that pages were in my hand, I know not her intentions! I read the words, though I had some difficult deciphering his scrawl. Erzsébet, in her cruelty, sought to instigate a brawl between two friends. But were we friends? I did not know. I could not know. As I finished reading, in my utter exhaustion, my firm grip on the pages loosened and the fell cascading to the floor. What were his intentions writing this story?

Mary Wollstonecraft Godwin's Journal

20 June. My Beloved had set the first piece of our luggage in the foyer. We planned to set out at first light for the nearby glacier we had had our hearts set on visiting all this this cruel, wet summer. The night had once again fallen faster than we expected having wiled away the evening packing our suitcases. The thunder continued its continuous cracking, but we would not find ourselves backtracking from our planned holiday to the glacier. No amount of storming could dissuade us from our intended weeklong expedition. The carriage had been commissioned with the horses pulling up at the cresting of the dawn. Our room in Hotel de Ville de Londres, itself situated at the foot of the glacier, had been rented in preparation for our arrival. However, Lord Bryon rapped upon our chamber door intent on persuading us for one more evening of ghost stories in our long, drawn out game. My own ghost of Dr Victor Frankenstein had gone quite queerly silent for countless long agonizing nights. I had become accustomed to his discussing his life with me. He no longer visits me in the small hours while my Beloved slumbers beside me. I want nothing more than to know more of the lumbering Creature he has created. My lust for his autobiography could not be sated. I hoped he could, by his preternatural nature, shadow our journey to visit me at the Hotel de Ville de Londres. I even left a note on the nightstand telling my dear Victor of our destination.

Lord Bryon stood before the hearth in the parlour holding ink-stained pages. In his eyes, the firelight blazed. There was no hint of authorly pride dancing in his eyes. Instead, I saw rage roiling. The veins on the backs on his hands boiled with hot blood as his fingers crunched the sheets of paper in his clinched fist. But his fists were not only clinched, but his teeth clenched as well. What manner of ghost story had he conjured to produce such fury. Clearly, I was no longer sure I wished to experience such a ghost of a story. Whatever spirit inspired this work was a foul fiend and I did not wish to be bedeviled on the eve of our holiday to the glacier.

And speaking of our holiday, my Beloved waltzed in from the foyer having set down the last of our luggage to take his customary chair. Poor Polidori sat beaming at his dearest friend as he prepared to continue our game. Lord Byron held out the pages to poor Polidori, who gracefully, but cautiously accepted the gift. The blood drained from his face and his fingers faltered to force a firm grasp on the pages. From my own seat, I did not recognize the little Lord's exquisite penmanship. The handwriting had the prevailing scrawl of a physician. Had the doctor written this particular, now peculiar, ghost story? Our little Lord had stepped towards the poor doctor and slowly, achingly, reached behind his back. Was there something concealed in his belt? I caught the gaze of my Beloved as the fire blazed and his eyes widened with genuine fear as he watched our little Lord retrieve a pistol from his belt at the small of his back. Byron's breath seethed in the cool night air, hot with smoke-like puffs. He pressed the barrel of the pistol into poor Polidori's temple. The cool steel could quickly become seeringly hot. Byron's hand did not tremble in the slightest, but held the pistol with a steeled grip. 'Read,' Lord Byron said, enunciating the single syllable with the intensity of a Catholic priest transubstantiating bread and wine into the Body and Blood of Jesus the Christ.

'What?' poor Polidori inquired, but the Lord no longer required Polidori to understand. He instead clicked back the hammer on the flintlock.

'Read.'

Poor Polidori pleaded, 'Why?'

'Read,' Lord Byron said. 'Or die!'

'Wh-what?'

'Confess your crime. I require no poetry nor rhymes. We are all writers seated here in the parlour, surrounding by books. Books, Polidori. The sacred scriptures of our profession. The ghosts of these authors haunt this very room. Had we not conjured our game of ghost stories... in this very room? Were we not so bored that I read from a poorly written translated book of poorly written German ghost stories? Had I not been the first to continue to the game? My dearest Shelley himself refused to play, while Claire has chosen not to share hers and, despite our constant cruel and keen mockery, Mary has surpassed us all with the creativity of her Creation. But you, my dear doctor, have chosen to commit the gravest sin of our chosen profession. You may not have stolen my words, but you have stolen into my very words. You have taken what was never yours. Ms. Mary's queerest doctor may have the stolen corpse of a man, one society left abandoned in death, and utilizing forbidden scientific practices reanimated it into an abomination of science, but you, my dearest doctor, have taken the corpse of my story, one that I left abandoned in death, and utilizing forbidden literary techniques reanimated it into an abomination of literature.'

'Lord Byron, let me explain.'

'Read your ghost story.'

Now, Lord Byron's finger trembled upon the trigger with the boiling of his pulse. Not the condition one wishes to possess next to a trigger designed retract with the slightest pressure and react with lethal intensity.

Poor Polidori gulped down the phlegm that had, no doubt, pooled at the top of his gullet. 'It happened that in the midst of the dissipations attendant upon a London winter, there appeared at the various parties of the leaders of the ton a nobleman, more remarkable for his singularities, than his rank. He gazed upon the mirth around him, as if he could not participate therein. Apparently, the light laughter of the fair only attracted his attention, that he might by a look quell it, and throw fear into those breasts where thoughtlessness reigned. Those who felt this sensation of awe, could not explain whence it arose: some attributed it to the dead grey eye, which, fixing upon the object's face, did not seem to penetrate, and at one glance to pierce through to the inward workings of the heart; but fell upon the cheek with a leaden ray that weighed upon the skin it could not pass. His peculiarities caused him to be invited to every house; all wished to see him, and those who had been accustomed to violent excitement, and now felt the weight of ennui, were pleased at having something in their presence capable of engaging their attention. In spite of the deadly hue of his face, which never gained a warmer tint, either from the blush of modesty, or from the strong emotion of passion, though its form and outline were beautiful, many of the female hunters after notoriety attempted to win his attentions, and gain, at least, some marks of what they might term affection: Lady Mercer, who had been the mockery of every monster shewn in drawing-rooms since her marriage, threw herself in his way, and did all but put on the dress of a mountebank, to attract his notice:— though in vain:— when she stood before him, though his eyes were apparently fixed upon her's, still it seemed as if they were unperceived;— even her unappalled impudence was baffled, and she left the field. But though the common adultress could not influence even the guidance of his eyes, it was not that the female sex was indifferent to him: yet such was the apparent caution with which he spoke to the virtuous wife and innocent daughter, that few knew he ever addressed himself to females. He had, however, the reputation of a winning tongue; and whether it was that it even overcame the dread of his singular character, or that they were moved by his apparent hatred of vice, he was as often among those females who form the boast of their sex from their domestic virtues, as among those who sully it by their vices.

'About the same time, there came to London a young gentleman of the name of Aubrey: he was an orphan left with an only sister in the possession of great wealth, by parents who died while he was yet in childhood. Left also to himself by guardians, who thought it their duty merely to take care of his fortune, while they relinquished the more important charge of his mind to the care of mercenary subalterns, he cultivated more his imagination than his judgment. He had, hence, that high romantic feeling of honour and candour, which daily ruins so many milliners' apprentices. He believed all to sympathise with virtue, and thought that vice was thrown in by Providence merely for the picturesque effect of the scene, as we see in romances: he thought that the misery of a cottage merely consisted in the vesting of clothes, which were as warm, but which were better adapted to the painter's eye by their irregular folds and various coloured patches. He thought, in fine, that the dreams of poets were the realities of life. He was handsome, frank, and rich: for these reasons, upon his entering into the gay circles, many mothers surrounded him, striving which should describe with least truth their languishing or romping favourites: the daughters at the same time, by their brightening countenances when he approached, and by their sparkling eyes, when he opened his lips, soon led him into false notions of his talents and his merit. Attached as he was to the romance of his solitary hours, he was startled at finding, that, except in the tallow and wax candles that flickered, not from the presence of a ghost, but from want of snuffing, there was no foundation in real life for any of that congeries of pleasing pictures and descriptions contained in those volumes, from which he had formed his study. Finding, however, some compensation in his gratified vanity, he was about to relinquish his dreams, when the extraordinary being we have above described, crossed him in his career.

'He watched him; and the very impossibility of forming an idea of the character of a man entirely absorbed in himself, who gave few other signs of his observation of external objects, than the tacit assent to their existence, implied by the avoidance of their contact: allowing his imagination to picture every thing that flattered its propensity to extravagant ideas, he soon formed this object into the hero of a romance, and determined to observe the offspring of his fancy, rather than the person before him. He became acquainted with him, paid him attentions, and so far advanced upon his notice, that his presence was always recognised. He gradually learnt that Lord Ruthven's affairs were embarrassed, and soon found, from the notes of preparation in — — Street, that he was about to travel. Desirous of gaining some information respecting this singular character, who, till now, had only whetted his curiosity, he hinted to his guardians, that it was time for him to perform the tour, which for many generations has been thought necessary to enable the young to take some rapid steps in the career of vice towards putting themselves upon an equality with the aged, and not allowing them to appear as if fallen from the skies, whenever scandalous intrigues are mentioned as the subjects of pleasantry or of praise, according to the degree of skill shewn in carrying them on. They consented: and Aubrey immediately mentioning his intentions to Lord Ruthven, was surprised to receive from him a proposal to join him. Flattered by such a mark of esteem from him, who, apparently, had nothing in common with other men, he gladly accepted it, and in a few days they had passed the circling waters.

'Hitherto, Aubrey had had no opportunity of studying Lord Ruthven's character, and now he found, that, though many more of his actions were exposed to his view, the results offered different conclusions from the apparent motives to his conduct. His companion was profuse in his liberality;— the idle, the vagabond, and the beggar, received from his hand more than enough to relieve their immediate wants. But Aubrey could not avoid remarking, that it was not upon the virtuous, reduced to indigence by the misfortunes attendant even upon virtue, that he bestowed his alms;— these were sent from the door with hardly suppressed sneers; but when the profligate came to ask something, not to relieve his wants, but to allow him to wallow in his lust, or to sink him still deeper in his iniquity, he was sent away with rich charity. This was, however,

attributed by him to the greater importunity of the vicious, which generally prevails over the retiring bashfulness of the virtuous indigent. There
was one circumstance about the charity of his Lordship, which was still
more impressed upon his mind: all those upon whom it was bestowed,
inevitably found that there was a curse upon it, for they were all either
led to the scaffold, or sunk to the lowest and the most abject misery.
At Brussels and other towns through which they passed, Aubrey was
surprized at the apparent eagerness with which his companion sought
for the centres of all fashionable vice; there he entered into all the spirit
of the faro table: he betted, and always gambled with success, except
where the known sharper was his antagonist, and then he lost even more
than he gained; but it was always with the same unchanging face, with
which he generally watched the society around: it was not, however, so
when he encountered the rash youthful novice, or the luckless father of
a numerous family; then his very wish seemed fortune's law— this apparent abstractedness of mind was laid aside, and his eyes sparkled with
more fire than that of the cat whilst dallying with the half-dead mouse. In
every town, he left the formerly affluent youth, torn from the circle he
adorned, cursing, in the solitude of a dungeon, the fate that had drawn
him within the reach of this fiend; whilst many a father sat frantic, amidst
the speaking looks of mute hungry children, without a single farthing of
his late immense wealth, wherewith to buy even sufficient to satisfy their
present craving. Yet he took no money from the gambling table; but immediately lost, to the ruiner of many, the last gilder he had just snatched
from the convulsive grasp of the innocent: this might but be the result
of a certain degree of knowledge, which was not, however, capable of
combating the cunning of the more experienced. Aubrey often wished to
represent this to his friend, and beg him to resign that charity and pleasure which proved the ruin of all, and did not tend to his own profit;— but
he delayed it— for each day he hoped his friend would give him some
opportunity of speaking frankly and openly to him; however, this never
occurred. Lord Ruthven in his carriage, and amidst the various wild and
rich scenes of nature, was always the same: his eye spoke less than his
lip; and though Aubrey was near the object of his curiosity, he obtained
no greater gratification from it than the constant excitement of vainly
wishing to break that mystery, which to his exalted imagination began to
assume the appearance of something supernatural.

'They soon arrived at Rome, and Aubrey for a time lost sight of his
companion; he left him in daily attendance upon the morning circle of
an Italian countess, whilst he went in search of the memorials of another
almost deserted city. Whilst he was thus engaged, letters arrived from
England, which he opened with eager impatience; the first was from his

sister, breathing nothing but affection; the others were from his guardians, the latter astonished him; if it had before entered into his imagination that there was an evil power resident in his companion, these seemed to give him sufficient reason for the belief. His guardians insisted upon his immediately leaving his friend, and urged, that his character was dreadfully vicious, for that the possession of irresistible powers of seduction, rendered his licentious habits more dangerous to society. It had been discovered, that his contempt for the adultress had not originated in hatred of her character; but that he had required, to enhance his gratification, that his victim, the partner of his guilt, should be hurled from the pinnacle of unsullied virtue, down to the lowest abyss of infamy and degradation: in fine, that all those females whom he had sought, apparently on account of their virtue, had, since his departure, thrown even the mask aside, and had not scrupled to expose the whole deformity of their vices to the public gaze.

'Aubrey determined upon leaving one, whose character had not yet shown a single bright point on which to rest the eye. He resolved to invent some plausible pretext for abandoning him altogether, purposing, in the mean while, to watch him more closely, and to let no slight circumstances pass by unnoticed. He entered into the same circle, and soon perceived, that his Lordship was endeavouring to work upon the inexperience of the daughter of the lady whose house he chiefly frequented. In Italy, it is seldom that an unmarried female is met with in society; he was therefore obliged to carry on his plans in secret; but Aubrey's eye followed him in all his windings, and soon discovered that an assignation had been appointed, which would most likely end in the ruin of an innocent, though thoughtless girl. Losing no time, he entered the apartment of Lord Ruthven, and abruptly asked him his intentions with respect to the lady, informing him at the same time that he was aware of his being about to meet her that very night. Lord Ruthven answered, that his intentions were such as he supposed all would have upon such an occasion; and upon being pressed whether he intended to marry her, merely laughed. Aubrey retired; and, immediately writing a note, to say, that from that moment he must decline accompanying his Lordship in the remainder of their proposed tour, he ordered his servant to seek other apartments, and calling upon the mother of the lady, informed her of all he knew, not only with regard to her daughter, but also concerning the character of his Lordship. The assignation was prevented. Lord Ruthven next day merely sent his servant to notify his complete assent to a separation; but did not hint any suspicion of his plans having been foiled by Aubrey's interposition.

'Having left Rome, Aubrey directed his steps towards Greece, and crossing the Peninsula, soon found himself at Athens. He then fixed his residence in the house of a Greek; and soon occupied himself in tracing the faded records of ancient glory upon monuments that apparently, ashamed of chronicling the deeds of freemen only before slaves, had hidden themselves beneath the sheltering soil or many coloured lichen. Under the same roof as himself, existed a being, so beautiful and delicate, that she might have formed the model for a painter wishing to pourtray on canvass the promised hope of the faithful in Mahomet's paradise, save that her eyes spoke too much mind for any one to think she could belong to those who had no souls. As she danced upon the plain, or tripped along the mountain's side, one would have thought the gazelle a poor type of her beauties; for who would have exchanged her eye, apparently the eye of animated nature, for that sleepy luxurious look of the animal suited but to the taste of an epicure. The light step of Ianthe often accompanied Aubrey in his search after antiquities, and often would the unconscious girl, engaged in the pursuit of a Kashmere butterfly, show the whole beauty of her form, floating as it were upon the wind, to the eager gaze of him, who forgot the letters he had just decyphered upon an almost effaced tablet, in the contemplation of her sylph-like figure. Often would her tresses falling, as she flitted around, exhibit in the sun's ray such delicately brilliant and swiftly fading hues, it might well excuse the forgetfulness of the antiquary, who let escape from his mind the very object he had before thought of vital importance to the proper interpretation of a passage in Pausanias. But why attempt to describe charms which all feel, but none can appreciate?— It was innocence, youth, and beauty, unaffected by crowded drawing-rooms and stifling balls. Whilst he drew those remains of which he wished to preserve a memorial for his future hours, she would stand by, and watch the magic effects of his pencil, in tracing the scenes of her native place; she would then describe to him the circling dance upon the open plain, would paint, to him in all the glowing colours of youthful memory, the marriage pomp she remembered viewing in her infancy; and then, turning to subjects that had evidently made a greater impression upon her mind, would tell him all the supernatural tales of her nurse. Her earnestness and apparent belief of what she narrated, excited the interest even of Aubrey; and often as she told him the tale of the living vampyre, who had passed years amidst his friends, and dearest ties, forced every year, by feeding upon the life of a lovely female to prolong his existence for the ensuing months, his blood would run cold, whilst he attempted to laugh her out of such idle and horrible fantasies; but Ianthe cited to him the names of old men, who had at last detected one living among themselves, after several of their near relatives and children had been found marked with the stamp of the fiend's appetite; and when she found him so incredulous, she begged of him to believe her, for it had been, remarked, that those who had dared to question their existence, always had some proof given, which obliged them, with grief and heartbreaking, to confess it was true. She detailed to him the traditional appearance of these monsters, and his horror was increased, by hearing a pretty accurate description of Lord Ruthven; he, however, still persisted in persuading her, that there could be no truth in her fears, though at the same time he wondered at the many coincidences which had all tended to excite a belief in the supernatural power of Lord Ruthven.

'Aubrey began to attach himself more and more to Ianthe; her innocence, so contrasted with all the affected virtues of the women among whom he had sought for his vision of romance, won his heart; and while he ridiculed the idea of a young man of English habits, marrying an uneducated Greek girl, still he found himself more and more attached to the almost fairy form before him. He would tear himself at times from her, and, forming a plan for some antiquarian research, he would depart, determined not to return until his object was attained; but he always found it impossible to fix his attention upon the ruins around him, whilst in his mind he retained an image that seemed alone the rightful possessor of his thoughts. Ianthe was unconscious of his love, and was ever the same frank infantile being he had first known. She always seemed to part from him with reluctance; but it was because she had no longer any one with whom she could visit her favourite haunts, whilst her guardian was occupied in sketching or uncovering some fragment which had yet escaped the destructive hand of time. She had appealed to her parents on the subject of Vampyres, and they both, with several present, affirmed their existence, pale with horror at the very name. Soon after, Aubrey determined to proceed upon one of his excursions, which was to detain him for a few hours; when they heard the name of the place, they all at once begged of him not to return at night, as he must necessarily pass through a wood, where no Greek would ever remain, after the day had closed, upon any consideration. They described it as the resort of the vampyres in their nocturnal orgies, and denounced the most heavy evils as impending upon him who dared to cross their path. Aubrey made light of their representations, and tried to laugh them out of the idea; but when he saw them shudder at his daring thus to mock a superior, infernal power, the very name of which apparently made their blood freeze, he was silent.

'Next morning Aubrey set off upon his excursion unattended; he was surprised to observe the melancholy face of his host, and was concerned to find that his words, mocking the belief of those horrible fiends, had inspired them with such terror. When he was about to depart, Ianthe came to the side of his horse, and earnestly begged of him to return, ere night allowed the power of these beings to be put in action;— he promised. He was, however, so occupied in his research, that he did not perceive that day-light would soon end, and that in the horizon there was one of those specks which, in the warmer climates, so rapidly gather into a tremendous mass, and pour all their rage upon the devoted country.— He at last, however, mounted his horse, determined to make up by speed for his delay: but it was too late. Twilight, in these southern climates, is almost unknown; immediately the sun sets, night begins: and ere he had advanced far, the power of the storm was above— its echoing thunders had scarcely an interval of rest— its thick heavy rain forced its way through the canopying foliage, whilst the blue forked lightning seemed to fall and radiate at his very feet. Suddenly his horse took fright, and he was carried with dreadful rapidity through the entangled forest. The animal at last, through fatigue, stopped, and he found, by the glare of lightning, that he was in the neighbourhood of a hovel that hardly lifted itself up from the masses of dead leaves and brushwood which surrounded it. Dismounting, he approached, hoping to find some one to guide him to the town, or at least trusting to obtain shelter from the pelting of the storm. As he approached, the thunders, for a moment silent, allowed him to hear the dreadful shrieks of a woman mingling with the stifled, exultant mockery of a laugh, continued in one almost unbroken sound;— he was startled: but, roused by the thunder which again rolled over his head, he, with a sudden effort, forced open the door of the hut. He found himself in utter darkness: the sound, however, guided him. He was apparently unperceived; for, though he called, still the sounds continued, and no notice was taken of him. He found himself in contact with some one, whom he immediately seized; when a voice cried, "Again baffled!" to which a loud laugh succeeded; and he felt himself grappled by one whose strength seemed superhuman: determined to sell his life as dearly as he could, he struggled; but it was in vain: he was lifted from his feet and hurled with enormous force against the ground:— his enemy threw himself upon him, and kneeling upon his breast, had placed his hands upon his throat— when the glare of many torches penetrating through the hole that gave light in the day, disturbed him;— he instantly rose, and, leaving his prey, rushed through the door, and in a moment the crashing of the branches, as he broke through the wood, was no longer heard. The storm was now still; and Aubrey, incapable of moving, was soon heard by those without. They entered; the light of their torches fell upon the mud walls, and the thatch loaded on every individual

straw with heavy flakes of soot. At the desire of Aubrey they searched
for her who had attracted him by her cries; he was again left in darkness;
but what was his horror, when the light of the torches once more burst
upon him, to perceive the airy form of his fair conductress brought in
a lifeless corse. He shut his eyes, hoping that it was but a vision arising
from his disturbed imagination; but he again saw the same form, when
he unclosed them, stretched by his side. There was no colour upon her
cheek, not even upon her lip; yet there was a stillness about her face that
seemed almost as attaching as the life that once dwelt there:— upon her
neck and breast was blood, and upon her throat were the marks of teeth
having opened the vein:— to this the men pointed, crying, simultaneously struck with horror, "A Vampyre! a Vampyre!" A litter was quickly
formed, and Aubrey was laid by the side of her who had lately been to
him the object of so many bright and fairy visions, now fallen with the
flower of life that had died within her. He knew not what his thoughts
were— his mind was benumbed and seemed to shun reflection, and take
refuge in vacancy— he held almost unconsciously in his hand a naked
dagger of a particular construction, which had been found in the hut.
They were soon met by different parties who had been engaged in the
search of her whom a mother had missed. Their lamentable cries, as
they approached the city, forewarned the parents of some dreadful catastrophe. — To describe their grief would be impossible; but when they
ascertained the cause of their child's death, they looked at Aubrey, and
pointed to the corse. They were inconsolable; both died broken-hearted.

'Aubrey being put to bed was seized with a most violent fever, and
was often delirious; in these intervals he would call upon Lord Ruthven
and upon Ianthe— by some unaccountable combination he seemed to
beg of his former companion to spare the being he loved. At other times
he would imprecate maledictions upon his head, and curse him as her
destroyer. Lord Ruthven, chanced at this time to arrive at Athens, and,
from whatever motive, upon hearing of the state of Aubrey, immediately
placed himself in the same house, and became his constant attendant.
When the latter recovered from his delirium, he was horrified and startled at the sight of him whose image he had now combined with that of a
Vampyre; but Lord Ruthven, by his kind words, implying almost repentance for the fault that had caused their separation, and still more by the
attention, anxiety, and care which he showed, soon reconciled him to his
presence. His lordship seemed quite changed; he no longer appeared
that apathetic being who had so astonished Aubrey; but as soon as his
convalescence began to be rapid, he again gradually retired into the same
state of mind, and Aubrey perceived no difference from the former man,
except that at times he was surprised to meet his gaze fixed intently upon

him, with a smile of malicious exultation playing upon his lips: he knew not why, but this smile haunted him. During the last stage of the invalid's recovery, Lord Ruthven was apparently engaged in watching the tideless waves raised by the cooling breeze, or in marking the progress of those orbs, circling, like our world, the moveless sun;— indeed, he appeared to wish to avoid the eyes of all.

'Aubrey's mind, by this shock, was much weakened, and that elasticity of spirit which had once so distinguished him now seemed to have fled for ever. He was now as much a lover of solitude and silence as Lord Ruthven; but much as he wished for solitude, his mind could not find it in the neighbourhood of Athens; if he sought it amidst the ruins he had formerly frequented, Ianthe's form stood by his side— if he sought it in the woods, her light step would appear wandering amidst the underwood, in quest of the modest violet; then suddenly turning round, would show, to his wild imagination, her pale face and wounded throat, with a meek smile upon her lips. He determined to fly scenes, every feature of which created such bitter associations in his mind. He proposed to Lord Ruthven, to whom he held himself bound by the tender care he had taken of him during his illness, that they should visit those parts of Greece neither had yet seen. They travelled in every direction, and sought every spot to which a recollection could be attached: but though they thus hastened from place to place, yet they seemed not to heed what they gazed upon. They heard much of robbers, but they gradually began to slight these reports, which they imagined were only the invention of individuals, whose interest it was to excite the generosity of those whom they defended from pretended dangers. In consequence of thus neglecting the advice of the inhabitants, on one occasion they travelled with only a few guards, more to serve as guides than as a defence. Upon entering, however, a narrow defile, at the bottom of which was the bed of a torrent, with large masses of rock brought down from the neighbouring precipices, they had reason to repent their negligence; for scarcely were the whole of the party engaged in the narrow pass, when they were startled by the whistling of bullets close to their heads, and by the echoed report of several guns. In an instant their guards had left them, and, placing themselves behind rocks, had begun to fire in the direction whence the report came. Lord Ruthven and Aubrey, imitating their example, retired for a moment behind the sheltering turn of the defile: but ashamed of being thus detained by a foe, who with insulting shouts bade them advance, and being exposed to unresisting slaughter, if any of the robbers should climb above and take them in the rear, they determined at once to rush forward in search of the enemy. Hardly had they lost the shelter of the rock, when Lord Ruthven received a shot in the shoulder, which brought him to the ground. Aubrey hastened to his assistance; and, no longer heeding the contest or his own peril, was soon surprised by seeing the robbers' faces around him— his guards having, upon Lord Ruthven's being wounded, immediately thrown up their arms and surrendered.

'By promises of great reward, Aubrey soon induced them to convey his wounded friend to a neighbouring cabin; and having agreed upon a ransom, he was no more disturbed by their presence— they being content merely to guard the entrance till their comrade should return with the promised sum, for which he had an order. Lord Ruthven's strength rapidly decreased; in two days mortification ensued, and death seemed advancing with hasty steps. His conduct and appearance had not changed; he seemed as unconscious of pain as he had been of the objects about him: but towards the close of the last evening, his mind became apparently uneasy, and his eye often fixed upon Aubrey, who was induced to offer his assistance with more than usual earnestness— "Assist me! you may save me— you may do more than that— I mean not my life, I heed the death of my existence as little as that of the passing day; but you may save my honour, your friend's honour."— "How? tell me how? I would do any thing," replied Aubrey.— "I need but little— my life ebbs apace— I cannot explain the whole— but if you would conceal all you know of me, my honour were free from stain in the world's mouth— and if my death were unknown for some time in England— I— I— but life."— "It shall not be known."— "Swear!" cried the dying man, raising himself with exultant violence, "Swear by all your soul reveres, by all your nature fears, swear that, for a year and a day you will not impart your knowledge of my crimes or death to any living being in any way, whatever may happen, or whatever you may see. "— His eyes seemed bursting from their sockets: "I swear!" said Aubrey; he sunk laughing upon his pillow, and breathed no more.

'Aubrey retired to rest, but did not sleep; the many circumstances attending his acquaintance with this man rose upon his mind, and he knew not why; when he remembered his oath a cold shivering came over him, as if from the presentiment of something horrible awaiting him. Rising early in the morning, he was about to enter the hovel in which he had left the corpse, when a robber met him, and informed him that it was no longer there, having been conveyed by himself and comrades, upon his retiring, to the pinnacle of a neighbouring mount, according to a promise they had given his lordship, that it should be exposed to the first cold ray of the moon that rose after his death. Aubrey astonished, and taking several of the men, determined to go and bury it upon the spot where it lay. But, when he had mounted to the summit he found no trace of either the corpse or the clothes, though the robbers swore they pointed out the identical rock on which they had laid the body. For a time his mind was bewildered in conjectures, but he at last returned, convinced that they had buried the corpse for the sake of the clothes.

'Weary of a country in which he had met with such terrible misfortunes, and in which all apparently conspired to heighten that superstitious melancholy that had seized upon his mind, he resolved to leave it, and soon arrived at Smyrna. While waiting for a vessel to convey him to Otranto, or to Naples, he occupied himself in arranging those effects he had with him belonging to Lord Ruthven. Amongst other things there was a case containing several weapons of offence, more or less adapted to ensure the death of the victim. There were several daggers and ataghans. Whilst turning them over, and examining their curious forms, what was his surprise at finding a sheath apparently ornamented in the same style as the dagger discovered in the fatal hut— he shuddered— hastening to gain further proof, he found the weapon, and his horror may be imagined when he discovered that it fitted, though peculiarly shaped, the sheath he held in his hand. His eyes seemed to need no further certainty— they seemed gazing to be bound to the dagger; yet still he wished to disbelieve; but the particular form, the same varying tints upon the haft and sheath were alike in splendour on both, and left no room for doubt; there were also drops of blood on each.

'He left Smyrna, and on his way home, at Rome, his first inquiries were concerning the lady he had attempted to snatch from Lord Ruthven's seductive arts. Her parents were in distress, their fortune ruined, and she had not been heard of since the departure of his lordship. Aubrey's mind became almost broken under so many repeated horrors; he was afraid that this lady had fallen a victim to the destroyer of Ianthe. He became morose and silent; and his only occupation consisted in urging the speed of the postilions, as if he were going to save the life of some one he held dear. He arrived at Calais; a breeze, which seemed obedient to his will, soon wafted him to the English shores; and he hastened to the mansion of his fathers, and there, for a moment, appeared to lose, in the embraces and caresses of his sister, all memory of the past. If she before, by her infantine caresses, had gained his affection, now that the woman began to appear, she was still more attaching as a companion.

'Miss Aubrey had not that winning grace which gains the gaze and applause of the drawing-room assemblies. There was none of that light brilliancy which only exists in the heated atmosphere of a crowded apartment. Her blue eye was never lit up by the levity of the mind beneath. There was a melancholy charm about it which did not seem to arise from misfortune, but from some feeling within, that appeared to indicate a soul conscious of a brighter realm. Her step was not that light footing, which strays where'er a butterfly or a colour may attract— it was sedate and pensive. When alone, her face was never brightened by the smile of joy; but when her brother breathed to her his affection, and would in her presence forget those griefs she knew destroyed his rest, who would have exchanged her smile for that of the voluptuary? It seemed as if those eyes,— that face were then playing in the light of their own native sphere. She was yet only eighteen, and had not been presented to the world, it having been thought by her guardians more fit that her presentation should be delayed until her brother's return from the continent, when he might be her protector. It was now, therefore, resolved that the next drawing-room, which was fast approaching, should be the epoch of her entry into the "busy scene." Aubrey would rather have remained in the mansion of his fathers, and fed upon the melancholy which overpowered him. He could not feel interest about the frivolities of fashionable strangers, when his mind had been so torn by the events he had witnessed; but he determined to sacrifice his own comfort to the protection of his sister. They soon arrived in town, and prepared for the next day, which had been announced as a drawing-room.

'The crowd was excessive— a drawing-room had not been held for a long time, and all who were anxious to bask in the smile of royalty, hastened thither. Aubrey was there with his sister. While he was standing in a corner by himself, heedless of all around him, engaged in the remembrance that the first time he had seen Lord Ruthven was in that very place— he felt himself suddenly seized by the arm, and a voice he recognized too well, sounded in his ear— "Remember your oath." He had hardly courage to turn, fearful of seeing a spectre that would blast him, when he perceived, at a little distance, the same figure which had attracted his notice on this spot upon his first entry into society. He gazed till his limbs almost refusing to bear their weight, he was obliged to take the arm of a friend, and forcing a passage through the crowd, he threw himself into his carriage, and was driven home. He paced the room with hurried steps, and fixed his hands upon his head, as if he were afraid his thoughts were bursting from his brain. Lord Ruthven again before him— circumstances started up in dreadful array— the dagger— his oath.— He roused himself, he could not believe it possible— the dead rise again!— He thought his imagination had conjured up the image his mind was resting upon. It was impossible that it could be real— he determined, therefore, to go again into society; for though he attempted to ask concerning Lord Ruthven, the name hung upon his lips, and he could not succeed in gaining information. He went a few nights after with his sister to the assembly of a near relation. Leaving her under the protection of a matron, he retired into a recess, and there gave himself up to his own devouring thoughts. Perceiving, at last, that many were leaving, he roused himself, and entering another room, found his sister surrounded by several, apparently in earnest conversation; he attempted to pass and get near her, when one, whom he requested to move, turned round, and revealed to him those features he most abhorred. He sprang forward, seized his sister's arm, and, with hurried step, forced her towards the street: at the door he found himself impeded by the crowd of servants who were waiting for their lords; and while he was engaged in passing them, he again heard that voice whisper close to him— "Remember your oath!"— He did not dare to turn, but, hurrying his sister, soon reached home.

'Aubrey became almost distracted. If before his mind had been absorbed by one subject, how much more completely was it engrossed, now that the certainty of the monster's living again pressed upon his thoughts. His sister's attentions were now unheeded, and it was in vain that she intreated him to explain to her what had caused his abrupt conduct. He only uttered a few words, and those terrified her. The more he thought, the more he was bewildered. His oath startled him;— was he then to allow this monster to roam, bearing ruin upon his breath, amidst all he held dear, and not avert its progress? His very sister might have been touched by him. But even if he were to break his oath, and disclose his suspicions, who would believe him? He thought of employing his own hand to free the world from such a wretch; but death, he remembered, had been already mocked. For days he remained in this state; shut up in his room, he saw no one, and ate only when his sister came, who, with eyes streaming with tears, besought him, for her sake, to support nature. At last, no longer capable of bearing stillness and solitude, he left his house, roamed from street to street, anxious to fly that image which haunted him. His dress became neglected, and he wandered, as often exposed to the noon-day sun as to the midnight damps. He was no longer to be recognized; at first he returned with the evening to the house; but at last he laid him down to rest wherever fatigue overtook him. His sister, anxious for his safety, employed people to follow him; but they were soon distanced by him who fled from a pursuer swifter than any— from thought. His conduct, however, suddenly changed. Struck with the idea that he left by his absence the whole of his friends, with a fiend amongst them, of whose presence they were unconscious, he determined to enter again into society, and watch him closely, anxious to forewarn, in spite of his oath, all whom Lord Ruthven approached with intimacy. But when he entered into a room, his haggard and suspicious looks were so striking, his inward shudderings so visible, that his sister was at last obliged to beg of him to abstain from seeking, for her sake, a society which affected him so strongly. When, however, remonstrance proved unavailing, the guardians thought proper to interpose, and, fearing that his mind was becoming alienated, they thought it high time to resume again that trust which had been before imposed upon them by Aubrey's parents.

'Desirous of saving him from the injuries and sufferings he had daily encountered in his wanderings, and of preventing him from exposing to the general eye those marks of what they considered folly, they engaged a physician to reside in the house, and take constant care of him. He hardly appeared to notice it, so completely was his mind absorbed by one terrible subject. His incoherence became at last so great, that he was confined to his chamber. There he would often lie for days, incapable of being roused. He had become emaciated, his eyes had attained a glassy lustre;— the only sign of affection and recollection remaining displayed itself upon the entry of his sister; then he would sometimes start, and, seizing her hands, with looks that severely afflicted her, he would desire her not to touch him. "Oh, do not touch him— if your love for me is aught, do not go near him!" When, however, she inquired to whom he referred, his only answer was, "True! true!" and again he sank into a state, whence not even she could rouse him. This lasted many months: gradually, however, as the year was passing, his incoherences became less frequent, and his mind threw off a portion of its gloom, whilst his guardians observed, that several times in the day he would count upon his fingers a definite number, and then smile.

'The time had nearly elapsed, when, upon the last day of the year, one of his guardians entering his room, began to converse with his physician upon the melancholy circumstance of Aubrey's being in so awful a situation, when his sister was going next day to be married. Instantly Aubrey's attention was attracted; he asked anxiously to whom. Glad of this mark of returning intellect, of which they feared he had been deprived, they mentioned the name of the Earl of Marsden. Thinking this was a young Earl whom he had met with in society, Aubrey seemed pleased, and astonished them still more by his expressing his intention to be present at the nuptials, and desiring to see his sister. They answered not, but in a few minutes his sister was with him. He was apparently again capable of being affected by the influence of her lovely smile; for he pressed her to his breast, and kissed her cheek, wet with tears, flowing at the thought of her brother's being once more alive to the feelings of affection. He began to speak with all his wonted warmth, and to congratulate her upon her marriage with a person so distinguished for rank and every accomplishment; when he suddenly perceived a locket upon her breast; opening it, what was his surprise at beholding the features of the monster who had so long influenced his life. He seized the portrait in a paroxysm of rage, and trampled it under foot. Upon her asking him why he thus destroyed the resemblance of her future husband, he looked as if he did not understand her— then seizing her hands, and gazing on her with a frantic expression of countenance, he bade her swear that she would never wed this monster, for he— — But he could not advance— it seemed as if that voice again bade him remember his oath— he turned suddenly round, thinking Lord Ruthven was near him but saw no one. In the meantime the guardians and physician, who had heard the whole, and thought this was but a return of his disorder, entered, and forcing him from Miss Aubrey, desired her to leave him. He fell upon his knees to them, he implored, he begged of them to delay but for one day. They, attributing this to the insanity they imagined had taken possession of his mind, endeavoured to pacify him, and retired.

'Lord Ruthven had called the morning after the drawing-room, and had been refused with every one else. When he heard of Aubrey's ill health, he readily understood himself to be the cause of it; but when he learned that he was deemed insane, his exultation and pleasure could hardly be concealed from those among whom he had gained this information. He hastened to the house of his former companion, and, by constant attendance, and the pretence of great affection for the brother and interest in his fate, he gradually won the ear of Miss Aubrey. Who could resist his power? His tongue had dangers and toils to recount— could speak of himself as of an individual having no sympathy with any being on the crowded earth, save with her to whom he addressed himself;— could tell how, since he knew her, his existence, had begun to seem worthy of preservation, if it were merely that he might listen to her soothing accents;— in fine, he knew so well how to use the serpent's art, or such was the will of fate, that he gained her affections. The title of the elder branch falling at length to him, he obtained an important embassy, which served as an excuse for hastening the marriage, (in spite of her brother's deranged state,) which was to take place the very day before his departure for the continent.

'Aubrey, when he was left by the physician and his guardians, attempted to bribe the servants, but in vain. He asked for pen and paper; it was given him; he wrote a letter to his sister, conjuring her, as she valued her own happiness, her own honour, and the honour of those now in the grave, who once held her in their arms as their hope and the hope of their house, to delay but for a few hours that marriage, on which he denounced the most heavy curses. The servants promised they would deliver it; but giving it to the physician, he thought it better not to harass any more the mind of Miss Aubrey by, what he considered, the ravings of a maniac. Night passed on without rest to the busy inmates of the house;

and Aubrey heard, with a horror that may more easily be conceived than described, the notes of busy preparation. Morning came, and the sound of carriages broke upon his ear. Aubrey grew almost frantic. The curiosity of the servants at last overcame their vigilance, they gradually stole away, leaving him in the custody of an helpless old woman. He seized the opportunity, with one bound was out of the room, and in a moment found himself in the apartment where all were nearly assembled. Lord Ruthven was the first to perceive him: he immediately approached, and, taking his arm by force, hurried him from the room, speechless with rage. When on the staircase, Lord Ruthven whispered in his ear— "Remember your oath, and know, if not my bride to day, your sister is dishonoured. Women are frail!" So saying, he pushed him towards his attendants, who, roused by the old woman, had come in search of him. Aubrey could no longer support himself; his rage not finding vent, had broken a blood-vessel, and he was conveyed to bed. This was not mentioned to his sister, who was not present when he entered, as the physician was afraid of agitating her. The marriage was solemnized, and the bride and bridegroom left London.

'Aubrey's weakness increased; the effusion of blood produced symptoms of the near approach of death. He desired his sister's guardians might be called, and when the midnight hour had struck, he related composedly what the reader has perused— he died immediately after.

'The guardians hastened to protect Miss Aubrey; but when they arrived, it was too late. Lord Ruthven had disappeared, and Aubrey's sister had glutted the thirst of a VAMPYRE!'

Poor Polidori, the plagiarist exposed, collapsed into his chair, sweat having poured from his brow, dripping onto the now ink-smudged exquisite pages torn from a– no doubt– equally exquisite journal. Lord Byron let the pistol drop from his firm, shaking grip onto the floor below. Just as the pistol met with the rug-covered floor, a crack of thunder so loud shot off like gunfire, startling all who heard it, include dearest Claire, who fainted. My Beloved yelped, though he could not help it. And Poor Polidori cringed into his chair, lifting his legs into the foetal. This particular phase of our game of ghost stories could not be ended soon enough.

Note by John Polidori Protesting Publication of The Vampyre, 1819

The tale which lately appeared, and to which his lordship's name was wrongfully attached, was founded upon the ground-work upon which this fragment was to have been continued. Two friends were to travel from

England into Greece; while there, one of them should die, but before his death, should obtain from his friend an oath of secrecy with regard to his decease. Some short time after, the remaining traveller returning to his native country, should be startled at perceiving his former companion moving about in society, and should be horrified at finding that he made love to his former friend's sister. Upon this foundation I built the *Vampyre*, at the request of a lady, who denied the possibility of such a ground-work forming the outline of a tale which should bear the slightest appearance of probability. In the course of three mornings, I produced that tale, and left it with her. From thence it appears to have fallen into the hands of some person, who sent it to the Editor in such a way, as to leave it so doubtful from his words, whether it was his lordship's or not, that I found some difficulty in vindicating it to myself. These circumstances were stated in a letter sent to the *Morning Chronicle* three days after the publication of the tale, but in consequence of the publishers representing to me that they were compromised as well as myself, and that immediately they were certain it was mine, that they themselves would wish to make the *amende honorable* to the public, I allowed them to recall the letter which had lain some days at that paper's office. (J.W.P.) [33]

---

33 From a footnote in the Introduction to *Ernestus Berchtold; or, The Modern Oedipus: A Tale.*

Chapter Fifteen[34]
Frankenstein (Encircled in the Arctic)

P.B. Shelley Writing to Lord Byron

Chamouni, Hotel de Ville de Londres
July 22, 1816

My dear Lord Byron,

We have this moment arrived at Chamouni – the evening of the day after our departure. An opportunity chances to offer itself of sending a letter. I shall not attempt to describe to you the scenes through which we have passed. I hope soon to see in poetry the feelings with which they will inspire you.3 The Valley of the Arve (strictly speaking it extends to that of Chamouni) gradually increases in magnificence and beauty, until, at a place called Servoz, where Mont Blanc and its connected mountains limit one side of the valley, it exceeds and renders insignificant all that I had before seen, or imagined. It is not alone that these mountains are immense in size, that their forests are of so immeasurable an extent; there is grandeur in the very shapes and colours which could not fail to impress, even on a smaller scale. I write in the hope – may I say so? – that we possibly shall see you here before our return. No sooner had we entered this magnificent valley than we decided to remain several days. An avalanche fell as we entered it. We heard the thunder of its fall, and in a few minutes more the smoke of its path was visible, and a torrent which it had forced from its bed overflowed the ravine which enclosed it. I wish the wonders and graces of these 'palaces of Nature' would induce you to visit them whilst we, who so much value your society, remain yet near them. How is our little William? Is he well?

Clare sends her love to you, and Mary desires to be kindly remembered.

Yours faithfully,
P. B. Shelley.

P.S. The roads are excellent, and every facility is accumulated for the traveller. You can go as far as Sallanches in a carriage, after which, although it is possible to accomplish the rest of the journey in a *char du pays*, I would advise you, as we have done, to hire mules. A guide is not absolutely necessary, although we took one; for the road, with one insig-

---

34 From *Frankenstein; or the Modern Prometheus* by Mary Wollstonecraft Shelley, published by Lackington, Hughes, Harding, Mavor & Jones, 1818

nificant exception, is perfectly plain and good. There is apparently a very trifling ascent from Geneva to Chamouni.

P.B. Shelley Writing In Mary Wollstonecraft Godwin's Journal

Fôtel de Londres, Chamouni, July 22d, 1816. Whilst you, my friend, are engaged in securing a home for us, we are wandering in search of recollections to embellish it. I do not err in conceiving that you are interested in details of all that is majestic or beautiful in nature; but how shall I describe to you the scenes by which I am now surrounded? To exhaust the epithets which express the astonishment and the admiration—the very excess of satisfied astonishment, where expectation scarcely acknowledged any boundary, is this, to impress upon your mind the images which fill mine now even till it overflow? I too have read the raptures of travellers; I will be warned by their example; I will simply detail to you all that I can relate, or all that, if related, would enable you to conceive of what we have done or seen since the morning of the 20th, when we left Geneva.

We commenced our intended journey to Chamouni at half-past eight in the morning. We passed through the champain country, which extends from Mont Salève to the base of the higher Alps. The country is sufficiently fertile, covered with corn fields and orchards, and intersected by sudden acclivities with flat summits. The day was cloudless and excessively hot, the Alps were perpetually in sight, and as we advanced, the mountains, which form their outskirts, closed in around us. We passed a bridge over a stream, which discharges itself into the Arve. The Arve itself, much swollen by the rains, flows constantly to the right of the road.

As we approached Bonneville through an avenue composed of a beautiful species of drooping poplar, we observed that the corn fields on each side were covered with inundation. Bonneville is a neat little town, with no conspicuous peculiarity, except the white towers of the prison, an extensive building overlooking the town. At Bonneville the Alps commence, one of which, clothed by forests, rises almost immediately from the opposite bank of the Arve.

From Bonneville to Cluses the road conducts through a spacious and fertile plain, surrounded on all sides by mountains, covered like those of Mellerie with forests of intermingled pine and chesnut. At Cluses the road turns suddenly to the right, following the Arve along the chasm, which it seems to have hollowed for itself among the perpendicular mountains. The scene assumes here a more savage and colossal character; the valley becomes narrow, affording no more space than is sufficient for the river and the road. The pines descend to the banks, imitating with their irregular spires, the pyramidal crags which lift themselves far above the regions of forest into the deep azure of the sky, and among the white dazzling clouds. The scene, at the distance of half a mile from Cluses, differs from that of Matlock in little else than in the immensity of its proportions, and in its untameable, inaccessible solitude, inhabited only by the goats which we saw browsing on the rocks.

Near Maglans, within a league of each other, we saw two waterfalls. They were no more than mountain rivulets, but the height from which they fell, at least of twelve hundred feet, made them assume a character inconsistent with the smallness of their stream. The first fell from the overhanging brow of a black precipice on an enormous rock, precisely resembling some colossal Egyptian statue of a female deity. It struck the head of the visionary image, and gracefully dividing there, fell from it in folds of foam more like to cloud than water, imitating a veil of the most exquisite woof. It then united, concealing the lower part of the statue, and hiding itself in a winding of its channel, burst into a deeper fall, and crossed our route in its path towards the Arve.

The other waterfall was more continuous and larger. The violence with which it fell made it look more like some shape which an exhalation had assumed, than like water, for it streamed beyond the mountain, which appeared dark behind it, as it might have appeared behind an evanescent cloud.

The character of the scenery continued the same until we arrived at St. Martin (called in the maps Sallanches) the mountains perpetually becoming more elevated, exhibiting at every turn of the road more craggy summits, loftier and wider extent of forests, darker and more deep recesses.

The following morning we proceeded from St. Martin on mules to Chamouni, accompanied by two guides. We proceeded, as we had done the preceding day, along the valley of the Arve, a valley surrounded on all sides by immense mountains, whose rugged precipices are intermixed on high with dazzling snow. Their bases were still covered with the eternal forests, which perpetually grew darker and more profound as we approached the inner regions of the mountains.

On arriving at a small village, at the distance of a league from St. Martin, we dismounted from our mules, and were conducted by our guides to view a cascade. We beheld an immense body of water fall two hundred and fifty feet, dashing from rock to rock, and casting a spray which formed a mist around it, in the midst of which hung a multitude of sunbows, which faded or became unspeakably vivid, as the inconstant sun shone through the clouds. When we approached near to it, the rain of the spray reached us, and our clothes were wetted by the quick-falling but minute particles of water. The cataract fell from above into a deep craggy chasm at our feet, where, changing its character to that of a mountain stream, it pursued its course towards the Arve, roaring over the rocks that impeded its progress.

As we proceeded, our route still lay through the valley, or rather, as it had now become, the vast ravine, which is at once the couch and the creation of the terrible Arve. We ascended, winding between mountains whose immensity staggers the imagination. We crossed the path of a torrent, which three days since had descended from the thawing snow, and torn the road away.

We dined at Servoz, a little village, where there are lead and copper mines, and where we saw a cabinet of natural curiosities, like those of Keswick and Bethgelert. We saw in this cabinet some chamois' horns, and the horns of an exceedingly rare animal called the bouquetin, which inhabits the desarts of snow to the south of Mont Blanc: it is an animal of the stag kind; its horns weigh at least twenty-seven English pounds. It is inconceivable how so small an animal could support so inordinate a weight. The horns are of a very peculiar conformation, being broad, massy, and pointed at the ends, and surrounded with a number of rings, which are supposed to afford an indication of its age: there were seventeen rings on the largest of these horns.

From Servoz three leagues remain to Chamouni.—Mont Blanc was before us—the Alps, with their innumerable glaciers on high all around, closing in the complicated windings of the single vale—forests inexpressibly beautiful, but majestic in their beauty—intermingled beech and pine, and oak, overshadowed our road, or receded, whilst lawns of such verdure as I have never seen before occupied these openings, and gradually became darker in their recesses. Mont Blanc was before us, but it was covered with cloud; its base, furrowed with dreadful gaps, was seen above. Pinnacles of snow intolerably bright, part of the chain connected with Mont Blanc, shone through the clouds at intervals on high. I never knew—I never imagined what mountains were before. The immensity of these aerial summits excited, when they suddenly burst upon the sight, a sentiment of extatic wonder, not unallied to madness. And remember this was all one scene, it all pressed home to our regard and our imagination. Though it embraced a vast extent of space, the snowy pyramids which shot into the bright blue sky seemed to overhang our path; the ravine, clothed with gigantic pines, and black with its depth below, so deep that the very roaring of the untameable Arve, which rolled through it, could not be heard above—all was as much our own, as if we had been the creators of such impressions in the minds of others as now occupied our own. Nature was the poet, whose harmony held our spirits more breathless than that of the divinest.

As we entered the valley of Chamouni (which in fact may be considered as a continuation of those which we have followed from Bonneville and Cluses) clouds hung upon the mountains at the distance perhaps of 6000 feet from the earth, but so as effectually to conceal not only Mont Blanc, but the other aiguilles, as they call them here, attached and subordinate to it. We were travelling along the valley, when suddenly we heard a sound as of the burst of smothered thunder rolling above; yet there was something earthly in the sound, that told us it could not be thunder. Our guide hastily pointed out to us a part of the mountain opposite, from whence the sound came. It was an avalanche. We saw the smoke of its path among the rocks, and continued to hear at intervals the bursting of its fall. It fell on the bed of a torrent, which it displaced, and presently we saw its tawny-coloured waters also spread themselves over the ravine, which was their couch.

We did not, as we intended, visit the Glacier de Boisson to-day, although it descends within a few minutes' walk of the road, wishing to survey it at least when unfatigued. We saw this glacier which comes close to the fertile plain, as we passed, its surface was broken into a thousand unaccountable figures: conical and pyramidical crystallizations, more than fifty feet in height, rise from its surface, and precipices of ice, of dazzling splendour, overhang the woods and meadows of the vale. This glacier winds upwards from the valley, until it joins the masses of frost from which it was produced above, winding through its own ravine like a bright belt flung over the black region of pines. There is more in all these scenes than mere magnitude of proportion: there is a majesty of outline; there is an awful grace in the very colours which invest these wonderful shapes—a charm which is peculiar to them, quite distinct even from the reality of their unutterable greatness.

I.

The everlasting universe of things
Flows through the mind, and rolls its rapid waves,
Now dark—now glittering—now reflecting gloom—
Now lending splendour, where from secret springs
The source of human thought its tribute brings
Of waters,—with a sound but half its own,
Such as a feeble brook will oft assume
In the wild woods, among the mountains lone,
Where waterfalls around it leap for ever,
Where woods and winds contend, and a vast river

Over its rocks ceaselessly bursts and raves.

II.

Thus thou, Ravine of Arve—dark, deep Ravine—
Thou many-coloured, many-voiced vale,
Over whose pines, and crags, and caverns sail
Fast cloud shadows and sunbeams: awful scene,
Where Power in likeness of the Arve comes down
From the ice gulphs that gird his secret throne,
Bursting through these dark mountains like the flame
Of lightning thro' the tempest;—thou dost lie,
Thy giant brood of pines around thee clinging,
Children of elder time, in whose devotion
The chainless winds still come and ever came
To drink their odours, and their mighty swinging
To hear—an old and solemn harmony;
Thine earthly rainbows stretched across the sweep
Of the ethereal waterfall, whose veil
Robes some unsculptured image; the strange sleep
Which when the voices of the desart fail
Wraps all in its own deep eternity;—
Thy caverns echoing to the Arve's commotion,
A loud, lone sound no other sound can tame;
Thou art pervaded with that ceaseless motion,
Thou art the path of that unresting sound—
Dizzy Ravine! and when I gaze on thee
I seem as in a trance sublime and strange
To muse on my own separate phantasy,
My own, my human mind, which passively
Now renders and receives fast influencings,
Holding an unremitting interchange
With the clear universe of things around;
One legion of wild thoughts, whose wandering wings
Now float above thy darkness, and now rest
Where that or thou art no unbidden guest,
In the still cave of the witch Poesy,
Seeking among the shadows that pass by
Ghosts of all things that are, some shade of thee,
Some phantom, some faint image; till the breast
From which they fled recalls them, thou art there!

III.

Some say that gleams of a remoter world
Visit the soul in sleep,—that death is slumber,
And that its shapes the busy thoughts outnumber
Of those who wake and live.—I look on high;
Has some unknown omnipotence unfurled
The veil of life and death? or do I lie
In dream, and does the mightier world of sleep
Spread far around and inaccessibly
Its circles? For the very spirit fails,
Driven like a homeless cloud from steep to steep
That vanishes among the viewless gales!
Far, far above, piercing the infinite sky,
Mont Blanc appears,—still, snowy, and serene—
Its subject mountains their unearthly forms
Pile around it, ice and rock; broad vales between
Of frozen floods, unfathomable deeps,
Blue as the overhanging heaven, that spread
And wind among the accumulated steeps;
A desart peopled by the storms alone,
Save when the eagle brings some hunter's bone,
And the wolf tracts her there—how hideously
Its shapes are heaped around! rude, bare, and high,
Ghastly, and scarred, and riven.—Is this the scene
Where the old Earthquake-dœmon taught her young
Ruin? Were these their toys? or did a sea
Of fire, envelope once this silent snow?
None can reply—all seems eternal now.
The wilderness has a mysterious tongue
Which teaches awful doubt, or faith so mild,
So solemn, so serene, that man may be
But for such faith with nature reconciled;
Thou hast a voice, great Mountain, to repeal
Large codes of fraud and woe; not understood
By all, but which the wise, and great, and good
Interpret, or make felt, or deeply feel.

IV.

The fields, the lakes, the forests, and the streams,
Ocean, and all the living things that dwell
Within the dœdal earth; lightning, and rain,
Earthquake, and fiery flood, and hurricane,

The torpor of the year when feeble dreams
Visit the hidden buds, or dreamless sleep
Holds every future leaf and flower;—the bound
With which from that detested trance they leap;
The works and ways of man, their death and birth,
And that of him and all that his may be;
All things that move and breathe with toil and sound
Are born and die; revolve, subside and swell.
Power dwells apart in its tranquillity
Remote, serene, and inaccessible:
And this, the naked countenance of earth,
On which I gaze, even these primæval mountains
Teach the adverting mind. The glaciers creep
Like snakes that watch their prey, from their far fountains,
Slow rolling on; there, many a precipice,
Frost and the Sun in scorn of mortal power
Have piled: dome, pyramid, and pinnacle,
A city of death, distinct with many a tower
And wall impregnable of beaming ice.
Yet not a city, but a flood of ruin
Is there, that from the boundaries of the sky
Rolls its perpetual stream; vast pines are strewing
Its destined path, or in the mangled soil
Branchless and shattered stand; the rocks, drawn down
From yon remotest waste, have overthrown
The limits of the dead and living world,
Never to be reclaimed. The dwelling-place
Of insects, beasts, and birds, becomes its spoil;
Their food and their retreat for ever gone,
So much of life and joy is lost. The race
Of man, flies far in dread; his work and dwelling
Vanish, like smoke before the tempest's stream,
And their place is not known. Below, vast caves
Shine in the rushing torrent's restless gleam,
Which from those secret chasms in tumult welling
Meet in the vale, and one majestic River,
The breath and blood of distant lands, for ever
Rolls its loud waters to the ocean waves.
Breathes its swift vapours to the circling air.

V.

Mont Blanc yet gleams on high:—the power is there,
The still and solemn power of many sights,
And many sounds, and much of life and death.
In the calm darkness of the moonless nights,
In the lone glare of day, the snows descend
Upon that Mountain; none beholds them there,
Nor when the flakes burn in the sinking sun,
Or the star-beams dart through them:—Winds contend
Silently there, and heap the snow with breath
Rapid and strong, but silently! Its home
The voiceless lightning in these solitudes
Keeps innocently, and like vapour broods
Over the snow. The secret strength of things
Which governs thought, and to the infinite dome
Of heaven is as a law, inhabits thee!
And what were thou, and earth, and stars, and sea,
If to the human mind's imaginings
Silence and solitude were vacancy?

July 24, 1816

Yesterday morning we went to the source of the Arveiron. It is about a league from this village; the river rolls forth impetuously from an arch of ice, and spreads itself in many streams over a vast space of the valley, ravaged and laid bare by its inundations. The glacier by which its waters are nourished, overhangs this cavern and the plain, and the forests of pine which surround it, with terrible precipices of solid ice. On the other side rises the immense glacier of Montanvert, fifty miles in extent, occupying a chasm among mountains of inconceivable height, and of forms so pointed and abrupt, that they seem to pierce the sky. From this glacier we saw as we sat on a rock, close to one of the streams of the Arveiron, masses of ice detach themselves from on high, and rush with a loud dull noise into the vale. The violence of their fall turned them into powder, which flowed over the rocks in imitation of waterfalls, whose ravines they usurped and filled.

In the evening I went with Ducrée, my guide, the only tolerable person I have seen in this country, to visit the glacier of Boisson. This glacier, like that of Montanvert, comes close to the vale, overhanging the green meadows and the dark woods with the dazzling whiteness of its precipices and pinnacles, which are like spires of radiant crystal, covered with a net-work of frosted silver. These glaciers flow perpetually into the valley, ravaging in their slow but irresistible progress the pastures and the forests which surround them, performing a work of desolation in ages, which a river of lava might accomplish in an hour, but far more irretrievably; for where the ice has once descended, the hardiest plant refuses to grow; if even, as in some extraordinary instances, it should recede after its progress has once commenced. The glaciers perpetually move onward, at the rate of a foot each day, with a motion that commences at the spot where, on the boundaries of perpetual congelation, they are produced by the freezing of the waters which arise from the partial melting of the eternal snows. They drag with them from the regions whence they derive their origin, all the ruins of the mountain, enormous rocks, and immense accumulations of sand and stones. These are driven onwards by the irresistible stream of solid ice; and when they arrive at a declivity of the mountain, sufficiently rapid, roll down, scattering ruin. I saw one of these rocks which had descended in the spring, (winter here is the season of silence and safety) which measured forty feet in every direction.

The verge of a glacier, like that of Boisson, presents the most vivid image of desolation that it is possible to conceive. No one dares to approach it; for the enormous pinnacles of ice which perpetually fall, are perpetually reproduced. The pines of the forest, which bound it at one extremity, are overthrown and shattered to a wide extent at its base. There is something inexpressibly dreadful in the aspect of the few branchless trunks, which, nearest to the ice rifts, still stand in the uprooted soil. The meadows perish, overwhelmed with sand and stones. Within this last year, these glaciers have advanced three hundred feet into the valley. Saussure, the naturalist, says, that they have their periods of increase and decay: the people of the country hold an opinion entirely different; but as I judge, more probable. It is agreed by all, that the snow on the summit of Mont Blanc and the neighbouring mountains perpetually augments, and that ice, in the form of glaciers, subsists without melting in the valley of Chamouni during its transient and variable summer. If the snow which produces this glacier must augment, and the heat of the valley is no obstacle to the perpetual existence of such masses of ice as have already descended into it, the consequence is obvious; the glaciers must augment and will subsist, at least until they have overflowed this vale.

I will not pursue Buffon's sublime but gloomy theory—that this globe which we inhabit will at some future period be changed into a mass of frost by the encroachments of the polar ice, and of that produced on the most elevated points of the earth. Do you, who assert the supremacy of Ahriman, imagine him throned among these desolating snows, among these palaces of death and frost, so sculptured in this their terrible magnificence by the adamantine hand of necessity, and that he casts

around him, as the first essays of his final usurpation, avalanches, torrents, rocks, and thunders, and above all these deadly glaciers, at once
the proof and symbols of his reign;—add to this, the degradation of the
human species—who in these regions are half deformed or idiotic, and
most of whom are deprived of any thing that can excite interest or admiration. This is a part of the subject more mournful and less sublime; but
such as neither the poet nor the philosopher should disdain to regard.

This morning we departed, on the promise of a fine day, to visit the
glacier of Montanvert. In that part where it fills a slanting valley, it is
called the Sea of Ice. This valley is 950 toises, or 7600 feet above the level
of the sea. We had not proceeded far before the rain began to fall, but we
persisted until we had accomplished more than half of our journey, when
we returned, wet through.

Chamouni, July 25th.

We have returned from visiting the glacier of Montanvert, or as it
is called, the Sea of Ice, a scene in truth of dizzying wonder. The
path that winds to it along the side of a mountain, now clothed
with pines, now intersected with snowy hollows, is wide and steep. The
cabin of Montanvert is three leagues from Chamouni, half of which distance is performed on mules, not so sure footed, but that on the first day
the one which I rode fell in what the guides call a mauvais pas, so that I
narrowly escaped being precipitated down the mountain. We passed over
a hollow covered with snow, down which vast stones are accustomed to
roll. One had fallen the preceding day, a little time after we had returned:
our guides desired us to pass quickly, for it is said that sometimes the
least sound will accelerate their descent. We arrived at Montanvert, however, safe.

On all sides precipitous mountains, the abodes of unrelenting frost,
surround this vale: their sides are banked up with ice and snow, broken, heaped high, and exhibiting terrific chasms. The summits are sharp
and naked pinnacles, whose overhanging steepness will not even permit
snow to rest upon them. Lines of dazzling ice occupy here and there
their perpendicular rifts, and shine through the driving vapours with inexpressible brilliance: they pierce the clouds like things not belonging
to this earth. The vale itself is filled with a mass of undulating ice, and
has an ascent sufficiently gradual even to the remotest abysses of these
horrible deserts. It is only half a league (about two miles) in breadth,
and seems much less. It exhibits an appearance as if frost had suddenly
bound up the waves and whirlpools of a mighty torrent. We walked some
distance upon its surface. The waves are elevated about 12 or 15 feet
from the surface of the mass, which is intersected by long gaps of un-

fathomable depth, the ice of whose sides is more beautifully azure than the sky. In these regions every thing changes, and is in motion. This vast mass of ice has one general progress, which ceases neither day nor night; it breaks and bursts for ever: some undulations sink while others rise; it is never the same. The echo of rocks, or of the ice and snow which fall from their overhanging precipices, or roll from their aerial summits, scarcely ceases for one moment. One would think that Mont Blanc, like the god of the Stoics, was a vast animal, and that the frozen blood for ever circulated through his stony veins.

We dined (M., C., and I) on the grass, in the open air, surrounded by this scene. The air is piercing and clear. We returned down the mountain, sometimes encompassed by the driving vapours, sometimes cheered by the sunbeams, and arrived at our inn by seven o'clock.

Montalegre, July 28th.

The next morning we returned through the rain to St. Martin. The scenery had lost something of its immensity, thick clouds hanging over the highest mountains; but visitings of sunset intervened between the showers, and the blue sky shone between the accumulated clouds of snowy whiteness which brought them; the dazzling mountains sometimes glittered through a chasm of the clouds above our heads, and all the charm of its grandeur remained. We repassed Pont Pellisier, a wooden bridge over the Arve, and the ravine of the Arve. We repassed the pine forests which overhang the defile, the chateau of St. Michel, a haunted ruin, built on the edge of a precipice, and shadowed over by the eternal forest. We repassed the vale of Servoz, a vale more beautiful, because more luxuriant, than that of Chamouni. Mont Blanc forms one of the sides of this vale also, and the other is inclosed by an irregular amphitheatre of enormous mountains, one of which is in ruins, and fell fifty years ago into the higher part of the valley: the smoke of its fall was seen in Piedmont, and people went from Turin to investigate whether a volcano had not burst forth among the Alps. It continued falling many days, spreading, with the shock and thunder of its ruin, consternation into the neighbouring vales. In the evening we arrived at St. Martin. The next day we wound through the valley, which I have described before, and arrived in the evening at our home.

We have bought some specimens of minerals and plants, and two or three crystal seals, at Mont Blanc, to preserve the remembrance of having approached it. There is a cabinet of Histoire Naturelle at Chamouni, just as at Keswick, Matlock, and Clifton; the proprietor of which is the very vilest specimen of that vile species of quack that, together with the whole army of aubergistes and guides, and indeed the entire mass of the population, subsist on the weakness and credulity of travellers as leaches subsist on the sick. The most interesting of my purchases is a large collection of all the seeds of rare alpine plants, with their names written upon the outside of the papers that contain them. These I mean to colonize in my garden in England, and to permit you to make what choice you please from them. They are companions which the Celandine—the classic Celandine, need not despise; they are as wild and more daring than he, and will tell him tales of things even as touching and sublime as the gaze of a vernal poet.

Did I tell you that there are troops of wolves among these mountains? In the winter they descend into the vallies, which the snow occupies six months of the year, and devour every thing that they can find out of doors. A wolf is more powerful than the fiercest and strongest dog. There are no bears in these regions. We heard, when we were at Lucerne, that they were occasionally found in the forests which surround that lake. Adieu. [35]

Mary Wollstonecraft Godwin's Journal

23July, Tuesday (Chamounix)— My scamp of a husband wrote in of Chamonix's Hôtel de Londres described– Nay! Faith! Declared– himself thus: 'I am a lover of mankind, democrat, and atheist'. The scandal that would beset us on all sides, but his joviality at this little prank had him in stitches. When the register inquired what his destination was, he wrote, '*L'Enfer*'. Dante's *Inferno*! My Beloved's Greek is poor; he is practically illiterate in the language! But he cares not for the poverty of his eloquence nor for the scandal that shall beset us. He never cares for the thoughts of others when scandalizing. One can only hope and wish and desire that our Little Lord on a future journey to Chamonix will scratch out the inscription thus saving my Beloved's reputation and my embarrassment.

In the morning, after breakfast, we mount our mules to see the source of the Arveiron. When we had gone about three parts of the way, we descended and continued our route on foot, over loose stones, many of which were an enormous size. We came to the source, which lies (like a stage) surrounded on the three sides by mountains and glaciers. We sat on a rock, which formed the fourth, gazing on the scene before us. An immense glacier was on our left, which continually rolled stones to its foot. It is very dangerous to be directly under this. Our guide told us a

---

35 From *History of a Six Weeks Tour* by Mary Wollstonecraft Shelley and Percy Bysshe Shelley, published by T Thomas Hookham, Jr. and Charles and James Ollier, 1817

story of two Hollanders who went, without any guide, into a cavern of the glacier, and fired a pistol there, which drew down a large piece on them. We see several avalanches, some very small, others of great magnitude, which roared and smoked, overwhelming everything as it passed along, and precipitating great pieces of ice into the valley below. This glacier is increasing every day a foot, closing up the valley. We drink some water of the Arveiron and return. After dinner think it will rain, and Shelley goes alone to the glacier of Boison. I stay at home. Read several tales of Voltaire. In the evening I copy Shelley's letter to Peacock.

Wednesday, July 24— To-day is rainy; therefore we cannot go to Col de Balme. About 10 the weather appears clearing up. Shelley and I begin our journey to Montanvert. Nothing can be more desolate than the ascent of this mountain; the trees in many places having been torn away by avalanches, and some half leaning over others, intermingled with stones, present the appearance of vast and dreadful desolation. It began to rain almost as soon as we left our inn. When we had mounted considerably we turned to look on the scene. A dense white mist covered the vale, and tops of scattered pines peeping above were the only objects that presented themselves. The rain continued in torrents. We were wetted to the skin; so that, when we had ascended halfway, we resolved to turn back. As we descended, Shelley went before, and, tripping up, fell upon his knee. This added to the weakness occasioned by a blow on his ascent; he fainted, and was for some minutes incapacitated from continuing his route.

We arrived wet to the skin. I read *Nouvelles Nouvelles*, and write my story. Shelley writes part of letter.

27 July, Saturday— It is a most beautiful day, without a cloud. We set off at 12. The day is hot, yet there is a fine breeze. We pass by the Great Waterfall, which presents an aspect of singular beauty. The wind carries it away from the rock, and on towards the north, and the fine spray into which it is entirely dissolved passes before the mountain like a mist.

The other cascade has very little water, and is consequently not so beautiful as before. The evening of the day is calm and beautiful. Evening is the only time I enjoy travelling. The horses went fast, and the plain opened before us. We saw Jura and the Lake like old friends. I longed to see my pretty babe. At 9, after much inquiring and stupidity, we find the road, and alight at Diodati. We converse with Lord Byron till 12, and then go down to Chapuis, kiss our babe, and go to bed.[36]

---

36 From Mary Wollstonecraft Shelley's journals dated 1816.

***

[Date unrecorded]— The glacier at Montanvert is a natural phenomenon to behold! I sat upon a rock that overlooks the sea of ice. A mist covered both that and the surrounding mountains. Presently a breeze dissipated the cloud. The surface is very uneven, rising like the waves of a troubled sea, descending low, and interspersed by rifts that sink deep. The field of ice is almost a league in width, and one could spend nearly two hours in crossing it. The opposite mountain is a bare perpendicular rock. From the side where I now stood Montanvert was exactly opposite, at the distance of a league; and above it rose Mont Blânc, in awful majesty. I remained in a recess of the rock, gazing on this wonderful and stupendous scene. The sea, or rather the vast river of ice, wound among its dependent mountains, whose aërial summits hung over its recesses. Their icy and glittering peaks shone in the sunlight over the clouds. These sights were just as my pale student of the unhallowed arts had described Montanvert to me weeks before while in my bedchamber at the Villa Diodati. How is it possible to have had my pale student describe something to me I had not yet seen or experienced? Was not my pale student a figment of my authorial imagination? I then looked across the vastness of the glacier and saw the queerest sight... a low carriage, fixed on a sledge and drawn by dogs, pass on towards the north, at the distance of half a mile: a being which and the shape of a man, but apparently of gigantic stature, sat in the sledge, and guided the dogs. I watched the rapid progress of the Creature without the need for telescopes, for my mind's eye perceived all, until he was lost among the distant inequalities of the ice. The Creature, as my pale student of the unhallowed arts had told me of, appeared frightened and being chased. Why was the Creature in fear for his every existence? I wonder what —or who— was stalking this poor Creature across the frozen wasteland of Montanvert? Or was it no longer Montanvert? Was I seeing the Arctic? I could not stop my mind's eye from picturing the Arctic with its endless sheets of ice that can easily surround a ship on all sides, port and starboard, bow and stern, scarcely leaving her the sea room and compassed round by a thick fog. How could the Arctic exist in the centre of the Continent? With mountains and a pleasant vale surrounding the glacier on all sides. One did not have to search for the North Pole or seek a northern route to the Pacific to see the wonders of the Arctic. In fact, it was a far safer holiday to visit a glacier than the Arctic. But whether the Creature sledged across the Arctic or the glacier, again I must ponder what —or who— was stalking this poor Creature?

After our exciting and exhausting tour of the glacier, we returned to our hotel at the bottom of the glacier in the vale below; the desk clerk handed me four envelopes addressed to a 'Mrs Saville, England'. As my Beloved disappeared up the stairs towards our room, I began to protest. I was not 'Mrs Saville'. She must be staying at another hotel in Chamonix. But the desk clerk insisted that his instructions were clear; the letters were to be delivered to a woman matching my very description. Whether or not I was 'Mrs Saville' was beside the point. I accepted the letters begrudgingly. Once in our room, I placed the letters on the bedside table and joined my Beloved for dinner in the hotel restaurant. We ate a lovely meal and back in our room, we were soon disposed to marital sport. Distracted, I could not stop glancing at the envelopes on the bedside table. After my Beloved had drifted off into a deep, dreamful, postcoital slumber, I picked up the envelopes. Three of which had been postmarked quite clearly and quite queerly as having travelled from Russia, all with a destination mark to London. How had the letters reached the Alps without nary a postmark in-between? No post office seemed to acknowledge their receipt or their transportation through their territory with a stamp. Not only did these letters come from across the great vastness of distance, but the great vastness of time! First two letters addressed to my pale student of the unhallowed arts arrived mysteriously at the door of the Villa Diodati on the eve of winter, one from his cousin, Elizabeth, and the other from his father, Alphonse. And now four letters find their way to the base of the glacier at Chamonix. Who is this preternatural— nay! psychological— postman who delivers letters to me. My name is not Mrs Saville and my pale student has yet to mention her name at any time during his recitation of his life to me. I sliced open– with the sudden violence of a murderer stalking the seedy streets of White Chapel– the envelope stamped as having come from St. Petersburgh. The letter enclosed was dated... Dec. 11th, 1798! The turn of nineteenth century? Eighteen years ago?

Letter 1 From R. Walton To Mrs Saville

To Mrs Saville, *England.*

St. Petersburgh, Dec. 11th, 1798.

You will rejoice to hear that no disaster has accompanied the commencement of an enterprise which you have regarded with such evil forebodings. I arrived here yesterday; and my first task is to assure my dear sister of my welfare, and increasing confidence in the success of my undertaking.

I am already far north of London; and as I walk in the streets of Petersburgh, I feel a cold northern breeze play upon my cheeks, which braces my nerves, and fills me with delight. Do you understand this feeling? This breeze, which has travelled from the regions towards which I am advancing, gives me a foretaste of those icy climes. Inspirited by this wind of promise, my day dreams become more fervent and vivid. I try in vain to be persuaded that the pole is the seat of frost and desolation; it ever presents itself to my imagination as the region of beauty and delight. There, Margaret, the sun is for ever visible; its broad disk just skirting the horizon, and diffusing a perpetual splendour. There— for with your leave, my sister, I will put some trust in preceding navigators— there snow and frost are banished; and, sailing over a calm sea, we may be wafted to a land surpassing in wonders and in beauty every region hitherto discovered on the habitable globe. Its productions and features may be without example, as the phænomena of the heavenly bodies undoubtedly are in those undiscovered solitudes. What may not be expected in a country of eternal light? I may there discover the wondrous power which attracts the needle; and may regulate a thousand celestial observations, that require only this voyage to render their seeming eccentricities consistent for ever. I shall satiate my ardent curiosity with the sight of a part of the world never before visited, and may tread a land never before imprinted by the foot of man. These are my enticements, and they are sufficient to conquer all fear of danger or death, and to induce me to commence this laborious voyage with the joy a child feels when he embarks in a little boat, with his holiday mates, on an expedition of discovery up his native river. But, supposing all these conjectures to be false, you cannot contest the inestimable benefit which I shall confer on all mankind to the last generation, by discovering a passage near the pole to those countries, to reach which at present so many months are requisite; or by ascertaining the secret of the magnet, which, if at all possible, can only be effected by an undertaking such as mine.

These reflections have dispelled the agitation with which I began my letter, and I feel my heart glow with an enthusiasm which elevates me to heaven; for nothing contributes so much to tranquillize the mind as a steady purpose,— a point on which the soul may fix its intellectual eye. This expedition has been the favourite dream of my early years. I have read with ardour the accounts of the various voyages which have been made in the prospect of arriving at the North Pacific Ocean through the seas which surround the pole. You may remember, that a history of all the voyages made for purposes of discovery composed the whole of our good uncle Thomas's library. My education was neglected, yet I was passionately fond of reading. These volumes were my study day and night, and my familiarity with them increased that regret which I had felt, as a child, on learning that my father's dying injunction had forbidden my uncle to allow me to embark in a sea-faring life.

These visions faded when I perused, for the first time, those poets whose effusions entranced my soul, and lifted it to heaven. I also became a poet, and for one year lived in a Paradise of my own creation; I imagined that I also might obtain a niche in the temple where the names of Homer and Shakespeare are consecrated. You are well acquainted with my failure, and how heavily I bore the disappointment. But just at that time I inherited the fortune of my cousin, and my thoughts were turned into the channel of their earlier bent.

Six years have passed since I resolved on my present undertaking. I can, even now, remember the hour from which I dedicated myself to this great enterprise. I commenced by inuring my body to hardship. I accompanied the whale-fishers on several expeditions to the North Sea; I voluntarily endured cold, famine, thirst, and want of sleep; I often worked harder than the common sailors during the day, and devoted my nights to the study of mathematics, the theory of medicine, and those branches of physical science from which a naval adventurer might derive the greatest practical advantage. Twice I actually hired myself as an under-mate in a Greenland whaler, and acquitted myself to admiration. I must own I felt a little proud, when my captain offered me the second dignity in the vessel, and entreated me to remain with the greatest earnestness; so valuable did he consider my services.

And now, dear Margaret, do I not deserve to accomplish some great purpose. My life might have been passed in ease and luxury; but I preferred glory to every enticement that wealth placed in my path. Oh, that some encouraging voice would answer in the affirmative! My courage and my resolution is firm; but my hopes fluctuate, and my spirits are often depressed. I am about to proceed on a long and difficult voyage; the emergencies of which will demand all my fortitude: I am required not only to raise the spirits of others, but sometimes to sustain my own, when their's are failing.

This is the most favourable period for travelling in Russia. They fly quickly over the snow in their sledges; the motion is pleasant, and, in my opinion, far more agreeable than that of an English stage-coach. The cold is not excessive, if you are wrapt in furs, a dress which I have already adopted; for there is a great difference between walking the deck and remaining seated motionless for hours, when no exercise prevents the blood from actually freezing in your veins. I have no ambition to lose my life on the post-road between St. Petersburgh and Archangel.

I shall depart for the latter town in a fortnight or three weeks; and my intention is to hire a ship there, which can easily be done by paying the insurance for the owner, and to engage as many sailors as I think necessary among those who are accustomed to the whale-fishing. I do not intend to sail until the month of June: and when shall I return? Ah, dear sister, how can I answer this question? If I succeed, many, many months, perhaps years, will pass before you and I may meet. If I fail, you will see me again soon, or never.

Farewell, my dear, excellent, Margaret. Heaven shower down blessings on you, and save me, that I may again and again testify my gratitude for all your love and kindness.

Your affectionate brother,
R. Walton.

Mary Wollstonecraft Godwin's Journal

24 July. Glacier Montanvert— Curious. It is not only curious how this letter has made it into my possession and not Mrs Saville's, but I have grown curious concerning this expedition Mr Walton seeks to undertake. This description of his destination at the crown of the world is so near to my own description of the wonder of this glacier my Beloved and I now sit at the feet of. While I make no bones to visit a 'land never before imprinted by the foot of man', the sheer joy of this glacier harkens me back to when my ancestors lived in caves and hunted the woolly mammoths and were hunted by the sabre-toothed cats.

His own joys at seeking a 'steady purpose' I feel in my heart. I had fixed my own intellectual eye upon the story my pale student of the unhallowed arts has been relating to me. Whether he be real phantasm haunting my nights or my projection of my own creativity, I know not. But as of late, he has grown quite quiet. How fond this Mr Walton was studying the history of all the voyages made for purposes of discovery. How fond was I, are all authors, of reading the volumes of poetry and prose when disposed to the mirth of a library? He had been forbidden by parental degree from pursuing his dreams. How many of my fellow travellers to the grave had been so forbidden. My own father, thankfully, has never begrudged me my fancies in any of my pursuits whether they be poetry, literature, or the sciences; only the subject of religion, particularly Christianity, was discouraged unless prefaced under the study of mythology. To my father, Jesus was no more real or desiring the worship of than the pantheons of the Greeks or Egyptians.

It is most fascinating that this man who longs for the physical exploration of the world also reads from Homer and Shakespeare. To my mind, I am afraid to admit, I have often reserved *The Illiad* and *The Odyssey* to the enjoyment of the creative souls but knowing that explorers draw equal inspiration from the great works brings my heart so much joy. And how can I not share his endurance of literal 'cold, famine, thirst, and want of sleep' to fulfil his dreams. An author in the creation of his work will endure metaphorical 'cold, famine, thirst, and want of sleep.' I know well the devotion of my nights to the 'study of mathematics, the theory of medicine, and those branches of the physical science' that an author might derive the greatest practical advantage. Have these studies not benefitted me of late when my pale student of the unhallowed arts relates his story to me?

Letter 2 From R. Walton To Mrs Saville

To Mrs Saville, England.
                                        Archangel, 28th March, 1799.

How slowly the time passes here, encompassed as I am by frost and snow; yet a second step is taken towards my enterprise. I have hired a vessel, and am occupied in collecting my sailors; those whom I have already engaged appear to be men on whom I can depend, and are certainly possessed of dauntless courage.

But I have one want which I have never yet been able to satisfy; and the absence of the object of which I now feel as a most severe evil. I have no friend, Margaret: when I am glowing with the enthusiasm of success, there will be none to participate my joy; if I am assailed by disappointment, no one will endeavour to sustain me in dejection. I shall commit my thoughts to paper, it is true; but that is a poor medium for the communication of feeling. I desire the company of a man who could sympathize with me; whose eyes would reply to mine. You may deem me romantic, my dear sister, but I bitterly feel the want of a friend. I have no one near me, gentle yet courageous, possessed of a cultivated as well as of a capacious mind, whose tastes are like my own, to approve or amend my plans. How would such a friend repair the faults of your poor brother! I am too ardent in execution, and too impatient of difficulties. But it is a still greater evil to me that I am self-educated: for the first fourteen years of my life I ran wild on a common, and read nothing but our uncle Thomas's books of voyages. At that age I became acquainted with the celebrated poets of our own country; but it was only when it had ceased to be in my power to derive its most important benefits from such a conviction, that I perceived the necessity of becoming acquainted with more languages than that of my native country. Now I am twenty-eight, and am in reality more illiterate than many school-boys of fifteen. It is true that I have thought more, and that my day dreams are more extended and magnificent; but they want (as the painters call it) *keeping*; and I greatly need a friend who would have sense enough not to despise me as romantic, and affection enough for me to endeavour to regulate my mind.

Well, these are useless complaints; I shall certainly find no friend on the wide ocean, nor even here in Archangel, among merchants and seamen. Yet some feelings, unallied to the dross of human nature, beat even in these rugged bosoms. My lieutenant, for instance, is a man of wonderful courage and enterprise; he is madly desirous of glory. He is an Englishman, and in the midst of national and professional prejudices, unsoftened by cultivation, retains some of the noblest endowments of humanity. I first became acquainted with him on board a whale vessel: finding that he was unemployed in this city, I easily engaged him to assist in my enterprise.

The master is a person of an excellent disposition, and is remark-able in the ship for his gentleness, and the mildness of his discipline. He is, indeed, of so amiable a nature, that he will not hunt (a favourite, and almost the only amusement here), because he cannot endure to spill blood. He is, moreover, heroically generous. Some years ago he loved a young Russian lady, of moderate fortune; and having amassed a consid-erable sum in prize-money, the father of the girl consented to the match. He saw his mistress once before the destined ceremony; but she was bathed in tears, and, throwing herself at his feet, entreated him to spare her, confessing at the same time that she loved another, but that he was poor, and that her father would never consent to the union. My generous friend reassured the suppliant, and on being informed of the name of her lover instantly abandoned his pursuit. He had already bought a farm with his money, on which he had designed to pass the remainder of his life; but he bestowed the whole on his rival, together with the remains of his prize-money to purchase stock, and then himself solicited the young woman's father to consent to her marriage with her lover. But the old man decidedly refused, thinking himself bound in honour to my friend; who, when he found the father inexorable, quitted his country, nor re-turned until he heard that his former mistress was married according to her inclinations. 'What a noble fellow!' you will exclaim. He is so; but then he has passed all his life on board a vessel, and has scarcely an idea beyond the rope and the shroud.

But do not suppose that, because I complain a little, or because I can conceive a consolation for my toils which I may never know, that I am wavering in my resolutions. Those are as fixed as fate; and my voy-age is only now delayed until the weather shall permit my embarkation. The winter has been dreadfully severe; but the spring promises well, and it is considered as a remarkably early season; so that, perhaps, I may sail sooner than I expected. I shall do nothing rashly; you know me sufficiently to confide in my prudence and considerateness whenever the safety of others is committed to my care.

I cannot describe to you my sensations on the near prospect of my undertaking. It is impossible to communicate to you a conception of the trembling sensation, half pleasurable and half fearful, with which I am preparing to depart. I am going to unexplored regions, to 'the land of mist and snow;' but I shall kill no albatross, therefore do not be alarmed for my safety.

Shall I meet you again, after having traversed immense seas, and returned by the most southern cape of Africa or America? I dare not expect such success, yet I cannot bear to look on the reverse of the picture. Continue to write to me by every opportunity: I may receive your letters (though the chance is very doubtful) on some occasions when I need them most to support my spirits. I love you very tenderly. Remember me with affection, should you never hear from me again.

Your affectionate brother,
Robert Walton.

Mary Wollstonecraft Godwin's Journal

[Continued]— My! How I feel his longing for a friend. True, I have the friendship of my Beloved, our little Lord, poor Polidori, and my sister Claire, who will participate in my joy. If I am assailed with disappointment, they will, no doubt, endeavour to sustain me in dejection. I too commit my thoughts to paper, but I disagree with Mr Walton, the medium is exquisite for the communication of feeling! This very summer has proven to my companions and myself to be rife with the inspiration of the communication of feeling! But Mr Walton's words do mirror my own longing for my pale student of the unhallowed arts. His desire for a friend to share this journey to the crown of the world is my desire for my pale student to share with me his own story. Why has my pale student abandoned me? He may not have desired to journey to foot of the glacier here at Chamonix, but since he exists as a phantasm, the journey should not have been arduous. He could have made the journey in the safety of my own carriage, in the safety of my own head. But he hasn't made the journey to Chamonix. He hasn't made an appearance in my bedchamber in the Villa Diodati in a fortnight.

* * *

Letter 3 From R. Walton To Mrs Saville

To Mrs Saville, England.

July 7th, 1799.

My Dear Sister,

I write a few lines in haste, to say that I am safe, and well advanced on my voyage. This letter will reach England by a merchant-man now on its homeward voyage from Archangel; more fortunate than I, who may not see my native land, perhaps, for many years. I am, however, in good spirits: my men are bold, and apparently firm of purpose; nor do the floating sheets of ice that continually pass us, indicating the dangers of the region towards which we are advancing, appear to dismay them. We have already reached a very high latitude; but it is the height of summer, and although not so warm as in England, the southern gales, which blow us speedily towards those shores which I so ardently desire to attain, breathe a degree of renovating warmth which I had not expected.

No incidents have hitherto befallen us, that would make a figure in a letter. One or two stiff gales, and the breaking of a mast, are accidents which experienced navigators scarcely remember to record; and I shall be well content, if nothing worse happen to us during our voyage.

Adieu, my dear Margaret. Be assured, that for my own sake, as well as your's, I will not rashly encounter danger. I will be cool, persevering, and prudent.

Remember me to all my English friends.

Most affectionately yours,'

R. W.

Letter 4 From R. Walton To Mrs Saville

To Mrs Saville, England.

August 5th, 1799.

So strange an accident has happened to us, that I cannot forbear recording it, although it is very probable that you will see me before these papers can come into your possession.

Last Monday (July 31st), we were nearly surrounded by ice, which closed in the ship on all sides, scarcely leaving her the sea room in which she floated. Our situation was somewhat dangerous, especially as we were compassed round by a very thick fog. We accordingly lay to, hoping that some change would take place in the atmosphere and weather.

About two o'clock the mist cleared away, and we beheld, stretched out in every direction, vast and irregular plains of ice, which seemed to have no end. Some of my comrades groaned, and my own mind began to

grow watchful with anxious thoughts, when a strange sight suddenly attracted our attention, and diverted our solicitude from our own situation.
We perceived a low carriage, fixed on a sledge and drawn by dogs, pass
on towards the north, at the distance of half a mile: a being which had
the shape of a man, but apparently of gigantic stature, sat in the sledge,
and guided the dogs. We watched the rapid progress of the traveller with
our telescopes, until he was lost among the distant inequalities of the ice.

This appearance excited our unqualified wonder. We were, as we believed, many hundred miles from any land; but this apparition seemed
to denote that it was not, in reality, so distant as we had supposed. Shut
in, however, by ice, it was impossible to follow his track, which we had
observed with the greatest attention.

About two hours after this occurrence, we heard the ground sea; and
before night the ice broke, and freed our ship. We, however, lay to until
the morning, fearing to encounter in the dark those large loose masses
which float about after the breaking up of the ice. I profited of this time
to rest for a few hours.

In the morning, however, as soon as it was light, I went upon deck,
and found all the sailors busy on one side of the vessel, apparently talking to some one in the sea. It was, in fact, a sledge, like that we had seen
before, which had drifted towards us in the night, on a large fragment of
ice. Only one dog remained alive; but there was a human being within
it, whom the sailors were persuading to enter the vessel. He was not, as
the other traveller seemed to be, a savage inhabitant of some undiscovered island, but an European. When I appeared on deck, the master said,
'Here is our captain, and he will not allow you to perish on the open sea.'

On perceiving me, the stranger addressed me in English, although
with a foreign accent. 'Before I come on board your vessel,' said he, 'will
you have the kindness to inform me whither you are bound?'

You may conceive my astonishment on hearing such a question addressed to me from a man on the brink of destruction, and to whom I
should have supposed that my vessel would have been a resource which
he would not have exchanged for the most precious wealth the earth can
afford. I replied, however, that we were on a voyage of discovery towards
the northern pole.

Upon hearing this he appeared satisfied, and consented to come on
board. Good God! Margaret, if you had seen the man who thus capitu-
lated for his safety, your surprise would have been boundless. His limbs
were nearly frozen, and his body dreadfully emaciated by fatigue and
suffering. I never saw a man in so wretched a condition. We attempted to
carry him into the cabin; but as soon as he had quitted the fresh air, he
fainted. We accordingly brought him back to the deck, and restored him

to animation by rubbing him with brandy, and forcing him to swallow a small quantity. As soon as he shewed signs of life, we wrapped him up in blankets, and placed him near the chimney of the kitchen-stove. By slow degrees he recovered, and ate a little soup, which restored him wonderfully.

Two days passed in this manner before he was able to speak; and I often feared that his sufferings had deprived him of understanding. When he had in some measure recovered, I removed him to my own cabin, and attended on him as much as my duty would permit. I never saw a more interesting creature: his eyes have generally an expression of wildness, and even madness; but there are moments when, if any one performs an act of kindness towards him, or does him any the most trifling service, his whole countenance is lighted up, as it were, with a beam of benevolence and sweetness that I never saw equalled. But he is generally melancholy and despairing; and sometimes he gnashes his teeth, as if impatient of the weight of woes that oppresses him.

When my guest was a little recovered, I had great trouble to keep off the men, who wished to ask him a thousand questions; but I would not allow him to be tormented by their idle curiosity, in a state of body and mind whose restoration evidently depended upon entire repose. Once, however, the lieutenant asked, Why he had come so far upon the ice in so strange a vehicle?

His countenance instantly assumed an aspect of the deepest gloom; and he replied, 'To seek one who fled from me.'

'And did the man whom you pursued travel in the same fashion?'

'Yes.'

'Then I fancy we have seen him; for, the day before we picked you up, we saw some dogs drawing a sledge, with a man in it, across the ice.'

This aroused the stranger's attention; and he asked a multitude of questions concerning the route which the dæmon, as he called him, had pursued. Soon after, when he was alone with me, he said, 'I have, doubtless, excited your curiosity, as well as that of these good people; but you are too considerate to make inquiries.'

'Certainly; it would indeed be very impertinent and inhuman in me to trouble you with any inquisitiveness of mine.'

'And yet you rescued me from a strange and perilous situation; you have benevolently restored me to life.'

Soon after this he inquired, if I thought that the breaking up of the ice had destroyed the other sledge? I replied, that I could not answer with any degree of certainty; for the ice had not broken until near midnight, and the traveller might have arrived at a place of safety before that time; but of this I could not judge.

From this time the stranger seemed very eager to be upon deck, to watch for the sledge which had before appeared; but I have persuaded him to remain in the cabin, for he is far too weak to sustain the rawness of the atmosphere. But I have promised that some one should watch for him, and give him instant notice if any new object should appear in sight.

Such is my journal of what relates to this strange occurrence up to the present day. The stranger has gradually improved in health, but is very silent, and appears uneasy when any one except myself enters his cabin. Yet his manners are so conciliating and gentle, that the sailors are all interested in him, although they have had very little communication with him. For my own part, I begin to love him as a brother; and his constant and deep grief fills me with sympathy and compassion. He must have been a noble creature in his better days, being even now in wreck so attractive and amiable.

I said in one of my letters, my dear Margaret, that I should find no friend on the wide ocean; yet I have found a man who, before his spirit had been broken by misery, I should have been happy to have possessed as the brother of my heart.

I shall continue my journal concerning the stranger at intervals, should I have any fresh incidents to record.

August 13th, 1799.

My affection for my guest increases every day. He excites at once my admiration and my pity to an astonishing degree. How can I see so noble a creature destroyed by misery without feeling the most poignant grief? He is so gentle, yet so wise; his mind is so cultivated; and when he speaks, although his words are culled with the choicest art, yet they flow with rapidity and unparalleled eloquence.

He is now much recovered from his illness, and is continually on the deck, apparently watching for the sledge that preceded his own. Yet, although unhappy, he is not so utterly occupied by his own misery, but that he interests himself deeply in the employments of others. He has asked me many questions concerning my design; and I have related my little history frankly to him. He appeared pleased with the confidence, and suggested several alterations in my plan, which I shall find exceedingly useful. There is no pedantry in his manner; but all he does appears to spring solely from the interest he instinctively takes in the welfare of those who surround him. He is often overcome by gloom, and then he sits by himself, and tries to overcome all that is sullen or unsocial in his humour. These paroxysms pass from him like a cloud from before the sun, though his dejection never leaves him. I have endeavoured to win his confidence; and I trust that I have succeeded. One day I mentioned to him the desire I had always felt of finding a friend who might sympathize with me, and direct me by his counsel. I said, I did not belong to that class of men who are offended by advice. 'I am self-educated, and perhaps I hardly rely sufficiently upon my own powers. I wish therefore that my companion should be wiser and more experienced than myself, to confirm and support me; nor have I believed it impossible to find a true friend.'

'I agree with you,' replied the stranger, 'in believing that friendship is not only a desirable, but a possible acquisition. I once had a friend, the most noble of human creatures, and am entitled, therefore, to judge respecting friendship. You have hope, and the world before you, and have no cause for despair. But I— — I have lost every thing, and cannot begin life anew.'

As he said this, his countenance became expressive of a calm settled grief, that touched me to the heart. But he was silent, and presently retired to his cabin.

Even broken in spirit as he is, no one can feel more deeply than he does the beauties of nature. The starry sky, the sea, and every sight afforded by these wonderful regions, seems still to have the power of elevating his soul from earth. Such a man has a double existence: he may suffer misery, and be overwhelmed by disappointments; yet when he has retired into himself, he will be like a celestial spirit, that has a halo around him, within whose circle no grief or folly ventures.

Will you laugh at the enthusiasm I express concerning this divine wanderer? If you do, you must have certainly lost that simplicity which was once your characteristic charm. Yet, if you will, smile at the warmth of my expressions, while I find every day new causes for repeating them.

August 19th, 1799.

Yesterday the stranger said to me, 'You may easily perceive, Captain Walton, that I have suffered great and unparalleled misfortunes. I had determined, once, that the memory of these evils should die with me; but you have won me to alter my determination. You seek for knowledge and wisdom, as I once did; and I ardently hope that the gratification of your wishes may not be a serpent to sting you, as mine has been. I do not know that the relation of my misfortunes will be useful to you, yet, if you are inclined, listen to my tale. I believe that the strange incidents connected with it will afford a view of nature, which may enlarge your faculties and understanding. You will hear of powers and occurrences, such as you have been accustomed to believe impossible: but I do not doubt that my tale conveys in its series internal evidence of the truth of the events of which it is composed.'

You may easily conceive that I was much gratified by the offered communication; yet I could not endure that he should renew his grief by a recital of his misfortunes. I felt the greatest eagerness to hear the promised narrative, partly from curiosity, and partly from a strong desire to ameliorate his fate, if it were in my power. I expressed these feelings in my answer.

'I thank you,' he replied, 'for your sympathy, but it is useless; my fate is nearly fulfilled. I wait but for one event, and then I shall repose in peace. I understand your feeling,' continued he, perceiving that I wished to interrupt him; 'but you are mistaken, my friend, if thus you will allow me to name you; nothing can alter my destiny: listen to my history, and you will perceive how irrevocably it is determined.'

He then told me, that he would commence his narrative the next day when I should be at leisure. This promise drew from me the warmest thanks. I have resolved every night, when I am not engaged, to record, as nearly as possible in his own words, what he has related during the day. If I should be engaged, I will at least make notes. This manuscript will doubtless afford you the greatest pleasure: but to me, who know him, and who hear it from his own lips, with what interest and sympathy shall I read it in some future day!

"I am by birth a Genevese,' he began.

Mary Wollstonecraft Godwin's Journal

[Continued]— My pale student! How he found me. He has not abandoned me. For this past fortnight I have not been abandoned. He has been on the arduous journey to the crown of the world! There to converse with Mr Walton and via letters to Mrs Saville inform me of his adventures. How I feared that he would not be able to find me at such a great distance from the Villa Diodati. It is a childlike fear that Father Christmas would not be able to find me if the family Christmased away from home and hearth. But I feared for nought.

Chapter Sixteen
Childe Harold's Pilgrimage (3rd Canto);[37]

Lord Byron's Diary

Date unrecorded]... 'Begun at sea.' With these words scrawl on my manuscript, I have begun the third canto of *Childe Harold's Pilgrimage*. With the first two cantos having seen publication thanks to John Murray and associates, I thought the pilgrimage was done. But I've fled my home and my country due to 'dark rumours'. Shall I repeat the rumours here for I know the truth and the rumour-mongering of gossiping hens are not content with their own marriage and their own affairs and their own scandals. Was King Oedipus so assaulted with the outright slander committed at dinner parties and the libel printing in the newspaper and magazines? How would Oedipus answer the assault on his character for the supposition of an improper relationship with his own mother? Would Oedipus have been forced to flee his homeland like I am being banished from my own island? There is no answer to these quite loud whispers that will satisfy the rumourmongers. Being shunned by the very society and high society that had once flocked to my poetry and gifted me with immeasurable fame. Where once I would stand in the parlours of the richest men and women in the country, reciting my poetry to their evening's guests, now I am expelled from their circles for rumours and rumours of rumours of... I cannot bear to say. I composed this *Pilgrimage* as I journeyed through Belgium, German, and finally landing on the shores of Lake Geneva at Cologny. My mind alight with the creative spark that gave birth to the first two cantos. The words flow onto the page effortlessly. I find it more a travelogue than a poem. And travelogues are all the rage back on my island, but will a publisher even be found to print this book given my scandal? Or will my infamy push copies out at the booksellers? I have permitted P.B.S. the honour of reading these stanzas as I have written them, including other works of darkness (pun intended). I have left him an inkpot filled with ink the colour of human blood having instructed him to 'Kill my darlings. Kill Kill. Kill my darlings'. If the pages do not return to be bloodied, then how can I, through the alchemy of editing, resurrect my poem or prose into a

---

37 From *Childe Harold's Pilgrimage, a Romaunt* by Lord Byron, published by John Murray. "Stanzas I through XXV are included in this chapter. The remaining stanzas can be found in Appendix 2"— R.D.B.

publishable work worthy of entering society? The first draft must be murdered, mercilessly cut, sliced, and maimed beyond all recognition to produce the final work. And this is what friends are for!

I.

Is thy face like thy mother's, my fair child!
Ada! sole daughter of my house and heart?
When last I saw thy young blue eyes, they smiled,
And then we parted,—not as now we part,
But with a hope.—
                Awaking with a start,
The waters heave around me; and on high
The winds lift up their voices: I depart,
Whither I know not; but the hour's gone by,
When Albion's lessening shores could grieve or glad mine eye.

II.

Once more upon the waters! yet once more!
And the waves bound beneath me as a steed
That knows his rider. Welcome to their roar!
Swift be their guidance, wheresoe'er it lead!
Though the strained mast should quiver as a reed,
And the rent canvas fluttering strew the gale,
Still must I on; for I am as a weed,
Flung from the rock, on Ocean's foam, to sail
Where'er the surge may sweep, the tempest's breath prevail.

III.

In my youth's summer I did sing of One,
The wandering outlaw of his own dark mind;
Again I seize the theme, then but begun,
And bear it with me, as the rushing wind
Bears the cloud onwards: in that tale I find
The furrows of long thought, and dried-up tears,
Which, ebbing, leave a sterile track behind,
O'er which all heavily the journeying years
Plod the last sands of life—where not a flower appears.

IV.

Since my young days of passion—joy, or pain,
Perchance my heart and harp have lost a string,
And both may jar: it may be, that in vain

I would essay as I have sung to sing.
Yet, though a dreary strain, to this I cling,
So that it wean me from the weary dream
Of selfish grief or gladness—so it fling
Forgetfulness around me—it shall seem
To me, though to none else, a not ungrateful theme.

V.

He who, grown aged in this world of woe,
In deeds, not years, piercing the depths of life,
So that hno wonder waits him; nor below
Can love or sorrow, fame, ambition, strife,
Cut to his heart again with the keen knife
Of silent, sharp endurance: he can tell
Why thought seeks refuge in lone caves, yet rife
With airy images, and shapes which dwell
Still unimpaired, though old, in the soul's haunted cell.

VI.

'Tis to create, and in creating live
A being more intense, that we endow
With form our fancy, gaining as we give
The life we image, even as I do now.
What am I? Nothing: but not so art thou,
Soul of my thought! with whom I traverse earth,
Invisible but gazing, as I glow
Mixed with thy spirit, blended with thy birth,
And feeling still with thee in my crushed feelings' dearth.

VII.

Yet must I think less wildly: I HAVE thought
Too long and darkly, till my brain became,
In its own eddy boiling and o'erwrought,
A whirling gulf of phantasy and flame:
And thus, untaught in youth my heart to tame,
My springs of life were poisoned. 'Tis too late!
Yet am I changed; though still enough the same
In strength to bear what time cannot abate,
And feed on bitter fruits without accusing fate.

VIII.

Something too much of this: but now 'tis past,
And the spell closes with its silent seal.
Long-absent Harold reappears at last;
He of the breast which fain no more would feel,
Wrung with the wounds which kill not, but ne'er heal;
Yet Time, who changes all, had altered him
In soul and aspect as in age: years steal
Fire from the mind as vigour from the limb;
And life's enchanted cup but sparkles near the brim.

IX.

His had been quaffed too quickly, and he found
The dregs were wormwood; but he filled again,
And from a purer fount, on holier ground,
And deemed its spring perpetual; but in vain!
Still round him clung invisibly a chain
Which galled for ever, fettering though unseen,
And heavy though it clanked not; worn with pain,
Which pined although it spoke not, and grew keen,
Entering with every step he took through many a scene.

X.

Secure in guarded coldness, he had mixed
Again in fancied safety with his kind,
And deemed his spirit now so firmly fixed
And sheathed with an invulnerable mind,
That, if no joy, no sorrow lurked behind;
And he, as one, might midst the many stand
Unheeded, searching through the crowd to find
Fit speculation; such as in strange land
He found in wonder-works of God and Nature's hand.

XI.

But who can view the ripened rose, nor seek
To wear it? who can curiously behold
The smoothness and the sheen of beauty's cheek,
Nor feel the heart can never all grow old?
Who can contemplate fame through clouds unfold
The star which rises o'er her steep, nor climb?
Harold, once more within the vortex rolled
On with the giddy circle, chasing Time,

Yet with a nobler aim than in his youth's fond prime.

XII.

But soon he knew himself the most unfit
Of men to herd with Man; with whom he held
Little in common; untaught to submit
His thoughts to others, though his soul was quelled,
In youth by his own thoughts; still uncompelled,
He would not yield dominion of his mind
To spirits against whom his own rebelled;
Proud though in desolation; which could find
A life within itself, to breathe without mankind.

XIII.

Where rose the mountains, there to him were friends;
Where rolled the ocean, thereon was his home;
Where a blue sky, and glowing clime, extends,
He had the passion and the power to roam;
The desert, forest, cavern, breaker's foam,
Were unto him companionship; they spake
A mutual language, clearer than the tome
Of his land's tongue, which he would oft forsake
For nature's pages glassed by sunbeams on the lake.

XIV.

Like the Chaldean, he could watch the stars,
Till he had peopled them with beings bright
As their own beams; and earth, and earth-born jars,
And human frailties, were forgotten quite:
Could he have kept his spirit to that flight,
He had been happy; but this clay will sink
Its spark immortal, envying it the light
To which it mounts, as if to break the link
That keeps us from yon heaven which woos us to its brink.

XV.

But in Man's dwellings he became a thing
Restless and worn, and stern and wearisome,
Drooped as a wild-born falcon with clipt wing,
To whom the boundless air alone were home:
Then came his fit again, which to o'ercome,
As eagerly the barred-up bird will beat

His breast and beak against his wiry dome
Till the blood tinge his plumage, so the heat
Of his impeded soul would through his bosom eat.

XVI.

Self-exiled Harold wanders forth again,
With naught of hope left, but with less of gloom;
The very knowledge that he lived in vain,
That all was over on this side the tomb,
Had made Despair a smilingness assume,
Which, though 'twere wild—as on the plundered wreck
When mariners would madly meet their doom
With draughts intemperate on the sinking deck—
Did yet inspire a cheer, which he forbore to check.

Stop! for thy tread is on an empire's dust!
An earthquake's spoil is sepulchred below!
Is the spot marked with no colossal bust?
Nor column trophied for triumphal show?
None; but the moral's truth tells simpler so,
As the ground was before, thus let it be;—
How that red rain hath made the harvest grow!
And is this all the world has gained by thee,
Thou first and last of fields! king-making Victory?

XVIII.

And Harold stands upon this place of skulls,
The grave of France, the deadly Waterloo!
How in an hour the power which gave annuls
Its gifts, transferring fame as fleeting too!
In 'pride of place' here last the eagle flew,
Then tore with bloody talon the rent plain,
Pierced by the shaft of banded nations through:
Ambition's life and labours all were vain;
He wears the shattered links of the world's broken chain.

XIX.

Fit retribution! Gaul may champ the bit,
And foam in fetters, but is Earth more free?
Did nations combat to make ONE submit;
Or league to teach all kings true sovereignty?
What! shall reviving thraldom again be

The patched-up idol of enlightened days?
Shall we, who struck the Lion down, shall we
Pay the Wolf homage? proffering lowly gaze
And servile knees to thrones? No; PROVE before ye praise!

XX.

If not, o'er one fall'n despot boast no more!
In vain fair cheeks were furrowed with hot tears
For Europe's flowers long rooted up before
The trampler of her vineyards; in vain years
Of death, depopulation, bondage, fears,
Have all been borne, and broken by the accord
Of roused-up millions: all that most endears
Glory, is when the myrtle wreathes a sword
Such as Harmodius drew on Athens' tyrant lord.

XXI.

There was a sound of revelry by night,
And Belgium's capital had gathered then
Her Beauty and her Chivalry, and bright
The lamps shone o'er fair women and brave men;
A thousand hearts beat happily; and when
Music arose with its voluptuous swell,
Soft eyes looked love to eyes which spake again,
And all went merry as a marriage bell;
But hush! hark! a deep sound strikes like a rising knell!

XXII.

Did ye not hear it?—No; 'twas but the wind,
Or the car rattling o'er the stony street;
On with the dance! let joy be unconfined;
No sleep till morn, when Youth and Pleasure meet
To chase the glowing Hours with flying feet.
But hark!—that heavy sound breaks in once more,
As if the clouds its echo would repeat;
And nearer, clearer, deadlier than before!
Arm! arm! it is—it is—the cannon's opening roar!

XXIII.

Within a windowed niche of that high hall
Sate Brunswick's fated chieftain; he did hear
That sound, the first amidst the festival,

And caught its tone with Death's prophetic ear;
And when they smiled because he deemed it near,
His heart more truly knew that peal too well
Which stretched his father on a bloody bier,
And roused the vengeance blood alone could quell:
He rushed into the field, and, foremost fighting, fell.

XXIV.

Ah! then and there was hurrying to and fro,
And gathering tears, and tremblings of distress,
And cheeks all pale, which but an hour ago
Blushed at the praise of their own loveliness;
And there were sudden partings, such as press
The life from out young hearts, and choking sighs
Which ne'er might be repeated: who would guess
If ever more should meet those mutual eyes,
Since upon night so sweet such awful morn could rise!

XXV.

And there was mounting in hot haste: the steed,
The mustering squadron, and the clattering car,
Went pouring forward with impetuous speed,
And swiftly forming in the ranks of war;
And the deep thunder peal on peal afar;
And near, the beat of the alarming drum
Roused up the soldier ere the morning star;
While thronged the citizens with terror dumb,
Or whispering, with white lips—'The foe! They come! they come!'

Chapter Seventeen
Frankenstein[38]
(The Death of the Creature)

Chapter I

In the very same, now utterly abandoned, chair that the Creature had sat just weeks previous, now had a new occupant: my pale student of the unhallowed arts. Victor had returned to me! And quite queerly, he sat as flummoxed as I had been just having been told the Creature's tale.

'The being finished speaking, and fixed his looks upon me in expectation of a reply. But I was bewildered, perplexed, and unable to arrange my ideas sufficiently to understand the full extent of his proposition.'

Oh! Ho! So, Victor has just been told the Creature's tale just as I had been. So, the Creature had not been addressing me as its Creator at all. It had been Victor Frankenstein to whom was the Creature's audience all along. When the Creature looked upon me those handful a weeks ago, did he see my pale student of the unhallowed arts lying in bed beside my Beloved? And now that I contemplate this, had Victor seen me as the ship's captain Robert Walton all along? And my bedchamber as the captain's quarters on his ice-locked ship? What manner of lunacy have I been suffering from to hallucinate my own characters?

He continued— ' "You must create a female for me, with whom I can live in the interchange of those sympathies necessary for my being. This you alone can do; and I demand it of you as a right which you must not refuse."

So the Creation desires a mate? Again and again this tale of Victor's and his Creature's prove to me at least to be an allegory for Adam and Eve? Why haven't I heard a name given to the Creature? I have been forced by a lack of evidence to call him 'The Creation', until he murdered poor William and framed poorer Justine. From this point onward, he is nothing more that 'The Creature', a monster that I am ashamed my mind has given birth to. But if this is an allegory for Adam and Eve, should his name not be 'Adam' and his bride 'Eve'? And if this is an allegory, one most contemplate the source of the myth.

---

38 From *Frankenstein; or the Modern Prometheus* by Mary Wollstonecraft Shelley, published by Lackington, Hughes, Harding, Mavor & Jones, 1818

*Did not the Lord God say, 'It is not good that the man should be alone;
I will make him an help meet for him.' And did not, out of the ground
the Lord God form every beast of the field, and every fowl of the air; and
brought them unto Adam to see what he would call them: and whatsoever
Adam called every living creature, that was the name thereof? And did not
Adam give names to all cattle, and to the fowl of the air, and to every beast
of the field; but for Adam there was not found an help meet for him. Did
not the Lord God cause a deep sleep to fall upon Adam, and he slept: and
he take one of his ribs, and close up the flesh instead thereof; and the rib,
which the Lord God had taken from man, made he a woman, and brought
her unto the man? Did not Adam say, 'This is now bone of my bones, and
flesh of my flesh: she shall be called Woman, because she was taken out
of Man.'? Is not the intention of God that therefore shall a man leave his
father and his mother, and shall cleave unto his wife: and they shall be one
flesh?*[39] Should not the Creature have a wife to cleave to? Where *the
Lord God formed man of the dust of the ground, and breathed into his nostrils the breath of life; and man became a living soul*[40], Victor made his
Creature of the flesh of many men; should he not have a wife made of
many women? If I was the author of this tale and not an audience for
its telling, I would acquiesce to the Creature's desire.

The latter part of his tale had kindled anew in me the anger that had
died away while he narrated his peaceful life among the cottagers, and,
as he said this, I could no longer suppress the rage that burned within
me.

' "I do refuse it," I replied; "and no torture shall ever extort a consent
from me. You may render me the most miserable of men, but you shall
never make me base in my own eyes. Shall I create another like yourself,
whose joint wickedness might desolate the world. Begone! I have answered you; you may torture me, but I will never consent."

Is my pale student of the unhallowed arts feeling the same pangs
of regret that the Lord God did when Adam and Eve ate of the fruit of
the Tree of the Knowledge of Good and Evil? Just like the Lord God,
Victor had created his Creature out of a longing to do good, but the
Creature by its very nature as a manufactured and not created being.
While the De Lacys educated him with the knowledge of good, the
Creature possesses a little too much of the knowledge of evil from the
remainder of humanity. Is this through no fault of his own, for his interactions with the fallen Creations of the Lord God have been... well,
unfortunate.

---

39 From Genesis 2:18-24, from the Authorized King James Translation of the Holy Bible.
40 From Genesis 2:7, from the Authorized King James Translation of the Holy Bible.

' "You are in the wrong," replied the fiend; "and, instead of threatening, I am content to reason with you. I am malicious because I am miserable; am I not shunned and hated by all mankind? You, my creator, would tear me to pieces, and triumph; remember that, and tell me why I should pity man more than he pities me? You would not call it murder, if you could precipitate me into one of those ice-rifts, and destroy my frame, the work of your own hands. Shall I respect man, when he contemns me? Let him live with me in the interchange of kindness, and, instead of injury, I would bestow every benefit upon him with tears of gratitude at his acceptance. But that cannot be; the human senses are insurmountable barriers to our union.'

The Creature errs. If there was a man born of sharp deformity, could he not be accepted by our society? Would his man be seen as a curiosity for mockery and scorn? Or should he be celebrated and his company sought after? What if both could be simultaneously true? And if there was a man born of sharp deformity, would his mind not be still so keen that he could and should adapt Isaac Watt's 'False Greatness' with his own opening lines?

> *'Tis true my form is something odd,*
> *But blaming me is blaming God,*
> *Could I create myself anew*
> *I would not fail in pleasing you.*
>
> *If I could reach from pole to pole,*
> *Or grasp the ocean with a span,*
> *I would be measured by the soul;*
> *The Mind's the standard of man.'*[41]

I possess the strongest of convictions that humanity could and would and should be much more welcoming of the Creature if given the proper opportunities and platform. While the religious may attempt to condemn and crucify Victor for dabbling in the realm reserved for God alone, such an articulate Creature could easily be welcomed into proper society as a wonder of the modern world?

Or am I being a fool?

'Yet mine shall not be the submission of abject slavery. I will revenge my injuries: if I cannot inspire love, I will cause fear; and chiefly towards you my arch-enemy, because my creator, do I swear inextinguishable

---

41 From an adaptation of Isaac Watt's poem, 'Fales Greatness', by Joseph Merrick, known as the 'Elephant Man'.

hatred. Have a care: I will work at your destruction, nor finish until I desolate your heart, so that you curse the hour of your birth."

'A fiendish rage animated him as he said this; his face was wrinkled into contortions too horrible for human eyes to behold; but presently he calmed himself, and proceeded—

' "I intended to reason. This passion is detrimental to me; for you do not reflect that you are the cause of its excess. If any being felt emotions of benevolence towards me, I should return them an hundred and an hundred fold; for that one creature's sake, I would make peace with the whole kind! But I now indulge in dreams of bliss that cannot be realized. What I ask of you is reasonable and moderate; I demand a creature of another sex, but as hideous as myself: the gratification is small, but it is all that I can receive, and it shall content me. It is true, we shall be monsters, cut off from all the world; but on that account we shall be more attached to one another. Our lives will not be happy, but they will be harmless, and free from the misery I now feel. Oh! my creator, make me happy; let me feel gratitude towards you for one benefit! Let me see that I excite the sympathy of some existing thing; do not deny me my request!"

'I was moved.' As am I! 'I shuddered when I thought of the possible consequences of my consent; but I felt that there was some justice in his argument. His tale, and the feelings he now expressed, proved him to be a creature of fine sensations; and did I not, as his maker, owe him all the portion of happiness that it was in my power to bestow?' So articulate and compassionate is the Creature and full of reason that I am so moved that I must return to calling him 'Creation'.

'He saw my change of feeling, and continued—

' "If you consent, neither you nor any other human being shall ever see us again: I will go to the vast wilds of South America. My food is not that of man; I do not destroy the lamb and the kid, to glut my appetite; acorns and berries afford me sufficient nourishment. My companion will be of the same nature as myself, and will be content with the same fare. We shall make our bed of dried leaves; the sun will shine on us as on man, and will ripen our food. The picture I present to you is peaceful and human, and you must feel that you could deny it only in the wantonness of power and cruelty. Pitiless as you have been towards me, I now see compassion in your eyes: let me seize the favourable moment, and persuade you to promise what I so ardently desire."

How this very much reminds me of my Beloved's own essays and poems vindicating a natural diet:

> 'My brethren, we are free! The fruits are glowing
> Beneath the stars, and the night-winds are flowing

O'er the ripe corn, the birds and beasts are dreaming–
Never again may blood of bird or beast
Stain with its venomous stream a human feast...
Reclining, as they ate, of Liberty,
And Hope, and Justice, and Laone's name,
Earth's children did a woof of happy converse frame...
Might share in peace and innocence, for gore
Or poison none this festal did pollute,
But, piled on high, an overflowing store
Of pomegranates and citrons, fairest fruit,
Melons, and dates, and figs, and many a root
Sweet and sustaining, and bright grapes ere yet
Accursed fire their mild juice could transmute
Into a mortal bane, and brown corn set
In baskets; with pure streams their thirsting lips they wet.[42]

Shall I share my own defence of my Beloved's beliefs? He chose for his hero a youth nourished in dreams of liberty, some of whose actions are in direct opposition to the opinions of the world, but who is animated throughout by an ardent love of virtue, and a resolution to confer the boons of political and intellectual freedom on his fellow-creatures. He created for this youth a woman such as he delighted to imagine—full of enthusiasm for the same objects; and they both, with will unvanquished and the deepest sense of the justice of their cause, met adversity and death. There exists in this poem a memorial of a friend of his youth. The character of the old man who liberates Laon from his tower prison, and tends on him in sickness, is founded on that of Doctor Lind, who, when Shelley was at Eton, had often stood by to befriend and support him, and whose name he never mentioned without love and veneration.

And again my own digressions now distract me from Victor's story: ' "You propose," replied I, "to fly from the habitations of man, to dwell in those wilds where the beasts of the field will be your only companions. How can you, who long for the love and sympathy of man, persevere in this exile? You will return, and again seek their kindness, and you will meet with their detestation; your evil passions will be renewed, and you will then have a companion to aid you in the task of destruction. This may not be; cease to argue the point, for I cannot consent."

' "How inconstant are your feelings!' I concur, dearest Creation. 'But a moment ago you were moved by my representations, and why do you again harden yourself to my complaints? I swear to you, by the

---

42 From *The Revolt of Islam*, canto 5, by Percy Bysshe Shelley, written between April and September 1817, but close enough for my purposes.

earth which I inhabit, and by you that made me, that, with the companion you bestow, I will quit the neighbourhood of man, and dwell, as it may chance, in the most savage of places. My evil passions will have fled, for I shall meet with sympathy; my life will flow quietly away, and, in my dying moments, I shall not curse my maker."

'His words had a strange effect upon me. I compassionated him, and sometimes felt a wish to console him; but when I looked upon him, when I saw the filthy mass that moved and talked, my heart sickened, and my feelings were altered to those of horror and hatred. I tried to stifle these sensations; I thought, that as I could not sympathize with him, I had no right to withhold from him the small portion of happiness which was yet in my power to bestow.'

How inconstant are your feelings, my pale student of the unhallowed arts!

' "You swear," I said, "to be harmless; but have you not already shewn a degree of malice that should reasonably make me distrust you? May not even this be a feint that will increase your triumph by affording a wider scope for your revenge?"

How constant are your feelings, my pale student of the unhallowed arts!

' "How is this? I thought I had moved your compassion, and yet you still refuse to bestow on me the only benefit that can soften my heart, and render me harmless. If I have no ties and no affections, hatred and vice must be my portion; the love of another will destroy the cause of my crimes, and I shall become a thing, of whose existence every one will be ignorant. My vices are the children of a forced solitude that I abhor; and my virtues will necessarily arise when I live in communion with an equal. I shall feel the affections of a sensitive being, and become linked to the chain of existence and events, from which I am now excluded."

Chain of existence? I recall these words, but from whence have I heard them. Victor would continue telling his tale unabetted, but I needed to know where I had heard these words. Ah!

> *Is the great chain, that draws all to agree,*
> *And drawn supports, upheld by God, or thee?*
>
> *Vast chain of being! which from God began,*
> *Natures ethereal, human, angel, man,*
> *Beast, bird, fish, insect, what no eye can see,*
> *No glass can reach; from Infinite to thee,*
> *From thee to nothing.*[43]

---

43 From *Essay of Man* by Alexander Pope, published in 1732.

* * *

'I paused some time to reflect on all he had related, and the various arguments which he had employed. I thought of the promise of virtues which he had displayed on the opening of his existence, and the subsequent blight of all kindly feeling by the loathing and scorn which his protectors had manifested towards him. His power and threats were not omitted in my calculations: a creature who could exist in the ice caves of the glaciers, and hide himself from pursuit among the ridges of inaccessible precipices, was a being possessing faculties it would be vain to cope with. After a long pause of reflection, I concluded, that the justice due both to him and my fellow-creatures demanded of me that I should comply with his request. Turning to him, therefore, I said—

' "I consent to your demand, on your solemn oath to quit Europe for ever, and every other place in the neighbourhood of man, as soon as I shall deliver into your hands a female who will accompany you in your exile."

' "I swear," he cried, "by the sun, and by the blue sky of heaven,'— and the fire of love that burns in his heart– 'that if you grant my prayer, while they exist you shall never behold me again. Depart to your home, and commence your labours: I shall watch their progress with unutterable anxiety; and fear not but that when you are ready I shall appear."

'Saying this, he suddenly quitted me, fearful, perhaps, of any change in my sentiments. I saw him descend the mountain with greater speed than the flight of an eagle, and quickly lost him among the undulations of the sea of ice.

'His tale had occupied the whole day; and the sun was upon the verge of the horizon when he departed. I knew that I ought to hasten my descent towards the valley, as I should soon be encompassed in darkness; but my heart was heavy, and my steps slow. The labour of winding among the little paths of the mountains, and fixing my feet firmly as I advanced, perplexed me, occupied as I was by the emotions which the occurrences of the day had produced. Night was far advanced, when I came to the half-way resting-place, and seated myself beside the fountain. The stars shone at intervals, as the clouds passed from over them; the dark pines rose before me, and every here and there a broken tree lay on the ground: it was a scene of wonderful solemnity, and stirred strange thoughts within me. I wept bitterly; and, clasping my hands in agony, I exclaimed, "Oh! stars, and clouds, and winds, ye are all about to mock me: if ye really pity me, crush sensation and memory; let me become as nought; but if not, depart, depart and leave me in darkness."

'These were wild and miserable thoughts; but I cannot describe to you how the eternal twinkling of the stars weighed upon me, and how I listened to every blast of wind, as if it were a dull ugly siroc on its way to consume me.

I heard the final words that Victor related unto me concluding this volume of his life, before he proceeds onto the next volume, but my mind constantly revised his words into those of my own: 'Morning dawned before I arrived at the village of Chamounix; I took no rest, but returned immediately to Geneva. Even in my own heart I could give no expression to my sensations—they weighed on me with a mountain's weight, and their excess destroyed my agony beneath them. Thus I returned home, and entering the house, presented myself to the family. My haggard and wild appearance awoke intense alarm; but I answered no question, scarcely did I speak. I felt as if I were placed under a ban—as if I had no right to claim their sympathies—as if never more might I enjoy companionship with them. Yet even thus I loved them to adoration; and to save them, I resolved to dedicate myself to my most abhorred task. The prospect of such an occupation made every other circumstance of existence pass before me like a dream; and that thought only had to me the reality of life.'

Chapter II

Day after day, week after week, passed away on my return to Geneva; and I could not collect the courage to recommence my work.' Oh, dearest Victor, you promised your Creation you would deliver him a companion! 'I feared the vengeance of the disappointed fiend, yet I was unable to overcome my repugnance to the task which was enjoined me. I found that I could not compose a female without again devoting several months to profound study and laborious disquisition. I had heard of some discoveries having been made by an English philosopher, the knowledge of which was material to my success,'— who would be English philosopher be is most uncertain? I know many! Erasmus Darwin is the most likely candidate. Truly the feminine creature is much more a complex physiological form than the masculine machinery. My Beloved has often said that *Man is mechanical, Woman is art!* Is there where Victor's consternation lies? Even Leonardo DaVinci, so astute in his observations of human anatomy avoided autopsying the female corpse. So repulsed was he of the feminine form and the unfathomable mysteries of 'wandering womb' that he refused any such study. A consummate observer may observe that obtaining female corpses proved far too difficult, but I believe he was truly horrified of *every* aspect of the feminine reproduction from birth itself to the very act of copulation. 'And I sometimes thought of obtaining my father's consent to visit England for this purpose; but I clung to every pretence of delay, and could not resolve to interrupt my returning tranquillity. My health, which had hitherto declined, was now much restored; and my spirits, when unchecked by the memory of my unhappy promise, rose proportionably. My father saw this change with pleasure, and he turned his thoughts towards the best method of eradicating the remains of my melancholy, which every now and then would return by fits, and with a devouring blackness overcast the approaching sunshine. At these moments I took refuge in the most perfect solitude. I passed whole days on the lake alone in a little boat, watching the clouds, and listening to the rippling of the waves, silent and listless. But the fresh air and bright sun seldom failed to restore me to some degree of composure; and, on my return, I met the salutations of my friends with a readier smile and a more cheerful heart.

'It was after my return from one of these rambles that my father, calling me aside, thus addressed me:—

' "I am happy to remark, my dear son, that you have resumed your former pleasures, and seem to be returning to yourself. And yet you are still unhappy, and still avoid our society. For some time I was lost in conjecture as to the cause of this; but yesterday an idea struck me, and if it is well founded, I conjure you to avow it. Reserve on such a point would be not only useless, but draw down treble misery on us all."

'I trembled violently at this exordium, and my father continued—

' "I confess, my son, that I have always looked forward to your marriage with your cousin as the tie of our domestic comfort, and the stay of my declining years. You were attached to each other from your earliest infancy; you studied together, and appeared, in dispositions and tastes, entirely suited to one another. But so blind is the experience of man, that what I conceived to be the best assistants to my plan may have entirely destroyed it. You, perhaps, regard her as your sister, without any wish that she might become your wife. Nay, you may have met with another whom you may love; and, considering yourself as bound in honour to your cousin, this struggle may occasion the poignant misery which you appear to feel."

' "My dear father, re-assure yourself. I love my cousin tenderly and sincerely. I never saw any woman who excited, as Elizabeth does, my warmest admiration and affection. My future hopes and prospects are entirely bound up in the expectation of our union."

' "The expression of your sentiments on this subject, my dear Victor, gives me more pleasure than I have for some time experienced. If you feel thus, we shall assuredly be happy, however present events may cast a gloom over us. But it is this gloom, which appears to have taken so strong a hold of your mind, that I wish to dissipate. Tell me, therefore, whether you object to an immediate solemnization of the marriage. We have been unfortunate, and recent events have drawn us from that every-day tranquillity befitting my years and infirmities. You are younger; yet I do not suppose, possessed as you are of a competent fortune, that an early marriage would at all interfere with any future plans of honour and utility that you may have formed. Do not suppose, however, that I wish to dictate happiness to you, or that a delay on your part would cause me any serious uneasiness. Interpret my words with candour, and answer me, I conjure you, with confidence and sincerity."

'I listened to my father in silence, and remained for some time in-capable of offering any reply. I revolved rapidly in my mind a multitude of thoughts, and endeavoured to arrive at some conclusion. Alas! to me the idea of an immediate union with my cousin was one of horror and dismay. I was bound by a solemn promise, which I had not yet fulfilled, and dared not break; or, if I did, what manifold miseries might not im-pend over me and my devoted family! Could I enter into a festival with this deadly weight yet hanging round my neck, and bowing me to the ground. I must perform my engagement, and let the monster depart with his mate, before I allowed myself to enjoy the delight of an union from which I expected peace.

'I remembered also the necessity imposed upon me of either journey-ing to England, or entering into a long correspondence with those philos-ophers of that country, whose knowledge and discoveries were of indis-pensable use to me in my present undertaking— my hand again revised his own words as I recorded them into my journal— The latter method of obtaining the desired intelligence was dilatory and unsatisfactory: be-sides, I had an insurmountable aversion to the idea of engaging myself in my loathsome task in my father's house, while in habits of familiar intercourse with those I loved. I knew that a thousand fearful accidents might occur, the slightest of which would disclose a tale to thrill all con-nected with me with horror. I was aware also that I should often lose all self-command, all capacity of hiding the harrowing sensations that would possess me during the progress of my unearthly occupation. I must ab-sent myself from all I loved while thus employed. Once commenced, it would quickly be achieved, and I might be restored to my family in peace and happiness. My promise fulfilled, the monster would depart for ever. Or (so my fond fancy imaged) some accident might meanwhile occur to destroy him, and put an end to my slavery for ever.

'These feelings dictated my answer to my father. I expressed a wish to visit England; but, concealing the true reasons of this request, I clothed my desires under a guise— again my hand recorded other words— which excited no suspicion, while I urged my desire with an earnestness that easily induced my father to comply. After so long a period of an absorbing melancholy, that resembled madness in its intensity and effects, he was glad to find that I was capable of taking pleasure in the idea of such a journey, and he hoped that change of scene and varied amusement would, before my return, have restored me entirely to myself.

'The duration of my absence was left to my own choice; a few months, or at most a year, was the period contemplated. One paternal kind precaution he had taken to ensure my having a companion. Without previously communicating with me, he had, in concert with Elizabeth, arranged that Clerval should join me at Strasburgh. This interfered with the solitude I coveted for the prosecution of my task; yet at the commencement of my journey the presence of my friend could in no way be an impediment, and truly I rejoiced that thus I should be saved many hours of lonely, maddening reflection. Nay, Henry might stand between me and the intrusion of my foe. If I were alone, would he not at times force his abhorred presence on me, to remind me of my task, or to contemplate its progress?

'To England, therefore, I was bound, and it was understood that my union with Elizabeth should take place immediately on my return. My father's age rendered him extremely averse to delay. For myself, there was one reward I promised myself from my detested toils—one consolation for my unparalleled sufferings; it was the prospect of that day when, enfranchised from my miserable slavery, I might claim Elizabeth, and forget the past in my union with her.

'I now made arrangements for my journey; but one feeling haunted me, which filled me with fear and agitation. During my absence I should leave my friends unconscious of the existence of their enemy, and unprotected from his attacks, exasperated as he might be by my departure. But he had promised to follow me wherever I might go; and would he not accompany me to England? This imagination was dreadful in itself, but soothing, inasmuch as it supposed the safety of my friends. I was agonized with the idea of the possibility that the reverse of this might happen. But through the whole period during which I was the slave of my creature, I allowed myself to be governed by the impulses of the moment; and my present sensations strongly intimated that the fiend would follow me, and exempt my family from the danger of his machinations.

Again and again my hand revises his words. Why? When will this madness end?

'It was in the latter end of September that I again quitted my native country. My journey had been my own suggestion, and Elizabeth, therefore, acquiesced: but she was filled with disquiet at the idea of my suffering, away from her, the inroads of misery and grief. It had been her care which provided me a companion in Clerval—and yet a man is blind to a thousand minute circumstances, which call forth a woman's sedulous attention. She longed to bid me hasten my return,—a thousand conflicting emotions rendered her mute, as she bade me a tearful silent farewell.

'I threw myself into the carriage that was to convey me away, hardly knowing whither I was going, and careless of what was passing around. I remembered only, and it was with a bitter anguish that I reflected on it, to order that my chemical instruments should be packed to go with me: for I resolved to fulfil my promise while abroad, and return, if possible, a free man. Filled with dreary imaginations, I passed through many beautiful and majestic scenes; but my eyes were fixed and unobserving. I could only think of the bourne of my travels, and the work which was to occupy me whilst they endured.

'After some days spent in listless indolence, during which I traversed many leagues, I arrived at Strasburgh, where I waited two days for Clerval. He came. Alas, how great was the contrast between us! He was alive to every new scene; joyful when he saw the beauties of the setting sun, and more happy when he beheld it rise, and recommence a new day. He pointed out to me the shifting colours of the landscape, and the appearances of the sky. "This is what it is to live;" he cried, "now I enjoy existence! But you, my dear Frankenstein, wherefore are you desponding and sorrowful?" In truth, I was occupied by gloomy thoughts, and neither saw the descent of the evening star, nor the golden sun-rise reflected in the Rhine.— And you, my friend would be far more amused with the journal of Clerval, who observed the scenery with an eye of feeling and delight, than to listen to my reflections. I, a miserable wretch, haunted by a curse that shut up every avenue to enjoyment'— is he addressing me directly or Walton? Curious!

'We had agreed to descend the Rhine in a boat from Strasburgh to Rotterdam, whence we might take shipping for London. During this voyage, we passed by many willowy islands, and saw several beautiful towns. We staid a day at Manheim, and, on the fifth from our departure from Strasburgh, arrived at Mayence. The course of the Rhine below Mayence becomes much more picturesque. The river descends rapidly, and winds between hills, not high, but steep, and of beautiful forms. We saw many ruined castles standing on the edges of precipices, surrounded by black woods, high and inaccessible.'

Oh! Ho! I know this place. My Beloved wished to tarry at this very castle because he personally knew several members of the 'Kreis der Empfindsamen', a literary circle from Darmstadt, who used the castle for their readings. Did they believe they were a Hellfire Club reciting their poems as if spells to summon the Great Dragon himself, that old serpent, called the Devil, and Satan, who deceives the whole world? At the Castle Frankenstein, we encountered students from the University of Strasbourg, of which Johann Konrad Dippel was an infamous alumnus. We learned from them of Dippel's discovery of the 'Elixir of Life', as evidenced by his *Maladies and Remedies of the Life of the Flesh*. He made this dark, viscous, tar-like, and putrid oil through the destructive distillation of bones. How could rotting death ever be an 'elixir of life'? The students spoke quiet highly of the Pietist theologian, physician, and alchemist, though they admitted that one Emanuel Swedenborg, both once a devoted disciple and then staunch critic had dismissed him as 'bound to no principles, but was in general opposed to all, whoever they may be, of whatever principle or faith ... becoming angry with any one for contradicting him.' How Swedenborg had fallen from once being enamoured to then being repulsed by 'a most vile devil... who attempted wicked things.' But the students hailed the glorious alchemist (though locals remembered him as notorious graverobber), who experimented in anatomy and supposedly transferred the souls from one cadaver to another with a funnel, as an exorcist and a saint! Did he not, they claimed, create an alchemic potion concocted from boiled animal bones and their flesh to supplant the *Rituale Romanum*, and therefore the Vatican, in the exorcising of demons? 'How my mind has born so many curious parts of this tale being related to me by my pale student of the unhallowed arts!

'This part of the Rhine, indeed, presents a singularly variegated landscape. In one spot you view rugged hills, ruined castles overlooking tremendous precipices, with the dark Rhine rushing beneath; and, on the sudden turn of a promontory, flourishing vineyards, with green sloping banks, and a meandering river, and populous towns, occupy the scene.

'We travelled at the time of the vintage, and heard the song of the labourers, as we glided down the stream. Even I, depressed in mind, and my spirits continually agitated by gloomy feelings, even I was pleased. I lay at the bottom of the boat, and, as I gazed on the cloudless blue sky, I seemed to drink in a tranquillity to which I had long been a stranger. And if these were my sensations, who can describe those of Henry? He felt as if he had been transported to Fairy-land, and enjoyed a happiness seldom tasted by man. "I have seen," he said, "the most beautiful scenes of my own country; I have visited the lakes of Lucerne and Uri, where the snowy mountains descend almost perpendicularly to the water, casting black and impenetrable shades, which would cause a gloomy and mournful appearance, were it not for the most verdant islands that relieve the eye by their gay appearance; I have seen this lake agitated by a tempest, when the wind tore up whirlwinds of water, and gave you an idea of what the water-spout must be on the great ocean, and the waves dash with fury the base of the mountain, where the priest and his mistress were overwhelmed by an avalanche, and where their dying voices are still said to be heard amid the pauses of the nightly wind; I have seen the mountains of La Valais, and the Pays de Vaud: but this country, Victor, pleases me more than all those wonders. The mountains of Switzerland are more majestic and strange; but there is a charm in the banks of this divine river, that I never before saw equalled. Look at that castle which overhangs yon precipice; and that also on the island, almost concealed amongst the foliage of those lovely trees; and now that group of labourers coming from among their vines; and that village half-hid in the recess of the mountain. Oh, surely, the spirit that inhabits and guards this place has a soul more in harmony with man, than those who pile the glacier, or retire to the inaccessible peaks of the mountains of our own country."

'Clerval! beloved friend! even now it delights me to record your words, and to dwell on the praise of which you are so eminently deserving. He was a being formed in the "very poetry of nature." His wild and enthusiastic imagination was chastened by the sensibility of his heart. His soul overflowed with ardent affections, and his friendship was of that devoted and wondrous nature that the worldly-minded teach us to look for only in the imagination. But even human sympathies were not sufficient to satisfy his eager mind. The scenery of external nature, which others regard only with admiration, he loved with ardour:

> *"The sounding cataract*
> *Haunted him* like a passion: the tall rock,
> *The mountain, and the deep and gloomy wood,*
> *Their colours and their forms, were then to him*
> *An appetite; a feeling, and a love,*
> *That had no need of a remoter charm,*
> *By thought supplied, or any interest*
> *Unborrowed from the eye."*

Oh! William Wordsworth! His words are worth their weight in gold! But another anachronism. I believe this poem was written after the dates related to me in this tale of Victor's. Again, my mind plays tricks upon me. Curious.

'And where does he now exist? Is this gentle and lovely being lost for ever? Has this mind so replete with ideas, imaginations fanciful and magnificent, which formed a world, whose existence depended on the life of its creator; has this mind perished? Does it now only exist in my memory? No, it is not thus; your form so divinely wrought, and beaming with beauty, has decayed, but your spirit still visits and consoles your unhappy friend.

'Pardon this gush of sorrow; these ineffectual words are but a slight tribute to the unexampled worth of Henry, but they soothe my heart, overflowing with the anguish which his remembrance creates. I will proceed with my tale.

'Beyond Cologne we descended to the plains of Holland; and we resolved to post the remainder of our way; for the wind was contrary, and the stream of the river was too gentle to aid us.

'Our journey here lost the interest arising from beautiful scenery; but we arrived in a few days at Rotterdam, whence we proceeded by sea to England. It was on a clear morning, in the latter days of December, that I first saw the white cliffs of Britain. The banks of the Thames presented a new scene; they were flat, but fertile, and almost every town was marked by the remembrance of some story. We saw Tilbury Fort, and remembered the Spanish armada; Gravesend, Woolwich, and Greenwich, places which I had heard of even in my country.

'At length we saw the numerous steeples of London, St. Paul's towering above all, and the Tower famed in English history.'

How I know them all so well! Curious!

Chapter III

London was our present point of rest; we determined to remain several months in this wonderful and celebrated city. Clerval desired the intercourse of the men of genius and talent who flourished at this time; but this was with me a secondary object; I was principally occupied with the means of obtaining the information necessary for the completion of my promise, and quickly availed myself of the letters of introduction that I had brought with me, addressed to the most distinguished natural philosophers.

'If this journey had taken place during my days of study and happiness, it would have afforded me inexpressible pleasure. But a blight had come over my existence, and I only visited these people for the sake of the information they might give me on the subject in which my interest was so terribly profound. Company was irksome to me; when alone, I could fill my mind with the sights of heaven and earth; the voice of Henry soothed me, and I could thus cheat myself into a transitory peace. But busy uninteresting joyous faces brought back despair to my heart. I saw an insurmountable barrier placed between me and my fellow-men; this barrier was sealed with the blood of William and Justine; and to reflect on the events connected with those names filled my soul with anguish.

'But in Clerval I saw the image of my former self; he was inquisitive, and anxious to gain experience and instruction. The difference of manners which he observed was to him an inexhaustible source of instruction and amusement. He was also pursuing an object he had long had in view. His design was to visit India, in the belief that he had in his knowledge of its various languages, and in the views he had taken of its society, the means of materially assisting the progress of European colonisation and trade. In Britain only could he further the execution of his plan. He was for ever busy; and the only check to his enjoyments was my sorrowful and dejected mind. I tried to conceal this as much as possible, that I might not debar him from the pleasures natural to one, who was entering on a new scene of life, undisturbed by any care or bitter recollection. I often refused to accompany him, alleging another engagement, that I might remain alone. I now also began to collect the materials necessary for my new creation'— Oh! Ho! He does intend to create a feminine creature for his Creation, but where-oh-where would he store these body parts, if this is what his intention is with these words?— 'and this was to me like the torture of single drops of water continually falling on the head. Every thought that was devoted to it was an extreme anguish, and every word that I spoke in allusion to it caused my lips to quiver, and my heart to palpitate.

'After passing some months in London, we received a letter from a person in Scotland, who had formerly been our visitor at Geneva. He mentioned the beauties of his native country, and asked us if those were not sufficient allurements to induce us to prolong our journey as far north as Perth, where he resided. Clerval eagerly desired to accept this invitation; and I, although I abhorred society, wished to view again mountains and streams, and all the wondrous works with which Nature adorns her chosen dwelling-places.

'We had arrived in England at the beginning of October'— how I believed he said 'December'. If Victor give me pause to flip back through my journal I can see... ah... yes, he did say 'December'! Curious! This error must be corrected— 'and it was now February. We accordingly determined to commence our journey towards the north at the expiration of another month. In this expedition we did not intend to follow the great road to Edinburgh, but to visit Windsor, Oxford, Matlock, and the Cumberland lakes, resolving to arrive at the completion of this tour about the end of July. I packed my chemical instruments, and the materials I had collected, resolving to finish my labours in some obscure nook in the northern highlands of Scotland.

'We quitted London on the 27th of March, and remained a few days at Windsor, rambling in its beautiful forest. This was a new scene to us mountaineers; the majestic oaks, the quantity of game, and the herds of stately deer, were all novelties to us.

'From thence we proceeded to Oxford. As we entered this city, our minds were filled with the remembrance of the events that had been transacted there more than a century and a half before. It was here that Charles I. had collected his forces. This city had remained faithful to him, after the whole nation had forsaken his cause to join the standard of parliament and liberty. The memory of that unfortunate king, and his companions, the amiable Falkland, the insolent Gower, his queen, and son, gave a peculiar interest to every part of the city, which they might be supposed to have inhabited. The spirit of elder days found a dwelling here, and we delighted to trace its footsteps. If these feelings had not found an imaginary gratification, the appearance of the city had yet in itself sufficient beauty to obtain our admiration. The colleges are ancient and picturesque; the streets are almost magnificent; and the lovely Isis, which flows beside it through meadows of exquisite verdure, is spread forth into a placid expanse of waters, which reflects its majestic assemblage of towers, and spires, and domes, embosomed among aged trees.

'I enjoyed this scene; and yet my enjoyment was embittered both by the memory of the past, and the anticipation of the future. I was formed for peaceful happiness. During my youthful days discontent never visited my mind; and if I was ever overcome by *ennui*, the sight of what is beautiful in nature, or the study of what is excellent and sublime in the productions of man, could always interest my heart, and communicate elasticity to my spirits. But I am a blasted tree; the bolt has entered my soul; and I felt then that I should survive to exhibit, what I shall soon cease to be— a miserable spectacle of wrecked humanity, pitiable to others, and abhorrent to myself.

'We passed a considerable period at Oxford, rambling among its environs, and endeavouring to identify every spot which might relate to the most animating epoch of English history. Our little voyages of discovery were often prolonged by the successive objects that presented themselves. We visited the tomb of the illustrious Hampden, and the field on which that patriot fell. For a moment my soul was elevated from its debasing and miserable fears to contemplate the divine ideas of liberty and self-sacrifice, of which these sights were the monuments and the remembrancers. For an instant I dared to shake off my chains, and look around me with a free and lofty spirit; but the iron had eaten into my flesh, and I sank again, trembling and hopeless, into my miserable self.

'We left Oxford with regret, and proceeded to Matlock, which was our next place of rest. The country in the neighbourhood of this village resembled, to a greater degree, the scenery of Switzerland; but every thing is on a lower scale, and the green hills want the crown of distant white Alps, which always attend on the piny mountains of my native country. We visited the wondrous cave, and the little cabinets of natural history, where the curiosities are disposed in the same manner as in the collections at Servox and Chamounix. The latter name made me tremble, when pronounced by Henry; and I hastened to quit Matlock, with which that terrible scene was thus associated.

'From Derby still journeying northward, we passed two months in Cumberland and Westmoreland. I could now almost fancy myself among the Swiss mountains. The little patches of snow which yet lingered on the northern sides of the mountains, the lakes, and the dashing of the rocky streams, were all familiar and dear sights to me. Here also we made some acquaintances, who almost contrived to cheat me into happiness. The delight of Clerval was proportionably greater than mine; his mind expanded in the company of men of talent, and he found in his own nature greater capacities and resources than he could have imagined himself to have possessed while he associated with his inferiors. "I could pass my life here," said he to me; "and among these mountains I should scarcely regret Switzerland and the Rhine."

'But he found that a traveller's life is one that includes much pain amidst its enjoyments. His feelings are for ever on the stretch; and when he begins to sink into repose, he finds himself obliged to quit that on which he rests in pleasure for something new, which again engages his attention, and which also he forsakes for other novelties.

'We had scarcely visited the various lakes of Cumberland and Westmoreland, and conceived an affection for some of the inhabitants, when the period of our appointment with our Scotch friend approached, and we left them to travel on. For my own part I was not sorry. I had now neglected my promise for some time, and I feared the effects of the dæmon's disappointment. He might remain in Switzerland, and wreak his vengeance on my relatives. This idea pursued me, and tormented me at every moment from which I might otherwise have snatched repose and peace. I waited for my letters with feverish impatience: if they were delayed, I was miserable, and overcome by a thousand fears; and when they arrived, and I saw the superscription of Elizabeth or my father, I hardly dared to read and ascertain my fate.'

How I have been enjoying this travelogue of dear Victor's! Its reminisces reminds me of the one I and my Beloved are composing of our present tour and that of last year. I have been drawn into my own memories of these lands so completely that—

'Sometimes I thought that the fiend followed me, and might expedite my remissness by murdering my companion. When these thoughts possessed me, I would not quit Henry for a moment, but followed him as his shadow, to protect him from the fancied rage of his destroyer. I felt as if I had committed some great crime, the consciousness of which haunted me. I was guiltless, but I had indeed drawn down a horrible curse upon my head, as mortal as that of crime.

— Damn Victor to Hellfire Eternal for breaking me out of my complacency! And now his excepts his travelogue to resume? Damn him!

'I visited Edinburgh with languid eyes and mind; and yet that city might have interested the most unfortunate being. Clerval did not like it so well as Oxford; for the antiquity of the latter city was more pleasing to him. But the beauty and regularity of the new town of Edinburgh, its romantic castle, and its environs, the most delightful in the world, Arthur's Seat, St. Bernard's Well, and the Pentland Hills, compensated him for the change, and filled him with cheerfulness and admiration. But I was impatient to arrive at the termination of my journey.

'We left Edinburgh in a week, passing through Coupar, St. Andrews, and along the banks of the Tay, to Perth, where our friend expected us. But I was in no mood to laugh and talk with strangers, or enter into their feelings or plans with the good humour expected from a guest; and accordingly I told Clerval that I wished to make the tour of Scotland alone. "Do you," said I, "enjoy yourself, and let this be our rendezvous. I may be absent a month or two; but do not interfere with my motions, I entreat you: leave me to peace and solitude for a short time; and when I return, I hope it will be with a lighter heart, more congenial to your own temper."

'Henry wished to dissuade me; but, seeing me bent on this plan, ceased to remonstrate. He entreated me to write often. "I had rather be with you," he said, "in your solitary rambles, than with these Scotch people, whom I do not know: hasten then, my dear friend, to return, that I may again feel myself somewhat at home, which I cannot do in your absence."

'Having parted from my friend, I determined to visit some remote spot of Scotland, and finish my work in solitude. I did not doubt but that the monster followed me, and would discover himself to me when I should have finished, that he might receive his companion.

'With this resolution I traversed the northern highlands, and fixed on one of the remotest of the Orkneys as the scene labours. It was a place fitted for such a work, being hardly more than a rock, whose high sides were continually beaten upon by the waves. The soil was barren, scarcely affording pasture for a few miserable cows, and oatmeal for its inhabitants, which consisted of five persons, whose gaunt and scraggy limbs gave tokens of their miserable fare. Vegetables and bread, when they indulged in such luxuries, and even fresh water, was to be procured from the main land, which was about five miles distant.

'On the whole island there were but three miserable huts, and one of these was vacant when I arrived. This I hired. It contained but two rooms, and these exhibited all the squalidness of the most miserable penury. The thatch had fallen in, the walls were unplastered, and the door was off its hinges. I ordered it to be repaired, bought some furniture, and took possession; an incident which would, doubtless, have occasioned some surprise, had not all the senses of the cottagers been benumbed by want and squalid poverty. As it was, I lived ungazed at and unmolested, hardly thanked for the pittance of food and clothes which I gave; so much does suffering blunt even the coarsest sensations of men.

'In this retreat I devoted the morning to labour; but in the evening, when the weather permitted, I walked on the stony beach of the sea, to listen to the waves as they roared, and dashed at my feet. It was a monotonous, yet ever-changing scene. I thought of Switzerland; it was far different from this desolate and appalling landscape. Its hills are covered with vines, and its cottages are scattered thickly in the plains. Its fair lakes reflect a blue and gentle sky; and, when troubled by the winds, their tumult is but as the play of a lively infant, when compared to the roarings of the giant ocean.

'In this manner I distributed my occupations when I first arrived; but, as I proceeded in my labour, it became every day more horrible and irksome to me. Sometimes I could not prevail on myself to enter my laboratory for several days; and at other times I toiled day and night in order to complete my work. It was indeed a filthy process in which I was engaged.' Again I am reminded of Leonardo's own revulsion towards the feminine creature. 'During my first experiment, a kind of enthusiastic frenzy had blinded me to the horror of my employment; my mind was intently fixed on the consummation of my labour, and my eyes were shut to the horror of my proceedings. But now I went to it in cold blood, and my heart often sickened at the work of my hands.

'Thus situated, employed in the most detestable occupation, immersed in a solitude where nothing could for an instant call my attention from the actual scene in which I was engaged, my spirits became unequal; I grew restless and nervous. Every moment I feared to meet my persecutor. Sometimes I sat with my eyes fixed on the ground, fearing to raise them lest they should encounter the object which I so much dreaded to behold. I feared to wander from the sight of my fellow-creatures, lest when alone he should come to claim his companion.

'In the mean time I worked on, and my labour was already considerably advanced. I looked towards its completion with a tremulous and eager hope, which I dared not trust myself to question, but which was intermixed with obscure forebodings of evil, that made my heart sicken in my bosom.

Chapter IV

I sat one evening in my laboratory; the sun had set, and the moon was just rising from the sea; I had not sufficient light for my employment, and I remained idle, in a pause of consideration of whether I should leave my labour for the night, or hasten its conclusion by an unremitting attention to it. As I sat, a train of reflection occurred to me, which led me to consider the effects of what I was now doing. Three years before I was engaged in the same manner, and had created a fiend whose unparalleled barbarity had desolated my heart, and filled it for ever with the bitterest remorse. I was now about to form another being, of whose dispositions I was alike ignorant; she might become ten thousand times more malignant than her mate, and delight, for its own sake, in murder and wretchedness. He had sworn to quit the neighbourhood of man, and hide himself in deserts; but she had not; and she, who in all probability was to become a thinking and reasoning animal, might refuse to comply with a compact made before her creation. They might even hate each other; the creature who already lived loathed his own deformity, and might he not conceive a greater abhorrence for it when it came before his eyes in the female form? She also might turn with disgust from him to the superior beauty of man; she might quit him, and he be again alone, exasperated by the fresh provocation of being deserted by one of his own species.'

Is my mind foreshadowing the clear eventuality of this tale of Victor's?

'Even if they were to leave Europe, and inhabit the deserts of the new world, yet one of the first results of those sympathies for which the dæmon thirsted would be children, and a race of devils would be propagated upon the earth, who might make the very existence of the species of man a condition precarious and full of terror. Had I a right, for my own benefit, to inflict this curse upon everlasting generations? I had before been moved by the sophisms of the being I had created; I had been struck senseless by his fiendish threats: but now, for the first time, the wickedness of my promise burst upon me; I shuddered to think that future ages might curse me as their pest, whose selfishness had not hesitated to buy its own peace at the price perhaps of the existence of the whole human race.

'I trembled, and my heart failed within me; when, on looking up, I saw, by the light of the moon, the dæmon at the casement. A ghastly grin wrinkled his lips as he gazed on me, where I sat fulfilling the task which he had allotted to me. Yes, he had followed me in my travels; he had loitered in forests, hid himself in caves, or taken refuge in wide and desert heaths; and he now came to mark my progress, and claim the fulfilment of my promise.

'As I looked on him, his countenance expressed the utmost extent of malice and treachery. I thought with a sensation of madness on my promise of creating another like to him, and, trembling with passion, tore to pieces the thing on which I was engaged. The wretch saw me destroy the creature on whose future existence he depended for happiness, and, with a howl of devilish despair and revenge, withdrew.'

No! Do not destroy the last vestiges of your Creation's hopes and dreams? You rend the flesh freshly sewn together apart, casting one limb against this unplastered wall and the other limb against the other. Her head is torn from her neck; the stitches tearing apart with the mouth agape in horror as if to scream if only the lungs had any strength to draw breath. You reach into the birth canal of his failed experiment and tear out the very womb that might give birth to an entire race of Creatures bent on the destruction of the parent species. You squeeze into your fist the very womb you have so carefully, horrifyingly constructed that will never now know life growing within it! The puss and blood dripped onto the floor of our apartment. The seed, if the Creation possesses any semen in his own dried stones, will never now know the freedom of swimming with the rich, lifegiving waters of the female Creation's birth canal. There will be no egg to greet the seed in this once carefully, horrifyingly constructed womb. With teeth clenched and blood dripping from a bitten lip, you invite your own destruction!

How I long to be no longer haunted by my pale student of the unhallowed arts. I am done with him! His soul is as rotten and worm infested as an apple left on the windowsill to fester in the sun. My pale student of the unhallowed arts, whom I longed to know more about from our first chance encounter during that thunderstorm-and-lightning-fuelled nightmare after a spirited and galvanising debate, was shown to me to be nothing more than failed student with a hollow heart.

And why did the Creation flee? Why should he not attempt to halt the destruction of his Bride? Mary, this does not make any sense! Victor's Creation should thrash him within an inch of his miserable life! But instead, your mind, he is out in the world doing what? Paddling about in his little boat? Mary, I am disgusted by your own literary decisions. But who am I to alter the story being related to me by my failed student with a hollow heart?

'I left the room, and, locking the door, made a solemn vow in my own heart never to resume my labours; and then, with trembling steps, I sought my own apartment. I was alone; none were near me to dissipate the gloom, and relieve me from the sickening oppression of the most terrible reveries.

'Several hours past, and I remained near my window gazing on the sea; it was almost motionless, for the winds were hushed, and all nature reposed under the eye of the quiet moon. A few fishing vessels alone specked the water, and now and then the gentle breeze wafted the sound of voices, as the fishermen called to one another. I felt the silence, although I was hardly conscious of its extreme profundity until my ear was suddenly arrested by the paddling of oars near the shore, and a person landed close to my house.

'In a few minutes after, I heard the creaking of my door, as if some one endeavoured to open it softly. I trembled from head to foot; I felt a presentiment of who it was, and wished to rouse one of the peasants who dwelt in a cottage not far from mine; but I was overcome by the sensation of helplessness, so often felt in frightful dreams, when you in vain endeavour to fly from an impending danger, and was rooted to the spot.

'Presently I heard the sound of footsteps along the passage; the door opened, and the wretch whom I dreaded appeared. Shutting the door, he approached me, and said, in a smothered voice—

I shall tear all these four paragraphs out of my journal and cast them into the fire beside which Victor sits and jump straight away with the trashing of the failed student with a hollow heart! Why are these words still present in my journal? Why haven't I struck them out with violent slashes of my pen? Blotted out of existence with ink. But this is *not* my tale which is being told. It is Victor's and Victor had told it in his own fashion and in his own time. Sometimes the author of the work is not truly the author but merely taking dictation. And yes, I am merely taking dictation!

' "You have destroyed the work which you began; what is it that you intend? Do you dare to break your promise? I have endured toil and misery: I left Switzerland with you; I crept along the shores of the Rhine, among its willow islands, and over the summits of its hills. I have dwelt many months in the heaths of England, and among the deserts of Scotland. I have endured incalculable fatigue, and cold, and hunger; do you dare destroy my hopes?"

' "Begone! I do break my promise; never will I create another like yourself, equal in deformity and wickedness."

' "Slave, I before reasoned with you, but you have proved yourself unworthy of my condescension. Remember that I have power; you believe yourself miserable, but I can make you so wretched that the light of day will be hateful to you. You are my creator, but I am your master;— obey!"

' "The hour of my weakness is past, and the period of your power is arrived. Your threats cannot move me to do an act of wickedness; but they confirm me in a resolution of not creating you a companion in vice. Shall I, in cool blood, set loose upon the earth a dæmon, whose delight is in death and wretchedness. Begone! I am firm, and your words will only exasperate my rage."

The monster saw my determination in my face, and gnashed his teeth in the impotence of anger. "Shall each man," cried he, "find a wife for his bosom, and each beast have his mate, and I be alone?' Ah! Does not God command the man and the women whom He has creating saying, *Be fruitful, and multiply, and replenish the earth, and subdue it: and have dominion over the fish of the sea, and over the fowl of the air, and over every living thing that moveth upon the earth.*[44] Little does the Creation know that Gods command, here, seals his fate! 'I had feelings of affection, and they were requited by detestation and scorn. Man, you may hate; but beware! Your hours will pass in dread and misery, and soon the bolt will fall which must ravish from you your happiness for ever. Are you to be happy, while I grovel in the intensity of my wretchedness? You can blast my other passions; but revenge remains— revenge, henceforth dearer than light or food! I may die; but first you, my tyrant and tormentor, shall curse the sun that gazes on your misery. Beware; for I am fearless, and therefore powerful. I will watch with the wiliness of a snake, that I may sting with its venom. Man, you shall repent of the injuries you inflict."

' "Devil, cease; and do not poison the air with these sounds of malice. I have declared my resolution to you, and I am no coward to bend beneath words. Leave me; I am inexorable."

' "It is well. I go; but remember, I shall be with you on your wedding-night."

'I started forward, and exclaimed, "Villain! before you sign my death-warrant, be sure that you are yourself safe."

'I would have seized him; but he eluded me, and quitted the house with precipitation: in a few moments I saw him in his boat, which shot across the waters with an arrowy swiftness, and was soon lost amidst the waves.

'All was again silent; but his words rung in my ears. I burned with rage to pursue the murderer of my peace, and precipitate him into the ocean. I walked up and down my room hastily and perturbed, while my imagination conjured up a thousand images to torment and sting me.

---

44 From Genesis 1:28 from the Authorized King James Translation of the Holy Bible, published in 1611.

Why had I not followed him, and closed with him in mortal strife? But I had suffered him to depart, and he had directed his course towards the main land. I shuddered to think who might be the next victim sacrificed to his insatiate revenge. And then I thought again of his words— "*I WILL BE WITH YOU ON YOUR WEDDING-NIGHT!*" That then was the period fixed for the fulfilment of my destiny. In that hour I should die, and at once satisfy and extinguish his malice. The prospect did not move me to fear; yet when I thought of my beloved Elizabeth,— of her tears and endless sorrow, when she should find her lover so barbarously snatched from her,— tears, the first I had shed for many months, streamed from my eyes, and I resolved not to fall before my enemy without a bitter struggle.

'The night passed away, and the sun rose from the ocean; my feelings became calmer, if it may be called calmness, when the violence of rage sinks into the depths of despair. I left the house, the horrid scene of the last night's contention, and walked on the beach of the sea, which I almost regarded as an insuperable barrier between me and my fellow-creatures; nay, a wish that such should prove the fact stole across me. I desired that I might pass my life on that barren rock, wearily it is true, but uninterrupted by any sudden shock of misery. If I returned, it was to be sacrificed, or to see those whom I most loved die under the grasp of a dæmon whom I had myself created.

'I walked about the isle like a restless spectre, separated from all it loved, and miserable in the separation. When it became noon, and the sun rose higher, I lay down on the grass, and was overpowered by a deep sleep. I had been awake the whole of the preceding night, my nerves were agitated, and my eyes inflamed by watching and misery. The sleep into which I now sunk refreshed me; and when I awoke, I again felt as if I belonged to a race of human beings like myself, and I began to reflect upon what had passed with greater composure; yet still the words of the fiend rung in my ears like a death-knell, they appeared like a dream, yet distinct and oppressive as a reality.

'The sun had far descended, and I still sat on the shore, satisfying my appetite, which had become ravenous, with an oaten cake, when I saw a fishing-boat land close to me, and one of the men brought me a packet; it contained letters from Geneva, and one from Clerval, entreating me to join him. He said that he was wearing away his time fruitlessly where he was; that letters from the friends he had formed in London desired his return to complete the negotiation they had entered into for his Indian enterprise. He could not any longer delay his departure; but as his journey to London might be followed, even sooner than he now conjectured, by his longer voyage, he entreated me to bestow as much of my society on him as I could spare. He besought me, therefore, to leave my solitary isle, and to meet him at Perth, that we might proceed southwards together. This letter in a degree recalled me to life, and I determined to quit my island at the expiration of two days.

'Yet, before I departed, there was a task to perform, on which I shuddered to reflect: I must pack my chemical instruments; and for that purpose I must enter the room which had been the scene of my odious work, and I must handle those utensils, the sight of which was sickening to me. The next morning, at day-break, I summoned sufficient courage, and unlocked the door of my laboratory. The remains of the half-finished creature, whom I had destroyed, lay scattered on the floor, and I almost felt as if I had mangled the living flesh of a human being. I paused to collect myself, and then entered the chamber. With trembling hand I conveyed the instruments out of the room; but I reflected that I ought not to leave the relics of my work to excite the horror and suspicion of the peasants, and I accordingly put them into a basket, with a great quantity of stones, and laying them up, determined to throw them into the sea that very night; and in the mean time I sat upon the beach, employed in cleaning and arranging my chemical apparatus.

'Nothing could be more complete than the alteration that had taken place in my feelings since the night of the appearance of the dæmon. I had before regarded my promise with a gloomy despair, as a thing that, with whatever consequences, must be fulfilled; but I now felt as if a film had been taken from before my eyes, and that I, for the first time, saw clearly. The idea of renewing my labours did not for one instant occur to me; the threat I had heard weighed on my thoughts, but I did not reflect that a voluntary act of mine could avert it. I had resolved in my own mind, that to create another like the fiend I had first made would be an act of the basest and most atrocious selfishness; and I banished from my mind every thought that could lead to a different conclusion.

'Between two and three in the morning the moon rose; and I then, putting my basket aboard a little skiff, sailed out about four miles from the shore. The scene was perfectly solitary: a few boats were returning towards land, but I sailed away from them. I felt as if I was about the commission of a dreadful crime, and avoided with shuddering anxiety any encounter with my fellow-creatures. At one time the moon, which had before been clear, was suddenly overspread by a thick cloud, and I took advantage of the moment of darkness, and cast my basket into the sea; I listened to the gurgling sound as it sunk, and then sailed away from the spot.' And in an instant, my failed student with a hollow heart believes he had rid not only himself but all of humanity of his crimes against humanity. The evidence may have been cast to the bottom of the sea, but it will live in your heart forever, Victor. 'The sky became clouded; but the air was pure, although chilled by the north-east breeze that was then rising. But it refreshed me, and filled me with such agreeable sensations, that I resolved to prolong my stay on the water, and fixing the rudder in a direct position, stretched myself at the bottom of the boat. Clouds hid the moon, every thing was obscure, and I heard only the sound of the boat, as its keel cut through the waves; the murmur lulled me, and in a short time I slept soundly.

'I do not know how long I remained in this situation, but when I awoke I found that the sun had already mounted considerably. The wind was high, and the waves continually threatened the safety of my little skiff. I found that the wind was north-east, and must have driven me far from the coast from which I had embarked. I endeavoured to change my course, but quickly found that if I again made the attempt the boat would be instantly filled with water. Thus situated, my only resource was to drive before the wind. I confess that I felt a few sensations of terror. I had no compass with me, and was so little acquainted with the geography of this part of the world that the sun was of little benefit to me. I might be driven into the wide Atlantic, and feel all the tortures of starvation, or be swallowed up in the immeasurable waters that roared and buffeted around me. I had already been out many hours, and felt the torment of a burning thirst, a prelude to my other sufferings. I looked on the heavens, which were covered by clouds that flew before the wind only to be replaced by others: I looked upon the sea, it was to be my grave. "Fiend," I exclaimed, "your task is already fulfilled!" I thought of Elizabeth, of my father, and of Clerval; all left behind, on whom the monster might satisfy his sanguinary and merciless passions. This idea plunged me into a reverie, so despairing and frightful, that even now, when the scene is on the point of closing before me for ever, I shudder to reflect on it.

'Some hours passed thus; but by degrees, as the sun declined towards the horizon, the wind died away into a gentle breeze, and the sea became free from breakers. But these gave place to a heavy swell; I felt sick, and hardly able to hold the rudder, when suddenly I saw a line of high land towards the south.

'Almost spent, as I was, by fatigue, and the dreadful suspense I endured for several hours, this sudden certainty of life rushed like a flood of warm joy to my heart, and tears gushed from my eyes.

'How mutable are our feelings, and how strange is that clinging love we have of life even in the excess of misery! I constructed another sail with a part of my dress, and eagerly steered my course towards the land. It had a wild and rocky appearance; but as I approached nearer, I easily perceived the traces of cultivation. I saw vessels near the shore, and

found myself suddenly transported back to the neighbourhood of civilized man. I eagerly traced the windings of the land, and hailed a steeple
which I at length saw issuing from behind a small promontory. As I was
in a state of extreme debility, I resolved to sail directly towards the town
as a place where I could most easily procure nourishment. Fortunately I
had money with me. As I turned the promontory, I perceived a small neat
town and a good harbour, which I entered, my heart bounding with joy
at my unexpected escape.

'As I was occupied in fixing the boat and arranging the sails, several
people crowded towards the spot. They seemed very much surprised at
my appearance; but, instead of offering me any assistance, whispered
together with gestures that at any other time might have produced in
me a slight sensation of alarm. As it was, I merely remarked that they
spoke English; and I therefore addressed them in that language: "My
good friends," said I, "will you be so kind as to tell me the name of this
town, and inform me where I am?"

' "You will know that soon enough," replied a man with a gruff voice.
"May be you are come to a place that will not prove much to your taste;
but you will not be consulted as to your quarters, I promise you."

'I was exceedingly surprised on receiving so rude an answer from
a stranger; and I was also disconcerted on perceiving the frowning and
angry countenances of his companions. "Why do you answer me so
roughly?" I replied: "surely it is not the custom of Englishmen to receive
strangers so inhospitably."

' "I do not know," said the man, "what the custom of the English may
be; but it is the custom of the Irish to hate villains."

'While this strange dialogue continued, I perceived the crowd rapidly
increase. Their faces expressed a mixture of curiosity and anger, which
annoyed, and in some degree alarmed me. I inquired the way to the inn;
but no one replied. I then moved forward, and a murmuring sound arose
from the crowd as they followed and surrounded me; when an ill-looking
man approaching, tapped me on the shoulder, and said, "Come, Sir, you
must follow me to Mr. Kirwin's, to give an account of yourself."

' "Who is Mr Kirwin? Why am I to give an account of myself? Is not
this a free country?"

' "Aye, Sir, free enough for honest folks. Mr Kirwin is a magistrate;
and you are to give an account of the death of a gentleman who was found
murdered here last night."

'This answer startled me; but I presently recovered myself. I was innocent; that could easily be proved: accordingly I followed my conductor
in silence, and was led to one of the best houses in the town. I was ready
to sink from fatigue and hunger; but, being surrounded by a crowd, I

thought it politic to rouse all my strength, that no physical debility might be construed into apprehension or conscious guilt. Little did I then expect the calamity that was in a few moments to overwhelm me, and extinguish in horror and despair all fear of ignominy or death.

'I must pause here; for it requires all my fortitude to recall the memory of the frightful events which I am about to relate, in proper detail, to my recollection.

What in the name of the Good Lord is happening? Victor? Victor? Answer me!

Chapter V

And then he answered my fears with even greater fears!

'I was soon introduced into the presence of the magistrate, an old benevolent man, with calm and mild manners. He looked upon me, however, with some degree of severity; and then, turning towards my conductors, he asked who appeared as witnesses on this occasion.

'About half a dozen men came forward; and one being selected by the magistrate, he deposed, that he had been out fishing the night before with his son and brother-in-law, Daniel Nugent, when, about ten o'clock, they observed a strong northerly blast rising, and they accordingly put in for port. It was a very dark night, as the moon had not yet risen; they did not land at the harbour, but, as they had been accustomed, at a creek about two miles below. He walked on first, carrying a part of the fishing tackle, and his companions followed him at some distance. As he was proceeding along the sands, he struck his foot against something, and fell all his length on the ground. His companions came up to assist him; and, by the light of their lantern, they found that he had fallen on the body of a man, who was to all appearance dead. Their first supposition was, that it was the corpse of some person who had been drowned, and was thrown on shore by the waves; but, upon examination, they found that the clothes were not wet, and even that the body was not then cold. They instantly carried it to the cottage of an old woman near the spot, and endeavoured, but in vain, to restore it to life. He appeared to be a handsome young man, about five and twenty years of age. He had apparently been strangled; for there was no sign of any violence, except the black mark of fingers on his neck.'

'The first part of this deposition did not in the least interest me; but when the mark of the fingers was mentioned, I remembered the murder of my brother, and felt myself extremely agitated; my limbs trembled, and a mist came over my eyes, which obliged me to lean on a chair for support. The magistrate observed me with a keen eye, and of course drew an unfavourable augury from my manner.

'The son confirmed his father's account: but when Daniel Nugent was called, he swore positively that, just before the fall of his companion, he saw a boat, with a single man in it, at a short distance from the shore; and, as far as he could judge by the light of a few stars, it was the same boat in which I had just landed.

'A woman deposed, that she lived near the beach, and was standing at the door of her cottage, waiting for the return of the fishermen, about an hour before she heard of the discovery of the body, when she saw a boat, with only one man in it, push off from that part of the shore where the corpse was afterwards found.

'Another woman confirmed the account of the fishermen having brought the body into her house; it was not cold. They put it into a bed, and rubbed it; and Daniel went to the town for an apothecary, but life was quite gone.

'Several other men were examined concerning my landing; and they agreed, that, with the strong north wind that had arisen during the night, it was very probable that I had beaten about for many hours, and had been obliged to return nearly to the same spot from which I had departed. Besides, they observed that it appeared that I had brought the body from another place, and it was likely, that as I did not appear to know the shore, I might have put into the harbour ignorant of the distance of the town of —— from the place where I had deposited the corpse.

'Mr Kirwin, on hearing this evidence, desired that I should be taken into the room where the body lay for interment that it might be observed what effect the sight of it would produce upon me. This idea was probably suggested by the extreme agitation I had exhibited when the mode of the murder had been described. I was accordingly conducted, by the magistrate and several other persons, to the inn. I could not help being struck by the strange coincidences that had taken place during this eventful night; but, knowing that I had been conversing with several persons in the island I had inhabited about the time that the body had been found, I was perfectly tranquil as to the consequences of the affair.

'I entered the room where the corpse lay, and was led up to the coffin. How can I describe my sensations on beholding it? I feel yet parched with horror, nor can I reflect on that terrible moment without shuddering and agony, that faintly reminds me of the anguish of the recognition. The trial, the presence of the magistrate and witnesses, passed like a dream from my memory, when I saw the lifeless form of Henry Clerval stretched before me. I gasped for breath; and, throwing myself on the body, I exclaimed, "Have my murderous machinations deprived you also, my dearest Henry, of life? Two I have already destroyed; other victims await their destiny: but you, Clerval, my friend, my benefactor"—

Victor, am I to believe that Clerval put up no struggle against your Creati— nay! faith! Creature! Creature!— when attacked? The Creature stands eight-feet tall and must weigh, I don't know how much! I say. I say! That it was you that murdered your own friend. Why not? You would have been able to approach your dearest compatriot with his arms wide open in welcoming, only to have your own hands wrapped around his neck. And if your Creature is as large as you have proposed to me during this tale, should not the black mark of fingers be grotesquely large to a magistrate who regularly sees signs of violence marked on the bodies of the dead?

The human frame could no longer support the agonizing suffering that I endured, and I was carried out of the room in strong convulsions... of madness!

'A fever succeeded to this. I lay for two months on the point of death: my ravings, as I afterwards heard, were frightful; I called myself the murderer of William, of Justine, and of Clerval. Sometimes I entreated my attendants to assist me in the destruction of the fiend by whom I was tormented; and, at others, I felt the fingers of the monster already grasping my neck, and screamed aloud with agony and terror. Fortunately, as I spoke my native language, Mr Kirwin alone understood me; but my gestures and bitter cries were sufficient to affright the other witnesses.

'Why did I not die? More miserable than man ever was before, why did I not sink into forgetfulness and rest? Death snatches away many blooming children, the only hopes of their doating parents: how many brides and youthful lovers have been one day in the bloom of health and hope, and the next a prey for worms and the decay of the tomb! Of what materials was I made, that I could thus resist so many shocks, which, like the turning of the wheel, continually renewed the torture.

'But I was doomed to live; and, in two months, found myself as awaking from a dream, in a prison, stretched on a wretched bed, surrounded by gaolers, turnkeys, bolts, and all the miserable apparatus of a dungeon. It was morning, I remember, when I thus awoke to understanding: I had forgotten the particulars of what had happened, and only felt as if some great misfortune had suddenly overwhelmed me; but when I looked around, and saw the barred windows, and the squalidness of the room in which I was, all flashed across my memory, and I groaned bitterly... with madness!

I greatly fear for your sanity, Victor. This entire tale bares the marks of the ravings of a lunatic in Bedlam! If you were not a figment of my overactive imagination I would commit you to the Bethlehem Hospital in St George's Fields in Southwark, where it only recently moved. Or! The horror of the realization strips all colour from my face. Should I commit *myself* to Bedlam for having conjured this horrifying tale from my own mind? What kind of woman would I be if I shared this tale with my Beloved, our little Lord, poor Polidori, and dearest Claire?

The winner of our little game of ghost stories is what!

'This sound disturbed an old woman who was sleeping in a chair beside me. She was a hired nurse, the wife of one of the turnkeys, and her countenance expressed all those bad qualities which often characterize that class. The lines of her face were hard and rude, like that of persons accustomed to see without sympathizing in sights of misery. Her tone expressed her entire indifference; she addressed me in English, and the voice struck me as one that I had heard during my sufferings:

' "Are you better now, Sir?" said she.

'I replied in the same language, with a feeble voice, "I believe I am; but if it be all true, if indeed I did not dream, I am sorry that I am still alive to feel this misery and horror."

' "For that matter," replied the old woman, "if you mean about the gentleman you murdered, I believe that it were better for you if you were dead, for I fancy it will go hard with you; but you will be hung when the next sessions come on. However, that's none of my business, I am sent to nurse you, and get you well; I do my duty with a safe conscience, it were well if every body did the same."

'I turned with loathing from the woman who could utter so unfeeling a speech to a person just saved, on the very edge of death; but I felt languid, and unable to reflect on all that had passed. The whole series of my life appeared to me as a dream; I sometimes doubted if indeed it were all true, for it never presented itself to my mind with the force of reality.

'As the images that floated before me became more distinct, I grew feverish; a darkness pressed around me; no one was near me who soothed me with the gentle voice of love; no dear hand supported me. The physician came and prescribed medicines, and the old woman prepared them for me; but utter carelessness was visible in the first, and the expression of brutality was strongly marked in the visage of the second. Who could be interested in the fate of a murderer, but the hangman who would gain his fee?

'These were my first reflections; but I soon learned that Mr Kirwin had shewn me extreme kindness. He had caused the best room in the prison to be prepared for me (wretched indeed was the best); and it was he who had provided a physician and a nurse. It is true, he seldom came to see me; for, although he ardently desired to relieve the sufferings of every human creature, he did not wish to be present at the agonies and miserable ravings of a murderer. He came, therefore, sometimes to see that I was not neglected; but his visits were short, and at long intervals.

'One day, when I was gradually recovering, I was seated in a chair, my eyes half open, and my cheeks livid like those in death, I was overcome by gloom and misery, and often reflected I had better seek death than remain miserably pent up only to be let loose in a world replete with wretchedness. At one time I considered whether I should not declare myself guilty, and suffer the penalty of the law, less innocent than poor Justine had been. Such were my thoughts, when the door of my apartment was opened, and Mr Kirwin entered. His countenance expressed sympathy and compassion; he drew a chair close to mine, and addressed me in French—

' "I fear that this place is very shocking to you; can I do any thing to make you more comfortable?"

' "I thank you; but all that you mention is nothing to me: on the whole earth there is no comfort which I am capable of receiving."

' "I know that the sympathy of a stranger can be but of little relief to one borne down as you are by so strange a misfortune. But you will, I hope, soon quit this melancholy abode; for, doubtless, evidence can easily be brought to free you from the criminal charge."— Wait! What? Exculpatory evidence 'can easily be brought' and yet why would have concluded that 'he did not wish to be present at the agonies and miserable ravings of a murderer'? Victor, your tale itself is descending into madness, unable to present its own argument sanely!

' "That is my least concern: I am, by a course of strange events, become the most miserable of mortals. Persecuted and tortured as I am and have been, can death be any evil to me?"

' "Nothing indeed could be more unfortunate and agonizing than the strange chances that have lately occurred. You were thrown, by some surprising accident, on this shore, renowned for its hospitality: seized immediately, and charged with murder. The first sight that was presented to your eyes was the body of your friend, murdered in so unaccountable a manner, and placed, as it were, by some fiend across your path."

— Madness. Shear madness! So many questions swim in my mind of 'questions raised by Clerval's murder: Where was he killed? Why did the Creature Bring Clerval's corpse to a small town in Ireland? The Creature certainly had no way of knowing that Victor would beach his craft here, and Clerval could not have been anywhere near the town— or Ireland, for that matter, for he had written to Victor asking him to meet up in Perth. Futhermore, the body was not yet cold when discovered. This suggests that the Creature actually took Clerval prisoner and transported him either in the boat in which they travelled or immediately on taking him ashore. All of this occurred in the short interval after the Creature departed from Victor's island laboratory. No explanation for these conundrums is put forward by the Creature or Victor'[45]— Madness I say! Madness!

'As Mr Kirwin said this, notwithstanding the agitation I endured on this retrospect of my sufferings, I also felt considerable surprise at the knowledge he seemed to possess concerning me. I suppose some astonishment was exhibited in my countenance; for Mr Kirwin hastened to say—

' "It was not until a day or two after your illness that I thought of examining your dress, that I might discover some trace by which I could send to your relations an account of your misfortune and illness. I found several letters, and, among others, one which I discovered from its commencement to be from your father. I instantly wrote to Geneva: nearly two months have elapsed since the departure of my letter.— But you are ill; even now you tremble: you are unfit for agitation of any kind."

' "This suspense is a thousand times worse than the most horrible event: tell me what new scene of death has been acted, and whose murder I am now to lament."

' "Your family is perfectly well," said Mr Kirwin, with gentleness; "and some one, a friend, is come to visit you."

'I know not by what chain of thought the idea presented itself, but it instantly darted into my mind that the murderer had come to mock at my misery, and taunt me with the death of Clerval, as a new incitement for me to comply with his hellish desires. I put my hand before my eyes, and cried out in agony—

' "Oh! take him away! I cannot see him; for God's sake, do not let him enter!" — Madness I say! Madness!

'Mr Kirwin regarded me with a troubled countenance. He could not help regarding my exclamation as a presumption of my guilt, and said, in rather a severe tone—

' "I should have thought, young man, that the presence of your father would have been welcome, instead of inspiring such violent repugnance."

' "My father!" cried I, while every feature and every muscle was relaxed from anguish to pleasure. "Is my father, indeed, come? How kind, how very kind. But where is he, why does he not hasten to me?" — Madness I say! Madness!

'My change of manner surprised and pleased the magistrate; perhaps he thought that my former exclamation was a momentary return of delirium, and now he instantly resumed his former benevolence. He

---

45 From *The New Annotated Frankenstein* by Leslie S. Klinger, published in 2017.

rose, and quitted the room with my nurse, and in a moment my father entered it.

'Nothing, at this moment, could have given me greater pleasure than the arrival of my father. I stretched out my hand to him, and cried—

' "Are you then safe— and Elizabeth— and Ernest?"

'My father calmed me with assurances of their welfare, and endeavoured, by dwelling on these subjects so interesting to my heart, to raise my desponding spirits; but he soon felt that a prison cannot be the abode of cheerfulness. "What a place is this that you inhabit, my son!" said he, looking mournfully at the barred windows, and wretched appearance of the room. "You travelled to seek happiness, but a fatality seems to pursue you. And poor Clerval— "

'The name of my unfortunate and murdered friend was an agitation too great to be endured in my weak state; I shed tears.

' "Alas! yes, my father," replied I; "some destiny of the most horrible kind hangs over me, and I must live to fulfil it, or surely I should have died on the coffin of Henry."

'We were not allowed to converse for any length of time, for the precarious state of my health rendered every precaution necessary that could insure tranquillity. Mr Kirwin came in, and insisted that my strength should not be exhausted by too much exertion. But the appearance of my father was to me like that of my good angel, and I gradually recovered my health.

'As my sickness quitted me, I was absorbed by a gloomy and black melancholy, that nothing could dissipate. The image of Clerval was for ever before me, ghastly and murdered. More than once the agitation into which these reflections threw me made my friends dread a dangerous relapse. Alas! why did they preserve so miserable and detested a life? It was surely that I might fulfil my destiny, which is now drawing to a close. Soon, oh, very soon, will death extinguish these throbbings, and relieve me from the mighty weight of anguish that bears me to the dust; and, in executing the award of justice, I shall also sink to rest. Then the appearance of death was distant, although the wish was ever present to my thoughts; and I often sat for hours motionless and speechless, wishing for some mighty revolution that might bury me and my destroyer in its ruins. — Madness I say! Madness!

'The season of the assizes approached. I had already been three months in prison; and although I was still weak, and in continual danger of a relapse, I was obliged to travel nearly a hundred miles to the county-town, where the court was held. Mr Kirwin charged himself with every care of collecting witnesses, and arranging my defence. I was spared the disgrace of appearing publicly as a criminal, as the case was not brought before the court that decides on life and death. The grand jury rejected the bill, on its being proved that I was on the Orkney Islands at the hour the body of my friend was found, and a fortnight after my removal I was liberated from prison.

'My father was enraptured on finding me freed from the vexations of a criminal charge, that I was again allowed to breathe the fresh atmosphere, and allowed to return to my native country. I did not participate in these feelings; for to me the walls of a dungeon or a palace were alike hateful. The cup of life was poisoned for ever; and although the sun shone upon me, as upon the happy and gay of heart, I saw around me nothing but a dense and frightful darkness, penetrated by no light but the glimmer of two eyes that glared upon me. Sometimes they were the expressive eyes of Henry, languishing in death, the dark orbs nearly covered by the lids, and the long black lashes that fringed them; sometimes it was the watery clouded eyes of the monster, as I first saw them in my chamber at Ingolstadt. — The madness continues to grip his very soul. Bedlam awaits, dearest Victor, Bedlam awaits.

'My father tried to awaken in me the feelings of affection. He talked of Geneva, which I should soon visit— of Elizabeth, and Ernest; but these words only drew deep groans from me. Sometimes, indeed, I felt a wish for happiness; and thought, with melancholy delight, of my beloved cousin; or longed, with a devouring *maladie du pays*, to see once more the blue lake and rapid Rhone, that had been so dear to me in early childhood: but my general state of feeling was a torpor, in which a prison was as welcome a residence as the divinest scene in nature; and these fits were seldom interrupted, but by paroxysms of anguish and despair. At these moments I often endeavoured to put an end to the existence I loathed; and it required unceasing attendance and vigilance to restrain me from committing some dreadful act of violence.

'Yet one duty remained to me, the recollection of which finally triumphed over my selfish despair. It was necessary that I should return without delay to Geneva, there to watch over the lives of those I so fondly loved; and to lie in wait for the murderer, that if any chance led me to the place of his concealment, or if he dared again to blast me by his presence, I might, with unfailing aim, put an end to the existence of the monstrous Image which I had endued with the mockery of a soul still more monstrous. My father still desired to delay our departure, fearful that I could not sustain the fatigues of a journey: for I was a shattered wreck,—the shadow of a human being. My strength was gone. I was a mere skeleton; and fever night and day preyed upon my wasted frame.

'Still, as I urged our leaving Ireland with such inquietude and impatience, my father thought it best to yield. We took our passage on board a vessel bound for Havre-de-Grace, and sailed with a fair wind from the Irish shores. It was midnight. I lay on the deck, looking at the stars, and listening to the dashing of the waves. I hailed the darkness that shut Ireland from my sight; and my pulse beat with a feverish joy when I reflected that I should soon see Geneva. The past appeared to me in the light of a frightful dream; yet the vessel in which I was, the wind that blew me from the detested shore of Ireland, and the sea which surrounded me, told me too forcibly that I was deceived by no vision, and that Clerval, my friend and dearest companion, had fallen a victim to me and the monster of my creation. I repassed, in my memory, my whole life; my quiet happiness while residing with my family in Geneva, the death of my mother, and my departure for Ingolstadt. I remembered, shuddering, the mad enthusiasm that hurried me on to the creation of my hideous enemy, and I called to mind the night in which he first lived. I was unable to pursue the train of thought; a thousand feelings pressed upon me, and I wept bitterly.

'Ever since my recovery from the fever I had been in the custom of taking every night a small quantity of laudanum'

— for it is indeed *not* madness that you are suffering from, Victor! Is not opium at present in great esteem? And is one of the most valuable of all simple medicines. In its effects on the animal system, it is the most extraordinary substance in nature. It touches the nerves as it were by magic and irresistible power, and steeps the senses in forgetfulness; even in opposition to the determined will of the philosopher or physiologist, apprised of its narcotic effect. Opium is the most sovereign remedy in the *materia medica* for easing pain and procuring sleep, and also the most certain antispasmodic yet know; but like other powerful medicines, becomes highly noxious to the human constitution and even moral, when improperly administered[46]—

'For it was by means of this drug only that I was enabled to gain the rest necessary for the preservation of life. Oppressed by the recollection of my various misfortunes, I now took a double dose, and soon slept profoundly. But sleep did not afford me respite from thought and misery; my dreams presented a thousand objects that scared me. Towards morning I was possessed by a kind of night-mare; I felt the fiend's grasp in my neck, and could not free myself from it; groans and cries rung in my ears. My father, who was watching over me, perceiving my restlessness, awoke me, and pointed to the port of Holyhead, which we were now entering.'

---

46 From the third edition of the *Encylopædia Britannica*.

Chapter VI

The voyage came to an end. We landed, and proceeded to Paris. I soon found that I had overtaxed my strength, and that I must repose before I could continue my journey. My father's care and attentions were indefatigable; but he did not know the origin of my sufferings, and sought erroneous methods to remedy the incurable ill. He wished me to seek amusement in society. I abhorred the face of man. Oh, not abhorred! they were my brethren, my fellow beings, and I felt attracted even to the most repulsive among them, as to creatures of an angelic nature and celestial mechanism. But I felt that I had no right to share their intercourse. I had unchained an enemy among them, whose joy it was to shed their blood, and to revel in their groans. How they would, each and all, abhor me, and hunt me from the world, did they know my unhallowed acts, and the crimes which had their source in me!

'My father yielded at length to my desire to avoid society, and strove by various arguments to banish my despair. Sometimes he thought that I felt deeply the degradation of being obliged to answer a charge of murder, and he endeavoured to prove to me the futility of pride.

— Where once I had been so studious to record Victor's tale as he related it to me... verbatim. Now, I find myself revising his words with greater skill and efficacy. I no longer am aware of his voice, only the quiet scratching of the quill upon the page—

' "Alas! my father," said I, "how little do you know me. Human beings, their feelings and passions, would indeed be degraded if such a wretch as I felt pride. Justine, poor unhappy Justine, was as innocent as I, and she suffered the same charge; she died for it; and I am the cause of this—I murdered her. William, Justine, and Henry—they all died by my hands."'

The guilt of the guilty. Victor cries out to the Lord... or society... or nature to blot out his transgressions! This is the guilt of the guilty. There is too much obfuscation in this tale of Victor's, related to me by a mystical phantasm sitting beside my fire in my apartment, to know what crimes are the Creature's and what crimes are his!

'My father had often, during my imprisonment, heard me make the same assertion; when I thus accused myself, he sometimes seemed to desire an explanation, and at others he appeared to consider it as the offspring of delirium, and that, during my illness, some idea of this kind had presented itself to my imagination, the remembrance of which I preserved in my convalescence. I avoided explanation, and maintained a continual silence concerning the wretch I had created. I had a persuasion that I should be supposed mad; and this in itself would for ever have chained my tongue. But, besides, I could not bring myself to disclose a secret which would fill my hearer with consternation, and make fear and unnatural horror the inmates of his breast. I checked, therefore, my impatient thirst for sympathy, and was silent when I would have given the world to have confided the fatal secret. Yet still words like those I have recorded, would burst uncontrollably from me. I could offer no explanation of them; but their truth in part relieved the burden of my mysterious woe.'

Oh! Woe is upon you my failed student with a hollow heart. If your father knew of the crimes you should rightly be convicted of, disownment would surely commence, closely followed by a short trip up the steps to the gallows. To have your neck stretched. The crime of murder you may not be— legally— guilty of, but crimes against nature. You, sir, are guilty... guilty... guilty!

'Upon this occasion my father said, with an expression of unbounded wonder, "My dearest Victor, what infatuation is this? My dear son, I entreat you never to make such an assertion again."

' "I am not mad," I cried energetically; "the sun and the heavens, who have viewed my operations, can bear witness of my truth. I am the assassin of those most innocent victims; they died by my machinations. A thousand times would I have shed my own blood, drop by drop, to have saved their lives; but I could not, my father, indeed I could not sacrifice the whole human race."'

They say confession is good for the soul. Confess!

'The conclusion of this speech'— speech? Oh, Victor, how I wish you would make a speech, but merely a choice words— 'convinced my father that my ideas were deranged, and he instantly changed the subject of our conversation, and endeavoured to alter the course of my thoughts. He wished as much as possible to obliterate the memory of the scenes that had taken place in Ireland, and never alluded to them, or suffered me to speak of my misfortunes.

'As time passed away I became more calm: misery had her dwelling in my heart, but I no longer talked in the same incoherent manner of my own crimes; sufficient for me was the consciousness of them. By the utmost self-violence, I curbed the imperious voice of wretchedness, which sometimes desired to declare itself to the whole world; and my manners were calmer and more composed than they had ever been since my journey to the sea of ice.

'A few days before we left Paris on our way to Switzerland, I received the following letter from Elizabeth:—

Letter to Victor Frankenstein

' "My dear Friend,

It gave me the greatest pleasure to receive a letter from my uncle dated at Paris; you are no longer at a formidable distance, and I may hope to see you in less than a fortnight. My poor cousin, how much you must have suffered! I expect to see you looking even more ill than when you quitted Geneva. This winter has been passed most miserably, tortured as I have been by anxious suspense; yet I hope to see peace in your countenance, and to find that your heart is not totally void of comfort and tranquillity.

' "Yet I fear that the same feelings now exist that made you so miserable a year ago, even perhaps augmented by time. I would not disturb you at this period, when so many misfortunes weigh upon you; but a conversation that I had with my uncle previous to his departure renders some explanation necessary before we meet.

' "Explanation! you may possibly say; what can Elizabeth have to explain? If you really say this, my questions are answered, and all my doubts satisfied. But you are distant from me, and it is possible that you may dread, and yet be pleased with this explanation; and, in a probability of this being the case, I dare not any longer postpone writing what, during your absence, I have often wished to express to you, but have never had the courage to begin.

' "You well know, Victor, that our union had been the favourite plan of your parents ever since our infancy. We were told this when young, and taught to look forward to it as an event that would certainly take place. We were affectionate playfellows during childhood, and, I believe, dear and valued friends to one another as we grew older. But as brother and sister often entertain a lively affection towards each other, without desiring a more intimate union, may not such also be our case? Tell me, dearest Victor. Answer me, I conjure you, by our mutual happiness, with simple truth—Do you not love another?

' "You have travelled; you have spent several years of your life at Ingolstadt; and I confess to you, my friend, that when I saw you last autumn so unhappy, flying to solitude, from the society of every creature'"—Oh! Elizabeth if you only the knew true natural of this Creature Victor flies from— ' "I could not help supposing that you might regret our connection, and believe yourself bound in honour to fulfil the wishes of your parents, although they opposed themselves to your inclinations. But this is false reasoning. I confess to you, my cousin, that I love you, and that in my airy dreams of futurity you have been my constant friend and companion. But it is your happiness I desire as well as my own, when I declare to you, that our marriage would render me eternally miserable, unless it were the dictate of your own free choice. Even now I weep to think, that, borne down as you are by the cruellest misfortunes, you may stifle, by the word honour, all hope of that love and happiness which would alone restore you to yourself. I, who have so disinterested an affection for you, may increase your miseries tenfold, by being an obstacle to your wishes. Ah! Victor, be assured that your cousin and playmate has too sincere a love for you not to be made miserable by this supposition. Be happy, my friend; and if you obey me in this one request, remain satisfied that nothing on earth will have the power to interrupt my tranquillity.

‘ "Do not let this letter disturb you; do not answer to-morrow, or the next day, or even until you come, if it will give you pain. My uncle will send me news of your health; and if I see but one smile on your lips when we meet, occasioned by this or any other exertion of mine, I shall need no other happiness.

Elizabeth Lavenza.
Geneva, May 18th, 17—.

Oh! The love that your cousin has for you is immense, Victor. She will fly from their arrangement if it makes you so miserable, but little does this know that you are miserable to your very soul. A miserable wretch that knows not happiness nor love... cannot know happiness nor love... should not know happiness nor love. If there is a Lord above in Heaven, of which I surely have my doubts.

'This letter revived in my memory what I had before forgotten, the threat of the fiend— "I WILL BE WITH YO ON YOUR WEDDING NIGHT!" Such was my sentence, and on that night would the dæmon employ every art to destroy me, and tear me from the glimpse of happiness which promised partly to console my sufferings. On that night he had determined to consummate his crimes by my death. Well, be it so; a deadly struggle would then assuredly take place, in which if he were victorious I should be at peace, and his power over me be at an end. If he were vanquished, I should be a free man. Alas! what freedom? such as the peasant enjoys when his family have been massacred before his eyes, his cottage burnt, his lands laid waste, and he is turned adrift, homeless, penniless, and alone, but free. Such would be my liberty, except that in my Elizabeth I possessed a treasure; alas! balanced by those horrors of remorse and guilt, which would pursue me until death.'

But in this analogy, this peasant is guilty of insurrection against his feudal lord, just as you're are guilty of insurrection against Nature herself! Nature has massacred your family before your eyes, burnt your cottage, laid waste to your lands. You are turned adrift, homeless, penniless, and alone, because of your crimes! If you have only embraced your Creation when you animated life into an amalgamated corpse, then there would be no deaths visited upon you. If your Creation had studied at your teat, then perchance fate would have been different, but you chose to flee from your Creation, considering it nothing more than a loathsome Creature to be abandoned. A babe abandoned in the woods will die by exposure or by wolves harkening to its cries; but the babe you abandoned in your laboratory did not die by exposure but was threatened by the wolves of mankind. And you are shocked and dismayed when he reactions from these threats? Oh, my failed student with a hollow heart, how wish to be done with your tale. But curiosity to its end is the only thing keeping me from truly dismissing you as a blot of mustard, a crumb of cheese, a fragment of an underdone potato.

'Sweet and beloved Elizabeth! I read and re-read her letter, and some softened feelings stole into my heart, and dared to whisper paradisiacal dreams of love and joy; but the apple was already eaten, and the angel's arm bared to drive me from all hope. Yet I would die to make her happy. If the monster executed his threat, death was inevitable; yet, again, I considered whether my marriage would hasten my fate. My destruction might indeed arrive a few months sooner; but if my torturer should suspect that I postponed it, influenced by his menaces, he would surely find other, and perhaps more dreadful means of revenge. He had vowed TO BE WITH ME ON MY WEDDING-NIGHT, yet he did not consider that threat as binding him to peace in the mean time; for, as if to show me that he was not yet satiated with blood, he had murdered Clerval immediately after the enunciation of his threats. I resolved, therefore, that if my immediate union with my cousin would conduce either to hers or my father's happiness, my adversary's designs against my life should not retard it a single hour.

'In this state of mind I wrote to Elizabeth. My letter was calm and affectionate. "I fear, my beloved girl," I said, "little happiness remains for us on earth; yet all that I may one day enjoy is centred in you. Chase away your idle fears; to you alone do I consecrate my life, and my endeavours for contentment. I have one secret, Elizabeth, a dreadful one; when revealed to you, it will chill your frame with horror, and then, far from being surprised at my misery, you will only wonder that I survive what I have endured. I will confide this tale of misery and terror to you the day after our marriage shall take place; for, my sweet cousin, there must be perfect confidence between us. But until then, I conjure you, do not mention or allude to it. This I most earnestly entreat, and I know you will comply."

'In about a week after the arrival of Elizabeth's letter, we returned to Geneva. My cousin welcomed me with warm affection; yet tears were in her eyes, as she beheld my emaciated frame and feverish cheeks. I saw a change in her also. She was thinner, and had lost much of that heavenly vivacity that had before charmed me; but her gentleness, and soft looks of compassion, made her a more fit companion for one blasted and miserable as I was.

'The tranquillity which I now enjoyed did not endure. Memory brought madness with it; and when I thought of what had passed, a real insanity possessed me; sometimes I was furious, and burnt with rage; sometimes low and despondent. I neither spoke, nor looked at any one, but sat motionless, bewildered by the multitude of miseries that overcame me.

'Elizabeth alone had the power to draw me from these fits; her gentle voice would soothe me when transported by passion, and inspire me with human feelings when sunk in torpor. She wept with me, and for me. When reason returned, she would remonstrate, and endeavour to inspire me with resignation. Ah! it is well for the unfortunate to be resigned, but for the guilty there is no peace. The agonies of remorse poison the luxury there is otherwise sometimes found in indulging the excess of grief.

'Soon after my arrival, my father spoke of my immediate marriage with my cousin. I remained silent.

' "Have you, then, some other attachment?"

' "None on earth. I love Elizabeth, and look forward to our union with delight. Let the day therefore be fixed; and on it I will consecrate myself, in life or death, to the happiness of my cousin."

' "My dear Victor, do not speak thus. Heavy misfortunes have befallen us; but let us only cling closer to what remains, and transfer our love for those whom we have lost, to those who yet live. Our circle will be small, but bound close by the ties of affection and mutual misfortune. And when time shall have softened your despair, new and dear objects of care will be born to replace those of whom we have been so cruelly deprived."

'Such were the lessons of my father. But to me the remembrance of the threat returned: nor can you wonder, that, omnipotent as the fiend had yet been in his deeds of blood, I should almost regard him as invincible; and that when he had pronounced the words, "I SHALL BE WITH YOU ON YOUR WEDDING-NIGHT."'

My! I heard those words, not in Victor's voice, but the voice of the Creature. Curious. Has the phantasm of the Creature returned to visit me as well? I see him not. But I hear his deep resonate unnatural bass speaking from the ether.

'I should regard the threatened fate as unavoidable. But death was no evil to me, if the loss of Elizabeth were balanced with it; and I therefore, with a contented and even cheerful countenance, agreed with my father, that if my cousin would consent, the ceremony should take place in ten days, and thus put, as I imagined, the seal to my fate.

'Great God! if for one instant I had thought what might be the hellish intention of my fiendish adversary, I would rather have banished myself for ever from my native country, and wandered a friendless outcast over the earth, than have consented to this miserable marriage. But, as if possessed of magic powers, the monster had blinded me to his real intentions; and when I thought that I had prepared only my own death, I hastened that of a far dearer victim.

'As the period fixed for our marriage drew nearer, whether from cowardice or a prophetic feeling, I felt my heart sink within me. But I concealed my feelings by an appearance of hilarity, that brought smiles and joy to the countenance of my father, but hardly deceived the ever-watchful and nicer eye of Elizabeth. She looked forward to our union with placid contentment, not unmingled with a little fear, which past misfortunes had impressed, that what now appeared certain and tangible happiness, might soon dissipate into an airy dream, and leave no trace but deep and everlasting regret.

'Preparations were made for the event; congratulatory visits were received; and all wore a smiling appearance. I shut up, as well as I could, in my own heart the anxiety that preyed there, and entered with seeming earnestness into the plans of my father, although they might only serve as the decorations of my tragedy. A house was purchased for us near Cologny, by which we should enjoy the pleasures of the country, and yet be so near Geneva as to see my father every day; who would still reside within the walls, for the benefit of Ernest, that he might follow his studies at the schools.'

Cologny? Perchance Victor is the owner of the Villa Diodati, for it is so near Cologny, sitting on the shores of Lake Geneva. If not for the unnatural nature of the thunderstorms and the snow, my Beloved, our little Lord, poor Polidori, dearest Claire, and I should have enjoyed the pleasures of the country. Perchance, this very room proved to be the bridal suite. But I cannot bring myself to believe Victor found happiness in the Villa Diodati, because the words of the Creature still echo in my ears: "I SHALL BE WITH YOU ON YOUR WEDDING-NIGHT."

'In the mean time I took every precaution to defend my person, in case the fiend should openly attack me. I carried pistols and a dagger constantly about me, and was ever on the watch to prevent artifice; and by these means gained a greater degree of tranquillity. Indeed, as the period approached, the threat appeared more as a delusion, not to be regarded as worthy to disturb my peace, while the happiness I hoped for in my marriage wore a greater appearance of certainty, as the day fixed for its solemnisation drew nearer, and I heard it continually spoken of as an occurrence which no accident could possibly prevent.

'Elizabeth seemed happy; my tranquil demeanour contributed greatly to calm her mind. But on the day that was to fulfil my wishes and my destiny, she was melancholy, and a presentiment of evil pervaded her; and perhaps also she thought of the dreadful secret which I had promised to reveal to her on the following day. My father was in the mean time overjoyed, and, in the bustle of preparation, only recognised in the melancholy of his niece the diffidence of a bride.

'After the ceremony was performed, a large party assembled at my father's; but it was agreed that Elizabeth and I should pass the afternoon and night at Evian, and return to Cologny the next morning. As the day was fair, and the wind favourable, we resolved to go by water.'

Oh! Evian! I recall transcribing the words of my Beloved in my journal: "The appearance of the inhabitants of Evian is more wretched, diseased and poor, than I ever recollect to have seen. The contrast indeed between the subjects of the King of Sardinia and the citizens of the independent republics of Switzerland, affords a powerful illustration of the blighting mischiefs of despotism, within the space of a few miles. They have mineral waters here, *eaux savonneuses*, they call them. In the evening we had some difficulty about our passports, but so soon as the syndic heard my companion's rank and name, he apologized for the circumstance. The inn was good. During our voyage, on the distant height of a hill, covered with pine-forests, we saw a ruined castle, which reminded me of those on the Rhine."[47]

'Those were the last moments of my life during which I enjoyed the feeling of happiness. We passed rapidly along: the sun was hot, but we were sheltered from its rays by a kind of canopy, while we enjoyed the beauty of the scene, sometimes on one side of the lake, where we saw Mont Salêve, the pleasant banks of Montalègre, and at a distance, surmounting all, the beautiful Mont Blanc, and the assemblage of snowy mountains that in vain endeavour to emulate her; sometimes coasting the opposite banks, we saw the mighty Jura opposing its dark side to the ambition that would quit its native country, and an almost insurmountable barrier to the invader who should wish to enslave it.'

Curious! A mere year or more from the dates of Victor's tale, it is not half the invasion of the French when they overran Old Swiss Confederation and established the Helvetic Republic! Though they only

---

47 From the *History of a Six Weeks Tour Through a Part of France, Germany, Switzerland, and Holland* by Mary Shelley, published by T. Hookham, Jun. Old Bond Street, and C. and J. Ollier, Welback Street, 1817

held these lands for half a decade, allowing our holiday on these shores possible.

'I took the hand of Elizabeth: "You are sorrowful, my love. Ah! if you knew what I have suffered, and what I may yet endure, you would endeavour to let me taste the quiet and freedom from despair, that this one day at least permits me to enjoy."

' "Be happy, my dear Victor," replied Elizabeth; "there is, I hope, nothing to distress you; and be assured that if a lively joy is not painted in my face, my heart is contented. Something whispers to me not to depend too much on the prospect that is opened before us; but I will not listen to such a sinister voice. Observe how fast we move along, and how the clouds, which sometimes obscure and sometimes rise above the dome of Mont Blanc, render this scene of beauty still more interesting. Look also at the innumerable fish that are swimming in the clear waters, where we can distinguish every pebble that lies at the bottom. What a divine day! how happy and serene all nature appears!"

'Thus Elizabeth endeavoured to divert her thoughts and mine from all reflection upon melancholy subjects. But her temper was fluctuating; joy for a few instants shone in her eyes, but it continually gave place to distraction and reverie.

'The sun sunk lower in the heavens; we passed the river Drance,'

— Again my memory serves up the transcription I made of my Beloved's words before we approached Evian and the mountains descended more precipitously to the lake, and masses of intermingled wood and rock overhung its shining spire: "As soon as we had passed the opposite promontory, we saw the river Drance, which descends from between a chasm in the mountains, and makes a plain near the lake, intersected by its divided streams. Thousands of *besolets*, beautiful water-birds, like sea-gulls, but smaller, with purple on their backs, take their station on the shallows, where its waters mingle with the lake."[48] —

'And observed its path through the chasms of the higher, and the glens of the lower hills. The Alps here come closer to the lake, and we approached the amphitheatre of mountains which forms its eastern boundary. The spire of Evian shone under the woods that surrounded it, and the range of mountain above mountain by which it was overhung.

'The wind, which had hitherto carried us along with amazing rapidity, sunk at sunset to a light breeze; the soft air just ruffled the water, and caused a pleasant motion among the trees as we approached the shore, from which it wafted the most delightful scent of flowers and hay. The sun sunk beneath the horizon as we landed; and as I touched the shore, I

---

48 From the *History of a Six Weeks Tour Through a Part of France, Germany, Switzerland, and Holland* by Mary Shelley, published by T. Hookham, Jun. Old Bond Street, and C. and J. Ollier, Welback Street, 1817

felt those cares and fears revive, which soon were to clasp me, and cling to me for ever.'

Chapter VII

It was eight o'clock when we landed; we walked for a short time on the shore, enjoying the transitory light, and then retired to the inn, and contemplated the lovely scene of waters, woods, and mountains, obscured in darkness, yet still displaying their black outlines.

'The wind, which had fallen in the south, now rose with great violence in the west. The moon had reached her summit in the heavens, and was beginning to descend; the clouds swept across it swifter than the flight of the vulture, and dimmed her rays, while the lake reflected the scene of the busy heavens, rendered still busier by the restless waves that were beginning to rise. Suddenly a heavy storm of rain descended.

'I had been calm during the day; but so soon as night obscured the shapes of objects, a thousand fears arose in my mind. I was anxious and watchful, while my right hand grasped a pistol which was hidden in my bosom; every sound terrified me; but I resolved that I would sell my life dearly, and not shrink from the conflict until my own life, or that of my adversary, was extinguished.

'Elizabeth observed my agitation for some time in timid and fearful silence; but there was something in my glance which communicated terror to her, and trembling she asked, "What is it that agitates you, my dear Victor? What is it you fear?"

' "Oh! peace, peace, my love," replied I; "this night, and all will be safe: but this night is dreadful, very dreadful."

'I passed an hour in this state of mind, when suddenly I reflected how fearful the combat which I momentarily expected would be to my wife, and I earnestly entreated her to retire, resolving not to join her until I had obtained some knowledge as to the situation of my enemy.

'She left me, and I continued some time walking up and down the passages of the house, and inspecting every corner that might afford a retreat to my adversary. But I discovered no trace of him, and was beginning to conjecture that some fortunate chance had intervened to prevent the execution of his menaces; when suddenly I heard a shrill and dreadful scream.'

I hear, quite audibly, the voice of the Creature saying: 'I SHALL BE WITH YOU ON YOUR WEDDING-NIGHT!' I shuddered uncontrollably. The flashes of lightning outside the windows to our apartment seemed to strike my spine, uncontrollable electric shots shooting up my spine into my brain. Proof of animal electricity fuelled by lightning! I could feel the blood trickling in my veins. The undersides of my arms and lesser two fingers on my hands went numb, tingling madly. Please, let this be a dream. Please, Victor, tell me this is a product... a project of your imagination and not a reality. I cannot accept it if your Creature has murdered unfortunate Elizabeth.

'It came from the room into which Elizabeth had retired. As I heard it, the whole truth rushed into my mind, my arms dropped, the motion of every muscle and fibre was suspended; I could feel the blood trickling in my veins, and tingling in the extremities of my limbs. This state lasted but for an instant; the scream was repeated, and I rushed into the room.

'Great God! why did I not then expire! Why am I here to relate the destruction of the best hope, and the purest creature of earth? She was there, lifeless and inanimate, thrown across the bed, her head hanging down, and her pale and distorted features half covered by her hair.'

Where had I seen this scene before? I know I have seen it with my own eyes! But where? My father's grand parlour perhaps. Was he hosting an artist, a fixture of radical artists and thinkers that were as commonplace to our home as rats and roaches are to the poor houses. William Godwin and Mary Wollstonecraft were counted among this circle of radical artists and thinkers. My father, with his anarchistic politics and atheistic rationales, and my mother, with the feminist philosophies, were bound together in more than love and marriage. How did the respectable of society and nobility loath and revile them. The memory is becoming clearer and clearer. I see the painting upon its easel in the centre of my father's parlour from my favourite hiding place where I could easily drop eaves on my father's salons. I saw the ladies and their gentlemen, who cherished invitations to Godwin's home on a Saturday. My father hosted many literary, scientific, and philosophical salons. Dinner was served promptly at eight, usually of four courses, but sometimes of seven, and rarely of anything more. These evenings were not intended for nourishment or merriment, but for enlightenment, though guests often left with all three. Esteemed and interesting persons were brought in to speak on any subject that struck my father's fancy this week or that week. Many critics would accuse my father of atheism, anarchism, anti-monarchism, feminism, utilitarianism, and radicalism inspired by the revolutionaries of France. My father was nothing if not outspoken.

This night, when I was five, my father had invited one Henry Fuseli, a Swiss, who lived in England and was counted amongst the circle with my father and my late mother. The painting that sat on the easel was his most famous painting named *The Nightmare*. The woman that lies upon her bed are as Victor described his Elizabeth: 'She was there, lifeless and inanimate, thrown across the bed, her head hanging down, and her pale and distorted features half covered by her hair.' And sitting upon the belly of the woman sat a stone-faced incubus peering and searing into the soul of the observer. A mysterious wild-eyed mare is the voyeur during this scene at night. Is this horse literally a night-mare? There were whispers from the titillated gossiping hens in my father's parlour concerning Fuseli having fallen madly and deeply in love with Anna Landholdt, the niece of his friend, the Swiss physiognomist Johann Kaspar Lavater. Such a scandal would have been exaserbated if the gossiping hens had been aware Fuseli had written to a friend: 'Last night I had her in bed with me— tossed my bedclothes hugger-mugger—wound my hot and tight-clasped hands about her— fused her body and soul together with my own—poured into her my spirit, breath and strength. Anyone who touches her now commits adultery and incest! She is mine, and I am hers. And have her I will....' Was Anna the woman having the nightmare, the hens gossiped. But I know the truth! The incubus had peered into me as a child and seared this painting onto my memory, a memory that Victor has drawn upon to describe his

'Every where I turn I see the same figure—her bloodless arms and relaxed form flung by the murderer on its bridal bier. Could I behold this, and live? Alas! life is obstinate, and clings closest where it is most hated. For a moment only did I lose recollection; I fell senseless on the ground.

'When I recovered, I found myself surrounded by the people of the inn; their countenances expressed a breathless terror: but the horror of others appeared only as a mockery, a shadow of the feelings that oppressed me. I escaped from them to the room where lay the body of Elizabeth, my love, my wife, so lately living, so dear, so worthy. She had been moved from the posture in which I had first beheld her; and now, as she lay, her head upon her arm, and a handkerchief thrown across her face and neck, I might have supposed her asleep. I rushed towards her, and embraced her with ardour; but the deadly languor and coldness of the limbs told me, that what I now held in my arms had ceased to be the Elizabeth whom I had loved and cherished. The murderous mark of the fiend's grasp was on her neck, and the breath had ceased to issue from her lips.

'While I still hung over her in the agony of despair, I happened to look up. The windows of the room had before been darkened, and I felt a kind of panic on seeing the pale yellow light of the moon illuminate the chamber. The shutters had been thrown back.'

And the apocalyptic thunderstorm that raged a war in the heavens seemingly between the armies of Heaven and the hordes of Hell buffeted the windowpanes with winds and rains of such force and ferocity that the panes shattered into a hail of glass. My Beloved slumbered so deeply that he did not stir. The wind and rain tore the curtains from their rings and their rod.

'And, with a sensation of horror not to be described, I saw at the open window a figure the most hideous and abhorred. A grin was on the face of the monster; he seemed to jeer, as with his fiendish finger he pointed towards the corpse of my wife.'

And I saw this with my own eyes! The Creature, who had sat in the same chair where Victor how sits, stood at the open widow, despite or in spite of the fact our apartment sat on an upper floor of the Villa Diodati. The lightning flashed illuminating his silhouette. His form and figure were the same as I remember a grotesque amalgamation of human cadavers and animal carrion, switched together in a quilt of death and decay.

'I rushed towards the window, and drawing a pistol from my bosom, fired; but he eluded me, leaped from his station, and, running with the swiftness of lightning, plunged into the lake.'

I too rushed towards the window, but possessed no pistol to draw from my bosom, but the Creature eluded me, leaped from his station, and running with the swiftness of lightning, plunged into Lake Geneva below! Only when Victor commanded my attention by continuing his tale unabetted.

'The report of the pistol brought a crowd into the room. I pointed to the spot where he had disappeared, and we followed the track with boats; nets were cast, but in vain. After passing several hours, we re-turned hopeless, most of my companions believing it to have been a form conjured up by my fancy. After having landed, they proceeded to search the country, parties going in different directions among the woods and vines.

'I attempted to accompany them, and proceeded a short distance from the house; but my head whirled round, my steps were like those of a drunken man, I fell at last in a state of utter exhaustion; a film covered my eyes, and my skin was parched with the heat of fever. In this state I was carried back, and placed on a bed, hardly conscious of what had happened; my eyes wandered round the room, as if to seek something that I had lost.

'After an interval, I arose, and, as if by instinct, crawled into the room where the corpse of my beloved lay. There were women weeping around—I hung over it, and joined my sad tears to theirs—all this time no distinct idea presented itself to my mind; but my thoughts rambled to various subjects, reflecting confusedly on my misfortunes, and their cause. I was bewildered in a cloud of wonder and horror. The death of

William, the execution of Justine, the murder of Clerval, and lastly of my wife; even at that moment I knew not that my only remaining friends were safe from the malignity of the fiend; my father even now might be writhing under his grasp, and Ernest might be dead at his feet. This idea made me shudder, and recalled me to action. I started up, and resolved to return to Geneva with all possible speed.

'There were no horses to be procured, and I must return by the lake; but the wind was unfavourable, and the rain fell in torrents. However, it was hardly morning, and I might reasonably hope to arrive by night. I hired men to row, and took an oar myself; for I had always experienced relief from mental torment in bodily exercise. But the overflowing misery I now felt, and the excess of agitation that I endured, rendered me incapable of any exertion. I threw down the oar; and leaning my head upon my hands, gave way to every gloomy idea that arose. If I looked up, I saw the scenes which were familiar to me in my happier time, and which I had contemplated but the day before in the company of her who was now but a shadow and a recollection. Tears streamed from my eyes. The rain had ceased for a moment, and I saw the fish play in the waters as they had done a few hours before; they had then been observed by Elizabeth. Nothing is so painful to the human mind as a great and sudden change. The sun might shine, or the clouds might lower: but nothing could appear to me as it had done the day before. A fiend had snatched from me every hope of future happiness: no creature had ever been so miserable as I was; so frightful an event is single in the history of man.

'But why should I dwell upon the incidents that followed this last overwhelming event? Mine has been a tale of horrors; I have reached their acme, and what I must now relate can but be tedious to you. Know that, one by one, my friends were snatched away; I was left desolate. My own strength is exhausted; and I must tell, in a few words, what remains of my hideous narration.

'I arrived at Geneva. My father and Ernest yet lived; but the former sunk under the tidings that I bore. I see him now, excellent and venerable old man! his eyes wandered in vacancy, for they had lost their charm and their delight—his niece, his more than daughter, whom he doated on with all that affection which a man feels, who in the decline of life, having few affections, clings more earnestly to those that remain. Cursed, cursed be the fiend that brought misery on his grey hairs, and doomed him to waste in wretchedness! He could not live under the horrors that were accumulated around him; the springs of existence suddenly gave way: he was unable to rise from his bed, and in a few days he died in my arms.'

No! Victor is now an orphan. Just as Robert Walton is an orphan. And the Creature himself is an orphan by the abandonment of my failed student with the hollow heart. All three are alone! All three are on their own! All three are lost! All are without roots of any kind! What manner of tragedy is this tale?

'What then became of me? I know not; I lost sensation, and chains and darkness were the only objects that pressed upon me. Sometimes, indeed, I dreamt that I wandered in flowery meadows and pleasant vales with the friends of my youth; but I awoke, and found myself in a dungeon. Melancholy followed, but by degrees I gained a clear conception of my miseries and situation, and was then released from my prison. For they had called me mad; and during many months, as I understood, a solitary cell had been my habitation.'

Again and again he is called mad! Again and again a solitary cell became his habitation! First in Ireland accused of murder and again in Geneva accused of madness! Murder and madness stalk Victor like creatures on the prowl. A Creature on the prowl.

'Liberty, however, had been an useless gift to me, had I not, as I awakened to reason, at the same time awakened to revenge. As the memory of past misfortunes pressed upon me, I began to reflect on their cause—the monster whom I had created, the miserable dæmon whom I had sent abroad into the world for my destruction. I was possessed by a maddening rage when I thought of him, and desired and ardently prayed that I might have him within my grasp to wreak a great and signal revenge on his cursed head.

'Nor did my hate long confine itself to useless wishes; I began to reflect on the best means of securing him; and for this purpose, about a month after my release, I repaired to a criminal judge in the town, and told him that I had an accusation to make; that I knew the destroyer of my family; and that I required him to exert his whole authority for the apprehension of the murderer.

'The magistrate listened to me with attention and kindness:— "Be assured, sir," said he, "no pains or exertions on my part shall be spared to discover the villain."

' "I thank you," replied I; "listen, therefore, to the deposition that I have to make. It is indeed a tale so strange, that I should fear you would not credit it, were there not something in truth which, however wonderful, forces conviction. The story is too connected to be mistaken for a dream, and I have no motive for falsehood." My manner, as I thus addressed him, was impressive, but calm; I had formed in my own heart a resolution to pursue my destroyer to death; and this purpose quieted my agony, and for an interval reconciled me to life. I now related my history, briefly, but with firmness and precision, marking the dates with accuracy, and never deviating into invective or exclamation.

'The magistrate appeared at first perfectly incredulous, but as I continued he became more attentive and interested; I saw him sometimes shudder with horror, at others a lively surprise, unmingled with disbelief, was painted on his countenance.

'When I had concluded my narration, I said, "This is the being whom I accuse, and for whose seizure and punishment I call upon you to exert your whole power. It is your duty as a magistrate, and I believe and hope that your feelings as a man will not revolt from the execution of those functions on this occasion."'

Was Victor as thorough with the telling of his tale to the magistrate as he has been with me over the course of his cataclysmic summer? Would the magistrate have sat as enraptured as I have at the telling of this tale? Or did his abridge the tale for the sake of brevity in his bereavement because he wanted to pursue the Creature into the wilds?

'This address caused a considerable change in the physiognomy of my own auditor. He had heard my story with that half kind of belief that is given to a tale of spirits and supernatural events; but when he was called upon to act officially in consequence, the whole tide of his incredulity returned. He, however, answered mildly, "I would willingly afford you every aid in your pursuit; but the creature of whom you speak appears to have powers which would put all my exertions to defiance. Who can follow an animal which can traverse the sea of ice, and inhabit caves and dens where no man would venture to intrude? Besides, some months have elapsed since the commission of his crimes, and no one can conjecture to what place he has wandered, or what region he may now inhabit."

' "I do not doubt that he hovers near the spot which I inhabit; and if he has indeed taken refuge in the Alps, he may be hunted like the chamois, and destroyed as a beast of prey. But I perceive your thoughts: you do not credit my narrative, and do not intend to pursue my enemy with the punishment which is his desert."

'As I spoke, rage sparkled in my eyes; the magistrate was intimidated:— "You are mistaken," said he, "I will exert myself; and if it is in my power to seize the monster, be assured that he shall suffer punishment proportionate to his crimes. But I fear, from what you have yourself described to be his properties, that this will prove impracticable; and thus, while every proper measure is pursued, you should make up your mind to disappointment."

' "That cannot be; but all that I can say will be of little avail. My revenge is of no moment to you; yet, while I allow it to be a vice, I confess that it is the devouring and only passion of my soul. My rage is unspeakable, when I reflect that the murderer, whom I have turned loose upon society, still exists. You refuse my just demand: I have but one resource; and I devote myself, either in my life or death, to his destruction."

Why was I suddenly trembling with an excess of agitation with a frenzy in my manner, of that haughty fierceness which the martyrs of old are said to have been possessed? I know not!

'I trembled with excess of agitation as I said this; there was a frenzy in my manner, and something, I doubt not, of that haughty fierceness which the martyrs of old are said to have possessed.'

Now I know! I am feeling the feelings of my pale student of the unhallowed arts. We are becoming of one body and one mind!

'But to a Genevan magistrate, whose mind was occupied by far other ideas than those of devotion and heroism, this elevation of mind had much the appearance of madness. He endeavoured to soothe me as a nurse does a child, and reverted to my tale as the effects of delirium.

' "Man," I cried, "how ignorant art thou in thy pride of wisdom! Cease; you know not what it is you say."

'I broke from the house angry and disturbed, and retired to meditate on some other mode of action.'

Chapter VIII

I have grown numb. My fingers ache from transcribing this tale of Victor's into my journal. My mind is exhausted. Why has this tale affected me thus? Is it the horror of it? Is it the lingering effects of science upon fiction, from which nary the twain have been stitched together like that amalgamation of human cadavers and animal carrion which I called both the Creation and, now and forever, The Creature. Who would have thought to form a plotline involving science so inextricably woven into the fiction that pulling out science and the entire novel collapses without its foundation as bedrock. But as his tale continues. I know not how much I can continue to give my annotations. I feel these comments of mine benefit the publication of Victor's and the Creature's tales, which I will seek as its 'author'. With the assistance of my Beloved, of course. Why the assistance of my Beloved? Who would publish a work of science and of fiction written by an eighteen-year-old girl without the assistance of a man. That is the world I was born into just as my mother was exiting.

'My present situation was one in which all voluntary thought was swallowed up and lost. I was hurried away by fury; revenge alone endowed me with strength and composure; it moulded my feelings, and allowed me to be calculating and calm, at periods when otherwise delirium or death would have been my portion.

'My first resolution was to quit Geneva for ever; my country, which, when I was happy and beloved, was dear to me, now, in my adversity, became hateful. I provided myself with a sum of money, together with a few jewels which had belonged to my mother, and departed.

'And now my wanderings began, which are to cease but with life. I have traversed a vast portion of the earth, and have endured all the hardships which travellers, in deserts and barbarous countries, are wont to meet. How I have lived I hardly know; many times have I stretched my failing limbs upon the sandy plain, and prayed for death. But revenge kept me alive; I dared not die, and leave my adversary in being.

'When I quitted Geneva, my first labour was to gain some clue by which I might trace the steps of my fiendish enemy. But my plan was unsettled; and I wandered many hours round the confines of the town, uncertain what path I should pursue. As night approached, I found my-self at the entrance of the cemetery where William, Elizabeth, and my father reposed. I entered it, and approached the tomb which marked their graves. Every thing was silent, except the leaves of the trees, which were gently agitated by the wind; the night was nearly dark; and the scene would have been solemn and affecting even to an uninterested observer. The spirits of the departed seemed to flit around, and to cast a shadow, which was felt but not seen, around the head of the mourner.

'The deep grief which this scene had at first excited quickly gave way to rage and despair. They were dead, and I lived; their murderer also lived, and to destroy him I must drag out my weary existence. I knelt on the grass, and kissed the earth, and with quivering lips exclaimed, "By the sacred earth on which I kneel, by the shades that wander near me, by the deep and eternal grief that I feel, I swear; and by thee, O Night, and the spirits that preside over thee, to pursue the dæmon, who caused this misery, until he or I shall perish in mortal conflict. For this purpose I will preserve my life: to execute this dear revenge, will I again behold the sun, and tread the green herbage of earth, which otherwise should vanish from my eyes for ever. And I call on you, spirits of the dead; and on you, wandering ministers of vengeance, to aid and conduct me in my work. Let the cursed and hellish monster drink deep of agony; let him feel the despair that now torments me."

'I had begun my adjuration with solemnity, and an awe which almost assured me that the shades of my murdered friends heard and approved my devotion; but the furies possessed me as I concluded, and rage choked my utterance.

'I was answered through the stillness of night by a loud and fiendish laugh. It rung on my ears long and heavily; the mountains re-echoed it, and I felt as if all hell surrounded me with mockery and laughter. Surely in that moment I should have been possessed by frenzy, and have destroyed my miserable existence, but that my vow was heard, and that I was reserved for vengeance. The laughter died away; when a well-known and abhorred voice, apparently close to my ear, addressed me in an audible whisper— "I am satisfied: miserable wretch! you have determined to live, and I am satisfied."

'I darted towards the spot from which the sound proceeded; but the devil eluded my grasp. Suddenly the broad disk of the moon arose, and shone full upon his ghastly and distorted shape, as he fled with more than mortal speed.

'I pursued him; and for many months this has been my task. Guided by a slight clue, I followed the windings of the Rhone, but vainly. The blue Mediterranean appeared; and, by a strange chance, I saw the fiend enter by night, and hide himself in a vessel bound for the Black Sea. I took my passage in the same ship; but he escaped, I know not how.

'Amidst the wilds of Tartary and Russia, although he still evaded me, I have ever followed in his track. Sometimes the peasants, scared by this horrid apparition, informed me of his path; sometimes he himself, who feared that if I lost all trace of him, I should despair and die, left some mark to guide me. The snows descended on my head, and I saw the print of his huge step on the white plain. To you first entering on life, to whom care is new, and agony unknown, how can you understand what I have felt, and still feel? Cold, want, and fatigue, were the least pains which I was destined to endure; I was cursed by some devil, and carried about with me my eternal hell; yet still a spirit of good followed and directed my steps; and, when I most murmured, would suddenly extricate me from seemingly insurmountable difficulties. Sometimes, when nature, overcome by hunger, sunk under the exhaustion, a repast was prepared for me in the desert, that restored and inspirited me. The fare was, indeed, coarse, such as the peasants of the country ate; but I will not doubt that it was set there by the spirits that I had invoked to aid me. Often, when all was dry, the heavens cloudless, and I was parched by thirst, a slight cloud would bedim the sky, shed the few drops that revived me, and vanish.

'I followed, when I could, the courses of the rivers; but the dæmon generally avoided these, as it was here that the population of the country chiefly collected. In other places human beings were seldom seen; and I generally subsisted on the wild animals that crossed my path. I had money with me, and gained the friendship of the villagers by distributing it; or I brought with me some food that I had killed, which, after taking a small part, I always presented to those who had provided me with fire and utensils for cooking.

'My life, as it passed thus, was indeed hateful to me, and it was during sleep alone that I could taste joy. O blessed sleep! often, when most miserable, I sank to repose, and my dreams lulled me even to rapture. The spirits that guarded me had provided these moments, or rather hours, of happiness, that I might retain strength to fulfil my pilgrimage. Deprived of this respite, I should have sunk under my hardships. During the day I was sustained and inspirited by the hope of night: for in sleep I saw my friends, my wife, and my beloved country; again I saw the benevolent countenance of my father, heard the silver tones of my Elizabeth's voice, and beheld Clerval enjoying health and youth. Often, when wearied by a toilsome march, I persuaded myself that I was dreaming until night should come, and that I should then enjoy reality in the arms of my dearest friends. What agonising fondness did I feel for them! how did I cling to their dear forms, as sometimes they haunted even my waking hours, and persuade myself that they still lived! At such moments vengeance, that burned within me, died in my heart, and I pursued my path towards the destruction of the dæmon, more as a task enjoined by heaven, as the mechanical impulse of some power of which I was unconscious, than as the ardent desire of my soul.

'What his feelings were whom I pursued I cannot know. Sometimes, indeed, he left marks in writing on the barks of the trees, or cut in stone, that guided me, and instigated my fury. "My reign is not yet over," (these words were legible in one of these inscriptions;) "you live, and my power is complete. Follow me; I seek the everlasting ices of the north, where you will feel the misery of cold and frost, to which I am impassive. You will find near this place, if you follow not too tardily, a dead hare; eat, and be refreshed. Come on, my enemy; we have yet to wrestle for our lives; but many hard and miserable hours must you endure until that period shall arrive."

'Scoffing devil! Again do I vow vengeance; again do I devote thee, miserable fiend, to torture and death. Never will I give up my search, until he or I perish; and then with what ecstasy shall I join my Elizabeth, and my departed friends, who even now prepare for me the reward of my tedious toil and horrible pilgrimage!

'As I still pursued my journey to the northward, the snows thickened, and the cold increased in a degree almost too severe to support. The peasants were shut up in their hovels, and only a few of the most hardy ventured forth to seize the animals whom starvation had forced from their hiding-places to seek for prey. The rivers were covered with ice, and no fish could be procured; and thus I was cut off from my chief article of maintenance.

'The triumph of my enemy increased with the difficulty of my labours. One inscription that he left was in these words:— "Prepare! your toils only begin: wrap yourself in furs, and provide food; for we shall soon enter upon a journey where your sufferings will satisfy my everlasting hatred."

'My courage and perseverance were invigorated by these scoffing words; I resolved not to fail in my purpose; and, calling on Heaven to support me, I continued with unabated fervour to traverse immense deserts, until the ocean appeared at a distance, and formed the utmost boundary of the horizon. Oh! how unlike it was to the blue seas of the south! Covered with ice, it was only to be distinguished from land by its superior wildness and ruggedness. The Greeks wept for joy when they beheld the Mediterranean from the hills of Asia, and hailed with rapture the boundary of their toils. I did not weep; but I knelt down, and, with a full heart, thanked my guiding spirit for conducting me in safety to the place where I hoped, notwithstanding my adversary's gibe, to meet and grapple with him.

'Some weeks before this period I had procured a sledge and dogs, and thus traversed the snows with inconceivable speed. I know not whether the fiend possessed the same advantages; but I found that, as before I had daily lost ground in the pursuit, I now gained on him: so much so, that when I first saw the ocean, he was but one day's journey in advance, and I hoped to intercept him before he should reach the beach. With new courage, therefore, I pressed on, and in two days arrived at a wretched hamlet on the sea-shore. I enquired of the inhabitants concerning the fiend, and gained accurate information. A gigantic monster, they said, had arrived the night before, armed with a gun and many pistols; putting to flight the inhabitants of a solitary cottage, through fear of his terrific appearance. He had carried off their store of winter food, and, placing it in a sledge, to draw which he had seized on a numerous drove of trained dogs, he had harnessed them, and the same night, to the joy of the horror-struck villagers, had pursued his journey across the sea in a direction that led to no land; and they conjectured that he must speedily be destroyed by the breaking of the ice, or frozen by the eternal frosts.

'On hearing this information, I suffered a temporary access of despair. He had escaped me; and I must commence a destructive and almost endless journey across the mountainous ices of the ocean,—amidst cold that few of the inhabitants could long endure, and which I, the native of a genial and sunny climate, could not hope to survive. Yet at the idea that the fiend should live and be triumphant, my rage and vengeance returned, and, like a mighty tide, overwhelmed every other feeling. After a slight repose, during which the spirits of the dead hovered round, and instigated me to toil and revenge, I prepared for my journey.

'I exchanged my land-sledge for one fashioned for the inequalities of the Frozen Ocean; and purchasing a plentiful stock of provisions, I departed from land.

'I cannot guess how many days have passed since then; but I have endured misery, which nothing but the eternal sentiment of a just retribution burning within my heart could have enabled me to support. Immense and rugged mountains of ice often barred up my passage, and I often heard the thunder of the ground sea, which threatened my destruction. But again the frost came, and made the paths of the sea secure.

'By the quantity of provision which I had consumed, I should guess that I had passed three weeks in this journey; and the continual protraction of hope, returning back upon the heart, often wrung bitter drops of despondency and grief from my eyes. Despair had indeed almost secured her prey, and I should soon have sunk beneath this misery. Once, after the poor animals that conveyed me had with incredible toil gained the summit of a sloping ice-mountain, and one, sinking under his fatigue, died, I viewed the expanse before me with anguish, when suddenly my eye caught a dark speck upon the dusky plain. I strained my sight to discover what it could be, and uttered a wild cry of ecstasy when I distinguished a sledge, and the distorted proportions of a well-known form within. Oh! with what a burning gush did hope revisit my heart! warm tears filled my eyes, which I hastily wiped away, that they might not intercept the view I had of the dæmon; but still my sight was dimmed by the burning drops, until, giving way to the emotions that oppressed me, I wept aloud.

'But this was not the time for delay: I disencumbered the dogs of their dead companion, gave them a plentiful portion of food; and, after an hour's rest, which was absolutely necessary, and yet which was bitterly irksome to me, I continued my route. The sledge was still visible; nor did I again lose sight of it, except at the moments when for a short time some ice-rock concealed it with its intervening crags. I indeed perceptibly gained on it; and when, after nearly two days' journey, I beheld my enemy at no more than a mile distant, my heart bounded within me.

'But now, when I appeared almost within grasp of my foe, my hopes were suddenly extinguished, and I lost all trace of him more utterly than I had ever done before. A ground sea was heard; the thunder of its progress, as the waters rolled and swelled beneath me, became every moment more ominous and terrific. I pressed on, but in vain. The wind arose; the sea roared; and, as with the mighty shock of an earthquake, it split, and cracked with a tremendous and overwhelming sound. The work was soon finished: in a few minutes a tumultuous sea rolled between me and my enemy, and I was left drifting on a scattered piece of ice, that was continually lessening, and thus preparing for me a hideous death.

'In this manner many appalling hours passed; several of my dogs died; and I myself was about to sink under the accumulation of distress, when I saw your vessel riding at anchor, and holding forth to me hopes of succour and life. I had no conception that vessels ever came so far north, and was astounded at the sight. I quickly destroyed part of my sledge to construct oars; and by these means was enabled, with infinite fatigue, to move my ice-raft in the direction of your ship. I had determined, if you were going southward, still to trust myself to the mercy of the seas rather than abandon my purpose. I hoped to induce you to grant me a boat with which I could pursue my enemy. But your direction was northward. You took me on board when my vigour was exhausted, and I should soon have sunk under my multiplied hardships into a death which I still dread—for my task is unfulfilled.

'Oh! when will my guiding spirit, in conducting me to the dæmon, allow me the rest I so much desire; or must I die, and he yet live? If I do, swear to me, Walton, that he shall not escape; that you will seek him, and satisfy my vengeance in his death. And do I dare to ask of you to undertake my pilgrimage, to endure the hardships that I have undergone? No; I am not so selfish. Yet, when I am dead, if he should appear; if the ministers of vengeance should conduct him to you, swear that he shall not live—swear that he shall not triumph over my accumulated woes, and survive to add to the list of his dark crimes. He is eloquent and persuasive; and once his words had even power over my heart: but trust him not. His soul is as hellish as his form, full of treachery and fiendlike malice. Hear him not; call on the manes of William, Justine, Clerval, Elizabeth, my father, and of the wretched Victor, and thrust your sword into his heart. I will hover near, and direct the steel aright.'

My failed student with the hollow art paused, pregnantly. I wept openly, but he either did not notice or did not care. He sat staring blankly at the wall as if it was not there. What was he staring at? His own mortality? His own death? Then the phantasm faded from my sight. Was his tale ended? Was there more to this story than what he related to me— to Walton— over the course of this calamitous, preternatural summer? I did not yet know, so I allowed myself to drift off. In the morning there came a rapping, a tapping on my chamber door. It was my dearest Claire announcing that a letter had arrived by post addressed to a 'Mrs. Saville.'

So the tale would, indeed, continue. Huzzah!

Continuation of Letter IV

Walton, *in continuation.*

August 26th, 17—.

You have read this strange and terrific story, Margaret; and do you not feel your blood congeal with horror, like that which even now curdles mine? Sometimes, seized with sudden agony, he could not continue his tale; at others, his voice broken, yet piercing, uttered with difficulty the words so replete with anguish. His fine and lovely eyes were now lighted up with indignation, now subdued to downcast sorrow, and quenched in infinite wretchedness. Sometimes he commanded his countenance and tones, and related the most horrible incidents with a tranquil voice, suppressing every mark of agitation; then, like a volcano bursting forth, his face would suddenly change to an expression of the wildest rage, as he shrieked out imprecations on his persecutor.

His tale is connected, and told with an appearance of the simplest truth; yet I own to you that the letters of Felix and Safie, which he showed me, and the apparition of the monster seen from our ship, brought to me a greater conviction of the truth of his narrative than his asseverations, however earnest and connected. Such a monster has then really existence! I cannot doubt it; yet I am lost in surprise and admiration. Sometimes I endeavoured to gain from Frankenstein the particulars of his creatures formation: but on this point he was impenetrable.

'Are you mad, my friend?' said he; 'or whither does your senseless curiosity lead you? Would you also create for yourself and the world a demoniacal enemy? Peace, peace! learn my miseries, and do not seek to increase your own.'

Frankenstein discovered that I made notes concerning his history: he asked to see them, and then himself corrected and augmented them in many places; but principally in giving the life and spirit to the conversations he held with his enemy. 'Since you have preserved my narration,' said he, 'I would not that a mutilated one should go down to posterity.'

Thus has a week passed away, while I have listened to the strangest tale that ever imagination formed. My thoughts, and every feeling of my soul, have been drunk up by the interest for my guest, which this tale, and his own elevated and gentle manners, have created. I wish to soothe him; yet can I counsel one so infinitely miserable, so destitute of every hope of consolation, to live? Oh, no! the only joy that he can now know will be when he composes his shattered spirit to peace and death. Yet he enjoys one comfort, the offspring of solitude and delirium: he believes, that, when in dreams he holds converse with his friends, and derives from that communion consolation for his miseries, or excitements to his vengeance, that they are not the creations of his fancy, but the beings themselves who visit him from the regions of a remote world. This faith gives a solemnity to his reveries that render them to me almost as imposing and interesting as truth.

Our conversations are not always confined to his own history and misfortunes. On every point of general literature he displays unbounded knowledge, and a quick and piercing apprehension. His eloquence is forcible and touching; nor can I hear him, when he relates a pathetic incident, or endeavours to move the passions of pity or love, without tears. What a glorious creature must he have been in the days of his prosperity, when he is thus noble and godlike in ruin! He seems to feel his own worth, and the greatness of his fall.

'When younger,' said he, 'I believed myself destined for some great enterprise. My feelings are profound; but I possessed a coolness of judgment that fitted me for illustrious achievements. This sentiment of the worth of my nature supported me, when others would have been oppressed; for I deemed it criminal to throw away in useless grief those talents that might be useful to my fellow-creatures. When I reflected on the work I had completed, no less a one than the creation of a sensitive and rational animal, I could not rank myself with the herd of common projectors. But this thought, which supported me in the commencement of my career, now serves only to plunge me lower in the dust. All my speculations and hopes are as nothing; and, like the archangel who aspired to omnipotence, I am chained in an eternal hell. My imagination was vivid, yet my powers of analysis and application were intense; by the union of these qualities I conceived the idea, and executed the creation of a man. Even now I cannot recollect, without passion, my reveries while the work was incomplete. I trod heaven in my thoughts, now exulting in my powers, now burning with the idea of their effects. From my infancy I was imbued with high hopes and a lofty ambition; but how am I sunk! Oh! my friend, if you had known me as I once was, you would not recognise me in this state of degradation. Despondency rarely visited my heart; a high destiny seemed to bear me on, until I fell, never, never again to rise.'

Must I then lose this admirable being? I have longed for a friend; I have sought one who would sympathise with and love me. Behold, on these desert seas I have found such a one; but, I fear, I have gained him only to know his value, and lose him. I would reconcile him to life, but he repulses the idea.

'I thank you, Walton,' he said, 'for your kind intentions towards so miserable a wretch; but when you speak of new ties, and fresh affections, think you that any can replace those who are gone? Can any man be to me as Clerval was; or any woman another Elizabeth? Even where the affections are not strongly moved by any superior excellence, the companions of our childhood always possess a certain power over our minds, which hardly any later friend can obtain. They know our infan- tine dispositions, which, however they may be afterwards modified, are never eradicated; and they can judge of our actions with more certain conclusions as to the integrity of our motives. A sister or a brother can never, unless indeed such symptoms have been shown early, suspect the other of fraud or false dealing, when another friend, however strongly he may be attached, may, in spite of himself, be contemplated with suspi- cion. But I enjoyed friends, dear not only through habit and association, but from their own merits; and wherever I am, the soothing voice of my Elizabeth, and the conversation of Clerval, will be ever whispered in my ear. They are dead; and but one feeling in such a solitude can persuade me to preserve my life. If I were engaged in any high undertaking or design, fraught with extensive utility to my fellow-creatures, then could I live to fulfil it. But such is not my destiny; I must pursue and destroy the being to whom I gave existence; then my lot on earth will be fulfilled, and I may die.'

September 2d.

My beloved Sister,

I write to you, encompassed by peril, and ignorant whether I am ever doomed to see again dear England, and the dearer friends that in- habit it. I am surrounded by mountains of ice, which admit of no es- cape, and threaten every moment to crush my vessel. The brave fellows, whom I have persuaded to be my companions, look towards me for aid; but I have none to bestow. There is something terribly appalling in our situation, yet my courage and hopes do not desert me. Yet it is terrible to reflect that the lives of all these men are endangered through me. If we are lost, my mad schemes are the cause.

And what, Margaret, will be the state of your mind? You will not hear of my destruction, and you will anxiously await my return. Years will pass, and you will have visitings of despair, and yet be tortured by hope. Oh! my beloved sister, the sickening failing of your heart-felt expecta- tions is, in prospect, more terrible to me than my own death. But you have a husband, and lovely children; you may be happy: Heaven bless you, and make you so!

My unfortunate guest regards me with the tenderest compassion. He endeavours to fill me with hope; and talks as if life were a possession which he valued. He reminds me how often the same accidents have happened to other navigators, who have attempted this sea, and, in spite of myself, he fills me with cheerful auguries. Even the sailors feel the power of his eloquence: when he speaks, they no longer despair; he rouses their energies, and, while they hear his voice, they believe these vast mountains of ice are mole-hills, which will vanish before the resolutions of man. These feelings are transitory; each day of expectation delayed fills them with fear, and I almost dread a mutiny caused by this despair.

September 5th.

A scene has just passed of such uncommon interest, that although it is highly probable that these papers may never reach you, yet I cannot forbear recording it.

We are still surrounded by mountains of ice, still in imminent danger of being crushed in their conflict. The cold is excessive, and many of my unfortunate comrades have already found a grave amidst this scene of desolation. Frankenstein has daily declined in health: a feverish fire still glimmers in his eyes; but he is exhausted, and, when suddenly roused to any exertion, he speedily sinks again into apparent lifelessness.

I mentioned in my last letter the fears I entertained of a mutiny. This morning, as I sat watching the wan countenance of my friend—his eyes half closed, and his limbs hanging listlessly,—I was roused by half a dozen of the sailors, who demanded admission into the cabin. They entered, and their leader addressed me. He told me that he and his companions had been chosen by the other sailors to come in deputation to me, to make me a requisition, which, in justice, I could not refuse. We were immured in ice, and should probably never escape; but they feared that if, as was possible, the ice should dissipate, and a free passage be opened, I should be rash enough to continue my voyage, and lead them into fresh dangers, after they might happily have surmounted this. They insisted, therefore, that I should engage with a solemn promise, that if the vessel should be freed I would instantly direct my course southward.

This speech troubled me. I had not despaired; nor had I yet conceived the idea of returning, if set free. Yet could I, in justice, or even in possibility, refuse this demand? I hesitated before I answered; when Frankenstein, who had at first been silent, and, indeed, appeared hardly to have force enough to attend, now roused himself; his eyes sparkled, and his cheeks flushed with momentary vigour. Turning towards the men, he said—

'What do you mean? What do you demand of your captain? Are you then so easily turned from your design? Did you not call this a glorious expedition? And wherefore was it glorious? Not because the way was smooth and placid as a southern sea, but because it was full of dangers and terror; because, at every new incident, your fortitude was to be called forth, and your courage exhibited; because danger and death surrounded it, and these you were to brave and overcome. For this was it a glorious, for this was it an honourable undertaking. You were hereafter to be hailed as the benefactors of your species; your names adored, as belonging to brave men who encountered death for honour, and the benefit of mankind. And now, behold, with the first imagination of danger, or, if you will, the first mighty and terrific trial of your courage, you shrink away, and are content to be handed down as men who had not strength enough to endure cold and peril; and so, poor souls, they were chilly, and returned to their warm fire-sides. Why, that requires not this preparation; ye need not have come thus far, and dragged your captain to the shame of a defeat, merely to prove yourselves cowards. Oh! be men, or be more than men. Be steady to your purposes, and firm as a rock. This ice is not made of such stuff as your hearts may be; it is mutable, and cannot withstand you, if you say that it shall not. Do not return to your families with the stigma of disgrace marked on your brows. Return, as heroes who have fought and conquered, and who know not what it is to turn their backs on the foe.'

He spoke this with a voice so modulated to the different feelings expressed in his speech, with an eye so full of lofty design and heroism, that can you wonder that these men were moved? They looked at one another, and were unable to reply. I spoke; I told them to retire, and consider of what had been said: that I would not lead them farther north, if they strenuously desired the contrary; but that I hoped that, with reflection, their courage would return.

They retired, and I turned towards my friend; but he was sunk in languor, and almost deprived of life.

How all this will terminate, I know not; but I had rather die than return shamefully,—my purpose unfulfilled. Yet I fear such will be my fate; the men, unsupported by ideas of glory and honour, can never willingly continue to endure their present hardships.

September 7th.

The die is cast; I have consented to return, if we are not destroyed. Thus are my hopes blasted by cowardice and indecision; I come back ignorant and disappointed. It requires more philosophy than I possess, to bear this injustice with patience.

September 12th.

It is past; I am returning to England. I have lost my hopes of utility and glory;—I have lost my friend. But I will endeavour to detail these bitter circumstances to you, my dear sister; and, while I am wafted towards England, and towards you, I will not despond.

September 9th, the ice began to move, and roarings like thunder were heard at a distance, as the islands split and cracked in every direction. We were in the most imminent peril; but, as we could only remain passive, my chief attention was occupied by my unfortunate guest, whose illness increased in such a degree, that he was entirely confined to his bed. The ice cracked behind us, and was driven with force towards the north; a breeze sprung from the west, and on the 11th the passage towards the south became perfectly free. When the sailors saw this, and that their return to their native country was apparently assured, a shout of tumultuous joy broke from them, loud and long-continued. Frankenstein, who was dozing, awoke, and asked the cause of the tumult. 'They shout,' I said, 'because they will soon return to England.'

'Do you then really return?'

'Alas! yes; I cannot withstand their demands. I cannot lead them unwillingly to danger, and I must return.'

'Do so, if you will; but I will not. You may give up your purpose, but mine is assigned to me by Heaven, and I dare not. I am weak; but surely the spirits who assist my vengeance will endow me with sufficient strength.' Saying this, he endeavoured to spring from the bed, but the exertion was too great for him; he fell back, and fainted.

It was long before he was restored; and I often thought that life was entirely extinct. At length he opened his eyes; he breathed with difficulty, and was unable to speak. The surgeon gave him a composing draught, and ordered us to leave him undisturbed. In the mean time he told me, that my friend had certainly not many hours to live.

His sentence was pronounced; and I could only grieve, and be patient. I sat by his bed, watching him; his eyes were closed, and I thought he slept; but presently he called to me in a feeble voice, and, bidding me come near, said— 'Alas! the strength I relied on is gone; I feel that I shall soon die, and he, my enemy and persecutor, may still be in being. Think not, Walton, that in the last moments of my existence I feel that burning hatred, and ardent desire of revenge, I once expressed; but I feel myself justified in desiring the death of my adversary. During these last days I have been occupied in examining my past conduct; nor do I find it blamable. In a fit of enthusiastic madness I created a rational creature, and was bound towards him, to assure, as far as was in my power, his happiness and well-being. This was my duty; but there was another still paramount to that. My duties towards the beings of my own species had greater claims to my attention, because they included a greater proportion of happiness or misery. Urged by this view, I refused, and I did right in refusing, to create a companion for the first creature. He showed unparalleled malignity and selfishness, in evil: he destroyed my friends;

he devoted to destruction beings who possessed exquisite sensations, happiness, and wisdom; nor do I know where this thirst for vengeance may end. Miserable himself, that he may render no other wretched, he ought to die. The task of his destruction was mine, but I have failed. When actuated by selfish and vicious motives, I asked you to undertake my unfinished work; and I renew this request now, when I am only induced by reason and virtue.

'Yet I cannot ask you to renounce your country and friends, to fulfil this task; and now, that you are returning to England, you will have little chance of meeting with him. But the consideration of these points, and the well balancing of what you may esteem your duties, I leave to you; my judgment and ideas are already disturbed by the near approach of death. I dare not ask you to do what I think right, for I may still be misled by passion.

'That he should live to be an instrument of mischief disturbs me; in other respects, this hour, when I momentarily expect my release, is the only happy one which I have enjoyed for several years. The forms of the beloved dead flit before me, and I hasten to their arms. Farewell, Walton! Seek happiness in tranquillity, and avoid ambition, even if it be only the apparently innocent one of distinguishing yourself in science and discoveries. Yet why do I say this? I have myself been blasted in these hopes, yet another may succeed.'

His voice became fainter as he spoke; and at length, exhausted by his effort, he sunk into silence. About half an hour afterwards he attempted again to speak, but was unable; he pressed my hand feebly, and his eyes closed for ever, while the irradiation of a gentle smile passed away from his lips.

Margaret, what comment can I make on the untimely extinction of this glorious spirit? What can I say, that will enable you to understand the depth of my sorrow? All that I should express would be inadequate and feeble. My tears flow; my mind is overshadowed by a cloud of disappointment. But I journey towards England, and I may there find consolation.

I am interrupted. What do these sounds portend? It is midnight; the breeze blows fairly, and the watch on deck scarcely stir. Again; there is a sound as of a human voice, but hoarser; it comes from the cabin where the remains of Frankenstein still lie. I must arise, and examine. Good night, my sister.

Great God! what a scene has just taken place! I am yet dizzy with the remembrance of it. I hardly know whether I shall have the power to detail it; yet the tale which I have recorded would be incomplete without this final and wonderful catastrophe.

I entered the cabin, where lay the remains of my ill-fated and admirable friend. Over him hung a form which I cannot find words to describe; gigantic in stature, yet uncouth and distorted in its proportions. As he hung over the coffin, his face was concealed by long locks of ragged hair; but one vast hand was extended, in colour and apparent texture like that of a mummy. When he heard the sound of my approach, he ceased to utter exclamations of grief and horror, and sprung towards the window. Never did I behold a vision so horrible as his face, of such loathsome, yet appalling hideousness. I shut my eyes involuntarily, and endeavoured to recollect what were my duties with regard to this destroyer. I called on him to stay.

He paused, looking on me with wonder; and, again turning towards the lifeless form of his creator, he seemed to forget my presence, and every feature and gesture seemed instigated by the wildest rage of some uncontrollable passion.

'That is also my victim!' he exclaimed: 'in his murder my crimes are consummated; the miserable series of my being is wound to its close! Oh, Frankenstein! generous and self-devoted being! what does it avail that I now ask thee to pardon me? I, who irretrievably destroyed thee by destroying all thou lovedst. Alas! he is cold, he cannot answer me.'

His voice seemed suffocated; and my first impulses, which had suggested to me the duty of obeying the dying request of my friend, in destroying his enemy, were now suspended by a mixture of curiosity and compassion. I approached this tremendous being; I dared not again raise my eyes to his face, there was something so scaring and unearthly in his ugliness. I attempted to speak, but the words died away on my lips. The monster continued to utter wild and incoherent self-reproaches. At length I gathered resolution to address him in a pause of the tempest of his passion: 'Your repentance,' I said, 'is now superfluous. If you had listened to the voice of conscience, and heeded the stings of remorse, before you had urged your diabolical vengeance to this extremity, Frankenstein would yet have lived.

'And do you dream?' said the dæmon; 'do you think that I was then dead to agony and remorse?—He,' he continued, pointing to the corpse, 'he suffered not in the consummation of the deed—oh! not the ten-thousandth portion of the anguish that was mine during the lingering detail of its execution. A frightful selfishness hurried me on, while my heart was poisoned with remorse. Think you that the groans of Clerval were music to my ears? My heart was fashioned to be susceptible of love and sympathy; and, when wrenched by misery to vice and hatred, it did not endure the violence of the change, without torture such as you cannot even imagine.

'After the murder of Clerval, I returned to Switzerland, heart-broken and overcome. I pitied Frankenstein; my pity amounted to horror: I abhorred myself. But when I discovered that he, the author at once of my existence and of its unspeakable torments, dared to hope for happiness; that while he accumulated wretchedness and despair upon me, he sought his own enjoyment in feelings and passions from the indulgence of which I was for ever barred, then impotent envy and bitter indignation filled me with an insatiable thirst for vengeance. I recollected my threat, and resolved that it should be accomplished. I knew that I was preparing for myself a deadly torture; but I was the slave, not the master, of an impulse, which I detested, yet could not disobey. Yet when she died!—nay, then I was not miserable. I had cast off all feeling, subdued all anguish, to riot in the excess of my despair. Evil thenceforth became my good. Urged thus far, I had no choice but to adapt my nature to an element which I had willingly chosen. The completion of my demoniacal design became an insatiable passion. And now it is ended; there is my last victim!'

I was at first touched by the expressions of his misery; yet, when I called to mind what Frankenstein had said of his powers of eloquence and persuasion, and when I again cast my eyes on the lifeless form of my friend, indignation was rekindled within me. 'Wretch!' I said, 'it is well that you come here to whine over the desolation that you have made. You throw a torch into a pile of buildings; and, when they are consumed, you sit among the ruins, and lament the fall. Hypocritical fiend! if he whom you mourn still lived, still would he be the object, again would he become the prey, of your accursed vengeance. It is not pity that you feel; you lament only because the victim of your malignity is withdrawn from your power.'

'Oh, it is not thus—not thus,' interrupted the being; 'yet such must be the impression conveyed to you by what appears to be the purport of my actions. Yet I seek not a fellow-feeling in my misery. No sympathy may I ever find. When I first sought it, it was the love of virtue, the feelings of happiness and affection with which my whole being overflowed, that I wished to be participated. But now, that virtue has become to me a shadow, and that happiness and affection are turned into bitter and loathing despair, in what should I seek for sympathy? I am content to suffer alone, while my sufferings shall endure: when I die, I am well satisfied that abhorrence and opprobrium should load my memory. Once my fancy was soothed with dreams of virtue, of fame, and of enjoyment. Once I falsely hoped to meet with beings, who, pardoning my outward form, would love me for the excellent qualities which I was capable of unfolding. I was nourished with high thoughts of honour and devotion. But now crime has degraded me beneath the meanest animal. No guilt, no mischief, no malignity, no misery, can be found comparable to mine. When I run over the frightful catalogue of my sins, I cannot believe that I am the same creature whose thoughts were once filled with sublime and transcendent visions of the beauty and the majesty of goodness. But it is even so; the fallen angel becomes a malignant devil. Yet even that enemy of God and man had friends and associates in his desolation; I am alone.

'You, who call Frankenstein your friend, seem to have a knowledge of my crimes and his misfortunes. But, in the detail which he gave you of them, he could not sum up the hours and months of misery which I endured, wasting in impotent passions. For while I destroyed his hopes, I did not satisfy my own desires. They were for ever ardent and craving; still I desired love and fellowship, and I was still spurned. Was there no injustice in this? Am I to be thought the only criminal, when all human kind sinned against me? Why do you not hate Felix, who drove his friend from his door with contumely? Why do you not execrate the rustic who sought to destroy the saviour of his child? Nay, these are virtuous and immaculate beings! I, the miserable and the abandoned, am an abortion, to be spurned at, and kicked, and trampled on. Even now my blood boils at the recollection of this injustice.

'But it is true that I am a wretch. I have murdered the lovely and the helpless; I have strangled the innocent as they slept, and grasped to death his throat who never injured me or any other living thing. I have devoted my creator, the select specimen of all that is worthy of love and admiration among men, to misery; I have pursued him even to that irremediable ruin. There he lies, white and cold in death. You hate me; but your abhorrence cannot equal that with which I regard myself. I look on the hands which executed the deed; I think on the heart in which the imagination of it was conceived, and long for the moment when these hands will meet my eyes, when that imagination will haunt my thoughts no more.

'Fear not that I shall be the instrument of future mischief. My work is nearly complete. Neither yours nor any man s death is needed to consummate the series of my being, and accomplish that which must be done; but it requires my own. Do not think that I shall be slow to perform this sacrifice. I shall quit your vessel on the ice-raft which brought me thither, and shall seek the most northern extremity of the globe; I shall collect my funeral pile,'— no doubt made of the sledges of Victor's and the Creature's. Does he cremate only himself but his Creator as well? I don't believe I shall over truly know— 'and consume to ashes this miserable frame, that its remains may afford no light to any curious and unhallowed wretch, who would create such another as I have been. I shall die. I shall no longer feel the agonies which now consume me, or be the prey of feelings unsatisfied, yet unquenched. He is dead who called me into being; and when I shall be no more, the very remembrance of us both will speedily vanish. I shall no longer see the sun or stars, or feel the winds play on my cheeks. Light, feeling, and sense will pass away; and in this condition must I find my happiness. Some years ago, when the images which this world affords first opened upon me, when I felt the cheering warmth of summer, and heard the rustling of the leaves and the warbling of the birds, and these were all to me, I should have wept to die; now it is my only consolation. Polluted by crimes, and torn by the bitterest remorse, where can I find rest but in death?

'Farewell! I leave you, and in you the last of human kind whom these eyes will ever behold. Farewell, Frankenstein! If thou wert yet alive, and yet cherished a desire of revenge against me, it would be better satiated in my life than in my destruction. But it was not so; thou didst seek my extinction, that I might not cause greater wretchedness; and if yet, in some mode unknown to me, thou hadst not ceased to think and feel, thou wouldst not desire against me a vengeance greater than that which I feel. Blasted as thou wert, my agony was still superior to thine; for the bitter sting of remorse will not cease to rankle in my wounds until death shall close them for ever.

'But soon,' he cried, with sad and solemn enthusiasm, 'I shall die, and what I now feel be no longer felt. Soon these burning miseries will be extinct. I shall ascend my funeral pile triumphantly, and exult in the agony of the torturing flames. The light of that conflagration will fade away; my ashes will be swept into the sea by the winds. My spirit will sleep in peace; or if it thinks, it will not surely think thus. Farewell.'

He sprung from the cabin-window, as he said this, upon the ice-raft which lay close to the vessel. He was soon borne away by the waves, and lost in darkness and distance.'

As I finished reciting the tales of Victor's and his Creature's own recitation, my dearest Claire flew into hysterics. These hysterics were fuelled by the child growing in her womb; the child growing in her womb caused her emotions to become practically preternatural. After being subdued with a drop or two of laudanum, Claire fell into a pharmaceutically induced slumber on the sofa. What was it about my ghost story that elicited such an extreme response? From the others there was nothing but silence.

I imagined their criticism that 'this is another anomalous story of the same race and family as Mandeville; and, if we are not misinformed, it is intimately connected with that strange performance, by more ties than one. In the present instance, it is true, we are presented with the mysteries of equivocal generation, instead of the metaphysics of a bed-lamite; but he who runs as he reads, might pronounce both novels to be similis farinæ. We are in doubt to what class we shall refer writings of this extravagent character; that they bear marks of considerable pow-er, it is impossible to deny; but this power is so abused and perverted, that we should almost prefer imbecility; however much, of late years, we have been wearied and ennuied by the languid whispers of gentle sen-timentality, they at least had the comfortable property of provoking no uneasy slumber; but we must protect against the waking dreams of hor-ror excited by the unnatural stimulants of this later school; and we feel ourselves as much harassed, after rising from the perusal of these three spirit-wearing volumes, as if we had been over-dosed with laudanum, or hag-ridden by the night-mare.

'No one can love a real good ghost story more heartily than we do; and we will toil through many a tedious duodecimo to get half a dozen pages of rational terror, provided always, that we keep company with spectres and skeletons, no longer than they maintain the just dignity of their spiritual character. Now and then too, we can tolerate a goule, so it be not at his dinnertime; and altogether, we profess to entertain a very due respect for the whole anierarchy of the dæmoniacal establish-ment. Our prejudices in favor of legitimacy, of course, are proportionably shocked by the pretensions of any pseudo-diabolism; and all our best feelings of ghostly loyalty are excited by the usurpations of an unauthor-ized hobgoblin, or a non-descript fee-fa-fum.

'We need scarcely say, that these volumes have neither principle, ob-ject, nor moral; the horror which abounds in them is too grotesque and *bizarre* ever to approach near the sublime, and when we did not hurry over the pages in disgust, we sometimes paused to laugh outright: and yet we suspect, that the diseased and wandering imagination, which has stepped out of all legitimate bounds, to frame these disjointed combina-tions and unnatural adventures, might be disciplined into something bet-ter. We heartily wish it were so, for there are occasional symptoms of no common powers of mind, struggling through a mass of absurdity, which well nigh overwhelms them; but it is a sort of absurdity that approaches so often the confines of what is wicked and immoral, that we dare hardly trust ourselves to bestow even this qualified praise. The writer of it is, we understand, a female; this is an aggravation of that which is the pre-vailing fault of the novel; but if our authoress can forget the gentleness of her sex, it is no reason why we should; and we shall therefore dismiss the novel without further comment.'[49]

OR

---

49 From a review in *The British Critic*, New Series, Vol. 9, April 1818, pp. 432-8.

'This novel is a feeble imitation of one that was very popular in its day,—the St. Leon of Mr. Godwin. It exhibits many characteristics of the school whence it proceeds; and occasionally puts forth indications of talent; but we have been very much disappointed in the perusal of it, from our expectations having been raised too high beforehand by injudicious praises; and it exhibits a strong tendency towards materialism.

'The main idea on which the story of Frankenstein rests, undoubtedly affords scope for the display of imagination and fancy, as well as knowledge of the human heart; and the anonymous author has not wholly neglected the opportunities which it presented to him: but the work seems to have been written in great haste, and on a very crude and ill-digested plan; and the detail is, in consequence, frequently filled with the most gross and obvious inconsistencies. We shall hereafter point out a few of those to which we allude.

'The story begins at the end. Walton, an enthusiastic traveller, bound on a voyage of discovery in the north seas, after having been for some time surrounded with ice, is astonished by the appearance of a human being of apparently savage character who passes the vessel at a distance, in a sledge drawn by dogs. The day after this extraordinary adventure the ice breaks up; but previously to the vessel sailing away from it, they encounter another human being, nearly exhausted with fatigue and privation. This last, who is taken into the vessel, proves to be Frankenstein, the hero of the tale; who at the time he had been nearly destroyed by the breaking up of the ice, was in pursuit of the being that had passed the vessel on the preceding day. After a time Frankenstein contracts a friendship with Walton, the Captain of the vessel, and relates to him his supernatural story.—In his youth he had been led by accident to study chemistry; and becoming deeply interested by the results of his experiments, he at length conceived the idea of its being possible to discover the principle of vital existence. Taking this possibility as the leading point of his studies, he pursues them with such effect as at last actually to gain the power of endowing inanimate matter with life!!! He instantly determines to put his newly acquired power into practice; and for this purpose collects the materials with which to form a living human being. From the difficulty of arranging some of the parts, arising from their minuteness, he determines to chuse them of more than ordinary size. In short, after incredible pains and perseverance, he at length succeeded in producing a living human being, eight feet high, and of proportionate powers. From this moment Frankenstein commences a life of unmixed and unceasing misery. The being which he has formed becomes his torment, and that of every one connected with him. He causes one by one the death of all Frankenstein's dearest connections; his brother, his friend, and lastly his wife— whom he murders on their wedding night. The fiend then quits the country where he has committed these horrors; and Frankenstein, in dispair, determines to pursue him until he shall either destroy him, or die by his hand. The story ends shortly after what we have related in the beginning. Frankenstein dies on board the vessel of Walton; and the fiend may, for any thing we know to be the contrary, be wandering about upon the ice in the neighbourhood of the North Pole to this day; and may, in that case, be among the wonderful discoveries to be made by the expedition which is destined there.

'We have mentioned that there are gross inconsistencies in the minor details of the story. They are such, for example, as the following: the moment Frankenstein has endowed with life the previously inanimate form of the being which he has made, he is so horror-struck with the hideousness of the form and features, when they are put in motion, that he remains fixed to the spot, while the gigantic monster runs from the horizontal posture in which he lay, and walks away; and Frankenstein never hears any more of him for nearly two years. The author supposes that his hero has the power of communicating life to dead matter: but what has the vital principle to do with habits, and actions which are dependent on the moral will? If Frankenstein could have endowed his creature with the vital principle of a hundred or a thousand human beings, it would no more have been able to walk without having previously acquired the habit of doing so, than it would be to talk, or to reason, or to judge. He does not pretend that he could endow it with faculties as well as life: and yet when it is about a year old we find it reading Werter, and Plutarch and Volney! The whole detail of the development of the creature's mind and faculties is full of these monstrous inconsistencies. After the creature leaves Frankenstein, on the night of its birth, it wanders for sometime in the woods, and then takes up its residence in a kind of shed adjoining to a cottage, where it remains for many months without the knowledge of the inhabitants; and learns to talk and read thro' a chink in the wall! "*Quod mihi ostendit,*" &c

'We have heard that this work is written by Mr. Shelley; but should be disposed to attribute it to even a less experienced writer than he is. In fact we have some idea that it is the production of a daughter of a celebrated living novelist.'[50]

A novelist cannot but create in her mind the most negative and critical of reviews! But the pregnant silence from my fellow players in our little game of ghost stories has my stomach twisted into knots. Then the Hear-hears came from all around. Our Little Lord declared

---

50 From a review in *The Literary Panorama, and National Register,* New Series. Vol. 8: June 1818, pp. 411–414.

me the winner the game of ghost stories he himself had a proposed. My Beloved's eyes shined with pride. And Poor Polidori, who himself possessed aspirations in the theatre, hailed the letters that I had *constructed* as theatrical brilliance. He took the letters from the small round table beside my chair and turned them over and over in his hands. How had I masked my naturally feminine handing writing in their construction? This is surely the haggard penmanship of the rough-hewn hands of a man at sea, he posed. And this is the mature and stable penmanship of the patriarch of the Frankenstein family, he questioned. But this the exquisite penmanship of the dainty hands of an educated woman, whom is cousin to the protagonist, he queried, countering his own argument with the realization that I possess the dainty hands of an educated woman.

The satisfaction I felt that their adulations and applause was an enormous burden lifted from my shoulders. Polidori, himself, had been so ruthless in his mockery of me at every breakfast for a week for not having found a ghost story yet. My Beloved sat stone-faced at my side at the kitchen table, neither supporting me nor condemning me for my lack of inspiration for a seemingly insipid game of ghost stories. Lord Byron, who had instigated said game, was quiet in his mockery, but it remained mockery still. But now, having related Victor's and his Creature's tales over the course of a handful of evenings in the parlour, while the thunderstorms buffets the windowpanes with calamitous wind and rain. If I had possessed Aladin's lamp straight out of *Arabian Nights*, I would not have wished for a suitable a backdrop as an author of a ghost story.

Curious. What tale would have composed this cruel summer if Lord Byron had selected that volume off the shelf instead of picking of *Fantasmagoriana*, that crude French translation of German ghost stories? Would he have proposed a game of additional Arabian Nights above and beyond the one-thousand-and-one? My mind reals as the possibilities spin in my mind. Of the hundred or more other works in his parlour, Lord Byron chose a poorly edited collection of poorly written ghost stories. And if my Beloved and Lord Byron had not engaged in their galvanising debate over electrified frog legs, then I would not have been seen my pale student of the unhallowed arts kneeling beside the thing he had put together. I would never have seen the hideous phantasm of a man stretched out, and then, on the working of some powerful engine, show signs of life, and stir with an uneasy, half vital motion. Frightful must it have been; for supremely frightful would be the effect of any human endeavour to mock the stupendous mechanism of the Creator of the world!

And now, once again, I bid my hideous progeny go forth and prosper. I have an affection for it, for it was the offspring of happy days, when death and grief were but words, which found no true echo in my heart. Its several pages speak of many a walk, many a drive, and many a conversation, when I was not alone; and my companion was one who, in this world, I shall never see more. But this is for myself; my readers have nothing to do with these associations.

I will add but one word as to the alterations I will eventually make. They are principally those of style. I shall change no portion of the story, nor introduce any new ideas or circumstances. I shall mend the language where it was so bald as to interfere with the interest of the narrative; and these changes occur almost exclusively in the beginning of the first volume. Throughout they shall be entirely confined to such parts as are mere adjuncts to the story, leaving the core and substance of it untouched.[51]

---

51 From the Introduction to the 1831 Edition of *Frankenstein; or, The Modern Prometheus,* published by Henry Colburn & Richard Bentley.

Epilogue
Matthew Gregory Lewis' Contributions
To the Game of Ghost Stories

P.B. Shelley Writing In Mary Wollstonecraft Godwin's Journal

> *A shovel of his ashes took*
> *From the hearth's obscurest nook,*
> *Muttering mysteries as she went.*
> *Helen and Henry knew that Granny*
> *Was as much afraid of ghosts as any,*
> *And so they followed hard—*
> *But Helen clung to her brother's arm,*
> *And her own spasm made her shake.*

Geneva, Sunday, 18th August, 1816. See Apollo's Sexton, who tells us many mysteries of his trade. We talk of Ghosts. Neither Lord Byron nor M.G.L. seem to believe in them; and they both agree, in the very face of reason, that none could believe in ghosts without believing in God. I do not think that all the persons who profess to discredit these visitations, really discredit them; or, if they do in the daylight, are not admonished by the approach of loneliness and midnight, to think more respectfully of the world of shadows.

Lewis recited a poem, which he had composed at the request of the Princess of Wales. The Princess of Wales, he premised, was not only a believer in ghosts, but in magic and witchcraft, and asserted, that prophecies made in her youth had been accomplished since. The tale was of a lady in Germany.

This lady, Minna, had been exceedingly attached to her husband, and they had made a vow that the one who died first, should return after death to visit the other as a ghost. She was sitting one day alone in her chamber, when she heard an unusual sound of footsteps on the stairs. The door opened, and her husband's spectre, gashed with a deep wound across the forehead, and in military habiliments, entered. She appeared startled at the apparition; and the ghost told her, that when he should visit her in future, she would hear a passing bell toll, and these words distinctly uttered close to her ear, 'Minna, I am here.' On inquiry, it was found that her husband had fallen in battle on the very day she was visited by the vision. The intercourse between the ghost and the woman continued for some time, until the latter laid aside all terror, and indulged herself in the affection which she had felt for him while living. One evening she went to a ball, and permitted her thoughts to be alienated by the attentions of a Florentine gentleman, more witty, more graceful, and more gentle, as it appeared to her, than any person she had ever seen. As he was conducting her through the dance, a death bell tolled. Minna, lost in the fascination of the Florentine's attentions, disregarded, or did not hear the sound. A second peal, louder and more deep, startled the whole company, when Minna heard the ghost's accustomed whisper, and raising her eyes, saw in an opposite mirror the reflexion of the ghost, standing over her. She is said to have died of terror.

Lewis told four other stories— all grim.

1

A young man who had taken orders, had just been presented with a living, on the death of the incumbent. It was in the Catholic part of Germany. He arrived at the parsonage on a Saturday night; it was summer, and waking about three o'clock in the morning, and it being broad day, he saw a venerable-looking man, but with an aspect exceedingly melancholy, sitting at a desk in the window, reading, and two beautiful boys standing near him, whom he regarded with looks of the profoundest grief. Presently he rose from his seat, the boys followed him, and they were no more to be seen. The young man, much troubled, arose, hesitating whether he should regard what he had seen as a dream, or a waking phantasy. To divert his dejection, he walked towards the church, which the sexton was already employed in preparing for the morning service. The first sight that struck him was a portrait, the exact resemblance of the man whom he had seen sitting in his chamber. It was the custom in this district to place the portrait of each minister, after his death, in the church.

He made the minutest inquiries respecting his predecessor, and learned that he was universally beloved, as a man of unexampled integrity and benevolence; but that he was the prey of a secret and perpetual sorrow. His grief was supposed to have arisen from an attachment to a young lady, with whom his situation did not permit him to unite himself. Others, however, asserted, that a connexion did subsist between them, and that even she occasionally brought to his house two beautiful boys, the offspring of their connexion.— Nothing further occurred until the cold weather came, and the new minister desired a fire to be lighted in the stove of the room where he slept. A hideous stench arose from the stove as soon as it was lighted, and, on examining it, the bones of two male children were found within.

2

Lord Lyttleton and a number of his friends were joined during the chase by a stranger. He was excellently mounted, and displayed such courage, or, rather so much desperate rashness, that no other person in the hunt could follow him. The gentlemen, when the chase was concluded, invited the stranger to dine with them. His conversation was something of a wonderful kind. He astonished, he interested, he commanded the attention of the most inert. As night came on, the company, being weary, began to retire one by one, much later than the usual hour: the most intellectual among them were retained latest by the stranger's fascination. As he perceived that they began to depart, he redoubled his efforts to retain them. At last, when few remained, he entreated them to stay with him; but all pleaded the fatigue of a hard day's chase, and all at last retired. They had been in bed about an hour, when they were awakened by the most horrible screams, which issued from the stranger's room. Every one rushed towards it. The door was locked. After a moment's deliberation they burst it open, and found the stranger stretched on the ground, writhing with agony, and weltering in blood. On their entrance he arose, and collecting himself, apparently with a strong effort, entreated them to leave him— not to disturb him, that he would give every possible explanation in the morning. They complied. In the morning, his chamber was found vacant, and he was seen no more.

3

Miles Andrews, a friend of Lord Lyttleton, was sitting one night alone when Lord Lyttleton came in, and informed him that he was dead, and that this was his ghost which he saw before him. Andrews pettishly told him not to play any ridiculous tricks upon him, for he was not in a temper to bear them. The ghost then departed. In the morning Andrews asked his servant at what hour Lord Lyttleton had arrived. The servant said he did not know that he had arrived, but that he would inquire. On inquiry it was found that Lord Lyttleton had not arrived, nor had the door been opened to any one during the whole night. Andrews sent to Lord Lyttleton, and discovered, that he had died precisely at the hour of the apparition.

4

A gentleman on a visit to a friend who lived on the skirts of an extensive forest in the east of Germany lost his way. He wandered for some hours among the trees, when he saw a light at a distance. On approaching it, he was surprised to observe, that it proceeded from the interior of a ruined monastery. Before he knocked he thought it prudent to look through the window. He saw a multitude of cats assembled round a small grave, four of whom were letting down a coffin with a crown upon it. The gentleman, startled at this unusual sight, and imagining that he had arrived among the retreats of fiends or witches, mounted his horse and rode away with the utmost precipitation. He arrived at his friend's house at a late hour, who had sate up for him. On his arrival his friend questioned as to the cause of the traces of trouble visible in his face. He began to recount his adventure, after much difficulty, knowing that it was scarcely possible that his friend should give faith to his relation. No sooner had he mentioned the coffin with a crown upon it, than his friend's cat, who seemed to have been lying asleep before the fire, leaped up, saying— 'Then I am the King of the Cats!' and scrambled up the chimney, and was seen no more.

-Appendix-
Ernestus Berchtold
& Childe Harold's Pilgrimage

Appendix 1
Ernestus Berchtold – Part One[1]

'Upon the left side of the lake of Thun lies the small village of Beatenberg, which, under the care of a simple pastor contains no individual above the rank of a peasant: it was in this village that I was born. Misfortune seemed to be anxious at my very birth to stamp me for its own.—Just at the termination of the short war between Austria and Prussia, of the year 1778, my mother arrived at this village in company with a gentleman severely wounded, as he said, in the slight skirmishes, which had alone formed the military display of this campaign. There was a mystery about them, which they seemed to wish should not be unravelled. The worthy pastor, therefore, whom I have since called father, did not make any inquiries of his guests, though it appeared to him very singular, that the most difficult and steep roads should have been preferred for the route of an invalid towards his home. The tender care of my mother towards this gentleman was exemplary; it seemed as if that courage and firmness, which was wanting in his breast, had taken refuge in her's. They were not Swiss, for the language they spoke was unknown to Berchtold the parish priest. They apparently understood German and French; but they said so very little, and that with such evident embarrassment, that nothing could be learnt from their conversation. There being no inn at the solitary Beatenberg, the pastor, with his usual kindness, on hearing of the arrival of strangers at the close of the evening, had immediately waited on them to offer his services and house. They were to have been his guests, only for the night; but the fatigue of the journey again forced open the wound in the gentleman's side; determined, however, to proceed, he attempted to walk to the litter prepared for him; the exertion proved too great, he fell into my mother's arms, and almost instantly expired.

'My mother was distracted; already far advanced in pregnancy, she fell upon the body, no longer capable of that firmness and resolution, which she had shown, when her companion's safety depended upon it. She listened to no one; but frantic, she sat by the dead body, alternately

---

1 Published by John William Polidori as *Ernestus Berchtold; or, The Modern Oedipus: A Tale* in 1819, publisher unknown. 'I am choosing to include parts one, three, and four in the appendix of this volume because *Berchtold* is a novella-length work and would too greatly disrupt the flow and detract from the other works that I prefer to have included in the main text. Since it is not the most easily obtainable work, so I have included parts one, three, and four in this appendix for completion's sake." — R.D.B.

shedding tears, and bursting into a loud laugh. Berchtold urged those soothing doctrines of which he was minister, but in vain; he spoke in vain of another world, of future hope; none could like him, soothe the pillow of the dying peasant, but here were miseries no hope could assuage. She at last fell exhausted upon the ground, she was conveyed to bed, and in a few hours I and a sister saw the light. But this did not allay her grief, she sunk into a silence that nothing could induce her to break; her eyes were fixed, and she at last died without a struggle. She was buried by him, whom Berchtold imagined, in spite of the disparity of his years, to have been her husband; and over their grave were placed those simple crosses, which you must have seen in the neighbouring church-yards. The pastor could not place any inscription upon their tomb, for he had been so engaged in attendance upon my mother, that he had not noticed the departure of her only servant, who took with him every thing of value belonging to his former mistress. He knew not what to do, there was no clue in his hands by which he could restore us to our family; for there was nothing to be found, except some linen and a locket, with my mother's portrait.

'Berchtold was a man whose humble endeavours had always been engaged in the attempt to fulfill those duties his profession imposed upon him. In these mountainous districts, the office of a parish priest is extremely arduous; he is often called up in the middle of the night, while the snow is falling, to go many miles over the frozen glaciers, to administer to the dying peasant the sacraments of the church. Berchtold never allowed the most distant hamlet to want religious comfort; he was old, yet often has he crossed to the foot of the Holgaut, merely to help the unfortunate in their attempt at resignation, under domestic calamity. He was not, therefore, likely to cast us from him; he immediately had us conveyed to the cottage of a married sister, and caused us to be brought up as luxuriously as an Alpine village allowed.

'I remember little of my early years, it seems, that I have vague visions of an age, when were spent whole days in gathering flowers, to adorn my sister's head and breast, from the precipitous bank that descends to the lake, when, at night, I was lulled half trembling, to sleep by the tales of my foster-mother concerning ogres and spirits from the dead. But all this is indistinct. When about six years of age, I was removed to the house of Berchtold. He called me son, and if the tenderest care and the greatest sacrifices could entitle him to the name of father, which I gave him, it was not wrongfully bestowed. One of the first circumstances which I can remember, is that one day, while sitting with him upon a bank, near the church-yard, gazing on the scene around, and watching the white sails which gleamed upon the lake beneath our feet; I threw my arms around his neck, and asked him, "Why they called me orphan?" He told me that my father and mother were dead. Retreating from him, I started, and trembling, asked him if he were then dead? He did not at first understand me; but upon my calling him by the name of father, he remembered that I had never heard the history of my birth. He took me to his breast, and weeping, told me, that I was indeed an orphan, that I was not his child. He then took me to the church-yard, and pointing to the raised sod, he told me my parents were there. I did not clearly understand him. I had then no idea of death; my mother, for so I called his sister, had told me tales of the dead, but these terrified without being understood. All the graves, save those of my parents, were adorned with flowers; upon my remarking this to him, he told me that they having died strangers there, none were bound to love them. I was hurt to see those flowers, which though faded, showed the attention of some living being, refused to my mother's tomb; it sunk deeply on my mind. And for years after, I felt a vague pleasure in strewing their graves with the fresh flowers that formerly were employed in adorning my sister's head. Often have I laid myself down looking upon their grassy covering, as if I expected that some of those tales of my mother would be realised with regard to myself, and that I should see them rising from their grave. My sister soon joined me in these meditations, and almost the first infantile communications which passed between us, rested upon another world. She would sit by me, and often the worthy pastor surprised us, after the sun had set, calling to our memory those tales we had heard when with our foster mother.

'We did not mingle with the other children of the village, for we delighted too much in each other's company; we spent hours together in talking about what had in a most unaccountable manner taken possession of our minds, or else we gamboled round Berchtold. He, debarred by his religion from the enjoyment of a domestic circle of his own children, had formed so strong an attachment to us, that his greatest delight was, when not engaged in his parochial duties, to join us in our games and infantile occupations. With all the simplicity of old age, he would lie down and allow us to play with his white locks, or tell us stories, which, though of a different nature from those of his sister, did not interest us the less. He was a good classical scholar, and was well versed in the history of his own country. From these sources he drew his tales, and at an early age he inspired me with an ardent love for independence and liberty, at the same time that he instilled into my heart, a burning thirst for the means of asserting a superiority over my equals. The anecdotes of Themistocles, Alcibiades and others, upon whom the fates of their country had depended, rested on my mind. Berchtold described to me the fallen glories of Rome, of that nation which once held sway over the known world. In short there was a material defect in my education, which is not uncommon, my imagination was stimulated, while my judgment was not called forth, and I was taught to admire public instead of private virtues. I rested upon those situations which one in the million attains, and in which the passions of others are to be guided, while I was not shown how to conduct myself, when my own inclinations and feelings might attempt to lead me astray in the common occurrences of life. With a strongly susceptible mind I imbibed deeply these first impressions, and throughout life this defect in my education has followed me. As I advanced in age, I gradually became acquainted with the Latin and Greek historians. Berchtold rashly, though innocently, took advantage of my thirst for relations of battles and deeds of renown, to induce me to learn. I consequently had Plutarch and Livy in my hands, long before I read any book tending to give man the power of regulating his passions.

'I joined the villagers only in those military exercises, which are constantly performed after the day's labour in every hamlet. Sometimes I would go with the chamois hunter, and reaching the higher ridges of the Alps, whose snowy summits were visible from the lake, I forced myself to follow him in his venturous pursuit. But it for a long time required a strong exertion of my mind to induce me to venture amidst the vast solitudes of eternal snows. I always felt an inward shuddering and awe at the sight of my native wildnesses. Even now I cannot bear to listen to those, who, amongst our magnificent scenes, which man has not yet overcome, and which mock his power, can talk of pleasure, and dwell upon the beauty of the scenery. I cannot feel this. I seem always to crouch beneath some invisible being whose power is infinite, and which I am conscious I cannot resist. It seems that I hear him laughing audibly at our vain attempts to encroach upon his dominion. It appears to me as if the avalanche were but the weapon of his impatience, while he insidiously steals upon those habitations he has covered with his snows, by the silent, gradual approach of the glaciers. Let mankind labour for ages upon these ribs of the world, and their work shall not be seen. The pyramids might rise unnoticed upon the rocks before my view, undistinguished from the fragment that falls unperceived with the passing torrent. I cannot bear that human strength should be unable to stamp its hand upon these towering memorials of convulsions we could not influence, could not hope to controul. This morbid feeling may have been excited by my foster mother constantly pointing to the Jungfrau, whose white peak forms so prominent a feature in the view from her house, while she related the peasant's tale of those mischievous spirits who dance upon its glittering icy coat, decked by the moon's ray. I gained, however, health and vigour from these excursions, and I became at last one of the most noted for activity in all the canton.

'I rapidly arrived at my twentieth year. My kind friend the pastor could not be induced to part with me. I was the only prop of his old age, I latterly, always accompanied him in his visits amongst the mountains, often joined him in his prayer over the dying, and frequently have I supported him at the brink of that grave, over which he was calling down the mercy of God, and which was soon to be his own refuge. My sister increased in beauty, and each day added some new charm to her person, and some additional accomplishment to her mind. I often represented to my father that I was of an age when I should begin to do something, and attempt to take the burthen of myself and my sister off his hands. He would agree with me in my arguments, but when the moment came, he was always so overpowered with sorrow, that I could not induce myself to leave him for the few remaining days he had to live.

'I seldom visited Thun or Interlaken; I did not feel pleasure in the society of men. I there found them engaged in all the petty interests, which pervade human breasts in the narrow sphere of a miserable provincial town. I found they could not sympathise with one whom they looked upon as a wild romantic mountaineer. About this time the French revolution began to exalt my imagination even more than the history of nations gone by, and I burnt with the desire of viewing nearer those actions, which in our solitary village, echoing only a softened sound of their horrors, seemed to wear a certain air of grandeur and glory. I ardently wished to join those soldiers who had driven back the foreign invaders from their native plains. I little thought then how soon I was to be engaged in resisting these very men, amidst my own native mountains.

'When the discussions between Berne and the French concerning the Pays de Vaud arrested the attention of all, anxious to be amongst men in action, and tired of my total want of employment, I again begged my friend to let me depart to the capital; but still, at his prayer, I remained with him. I laid myself down upon the snow, shining as it then was in the first rays of spring, and abandoned myself to visions of battle and renown. My spirits gradually left me, there was a craving for exertion about me, which I found it impossible to overcome. I seized my gun, and going amidst the eternal glaciers and rocks, I sought by forcing myself to exert my body, to lose this feeling of vacuity. But I often lost sight of the chamois, engaged in the thought of my country, and bounded from rock to rock, no longer occupied with what I imagined was before me. My sister would endeavour to sooth me by her caresses. I told her of my visions with regard to my country's cause, and at moments excited even in her breast the sparks of enthusiasm. But she generally echoed

Berchtold's sentiments with regard to the indecision and incapacity of the government.

'Tired one evening of listening to Berchtold, who attempted to repress my ardour, by representing to me that the country was betrayed, and that, in consequence of the tardiness and imbecility of the rulers of Switzerland, in spite of the courage and daring of its peasantry, it was doomed to become an easy prey to France, I left him determined again to seek refuge in the chase. I accordingly set out the next morning, intending to remain several days amongst the mountains; but I grew listless, and at the close of the second day, I still found myself upon the Wengern Alp. I issued forth from the chalet where I had taken some refreshment, and soon lost myself in reflection. I now looked with pleasure upon the Jungfrau's white head, glistening on the blue canopy of heaven. All the horrors of the Grindewald at my feet, the high summit of the Schrechorn, with the echoing thunders of the numerous avalanches, no longer appalled me. It seemed as if they now put on their terrors against a presumptuous foe, in defence of their children. There was no cloud upon the dark blue sky,—there was no mist upon the rocks; and though the snow still covered the whole surface of the mountains around, still there was a genial warmth and splendour in the sun's reflected ray, that vivified and strengthened. There was no sound, save that of the distant cataract, and falling avalanche. I stood a long time leaning upon my musket, to look upon this scene. How could avarice hope to find a resting place in the minds of those nursed amidst such objects? How could slavery expect to find its votaries resident amidst such fortresses? The tyrant could not dare to add these horrors of nature to those already revelling in his breast. A slave who shrinks before the frown of a despot, could not stand erect amidst these awful monuments of a power that mocks at human prowess. Upon this occasion, it seemed as if the sun threw its proudest ray upon these rocks; they had seen, might hope to see, men worthy of gazing upon that nature which, lifting unappalled its head amidst the thundering clouds, had snatched their weapon from their grasp, and had thrown it at its feet, while, with its snowy head, it struck in defiance the arching canopy of heaven. I was thus engaged in thought, which but served to increase my indignation at the conduct of men, who sacrificed to personal interest the safety of their country, when I was suddenly struck with the sound of a voice, which I shall never, never forget. In unison with my feelings at that moment, the notes sometimes broke out into the wildest tones of defiance; at others, suddenly sinking, they seemed uncertain and soothing. I dared not look around; I felt as if entranced, and I imagined I heard the voice of these mountains, mocking the invaders, then sinking into despondence. Gradually the voice approached,—I could distinguish words.—I heard footsteps. I suddenly turned round, and beheld a figure; I cannot describe it to you. Arrayed in a dress foreign to these mountains, her white drapery, breathed on by the wanton breeze, now betrayed the delicate form of her limbs,—now hid them from my sight. Her dark eye seemed exultingly to gaze upon my native rocks, while the wild notes of defiance played upon her lips. She suddenly saw me, and was silent. She looked around, as if for some one; and I then perceived, at a little distance, a man worn down more by grief than by age. I approached, and re-assured her. She blushed, and in that language which, in its very sound, breathes love, told me that she did not understand me. I could not answer; but, gazing on her, I seemed to be fascinated by her words. The old man approached, and we soon entered into conversation. I spoke Italian fluently; her surprize and pleasure cannot be painted, when she heard me address her father in her native language. I walked by her side, and I was often so lost in thought, that I was obliged to answer, by an unmeaning yes or no, the questions of the old man. Our conversation at last turned upon Switzerland; he seemed to be perfectly conversant with its situation. She entered with enthusiasm into its cause, and asked me, why I was idling amidst these valleys, when my country called me to the post of danger. These simple words from her lips caused an emotion in my breast that drew the blood to my cheeks. She thought of me. I at once promised to join my countrymen tomorrow. She then told me, that orders had arrived at the neighbouring towns for an instant levy to join the army of d'Erlach, which it was expected would be immediately brought into action.

'I was yet walking by her side, when we arrived at Lauterbrunnen. At the gate of a small cottage, after having asked me to take some refreshment, which I declined, they bade me farewell. There was a carriage waiting at the door. The thought rushed upon my mind that I might never see her again. I know not by what impulse, but, ignorant of the forms of the world, I summoned courage, at the moment of parting, to ask of her a ribbond with which she was playing; that, as I said, I might wear it in remembrance of her who had made me decide upon joining the patriots. Blushing, she looked at her father, who smiled consent, and she bound round my arm the scarf which she had worn during the morning. I have often heard that song again; I have often seen that form; and many are the years I have worn that scarf:—they have been years of misery and grief. Memory has no moment to look back to between the present and that happy day. Yet, for such another moment of enthusiasm I would undergo all my miseries afresh. I revert to it as the Arab, in the midst of the rising sands, turns to his visions of the green speck upon the desert's sandy ocean; amidst dangers, that is his hope; in anguish, that is his refuge. That moment seemed to bestow upon me the happiness which my fancy had so long pictured in the future. But every moment since has only served to weave closer round me the meshes of that net, which has shut me out from joy. I then, however, felt as if time no longer weighed upon me; and I was grieved, when arriving at my father's door, I found that the joys of hours had passed as those of a minute.

'I found my sister in tears; Berchtold, with his grey locks hiding the hands covering his face. Hearing my footsteps, my aged father rose, and taking me in his arms, with tears in his eyes, he told me, that he could no longer take upon himself to hinder me from joining my countrymen in the sacred cause of independence. He bade me take leave of my sister, and, while my courage remained, to surmount the pang of bidding her farewell. He told me, that he had caused my sister to prepare every thing for a parting, which he feared was to be our last. He embraced me, and rushed out of the house. My sister's eyes, wet with tears, now turned upon me, anxious to show the same resolution as my father had displayed, she hastened my departure. She gave me my gun and powder flask,—bound round my waist more than half the savings of Berchtold; and kissing me, bade me farewell. Bewildered by the rapidity of my different emotions, I hurried to the side of the lake, looked once more up the steep mountain, on the ascent of which Beatenberg raised its white cottages, and, turning the point of land which encroached upon the lake, I was soon wafted, in company with many others, towards the town of Thun. I did not heed the white sails hurrying along the blue rippling waves. I could not gaze upon the rich cultivated scenery of the lake. My mind was straying midst those wild glaciers, that once had been my horror,—which to-day had shewn me the unknown. Why does fate cause the approaches of misery to be decked with all the show of promised happiness? From this moment begins my eventful history; till now I had only been in the hands of the foul fiends that have tormented me, as plastic clay, which they formed in that manner, best fitted to contain the miseries they were preparing to pour upon it. You may think I have rested too much upon my early years, which passed without action; but those years saw deposited in my breast the seeds which have brought me to the state of apathy and misery you witness. That vision has proved to me the harbinger of more woes than it promised pleasures, and that scarf, which you see is yet bound round my heart, has felt it beat more violently through anguish, than it did even through hope, at the moment it first encircled my arm. My life till now had passed in dreams. I had not known the rude blast of worldly interests; I had been unconscious of the activity of the bad passions, and had only viewed man in the shape of my foster-father, breaking by his presence the shackles of grief that restrained the energies of his children, as the sun destroys the icy bonds that bind the vital powers of the spring. In the cause of charity and virtue, I had seen employed those powers and that activity which, exerted in a less degree, have often excited the admiration of the multitude, and concealed follies, nay, crimes, from even the philosopher in that halo of fame they bring around them. The earliest impressions, I received, were those from my foster-mother's tales, and they have not left me even at present; how much less, when but entering on manhood. I had so often gazed upon my mother's picture, which my sister wore round her neck from her earliest infancy, that, while sitting by her tomb, it seemed as if her image had haunted me in my sleep, for I frequently found myself arguing as if I had had actual proof of the existence of beings superior to ourselves.

'The evening had closed before I arrived at Thun. The town was crowded with the peasantry of the neighbouring mountains; there were fires throughout the streets, around which stood the aged and the boy, the mother and the virgin. They were all come to offer their arms in defence of their country. I approached the town-house; the door was crowded with petitioners, who were attempting to induce the sentinel to give them precedence in the enrolment of their names. I stood for some time watching the earnestness with which the aged laid hold of their very weakness and uselessness, as a reason why they should be preferred in the cause of death; while the young, elate with the hopes of youth, showing their sinewy limbs, appealed to their expectations of victory from their strength, as a reason why they should first be put upon the lists for battle. Their arms were more various than their ages; an iron wedge, sharpened and fastened to the end of a stick, served some as the substitute for a hatchet; burnt stakes and the chamois hunter's rifle mingled with the scythe rounded into a sabre, and the sickle straightened to a sword. While thus silently gazing upon the scene, a magistrate, a friend of Berchtold, going to his post, recognized me, and approaching, led me through a private entrance into the council chamber. My proffered services were immediately accepted, and I was directly ordered to put myself at the head of those villagers, who could be found in the town belonging to Berchtold's parish, avoiding, however, as much as possible the burthening myself with the infirm and women. I received orders to reach Berne in the shortest possible time, and to depart with the earliest dawn. I went out into the streets, a great part of the peasants had retired under the arcades which are on each side of the streets of Thun; they there formed one promiscuous mass, in which it was impossible to distinguish between man and woman. All was silent, save the dead sound of heavy footsteps and the hoarse voice of individuals like myself, treading amidst these sleepers, and calling out the name of that place, whose in-

habitants they sought. The night was damp and dark, there was no light
in the heavens, and often as I went, I stumbled over the body of some unseen person, who, uttering a note of impatience, again turned himself to
sleep. Imitating the example of the others, I called out the name of Beatenberg at every step, and soon mustered almost the whole population of
Berchtold's parish. I had a painful task, the old pointed to their children,
and with tears in their aged eyes, asked me if I intended to hinder them
from setting the example to their children, of dying for their native soil.
The women, pointing to their lovers, would take no refusal; they seemed
determined to witness their conduct on the day of battle, and see if they
were worthy of the love they claimed. I spoke separately to the young
men, and advised them to steal from their companions and meet me at a
certain hour about a mile from the town.

'They retired to rest, and I laid myself down in the street to sleep; I
was soon lost to all external objects, and I again saw hovering at my side,
her, who had seemed in the morning but a vision. She smiled upon me,
again urged me by those words;—but suddenly it seemed as if the earth
parted between us, and a huge chasm opened at my feet; we seemed
to stretch our hands towards each other; I threw myself into the gulph,
and awoke. Finding it but a dream, I again attempted to compose myself
to sleep, but in vain; her image still stood before me, and the moment I
rested upon it, the idea of my orphan state and her apparent affluence
startled me. I had not asked her name. I knew nothing of her; her form,
her face, her voice, and her words already began to appear to my memory as the recollections of an unsubstantial, supernatural vision; but at
this moment my hand fell upon the scarf, which I had now bound round
my chest. The touch roused me from my painful reveries, and hope pervaded my breast. I started from the ground convinced that she did exist,
I fell upon my knees, and uttered aloud a prayer to the Divinity to make
me worthy of her. Hardly had the words passed my lips, when a loud
hoarse laugh sounded on my ear. It was but a drunkard laughing at some
wild imagination of his own; but it made me shudder. I left the town; a
heavy thick rain was falling, there was no wind, nothing seemed stirring,
the shape of the distant mountains could be perceived by the white mass
they presented on the dark canopy of night, every thing else was of one
dead hue. I leant myself against the trunk of an old tree, and the dawn
had, unperceived by me, risen in the east, when I found myself roused by
the salutations of many of my comrades.

'I had in vain attempted to dissuade the old and the women from joining us; they were all with us at the appointed hour. I again as fruitlessly
endeavoured to show them the embarrassment they would prove to our
march; they would not listen, and I gave orders for the men to proceed.

In consequence of the exercise the peasants had been accustomed to in their native villages, I found no difficulty in forming them into something like a regular body. Towards night, as I had purposely pressed the march throughout the day, I was glad to perceive that the number of the old and infirm had much diminished. Next morning I again proceeded; it was with great difficulty that I could restrain myself and comrades from stopping to assist the women and old men who fell by the roadside through actual weakness and fatigue. Their cries imploring assistance from lovers, from sons, were heart-rending. I shut my ears and dared not listen. The nearer I approached Berne, the more deserted I found the country, all had flocked to the town or to the posts of danger. At last, with a body of two hundred men, not even yet entirely deserted by the women, I entered the capital. I read dismay and horror upon every face, even the peasantry, which here, as at Thun, crowded the streets, were silent; there were no signs of enthusiasm, but the glance of suspicion fell from every eye. Just as we were approaching the great place, we met a party of soldiers with their bayonets wet with blood. They seemed with hasty steps to be hurrying from a spot that brought something horrible to their mind. They did not speak, but we soon learnt that they were the murderers of Stetter and Ryhiner. They washed the blood of their countrymen from their weapons in the blood of their invaders, and at last bathed them with their own. Posterity may then spare their names the brand of infamy, for a momentary fit of rage against those they imagined traitors to their country.

'We were ordered immediately upon our arrival to reinforce the army at Frauenbrunnen, and were joined upon our departure by other militias, and by the venerable Steiguer, who had just thrown up the insignia of civil office in the determination of dying for his country. We arrived at a critical moment, the French having an advantage in cavalry and artillery, which the Swiss could not resist, were upon the point of surrounding the small army, the only impediment in their road to Berne. Steiguer immediately perceived the danger; ordering us to follow, he rushed forwards, and attacked the troops which, having already passed the right flank of General d'Erlach, were upon the point of gaining the road on his rear. The combat was obstinate, our chief attack was upon the artillery, with which the enemy was attempting to cross the road. Our women did not shrink, they rushed forward, threw themselves upon the wheels of the guns, and allowed themselves to be hewn to pieces ere they would quit their hold.

'The army under d'Erlach had in the meantime began its retreat to Grauholtz. We found ourselves surrounded and engaged amidst the very carriages of our enemy's guns, which we had taken. By great exertions at last we formed ourselves again into a compact body, and suddenly, as if by one impulse, falling upon our knees, we offered a prayer to the God of battle. The enemy thinking we were about to throw down our arms, checked themselves for a moment; we arose; the officers placed themselves at the head of the column, which set up a loud shout, ran upon the foe, and bearing all opposition down, soon reached Urteren, where we made a momentary stand, and then reached Grauholtz.

'The troops were immediately employed in raising an abbatis in front. While the men were thus engaged, Erlach and Steiguer met; at the instigation of the latter, the general came forward, and thanked my troop for the intrepidity it had shown during the whole combat. I was particularly noticed by them, and received from the aged general a medal he wore round his neck, as a token of his country's gratitude. "I have seen," he said, "the sun rise today upon freemen; I shall not see it set upon my countrymen. Our country is lost; it cannot thank its sons; let me, therefore, who have directed its last efforts for freedom, acknowledge the few hours' respite you have obtained to its fate, by presenting you with this mark of honour, which I obtained from a free nation." The loud roar of cannon burst upon our ears; he left me. I stood for a moment still; in one hand I held the medal, with the other I pressed the scarf of my unknown friend closer to my heart. Again we fought, but again their numbers enabled them to turn our flank, and, in spite of the strength of our position, we were obliged to retreat. One more struggle at the gates of Berne, and all was lost. The slaughter was horrible. Determined to sell my life as dear as I could, I rushed into the thickest of the fight; but my peasants followed me; they snatched me from danger, and bore me struggling through the town. I reproached them with having deprived me of an honourable death; one approached with aged steps; looking me in the face, he merely mentioned the name of Berchtold. I understood him; and, leaving Berne, we turned our steps towards Thun.

'Unfortunately, the slaughter by the enemy's sword was not the only horror that attended the dispersion of our troops. The peasants and soldiers never, in their legendary tales, having heard of a defeat accompanied by a retreat, on their native soil, imputed the whole to the treachery of their officers. The French had from the very beginning spread papers to this purport amongst them. As we proceeded, we therefore found the bodies of many of their officers hacked to pieces by the infuriate stragglers. Upon our arrival at Musingen, we found General d'Erlach in the hands of some of these men, who had determined to convey him to Berne. With him was his wife, who had accompanied him in his flight, and a young officer, whom I had remarked earnestly engaged in looking at my scarf, at the moment I was receiving the general's thanks at Grauholtz. I remonstrated with the soldiers, but in vain. I gradually, however, contrived to approach the general, and, when I thought myself sufficiently near to shield him, drawing my sword, I called upon the Beatenbergers to assist me, and instantly attacked them. The young officer, possessing himself in the struggle of a sword, was soon by my side. The peasants joined us; we drove the soldiers through the village; but in the meanwhile some stragglers issued from the houses, and striking the defenceless old man with their hatchets, left him for dead in the arms of his wife. When I returned, I found him apparently reviving through her care; it was only for a moment, he could not speak; it appeared, however, as if he recognised me, for he pressed my hand, and turned his closing eyes, first on his wife, then towards me. Thinking he recommended her to my care, I promised that I would protect her to the utmost of my power; his eye glistened, and he expired.

'At this moment I again heard the cries of the soldiers. As there was an unfrequented path over the mountains from this place towards Hoestetten, whence the young officer might easily get to Lucerne, I advised him to pursue it, and get immediately out of the canton of Berne. We parted. Gathering my peasants together, I directly set off with Madame Erlach in the cart towards Thun. She did not shriek or weep, she seemed stupified by the greatness of her loss, and, when arrived at the city, she without difficulty allowed herself to be taken from the body, and to be conveyed in a boat to Berchtold's, whence she retired in a short time to complete solitude, where she saw no one, and soon after died.

'I cannot paint to you the joy of Berchtold when he once more held me within his arms. My sister's tears flowed now as profusely as at our parting, but from a different cause. I had only been away a few days, yet the crowded events that took place in that short period made it appear as many weeks. The first spot I sought with my sister was my mother's grave. There I sat with her silently engaged in thought; after some time we began to converse, and as I had nothing hidden from her, I soon told the whole of my history from the morning of that day on which I had seen the unknown. She seemed disturbed, and upon my pressing her to explain to me what passed in her breast, she advised me to beware, for that it was probably one of the spirits of the Jungfrau's eternal frosts that had accosted me. I laughed at what I deemed her folly; but I soon perceived that there was something more on her mind than she was willing to confess. In vain I besought her to disclose it to me; she told me she durst not, and asked me as a favour not to speak to her any more on this subject. Alarmed, I knew not why, I looked at her with earnest attention. She could no longer bear it, but throwing herself into my arms, informed me that while I was away she had seen our mother, who had appeared to her, arrayed in mourning, announcing, that I was in the greatest danger, and that she must guard me, but that unless she wished to share my peril, she must conceal it from me. "Ernestus," my sister said, "I cannot obey, let your fate be mine, and I am content." Saying this, she again pressed me to her bosom, and wept. I was moved, I sat down by her side; bound in each other's arms, we gazed upon the green sod in silence, unwilling to disturb those thoughts which we knew must be the same in the breasts of both.

'Anxious to learn some tidings concerning the fate of my native country, I went every day to Thun. My indignation was excited by the recital of the cruelties and extortions of the French, and, when they dared to attempt disarming the inhabitants, determined not to submit to so base an insult, I was proscribed, and sought refuge amongst those mountains which had been the scenes of my prowess in the chase. I went and sat whole days by the rocks in the Wengern Alp, where I first saw that form which has since engrossed the whole of my thoughts. I made enquiries at Lauterbrunnen concerning the two strangers, but ineffectually; they had merely been there as other travellers, to view the sublime scenery of the mountains, and had not been heard of since. I remained a whole month amidst these rocks, only going to Beatenberg at night, when Berchtold and my sister would receive me, and supplying me with provisions for the ensuing days, tell me of all the insults that added to the shame of Switzerland. But at last they showed me the proclamation of Schwarenberg against the six eastern cantons. I immediately announced my determination to join them. Berchtold said nothing; my sister followed me out of the house, and begged to be permitted to accompany me. I refused, and upon her reminding me of her dream, told her, that, as it promised she should share my peril, it would prove impossible for me to go into any real danger without her, that therefore she need not follow me, or, if the fates decreed it, we should meet at that moment without any endeavours on our part to assist their fiat. I painted to her the horrors of the exterminating warfare that was carried on, and asserted that it was most likely not the peril of the sword in which she was to partake. In short, I forced her to promise me not to follow, by representing to her the misery Berchtold would undergo, if at once deprived of both of his adopted children. I led her back to the door, and left her in his arms.

'It is useless for me to give you an account of this campaign. It is recorded in history with even all the unsuccessful struggles for liberty, as one of those gleamings of that noble spirit in men, which, though generally hidden under the pressure of vice and corruption, at times bursts forth like the volcano's fire. I was taken prisoner, and could find no means of escaping, till the French, towards the end of June, after the restoration of Rapinat, became more lenient in their treatment of their prisoners, and less careful in their watch over them. I once more joined the Underwalders, and was again witness to the defeat of my country-men. I met the young officer I had saved from slaughter at Musingen. His name was Olivieri. We had no time for intercourse, always in action or on the march, we only saw one another in the field, where we often joined and tried to vie with each other in acts of daring and courage. We became at last noted in the army, and though only volunteers, we each soon found ourselves at the head of about ninety men, who always were ready to obey our commands.

'In the midst of our struggles in the Underwald, intelligence reached us of an insurrection having taken place in the upper Valais; it was deemed necessary by the leaders of our army to send them assistance, and thus cause a diversion in our favour. They proposed that one hun-dred men should be given to each of us, and that with this force we should be sent to aid the Valisians in their attempt. It was a hazardous undertaking, we had to cross upon the flanks of the enemy, and should be obliged, it was supposed, to pass through the Grimsel, which was in the possession of the French. When it was proposed, no one was found to volunteer; no Underwalder would leave his home in the hour of dan-ger. I had however remarked a number of Schweitzers, who had joined us singly, having left their dwellings, though not countenanced by their countrymen who were ranged on the other side, to partake in the dan-gers of the patriotic Underwalders. To these men we applied, and in a short time, two hundred men were selected. We kept almost upon the summit of the high ridge that joins the Furca from the Lake of Lucerne, and crossing the glaciers by rocks, that even in the chase of the chamois would have startled me, we arrived at Realp, and soon crossed into the Valais. At Obergesteln we learnt that some French troops had that very night crossed from the Grimsel, while the whole body of peasants were engaged in the lower part of the valley, amidst the fastnesses attempting to stop that force which was advancing by the bridge of Hochflue. They had committed great outrages, and had caused those, who were able, to fly behind the glaciers of the Rhone.

'Our undertaking now seemed desperate. The number of the French in the rear of our allies was greater than ours, and the end of the Valais through which we were to advance was flat and open, without any shel-ter, surrounded by steep mountains. Olivieri was however before me, we had each one hundred chosen men, and he seemed resolved on advanc-ing. Not knowing how to procure intelligence of the enemy, I immediate-ly offered to advance by myself and reconnoitre. As I well knew every part of this valley, I was certainly the fittest person in our body for such an undertaking; but my companion would not hear of ceding the post of danger to me; we were obliged to draw lots, and it fell upon him, and he departed.

'In the mean time the women, hearing of our arrival, came from their fastnesses, and joined us. They seized upon every thing which offered the semblance of a weapon, and resolved to follow us. As my companion did not return as soon as I expected, fearful of a surprise, I determined to advance, and, if possible, gain some of the passes before the enemy knew of our arrival. I, however, previously sent forward a young woman, to see if she could obtain any intelligence of Olivieri. I then ordered the men to follow in silence, and marching all the evening, we at last, towards night, reached the village of Blizingen, where the valley straightens, and becomes more inclosed and rocky. The river here runs through a deep-ly-cut channel, more resembling a ravine, than a common bed. As I knew there was but one path, and that very steep and dangerous, I ordered my men to rest upon their arms, while I went along the river's channel to learn something concerning the enemy, who I thought could not have advanced much farther. At last, being arrived opposite the village of Vietsch, I heard a great noise, and saw many lights; making no doubt but that these proceeded from the point where the enemy was stationed, I returned. I found my men asleep; arousing them I ascended at their head the steep sides of the mountain, and making them march parallel with the path, but much higher, I brought them above the village, and hid them in a wood of pines that stretches along the steep. I now no longer feared the superior numbers of the enemy, the ascent was so precipitous that we could not be attacked, except to great disadvantage, while we could either join the Valisians, or fall upon the foe with every prospect of victory.

'I determined once more to go and discover their exact position, giving the word that if I thought it a fit moment for an attack, I would fire my gun, and then sound my hunting horn, so that no mistake could occur from the firing of any drunken soldiers or guard. Wrapt up in my mantle I descended from the wood, and found the men lying securely asleep in the road between the houses. They were certainly all there; anxious to know something concerning my companion, I resolved, in spite of the risk, to awaken some straggler, and learn from him if any prisoner was amongst them. I accordingly approached one who, stretched along the edge of a precipice over the river, was sunk in a sleep that seemed that of the innocent. Putting my pistol to his breast, I awoke him. Alarmed, he was upon the point of calling out, when I threatened him with instant death. To my inquiries he answered, that a person had been surprized by some stragglers in the course of the day, and he added that he was then

lying bound in a cottage in the very centre of the village, destined to be
in the morning a butt for their muskets. It did not appear that his having
been found armed had excited suspicion, as he was taken for a common
peasant. Determined to save Olivieri, I knew not what to do with this
sleeper, to shoot him would alarm the enemy, they might immediately
dispatch my friend, and yet I could not leave this man to raise his comrades. I pushed him down the precipice, and directly entered the village.
All were asleep, I found the cottage, there was a light in the window. I
stole close to it, wrapping myself up in my mantle. I looked in; you may
imagine my alarm when I saw two soldiers awake in conversation, while
my friend, upon his back, was bound to a bench fastened to the floor.
There were several soldiers at my feet, with their arms by their sides, a
sudden thought struck me, I seized one of their guns and firing it, I instantly retreated to the other side of the cottage, where I had remarked a
window close to the fatal bench. As I expected, the two soldiers went out
to inquire about the report which they had heard; I took advantage of the
few moments, leapt into the room by the window, roused Olivieri, who
gazed upon me expecting death; I made a sign for silence, cut his bonds,
and was again out of the cottage with my companion, when I heard the
door open to admit the two soldiers. We hastened up the ascent, and
when, amidst the rocks I fired my own fowling piece, and blew a national
air upon my horn. Before the enemy, alarmed by the two soldiers, who
missed their prisoner, could form, we were amongst them, and morn
had hardly dawned before we had cut to pieces the whole of this detachment. I could have induced the men to give quarter, but the women were
outrageous, they followed our soldiers, and dispatched the wounded,
whom their more merciful companions had spared, while they excited
the Schweitzers to slaughter even those who threw up their arms; none
were saved. The Valisians who were making head against this body, hearing the report of so many guns, did not know what to believe; they however approached, and when they heard the Swiss war cry of liberty, they
immediately joined us. Their joy cannot be expressed by words; Olivieri
and myself had in the mean time met, and his thanks were profuse; but
what was my sorrow to find that the young woman had been seized and
bayoneted in cold blood, because she would not acknowledge the right
of the French to a superiority over her nation; she had pretended not to
know my companion, and thus avoided betraying us, by not being con-
fronted with him.

'We had gained a victory, but it only served to delay the subjection of
this noble peasantry; they were obliged to come at last to a capitulation.
We could not be included in it; the French asserted that the Schweitzers
were deserters. We therefore determined to attempt once more a pas-

sage over the most unfrequented Alps. To avoid the Grimsel, where the French might pass to interrupt our passage, we crossed at once into the valley of Formazza. Hidden in the day amidst the woods, or upon the tops of precipices, my few companions, for our numbers had been greatly diminished, journeyed in the night by a circuitous route into the Vadi Bedretto, and thence over the St. Gothard by the path we had come, towards the valley of Stantz. We had there expected to find our former companions yet struggling for life, if not for victory. We entered the valley, there was no living creature to be found, there was a silence unbroken by any sound of human labour, the hoarse ravens fluttered above us, as if they thought we also came to spread their banquet. We could find no one to guide us, no one even to tell us of our misfortune. Our imaginations pictured sufficient. The villages were burnt, the cattle lay slaughtered on the field, it seemed as if death, with one sweep of his scythe, had cut off the life of all. Creeping along the sides of the mountains, we approached Stantz, we expected to find the destroyers there; but when we were in sight, there was no town appearing. We found but sixteen straggling houses yet standing, all the rest were burnt; these also bore the Frenchmen's mark, they were billetted. We looked at one another in silence. The birds of prey were not disturbed by our presence, they continued feeding on the dead. While walking amidst these ruins, I at last heard the sound of a voice, it was the cry of sorrow. A mother had found words to call on heaven for strength to bear her individual grief, heedless of her country's death. I saw her amidst these ruins, her hands were tearing up the soil to give the last refuge her country could afford to her child,—a grave. She did not at first perceive me, when she did, her hand worked doubly quick, while, with her eyes fixed upon the corpse, her hurried lips uttered, "hold your hand, hold your hand for a moment, I shall soon be ready to follow." I dug her son's grave, and left her striking the sod as if she repented of having resigned the body to the earth.

'We assembled our few remaining companions, Olivieri and myself addressed them, we advised them to separate and seek singly a refuge in their homes. While yet speaking one of them brought before us a man, who seemed to have risen from the grave. His grey locks, thinly scattered on his head, were entangled, his eyes were sunk so deep within their sockets, that their lustre seemed the last glimmering of life before it sinks. He had sought death from the foes, and they, in mockery, had bade him live. They had fastened him to a table in the open air, with several days' provision within his reach, and had placed before his sight the corpses of his aged wife, his children, and grandchildren, all marked with the wanton infliction of their barbarous cruelty, not even excelled by the voracity of the vulture or beasts of prey. This wretched being told us that the Schweitzers had troops placed the whole length of the other side of the lake, to hinder the fugitives from this valley escaping. Upon this intelligence our men became dejected; the thoughts of dying ingloriously by the hands of their treacherous countrymen, weighed upon their mind. They spoke some time amongst themselves, and then begged of us not to desert them, assuring us that if we enabled them to reach the upper part of Schweitz unbroken, they then could disperse to their families without danger. We could not refuse them. We ordered them to go along the shore, and see if they could find any boats; they soon got together more than enough to convey us over. But they had been observed by an individual, who had immediately put off in his skiff, and crossed to the other side. This rendered greater caution necessary, as he would undoubtedly inform the enemy of our neighbourhood. We offered to take the old man with us; he refused; determined, not even in ruin, to desert those spots which had seen his birth, and infancy, and manhood, he returned to the bodies of his children, threw himself upon them, apparently resolved to breathe his last sigh in defending these mangled remnants from further insult: all that we could do was to lay a fresh stock of provisions by his side.

'Hoping to find the enemy unprepared, upon some point or other, we immediately entered our boats. They however watched us, and at the moment of our landing, appeared before us in a body so numerous, that it seemed impossible to escape. We formed our men in the very water into a wedge, and taking a gun and bayonet ourselves, we led them against the foes, determined either to cut our way through, or to fall upon the field of battle. After repeated charges we at last succeeded, but our numbers were reduced to fifty, and several were wounded. We mustered upon the very spot where the liberty of Switzerland had been sworn to by the three patriots; it was the valley of Brunnen. Fortunately the Schweitzers did not pursue us. Travelling night and day, we at last gained the higher parts of the canton, whence my companions came. We separated, and it was a proud moment when they brought their wives and children to thank us as the preservers of their husbands and fathers. Olivieri and myself were now alone amongst the mountains, as a reward was set upon our heads, and as we here depended entirely upon the fidelity of many who had shunned our cause, we determined to depart and seek some other refuge. My friend knew not where to go, being ignorant, as he said, where his family was; he having left it privately, while travelling, to join the Swiss. He however determined to go into the Austrian dominions, and there seek for information. We parted with mutual protestations of friendship, and a promise from him of letting me know by means of Berchtold, when he had found safety. We had had little communication; I therefore scarcely knew more than that Olivieri was not his family name, and that he was an Italian. I had often remarked his eyes to be fixed upon my scarf, but his delicacy preventing him from speaking upon a subject, he perceived I was not willing to converse on, was the cause of our parting without further communication. He was indeed the brother of that object, which had never deserted my thoughts, which, sleeping and waking, my lips had often called upon. No night passed, though dangers surrounded me on every side, without her image rising to cheer for a moment my wearied heart; but the dreams always ended unhappily. It seemed as if the fates were determined to embitter even those moments, in which I was engaged in a noble cause, thus to prepare my mind for those pangs which follow guilt. You may think I rest too much upon these instants of my life; but I dread to narrate my miseries; the recalling to memory anguish and grief racks my heart; but I have begun, and you shall hear the whole.

'Knowing the country well, and being acquainted with every pass, I found no difficulty in reaching the neighbourhood of Beatenberg, and I was soon locked in my sister's arms. Berchtold and Julia's anxiety about me had been great, they had heard by report of my being in action, and had seen in the papers the immense reward offered for my person. Seeing me safe they could not contain their joy; but morning came, and I was obliged to depart into the mountains, for who could be trusted? Treachery and avarice had proved at last the master passions in many breasts, though they had at first worn the mask of the noblest virtues. Promising to be back at night, I flew to the Wengern Alp, and there again visited the spot, which now began to appear sacred to my mind. At night I returned to the pastor's cottage; I only found my sister there, he was gone to Thun. Leaving the house, Julia led me to our mother's grave, and again begged of me to be cautious, for constantly while I had been absent the same admonition had been given. It did not seem to her to relate to a personal danger; it was a vague threat, that seemed the more terrific, because it could not be decidedly represented to the mind. She then begged of me to relate the dangers I had undergone; I gave her a minute account of the whole.

'Amongst other things which she mentioned to me, was the arrival of a stranger, who had taken up his abode at Interlaken, and who excited the wonder of his neighbours by the account his servants gave of his riches, and by their intimation of his having communication with an evil spirit. The source of his riches was unknown. Many were the tales related concerning him, and if but half were true, she said, he must certainly be possessed of a wonderful power. He was old and apparently wretched. His only daughter accompanied him, her beauty was as much the subject of conversation, as the riches of her father. These were the only rumours my sister had heard, for they had only arrived a few days before. I wish that I had never known more. I did not laugh at the idea of the supernatural part of the report. We were both too strongly imbued with the tales of our foster-mother not to attach some credit to them. My sister's dreams, in which our mother visited her, my own which always portended misfortune, had enforced upon our minds the belief of the interference of superior beings.

'For several nights I returned, but Berchtold was yet, as we imagined, at Thun. My sister and myself left entirely to ourselves, again talked over the feats of Olivieri, and she often asked me to repeat them, seeming with pleasure to rest upon every circumstance regarding him. Foolishly, I also took a pleasure in relating them, for though we had been constantly rivals, there was a frankness, a heedless daring about him, that excited admiration, at the same time, that the warmth of his expressions called forth a reciprocal feeling of love. I knew not then how to discover the sting protruding from the rich scales of the snake. We conversed upon our mother, and my enquiries were numerous about her person, her voice. I cannot explain it, but I wished even from Julia's dreams to aid the representation I had formed from her portrait of a being, who seemed even after life, to feel an interest in my fate. In the locket, there was a melancholy look about her dark blue eyes, that was rendered heavenly, by the soft smile playing upon her open lip. I had gazed upon it so often, that I had her image before me, even when far from home, but it was only distinct in the face, which appeared to be gazing on heaven, with the consciousness of having obtained a prayer for me. Since my sister's dreams, it seemed as if I knew a mother's care, and I often sighed, to think, that though thus thoughtful of me even in heaven, she did not think me worthy of enjoying her smile.

'One morning I left my sister, and retired to the wild borders of the Brientz lake. The sun rose, and with its glittering ray painted on the water, the reflected images of the wild rocks upon the other side. There is a point which juts into the lake, and on it are the ruins of an old church; I did not feel inclined to exert myself to reach a more distant spot, but I laid myself down by an arching gateway, round which the ivy clustered, as if by its tenacious grasp, it would hold together the monuments of another age, upon which the breath of time was acting with a destructive power, unheeded by man. I seemed to feel this breath of time acting upon me as upon these works of man, the wild joys of youth seemed sunk into the melancholy uniform feeling attendant upon age, when all joy is passed, all hope extinguished by the consciousness of the presence of death. I gazed upon the mists as they rolled slowly along the hills, veiling successively the various beauties of the banks, and watched the cloud's shadow, depriving the lake of its glittering sheen. I rested upon their passing powers, but did not notice, that the glow of the bright sun invariably returned upon the spots, before darkened by a shadow. The peasants' barge, and the light skiff, passed rapidly before me, but unheeded they passed in silence, for it appeared, as if, even they sympathized in my grief. It was mid-day, I rose to shelter myself from the sun's ray, and sought that side of the point towards Interlaken. There was a small light skiff upon the water, and in it was a female figure. It was at some distance, it gradually approached; my heart fluttered, my breathing became difficult, my eyes were fixed upon a form I seemed to recognise. Her face was not lit up, as I had seen it, by all the fire of her indignant eye; carried along by her small latin sail, she approached. Her eye was gazing upon the rippling wave, cut by her prow, it seemed as if joy did not dwell there, her eye-lash veiled its splendour, while her black locks curling on the breeze, floated playfully around. Her breast at times would heave as if the sorrow in her bosom was loath to grieve her, but she seemed unwilling it should go, for she rested upon it. I stood intently gazing, it seemed as if my least motion would have at once destroyed an illusion. The current brought her heedless close to the shore, and the boat struck the bank; she looked around and saw me. It was plain she recognised me, for her eyes fixed upon her scarf. To paint to you, the varying expressions of that eye, and the varied colour of that cheek, is impossible. With slow hesitating steps she approached, our eyes did not dare to meet, and I stood by her for some moments in silence; at last with a trembling voice, she asked me if my name were not Ernestus Berchtold? "If you own that name, fly instantly, you have been betrayed, and the blood-suckers are already, at Interlaken upon their way to Berchtold, do not go there to-night." I could hardly acknowledge my name, I was so moved by her voice; she offered to convey me to the other side of the lake, if I thought myself safer there. Unconscious of what I was doing, I entered her boat, and taking the oars, tried by violent exertions to rouse myself; we did not speak; when upon the other side, I landed. Farewell fell from her lips, and it seemed as if the echoes mocking me, repeated farewell. I stood still, watching her as entering the current of the Aar, she was gradually borne down towards Interlaken; even when she had passed the bridge, I gazed, and seemed to see a white speck, that I imagined was her.

'I turned away, and towards evening found myself upon the same spot on which I had first seen her. Again, she had appeared. At first, she had guided me into the path of honour, this day she ensured my safety. Was she then a vision? I asked myself. Was it my guardian angel, who invested that form? I did not think of pursuing my route to any place of greater safety, it seemed as if this spot where my protector had appeared, was secure, I laid me down beneath the rock, that had witnessed her presence, and offering up a prayer to heaven, I gave way to all the visions my imagination offered. She had recognised me, she knew my name, my rank, and still felt an interest in my safety. If you have ever known, what it is to be in love, you may judge what my feelings were, if not, my words are useless, I hardly slept the whole night.

'Next day I roamed restless over the Alpine heights around, I did not heed the horrors or the beauties of these solitudes. The cataract fell by my side, and yet I heard it not, wherever the valley wound, thither I followed; but as evening threw its stillness over nature, ere the light canopy of heaven was darkened, I found myself upon the covered bridge of Interlaken, I had forgotten my danger. The open spaces between the beams supporting the roof, enabled me to see the different houses which skirt the river's side. Mine eyes however gazed upon that one, in which I had heard, the new inhabitants of this neighbourhood had taken up their abode. I had imagined my unknown was the beautiful daughter I had heard of from my sister; and I had not long been upon my station, when I saw her come forth, supporting upon her arm the feeble steps of the old man I had seen with her upon the Wengern Alp. Her eyes, fixed upon his languid face, seemed anxiously to be watching the features of her invalid father. There was a bush not far from the door beneath the wide-spreading canopy of a lofty elm; she placed him there, and I saw reflected on her face, the smile which beamed upon the old man's, as he gazed upon the setting sun. I watched her slightest action, her every glance, it seemed as if her words soothed the pains of sickness, and lightened the languor attendant upon an invalid's inactivity. Oh, if that smile had fallen upon myself, as it then fell upon her father, if I had only felt its cheering influence without that burning passion it has excited in this breast; but I must not anticipate my narration. The sun sunk behind the mountains, she carefully shielded her sire from the damp. I watched her retiring steps, heard the door close after her, and at last turned away.

'Intending to depart again to some retired spot, I was advancing, when I perceived that there was some one at the end of the bridge apparently watching me, and then retiring as if to look up the road. Alarmed, I seized my hunting knife and approached him: seeing me advance, he came towards me, it was the servant of Berchtold. He had seen me from a neighbouring height, and anxious, as he said, for my safety, had immediately followed me, and finding me on the bridge, had several times spoken to me without my paying the least attention; perceiving at last how I was engaged in contemplating the beautiful object before me, he had contented himself with guarding the entrance to the bridge. I enquired about the French soldiers, he turned pale, but at that moment I hardly noticed it; he told me that they had been watching Berchtold's house during the whole of the night, apparently aware of my being in the habit of going there every evening. He informed me that there were only two remaining, whom he had supplied so abundantly with wine, that if I chose to venture towards the cottage, he would inform Berchtold and my sister where they could meet me, while he engaged the attention of my pursuers. How easily I was deceived; I have since known the value of men's professions; then I was young and confident in virtue. Berchtold and my sister met me, but there were other soldiers in the neighbour-hood; those the servant led to a pass by which I must descend on my return. It was but another instance of that venal boasted honour which so much stains the Swiss patriotic history.

'In the mean time I learnt from Berchtold that he had walked to Berne, hoping to cause my sentence of outlawry to be cancelled; that the French employers had lulled him with hope until he had been rash enough to acknowledge my being in this neighbourhood; when they would listen to him no longer, but sent the soldiers I have mentioned. Even Ochs, who had formerly been his school-fellow, had laughed when he reproached him for so vile a breach of confidence. I spoke with my sister apart, and informed her of my discovery, she was surprised, and seemed downcast; but Berchtold, who had gone to listen, and reported all silent, joining us, we could not proceed in our conversation. I em-braced them, and had begun to descend the steep, when I heard myself challenged; having my gun with me, I fired, and the challenger fell; but one leapt upon my back, it was my own servant, and I was surrounded. I struck upon every side, but it was in vain: determined, however, to be revenged, I threw myself upon the ground with the traitor; as we turned, I succeeded in getting him undermost, and plunged my hunting-knife up to the hilt in his chest. He groaned and died. I surrendered.

'I was hurried to Interlaken, put into a boat, and before the dawn of day, was locked in the prisons of Thun. I expected to be immediately taken out and shot. I was not, however, disturbed till night, when I was awakened from a sound sleep, and, guarded by a company of soldiers, was ordered to be conveyed to the castle of Chillon, upon the lake of Geneva. Entering into conversation with the soldier who marched by my side, I heard from him that Berchtold and my sister had in vain applied for admission to my dungeon, upon hearing of my misfortune; that the reason I was removed at this late hour arose from the magistrate's fear-ing a rescue by the people, who once or twice in the day had seemed, by their tumultuous meeting, inclined to force the prison of him whom they called their only remaining patriot. From him I first learnt that my name was in every mouth; that there were romantic tales printed about me, and spread over all the country in spite of the police which endeavoured to suppress them. I did not feel any vain exultation at this; I was too near death; but I certainly experienced some satisfaction in the thought, that for Louisa,—that—that was her name. For years locked up within my breast, it has not passed my lips. I have not dared to utter that name, not even whisper it to my own ear; but it has been deeply engraven here. It is now a spell that conjures up horrid thoughts; once it did not.

'But I must command myself. I had not visited this part of Switzerland yet, though beautiful, and perhaps richer than any I had seen, it passed unobserved before my eyes. The simple villagers, hearing my name, came round the inns at which we stopped, and looked upon me in silence. Mothers brought their children to me to kiss, as if my kiss could call down a blessing, or inspire heroism. I crossed the Dent de Jamanu, and soon saw the castle once the prison of Bonniva, now destined to be my own.

'The draw-bridge was up, and the sentinels were parading as if they esteemed the castle of importance. Upon my name being mentioned the bridge was lowered, and I soon heard the clash of the chains employed in raising it after me. It seemed to be accompanied by a voice that bade hope to leave me. The rude stare of the soldiers, and the bustling scene of the officers, running to and fro, did not tend to relieve the sorrow that weighed upon me. I had dared danger in the chase upon the Alps; death in battle; yet here the thoughts of leaving all, oppressed me. I did not think of the pain of parting with existence; but Berchtold, my sister, the vision of the Wengern Alp, all seemed to press upon my imagination with eyes, that, by their look, seemed to denote a breaking heart. My head fell upon my breast, while, with folded arms, I walked along the vaulted passage. I was searched, all was taken from me, my knife, the little money I had. The rude jailor already had his hand upon the scarf, retaining it with a firm grasp, I looked at him, and seeing his daughter close by his side,—"if that child," I said, "should be far—far from thee, and thou couldst not hope to see her but in heaven, couldst thou part with the only relic of her memory?" He looked upon his child, and let go his hold.

'I was taken into a room where several officers were deliberating concerning me. I had stood before them some time, when one asked me my name. "Ernestus Berchtold" was my answer. "It is the traitor;" fell from the lips of one. I looked upon him; he could not stand my glance, but sunk into silence. They were considering whether they should lead me to instant execution, or whether I should be confined till the pleasure of the government at Berne should be known, as it was thought that they might wish to make a more public exhibition of the punishment of him they so gratuitously called a traitor. I was respited by one voice, and was instantly ordered to my dungeon.

'To descend into the prison, which is below the level of the water, it is necessary to go down a narrow circular staircase. While descending it, we were stopped by that child upon whom I had rested my appeal to the jailor; to pass her we were obliged to go singly; when I came close to her, I felt something pressed into my hand, while at the same time she made a sign with her finger for silence. I put her present into my breast and followed her father, who was before me, while the others were at my back. I entered a long vault, its floor was the solid rock, and its high roof was supported by seven thick massy pillars. The waves of the lake dashed sullenly against the walls above my head, and the feeble light that pierced the high windows only showed me the damp black sides of this prison. There were the steps of a prisoner marked during a long imprisonment upon the very rock; I still heard the noise of bolts, but did not heed it, till I arrived at a narrow cell, partitioned off from the greater dungeon, which I had not perceived in the general obscurity. Into this narrow space I was forced to enter. It was not sufficiently long for me to lie down at full length, and the barred grating, which, far above my reach, was intended in mockery to represent a window, received no reflected light from the dark floor of Bonniva's prison. I heard the doors fastened one after another.

'Beneath the slowly sounding wave I was cut off from humanity; the monotonous dashing against the castle's base alone broke the dread silence; it seemed like the loud note of the moments in nature's last hour. My spirits fled, and I leant against the stones to which I was chained, with hands clasped, and my eyes painfully straining, as if they sought at least to see the real horrors of my dwelling. Fatigued by my long journey over the steep Jamanu, I sought to sit and sleep, but the damp floor for a long time kept my racking mind awake to all the torments of thought, while it hoped for a momentary oblivion of woe.

'At last I sunk into repose, and it was not until late the next morning that I awoke, but I awoke refreshed; I had seen the constant attendant upon my dreams, and I soon lost myself in thought upon her various appearances. The waves above me seemed silenced to a calm, and the sun's powerful meridian ray reflected upon the various sides of the greater vault, penetrated, though in a feeble glimmer, my solitary cell. Gradually stealing upon my ear, I heard a distant voice, which in melancholy notes seemed to sympathize with my sorrows. I listened; it approached; the measured strokes of an oar interrupted the heavenly strain; suddenly breaking into livelier notes it sung of hope; the voice was, they were Italian words, it was my vision's voice. It gradually sunk away into indistinct sounds. I seemed another being, hope breathed upon my heart, and Louisa wore the semblance of that enchanter; oh that I had died, that she had left me to myself to die! it was not the will of heaven. Again I heard the splashing sound of the oar, and again that voice sounded on my ear; it was no longer the thrilling notes of an air, but in slow recitative it bade me hope, it told me that a boat should be stationed at two or three stone throws distance from the castle, ready at all times to receive me if I could manage to get out, and that in the mean time endeavours were making at Berne, to gain a repeal of the sentence passed upon me. Again the song of hope sounded in my cell, losing itself gradually in the distance, it at last left me with nothing human within hearing.

'I now remembered the child's present; feeling in my breast, it proved to be a file and a knife; I instantly began to work at the wall, dividing me from the great dungeon; while thus busily employed I heard the bolts of the vault withdrawn; my jailor entered, he spoke not, but threw me my pittance of bread, and laid down my pitcher of water. Hardly was he gone, when I resumed my work, the dampness of my cell aided me. The mortar was soft, and the wall built of small stones; when therefore I had scraped the mortar away from the crevices, I did not find any difficulty in forcing them out. One by one I tore away many, and I had already almost pierced the wall, when, fearful of penetrating entirely through, lest the jailor might next day detect my attempt, I managed to replace most of the rubbish in its situation, and to push the rest into a corner. I now began with my file to cut the chain that surrounded my waist. The jailor came next morning, and told me, that at the dawn of the ensuing day I was to be conveyed to Berne. This gave me additional strength, the hopes of liberty, of seeing Louisa, spurred me on, and in a few moments I was free from my chains. With what impatience I waited for the night. It came; I forced a passage through the wall, and I found myself in the great vault without a manacle. The moon's ray seemed with a smile to seek the ground on which I trod, for its cold beams pierced the grated apertures above, and illumined some dreary spots. I was not yet free, the window was high above my reach; but I did not despair, taking the whole length of the dungeon to give me power, I leapt, and caught with my hands at one of the bars. I raised myself, and resting my knee upon the shelving sill, I immediately began to employ my file, and the rusty bars soon gave way to my arm.

'I paused a moment, the cool fresh air of the night, no longer poisoned by the noxious vapours of the subterranean dungeon, played amidst my hair; I seemed to inhale life. The moon's ray, decked with one glittering streak of light the whole breadth of the wide lake; it seemed the path of hope. Not far distant was a barge; in three or four hours my murderers would be at my prison door. The ground was covered with snow even to the water's edge; I leapt into the lake, and being a good swimmer I reached the boat numbed by the cold, I had hardly the strength to raise myself into it. There was no one to be found; there were some coarse provisions, a peasant's habit, and a letter; it had no direction, "if safe," it said, "proceed to Milan, you will hear of us there. Your sister is well, Berchtold ill, but do not go to him, he knows we are attempting to save you, and he shall immediately be informed of your escape. The daughter of Olivieri's father." It was now that I learnt that Olivieri was the brother of Louisa Doni. It was now explained why he so attentively examined my scarf.

'I could not resolve on leaving Switzerland without seeing Berchtold, there was a western breeze, I hoisted the latin sail, and in a few minutes I was free from immediate danger, and on my way towards Beatenberg. It was necessary that I should keep amongst the mountains, and I only dared approach the most solitary chalets. They were generally deserted, and it was with difficulty that I procured sufficient to support nature during the three days I was upon my way. Arriving at Œschi, I took a boat from the side of the lake, and crossing, was soon at the foot of the steep, on which stands Beatenberg. The stillness of the night was broken by the sound of voices chaunting, which, stealing down the mountain, sunk upon the wave. Alarmed I knew not why, I rushed up the path; before the church porch, around the great cross that stood upon the green sward, knelt Berchtold's parishioners arrayed in white. Though the red glare of the pine torch fell upon their faces, it did not allow me to distinguish any one. Breathless I stood incapable of motion. The chaunt ended, the minister of peace arose, it was not Berchtold; "he's dead," I cried, and rushed forward; alarmed, the peasants rose, they recognized me and were silent; my sister took my hand and bade me pray for him who had died. Incapable of any longer bearing the anxiety attendant upon my fate, I knew not what I did, I knelt, I heard the solemn chaunt sing Berchtold's requiem, and could not join it. The earth closed over him, and the minister led me to my former home.

'I was inconsolable, they talked to me of ensuring my safety; I was deaf to their remonstrances, and only listened to grief; my sister was left alone with me. She wept with me, and ere it was dawn, had persuaded me to depart. She told me that Louisa had been with her, had made her promise to join her, in case of Berchtold's death, so that I need not be under any anxiety on her account. She informed me that Louisa had walked with her over my haunts, had enquired after every minutest circumstance about me. My sister said, she thought she loved me. I could listen to no more, embracing her, I issued forth, visited my mother's and Berchtold's grave, and soon lost sight of Beatenberg.

'Louisa loved me! it was too true, if that love had fallen upon any one else it would have proved a blessing. On me; you see my withered lineaments, my sunken eye, my feeble step, think you, a common curse could thus blast the bloom of life? Berchtold was but the first victim to my love. My love has left me, a scattered pine amidst this desolate scene, but first it has destroyed all who were bound to me, my love has proved,—but I must preserve my strength,—I have horrors to relate,—going through the Simplon, then a road only passable by mules or on foot, I soon arrived at Milan.

'I was in safety, the city was in possession of the Austrians. I had hardly rested at the inn, at which I took up my abode and was making enquiries, in hopes of discovering the Donis, when Olivieri entered. We flew into one another's arms, he answered none of my enquiries, but leading me to his carriage, we arrived through the corso at a palace close to the gates. We got out, I knew not whither he was leading me, the doors of the saloon were thrown open, and I found myself in the presence of his father, his sister. The old man advanced, and taking my hand, which hung by my side, he thanked me for having twice saved the life of his son. I knew not what to say; conscious I owed my life to Louisa's interference, I could not find words to thank her. The father at last led me towards his daughter, and bade her attempt to thank me. Her eyes turned upon me, suffused with blushes she had some words upon her lips, when I forced myself to stop her. "Do not mock me, what do I owe to you? my life is nothing, when compared to that thirst of honour, you inspired in my breast." Again, she blushed and was silent. At that moment, another carriage arrived, it was my sister attended by two faithful domestics of my friend; locked in my arms, she was at last taken thence to be clasped in those of my preserver.

'After taking some refreshment, the father led me into another room, he there told me that Berchtold's last request was, that he should supply his place, and take my sister and myself to him, as his children. As he spoke, he showed me at the same time, the last lines which my foster-father had written a few moments before he died. They contained our history as far as he was acquainted with it; in them he bade me trust always in God, and recommended me to bow under that dispensation, which had made me an outcast on my native soil, and not to murmur at the will of him, who had deprived me of the feeble support a Swiss pastor could afford against the pressure of events, since he had raised me up a protector, so much more powerful in the father of him whose life I had saved. Doni took me by the hand, and perceiving the tear trembling in my eye, he begged of me to let him supply the place of Berchtold. He called me son; Louisa's father could not call me so in vain, I fell upon his neck, but could not speak.

Ernestus Berchtold – Part Three

'I HAD already undergone more than falls to the lot of most men in this valley of miseries; but I was not allowed repose; from this moment my heart was torn piece-meal, by fiends each more horrible than the other. Not many days had elapsed since Julia's death, when Olivieri's father received an anonymous warning to prepare himself for the worst news. The letter was dated Strasburgh. Next day he read in another letter, that his son, under an assumed name, had been taken with several others of a band of robbers, who had for a long time infested the banks of the Rhine. Doni had now become aged and infirm, he was not capable of undergoing the fatigues of a long journey, yet it was hardly possible to hinder him from setting off, to attempt saving his only son. He blessed me when I insisted upon performing that office. "You have twice saved his life in the field of honour, may you be as successful in snatching him from the death of infamy." He gave me unlimited power, and rushed into his daughter's apartment to seek there for the comfort all else seemed to deny him.

'I departed, travelled night and day, I saw Switzerland again, but did not even notice it, my mind was anxious, was alarmed; it seemed as if heaven wished by repeated inflictions of its bitterest curses, to humble to the dust the family circle of my protector. I was so rash, that for a moment I dared to question Providence. So weak is all mortal knowledge; misery is but the fruit of vice, virtue never feels the world's infamy; there is a heavenly beam of certainty in the merciful justice of their God that enables the just to look upon all the inflictions of this life, but as the most lenient atonement due to a tender, though offended father, for those weaknesses belonging even to our nature.

'I arrived at Strasburgh; its fretted spire, rising high above the houses, upon the far extended plain, for a long time marked the bourne to which I was tending, while the winding road that forms the approach, seemed to mock my endeavours to reach it. Justice had been summary, there had not even been a regular trial, but a court martial had been summoned, and instantly had condemned the prisoners to death. A respite had however been granted for a few days, in consequence of the hopes entertained of inducing some individual to betray the secret retreats of their comrades. I immediately proceeded to the prison and asked admission. Application being made to the governor, and it being evident that I was not one of the gang, I obtained it. I entered; bolt after bolt slowly sounded as they were forced from their rusty clasps, and I found myself in a low gallery, the damp was slowly falling in measured drops from the arched vault above, and the coldness of the chilly air made me shiver. The jailor bore a torch before me; its red light at last rested upon the strong fastenings to a narrow door. I gave him money, and seizing the torch, entered.

'Upon a little straw, covering a few loose stones in a corner, lay a form, which seemed reckless of all. The light of the torch did not cause it to move, its hands were upon its face, clenched; its whole posture was strained, as if by the convulsive stiffening of its limbs it would harden itself against the inflictions of the mind. I could not speak; thrice I strove to utter the name of Olivieri, and thrice it stuck in my throat. "Speak, I can listen to my fate," Olivieri at last said in a hurried voice, "Death they say silences all voices, if it can silence that which echoes through the chambers of my breast, scaring oblivion and repose, I shall be content to die, though on the wheel, waiting, when all my limbs are crushed, for that repose the iron bar may give." He did not move, but seemed to mutter this, addressing himself as much as me. "Olivieri," at last fell trembling from my lips. He with one exertion stood erect; his eyeballs straining in their sockets, seemed to seek the horrid certainty they knew would blast them. Berchtold appeared before him. He threw himself upon the straw, and with a hand clenching with furious grasp his long black hair, he seemed to force his head upon the ground, fearing his eyes should again turn upon me. I sate upon the stones at his side, laid my hand upon him, bade him be comforted. He shrunk as if my touch froze him. I told him of my hopes of obtaining his release, of the wealth I could employ in bribing his judges. He looked up; "You talk to me of mercy; Julia was seduced by me." "I know it," I replied, "it is your father, who acts by me, I am but my benefactor's agent. For him I am to attempt to save his son." "His son?" he echoed in a faltering voice, "true, I was his son." I in vain asked him for information on which to proceed; he would give me none. I left him.

'I applied to the court which had passed his sentence. I saw the members who had composed it in private. They gave me an account of the desperate gang to which he had belonged, and painted in horrid colours the devastations they had committed in the French territory. It appeared that Olivieri had put himself at the head of these outlaws, and had with the most daring rashness and carelessness of life, always eluded the numbers that often seemed to surround him. I made those who appeared favourable to my pleading great presents, under the pretence of enabling them to aid the furtherance of my objects. Amongst the others, the governor seemed to have the most influence. I gave him immense sums, which he promised to expend for the prisoner's advantage. The next day was appointed for the execution. I had not seen Olivieri again, I was anxious not to encourage too much his hopes of life, while all seemed uncertain. I called early in the morning, upon the governor; I saw him. He raised my expectations very high, he said, that if I could but find the slightest pretence for a respite, that it was determined to grant it. "If I were to judge by your riches, he and yourself must be of higher rank than you pretend." I had concealed both our names. "Now, if you can but show that some one of influence is interested in his fate, we will admit of an appeal." Rashly I was induced to utter the names of Olivieri Doni, and Ernestus Berchtold. I was surprised at seeing the man before me turn of a most deadly pale. His limbs seemed to fail him, but he in an instant recovered himself; his voice alone betrayed an emotion I could not understand. He assured me that he would instantly occupy himself about it, and I left him. An hour afterwards I received a note from him saying, that I should prepare a carriage and post horses upon the bridge, and as the clock struck the first hour of the morning, that I should present myself at the prison door, where I should meet my friend. That this had been thought the best means of allowing his escape. Passports were enclosed, which would allow us to pass the bridge, and we should then be in safety. I immediately prepared every thing, anxious for the arrival of the moment when I was again to save the brother of Louisa.

'Towards evening, restless, I issued out. I wandered up and down that part of the main street, which, covered by arcades, brought to my recollection the towns of my native country. Memory was rapidly crowded with the images of infancy, while the evening tints, and the stillness of nature soon enabled me to abstract myself entirely from the surrounding objects. I at last found myself in the cathedral. There was no one there, even devotion seemed for a while to have laid aside its pomp to enjoy the balmy freshness of an April evening. I had at last advanced into the most obscure part of the aisle; when turning round, a light figure dressed in the singular vestment of the neighbouring peasantry, caught my eye. Her step was hurried, and her head moved anxiously as if seeming to shun observation. Thinking that my presence might be painful, I was retiring, when she beckoned to me. I stood still, and she was immediately by my side. She hastily addressed me. "You are a friend of Olivieri Doni's, you perceive from my knowing his name, that I am in his confidence. He once professed love to me, he has probably done so to many more, who are now like me ashamed of their name; but even if I told it you, it would be useless. Hoping to be of service, and anxious to hear of him who still possesses my affection, though he has broken the peace of her, who loves him; but I deserve it, for I am guilty, he cannot love guilt; I am so lowered, that I was not ashamed to gain my object, by seeking one of the prison guard. I have just left him intoxicated. From him I learnt, while he was blabbing all, that he was called upon to perform a service this night in the course of his duty, that he disliked. I gained from him that he was to belong to a party, who were to lurk in one of the streets and seize my lover and yourself, at the moment you thought yourselves secure of freedom, for that the police were anxious to take you, who, they suspected belonged to the same gang, and therefore had resolved to arrest you, while engaged in aiding the escape of your friend, which alone will ensure your condemnation." I was astonished, could I then be so shamefully betrayed? I immediately remembered the sudden emotion of him, who had promised so much, when he heard our names, and it flashed upon my mind, that I had a faint recollection of his name as being that of an officer in the French troops opposed to us in the Underwald, who having been placed in a post of importance, had been surprized by Olivieri and myself, and had been, in consequence of his precipitate flight, broken and disgraced. It was now nearly dark, I could not think of deserting Olivieri without still attempting his rescue. The girl's information might be false. I spoke with her, she appeared sincere; I offered her money, she refused it; my case was desperate, I determined to confide in her, I got her to lead me to the neighbourhood of the prison, and show me all the turnings and secret cuts through the different streets. I soon gained a perfect idea of the plan of this part of the town, and I began to hope in consequence of the intricacy and number of turnings in this neighbourhood that I might elude the ambush, if I could at any point break through the guards. I did not entirely open my plan to my guide, but asked her if she knew of any certain place of refuge, whither I could retreat in case of need. She led me and showed me her apartment, it was miserable, but there was an air of neatness about it that seemed, in contradiction with the poverty, visible in every article. "If you can arrive here without being observed, you are safe."

'To avoid suspicion, I immediately left her and returned to my hotel, which was close to the river. The hour approached, I armed myself with a sabre and a pair of pistols, and hiding under my large Italian cloak another sword and pair of fire arms, I sauntered negligently out of the inn door, and calling my servant, I told him in a loud voice to take care the horses were ready, as I intended to set off the moment I had fixed on. This I did to blind any one, who might be watching my motions. Then turning down some of the most abrupt windings, I first went whither I had learnt the different parties were to be placed. By means of keeping close to a shaded part of the walls of the streets, which being lit by a single reverberating lamp1 suspended in the middle between the houses, were rather dark, I could approach very near them without being perceived. I discovered one point which I thought weaker than the rest, for the number of the men seemed smaller, the silence being greater. I then returned, entered the main street leading to the prison, and soon found myself at its gate, without meeting any one. The high narrow windowed walls, were suddenly illuminated by the moon bursting in all its splendour from behind a cloud, and high above my reach I perceived some one watching me, he retreated and I heard the gates open. I could not perceive who was there, for the hollow opening was in the dark shadow thrown over it by a salient buttress. My heart beat violently. It might not be Olivieri, a person was pushed out, I heard the words, "I am free," spoken in a voice that denoted the despair within. I approached, it was Olivieri. Throwing off my mantle, I stood before him; he did not notice me, though the moon's ray was full upon us. I roused him, thrust the sword and pistols into his hand, and bade him follow me. "We are not safe, we must baffle the traitors yet," said I, "be firm, we have escaped greater perils than these, follow me." His broken voice, merely answered, "To death."

'I hastened towards the point I thought the weakest. A shrill whistle sounded at our back, and we found ourselves surrounded. The first who approached, were dead at our feet. They retreated before us, we had broken their circle and were already free towards the street down which it was necessary to turn. "Now to the right," I cried to my companion. A shot struck him and he fell; I rushed to the spot hoping that he might rise. I struck on every side determined not to leave him in their hands, their numbers increased, but at the same time I heard a trampling of feet at my back; desperate, I rushed forward; a female shriek struck my ear, and at the same time I found myself joined by about twenty men. Their blows told, we caused the town-guard to retreat, I could not again find Olivieri's body. I rushed along the streets, and was soon at the young woman's door. I heard voices; alarmed, I listened, they were evidently from their conversation trying to console some one. I knocked, a female voice immediately exclaimed, "'Tis he," and the door was opened. I entered, Olivieri was extended upon a couch, attempting to write a few lines; he had just finished. Around him were many men in a strange uncouth garb. They were his former companions, who having received the same intelligence from the girl as myself, had resolved to attempt a rescue, and had stolen singly into the town. Olivieri gave me what he had written, it was to his father; his pale face was turned towards me, his feeble arm could hardly support its own weight. "Berchtold, I have not deserved the risking yourself for me; can, can you forgive me dying." "I do," was my answer, and I held his extended hand. He threw himself upon his bed, and in a stifled voice, "There is another, whose forgiveness I do not ask, but tell, oh! tell her, it was her shame that has damned me, that made me desperate, damned me." "She's dead, she too would have forgiven you; she died speaking of you, but not cursing you." His limbs were instantly relaxed, and moved no more.

'We were now aroused by the entry of another robber, the soldiers were approaching, I begged of them not to leave the body of my Louisa's brother to their insults; they lifted it from the couch, and placed it in a recess so artfully contrived, that it bid defiance to the most accurate search, and they promised me they would return and bury it. We took the young woman with us, and separating, we singly hastened to a spot by the river's side, where we hoped to find boats. Ten only reached it, we entered a small wherry. The town was in such confusion that the necessary orders had not been sent to the different boundaries. We let the boat float down the stream, and soon found ourselves beyond the fortifications. We landed on the German side, and presently reached one of the dwellings of the freebooters. I now learnt that it was this same girl, who had written the anonymous letter to her lover's father. I offered her a considerable sum of money, again offered to secure her an independence, she refused it all, and insisted upon remaining with those men amongst whom she had first known Olivieri. I remained with them a considerable time, anxious to see the body of my former friend secure against any insult, and before I left them, aided by the daring of these men, who managed to enter the town and take the body from its secret hiding place, I had the satisfaction of consigning him to the earth. I gave them all the loose money remaining with me, secure upon my letters of credit of having more than enough to convey me whither I liked.

'I reached Inspruck, not deeming myself safe in any part of the French territory, I determined to remain here, and I wrote to Doni merely mentioning that I had been unsuccessful, and telling him where I had stopped. I thought it best not to tell him more for fear of my letter being intercepted, and hoping that when I saw him I should be able to break the fatal news to him. My last hope was vain, for all the papers and public prints contained a full account of the daring attempt I had made to save a robber from the ignominious sentence of the law. Our real names were also mentioned, and at the same time that many rested upon the courage, they pretended had been shown in this attempt, many took advantage of the connection of our names with a gang of robbers to throw discredit upon our former conduct in the cause of Switzerland. It was soon known through my banker, at Inspruck, that I was the notorious Ernestus Berchtold, and I was surrounded by people, who were glad to seek some refuge from their ennui, in gazing upon one, whose name seemed to have something like romance attached to it.

'Count Doni arrived, Louisa too, though weak and feeble, still in better health than when I had last seen her, accompanied him. She had been
forced to exert herself to support her father under his anxiety for his
son, and then under the severe blow of seeing his own name in all the
prints, known to all as the father of Olivieri, "a captain of banditti." The
spring had given her the requisite strength, and I was glad, after so long
an absence, to see her once more sitting by my side with renovated life. I
could not take my eyes from her, and I rested upon her face so long, that
I gradually forced myself to hope that her hectic flush was but her natural
colour. We were constantly together, and tried in each other's presence
to forget the griefs that weighed upon us both. I had given the last lines
of my former friend to his father. He had read them in his own room, and
though when we next met I remarked that his eye turned upon me wet
with tears, as he evidently did not intimate the least inclination to expose
to me what his son had written, I did not seek to learn the substance of
Olivieri's note; though I was anxious to learn whether he had disclosed
his conduct towards Julia. We never after mentioned his name, and we
tried to keep the thoughts of his melancholy fate out of our minds, by
resting upon our hopes of Louisa's welfare.

'Count Wilhelm, whom I have before mentioned, found us on his way
to his native country; hearing of our being at the same hotel, he sent in
his name to my friend. Day after day he remained at Inspruck. The whole
of the evening was spent with us in our apartment, and he seemed to
seek more and more the means of showing attentions to Louisa. At first
I was not disturbed by them, but at last I became fretful and irritable, for
it appeared as if Louisa took a pleasure in his conversation. I had heard
so much of his power of attaching women, that it seemed impossible for
her to resist him. Every thing he did, though the most simple action,
was perverted in my mind, to a covert sneer at my poverty and insignif-
icance. I often answered him abruptly, and even insulted him. Louisa's
meek eye turned upon me, but it seemed to have lost its influence. I one
night found him by her side, he seemed to be earnestly pleading, he
had hold of her hand, and she smiled. Stung to the quick by so slight a
circumstance, I turned furiously away and retreated to my chamber. Had
Berchtold taught me to command my passions, had he but shown me as
models for my conduct, men, in the privacy of life, I might have escaped
much. It is vain to rest upon it. I had thought that Louisa's influence
over my mind, would have hindered me ever again losing myself, hurried
away by any passion. But here Louisa's form arose in all the hideousness
of jealousy's distorting mirror! I was mad. My clenched fist struck the
table, I could not command myself. I remained some time in this state,
when turning my eyes towards my bureau, I perceived an almanack; I

seized it in mockery; I counted up the days since she had told me she loved me. I was suddenly struck, it was the 28th day of the month, it was a combination of seven. It seemed as if by one exertion I might free myself from doubt, and be at once lost in the horrible certainty, or be for ever blest in the knowledge of Louisa's heart.

'I did not reflect; the hour struck; I seized my lamp, and rushing out was already close to the apartment of Doni, when wavering on the wick the flame suddenly sunk and expired. Yet nothing around was dark, it seemed as if I was surrounded by a mist formed by a dazzling light, too dazzling to allow me to view the objects round. I was a moment startled, but undismayed I strove to rush forward, my feet were bound to the floor. I strove but in vain to move. Gradually the light cleared, and gradually the features of that face, which I had so often gazed upon in my imagination, my mother's, appeared distinctly before me. Her form was majestic, but in her eye there was a softness, which was not even destroyed by the severity of her feeling. "Ernestus," were her words, "heaven has decreed at my prayer, that this crime shall be spared to you, you shall not act ungratefully."—She seemed to vanish with an expression of sorrow upon her face, as if she were not allowed to continue, and felt the horror that burst upon me in consequence of the ignorance in which I was left. My senses forsook me, and the dawn of day had already pierced the thick clouds before I recovered.

'I did not return to my room, I went into the open air, my thoughts were hurried; baffled, I was not subdued; jealousy still was not banished, I did not rest upon my mother's apparition, so strongly had the idea of Louisa's infidelity taken hold of me. While walking amidst the intricate windings of a public garden, I heard voices near me. One was Count Wilhelm, I heard him boasting of the favours of some lady, whom another thought loved him, and he suddenly presented himself before me; I grossly insulted him. He took a pleasure in torturing me with his pretended concern at my mistress's kindness to another. I struck him, we fought and he fell severely wounded. I stood by him and he was amply revenged. He told me that he had seen me entering the preceding evening, that being at that moment engaged in speaking about me, and Louisa having expressed her wish that I might be received into the Austrian service, he was offering his interest to forward my views, and that knowing how easily I was irritated, he had purposely taken her hand. He advised me to fly, I was obliged to do so for I was no longer safe where I was.

'Louisa was then innocent. I cursed that fate which seemed to hang about me, always shielding me from death. I had fought in battle, but never yet had received the slightest wound: I had escaped from prison while the axe was falling. My rashness seemed to be incapable of hurting me; for there was a shield around me, that snatched me from peril. I was preserved from worse than death. Even this last act could not divide me from Louisa. She loved me indeed. Alarmed at seeing my antagonist brought in wounded, she did not shriek; she did not give herself up to loud and weak lamentations; but conscious, that probably my life depended upon the event of his wound, she sacrificed herself entirely to the care of the invalid. With unremitting attention she watched by his bedside. But when he was declared free from danger, then the cold hand of strengthened disease made itself felt. She was obliged again to return to her sick chamber. But first she begged her father to inform me of the favourable result. I returned. Doni met me on the stairs,—embraced me; but no joy was visible on his face. He announced to me the dangerous state in which Louisa lay, but did not reproach me; she had forbidden it. I was introduced into her room. Consumption was ruining her system; she was faint and weak; her continued cough and the marked colour on her cheek, but too well denoted the power it had acquired. I could not even ask her how she felt; but the tears fell down my cheek on the moist hand that held mine. She allowed me to stay with her. Talked to me of that power, whose pleasure it was to strengthen the weak and console the wretched, she said that he had soothed the agony of death's visible approach, and until she saw me, that she had found relief in the thought of the short time we should be separated. But now she saw my grief, she was sorry I should be left alone, even for those few moments, without a being, to whom I was attached; that she again wished for life, if amidst all its miseries she could but hope for the power of consoling me through these inflictions. In fine, she did not speak of herself, but of me—of the wretch who had gradually broken the weak threads which bound her pure soul to life. Count Wilhelm perfectly recovered, left us. I had seen him, and as the only atonement in my power, had acknowledged my folly, and had begged he would pardon it, though it had been so severely felt by him. He returned a vague answer, and I saw him no more.

'Doni's interest was great; his wealth insured him friends, active in bringing back to their neighbourhood one whose riches fell in beneficent showers upon all. By their influence, he soon obtained a pardon for my resistance to the civil authorities in behalf of Olivieri, and I was granted permission to return to any part of the French territory. As the cold Alpine air seemed to hasten the rapid steps of his daughter's decline, he determined upon having her conveyed again to the borders of the Lago Maggiore, which had seemed last year to have possessed such renovating powers. We departed, and soon found ourselves fixed in our abode. Nature wore the same aspect as the year before. Palanza, with its white walls and glittering columns shone as brilliantly in the sun's ray;

the smile of heaven seemed to play upon the fairy islets of the Boromei, and the rich woods of Belgirato reflected in the blue surface of the water, seemed to put the beauty of this in competition with the sublimity of the wild rocks of the upper part of this long lake. But Louisa's health had faded. She could hardly hope, if the disease continued its hasty steps to see these scenes again. But still that fairy enchanter, hope, acted upon me, and as each day she gained some slight addition to her strength, I pictured to myself years of happiness united with her I had long so ardently loved. She would not undeceive me, but left me the illusion. She was again able to enjoy the freshness of the air, and to walk out, amidst the varying scenery around. I supported her, and felt the light pressure of her feeble form resting upon my arm. She would stop, and draw some reflections on the bounty of God, even while in pain, from the various pictures before her; always attempting to turn my mind towards those thoughts, which she well knew could alone give me consolation, and a resting place in this vale of miseries. But still she seemed to recover strength. I entreated her to hope, and not to give way to such desponding thoughts. Her father, who was deceived as well as myself, begged of her to console herself; talked to her when alone of me, and spoke of his hopes of seeing us united, of her forming the only prop to his old age, and that I, how could he say it? was alone worthy in his estimation of receiving from a father's hand so great a treasure.

'Unwilling to grieve her father, she yielded to my importunities, promised to be mine, if upon a certain day her acquired strength had not given signs of decay. You may imagine with what anxiety, with what hopes I watched each intervening moment. Every cold breeze made me shudder; every cloud that veiled the sun's ray caused me pain. I counted her breathings: whenever she moved, watched the firmness of her step. The day arrived. She was not weaker, but had seemed to find renewed energy in the thought of being mine. She was mine. I cannot paint to you the delirious state of mind, in which the next months passed over my head. I had a right to protect. I was something to that being; but I will not rest upon these feverish moments, you may imagine them; Louisa was mine—Louisa mine! But heaven had not smiled upon our union—no, no. It was but the anger of a God veiled under the brightest hues. Louisa was my,—but I must relate the whole. Her health, as the winter approached declined again, and we returned to Milan. We lived with her father.

'To engage my wife's attention, I resolved upon fitting up a part of the palace anew for our private use. Every thing was ordered, when it occurred to her that the best ornament we could add would be the portrait of her father. I had recovered from my sister our mother's locket, and shewing it to Louisa, we determined upon having it copied and hung opposite the Count's. To give Doni, as we thought an agreeable surprize, we determined upon having them privately executed, and placed in their situation without his cognizance. I sought for a painter, and spent whole mornings with him at his eazel, directing him how to paint my mother. I described to him, as well as I could, her appearance to me at Inspruck, and pretending that I had seen her in a dream, I insisted upon his representing her in such a situation. He executed it, and by the magic effect of his pencil, excited a most extraordinary impression of awe in my breast, whenever I turned my eyes upon the picture. She seemed starting from the canvass; the outline of her figure was lost in the blaze of light, and her face, meek amidst splendour, severe, though with features naturally mild, seemed speaking those words I had heard. I took Louisa to see it; she felt the same awe as myself, though she could not assign a reason for it, but she continued gazing, till I perceived her eyes wet with tears.

'The pictures were privately introduced into the house. We had succeeded in keeping them secret from Doni. In a few days was Louisa's birth day, we resolved therefore to make him our guest upon that occasion in our new apartment. We invited several of our most intimate friends. Every thing passed in gaiety. At last, all the company were gone, and we remained alone. We then, taking him each by one hand, led him into what we intended should be our private sitting room, telling him he should then see our best friends, the one in heaven, the other on earth. The door was opened; directly before him was his own portrait; he seemed surprized and pleased; he turned round; I had hardly announced to him that the one he then saw was my mother's, when he fell. Alarmed we raised him. "Your mother! did you say, your mother?" He threw himself upon the floor, and called upon God to free him from the consciousness of horror like to his. We knelt by him close together; he saw us, raised his aged hands, and with a fluttering voice bade us, if we dreaded heaven's most dreadful curse, to separate. But again he fell to the ground, crying, "It is too late, too late, the crime is consummated." We raised him, he turned hastily away, for he was opposite the portrait, and besought us to take him thence. We led him to his chamber; he motioned us to leave him.

'We retired in silence, we knew not what to understand; was it merely the greater effect of that portrait's power which had been exerted over us. We could not hope it, we were lost in conjectures. Louisa's health was so much broken that I was alarmed for the effects it might have upon her, and, therefore, strove to turn her mind from the subject; but in vain. She did not sleep the whole night, the anxiety concerning her father would not allow her to seek forgetfulness even for a moment. The effect may be imagined upon so weak a constitution. Her father refused to see us for several days, and each day I saw the mind acting upon my wife's health with alarming rapidity. When this reached the ears of her father, he could no longer resist our importunities, he saw us; but the sight of his haggard and wild countenance did not restore Louisa. He had evidently been engaged in writing. We pressed him to explain his conduct. He replied, I knew not what I wished to learn. "It will blast you, as it has done your friend. You must learn it, but it shall be when I am in the grave, and before him who has thus punished my crime; then, then, I may intercede for you, if I myself am sufficiently purified by suffering. He may hear a father's, though it be a criminal's, prayer." His words seemed almost incoherent, he at times called me son, but then with hurried impatience he corrected himself; he asked me whence I got that portrait, I put the locket into his hands. "'Twas mine, I gave it," he hurried, pressed it to his breast, and bade us leave him. We did; he saw us daily, but in silence; he seemed absorbed in one thought, and to that he could not give utterance. He took little, too little, nourishment; but always occupied in writing; he seemed but to find strength for that; when we saw him, he was hardly capable of motion. His task was at last finished. We had been with him as usual, when we were suddenly recalled. He was dying; he bade us kneel down by his side, he blessed us. He took the papers from his table, and putting them into my hands, he bade me read them when he was in the grave, and know the horrors that awaited me; he commanded us to trust in God's mercy, and he sunk, blessing us, upon his couch, breathed no more.

'I bore my Louisa from this scene, she was from this moment confined to her bed. I saw the Count laid in the vault of his ancestors, and then returned to my wife's chamber, whence I never issued till I had no longer a wife. It was evident that all art was unavailing. It was the undermining of a constitution, not by a common bodily disease, but by the griefs of a heart that had never lately found a moment's respite from the most bitter inflictions. Yet, even at this moment, she seemed to forget herself, in her attempts to console me. She alone broke the silence around; I sat in mute despair; I saw Louisa before me, and I was to be left isolated, scathed by divine anger, without consolation. She held my hand, spoke to me of another world; for a moment her words would even subdue my grief, and let me feel as if that hope were enough. At last, seeing the silent sorrow that was preying confined within my breast, she sought to rouse me, bade me read those papers; I did in a luckless moment; only hinted at the horrible mystery unfolded there, and saw the last convulsive throe I was destined to witness in any bound to me by love. I cannot tell you more; read that damning tale, and then you may know what I dare, nay, dare not rest upon. My history is quickly ended. I was dragged from the now lifeless Louisa; but I stole from my guards in the night, gained an entrance into the room, where death showed, as if boasting his beauteous victim, dressed in pomp. The wax tapers seemed to burn dimly, as if in unison with the solemn scene; the black walls, the felted ground, the corpse stretched out, arrayed in white, the stillness visible upon that beauteous face, stilled even the tumult in my breast. She did not seem dead but asleep, I had held her in my arms, upon my breast, looking as she then looked, I gazed upon her for moments, it seemed as if I believed the still appearance wronged my senses. I was about to press her to my heart, my lips were approaching hers, but I started; there were two flies already revelling on those lips, and she could not chase them. I hurried away, I could not remain any longer there. I followed her bier also, and I saw my dearest, my last bond to this earth deposited there, where peace seemed to invite me too. Religion, Louisa's words, however, had not lost all influence, I resisted that will, which would have led me to immolate myself a victim to the manes of those my love had slain. The hopes of a futurity, of Louisa in heaven, upheld me. I retired first to Beatenberg, there in the former house of Berchtold, I spent some time: it was too near the first scenes of memory. I left them and came hither; here, amidst these rocks, bound to me by no memory of the past, I spend the few hours allotted me by heaven, in penance; here each day, my prayer is offered up, that in mercy I might be taken to Louisa. My life has been a life of anguish, of vice, of crime; but still amidst these there have been moments, there has been a being, which, if life could be renewed, would cause me to dare all again, once more to go through those few moments. Often in my dreams I see that form, but now, if when in this mortal life her beauty could not be described, how can I now, that her form, her face, are decked with the smile of him, who glories in the glory of his children. When she now appears in my dreams, there is no longer that hideous chasm opening between us; she is always decked as if for another bridal day, and I awake confident in that day's approach without guilt.

'But leave me, depart to-morrow upon your intended journey, if that you stay, who knows but the curse which has attended me through life may yet be acting, and may fall upon you as well as all others whom I have loved. These papers will explain to you what I have withheld, the life of Doni. If that you return this way, you may find me dead. Drop not a tear over my grave, I shall be with Louisa. Farewell, but depart knowing that there exists a consolation, which man cannot take from you, which misfortune cannot destroy, the belief in a future state, in the mercy of a redeeming God. It is there I find refuge.

The Life of Count Filibero Doni

'The family to which I belong is one of the most noble in Lombardy; but I, being the son of the younger branch, did not enjoy many of those advantages which belong to high rank. I was sent at a very early age to a college of Jesuits, and soon distinguished myself so much, that all the allurements the society was in the habit of holding out to young men of promise, were employed to attach me to this community. I had, however, been educated amongst the mountains; and having been nursed by an old retainer of the family, I had conceived so high an idea of the importance and consequence attached to nobility, that I could not resolve upon putting on a dress, which bound me to forego all those advantages and pleasures, the early associations excited by my nurse, had taught me to believe, belonged to the entry of a nobleman into that very world, my venerable master endeavoured, in vain, to persuade me, was every thing horrible. In the mountains, a son of even the lateral descendants from the Lord, is always looked up to with so much respect and veneration by the poor inhabitants of these districts, that it is no wonder if I was deceived. When the religious began to flatter and distinguish me above my companions, as I was not conscious of any exertion in the acquisition of that mental superiority about which they talked, I attributed their attentions to the respect they felt for one of such exalted rank, as I imagined myself born to, having been left also for the whole of the time with the men, without having paid a single visit to my family, the distant memory of what I had seen at home, appeared to me in contrast with the plain life of my superiors, as something magnificent and passing comparison. My parents, hearing of the talents of their son, were anxious for his entry into an order, whose influence they well knew could be profitable in the greatest degree, not only to the individual, but to the whole of his family. When, therefore, they found that their son was determined not to bind himself by any bond which should hinder him from enjoying, what his imagination had pictured; they thought the best plan in such a case was to allow me to view nearer, that misery which attends nobility devoid of riches. I was accordingly sent for home.

'I arrived—I was astonished at not being led to one of those numerous palaces I met on my way to my father's, in the streets of Milan. My guide and myself came at last into the Corso; I began to reconcile myself, seeing the end of the city before me nothing but palaces on both sides; when suddenly, we turned down a narrow street, and I came to the gate of an obscure house. I did not speak, but my feelings were hurt. I

ascended a narrow staircase, and I found myself in the presence of my
mother. She was lying on a couch covered with leather, dressed in all
the dirty tawdry of one who glories in the past; she was playing with a
dog with one hand, while the other was stretched over an earthenware
brazier. A dirty servant, slip shod, with hair which had apparently never
been touched by a comb, led me into the room, and announced me. My
mother did not even move, she was too busily engaged by her puppy to
notice me. At last, tired of seeing only the same jumps, turning round in
the act of stretching her weary limbs, she saw my figure; imagining it to
be that of her son, she addressed herself to me. "Ah, Filiberto, so you
are really come home to load your parents with your expences, when
you might have become a jesuit with every prospect of power. Well, we
shall see how your father will bear it. For my part I will not sacrifice any
more first representations for your follies. I had already engaged a box
at the Scala, with the money I had spared from our very food; when your
father, hearing of it, went and sold the tickets because you were expected." These were the first words, I remember, my mother spoke to me.
I cannot describe to you the various feelings they excited in my breast.
I could not believe this to be my mother. I did not answer her; but engaged in thought, I sat down, and soon lost sight of the white cold walls
and brick floor, in the bitterness of my imaginations. My father entered,
throwing off his huge great coat, which, placed upon his shoulders, covered both his body and the clay vessel containing the heated charcoal; he
embraced me, and seemed really pleased to see me.

'I spent a miserable day, for it was the very one on which a new opera
was to be brought out, and all the usual companions of my mother, having, by intrigue and what not, secured places, she was left alone without
even her cavalier servente, in the company of her husband and son: this
was insupportable, and she did nothing the whole evening but vent her
bad emper upon me, sneering at my foolish ideas of rank. My father, who
seemed accustomed to these scenes, quietly took his seat in a retired
part of the room, and with his great coat confining the warm air arising
from his scaldino around his body, soon fell asleep. The servant came in
after the Caffè, and spinning at my mother's side, for a time diverted her
attention from me, by joining with the complete appearance of an equal in
all that mean criticism of their neighbours, which is esteemed the more
witty according to its ill-nature. I was at last glad to go to bed. You may
imagine what was the bed room of the son, when the receiving room of
the Padrona was such as I have described.

'As I passed by a door upon the staircase, I saw two heads put out to
look at me; they were my sisters; I cannot describe to you the sensation
I felt, when I found no one had thought it necessary to bring them to see

their brother, or even to mention them to him. I found them dressed in the most coarse clothes, and I had hardly been there a few minutes, before they began recounting to me the hardships and privations they had lately undergone in consequence of the anxiety of my mother to secure a box at the opera for this night. It is useless to paint more scenes of this nature; my mother was vain, and spent even what should have been given to feeding her children, in the most distant imitation of the rich, to whom she had the honour of being allied, and who condescended to laugh at her for her pains. My father loved quiet above all things; his income was small, very incompetent to supply the foolish vanity of my mother, he was therefore always in debt, and even obliged to be a mean hanger on upon the elder branch of the family.

'Next day I went with my father to visit the head of our family, and I there saw what my imagination had represented to me. The numerous servants seemed bustling about, as if their wills were too rapid for their limbs. The rich liveries, which were almost reflected in the burnished floors of marble and precious woods, the porphyry columns, the fresco paintings, and the silken coverings to even the footstools astonished me. I followed in silence the officious servant, who seemed amazed at my astonishment at that splendour, in which he had always bustled, though but the son of a cowherd. We were conducted into the boudoir of our relation. He was at his toilette, every thing breathed effeminacy, all was luxurious, the delicately coloured curtains let in the enfeebled light of the noon day. When I entered I could hardly distinguish the objects around, for coming from rooms illuminated by all the powers of the sun, my eyes could not feel the weaker impressions of this veiled obscurity. My relation struck with the astonishment I displayed at such magnificence, amused himself with calling forth signs of wonder from me. I was invited to stay with him, and I accordingly went from my mother's, who was glad to get rid of the inconvenience arising from the addition I caused to be made to the daily expences, at the same time that she was proud of having to talk about the notice I had excited at the Palazzo Doni. My relation conducted me every where. I was introduced by him to the casino of the nobles, and was always in his box at the theatre of La Scala. He advised me to attach myself to an old countess, whose cavalier servente was just dead. I did so, and soon had the honour of carrying her shawl, and whispering in her ear even to the exclusion of her superannuated husband, at all the places of public resort.

'I was now initiated into all the magic enjoyments of wealth and splendour. Without any riches or merit of my own, I enjoyed all the luxuries, which were not a little heightened by the visits I paid my father's house, where I saw poverty in its most appalling state, accompanied by pretensions to rank. I was intoxicated. The Countess had several daughters, these I seldom saw, though they were approaching rapidly to woman-hood. It however happened, that soon after I had obtained a footing in her house, that a birthday of her eldest child occurred. She resolved upon celebrating it by a little ball, chiefly composed of the immediate connections of the family. I was admitted by virtue of my office. I had nev-er before been in a ball-room. The splendid chandeliers, the gay dresses, and the beautiful women, surrounding me on every side, raised a scene before me, which even my most vivid fancy had never imagined.

· 'I could not dance, I was therefore a mere spectator; but I was not idle, I had never been accustomed to see unmarried females, for they are not admitted into the society to which I belonged. There appeared a charm about them I could not define; they fixed my attention, and as each moved in the light dance, with all the agility and grace attendant upon youth, while their retreating looks seemed to denote a fear that they excited observation; I attempted in vain to discover what fascinated me. My heart beat violently, it seemed as if I had never before witnessed beauty. Towards the end of the evening, a party of foreigners entered; they had come to reside in Milan; with them was a young lady. She en-tered into the dances. She had not the light airy step of her companions, she had not the same brilliancy of eye, but there was something so pow-erful in her meek glance, in her measured graceful step, that enchained the senses. From that moment I could gaze upon no one else. She alone seemed to be moving, she alone seemed to be the object worthy of atten-tion. I was yet gazing upon her, when the Countess called me to join her party at tre sette. I accompanied her, but it was in vain for me to attempt fixing my mind upon the cards before me. I saw nothing but that fig-ure which had been that moment before my sight. I made blunders that called forth impatient exclamations from my partners, and I was at last allowed to rise upon the plea of a headache. I instantly entered the other room, but she was gone.

'She had however left her image in my breast. For several days I did not see her again, but at last she began to appear in public, for being a foreigner, her parents did not confine her as is customary amongst Ital-ians. I often left the Countess in the Theatre, and placing myself in the pit, near the box in which she was, watched her slightest motion. There was a melancholy look about her that seemed to indicate an acquaint-ance with grief, that was extraordinary in so young a person. Her dark blue eye was seldom unveiled; her long modest eyelashes generally hid their splendour, and her silence, and her uninterested glance, added a charm to her figure I cannot describe. Her goodness and charity were spoken of by all, her beauty was not envied or denied by her own, while her gentle manners and winning smile, seemed to gain the heart of all the other sex. I accompanied the Countess to her house. I sat by her, but could not speak with her. It seemed as if the emotion in my breast, stifled the words I was about to utter. She however noticed me, and her parents in repeating their compliments to the lady I accompanied, included me in a general invitation to the house.

'As it was not the custom for ladies of rank to rise until a late hour, I had a great part of the day upon my own hands. I used generally to lounge about, and sometimes go to the Ambrosian Library, in quest of something to engage my attention. One morning I was there as usual, and I found the Ernachs there. Matilda was with them, they were just then occupied in viewing the manuscript of Virgil, with Petrarch's annotations. When the Cicerone pointed out the last note of this latter poet, in which he speaks of his love to Laura, I could not help remarking, a momentary emotion which passed across the face of Matilda. Her mother also observed it, and immediately taking her arm, accompanied her into the room containing pictures of several of the greatest masters. I followed them, and entered into conversation by pointing out the heads of the Milanese Raphael, which one cannot examine without feeling a stillness come over our senses foreign to our nature. There is so much beauty and heavenly quiet about them, that they indeed resemble representations of a poet's dream. Before we parted, I was accepted as the guide to the curiosities, which they had not yet seen, and my office was to begin the next day.

'It is useless to describe to you the gradual steps of love. I at last neglected the attentions due to the Countess, while sitting by the side of Matilda. At last, no longer capable of enduring the feelings within my bosom, I confessed my love to the object I adored. She was not angry, nor did she seem surprised; but in a voice that betrayed inward agitation, she begged of me to lay aside all hopes of gaining her hand, and conjured me not to mention it to her father. I was confused and abashed. I retired and returned to the palace, where I confined myself to my chamber. Not having appeared for several days in society, and enquiries being made concerning me, I was soon sought for by my kind relation. He seemed so anxious about the ill health, which he imagined was the cause of my absence from those gaieties in which I always seemed to delight, that I was induced to lay open to him the whole of my heart. He tried to administer consolation, but could not succeed; my vanity was mortified, and reflecting upon my poverty, I had imagined that I was despised for some richer rival. He seemed to know Matilda better, told me he could not believe it, but I dwelt so much upon the subject, that he saw it was useless to oppose my opinion any longer. He attempted to induce me to accompany him into society, but I refused, and for some days remained alone in my chamber.

'Sick with all the splendour around, which seemed to mock me, I determined in spite of the expected reproaches of my mother, to return to my father's house, where by long confinement I fell ill. My kind relation hearing of this came to me, and tried to represent to me the folly of my conduct; but disappointed love and mortified vanity, did not allow me to listen. Seeing me thus haunted by the idea of riches, he generously offered to advance me a considerable sum, and to give me letters to a friend at Alexandria, where I might he thought employ my capital to the greatest advantage in commercial speculations. I thanked him, and accepted his kind offer. I soon left Milan, determined never to return till those riches were mine, which should enable me to assert a rank equal to any in my native city. I arrived at Alexandria, and was soon engaged in mercantile speculations, with an eagerness that caused all my transactions to appear more like the ventures of a desperate gambler than the secure projects of a merchant. I found several Europeans established in this city, chiefly engaged in the commerce of grain.

'Amongst the rest, there was one who seemed to form a particular attachment to me; he was several years older than myself, and was noted amongst us for a certain avoidance of pleasure which did not appear natural to his years. He was always engaged, when not occupied in his business, either in reading or in a solitary ramble through the burnt neighbourhood of this ruined town. I was the only person he sought; he seemed to place his confidence in me, and made many enquiries, at first vaguely, concerning those I had known at Milan. Happening to name the Ernachs, his face immediately became anxious, and his questions evidently bore a stamp of interest they had not before shown. This excited my attention and caused me to make more particular enquiries concerning him. Little was known; he was a German, and it was thought he had been disappointed in love. He perceived the attention I began to show him, and one evening when we were alone, he told me that he had at first been induced to seek my society, from a letter he had received from Matilda. "You must have perceived the interest, with which I listened to your account of the family of the Ernachs; know that I love Matilda, that I have reason to believe my affection is returned, but that owing to my poverty, I have never dared to confess even to her the feelings of love I bear within my breast. We were together from earliest infancy, all our pleasures were in common, and though, when I grew to manhood, I no longer dared to use the familiarity of my earlier years with her, who began to vest the charms of woman, still we partook in the pleasures of each other's occupations. Many things we studied together. I read the lighter authors of literature to her while she was engaged in those occupations attendant, in our country, upon every female member of a family. I at last opened Petrarch, and read those sonnets in which love is so delicately pourtrayed. You cannot conceive my emotions, when I perceived that she felt them as I did myself, and that she often raised her modest eyes, while a blush mantled her cheek, to gaze upon me, while my trembling voice seemed not to be reading the sentiments of another, but speaking the feelings of my own breast. We seemed, indeed, not to want to comment upon what we were both sensible expressed only those truths which echoed in the breasts of both. When, however, I retired, I always upbraided myself for thus exposing, though indirectly, that love, of which I had no reason to think her parents would approve, for I had no profession, and was not born to riches. When, however, I saw her, and she again asked for the author whose delicate pencil only traced the most fading hues of love, I again read. We were thus engaged, when we were interrupted by her mother, who had stood unperceived some time watching the emotions but too visible in our countenances. She did not then speak, but taking another opportunity, when I was alone with her, she gently intimated, that I had not acted honourably in thus engaging the attention of Matilda to such poetry, as was but too powerful a seducer of the mind. I was but too conscious of it. I acknowledged my error, and promised to take no further occasion of thus acting upon her daughter's susceptible heart. She placed entire confidence in me, and was not deceived. I applied to my father, who, at my desire, sent me hither to push my fortune, and I have succeeded as well as I expected."

'How shall I convey to you an idea of what passed in my mind? Before me stood the unconscious cause of my being rejected by Matilda. He had told me, he loved her, that she loved him. I was silent when he ended, I could not rouse myself to speak to him; he, thinking that his narration had tired me, made an apology, to which I could only answer by monosyllables; he retired and left me to my own thoughts. It was evident Matilda preferred another. My feelings may be imagined,—cannot be described. It seemed as if some demon actuated me, I fell upon my knees, and dared even to call God to witness my vow of obtaining the object of my affections, in spite of all obstacles. It seemed as if I felt more at peace after having thus resolved upon not yielding even to him she loved, the possession I ambitioned.

'I sought Huldebrand, for so was my rival called, determined to worm into his confidence, and gain the whole of his secret. I told him not to impute my abstraction on the former evening to any thing but my mind being engaged in thought upon a circumstance, which I noticed at Milan, and which was now fully explained. I then mentioned to him the emotion I had noticed in Matilda's countenance, while listening to the memorial of Petrarch with regard to the duration of his love. This immediately secured his attention, and I soon learnt many circumstances with regard to their early years; and I became convinced, that there was really no engagement between them.

'In the mean time my speculations, which had been begun rashly, had for the greater part turned out badly, and I found myself with a capital considerably diminished. Huldebrand who could not remain ignorant of my losses proposed to me, as I seemed ignorant of the best means of securing a profitable commerce, to join him. I did so; but growing tired of the slow advantages to be obtained by the regular channels, I at last induced him to join me in a speculation that seemed to promise a certain and at the same time immense profit. We ventured, and lost all we risked. My loss did not grieve me much, for it had reduced my Matilda's favoured lover to the same want as myself. He was not however dismayed, nor did he reproach me, but immediately exerting himself to recover all that remained of our property, he proposed, that we should join some Armenians, who were about to leave Alexandria and penetrate into the interior of Asia, in hopes of finding some opportunity of bettering our small fortunes. I consented, and we accompanied them.

'We entered Persia, and travelled even into India. We soon found our capitals rapidly increasing, for, imitating the Armenians, we bought upon several occasions precious stones, which we resold almost immediately greatly to our advantage. It is, in no way necessary for me to give an account of these countries, towards the understanding the fatality that attended my life. I travelled through them careless about the scenery or inhabitants; the whole of my attention was engaged in my endeavours to acquire wealth. Matilda stood constantly before me as the bride of Huldebrand, and my father's house always appeared in contrast with the palace of the head of our family. I soon entered into the spirit of the traffic I was engaged in, and restrained as I was by Huldebrand's steadiness, we rapidly indeed accumulated an immense sum, which we carried always with us in precious stones.

'I had been particularly struck by the venerable appearance of one of our companions, he was aged, his head was white with the numbered years that had passed since his birth. This was the more remarkable from the contrast it offered with the jet black hair and beards of his countrymen. He was never engaged in their occupations, he never seemed to be concerned in any mercantile transaction, yet he seemed to be careless of his money, which he gave profusely to all. He seemed to delight in the society of strangers, and therefore sought ours; but Huldebrand not speaking his language did not gain the same hold of his affections as myself, he indeed treated me completely as his son, and often directed me in the conduct of our concerns; his advice was always advantageous.

'This stranger seemed to look upon me as his pupil, and he gradually turned my mind to the objects around me. But he did not improve my heart by the opening of my mind. He was himself extremely rich; when therefore he held forth upon the happiness of contented poverty, I thought he was but a mere visionary, imagining the Arabian delights of a sandy desert, while shaded by the canopying foliage of a grove, and surrounded by all the riches of a cultivated country. I looked around, and I saw the genius and the ideot both equally subservient to the will of the wealthy. I saw virtue trodden under foot, and vice, that monster in rags in the cottage, adored as a goddess in the temples of the gaudy palace. Wherever I went, it seemed as if gold, in the bustling of the whole of life, had the same effect as a few aspers thrown amidst the obstreperous crowd that immediately leaves off its hideous yell in haste to scramble for the miserable gain. Riches were a thirst upon me. I could not believe that Matilda or Ernach, her father, could resist the splendour of wealth. But Huldebrand was with me, half our common property was his. He loved,—was beloved. Whenever I looked upon him, my heart did not beat quicker; it seemed for a moment to pause, as if his sight blasted its vital action, but it beat again with redoubled violence, when Matilda's image rose upon my mind, and my former vow was again repeated.

'Though my appetite for riches was not sated, it was gratified; our speculations had been constantly doubling our capital, and we had already left the banks of the Euphrates, turning our steps towards Europe, when we gradually entered the vast desert that spreads its subtle sands from the Red Sea, almost to the Mediterranean. Having all our wealth about us in jewels and gold, we were anxious about our safety. Every night the cry of the watchful sentinel bidding us be upon the alert, while it called to the roaming Arab to depart, sounded on my waking ears, and often I arose in painful anxiety, to gaze upon the far spread horizon, lost sometimes in the misty light of the bright moon. I envied the sound sleep of the poor camel-driver, who lay extended by the animal entrusted to his care, as heedless of my wealth, as the brute about the fate of his burden. At last the ground seemed to acquire firmness to the foot, and the camel already began to browze upon the solitary stunted plants that here and there spread their parched growth to the no longer beneficent ray of an eastern sun. I thought myself secure, night came, and I was standing by my open tent, for I could not rest; I was gazing upon a long line which bounded the horizon, with a thin dark streak, indicating the palm boundary to our toilsome pilgrimages; there were slight clouds flitting before the moon, and as their shadows fled over the vast expanse, my heart beat quicker, for each, as it approached from the horizon, seemed to my hurried imagination, as the dark shadow formed by an Arab troop; one followed the other, always bearing deceit with it. At last from the long line of palms, a black speck seemed to move with great rapidity; I could trace no cloud upon the heavens, which could throw its dark shadow upon this track; I breathless called a sentinel, the alarm was given, but we were surrounded; I went about like a madman, encouraged the men to fight,—fought. The circle was gradually straightened round us; the men fell by the distant arrows at first, but the work of death was not slower, when the sword clashed against sword, and the robber's foot trod upon his antagonist's. I struggled, my riches were lost; while yet struggling amidst our very tents, I heard the old Armenian cry for help, he was combating with a young Arabian, who had thrown him to the ground. I rushed forward, bade the robber defend himself; we fought, I succeeded in disarming him, and was upon the point of thrusting my sword through his body, when he begged of me to spare his life, promising that both the Armenian and myself should be safe. I saw all resistance was at an end, I gave him back his weapon, and approached the old man who was wounded. He took my hand, thanked me for my attempt to save him, but he thought his wound was mortal; he bade me at the same time console myself for the loss of my accumulated wealth, saying that he would, ere he died, make me ample amends.

'Our lives, at the intercession of the Arab I had spared, who proved to be a man of rank amongst the robbers, were granted us. He conveyed the Armenian to his own tent, and I anxiously placed myself by the old man's side, watching, with the agitation of a desperate gambler, every various expression of his countenance; it was my last stake. Huldebrand I knew was not killed, but had been given, as part of the booty, to one of the robbers, in hopes of his ransoming himself, but he was ruined like myself, had lost every thing; I was however, if not deceived, to obtain riches as abundantly as before. Matilda might then be mine; I made no further enquiries about him who had partaken the vicissitudes of commerce and of life with me, who had been almost beggared by my rashness, and whose steadiness had enabled me to recover every thing, and to gain wealth. I sat by the old man; every sound that fell from his lips, seemed the announcement of his bequest, but he was silent on that subject.

'Five days elapsed, at last the sixth was passing, and his strength was evidently rapidly failing, his breath became hurried, and his eyes began to take that lustre, which seems to be the last exertion of the departing soul; he then spoke, "I wished," he said, "that my life had been spared but a short time longer, I could then have bestowed wealth upon you, without the conditions that may now startle you. Know, but how dare I tell it? you may look upon me with horror, and while I am wishing to bless you, may turn away from me. I have a power that is supposed to bring the curse of the Almighty upon it; I can,—I have the power of raising a spirit from the vast abyss, and make him lay at my feet, the infinite wealth enclosed within the earth's recesses. But if you would listen to one aged, who has borne this blasting power from early youth, you would refuse the dangerous gift. For there is a condition necessarily bound to that power, which will undoubtedly quell your ardent longing even for riches." It was in vain that he addressed me thus, Matilda and wealth connected rose to my imagination. I pressed him to explain himself. He did. He told me that either I could only call for a certain sum at a time, and that at each time, some human domestic infliction, worse than the preceding, would fall upon me, or that, I at once, could gain unlimited power, and constant domestic prosperity, on the condition of giving myself up for ever to the will of a malignant being. He had chosen the first, had called but once for the exertion of the demon's power, but his happiness had been withered by that once. I did not hesitate, I laughed in my own mind at domestic happiness, I had lived only in Italy, and in the East, I begged of him to disclose his secret; he did. I bound myself to the first condition.

'I impatiently rose, I left the old man upon his dying couch, and retreated to my own tent. I raised the spirit, his hideous form might have appalled a stronger heart than mine. I trembled, but his mocking laugh subdued my fears, and bending my knee, I acknowledged him as my superior through life. I cannot describe the scene, I could not without recording some part of the spells by which I raised this monster, and he has but too fully proved his power for me to be willing to put the least clue into the hands of any one which might bring the curse I have felt upon him. Besides riches, I gained other powers, but these are not connected with yours and my Louisa's fate, I shall not speak of them.

'I returned to the sick man's tent, the Armenian was dead. I did not feel sorry, how could I at that moment; I was exultant, my wealth was so enormous, I did not see a possibility of spending it. The next day the robbers buried my benefactor in the burning sands. I proposed a ransom for myself to the Arab, he insisted upon my accepting my freedom. I did, and we eat together; no longer fearing treachery, I made him a present to an enormous amount. He was surprized, but did not make even the smallest enquiry.

'I roamed about the encampment, for I was desirous of seeing these robbers in their native barren plain. While wandering about their black tents, I heard a voice of pain issuing from one of the most miserable. It was Huldebrand, he was calling, in the delirium of a fever, for a drop of water to allay his thirst. The well was close to me. The tent was open, no one was near, he was extended upon the sandy floor, with hardly any clothes to defend him from its hot touch. I, even I, could not resist this appeal, I seized a vessel lying by his side, and drew it from the well full. I was turning towards him, when suddenly his tones altered, he seemed to press his breast, while in the softest words he addressed some one. I approached, he was imagining Matilda stood by him. The words sounded on my ear,—"I know, Matilda, that you love me." The pitcher fell upon the sand, and the water was drank up by the burning dust, and I turned away with a raging heart, from the dying Huldebrand.

'I instantly determined upon leaving the spot. The noble Arab escorted me to the utmost boundary of the desert, and I was safe from danger. I hired camels and horses, and proceeded to Aleppo, spreading every where that I was a merchant, who had been very successful in my speculations. This was easy to me, for I could refer to people with whom I had had transactions, and my name was known. I hastened to Italy, and soon reached Milan, I entered with all the pomp of riches; I will not describe my entry, it was foolishly splendid, nor will I attempt to paint to you the daily display I made of some new folly; they were produced by the intoxication of a madman. Matilda, for she held no less a powerful influence over me than my avarice, was the object of the whole. I found her health much decayed, she had not heard of Huldebrand for more than two years. Yet there was perhaps a greater charm in that pale cheek and languid eye, than I had found in the delicate colouring of the one, or the splendour of the other. If I could gain her love now, it would, indeed, be an ample compensation for her former rejection. I began by spreading the report of her lover's death, though I was not certain of the fact, yet I thought, at any rate, that he could not re-appear so soon as not to allow me time to accomplish my end. I then went to her father's, and in the course of the conversation announced it.

'Matilda was inconsolable, but she took pleasure in my society, for I could talk to her of Huldebrand, I related indifferent particulars concerning him, the eagerness with which she listened reached my heart; I determined, however, to endure even these pangs, rather than lose the opportunities afforded me of sitting by her side. As in the course of narration, I introduced the relation of actions in which I had been his benefactor, she blessed me for it. I felt like a baffled demon. I gradually began to talk of myself. I sounded the father and mother with regard to a marriage; obtained their full consent and approbation. They gradually broke it to their daughter. She wondered at my seeking for a widowed heart; insisted upon my taking some months to consider of it, while she herself fulfilled the term of mourning she thought due to her lover's memory. I was anxious, and fearful of Huldebrand's appearance. I pressed my suit with earnestness; my relations, her father, her mother, used all the arts of persuasion to induce her to anticipate the day. She did, and we were married.

'It now seemed as if I could dare the world. I had Matilda, had wealth, the only objects my mind had ever rested upon were mine. I had two children, Louisa and Olivieri. You cannot imagine the splendour in which I lived. Where could the mortal be found who had greater supposed sources of happiness than mine? yet I was miserable; Matilda was mine, my wife, but her affections still rested upon the image of my rival. I doated upon her; it seemed as if the price of guilt I had paid bound her the more to me, as if she were to form the only happiness I was to know, and she did not love me. She differed entirely from my countrywomen; she enjoyed her domestic circle, she was modest; and while she stood amongst the abandoned wantons, who formed the only society around her, she stood erect, as if she were sent by Heaven to show deluded men the beauties of the virtues they despised.

'I had not enjoyed the society of my wife more than three years, when my momentary happiness was blasted. Matilda came home one day, as I imagined, from the Corso, flurried and violently agitated. She threw herself upon the sofa, and lost in thought, she did not perceive that I was near her. She drew from her breast a note: I could see over her shoulder; it struck me that it was Huldebrand's hand-writing. She seemed to look upon it as if she could not believe her eyes. She viewed it, her hands fell, and the movement of the eyelids over the fixed eyes seemed to denote the belief in a deceit of the senses. Her breath was still, her cheek pale, she did not move. I unavoidably discovered myself; she turned, looked at me, and the tears bursting from her eyes, rolled down her cheeks, as she rushed out of the room. I dared not follow her. Huldebrand might be stalking in my very house, might be close to me, his words of reproach might be already in the air, prepared to damn me with their sound. I should be proved in the world's face, a liar, a wretch without a spark of generosity, of gratitude, in Matilda's face—I hid myself in my chamber, for the consciousness of my guilt caused me at first to wish for concealment. But the thought of my rival roused me; was it not possible to remove him? I rushed out of my room, and was upon the point of going through the great gate, when I perceived a figure descending the staircase, wrapt closely in a large mantle. It was a woman—it was Matilda. Her hurried step and anxious glances thrown around caused me to watch her. She went out into the street, I followed her; there was an obstacle near the theatre, she cleared it, but I lost her in the crowd of carriages. In vain I tried every opening leading to the theatre, I could not recover a trace of her. At last I was obliged to lean exhausted against the wall, and Ernach, her father, coming from the theatre, discovered me. Perceiving my agitation at sight of him, he insisted upon escorting me home. He attempted to lead me to explain to him the cause of my trembling limbs, which weighed upon his arm. He did not know that he sought to know my shame; I insisted upon his leaving me, and I at last fell exhausted upon a chair in my saloon.

'I know not how long I had remained in this situation by myself; I at last heard Matilda's light step ascending the staircase. I did not move, my eyes remained still gazing on the ground when she entered. At sight of me she started, but she commanded herself—approached me with a faultering step. I attempted to clasp her to my bosom, as if—I know not what passed in my mind. She retreated. "You have a right to know where I have been in this clandestine manner." I hid my face with my hands, I was conscious she had been to see Huldebrand. She had been with him, she would say no more. I threw myself at her feet, she turned away. "I can no longer even esteem you," were the last words she said, when she left me.

'She went out several times in the course of next day; once I attempted to follow her. She perceived me at the door: "Filiberto," she said, "seek not to pursue my steps, I am but active in the cause of virtue. Retire and leave me. You must be aware of what hangs over your head. Would that heaven may grant I could avert it from my husband, my children's father." I was left in a state of mind that bordered upon phrenzy. I rushed out of the house, and turning my steps another way, I did not return towards my home till night. When I did return, I found every thing in the greatest confusion. There was a carriage with posthorses at the gate. The moment I approached, my valet came to me to tell me of my shame. Matilda had been seen leaving Milan, with a gentleman in her company. I jumped into the carriage, and followed upon the road they were reported to have taken.

'I did not speak during the whole time; I did not listen, though my servant, having entered with me, was telling me more of the circumstances. Night and day I travelled in pursuit. I seemed to be gaining on them. I at last overtook them just as I was entering a village in Savoy. They were upon the point of leaving it. I sprung out of my carriage, and with the speed of a demoniac I ran after them. In my furious haste, I fell. I did not attempt to rise, but instantly fired; my wife's shriek was heard: they, however, drove on. When my carriage with fresh horses overtook me, my servant tried to raise me, I had dislocated my ancle. Blood, my servant told me, could be traced upon the road, as if it had fallen from my wife's carriage. I could but look upon myself as Matilda's murderer, the shriek was her's. My emotions and feelings were so violent and various it would be impossible to portray them. The demon's power was upon me, and his curse proved a bitter one.

'I was conveyed home, where I was for a long time delirious; I became calm but not less miserable. My attendants then gave me a letter, which had been found upon my wife's dressing table, after my departure in chase of her. She was innocent, she had not fled with Huldebrand, but with her father. Huldebrand had upon that condition agreed to conceal my crime, my shame. She had left her home, her children; had sacrificed her own to shield my name from infamy. I did not at this intelligence relapse into the violent ravings I had undergone. I sunk into a state of apathy, whence nothing could rouse me. I refused even to see my children, and hardly ever leaving my chamber, I spent the night and day with short intervals to self-reproach in combating inflictions of the mind more dreadful than any corporeal penance of the holy anchorite.

'Many years had thus passed, I had not once seen my children, not even heard of them, for I would speak with no one. I at last saw them by accident. You know Olivieri's violent character. He had constantly enquired after me, always baffled by the servants in his wish of seeing me; he at last seized his opportunity, but Louisa had watched him, and they both appeared in my sight struggling with one another; for she was trying to hinder his disturbing me. If Matilda herself had stood before me she could not have affected me more; for Louisa, though her features are different, her eye dark, has the expression that gave such power to her mother's looks, playing upon her face. She at last, no longer capable of resisting her brother, threw herself at my feet, and earnestly begged me not to be offended with her dear Olivieri. I took her to my arms. From that moment I was aroused. I could not leave my daughter, but gave up all my time to the education of my children; but I brought another curse upon my head, for I neglected Olivieri; except in his literary studies I did not assist him, his mind was allowed to be biassed by any one who chose to trouble themselves with acting upon him. Louisa on the contrary was my constant companion, she rewarded my care. You know her, if ever a wretch like me might have hope, it must be in the prayers such a being can offer up for me to the throne of heaven. After some time I proposed journeying through the different countries of Europe, to show my children the different peculiarities of nations. We had already entered Switzerland when my son left me. I had been accustomed to his often quitting me for days together, and hardly noticed his departure. Louisa and myself proceeded to the different spots remarkable for their beauty or sublimity. On the Wengern Alp we saw you. We soon after heard daily of the feats of Ernestus Berchtold and Olivieri. I don't know why, but the thought of the chamois hunter we had seen being this Ernestus, first struck my daughter, and I soon joined in the belief. A letter from Olivieri appointed Interlaken as the place of meeting; we went there. Events in which you were concerned brought us again to Milan.

'The immense riches I had obtained from the spirit under my command, though much diminished, were yet more than sufficient to maintain us in sufficient splendour, not to fear any thing like a competition. But Olivieri and yourself were gamblers. Louisa forced me again to risk an infliction equally severe as the last, for your sake. I could not resist her prayers for you. I again called the spirit from his immortal haunts, and Olivieri's infamy was the consequence. Your debts had proved so enormous, that in my attempt at saving him from an ignominious death, I was again obliged, though I knew the horrible powers of the demon, to call upon him. I did so. He announced to me that I had exhausted my spells, and that after this infliction, as nothing round me would remain, on which he could breathe his pestilential breath, he would no longer obey my summons. I called upon him to take back his gold, he laughed and left me. I had no suspicion of Olivieri's seduction of your sister; when therefore his letter was put into my hands, you may imagine how your noble conduct affected me. I did not speak of it, for what could a father say? Must I even acknowledge it to you, I sometimes rested upon it with a feeling of consolation, for I hoped, that crime of my son's might be the infliction upon his father, meant by the demon as passing all others. Louisa I thought might then be spared, and you two might at least be happy.

'But you married; I dreamt of happiness, on Louisa's birth-day accompanied you to your room, and the demon's threat I found had indeed been fulfilled. Your mother's portrait was Matilda's. Olivieri had seduced, you married a daughter of Matilda, of Matilda's husband, and I was the murderer of her father.'

About the Author

To the popular imagination, paranoid schizophrenics hear the Devil instructing us to commit murder, or we crowd mental institutions believing we are Jesus Christ Himself. My mental condition has coloured my creativity in a variety of different ways. Many writers will often encounter their "characters" actively participating in the stories they are writing. This "inner-voice" instructing the writing process can be unsettling to nascent writers. For an author with my condition, the voices are audible and very, very communicative.

My voices, however, are not those of the characters I am writing, but of pseudonymous co-writers, actively and audibly participating in the writing process. Each of my books has a very different and unique co-writer. Ophelia T'Wat, the co-writer of *The Marquis de Sade's Wettest Midummer Night's Dream Conceivable*, is a 21 year-old college student who is stripping her way through college. The co-author of Satan's Study Bible: The Four Gospels is far more a nefarious personality, Satan himself, but instead of instructing me to murder, he wanted nothing more than a Study Bible written from his own point-of-view. Satan's Preacher Man manifested more as a dreamlike past life experience. And finally, the granddaddy of them all, God and His Only Begotten Son Jesus Christ spoke to me audibly and through dreams instructing and inspiring The Holy Bible Trilogy and its Next Testament.

But can a novelist, who was diagnosed schizophrenic as a teenager, actually hear the Voice of God tell him to continue the Word of God? As a dutiful Catholic, I sought the intersession of a priest for exorcism from demonic forces. He instructed me to see a psychiatrist to alleviate my hallucinations. I am caught in a spiritual conundrum, would I rather be a Prophet of God or crazy?

Over decades of constant psychoanalysis, I have come to peace with my rather unique creativity. I have embraced the quirks that come with my writer's voice, or voices as it were. I hope you, the Reader, can appreciate and enjoy my collaborations with my voices.

This is a major contributing factor to both the Pale Student of the Unhallowed Arts and his Creation/Creature haunting Mary as a hallucinogenic phantasm. Authors often describe to lay readers that their characters 'speak' to them, specifically telling the author what they are going to say and do. Readers are aghast at the idea that a creation of the author's brain can override the author's own intentions with 'their' story. But it is not the author's story, it is the characters. The Pale Student and the Creation/Creature may be products of Mary's imagination, but they are a real to the author (and reader) as if they were flesh and blood. It is a shocking experience for the nascent author when their characters 'speak' to them, often saying, 'No! This is my story now. I shall relate it the way I wish!.'

If writing is as schizophrenic an experience as I allege, then what about an author who is a diagnosed schizophrenic? When I said earlier that 'pseudonymous co-writers, actively and audibly participat[e] in the writing process', I was not exaggerating. I, more often than not, hear my characters speaking to me over my left shoulder while I type on a MacBook. It *is* like they are a co-writer looking over my shoulder saying, 'No. No. Say this.'

To me my characters are co-writers ,and I have, in the past, given them co-writing credits, like I did with Abigail K.C. Sterling, the co-author of *Alistair Strange & the Fan Friction*. She deserves the credit as much, if not more so, than I do.

Acknowledgement on the Galvanising Debate Chapter

While obtaining the texts of *Frankenstein*, *The Burial*, *The Vampyre*, and other works collected in this collection were as simple as copy-ing-and-pasting from the Internet (particularly Project Gutenberg), one chapter, in particular, needed to be an original story. The chapter on the galvanizing debate is so important to this collection because it was the very debate that inspired Mary Shelley's nightmare of the 'pale student of the unhallowed arts'. But this chapter would require intense research, and this research led me to a singular work: *Shocking Frogs: Galvani, Volta, and the electric origins of neuroscience* by Marco Piccolino and Marco Bresadola, with translation by Nicholas Wade. This $130 university-grade textbook required great investment, both financial and intellectual. I am indebted to this work. When the authors quote substantial quotations from Galvani, Volta, and others, I draw upon those quotations for Lord Byron's and Percy Shelley's arguments in their debate. Elsewhere, where they draw upon simpler quotations within the text, I admit to using the words and phrasings of Piccolino and Bresadola, not out of an attempt to plagiarize or diminish their work, but to communicate the scientific arguments between Shelley and Byron effectively. (I use the Adobe Caslon font to distinguish their words from either mine or those written in the late 17th or early 18th centuries). Part of the mission statement for this collection is to let the original work, whether *The Vampire*, *Ernestus Berchtold*, or *Frankenstein* stand on their own merits. And I wish to do the same with *Shocking Frogs*. If you have a spare $130, please purchase this textbook. It is well worth the read.

www.ingramcontent.com/pod-product-compliance
Lightning Source LLC
Chambersburg PA
CBHW020813060726
47498CB00017B/2853